JUST TO LAND IN TOKYO
AN INTRODUCTION

—

Rosa JH Berland

Just to Land in Tokyo is an evocation of feeling and involves themes of faces, masks, isolation and reincarnation. We also explore immigration, the crisis of European culture, and double standards. This is all imprinted in a jazz format in photographs as digital experiments. These visual stories reflect our artistic search, our thoughts on current events, circumstances and the society around us. (Ajuan Song) [1]

Kuzma Vostrikov and Ajuan Song's Neo-Surrealist photography series *Just to Land in Tokyo* is an illusionist narrative of bright color and strange vignettes of the problematics of contemporary identity and the diasporic experience. Drawing upon Vostrikov's novel of the same name, these photographs constitute a theatre of enigmatic fantasy, absurdity and inverted tropes of portraiture.

According to Song, the series expands beyond simply retelling the novel. Rather, it is an improvisation built on the imaginative process of producing the photographs themselves. Costumes and symbols are used to subvert their usual meaning, thereby unsettling the viewer. As such, many of the images play with repetition, evoking a sense of desperation, loss — and reinvention as well. At the same time the series offers a critical view of the commodified world. Photographs featuring cardboard cutouts and allegorical representation blur the lines between the real and the artificial. Motifs of politics, popular culture and art history are interspersed with images of the artist and strange if not unexpected company.

One group of brightly colored portraits recall the screeprints of Andy Warhol and function as explorations of notions of celebrity and artificiality. Overall, the artists' thoroughly symbiotic process allow the development of synergetic images that "speak to one another" and engage in both inventive artistic construction and critique.

From Novel to Image: A Place of Newness and Repetition

—

Notwithstanding the skeptical tongues that predicted the death of art, Hans used the destructive force of the irrational, which was able to deconstruct what was observed and compose it into a unique picture. (Just to Land in Tokyo, *Kuzma Vostrikov)* [2]

Vostrikov's writing of the novel *Just to Land in Tokyo* was inspired in part by Leo Tolstoy's *Anna Karenina*, and he notes "Andrei Platonov and his *Foundation Pit* and *Chevengur* also lurks between the lines of *Just to Land in Tokyo*. In an era of short text messages, literature can't be 'literary.' The speed of our times reduces word count." For Vostrikov there are further literary influences that inform the photographs, such as "the contrast seen in the writing style of Henry Miller, underlined by the conflict between the internal and external. I should also mention *Ulysses*, with its unbearable cluster of newness and repetition." [3]

This wondrous place of "newness and repetition" is at the center of Song and Vostrikov's explorations of portraiture and scenery that simultaneously construct and critique. [4] The novel's protagonist (the recurring figure of Vostrikov) in the photos is an allegory for the blunted contemporary experience and humankind's search for identity, particularly the phenomenon of displacement engendered by immigration. In some images there is an overriding sense of artificiality, a response of sorts to the problematics of globalization, technology and post-revolutionary culture.

In particular, the self-portraits included in the series somewhat irreverently juxtapose loss and reinvention with the absurd. For example, the portrait of Vostrikov functions as an interrogation of the construction of self. A red-suited figure holding a skull sits on a couch accompanied by a figure of Mao and a white sculpture of a rooster which "symbolizes leadership and a thirst for battle. In the novel, Hans becomes a bird, probably a rooster, which never gives up until it dies," Vostrikov explains. He continues, "The protagonist finds himself on the couch because he is inside his dreams. Some kind of strange, otherworldly reality. What do all these truly bourgeois, useless, diffuse decorations mean, that are so foreign to Hans, in the place where he wakes up? Spiritual illness gives rise to hallucinations of a branching maze where Hans gets lost." [5]

At the core of these photographs is the tragedy of immigration, a process too often accompanied by the loss of identity, the erasure of professional and familial connections and accomplishments, the rote processes of bureaucracy that tax the individual both personally and financially, a slow burn of forfeiture. "We see displacement between the generations, between geographies, in periods of revolution. *Just to Land in Tokyo* is the tragedy of a man tangled in the waves of revolution." [6]

—

Beyond Performance: The Evocation of Dissonance and Fantasy

—

If Song and Vostrikov's approach involves the critical use of portraiture, their practice also draws upon and extends the tenets of early twentieth-century Surrealism, namely in the pairing of the irrational with the analytic to create dissonant visual environments. This is not to say there is any derivative tendency, but rather an approach to creativity featuring non-linear time, characters and unexpected juxtapositions. Take, for example, the beatific portrait of Vostrikov, holding a guitar, his face covered in gold buttons recalling the sanguine face of Albrecht Dürer's iconic 1500 *Self Portrait*. In other images, the figure of Andy Warhol sits with the artist alongside Mao and a paper cut-out of the protagonist Hans' girlfriend (who has long since left his life, but still remains as a paper ghost, her absence indicated by her attenuated presence as a paper figure). The absurdity of such pairings serve as sociopolitical critiques, providing access to the uncanny, tapping into the hidden desires and fears of the viewer. Deepening this construction of dialogue and reception, there are also iconographic borrowings, such as the artists' frequent use of a lobster motif (referring to Dalí's 1936 sculpture *Lobster Telephone*). It is interesting to note here that Dalí's Telephone made for the magazine *American Weekly* included a picture with the caption "New York Dream-Man finds Lobster in Place of the Phone," perhaps an indication of the strangeness found in the American metropolis or the dissonance of modern life. [7]

Another important motif is the obscured eye. In a number of the portraits the subject's eyes or sight is obscured with objects such as dark or strange glasses. These images suggest an uncanny blindness, the intersection of innocence with immaturity, of processed automated self as opposed to authentic experience. The eye was a potent signifier in 19th-century Surrealist work, and in Song's and Vostrikov's imagery the ornamentation and manipulation of the subject's eye deepens the sense of strangeness within. One rather feels as if one has wandered into a room of dreams, the sitter's blindness representing the failure of modern experience and technological and capitalist culture to reflect true experience and identity. [8]

Song notes that our increasingly disparate and socially distanced world seems in part governed by social media and an automated and artificial way of relating to one another. As such contemporary experience is so often about artifice. "Life is an underlying theme in this project as are improvisation and simultaneity. In this live documentary, we experience life and death, joy and sorrow." [9] For Vostrikov, the story of his novel's protagonist occupies a central position in this absurd theatre of enigmatic fantasy. The fictional character's internal, invisible sorrows translate into a series of images that appear as masks speaking of irony and artificiality. These themes are intrinsically connected to the alienating experience of an increasingly technological world and systems of hierarchy and worth, which in turn deny and destabilize the immigrant experience. Vostrikov notes: "What we call the science and technology revolution makes its contribution here, too. The world has sped up and gone flat, uniform, and understandable. Think of the cult of consumption, globalization, and the information sphere, as well as the philosophy of money. The world is propped up on these three pillars." [10]

If this work suggests a disavowal of the harmful effects of rapid technological advances, it can be then said that the artists' striking layering of symbolism, imagery and narrative reveals contemporary experience and identity, particularly the phenomena of displacement engendered by immigration, globalization, technology and post-revolutionary culture. As such this diasporic tale also expresses a more universal theme — that of seriality, the ever evolving and often artificial nature of identity and masks. This series, then, exists along the edges of fantasy and reality, a collaborative expression of lived experience and imagined narrative.

—

About the Artists

—

Ajuan Song and Kuzma Vostrikov bring a unique worldview to their project which is in turn infused with influences and ideas from a diverse range of international sources including literature, political iconography, pop culture and fine art. An established Chinese multimedia artist, Song has widely exhibited work that examines the lyricism of the human body and responds to issues of isolation, identity and displacement. As such, her oeuvre alternates between contemplation and construction of narrative.

Kuzma Vostrikov has worked for over twenty years as a storyteller in film, fine art and literature. Vostrikov's own experience as an immigrant and artist contributes to the creation of an artistic dialogue that is both inclusive and experiential. A writer and philosopher, Vostrikov unites discourse on global politics, experience and fine art in his expansive oeuvre. The artist's photographs and films encounter and transform complex personal and socio-political stories and themes.

Together their vision invites dialogue about ideas of contemporary art, the intergenerational immigration experience, displacement, identity and offers an intersectional view of today's world.

—

1 Ajuan Song, Correspondence with the author, June 24th, 2020 (Archives of the Author).

2 Excerpt from Kuzma Vostrikov's novel *Just to Land in Tokyo*, p.25.

3 June 24th, 2020, Archives of the Author.

4 This approach connects work of Song and Vostrikov to the legacy of American photographer Cindy Sherman.

5 Vostrikov. June 24th, 2020, Archives of the Author. This image also refers to Luis Buñuel and Jean-Claude Carrière's 1972 surrealist film *Le Charme discret de la bourgeoisie*.

6 Ibid.

7 Other important sources include Luis Buñuel and Salvador Dali's 1926 film Un Chien Andalou. An additional theme of this series is that of a coercive culture of assimilation.

8 If we understand the development of this series within the context of the birth of Surrealism one hundred years ago we will see parallels. It has long been said that European Surrealism emerged from the great suffering endured during World War I. Of particular note are the expatriates whose displacement in America meant a certain dissonance between the prevalent culture and artistic movements with the experience of the artists.

9 June 24th, 2020, Archives of the Author.

10 Ibid.

HANS AND YUMA: A NEW YORK LOVE STORY

—

Jonathan Goodman

In *Just to Land in Tokyo*, Hans, a German photographer, and Yuma, a Japanese rock singer and bass player, meet in a Lower East Side bar where she is performing. Or at least that is the beginning of a scenario that may or may not be true, being the story of Hans' overheated imagination regarding a girl who may be completely imaginary. As the narrator of this idiosyncratic tale, Hans is given to wild flights of fancy, in which Yuma serves as an Oriental goddess and a siren of desire, and a friend in New York's postmodern hipster culture. The book's format comes close to that of a monologue involving events that may never have occurred – in the end, we are not entirely sure that Yuma ever existed at all. But the drinks and the flirtation at the bar seem real enough, even if Hans is never able to find Yuma again, although he knows where she lives. Much of the language seems both highly realistic and entirely imagined. Much of it is fantasy, as is the extended meditation on Yuma's body and underwear. Details are luminous, even hallucinatory, but they do not fully contribute to a believable story.

Even so, the believability does not matter, as this novel has been composed as a fable of love. Yuma disappears and is never seen again, although there are realistic scenes in which she sues Hans for money and is seen making love – or is the person screwing actually Yuma? There is a hostile exchange that occurs between the male stud making love to Yuma and a beleaguered Hans, who never fully identifies the girl as Yuma. Yuma is the key to the mystery of this contemporary morality play, appearing or not appearing as a real person according to the imagination of the reader. She allows Hans, who is a vehicle for the author Kuzma Vostrikov, to enter into an extended meditation on beauty and love, in the sense that her attractiveness, along with her ability to exist and not to exist in the narrative, becomes the subject of fantasy nearly philosophical in the distance between her description and the reality that originated it. The other major character of affection, beside Yuma herself, is the city of New York – a place rather than a person. Descriptions that particularly stand out are the wooded area in the boat basin, where Hans supposedly has hanged himself, and the beautiful, extended treatment of New York in winter, after a heavy snowfall.

Indeed, the kind of connection we find in the flash romance between Hans and Yuma is the kind of event that happens easily in New York, famous as it is for its many communities of different cultures, in which the pleasures of love occur across cultural, ethnicity, language, etc., often on a spontaneous basis. In actual life Kuzma Vostrikov works with the Mainland Chinese artist Ajuan Song on photographic collaborations that emphasize a fashionable Surrealism. One has the sense that the novel glides across a romantic narrative, in which different people from different cultures fall in love – even it the affair is a fiction of the mind. That said, the atmosphere is entirely believable, making it hard for the reader to separate truth from what is imagined – just like real life! Vostrikov knows that the imagination is the battlefield here – he suggests that the flights of fancy Hans seems to be employing are not entirely based in the mind; their reality is believable because of the details put into experiencing. Yet Yuma remains entirely elusive. Our unknowing – our need to suspend our disbelief in the face of events that seem mysterious and symbolic – also serves as a metaphor for a larger ignorance about why things happen the way they do.

The larger implicit issues of this novel don't have as much to do with the love story – which is of course deeply important – but about notions of creativity, both in the lives of the characters and as a general theme in and of itself. Hans is imagining things... He may well have met Yuma, but the extended meditations he engages in are free-fall examples of romantic thinking, close to hallucinatory in their particulars. After the first exchange in the bar, Yuma disappears, leaving Hans with his thoughts. She seems to be that once-in-a-lifetime girl who has slipped away. But Yuma is also the starting point for Hans' thinking on female beauty and desirability, as well as musicianship and singing. His speculation is inspired because of her erotic pull – pages are spent on her body and clothing. The details create an aura of truth that surrounds what looks like, by the end of the novel, an extended philosophical treatise on the transcendent gift of attraction – in a classically contemporary form. Hans suffers for his love, but that is not quite the point of the novel. It seems that he rises to the occasion of his obsessive feeling, writing in ways that do justice to a slightly shadowy figure with whom he seems to have only spent one evening. Yuma is gorgeous and exotic, and also unavailable and dangerously free – to the point where late in the book, someone unknown seems to be shagging her. (But she is never fully identified.)

Women's exoticism is part of the New York scenery. New York's streets, covered with strewn garbage, and inhabited by deracinated and nondescript, often surly people from all over the world, form the negative backdrop that contrasts with the slender beauty of the Japanese musician. Yuma may escape her surroundings, but for Hans, they are a part of his captivity in a romantic sense, which he eludes by making up stories. So in some ways this is a meta-novel: a novel about the imagination itself, with the right of the imagination to insist on a high road in contradistinction to the filthy, sodden streets and psychic indifference of a major city like New York. There is something deeper, more culturally dialectical as well: Yuma is a magnificent flower that occasions lust; one of the high psychological moments of the novel occurs when she asks Hans to kiss him, and for some reason he loses his nerve. But the desire is mostly originated by Hans, who falls completely for the otherness of a Japanese temptress (one wonders what Yuma herself feels in the situation). Desire, in this novel, becomes an occasion for its unreliability as a truth and Yuma's erotic evasiveness – Hans never beds down his Japanese girl, but only chases her without seeing her again. The hopeless but beautiful pursuit keeps the novel going, in large part because Hans never achieves his goal.

What else can be noted about a novel that delivers everything but the girl! Jessica Mroz's translation from the author's Russian is excellent, being abundant in unusual adjectives paired with less unusual nouns. Technically, the story hangs together very well, acknowledging high emotional points as a way of breaking through the meditative thinking of which the novel is often made. There is then the shift, back and forth, between the thoughtful atmosphere of Hans' musings and the moments that intrude: the extended futile searches to find Yuma, her decision (imaginary or not) to sue him, the shock of seeing her being loved in the apartment next to his – the one he rents in pursuit of finding her. Despite Hans' suffering – at one point, in another emotional crossroads, he is described as committing suicide, although a few pages later, it is made clear that this never took place – what comes across more than anything else is the sanctity of love, not idealized love but the love of a city convergence – not without erotic fervor – between two people coming from far away. This by itself is inherently romantic as an encounter, but author Vostrikov makes it clear that the interaction – if it is in fact real – would be difficult from the start. One might generalize and say that love always presents difficulties, but the two protagonists here seem poorly followed by the stars, that is, they succumb to a fate that consumes because it consists of unfulfilled love.

So what can be said about a novel that is not a novel, a beautiful girl that may well exist only in the imagination, and a current culture that regularly undercuts real feeling in favor of fantasy. You might think that sex would be the glue holding the narrative together, but eroticism in this story is an occasion for romantic wonder as much as it is an occasion for lust – we remember that in the middle of the book, the words "I love you" appear in as many languages as Vostrikov can fashion. Yet it is also true that the strength of the story turns on the tension between its melancholic realism and a place in the mind where love truly exists. Good realistic storytelling always encompasses the imagination in ways that do justice to the book's events, even if the events are mostly made up. But then fiction in general is an imaginary construction, is it not? The losses that occur in Hans' life and thoughts are of a piece; they cannot be separated. The event cannot be severed from the imaginative milieu and commentary surrounding it. As I have said, the realism of the novel comes from Vostrikov's sharp handling of details, which offset the less realistic tenor of the writing in marvelous ways. If it is true that the entire story of Hans and Yuma is a dream, we can only acknowledge its sharp images and closely detailed events. Perhaps, Vostrikov is implying, we are all living in a world of fantasy, offset only by the moments when the fantasy assumes, usually only momentarily, elements of truth.

So what can be made of a novel that is not a novel, a story that likely exists only in the mind, a narrative we are unable to believe in? In this sense, *Just to Land in Tokyo* is completely a contemporary novel, being an extended series of what ifs, buttressed by a fully believable realism that turns out not to be real. In the end of the novel, when Hans is arriving in Japan, his fantasies are immoderate and unstoppable. Even so, we cannot be sure that the landing actually took place. The gap between what might be and what really took place is Vostrikov's most comfortable theoretical site in this novel, engending doubt, which is surely the last emotion we could wish for in a love story. Sadly, though, this seems to be the way the times are going – we move into interstices of paralysis, in which our desire fails to open doors. Yuma is a sexually attractive young woman whom Hans cannot resist –who could? But on a deeper level she is a figment of the imagination. We do learn some new things in the novel – we learn a bit about music, a fair amount about New York as a platform for romance, and the complicated connection between our desire and the reality of fulfilling it. So *Just to Land in Tokyo* is a very sophisticated treatment of a very old theme: a love story between two people from vastly different, if not actively oppositional, cultures.

It isn't that Vostrikov very heavily accentuates the differences between the two lovers, although his erotic musings are predicated on the exoticism of an exquisite girl from Japan. Really, the novel is about desire, whose limitations and frustrated hopes lie at the center of the book. Hans is a young man without a woman – always a vulnerable circumstance. His feelings are occasioned by the distance Yuma assumes in her relations with him, emotionally and physically. The more troubling aspects of the novel – her supposed suit and the shagging episode – seem real enough, at least in Hans' mind. But Vostrikov allows for the possibility that this is untrue – and how can it be verified, if the entire story is something made up, being a work of fiction. We are living in a time of deliberate lying in politics, just as we are committing our personal lives to public scrutiny. One of the great strengths of *Just to Land in Tokyo* is its capacity to take these unattractive qualities of contemporary life and turn them into something imaginatively supple, so that the narrative thread achieves, at times, both the verisimilitude of actual life and a romantic view driven by love. Why would Vostrikov go to the lengths that he does in order to pass off the imagination as truth? It is part of the spirit of the time, when we take our visions, our visions of love and desire especially, as more genuine than the realities that originated them. Yuma may not exist, but that hardly matters. She is alive in Hans' mind, and in our own, due to the skills of the book.

GUEST ON
JUST TO LAND IN TOKYO

—

Anthony Haden-Guest

In the earlier years of the form photographers would often feel free to play around with the available bag of tricks, whether in the darkroom or in real life. Occasionally this would be so even while documenting historic event, as when the highly regarded American Civil War lensman, Alexander Gardner, hefted a soldier's corpse from the rather ordinary place where he had met his end into a more compelling setting to create *Home of a Rebel Sharpshooter*. Fast-forward to Henri Cartier-Bresson, who would sometimes shield his camera in duct tape so as to prevent his subjects' awareness of the process from tainting the product. Magnum, the group of photographers of which Cartier-Bresson had been a founder, was a secular priesthood: Reality ruled, and it was unalterable, that was their moral law.

But hello! The wave of iPhonery has come crashing in, along with the shape-shifting wizardry of high tech and the visual slanguage of social media. Together they have swept us into a time when the medium I grew up working in cahoots with has become so over-used, so weak and so mock stylish as to be terminally drained of effect. Or so it has seemed. Kuzma Vostrikov is proving me wrong.

Vostrikov, who is Russian, works with Ajuan Song, a multi-media artist born in China. Here I focus on their photo project, *Just to Land in Tokyo*, which has been chosen because Vostrikov has also given that name to a fat novel-in-progress (A very po-mo move this, by the way. Bjarne Melgaard, another artist/ disruptor, has also put out a novel as an art project).

The photograph chosen for the cover shows a man expressionlessly confronting the viewer. He has what looks like a four-day shadow and his explosive afro is the same unlikely crimson as his jacket. A lifesize golden lobster is dangling from his neck and his eyes are shielded by golden spectacles, which are slitted in a way that should remind fashion cognoscenti of the space-age eyewear of Andre Courreges, the French designer who went supernova in the 1960s.

That man represents "Hans," a German immigrant to New York who is the protagonist in the novel but in actual fact the man is Kuzma Vostrikov, likewise an immigrant, who came to New York in 2013. And he makes it clear that the 1960s references in the image – the afro, the eyewear – are no accident. "I feel I live in the 60s," Vostrikov says. "Even though I was born in 1977 the 1960s is my home. So I remember the time when everybody thought about space, about romanticism. You can wear a spaceman suit or Salvador Dali's lobster, it's all the same. We want to live on the moon, on Mars."

He and Ajuan put a year of work into this photo project. "Four months of preparation, two months shooting and a couple of months of post-production," Ajuan says. The disciplined energy required indicates that *Just to Land in Tokyo* is a thoroughly thought-through project and, given the goofily disparate elements which Vostrikov and Ajuan have yoked together to construct their images, it would be tempting to see it as a project in a Neo-Surrealist vein. Quite wrongly, I think. The Surrealists had sucked up what they needed from the then vibrant psychoanalytic culture and they had put together a program designed to release the powers of the unconscious by assembling a toolkit that included automatic writing, unsettling juxtapositions, pure chance and such potential random actions in the real world as firing a revolver into a crowd. The surreal was not about the real and Giacometti had been expelled from the movement – and, God, did they enjoy expulsions! – because he had had the effrontery to return to drawing from life.

Vostrikov's images are wholly differently made, otherwise intended. Like his words, they may be wild, but they are not irrational. He has a program, which is to explore the psycho-geography that he continues to inhabit as an immigrant. He always works from advance drawings so the images that he and Ajuan produce have been solidly pre-imagined in the round, although, as is the norm in art-making, changes can be made as work proceeds. The 19th-century Symbolists could be considered as temperamental ancestors, but, even more so, the fantasists of the late 19th and early 20th centuries, such as Lewis Carroll, George Melies, maker of *A Trip to the Moon* and E. Nesbit of *The Magic City*. And it's very much in keeping that the work of Vostrikov and Ajuan is painstakingly hand-crafted.

Another element in the work, and this is unusual in fantasy but a staple in advanced sci-fi, is the willingness of Vostrikov to indulge in socio-political messaging. In one such piece the man who confronts the viewer – and, yes, it's Kuzma again – is holding up a store mannequin, the demi-torso of a woman, which is headless and chalk-white, aside from the short lengths of pitch-black tape cut into an X that conceals each nipple. Identical black Xs cover his eyes. "They give us rules what to show and what not to show" he says. "So I make my own rules as to what I can see."

Indeed the thought of censorship, a tender area with anybody with even just inherited memories of the USSR, provokes a truly Kuzmatesque volley. "The institution of censorship never likes to fall behind the wave of technological advances," he says. "So it tries to weaponise its helplessness, pretending a wooden stick is an up-to-date laser weapon. Once upon a time, states just controlled newspapers, and that was enough. Then they decided to control the radio waves and they were quite effective at it.

"Then the internet appeared. And Instagram. How could anyone ban Instagram? It's a going concern. The shareholders would not be pleased. They need to eat too. Politicians figure they need to take care of morals but what can they do when everybody loves Instagram? That's why we see those delicious asses and boobs covered by small crosses. The cross is a deal between the masturbators and the guardians of order. Everyone is satisfied. Even the artist, because he has work to do, and he doesn't feel like jerking off. With these crossed-out eyes even the artist sees nothing he shouldn't, and the viewers barely notice him anyway because their eyes are distracted by yet another "censored" sticker on a rear end."

It figures that Vostrikov himself appears with some frequency in these images, as does Ajuan, and two other individuals also make a number of appearances: Andy Warhol and Chairman Mao. Indeed Warhol references crop up reliably every few pages in the book and in the photo project cut-out standing figures of Warhol himself or Warholesque references – platinum wigs, silver bananas and cut-outs of young Asian women, their heads reliably too large for their spindly bodies, and clothed in Campbell's Soup Can dresses – appear in different configurations in a dozen photographs.

This startles at first, then seems absolutely spot-on. Andy Warhol, like Pablo Picasso, Marcel Duchamp, Salvador Dali and Frida Kahlo, has become an artist whose image/images have become so much a part of the popular image bank that it seems to be assumed that they are fair game for others, including other artists to use. Indeed, in this context even the appearances of Mao, who appears both as a cut-out and as a bronze statue, and who certainly remains a powerful presence in Ajuan's native land, takes on a distinctly Warholesque resonance.

I wondered just how Vostrikov came to focus on Warhol. In 1987, the year of his death, the artist had been gossip-column famous, but he had been very much on the Art World B List. He was not considered in the same league as Roy Lichtenstein, Claes Oldenburg, James Rosenquist, nor was he fetching remotely the same prices. What kind of a figure had Warhol been as young Kuzma was growing up?

"He was big and well-known, of course, in Russia," Vostrikov told me. "But the most funny thing is that my father very much resembles Andy Warhol. And he did projects about that. He made himself up and then he and other artists did photo projects dedicated to Warhol."

This interest only intensified after they had arrived in Warhol's home town. "My father's problem was that he was an immigrant and he could not get used to this situation," Vostrikov says. So he took a role model. Warhol was an artist ... a businessman ... a socially active person ..." And Kuzma memorialized this in his own fashion. In one of the images in JTLIT Kuzma's father has a plump old-school crown in front of him and Kuzma is wearing a graffiti crown, a borrowing from Jean-Michel Basquiat.

"This is two Kings of Pop Art," he explains, capitalizing the words.

"Bonnie and Clyde, Kasparov and Karpov, Romeo and Juliet, Micky and Mouse, Cartier and Bresson, Lennon and McCartney. The list could go on forever. Two generations have met in Pop Art's full armor to pose one hard day's night in front of the cameras on the road to the fame they deserve. Le Roi est mort, vive le Roi!"

Other images swamp the Immigrant. A blonde, likewise wearing a Basquiat crown, blows him a kiss. He is wearing solid gold spectacles, a pink wig, that Daliesque lobster again, he sports toy baby hands on each finger and he is clutching a silvery toy duck. In another he wears Warholesque silver bananas, like learner horns, and in another holds two white balloons with protuberant fingers and thumbs. "It's just a kind of Pop Art noise. He doesn't know who he is .... he likes to watch TV, to watch elections. He doesn't know who he is. He's lost his identity, his aura."

This is Hans/Kuzma, this is The Immigrant. And who is his saving grace? *Andy Warhol was the first Don Quixote of the digital evolution, a Che Guevara of computer networks*, he has written elsewhere. And there's a set of images in *Just to Land in Tokyo* that hauls the Vostrikov/Ajuan vision center-stage, set-ups which feature multiple cut-outs of Warhol, Mao and a trio of young Asian woman, whose heads seem rather too big for their bodies and each of whom is wearing an identical Campbell's Soup Can dress.

"This is my circle. And Ajuan's circle too," says Vostrikov. "This is the world that the main character in *Just to Land in Tokyo* built. "Look! Andy ... Andy ... Andy ... There are three Andys."

"AND Three Maos," said Ajuan.

"Three Maos. It's a party!" Kuzma Vostrikov crowed. The soupcan dress is the real thing?

"It is. It is. Recently Ajuan saw that the dress was on sale for $3,000. From Campbel's Soup. I don't know how many copies they did,"

I pointed out the disproportionately large heads.

"Proportions here are not perfect. It doesn't matter. The heads *should* be bigger."

Kuzma Vostrikov has also written of Warhol: *Fifteen minutes of fame, it looks like an eternity.* So it does. And *Just to Land in Tokyo* is both agreeable evidence of that and a brilliant and provocative project in its own right.

Anthony Haden-Guest
New York
2018

Novel by
Kuzma Vostrikov

JUST LAND IN TOKYO

Photos by
Ajuan Song
Kuzma Vostrikov

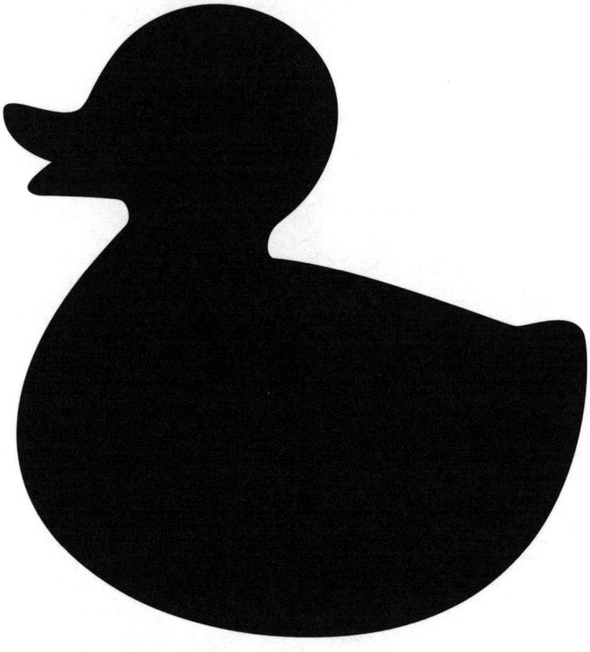

CHAPTER 1

Good evening, Yuma.

I'm writing to you as if you were the real Yuma and not just the paper decoration on an easel.

My uncle died while sitting on the couch in his house near Dubrovnik, his arms folded across his chest, under a window plastered over with newspaper. He fell asleep after lunch and never woke up. But why would you need to know that?

He was my father's brother. I spent a lot of time with his sons, my cousins. My uncle was an artist and a dreamer who lived among his books. His entire family had long been living in Dubrovnik when The Wall was built. They had settled in a two-story house for artists right on the mountain, in the forest among the pines, where city life, work, and the hustle and bustle gradually forgot about them. It seemed as if no war would ever make it there. But a shell did once land right in the courtyard, exploded, and blew out the window frame.

Despite his artistic talents, my uncle loved cars and would work on his old blue Volvo for days on end, all the while washing the business down with some alcoholic liquid to make it easier. The sea was just a few steps from his home. Three hundred yards, to be exact. In a big storm, you could hear the surf crashing against the shore through the window at night, while the house kept its inhabitants warm with the coziness of its inviolable walls.

But my uncle was uninterested in the sea; he didn't even know how to swim. One summer we were visiting for vacation, staying in a small house nearby. We soon moved into my uncle's house, though—untouched by time, idiosyncratic, with a yard full of scorched grass, and books with the smell of century-old pages in the library on the first floor. Outside sat a record player and speakers. Miles Davis was Uncle's favorite. He had a record that sizzled more than the trumpet. The music played straight into the forest. And the pines, dancing, threw their needles down onto the record, which made the music even more alive.

We spent all our days at the sea, among the military vessels and the civilian ships docked not so far from us. The salty sea air, the hard and stale wisps of seaweed burnt by the sun, the flour-white color of the marl on our clothes, and the aroma of the overheated cliffs. Uncle sat in his clothes on the shore, sketching in pencil. Not once did he touch the sea. But we never left it. The locals would go swimming, jumping off the pier, floating on truck tire inner tubes. The bigger the tube, the more authority was granted to its owner. The days weren't measured by any sort of time: they just stopped, stopped so that childhood would recognize no future. We placed hot white rocks on each other's backs after swimming and dried off in two minutes, dizzy from the heat. Streams of seawater poured from our noses: no matter how much we shook our head, the water wouldn't stop. And then there were the blackberry bushes and the thorns protecting their color and digging into your feet. The sweet, living, shiny, cloudy berries that settled on your tongue with their sugar-vanilla violet aroma. The flavor of dust, summer, the glaring sun and the sea's salt on your lips. Again, we made running jumps from the pier into what seemed to be icy waters, deafened by the silence of the underwater world, then resurfacing into boiling childhood. At night it seemed that a frost had fallen after the sun had retreated. Your body shivered, your knees and legs hurt. And from that bliss you disappeared into a dream of the longest and happiest fairy tale. And although we were only there in that house for a few weeks, these memories still have not left me.

Today is a very hot day; it must be about ninety-three degrees Fahrenheit. My friends have invited me out of town, to some suburb of New York. They themselves haven't come, hinting that they were too busy. It's easy to hint at things in New York. I'm not disappointed, and I revel in the solitude. There is beauty and timelessness here, just like thirty years ago. The flies and dragonflies moving through the air. The same grass burnt by the heat. The sun warming your head. Existence melts, devastating any initiative or effort. A dream of reason filled with the bliss of the heat. My skin turns golden, developed by the sun like a photograph. My muscles move under my skin and cease to feel weary. It's like I'm jumping off the pier again.

I feel like the past, while it is spinning above me, is at the same time abandoning me. This brings me relief. Can you carry the same suitcase for years and years? There's not even a slight breeze. Every leaf on the thin tree branches is paralyzed in a pose of tranquility. I'm swimming alone, reveling in the warm water of the blue pool, the splashes of water, the shadows of trees, the flight of the birds, and the merciless, scorching sun. There's no difference. Life stopped about thirty years ago and hasn't moved an inch. Only now you're alone. What is that strange feeling—being alone in this desert, once full of people? As if they had just closed the door behind them having promised to return soon, then forgot their promise. But you're still waiting for them.

I swim unhurriedly, enjoying each breath and each waft of the breeze, examining the trees hanging over me. I feel so good that I want to forget New York with its puffed-up and inflamed cheeks. I don't want to go back to city life, where reason serves trivialities and illusions. I want to merge with nature and give her all the rest of my time while I study the fireflies, grasshoppers, and dragonflies that fall into the water. I want to go to the ocean and watch the sunset, hearing the whirr and rasp of the armor of horseshoe crabs in the water, listening to the whining of the mosquitoes, and watching the lights on the ships burning far away on the horizon.

The days flicker by one after the other, converging into an endless stream of celluloid. The water slips through my fingers to the bottom of the pool. The wind running from the past rustles the trees above. Midnight immediately follows sundown. Predatory animals scream in the dark, hunting and defending their patch of life. The same stone road goes down to the sea and the glaring sun ruthlessly commands time over all distances between the living and over the entire landscape of inner turmoil of people, insects, and animals.

In my lazy thoughts, weary from the heat, four Yumas are dancing by the edge of the pool to songs from the eighties. I'm also playfully dancing along in the water, surrounded by them. I swim over to the edge and carefully grab one of the Yumas by her lovely leg. The girl, pleased by the joke, falls into the pool's cold water with a shriek of satisfaction, escaping from the burning day. Her friends also hurry to cool off, and with sympathetic squeals collapse into the water like dominoes. They are all maidservants of the past, created by me from photographs and cardboard. So many years have passed.

But, it seems, I'm not alone!

Yours,
Hans

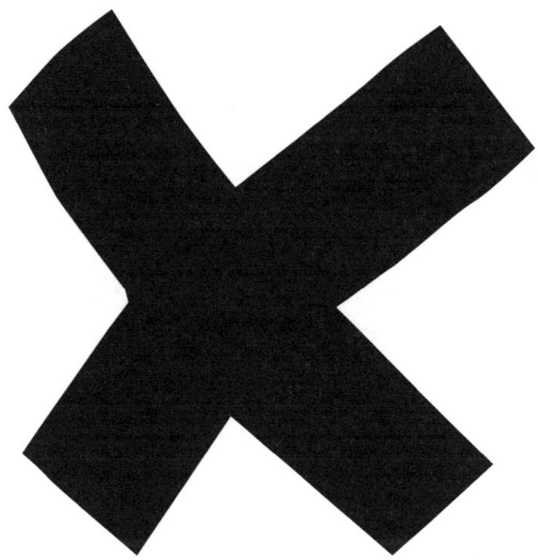

CHAPTER 2

Sometimes Hans would play soccer with his friends in Central Park. But they weren't really friends. They were more like new acquaintances to get together with and, instead of personal conversations that started with questions like "How are you doing?" or "How's the family?" which he didn't really like, he could juggle the soccer ball and use the useless energy of his sadness towards athletic achievement.

People, the sunlight in the evenings, his friends' weariness of bland adult life, the eccentric language, and the soccer field with its homemade goalposts connected Hans to the world, to a still-living network through which he plugged into the socket of life, accumulating hope. He needed people like he needed the air particles for breathing that flushed through his circulatory system. Usually, they kicked the ball around until they were utterly exhausted, or until twilight. Most often it was twilight; by that time their strength had been so depleted that they'd have to crawl off the field. And that was the inspiration. The addictive feeling of physical exhaustion was the true aim of playing soccer. Withered from the afternoon sun, running, whacking the ball, screaming, watched by skeptical onlookers, drenched in sweat, and embroiled in foot-to-foot combat, the players could barely make it home afterwards. Hans probably felt worse than the rest of them after a game, and because of that, each time, he would even more eagerly await the moment when he could give himself over fully to the exhaustion of his physical being, an insult to his shy nature.

Sometimes the ball flew at his face. It would hit him in the mouth or bash his nose, and the jolt from these boxer's punches would jolt his life as well, restarting the count from zero. Hans was not a weakling, but what separated him from many people was his determination to survive and his strange, stubborn essence. He was no soccer champion, but he would also never throw in the towel. He was always the last one off the field. And he always took the subway home, while some of the players were already calling taxis from the sidelines.

Hans was thirty-eight years old and weighed a hundred and thirty-eight pounds. On the whole, he was pretty well built, at least by the numbers. He was a bit naïve, a tad, it seemed, infantile, somewhat romantic, and a little shy. But he hid all these introverted qualities—they were imperceptible at first, thanks to which Hans gave off the initial impression of being soft, although secretive and maybe slightly neurotic. Instinctively, this last trait turned some people off at first. But, in general, Hans looked friendly and active, just as society required. A quick smile, enthusiasm for empty conversation, and a desire to participate in social activities at work and other routine things were sufficient to win people over. Hans kept all this up with ease if he wasn't being lazy, and soon doubters were convinced of his likability, never suspecting the other spaces behind his open eyes and digitally frozen smile.

Sometimes Hans' reactions seemed slow. The experiences he had had in his life would no longer allow him to be naïve and react too quickly to external events. He preferred to hide his true feelings, attempting to play the role of a kind of garrulous, open guy, whose shirt wasn't hiding a deep dark forest in his heart.

Hans could come off as an autistic, hard-hearted loser, choked by the weeds of his ideas about life. Like a beard that, bursting forth from inside him, has formed unintelligible hieroglyphs. People saw him as a lightweight character on a soap opera, who would play around just a little more annoyingly than his tired companions wanted to—his fellow soccer players, the rare friend, co-workers, his fifteen friends on Facebook…

They called him odd because Hans wasn't capable of relating to and communicating with people in the way that the rules of collective expectations demanded. He was brusque and paid for his brusqueness with the inevitable isolation. Reserved in speech, he also didn't much care about how people interpreted what he said. Hans played a tune that was incomprehensible, even inaudible, to those around him. He walked around like a hurdy-gurdy man, with an instrument that everyone could see but a melody that met the air without a sound, and no one knew exactly what it was that he was playing.

Hans' true, non-soccer face, hidden by the shutters of tiny, secret doors, was different. From his childhood, Hans had shown an ability for math, and when he was ten his parents put him in a math-focused school, where he developed his talents and soon became famous in East Berlin as the schoolkid who won the mathematics competition.

Had math brought anything useful to his life afterwards? Had it answered any questions for him? Hans had retained the ability that he had in school to concentrate and solve problems rationally—even when it concerned emotions. Math and science, in general, when combined with his reserved nature, often took the place of real, live feelings in his heart. But what made Hans' heart truly cold could not be easily explained by his tendency towards exactitude. It wasn't Hans' fault that it all turned out like this. It also wasn't his fault that he was hiding something important from the people around him. And he hid this with all his might and from his own memory too, which would sometimes come up, nibble away at him, threaten him, and torture him with that one solitary question.

Hans was utterly certain that everything didn't have to be like this. It didn't have to turn out this way. If it would have been possible to make time go in the opposite direction and change just one insignificant detail, the chain of events would have taken a different path. Sometimes he would turn this over in his mind a hundred, a thousand times. The regret he felt at not being able to go back and make the better, mathematically-verified decision ate away at his soul like poison. The white twin-screw coast guard boat, with its two spotlights, shone through the rain in the dead water. There was no chance to go even one second into the past, to not go outside in that icy weather, to refuse to swim in that cold water. It was only the past, having now become a reality, that knocked on Hans' present and had every right to, laughing at him all the way.

Everything that Hans hid from those people who couldn't understand, who were happy with their health, had to be hidden. He would often scream out in his sleep. He'd slam the door, locking all the locks and holding it closed tightly with his hands. But the unknown continued trying to bust it down.

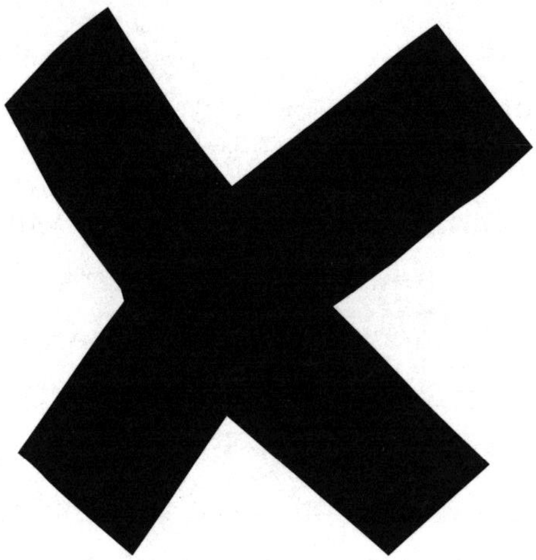

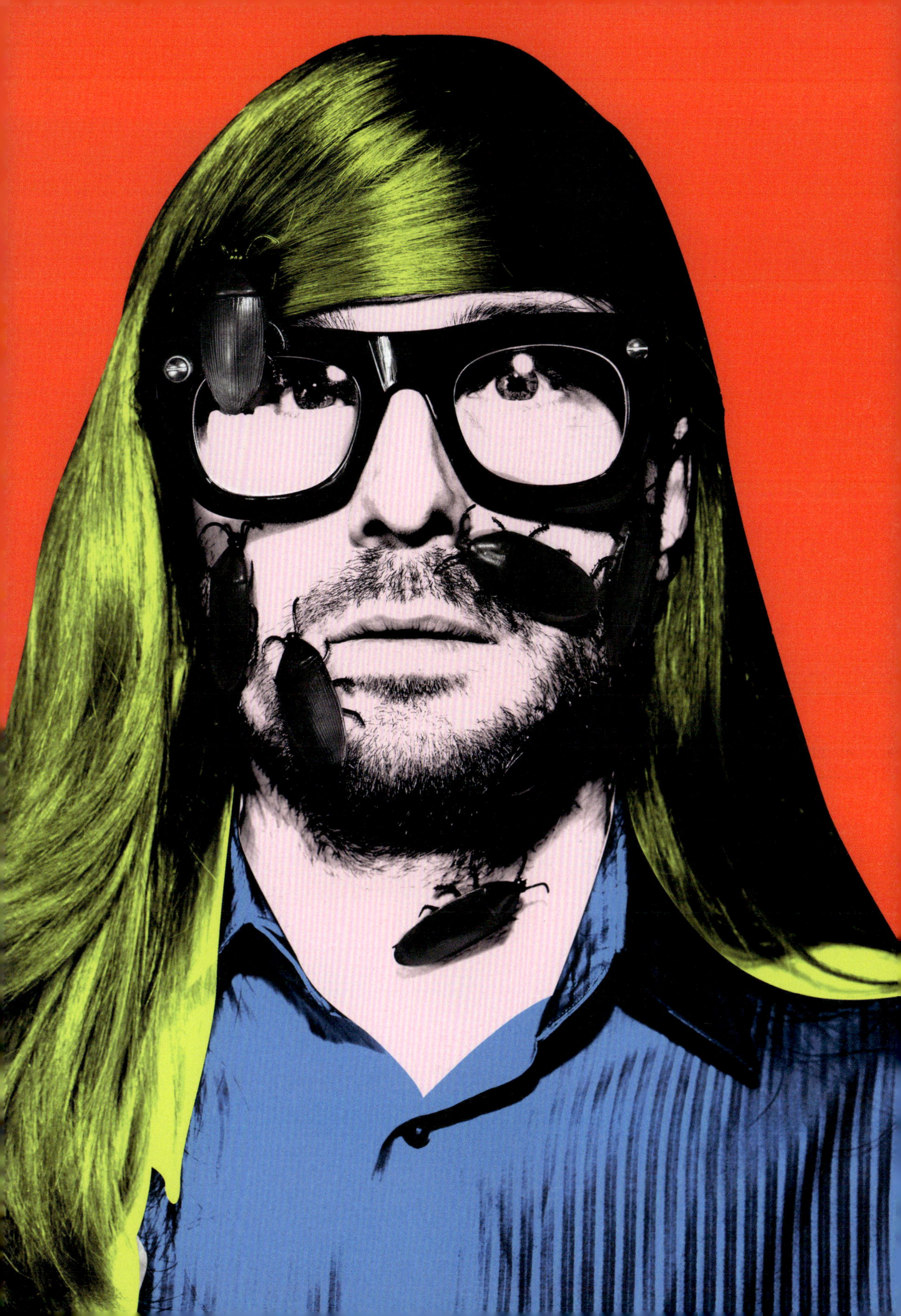

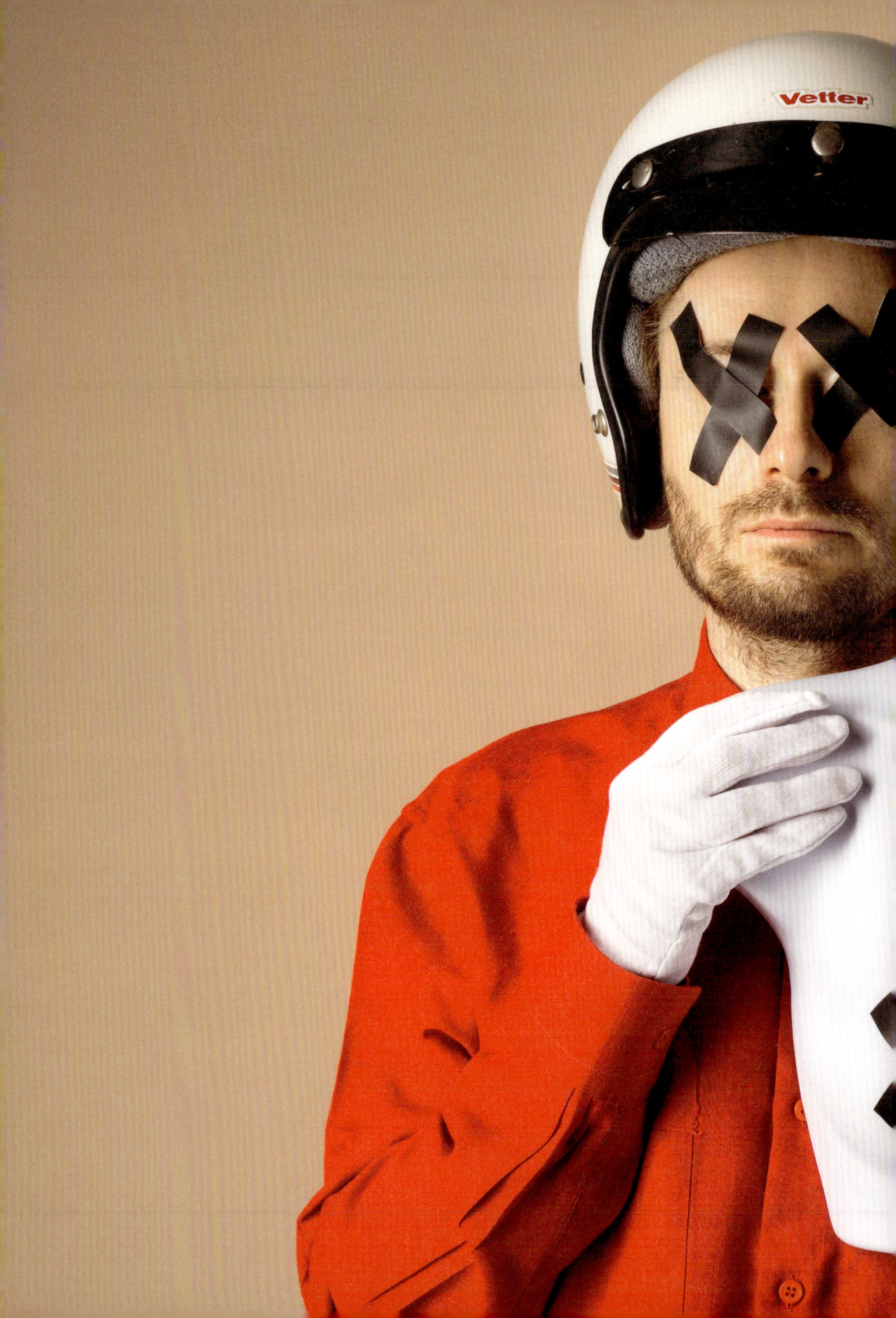
Vetter

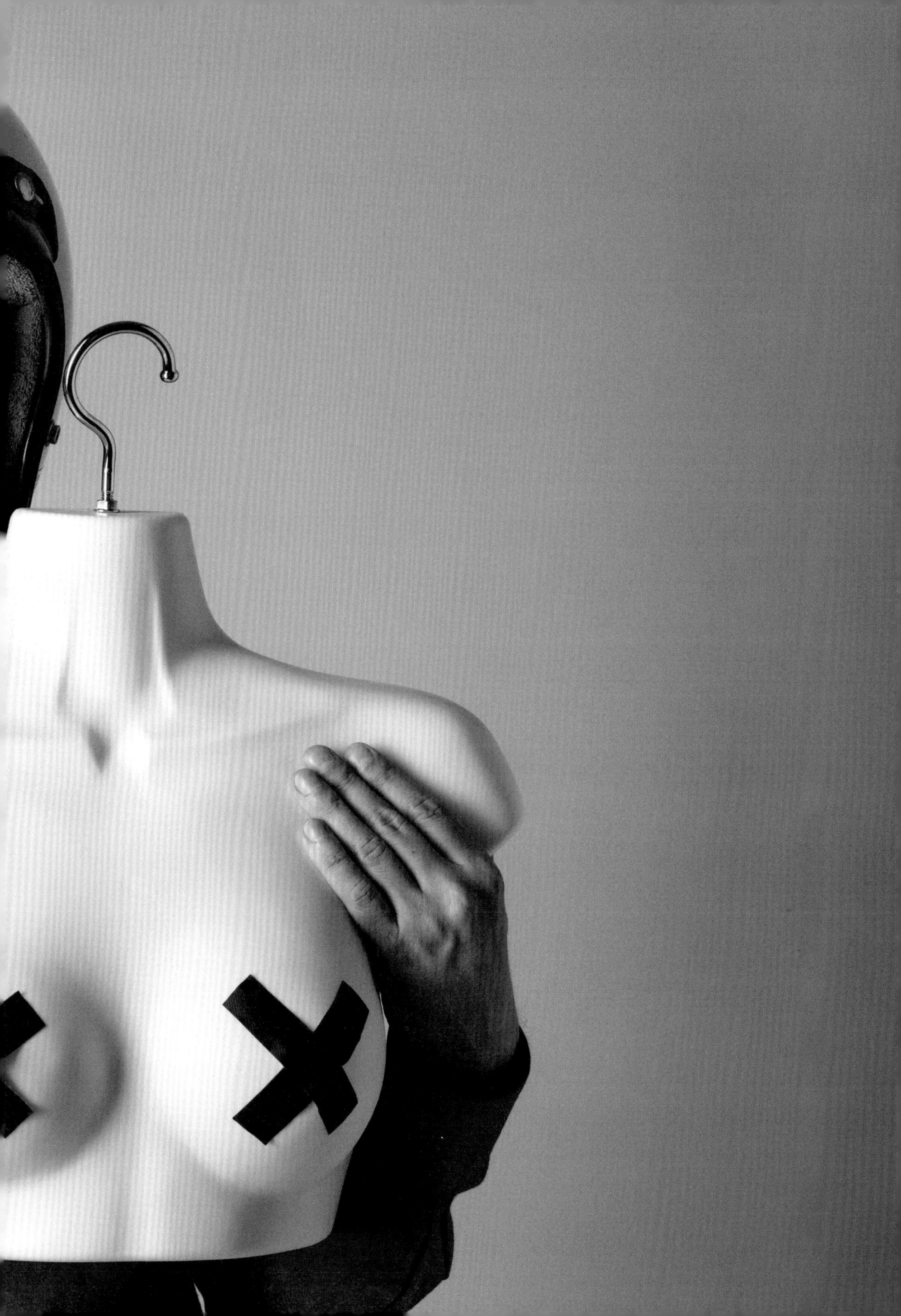

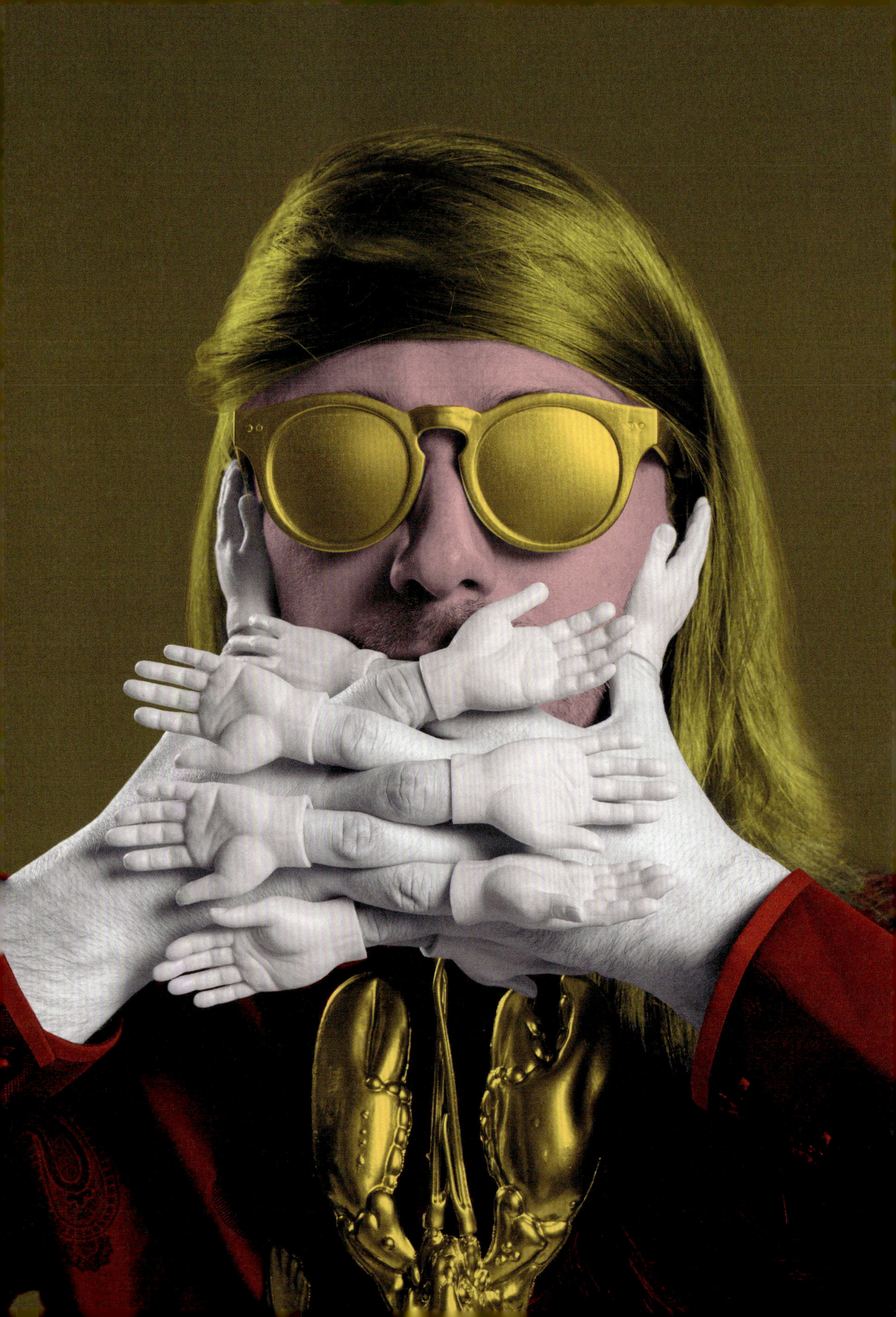

CHAPTER 3

It was the end of May. The hot and carefree spring evening was pushing nature to meet the sunset. The warm wind was ready to entice everyone into a happy summer with the possibility of swimming in the gentle turquoise ocean, salty air, and towels wet with seawater that took forever to dry and smelled like crabs.

Hans had gotten an e-mail that he was accepted. The joyful event jolted him, as was to be expected. It took his focus off everyday expectations. When sunrise and sunset become identical, daytime drowsiness becomes an eternity.

Hans was not an accountant or an engineer and didn't sit in an office selling paper or diesel generators. He was a photographer. A regular photographer, in terms of earnings. But he was a real photographer, in that he always served obscure lenses of the camera. He loved doing things that did not fall within the realm of necessity and were therefore seen as unnecessary for real life. Since he was in no way ashamed of this uselessness, he was able to express melancholy in a form and color that attracted viewers.

Hans sat on the veranda of his small wooden cabin in Florida and, as always, was writhing in anguish with his doubts. He tried to convince himself to feel emotions and taste life which, as time and the years slipped away, was pestering Hans with its uniformity. He would even use his fingers to shape his lips into a smile in front of the mirror. "If I can't stop time," thought Hans, "if I can't belong to myself… then why are we even given reason and comfort, which are only wasted in vain?"

The e-mail said that Hans was accepted to work as a commercial photographer at a well-known photo agency in New York—with no interview. All that was left now was to sign the contract and forget all the problems that were strewn across his floor in an even layer. Whatever was before, the remainder of his past life, Hans already could not remember. He packed his things.

The room in which he worked didn't seem to be part of his house. It wasn't particularly orderly and looked more like a studio. In the corner, there was a big photo enlarger on which Hans enlarged life and affixed it onto paper in black and white. Film cameras sat on a handmade wooden table like Russian nesting dolls, developing baths, film containers, chemicals, and packs of paper. The room was overloaded with frames, photo prints, and plaster casts, which Hans used for artistic photographs. He liked to draw sometimes too. The windows of the house were small, as is usually the case with cheap houses in the South. He had no air conditioner, so most of the time Hans didn't even wear a t-shirt, being used to the humid, warm, unchanging climate of velvety Florida. He didn't want to leave for good. Mostly he just wanted to jump to a change of scenery, leaving the reservoir of the past that so frightened him. The past was fixed to Hans with an invisible, loudly clattering chain.

Hans left all his things there, except for a few suit jackets, cameras, a portrait of his father sitting on a chair, and a box with photographs that were sent to him from Berlin ten years ago after The Wall had come down. He also shoved a few other insignificant trifles into his three large suitcases. And of course, the Andy Warhol album. He decided to toss everything else. Ronald, his redheaded friend and neighbor, promised to look after the house. But there was nothing much to look after—the house was tiny, and all the land around it was overgrown with eager tropical vegetation that occupied the territory of life, taking it from the weak people.

It was early in the morning. Hans went down to the ocean and spent some time on the beach looking far off into the horizon. The sun had not yet risen, and the cool of the morning promised calm to the day. Sanderlings were scooting along the sand bar. Hans could sit for hours watching their efficient and somewhat comical labors in their search for food. After Ronald, they were his best friends. He considered his character and lifestyle to be like that of these fragile little birds. Almost unable to fly, they preferred to run and keep to their tradition: scampering around on their feet in basically the same place for hours, days, years on end. Hans was just like them. He too would dart about, he was composed of thin bones, he preferred monotonous work, and he was drawn to the ocean. Maybe it was written in his DNA that he was a bird.

Afterwards, he went to see his father. But not for long. They didn't say their farewells then, though. Hans knew he would visit him many more times.

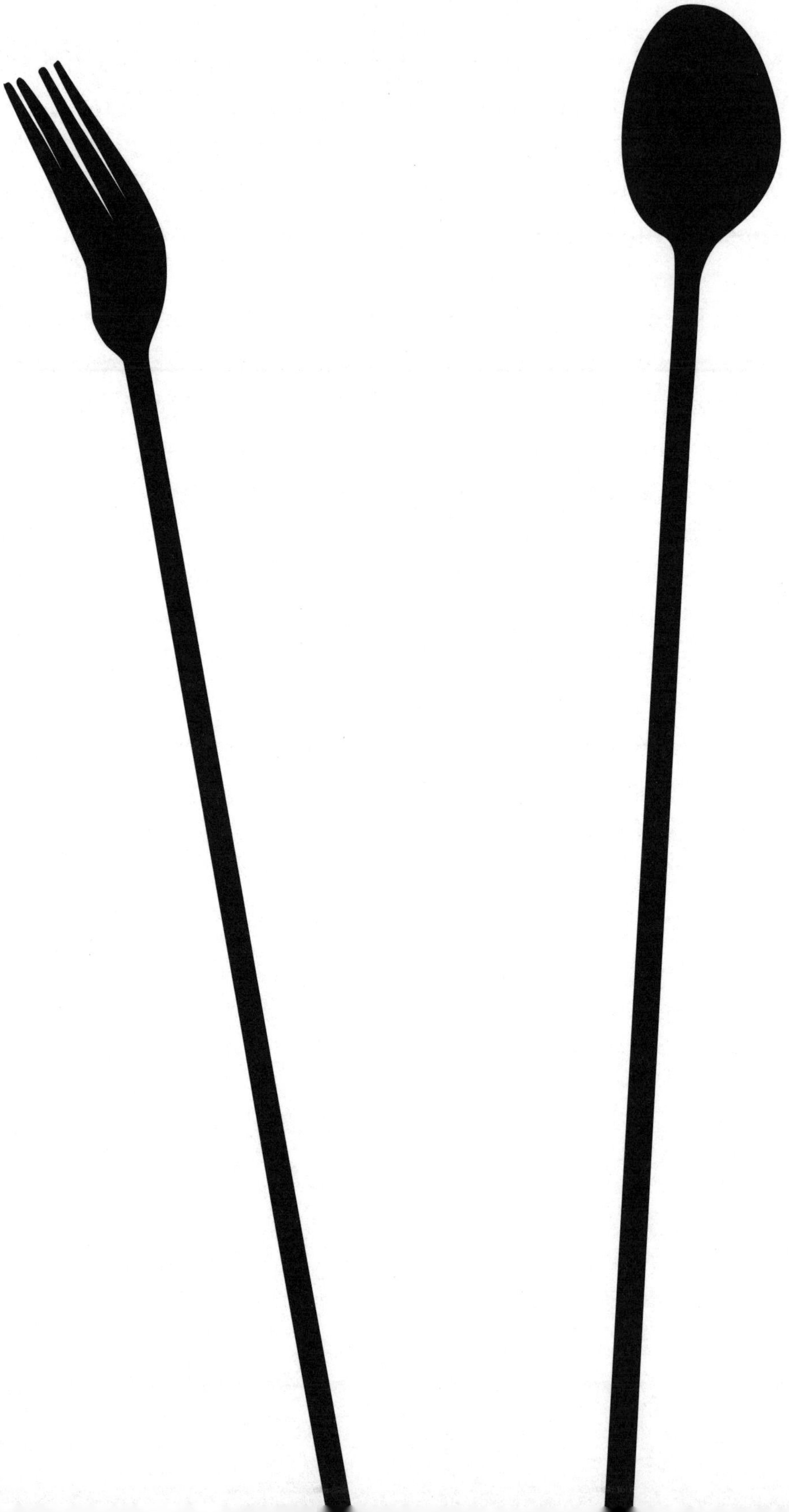

CHAPTER 4

Dear Yuma!

Greetings and, maybe, farewell. I want this last letter to be the most joyful one, the most intimate one.

Light travels from New York to Tokyo in just fifty milliseconds. I could read a book in that time and run out to get coffee and croissants. People these days are so lazy. But not me. Fifty milliseconds. Low latency. You can go through an entire life in that time, even having time to part company.

And still, with the power of teleportation, I'm right there next to you. I want to be with you. I would like to be with you. What could sound gentler?

And you in a dress.

But first, let's imagine those leather pants. I love putting clothes on you with the force of my mind. What else is left now?

I remember you walking around Manhattan in those leather pants, and your ass shone like a stoplight. I confess that I don't like leather pants much. But you look fantastic in them. Black, stretched tight—they allow me to get lost in contemplation of your legs and your rear end, hard and amazingly supple, like an Olympic trampoline. Your ass is tauter than the hardest baseball in the United States of America. It's so solid that Denver's Peyton Manning couldn't handle it. But at the same time, the tightness doesn't make it lose the weight of experience. I adore that.

The pants add a spark to you, and they spark an uncontrollable desire in me to follow you into any situation. Sometimes only pants can make a woman a woman. As if the rest is hiding in the shadows of her talents. But it's not like that with you. With you, everything glows.

But with me—I have nothing bright, no shining hope. I'm a pale engineer, an airplane designer. And the son of an airplane designer. My fantasies were always dull and flat. I was a student in glasses holding a slide rule when my fellow classmates were already walking around with their thickened little willies in their hands. All I could do was draw blueprints on the boards in the prison of my feeble-mindedness.

Even ten thousand pairs of binoculars couldn't have helped me see you from the hole that I was in. Let's say you even stripped, completely. Down to your soft, silky bush. The gardeners hadn't even given it its morning watering yet. And still, you would be just a tiny spot on the map of my retina. Only one of my cone cells, the nimblest of them, would have been able to discern you at all.

Yuma—faraway, wonderful, oscillating. With moon skin, glistening sorrow and tenderness. A passionate, eternal, young, reckless, reciprocal, aching harmonica that plays sadness on the front lines while sitting in the soldier's pocket. Stubborn Yuma. Take my prick in your hand. Make me say the word "prick." I'm shy. Breathe into me the breath of life. I was always afraid to get an F for those letters. Take my childhood, my virginity, Yuma. Pull me in up to my ears, into the dirtiest story.

Do you remember when I asked you to send me one of your eyelashes?

I made a mistake.

I love the hairs from your pussy. I suppose that phrase will be prohibited by the government. They're barbed wire, and everyone wants to cut their passionate lips on those sharp little spikes.

It's as if it's anointed. I'm ready to pursue you until I am utterly disgraced. I'm ready to humiliate myself, reveal the shame of my timid existence. That spot of yours pulls me in as if your bush were the only one in the world.

And it is, really. Just the thought of diving into it nose-first raises my temperature, and then immediately gives me chills. I imagine you abusing me and dominating me—in all the nonsenses of the word. You walk across my face in mud-covered boots, like an army of soldiers. When I imagine your chestnut grove, those hairs for me are like superconducting magnets. Each one of them gives off a thousand kilovolts, sucking me into Maxwell's equations. Everywhere, no matter where I am, no matter what I do, I feel the energy of your hair.

You are walking in front of me along the hot sands of the village river, and the swing of your hips traces Lissajous curves in black silhouette on the patches of sunlight. I crawl after you, like a wounded animal, hoping I won't miss your footprints at least.

At least to not be late for lunch?

Your legs could teach me everything that I have yet to experience. A woman is a how-to manual for someone drowning in a rippling sea. We men are mollusks, spineless fish swimming at your feet. Without you, I couldn't even conceive of a simple word. Just the presence of your flower gives birth to the possibility of my being brave enough to buzz.

I want you to be forever wet, and the best old person sex would be ours alone. Like tortoises, three hundred years old, shriveled in our shells from frailty, and the only thing we can still do is touch our bedsores together in the picturesque landscape of timeless Okinawa!

If you think that I was created for the entropy of physical energy, you're mistaken. I'm no fan of that shallow materialistic drivel. I am a scraggly fern, chosen by natural selection for extinction. There would be no difference between sex and going to the gym if not for the institution of creativity. Personal effort gives an engraving a meaning.

Dearest Yuma! I'm now again in Central Park, between the deep, noisy hairpieces of the trees, sitting at a table near the Metropolitan Museum, thinking of you for what I'm sure is the thousandth time. Stability calms me like nothing else. If I could, I would come here a million times. And that's indeed what I will do until, according to the theory of improbability, I meet you here with a bass guitar, walking along in red heels, delicately carrying your ass behind you. Sucking on a ruby rooster lollipop on a wooden stick. I would recognize you from afar since my eyes long ago turned into telescopes, polished clean by frustration. I, like Captain Hook, have been salted by life on the ocean, tensely peering into the maritime streets of New York in the hope of distinguishing your gait among the noise of the waves of life, seeing the springiness of your tanned legs. I remember well how they smell. It's October now. I hope to discover you before winter.

Yes, I'm going to walk around the streets of New York and look for you. In flea markets, in laundromats, in jewelry stores, and in the juvenile courts. At the opera, at the gynecologists, and at the fishpond. You're auspicious. Your figure is as noticeable as a queen on a chessboard who has lost her shriveled king.

Yuma! My knowledge of sex is so scanty and fragmented. I'm like a teenager who somewhere read about it in books, somewhere heard some stories of how it is done by the successful guys of the world, somewhere saw fragments of it happening—but, never participated in such good scenes himself. I mean, like a real procreating stag from the animal kingdom, with fantasies between my furry paws. Maybe this is because my face wasn't the most handsome, and I was bashful whenever I tried to come on to a woman? My world consisted of boring

undertakings and books laid away in floors and floors of dusty labyrinths.
I opened doors for female visitors who proceeded to run from me, like people running from a train coming towards them on a screen, billowing cigarette smoke from its chimney.

Can I say that something similar occurred with us? Of course not. The history of our love has only just begun. It exceeds all possible analogs of love, exceeds even the mass of the Universe!

Our love is more constant than Planck's constant!

Decrepit old Shakespeare, who has written himself tired, trembles from his Alzheimer's in the corner with a yellow puddle forming from the streams running down his legs. Sitting on the bedpan, like a depressing Nils on his geese, he envies the dramatic context of the fresh, shocking story that you and I are writing with our fountains of passion!

Romeo and Juliet are pubescent bedbugs that worked up a sweat by rubbing themselves together in the bushes at night. And that was considered the benchmark for love and the masterpiece of relationships enveloped in the history of literature. "Of course you know all of this." Their bleak fiddling about is simply absurd in the light of our comets. And do you not find the plight of young Werther humorous, who, looking at an old, dilapidated aunty with sagging breasts, began sniveling and wailing, hiding his pimpled, four-eyed face in a tiny German handkerchief soaked all the way through? And he just kept weeping till the end. Poor boy. I feel so sorry for him!

Our harmony is written on a hundred sheets of music. This symphony could be heard across continents, on the Llullaillaco volcano, in Fukushima, by schools of fish in the Pacific Ocean, in the clouds, between molecules of oxygen, in teacups filled with tea, under baobab trees in Africa, and under the hooves of antelopes throwing dust into the face of a tiger!

So, what is stopping this music from playing?

Me.

I let you get on the cheap train with the freight cars and scurry off to your fishing village. You were setting off for Tokyo, your cheap costume jewelry jingling. Going to a dirty flea market, behind which you couldn't see the foreign sun and shiny boutiques of New York. You were being baked, like bread rolls in a shabby country oven. The lines of perspective that divide the continents had shrunk New York to the size of an enchanted quark.

I didn't make you promise. I carelessly lost your e-mail. Out of spite, I wrote your telephone number down on the first losing lottery ticket I came across. I forgot and garbled your name, scattering the alphabets of three languages to the wind and tossing the suffixes in the water.

To you I seemed an ant the size of a match head, jumping on the threads of my legs in a tiny town. But I am a gigantic clod of a man, with an inner world that is developed beyond my years, and an intellect equal to a hundred and thirty chess players and eighty-one Immanuel Kants. I, whose octane number surpasses that of all automobiles. I, whose individuality is admired by cardiologists' oscillograms and psychiatrists all over the world! I, because of whom models break out in manicures. I, who make bearded hipsters in Keds get a sinking feeling in the pits of their stomachs! I, whose ski run stretches across the Kremlin and Putin's office, Central Park and Duke Ellington's piano, curves around Pyongyang's nuclear arsenal, goes through the Large Hadron Collider, penetrates Mount

Kazbek, makes its way through the pines of Sakhalin, and ends near the Japanese Imperial Palace. I, mighty and cunning, like a grasshopper, leaping, like a moon astronaut, persistent and ergodic, like the Dow Jones index. Full of sperm, like Hugh Hefner. Rattling the trumpet of my vinyl tongue, like the dead Miles Davis!

But I took you to the plane. Do you remember La Guardia airport? Do you remember how carefully you used your finger to support your suitcase so it wouldn't show more than fifty pounds on that small airport scale when you checked your bags before the flight? Do you remember how you used your charm to brainwash that Japanese lady-robot in her skirt costume? You little trickster! Do you remember how everything was all topsy-turvy, and I was standing right there?

Do you remember how you lied to me about the recording, when you went to the Blue Note Jazz Club with the first street cleaner you came across, just to get away from me? To drug yourself and vegetate away your starched royal beauty.

Do you remember how you blossomed bouquets in front of those New York macho men good at baseball, chess, and bullfighting? Wasn't it I who saw how you smiled even wider—not for me—when you were glancing at the tension of the plastic balls in their underwear that were resonating because of you?

I regret that I got cold feet.

If we were to stretch eternity out along a ruler and then place one inch of our history right in the line of vision, the whole of history wouldn't fit in that fractal. That means that your passion is not ready to cool down. The liquid nitrogen of male rationality has frozen your cheeks and eyelashes. Broken apart into myriads of shiny fragments, you, like a golden fly, have flown to a new, fluffier maggot. You dealt with me fairly, when you didn't even know or recall my name, address, height, taste, or color—your wings droning away somewhere at the other end of the galaxy. Like a true teacher, the likes of which I've seen thousands of times, so attractive during the lesson!

But we must sign the contract of eternal erotica. Your eyes would burn with the smoke of a thermonuclear explosion. You would look at me like a lioness, giving nature's victor your valuables. Like a female praying mantis, ready to bite off my head after I pull my tool from you! You heard correctly, Yuma. I love you. I love you as Mao taught. I love you wordlessly, directly. Without any intermediary cultures, plugs, sockets, or other electric stuff. I'm tired of waiting until these layers of cabbage leaves are removed from us. Until we hold in our hands bouquets and presents, fooling each other and creating an atmosphere of false reverence. Let me tear off your dress and corrupt you like the democracy of my personal fantasies! Like no man in any brothel has ever done!

Let me corrupt you in the worst way.

My memory whispers to me shamefully that I don't even remember how much calico material was used on your dresses and bras. I don't remember the true coordinates of your smile. My memories of you are hidden by the iron lattices of suffering that I hung over myself out of humaneness and languor. All that I forgot, in essence, was to take off your panties in time. You remained in that pseudo-chaste lampshade of a virgin, like a packaged scarecrow from a state institution.

But you didn't forget that evening, did you, when my teeth gripped the elastic of your panties, like a Viking hanging on a wild high cliff, ready to fall into the abyss? Do you remember the color and smell of that fluid that was longingly waiting for its hour to come to the surface and permeate the grass and mantle of the Earth in Central Park?

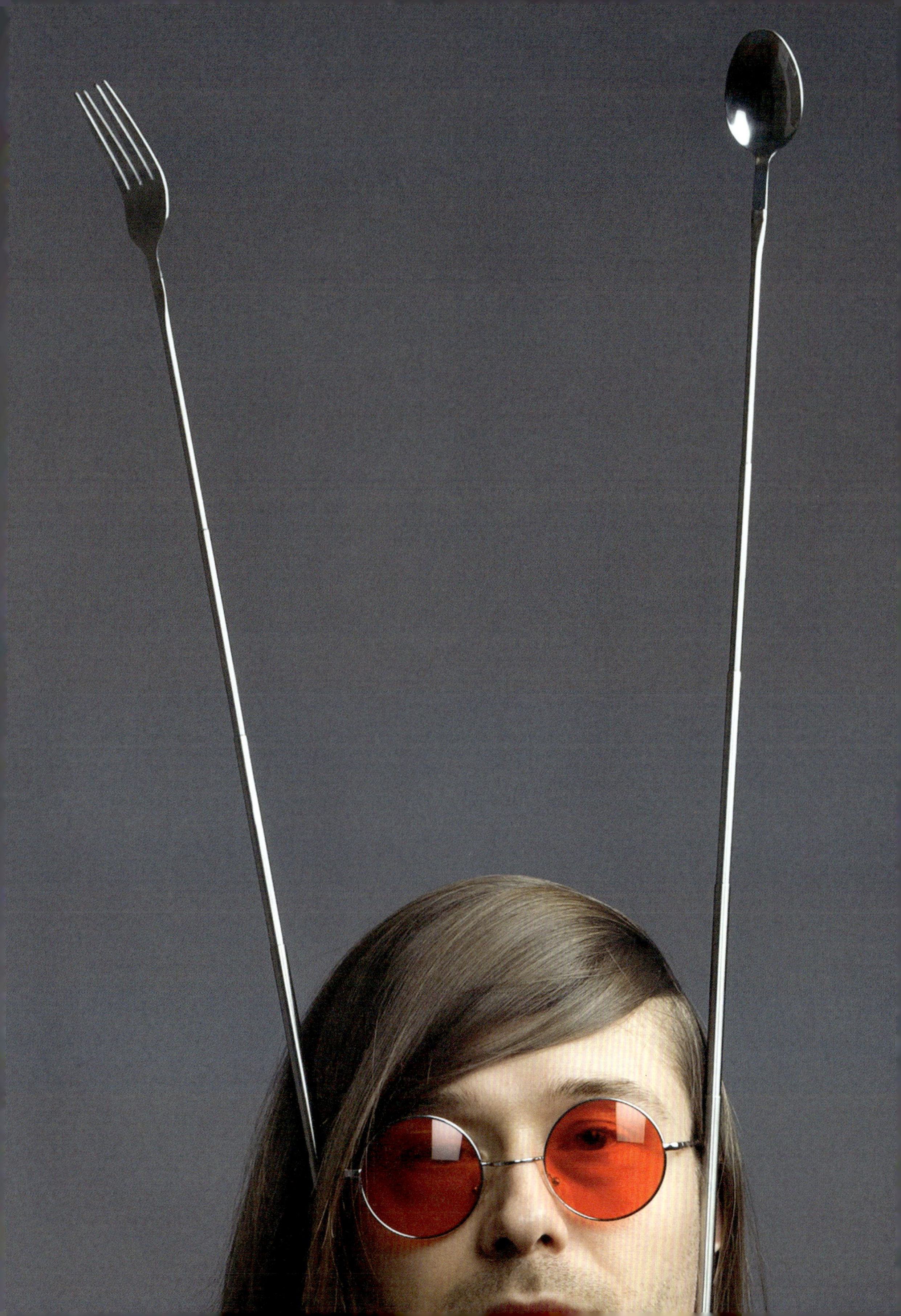

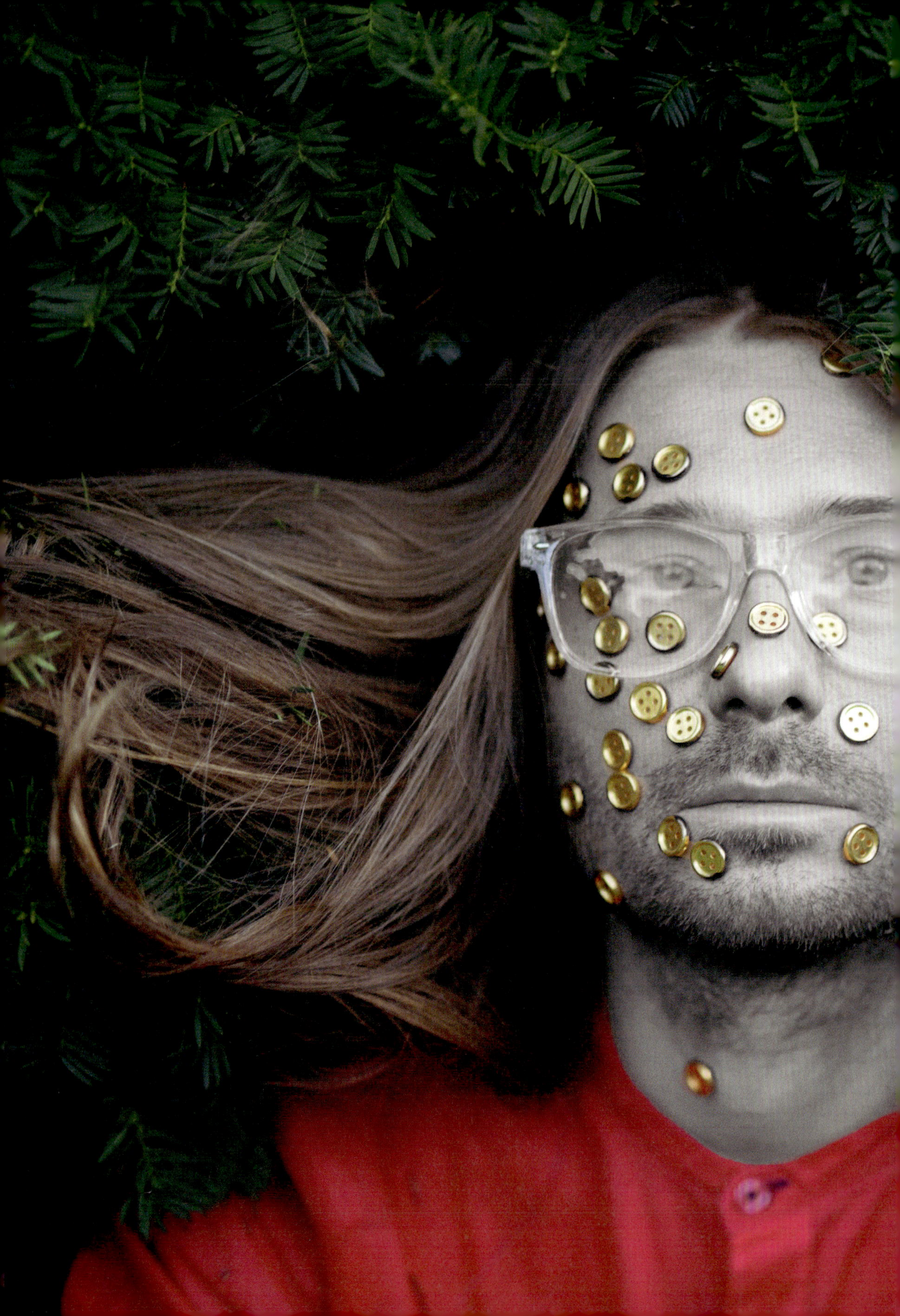

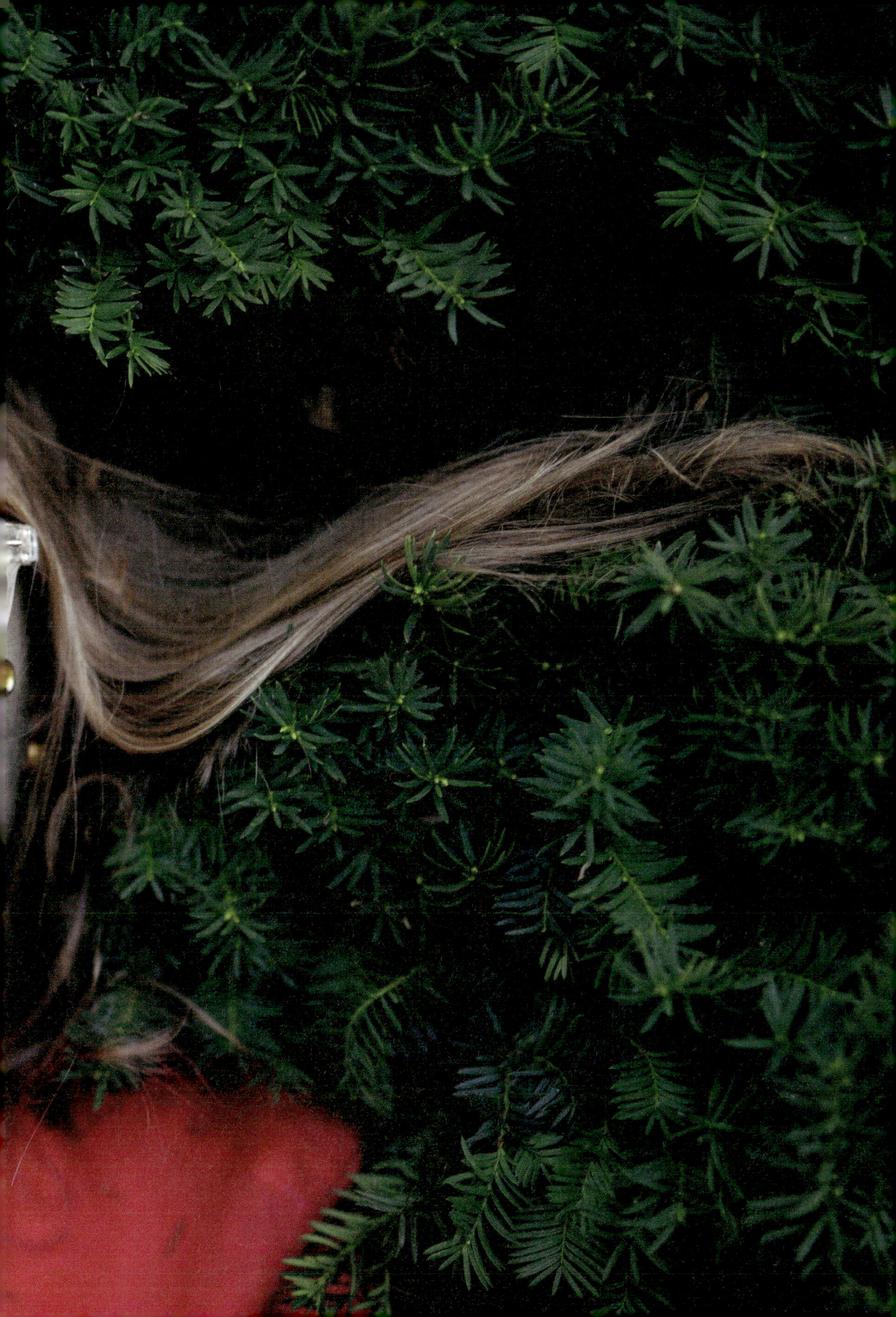

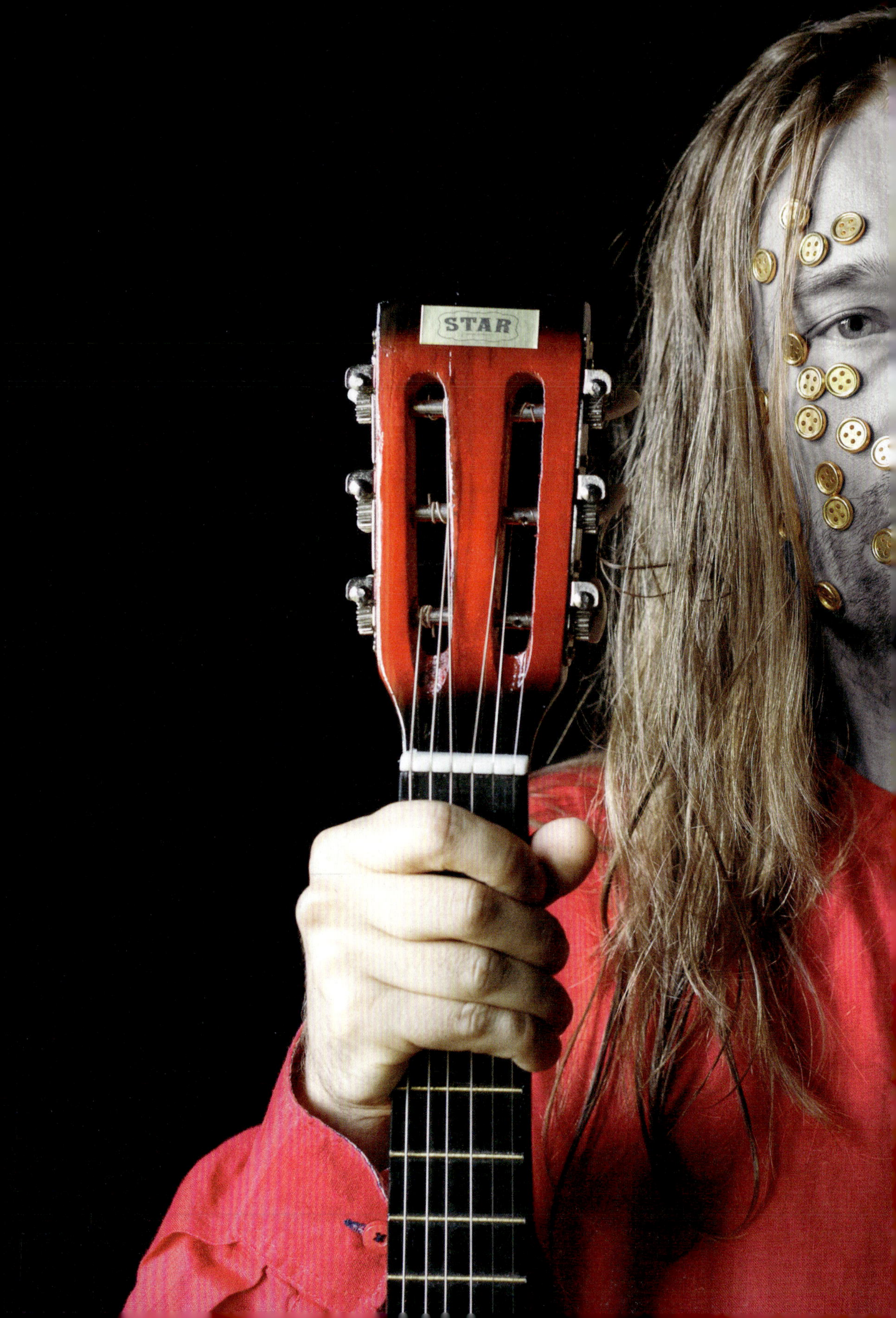
STAR

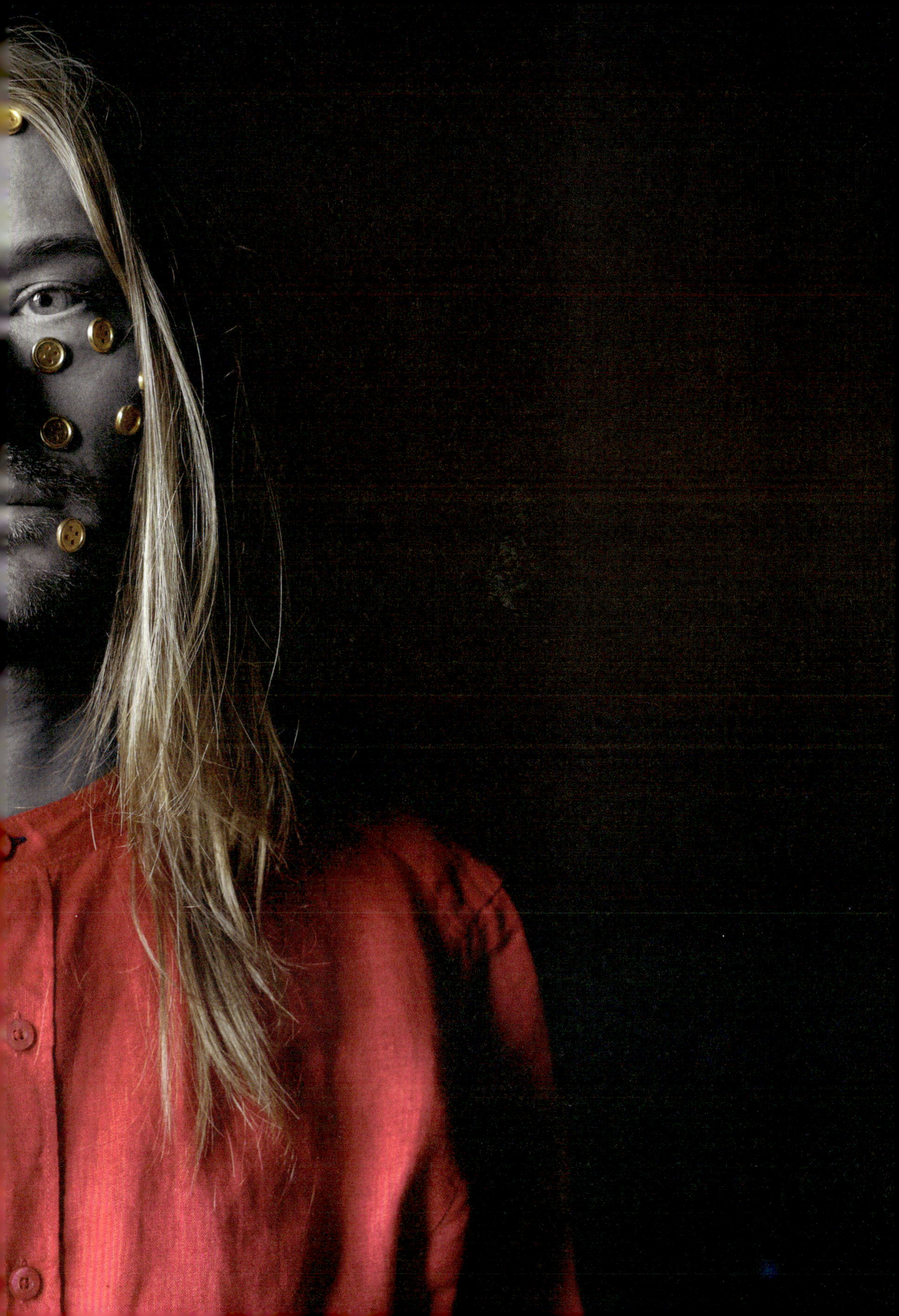

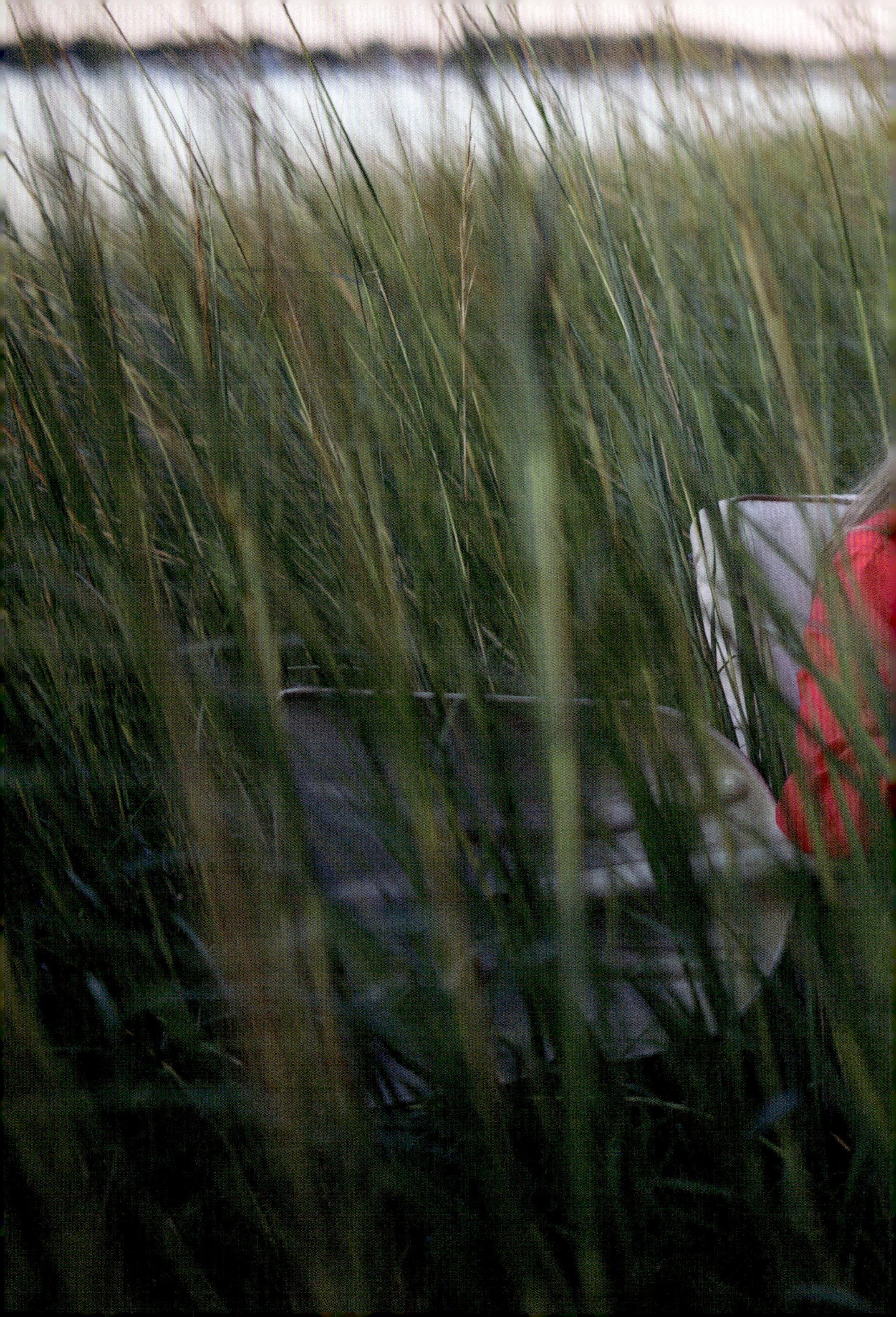

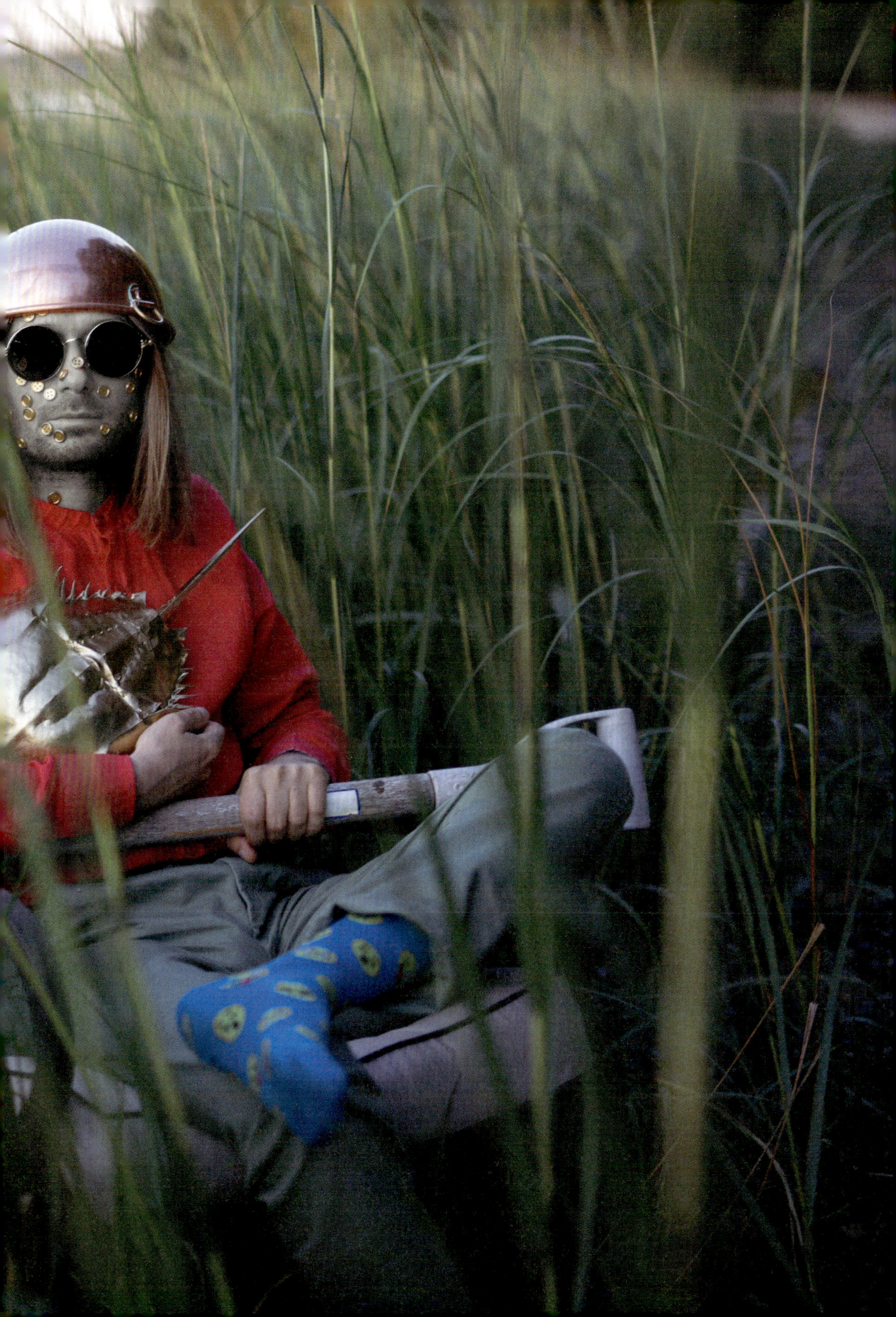

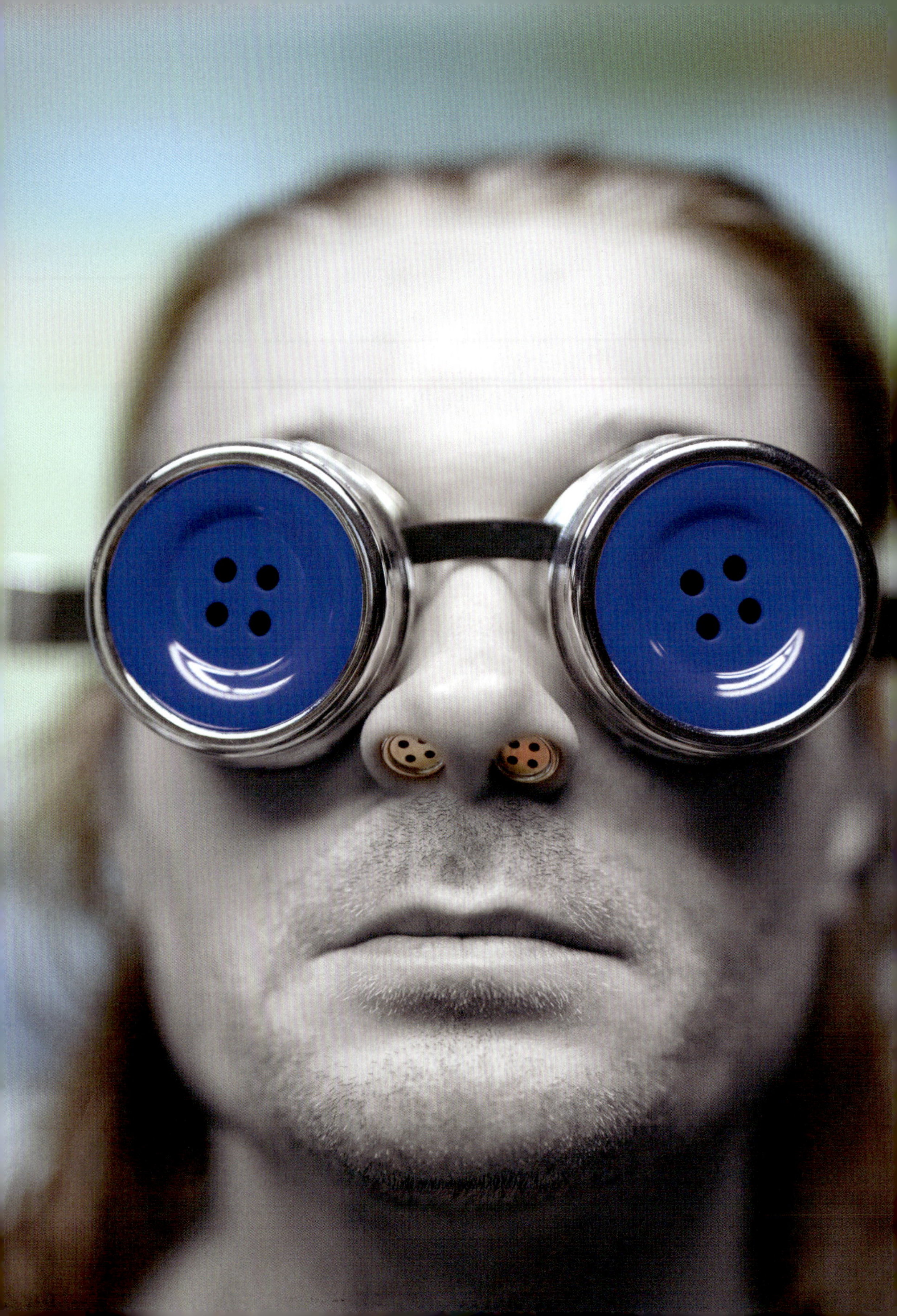

Do you remember how the pupils of your eyes pleaded with my corneas, that it was indecent? And how I, with the will of a cruel mathematician, tortured you? Do you remember that skirmish in the field of grass when I, having paralyzed you, stopped the hot workshop?

You disappeared into the six continents, crossing meridians parallel and parallels perpendicular so that I couldn't find you in a billion years. So that I couldn't decode the characters for the trajectories with any neural networks, arithmometers, or differential equations.

You wiped away all the traces of the lipstick and the hands of all the clocks, throwing a dynamite stick with a railroad-sized number of explosives into the memories.

You are earthy. You are unearthly. You with your odors. With your legs and your swaying buttocks. With your sparkles on your eyelashes, with all that hazy knick-knackery in your tiny chick purse. You are so concrete, so surprising. And I'm so indistinct. You slipped away from me, turning the pages of your fish scales around my fisherman's fingers.

Do you remember how you sang in the Japanese bar, your voice never turning from my gaze? Do you remember how concrete our feelings were, and how palpable you were in my hope to be you instead of myself?

I would have taught you the Argentinean tango of love on the broken gramophone of the coffee table, and together, with twirling feet, would whirl you like an Olympic champion spins the ice arena around his frozen girl. I would be the most famous mathematician in wild nature, a master of orgasms on tables in shitty New York cafes.

I would have showered you with the sparks from my motor so that you would beg me to do anything but stop. The moaning scream of intolerably greedy love, which we in our hysteria would make in the fury of our corpuscles. Ultra-low latency—that's us.

Me and my powerful gear, controlled by high technology over the internet. The smell of burnt things and smoke, these products of our crazy rhythm, would be so strong that all the axes of all the lumberjacks would hang on them in the air anywhere in the world. You would see how the real animal impulse of my spirit would create the absolute value of this young international family in a dark New York night, announced by me as the night of our astonishing wedding!

Yours,
Hans

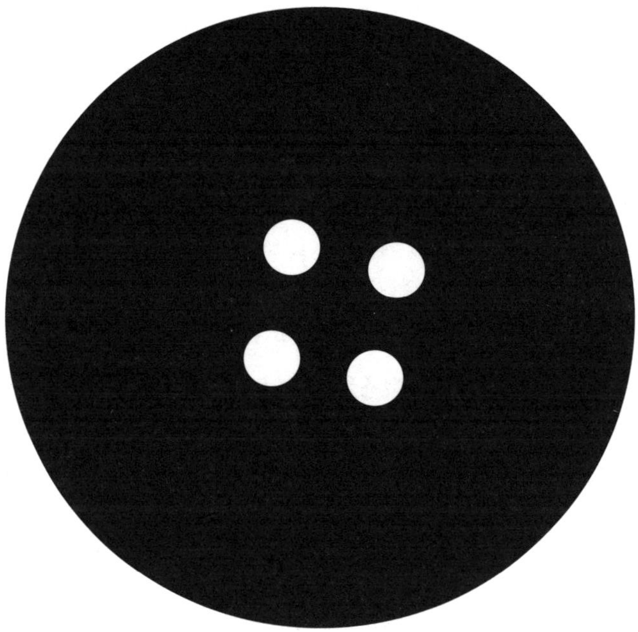

CHAPTER 3

Real, humongous, capricious, frightening, iron, noisy New York peeked at Hans in the plane, which tilted while circling towards Brighton Beach with its thousands of shacks, houses, and buildings. Although Hans was never that fond of the testosterone city that forged happiness, inflated with cubes of running-track streets, Hans and New York did have similar curiosity levels. The aircraft captain's voice calmed and inspired Hans. It was ninety degrees in New York, sunny, and no precipitation. And then they landed.

New York's airport met Hans with adolescent fellowship. The cabbies lined up in a long orange chain, a tangerine queue, with each one of the four-wheeled fruits going out of its way to hurry and plant some passenger seeds. And nothing was as easy as starting along the road to the city of dreams. Hans was enchanted on all sides—the alarm on the faces, the whiffs of hot, lightly humid air, and the living English, somewhat different from what was spoken down South, intoxicated his reason and tempted him with colorful pictures of a rainbow future. The stress of the joy required him to put off the rejoicing until later. In this stagnation, he turned stale and was less and less able to move. Now there was something bursting through to the surface, reaching its hand out to meet the new. Apparently, curiosity or passion will change when it encounters this dancing rhythm.

The impressive, even majestic, turbaned taxi driver symbolized for Hans the incarnation of a multicultural city and the stories of Scheherazade. A thousand and one nights in New York. Two thousand and eleven years in New York—and not a year less.

"I know all of New York like I know my five fingers," bragged the cabbie. "I used to drive Bloomberg around. I even humiliated him in an elevator. You want me to drive a mile with my eyes closed?" He coquettishly dropped his hands from the wheel and placed them on his knees. "Where are you headed, my friend? I forgot. Harlem?" "Modern technology—a driverless car," thought Hans in fear. "They're gonna show this accident on the news."

Hans had heard about Harlem, but, just in case, decided not to push the driver into a conversation about it and, instead, showed him again the sheet of paper with the address. It was an apartment in Soho that he was to live in at first, and in which living should be quite nice. Because Soho sounded like a decent place.

But Hans knew that Harlem was the birthplace of jazz, and jazz—like a wild animal, like a house of ill repute—had called to Hans throughout his entire youth, from the moment his father taught him how to listen to shortwave radio music programs on Radio Free Europe. Now Harlem was breathing the velvet of a saxophone somewhere so very close by, this time for real. Just a bit more and the drums would start to stir, to rock Hans' heart. And Hans said, "Take me through Harlem."

Life moves fast. Driving in the hired yellow vehicle through Midtown East, Hans, completely oblivious to where he was and dumbfounded by the scale of the life that was sweeping by him, tried to convince himself his surroundings were nothing very spectacular. As if he had lived in this city his whole life and was going to live here forever. Tall buildings? No big deal. In childhood, while curiosity has not yet lost the ability to fight gravity, kids grew upward too, like houses getting fat on money and the dreams of their obedient buyers.

The empty, unfurnished apartment still smelled like the paint from half-assed renovations, and the air conditioner was on full blast. Cars and air conditioners were the two whales of the American Dream, each incorporated into the other like Bruegel's fish. The romance of a new, colorful life! Hans joyfully and forcefully dumped the eight-pound album of Andy Warhol photographs on the floor. The floor rumbled like a bass drum in greeting, "Helllllo Hans. Welcome to New York!"

The neighbors' windows were so close, like the faces of solidified lovers looking at each other. Just a bit closer, and their glass-window eyes could meld together in an eternal kiss. Hans felt the joy and fullness of this new, completely incomprehensible emulsion of people's lives, skyscrapers, and cars. And the city of the future whispered tempting secrets to him about the fate of all of those packed into the concrete stories.

On his first night in New York, Hans fell asleep immediately, without even getting undressed, with a beatific smile, right on its floorboards, his head on the Andy Warhol album.

Cars and air conditioners
were the two whales
of the American Dream,
each incorporated into the
other like Bruegel's fish.

CHAPTER 6

June came. And, it seemed, made it even hotter. The whole of Manhattan was wasting power to cool the streets and make the temperature suitable for public use. New York had long ago learned to live the beautiful life, inviting foreign experts to dig its ditches. All the ditches had now been dug, and their owners shaved clean. Ever since Edison brought his first light bulb here, every building in Manhattan glowed at the windows and fanned the bonfire of life, ignoring all suffering. At night all the streets buzzed with people, like a multicolored patchwork flowerbed.

Hans covered musical events for his agency through the prism of artistic photography. This of course is said with some grandiloquence, but he did indeed place a special sapphire prism in front of his lens. Even though skeptical tongues predicted the death of art, Hans used the destructive force of the irrational, which was able to deconstruct what was observed and compose it into a unique picture. It was thanks to this ability of his that Hans was invited to work in this boiling point of the world—to this dream of everyone who had visited ten times and of those who had never—New York.

The city's magic quickly seeped into the alchemy of the photographs, and, after a month of working there, Hans had already been to many evening events of New York's cultural life, having explored Soho in a progression from square feet to inches. Although Hans was an introvert, he interacted with the world through the trunk of his camera; like a deaf-mute, the city opened itself to him through the narrow tube of this friendship. This doorway to reality gave Hans certainty like a cane gives the lame. When necessary, he could hide entirely behind the small box of the camera, hide the whole of his introverted body. And this interest in what was occurring around him began to become mutual and even filled him with a sense of comfort. What could be a better reward…? Hans didn't want to discuss this with himself, however. He was worried at the prospect of being worried.

Renting an apartment in Manhattan for a year required only a few trifling efforts on Hans' part. He was so pleased with his new life that these papers seemed to him child's play. The first thing that he had to do was fill out a thirty-page application containing a hundred and twenty-one questions. For this privilege, Hans was charged a purely symbolic fee of approximately half his monthly salary. Just a measly two thousand dollars. And it wasn't refunded.

No problem. Small potatoes. Agents need something to live on too. Without the agents, paper would have no reason to exist. It would stop being produced, and all the workers at the paper mills would lose their jobs. And then what about their families?

Hans had to pay another two thousand to process the application. That means that somebody would look at it. Their looking at it guaranteed exactly nothing, but what you could be sure of was that you could forget about seeing that other two thousand dollars again. Hans smiled and nodded. He didn't even suspect that it would be so good! New York—the city of opportunities.

In this city of ultimate democracy and privacy, the landlord's application asked, among other things, simply where Hans had rented his previous apartment in Manhattan. Then it wanted to know what kind of work Hans did in Manhattan, and how many decades he had been in that profession. Then the owner's interest moved on to how many times Hans had paid off loans, and how many times he had done so early. The landlord also desperately needed to know how many banks across the world Hans had open accounts in, and did he have in them a hundred and three thousand dollars, and how much of this money was in banks in Manhattan. Next—did Hans have life insurance in an insurance company with Manhattan headquarters? Then—did he know anything about the insurance on his insurance premiums, in case his insurance company went bankrupt? There were even some questions of insurance on the insurer's insurance. Another question probed him on whether he used the services of a Manhattan dentist because the building was a so-called "white house," in which all the residents were obligated to whiten their teeth. He also needed a letter from the fire department saying that he had a fire-safe background and had not been an arsonist in Manhattan for the past thirty years. After that, Hans had to sign a letter of commitment vowing that he would not cultivate any GMOs on the territory of his apartment, and would not bring in any animals to stay overnight. Furthermore, it was also prohibited to leave his bicycle anywhere within a mile radius of the street door.

You couldn't rent small rooms if your furniture was too big, and so you had to provide proof that you had furniture that could fit through the door. Moving furniture was permitted only for fifteen minutes a day, and it was prohibited to use packing material that could offend any particular groups of people. No images of women or dollar signs were permitted on the boxes, and they couldn't be too dark in color either. If he wanted to drill a hole in the wall, Hans had to call the handyman, and the handyman had to call the supervisor to check the type of wall and the quality of Hans' nail. Also, he had to leave the handyman a 50-dollar tip. Then, the handyman, the supervisor, and Hans had to call the landlord's office altogether and insure the nail against bending or breaking due to wall hangings, hammers, and time.

Also, for the Managing Office to consider Hans' application, he had to have his blood tested for HIV and whooping cough. For a pleasant young man in a white coat, Hans spilled his blood into what looked like a pot. This is Manhattan, where safety was the highest priority. Hans himself could not stand the sight of blood, and with all his strength he squinted his eyes when the cold, pleasant hand of the "blood technician" grasped his shoulder to wrap the tourniquet around his arm. Hans could only listen to the gurgle of the blood as it dripped into the bottom of the pot, which they delicately called a "professional medical receptacle" so as not to scare the other patients with the antique substantiality of the vessel.

They even asked Hans to get a test for fleas, because Hans had been in Germany where there were too many refugees. It didn't matter that when Hans had left Germany there were no fleas. No one really knows how infections are spread. Or how fleas spread. Maybe the refugees were running from the fleas? For the test, Hans chopped off a lock of his hair from around the nape of his neck and took it to the Mt. Sinai Hospital lab.

Yes, Manhattan is the island of the elite. A paradise where freedoms and the highest achievements of mankind flow like the wind in a perpetual celebration of labor, solidarity, and communism. Manhattan is the peak of democracy, the orgasm of the Revolution, the victory of Che Guevara. Manhattan is a pure, incorruptible Cuba.

Yes, Manhattan is the island of the elite. A paradise where freedoms and the highest achievements of mankind flow like the wind in a perpetual celebration of labor, solidarity, and communism. Manhattan is the peak of democracy, the orgasm of the Revolution, the victory of Che Guevara. Manhattan is a pure, incorruptible Cuba.

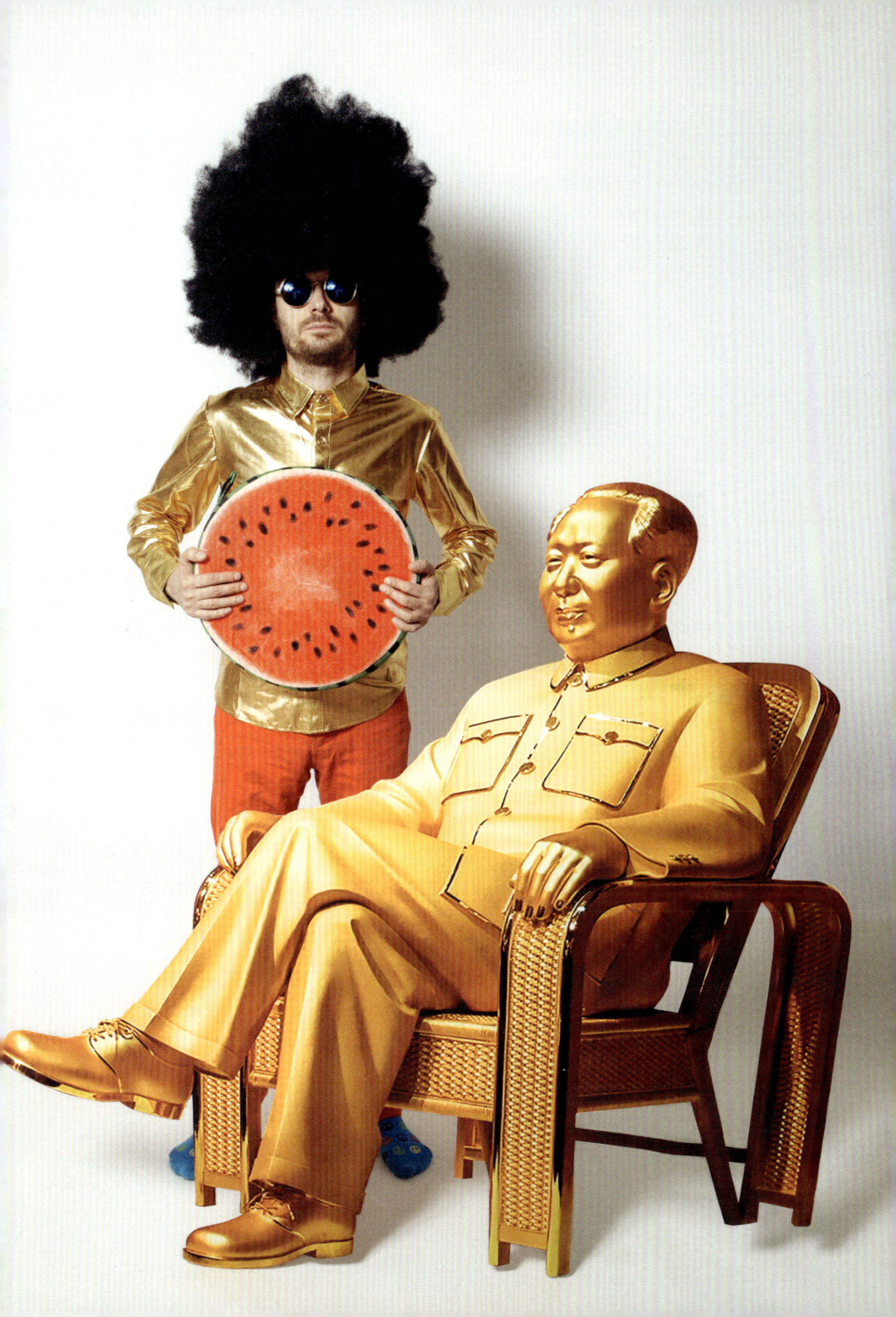

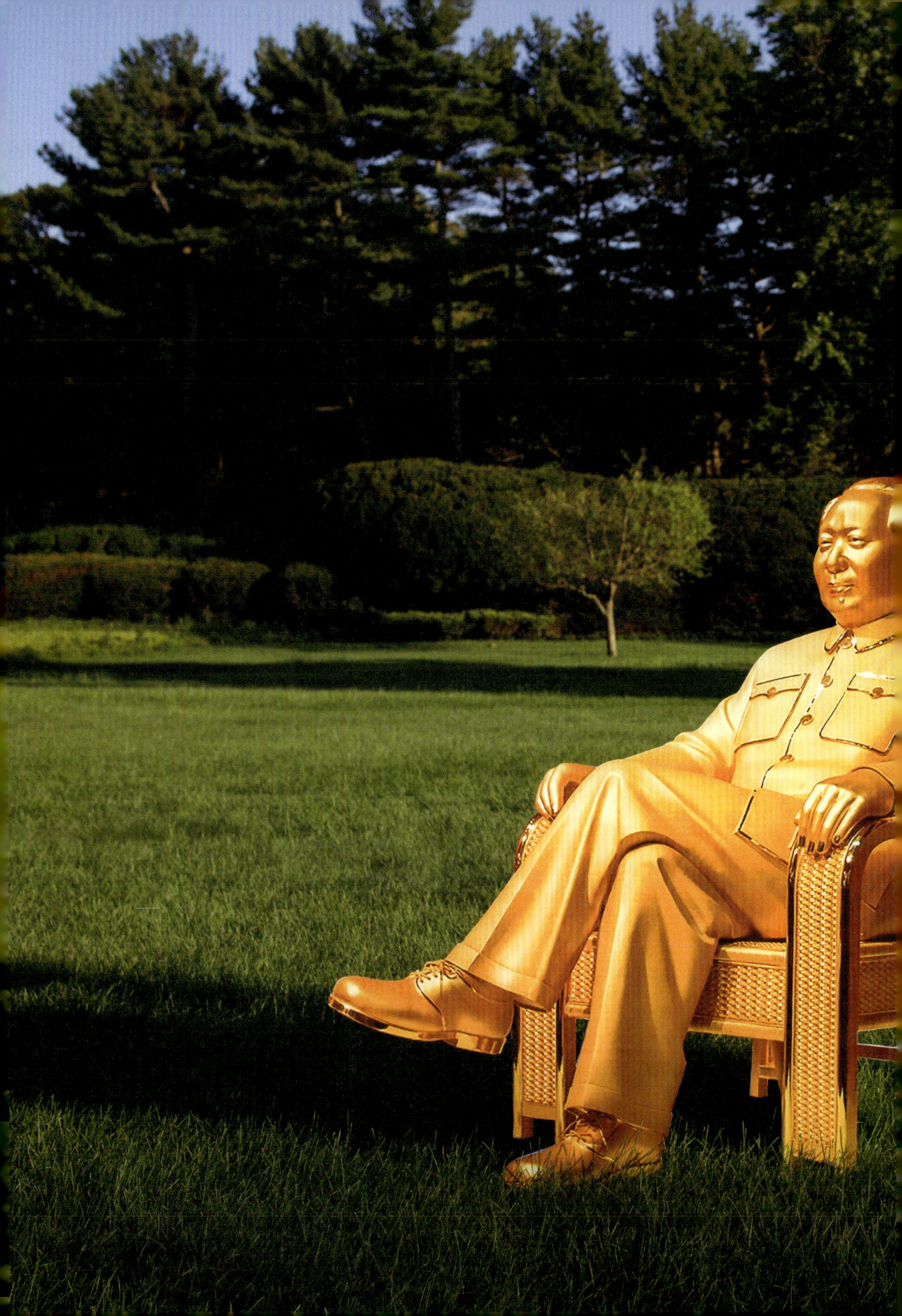

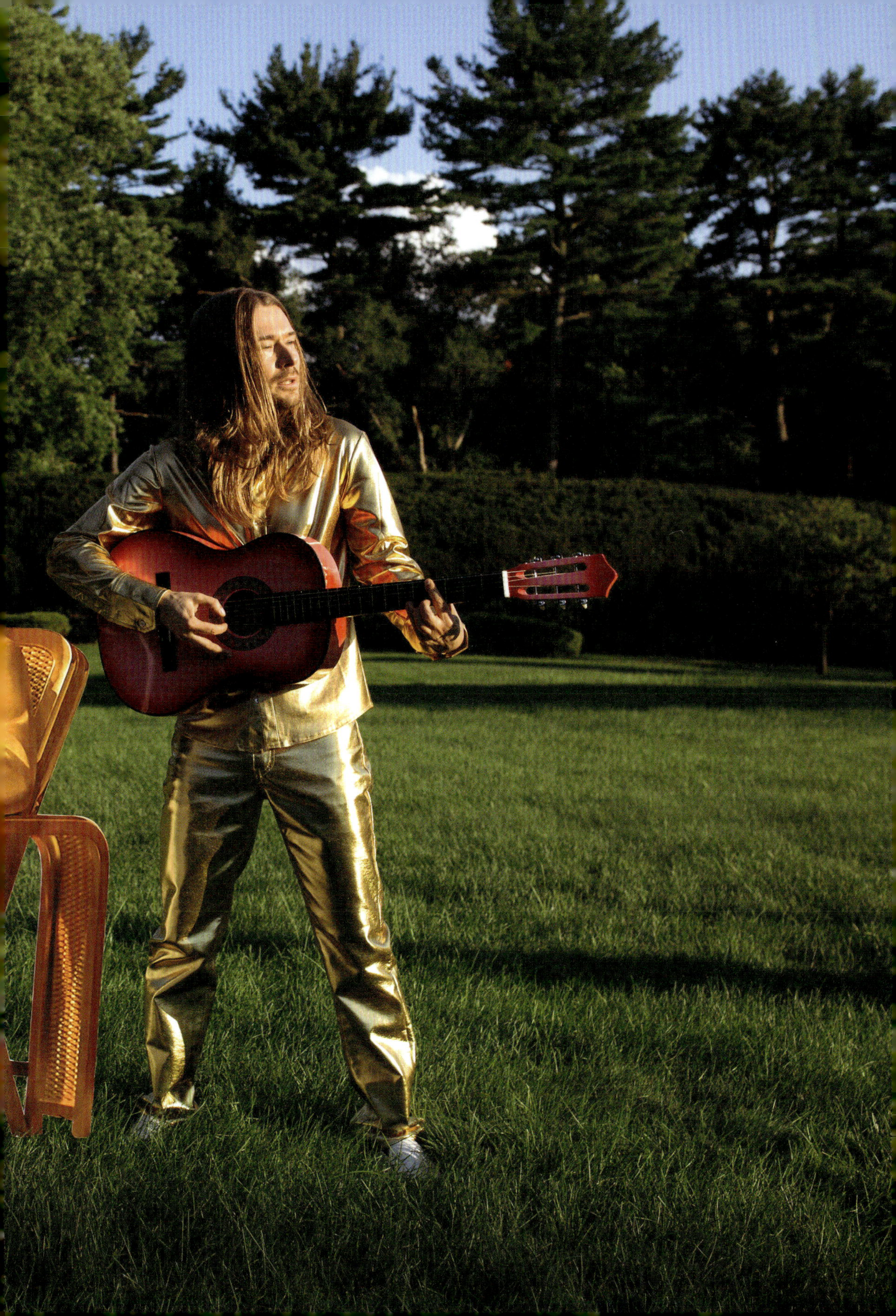

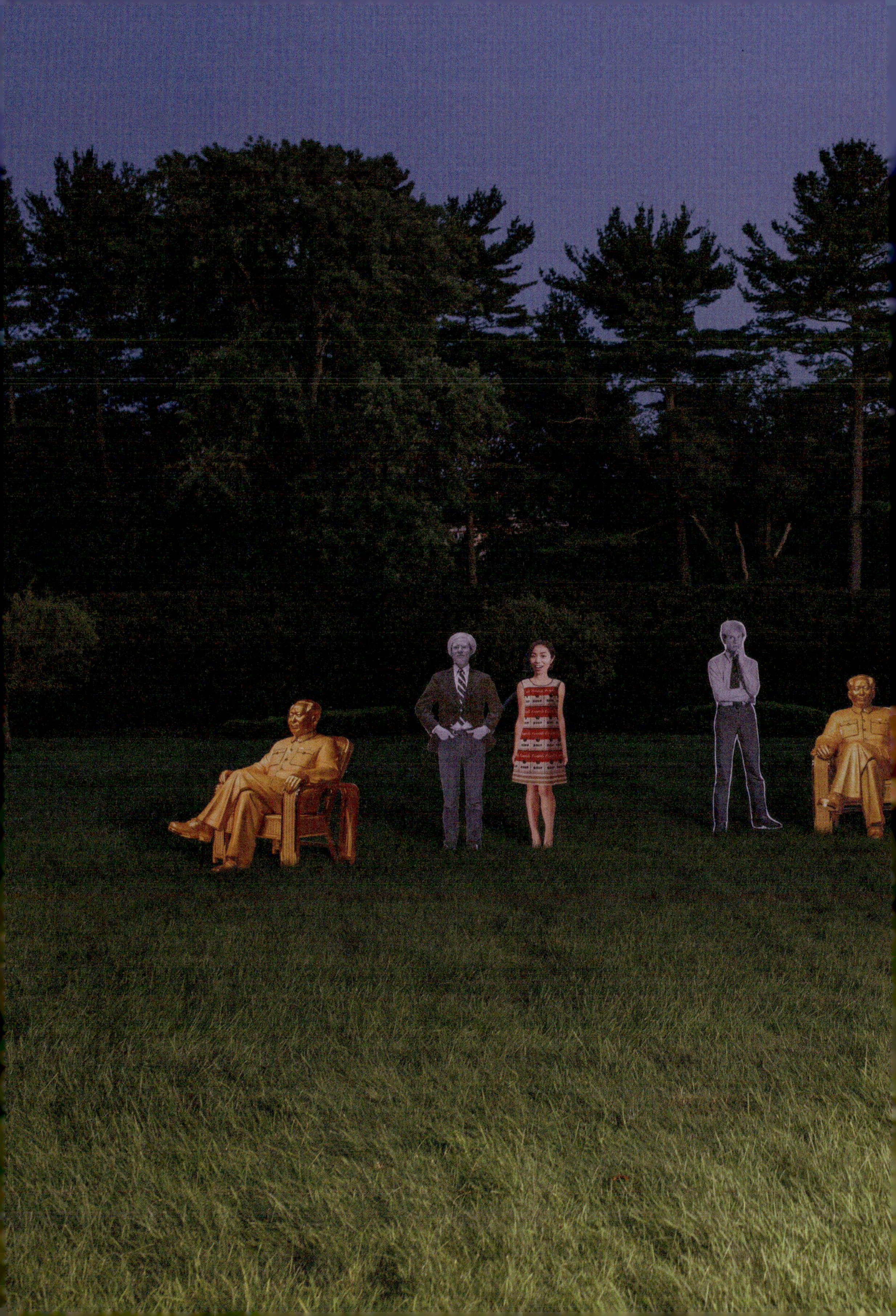

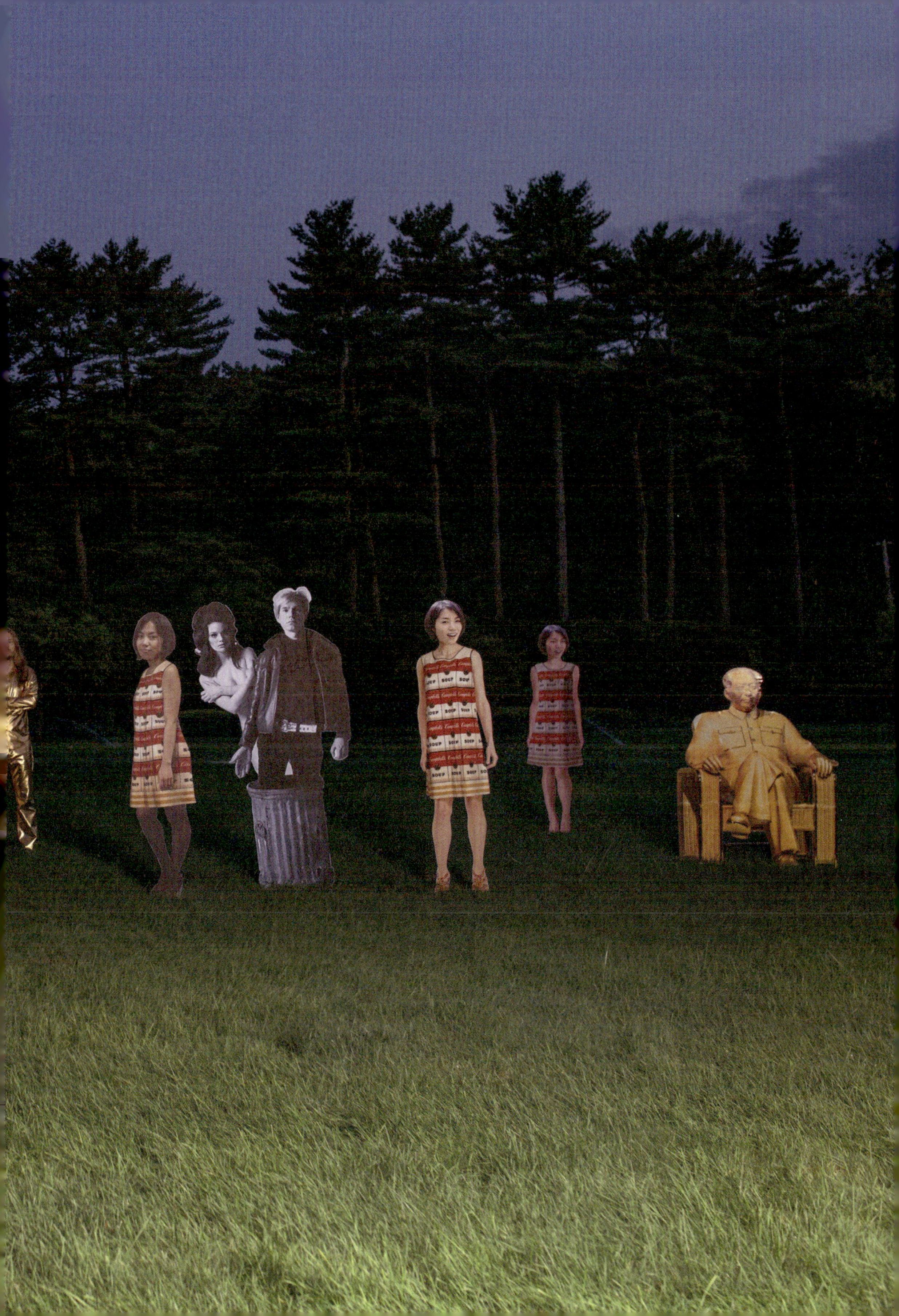

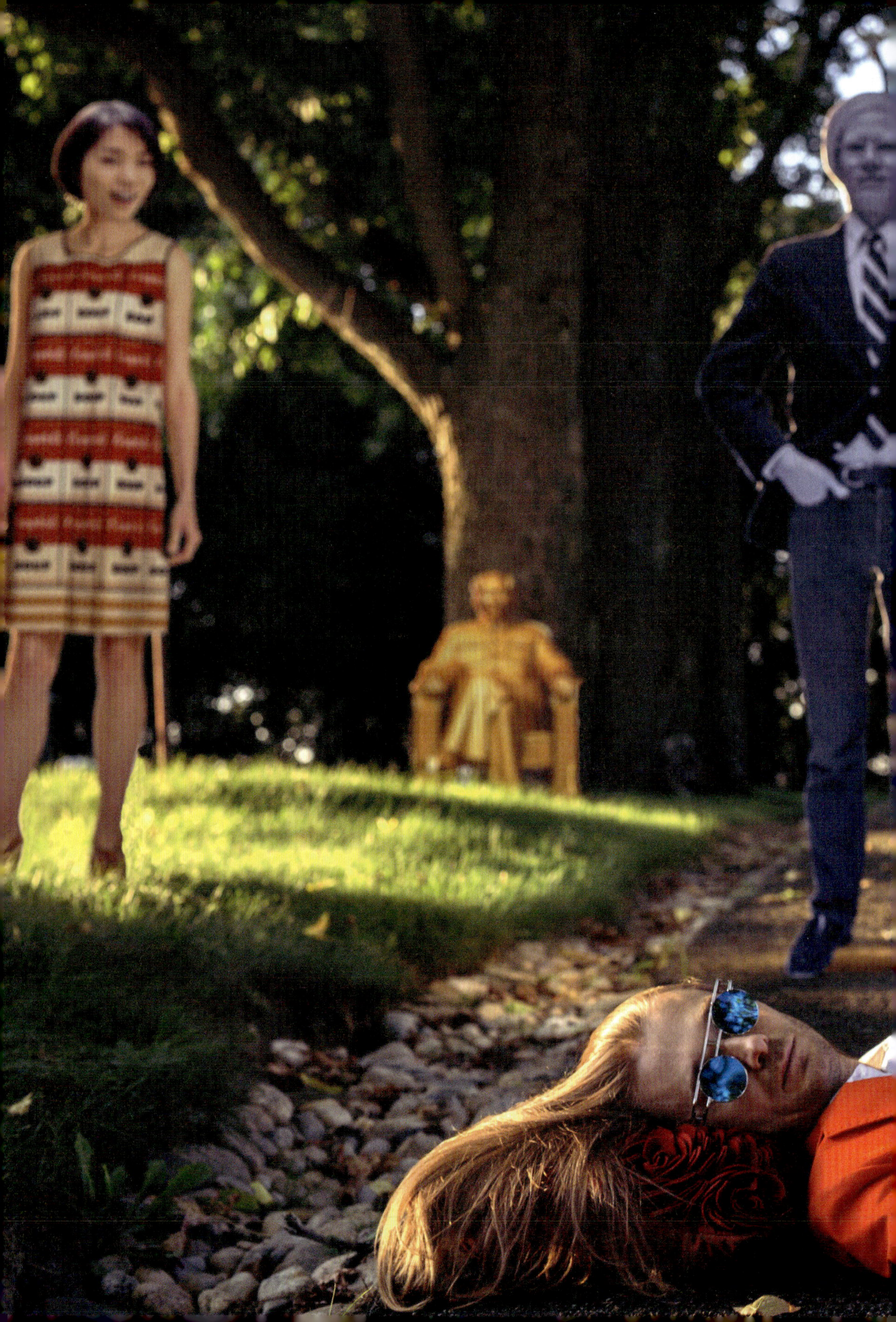

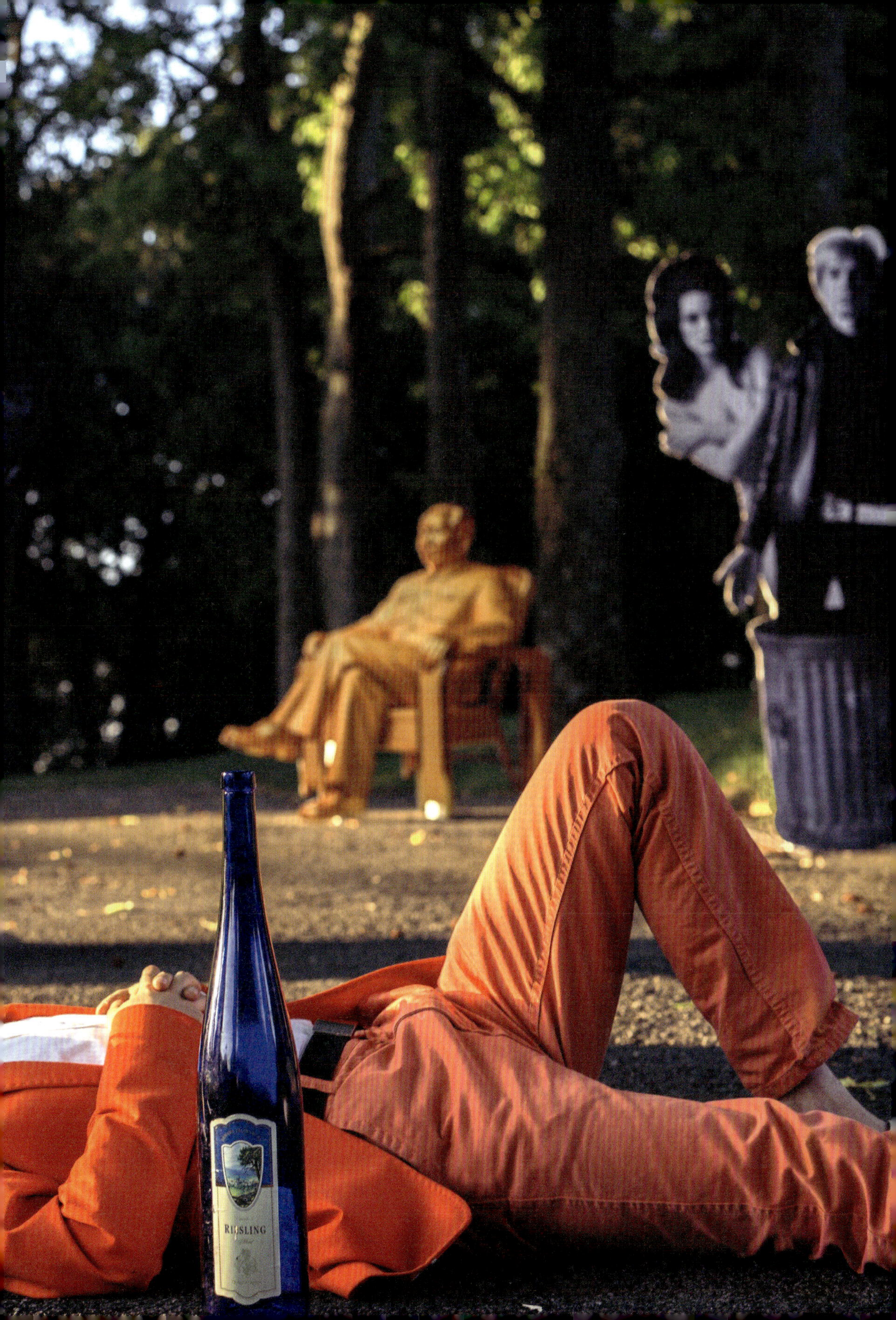

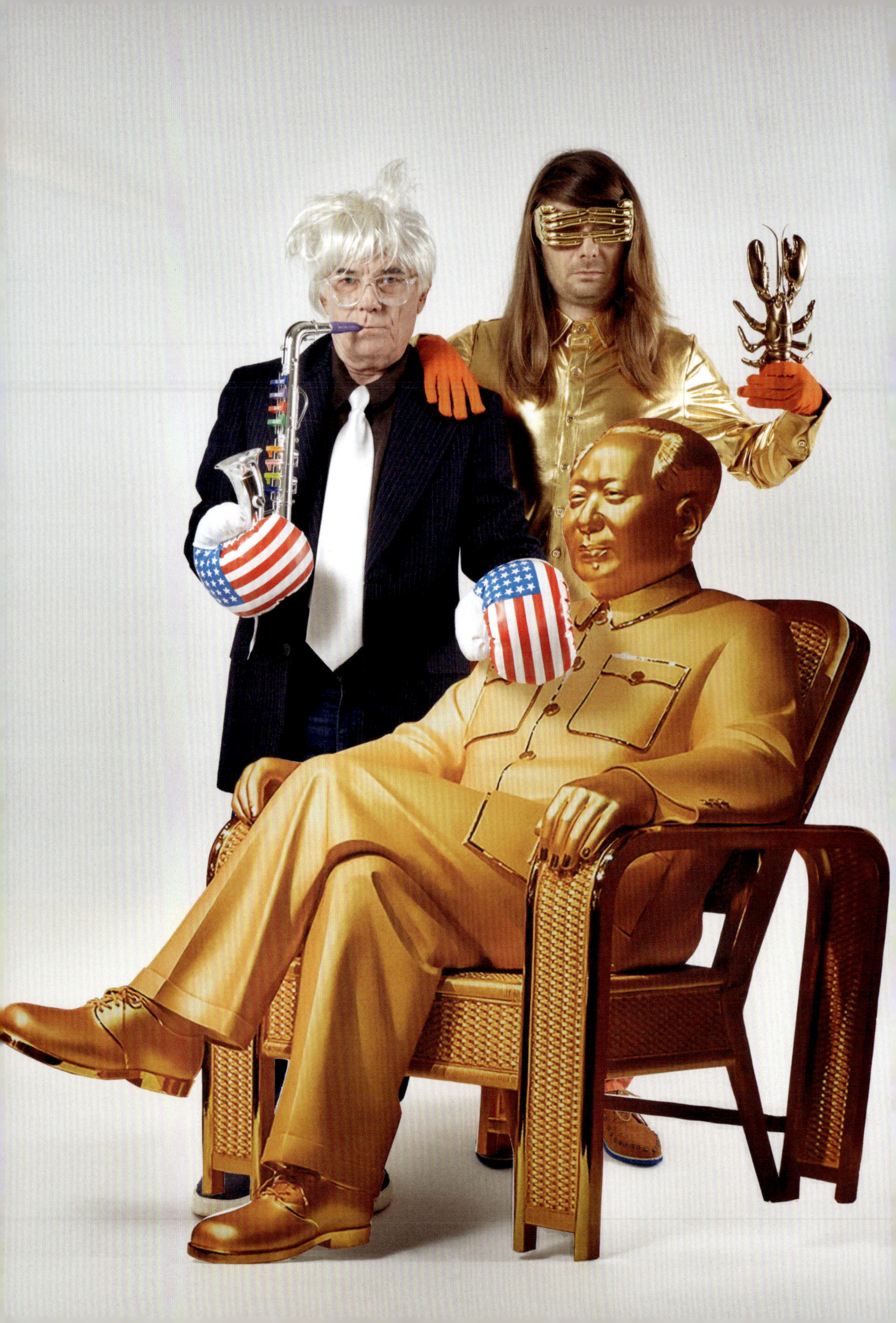

CHAPTER 7

Hans held a festive celebration for his thirty-ninth birthday, doing the work he loved—photographing musicians at the Blue Note Jazz Club. Tonight, a group of musicians calling themselves The Mirror Jazz Band were playing the famous jazz venue. To get a one-of-a-kind photograph in a jazz atmosphere, Hans was allowed to do basically anything he wanted, including using construction materials, structures, decorations, and a sick imagination, from a small space near stage right.

On the day of his irredeemable birth, Hans was hanging from a crane under the ceiling, like a twilight moth with his camera proboscis among the musician-flowers. Young women in sequined costumes with their bodies exposed to an almost impermissible extent ran out onto the stage. At one point during the performance, fireworks were set off in a magical fountain that lit up the dark hall. The audience oohed and aahed. It was a real furor, and the jazz itself was simply magnificent. The trumpet players, drummer, and bass player caused anaphylactic shock in people's ears. A frail, fidgety Japanese girl, who from afar seemed as if she were weightless, sang along with the musicians—sad words about an unfamiliar town and the coldness of a faraway land. She also played the bass guitar. The instrument was larger than she was, and its strings seemed like the thick steel cables of the Brooklyn Bridge.

Hans was flying through the air with his camera, under the

cupola of the jazz hall and above the performance, giving himself over to his work and his fantasy in thinking up frames and formats. The vibrations of the instruments and the voices inspired him. He recalled the nights he sat with his father around the shortwave radio, where, through unbearable whistles and the hiss of the station generators that were trying to suppress the signal, they listened to the magical jazz. If they couldn't hear all of it, they would finish the songs themselves by whistling along. Hans continued his work with doubled imagination, swinging from cable to cable like a monkey in the jungle, hanging upside down in the cosmic antipodal pose.

When the concert was over, the audience quickly headed for the exit, weary from the dinner, the wine, and the musical magic. For some reason, audiences always want to run away immediately after a show, as if they were running from a natural disaster. As if they were ashamed to meet the musicians offstage. Musicians are only alive when they're on stage. Hans' shoulders were covered in confetti. The waiters were removing empty wine bottles from the tables, most likely stuffing them with wish lists and setting them free into the Hudson. The wailing walls of music quieted down, and the space filled up with human words, the meaning of which was mostly finding out the fastest way to get, for example, from W. 4th to 63rd and Lexington. The musicians were all gathering their notes, instruments, and microphones. The bass player vocalist airily scuttled between the mike stands in her blue dress and skillfully wound up an unwieldy elephant trunk of microphone cords on her thin arms. Hans landed on the stage flipped like Neil Armstrong, crawled out of his basket, and started gathering his lenses and lighting equipment into large cases and bags. The stage lights shone into his eyes, and through the blueness of the vibrant, cool light of success radiated the silhouette of the weightless-in-zero-gravity statue of the musician girl.

Hans, bending down to his bags, closed the umbrella reflector with German accuracy. Suddenly something cold hugged and then burned his neck in a flowing stream. A microphone cord had slithered across a table holding a few cocktails and caught on one of them. The glass toppled, spilling the drink and the ice floating in it down Hans' neck.

A harrowing shout in the dark rang out, "Oh, I'm so sorry! Forgive me so much—it was a mistake!"

The figure in the blue dress ran to Hans' side, hoping to stop the remainder of the cold drink flow. The scene was a short one, the darkness was almost impenetrable, and the girl's trajectory was eccentric. Her character brought a certain quirkiness to everything. Her heels were high. With or without interference from the cord, she tripped and almost fell off the stage. As absurd and unlikely as it was, wet Hans obstructed her downward path.

"Oh my God, how awful, how clumsy! Forgive me! Oh God!" she repented, getting tangled up in his arms. "God can see everything, but I missed that stupid cocktail glass! Forgive me, please."

"No, no, you forgive me," Hans apologized just in case, even if there was nothing to apologize for. Even more so because, as she said, God sees everything anyway. "It wasn't your glass, and I was the one who knocked it over."

Which was not true. Hans' wet Hasselblad camera, which cost as much as a small house in Florida, wasn't afraid of moisture and was insured by the company. And even the three lenses that did sustain damage couldn't ruin his mood.

"What's your name?" Hans asked politely, shaking the spilled mystery drink from his white shirt and orange jacket.

"Yuma," the girl, for some reason, whispered.

"I'm Hans," Hans smiled awkwardly, hiding the introvert within him with a loud answer. "Nice to meet you."

"Nice—Hans!" she laughed.

Hans also laughed. That kind of unprepossessing humor was just up his alley.

"Are you on Facebook?" That girl Yuma got down to business. "You're a photographer. I suppose you post your photographs there?"

"Yes, I have Facebook, but I don't really... I don't know how to start a conversation..."

"Let's friend each other. How can I find you?" she pushed.

Hans didn't know how to use Facebook and didn't want to. He only had sixteen friends on Facebook, and only one from New York—a seller of second-rate junk in a Brooklyn shop. That was Otto, who was born in East Berlin. Otto, by the way, was quite clever, and his work in the shop didn't say much about him. Sales were, to put it mildly, not his thing. He did it with derision that quickly moved into contempt. He often said, "Hans, business is the worst form of prostitution. I would glue clothespins together tomorrow if I knew it would bring me more than this junk." He proudly swung his arm upward. Business is dissemblance, a facade for touching up your existential failures.

On top of that, Otto had a doctorate in radio signal detection, but ever since he left Germany looking for a better life, career success had completely turned its back on him. The fate of an engineer or scientist did not follow him across the ocean. Or maybe there was something wrong with the ocean? With the money he saved, Otto bought a small house in Brooklyn and began doing what was closest to his heart. At first, he sold carpets, and then switched to knick-knacks, Halloween bric-a-brac, and, rumor had it, weapons. Which Hans seriously doubted, knowing Otto's nature and past.

Yuma asked for a towel from the restaurant kitchen and brought it to the stage. Although the summer was hot and Hans was more comfortable thanks to the cool liquid from the glass, he thought that it was quite nice to feel cared for.

"Do you surrender?" asked Hans, increasing his intrigue rating.

"What does that mean?" she smiled, with all the rows of her multi-level smile.

"You were holding the towel like a white flag as if you were showing me that you no longer intended to fight."

"You're funny."

"Yeah, that's me."

"What does 'funny' mean to a singer?" thought Hans amicably and critically. "How could she use the situation as a source of amusement? Is it possible to formulate the dialogue to make it funny?" And so, the self-reflection began. It was a quality that Hans didn't like about himself. He knew it was splitting hairs.

He didn't want to express interest. Interest leaves no alternative. Interest makes boundary-crossing inevitable. Interest removes what is unspoken. Hans did not want to see or feel the results of this on unfamiliar territory. He tried to avoid the need for additional steps.

"My musicians don't listen to me. We have a very tight schedule these days: two concerts a day for two weeks. I mean, music is not just notes and a world of harmony. Like any work, it is stress, fatigue, and unwashed dishes. I even have to carry my bass guitar case around myself. And nobody wants to help."

"Even though you're beautiful?" Hans recklessly roused himself, flexing his imagination muscle. He had read about such conversations in books and just pulled the words up for fanciness and titillation. Yuma laughed.

"Ha! Are you serious? How can you say that after seeing me for just the first time?"

"I've seen you from different angles. You have harmonious proportions."

"You're an impudent New Yorker."

"I'm from Germany... Where are you from?" Hans looked at her.

But he knew everything: that the jazz band was from Japan and that their vocalist was not from Sweden. Suddenly she paused while Hans moved forward on his ice skates from inertia and ran into the rink wall. Her eyes shone in the dark with an unexpected benevolence, which burned away Hans' obduracy, his constant readiness for confrontation and formality, between which he always chose a quiet retreat when associating with people he didn't know. He didn't know Yuma, but she called him to living emotions, maybe even to a greater lyricism.

Her lips froze in a half-smile, which didn't seem to be due to an unnecessary acquaintance, the time of day, a foreign town, or maintaining a permitted level of openness. This made an impression on Hans, and his blind eyes looked her over more. She had a birthmark on her upper lip. A wonderful sign—a lighthouse for the heights of tuning forks. Her calmness was a rhythm: Storm. Pause. Tornado. Pause. Blizzard. This external look said of her that she was woven of feelings and tactility. Of movement and the heights of sound. Her cheeks were waiting for something. Almost unnoticeably, they were under the tension of a smile, making dimples thanks to which even heartless people like Hans had rediscovered some of their vision. Her face was made up of a surprising mix of the ironic and the naïve. The former she had from birth, while the latter was likely something from her youth. Her face was pale, slightly blue from the lighting and the walls. It was also prone to wanting to get closer, and it blinded with its teeth that thirsted for connection. In a skinny chicken body, the child sat, self-confident and disenchanted with the life of an adult and with a shade of trouble in her eyes, the origin of which was a mystery. Her eyes were trying to say something to Hans through the glimmering glass of a mutually accepted brilliance, like a prisoner knocking from the inside asking for help. The fear in her eyes synergized with her youth. This is what Hans noticed, what was flickering about in the back alleys of his universe, and so he preferred not to see that feeling.

"Well, I'm not interested in myself as a woman anymore," continued Yuma seriously. "I'm only hungry for musical and existential materials. Here, in New York, a magic city, a hero city, trying to occupy the stratosphere, it seems the focus is on the size of your wallet or under your skirt. Are men really men anymore? Just think, he's talking in words, but in his thoughts, his hands are undressing you from the first second."

"Isn't that what nature intended?" Hans tried to be unhackneyed.

"Has a man ever undressed you, Hans? Have you ever felt how vile it is to belong to a man?"

"Yes, my father undressed me before I would take a bath when I was about four years old. It was awful."

"You're a joker. But for a woman, it is much more important than a simple kid's bath. A woman always expects complications. She likes the head-spinning heights of experimentation. But if she already knows the answer..."

The sparkles on her eyelashes and eyes reflected a light blue sheen in the semi-darkness, pierced by the darker blue of the lights. She was like the planet Jupiter in the telescopes of stiff astronomers.

Night fell definitively over the club, with just the waiters clearing the tables left. The lights were almost out, and Yuma's blue dress no longer flickered with star rays. Only Hans' camera was able to capture some of the reflections and sparkles, saving them in the gelatin of old-fashioned film.

Hans was ready to leave. He had a lot of work that week—a few more concerts and a couple of projects he still had to think about. The riddle of women didn't interest him, nor did any reality outside his photography. The only thing he wanted was not to leave Yuma in that sad, disappointed state, as if he were the reason for the uneasiness that had settled upon her. He felt like he had to return her to her place, like a beautiful and expensive toy in a shop.

"What do you like?" inquired Hans.

"I love Duke Ellington. And I love… to sing," she said with strangeness in her voice.

Hans cast his glance around in the dark: the huge room was completely empty, and just one light remained, lighting a corner of the stage. Now in the complete blackness of the musical building, they were alone. A white towel, the smell of the spilled cocktail, and no one else around.

"Can you sing to me about what's bothering you right now?" For some reason, Hans reached for his camera cases.

"You really want me to?"

Her eyes began to glow and became the eyes of a lion that has overtaken a buffalo in the African steppe. She sat on the chair. She thought about it. It was awkward. She stood up from the chair and withdrew into the night. "I suppose I'll never see her again." Hans decided to think that nonsense just in case. Yuma returned from the night with a new cord and quickly plugged it into the combo, reopening her bass guitar case.

And without missing a beat, Hans got his cocktail-covered camera out, anticipating something. He wanted to somehow hide behind the camera from the growing unease. He wasn't used to sitting with a girl in a nightclub in the dark and emptiness. He should have made peace with that circumstance somehow, but he couldn't. He was raised in East Germany.

The bass guitar sounded beautiful. B-B-B-B-B-B-B-B-B-B-B-B-B-Bommm. Bom-Bom. Hans was frightened of this enchantment. Like Alice in Wonderland, afraid to go down the rabbit hole. His life experience always protected him from emotion—he could move forward only once he had raised himself above what he saw and when he could determine what was real. But despite his defenses, reality always found a way to get under Hans' skin.

Suddenly Yuma started singing without the microphone. Her voice sounded like hot sand on a steamy summer day, each grainy speck hitting Hans in the face, burning him. Her voice said more about her than her appearance. It seemed to Hans that some kind of live record was playing inside her. The song was a mix of bass, echo, and a subtle vocal, flowing out gently and inconspicuously, with a distinctive and idiosyncratic vinyl accent in a voice that shook Hans with its purity. This music was written within her before birth, her gramophone record that wanted to live outside of her. It was the seventies, when Hans was born. But how did she know about it, this young twenty-year-old girl? Hans burned with this question and with rapture from what he was hearing. The voice of Radio Free Europe and the rock programs returned to him from his childhood in shortwave snippets in which the song jammer was more audible than the song itself. Femininity and tension. She hid notes and certain letters in words, and Hans' hearing was magnetized to these scratches in her internal recording. There was a concentration in her voice, uncharacteristic of a young woman applying her angular adolescent figure to jazz. Yuma was standing delicately, wearily holding the bass but sure of herself, like a hooked fish. There was a poignancy in her voice that told Hans one thing: Yuma lived on her anguish.

Hans took in that concert. He wasn't a musician, but he carried shades of music in his inner jacket pocket and was now sad along with Yuma. He wanted to hear slowly, so beautiful was the sorrow in her soft, sibilant, lulling vowels, in the flowing touches to the stiff strings of the bass with child's hands.

Hans didn't know Japanese, and he had no additional locksmith's tools to unsheathe the words. Because of the accumulating darkness finding them in this place and because of the general tiredness of the lived day, the disquieting spark fanned a foreboding in him.

Yuma's face closed in to within five inches of Hans'. She was playing—in the full sense of the word—not suspecting Hans had already played out the chess game. Play was the largest part of her being. Artistry was not only essential to her as a means of survival—she needed people who were ready to give their whole game and leave nothing, burning out. And her nerve, the long snake wound around her thin neck, scorched Hans.

At this point, Yuma noticed nothing around her. And even human Hans was wiped away by the powerful wave of her extreme expression. Her voice, suspended in the night by acoustic resonance, moved closer to frozen Hans. He felt how the air flowed through the fur of her vocal cords like a trombone; he sensed the smell of her breathing, watched her half-open, tensed lips that looked like a small inflatable boat. He saw every sparkle of her pink lipstick. His first year in Florida, Hans worked selling perfume, and ever since, he remembered the shades of the smells of all of the popular French perfumes. Odors often substituted for his eyes and his words.

When the bass guitar buzzed its last solid note and gradually began to quiet down, Hans all of a sudden stood up:

"I'm sorry. Yuma, you know, I completely forgot," He was bothered by something. "I have film in a bath at home. And I didn't turn the water off. And I have downstairs neighbors… It was a magical evening. See you soon, Yuma!"

Hans grabbed all of his cases and stands, picked up his bag with the lenses, and made a beeline for the exit straight through the rows of empty night tables. "I have to go. I have to go," he said under his breath, for some reason trying to convince himself. On the street, he spasmodically waved down a taxi, jumped into its safe womb, and sped away as if in an ambulance.

Hans couldn't recall how he got into his apartment or what he did afterwards. There is a state in which you can't do anything and at the same time can't not do anything. You don't want to think or remember what is happening to you. Hans decided to kill some time, to the extent that was possible, so that tomorrow he could calmly return to his photographs and negatives. Glass after glass, he drank one gallon of water. What was happening to him? He picked up a hammer and thought about hanging a photograph on the wall but then remembered that you weren't allowed to put nails in the wall without permission.

While on his last glass of water, he received a text: "Dear Hans. You forgot your big lens. I had to take it with me. I can give it back to you tomorrow evening. Yuma."

Hans was not very happy that he had forgotten his best lens—a Carl Zeiss with a 1.2 f-stop. But on the other hand, he felt relieved. The awkward feeling that led to the evening ending in complete embarrassment suddenly melted away. Hans even began to hover over the parquet floor, or so it seemed to him. He knew that when writing to people, he often showed them an unnecessary side of his illusions and, therefore, spent a few minutes thinking up the proper reply. "No problem. I can just buy a new lens. See you next year." Delete. "My heartfelt thanks for tonight. Please forgive me for running away. I was scared. It must have looked so infantile." Delete. "Your kindness knows no bounds. How could I forget such an expensive lens? Please hold it for me until tomorrow." Better. Delete.

"I objectively forgot my objective lens. I'll pick it up tomorrow." Too conceptual. Stinks of insecurity. Delete. "Yuma, Thank you! Until we meet again tomorrow!" Sent.

"OK. It's a bit formal but quite friendly," thought Hans. He had never learned to write messages to girls. However, he was quite proud of the result for now.

The white stain of the moon peeped into Hans' bedroom through the gloomy clouds. Its beams, like a cosmic schoolteacher, painted rectangles and trapezoids on the floor. Hans opened the window to dilute the dust with some air. The wind quickly found an entrance to the apartment, blowing the drapes to the side, and the draft began tidying up the things in his room, the books, the photos, both on the shelves and under the table. Hans shivered, exulting in his feeling of sudden chilly freshness in the warm July night. The rustling of the wind calmed him down.

He reclined on the couch and began reading Warhol's diaries. Everything in them was quite clear. Warhol walked around, called people, got up, met people, ate. The written documentation of his life covered a lot more than did the trivial utterance of life itself, the body and the biology. Hans, fading into the dream world, thought about Andy Warhol. He thought, maybe, like a man about another man, or maybe even like Warhol about Warhol, realizing that there were light years between a work of art and its subject.

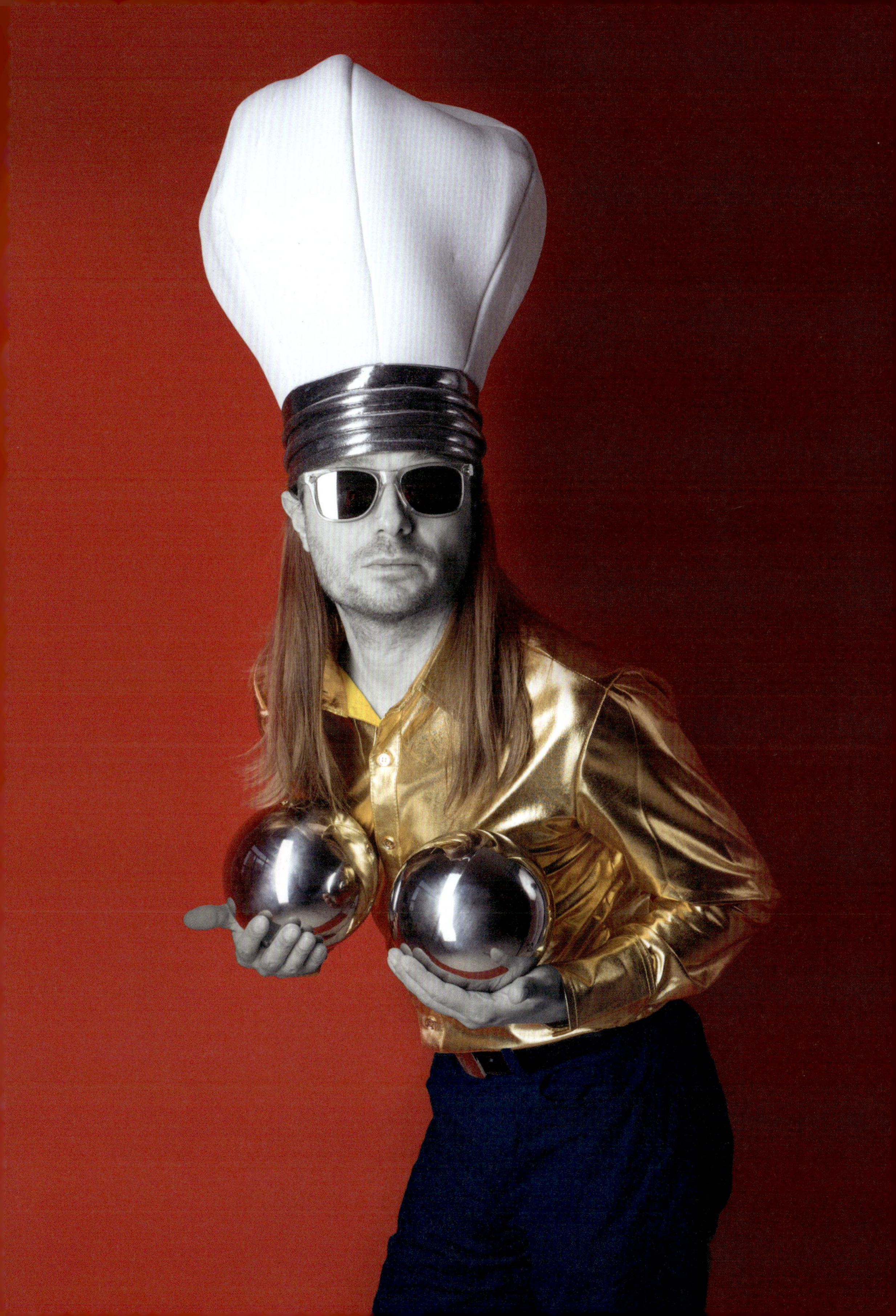

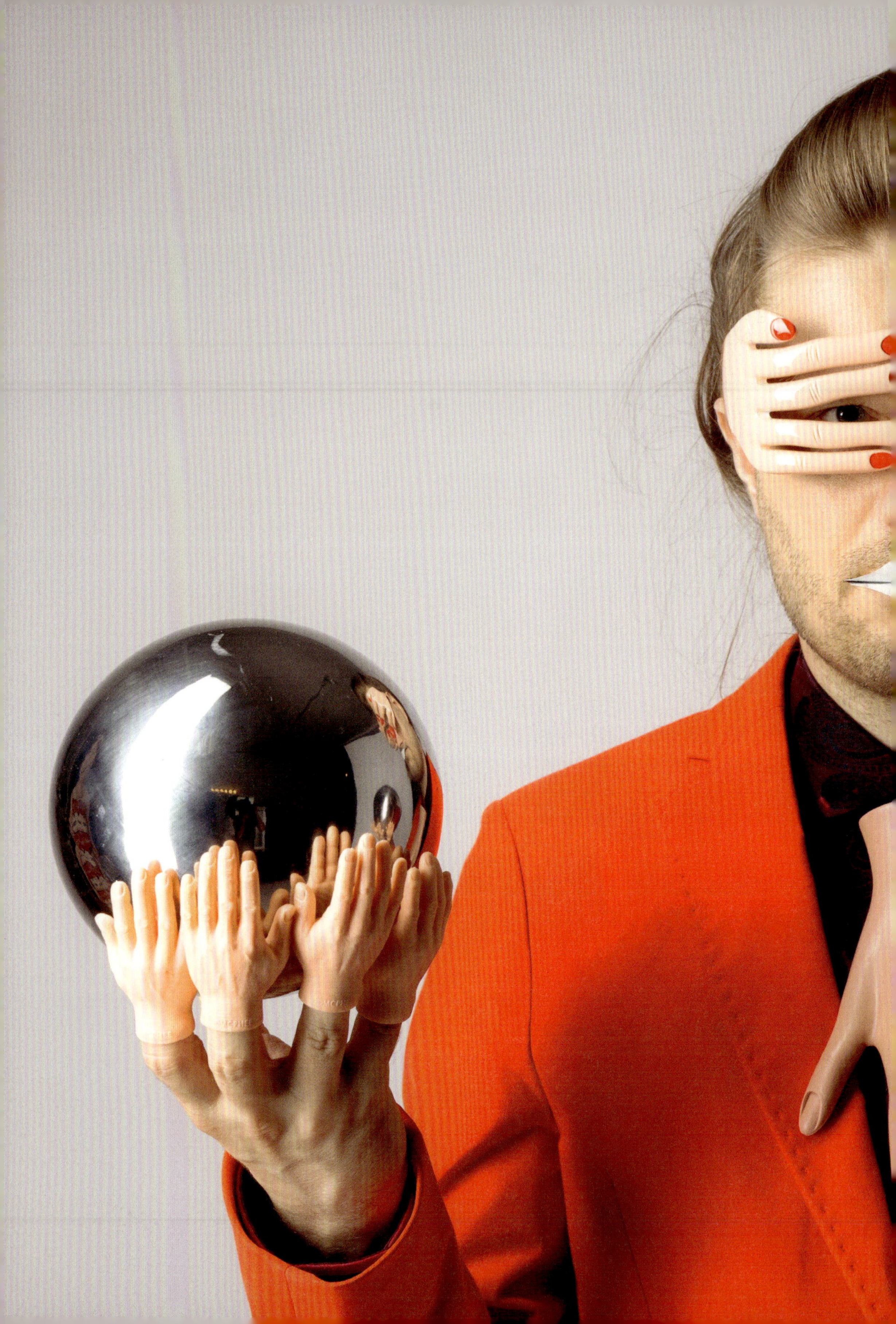

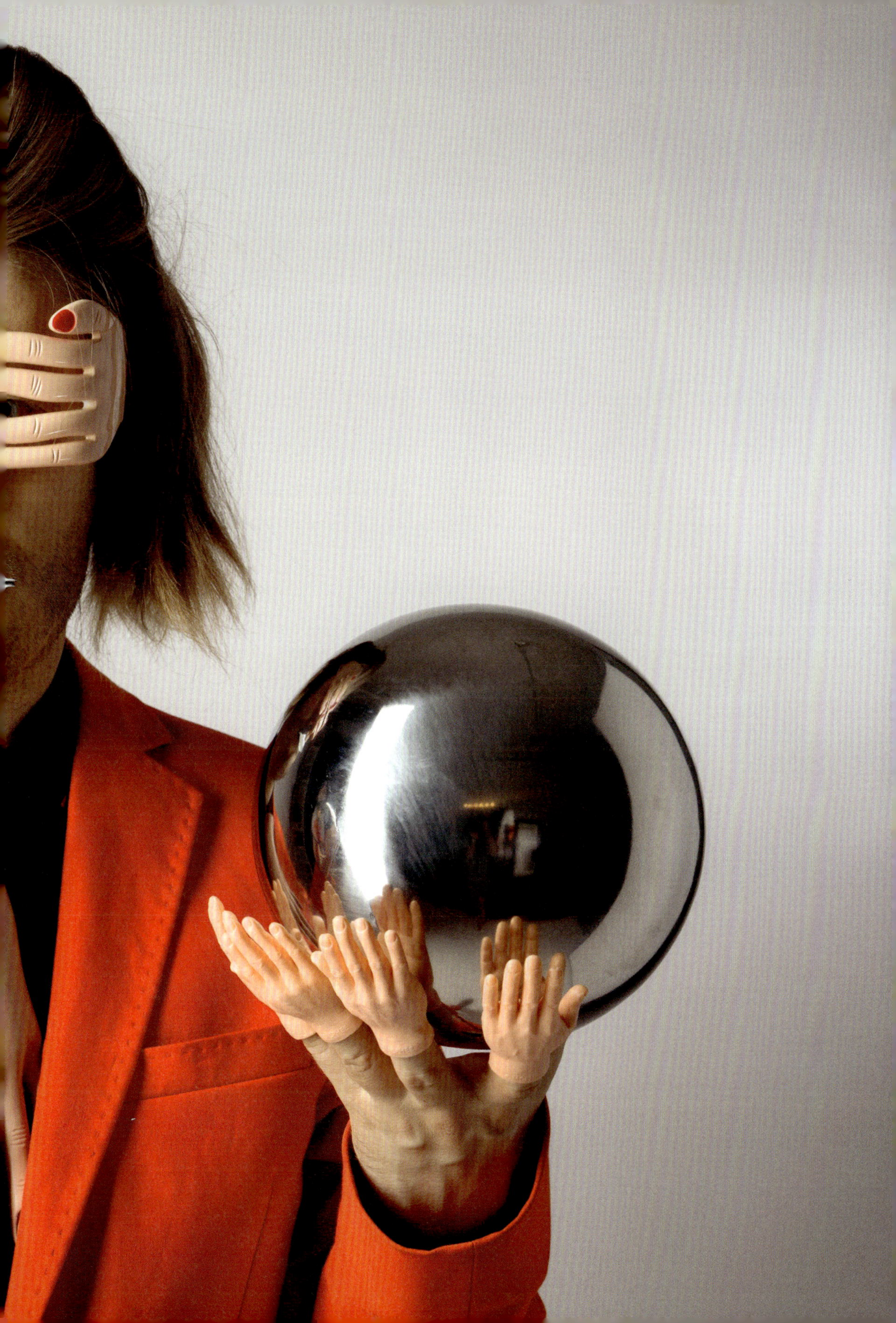

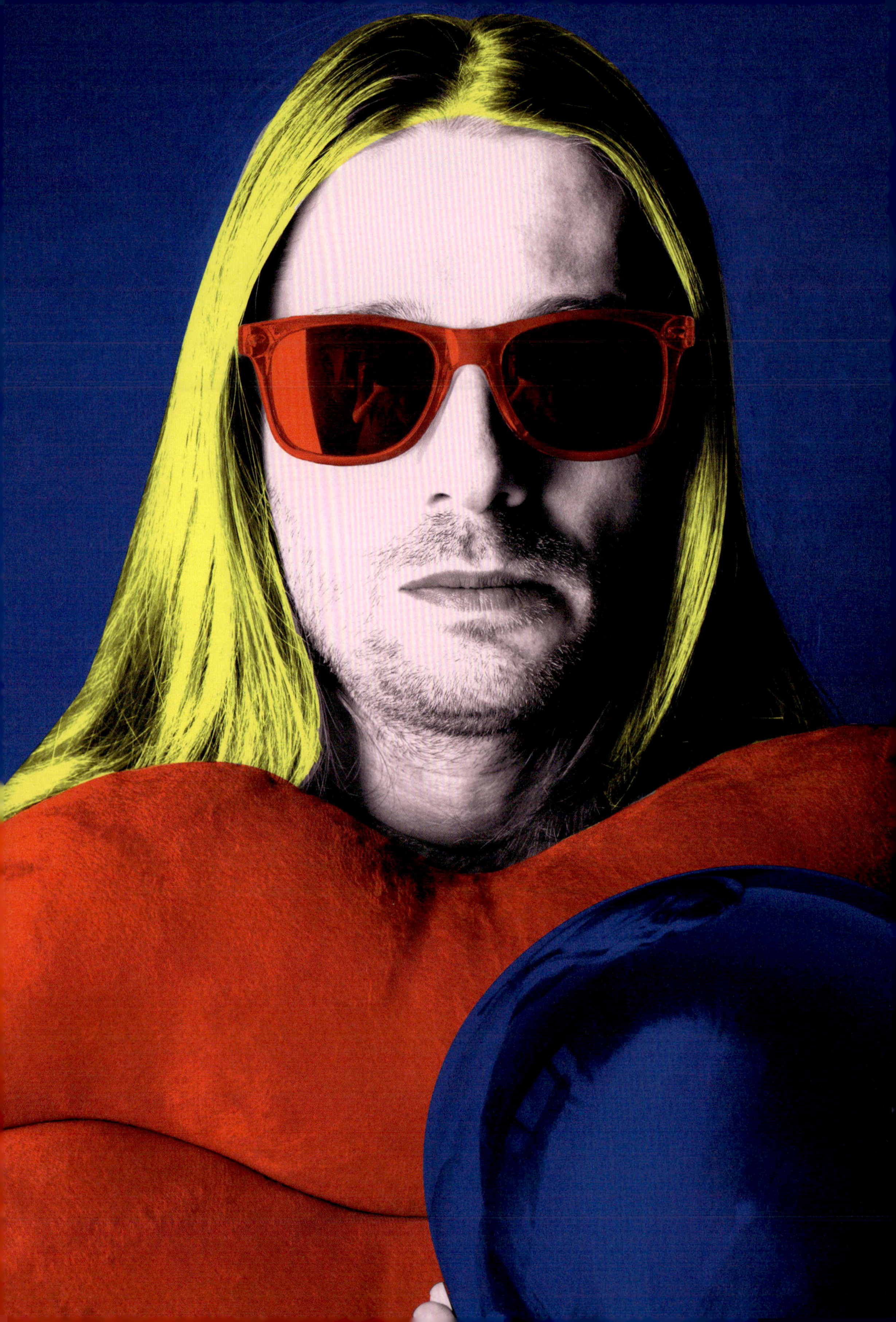

CHAPTER U

For the first half of the day, Hans was printing photographs for the agency's editorial board. July peeked into the window like a schoolkid. The sunlight was aching to infiltrate the photo paper and leave the tracks of its jovial, artistic black light. After printing, Hans immediately headed to the West Side to hand over yesterday's film for developing. The agency needed these photos this week. Hans had wanted to develop last night's occurrences himself. Film helped him reconstruct parts he had missed.

He decided to walk to the lab. July was warming the streets as much as it could; the heat exceeded ninety degrees. Hans liked to walk among the streams of heated wind. When his thoughts stopped, his legs kept going. Time disappeared, not even turning into a constant. For a spell, the concrete city became a liquefied and timeless Southern town. Soho was once a place that artists called home. Now the stores sold slippers for five thousand dollars and condoms for a buck. Lingerie, perfume, hats, boots, ties, and antiques. Soho made money while the young bearded hipsters took pictures against the background of the shops filled with goods and people. "I adore New York," everyone repeated. And then bought some piece of trash. Hans liked this romanticism, and he loved New York for the same reason others did—the heat, the walls that can bake "dough," the thousands of stoplights, and the summer dust.

Hans photographed all the decorations that occluded his camera's visual field. Little Italy, a sad parody of the real Italy, shriveled in the narrow openings of its checkered streets. The dingy houses stood like clones dreaming of returning to the motherland. Everything in Little Italy longed for the real Italy: even the restaurants, weeping, offered hamburgers and fries. Sheathed like dolls and almost bursting from their fashionably skinny suits and blouses, an unnoticeable number of office workers detoured around the happiness found on the worn tourist trails. People were running from one place to another with no rhyme or reason, with the understanding that soon they'll have enough money to take a vacation to someplace exactly as hot but far away from Soho. This idea kept them warm in the heat and sprung their muscles into action. They called their clients right in the middle of the street and told them that they'd be there soon.

"I'll call you right back!"

"You know the beneficiary didn't set up that trust!"

"Our company can offer you a promissory note!"

They ran even harder, even sadder. The faces glued to smartphones were concentrated and stressed.

Welcome to the city of dreams. Hans had lived here for two months now. It seemed to him like ten years. And he liked it—contradictions, people, emotions, disappointments, meetings, hopes, crimes, taxis, stoplights, heat. It all swarmed into a drunken cocktail, making each little sand-grain person in some way joyful thanks to the abyss of storming high and low energies. The film would be ready the next day.

On the way back, Hans walked through Central Park, by the field where he played soccer with his friends from work. It was a deviation from his planned route. Hans wanted to get to know Central Park better, to feel like a tourist and a local. Like a child running naked in the concrete fountain with the buttons. Push the button, and the fountain turned on, and the kids, running circles around their well-to-do parents, caught the summer streams with their thin hands. Across from Belvedere Castle, you could see a small island. Hans decided to move closer to the edge of the pond and noticed an uncountable family of turtles of all sizes slowly swimming in the loamy emerald water.

In one day, Hans walked around the entirety of Manhattan three times, it seemed. Like Yuri Gagarin flying over America, dropping celebratory welcoming telegrams for all the American people.

Hans took many documentary shots to get himself accustomed to life in the city, soak in the heat and the summer he loved. He was moved by the curiosity and passion of a researcher. When he had finished his tenth mile and was already close to home, exhausted and dried out by the sun, his telephone rang.

Yuma and Hans met late in the evening when all the streetlights were lit, taking the electricity from the sun, rivers, and winds. New York, taking life into its stony hands and dispersing doubt high into the heavens between the boxes of the avenues and streets. New York, handing its victory over nature to the bridges, roads, and subway lines.

Soho began to seethe even more from the happiness of the collectives of young people headed into the streets to celebrate their youth and eat time in cozy restaurants. Even the words "New York" excited every visitor, and flash froze the city's discreet charm.

Yuma leaped out of the subway underground to the street lit up like a stadium. Trillions of electrons worked hard to allow Hans to look at her for the first time without the filter of the lens of a tired camera. Like a camera flash, her flesh appeared in a thin burgundy dress. The dress was jealous of her figure, perfume, manner, youth, and brightness.

Hans didn't recognize her. He woke up just a bit more. It was all much worse. She was better than yesterday. And frankly speaking, that was impossible. Hans wanted to grab his lens and take off immediately in a cab.

Her eyes shone like nuclear power plants. She was full of curiosity. Her legs were bare—no pantyhose. Her hair was down like a spider web waiting for prey. She exuded shades of a smell that was impossible to decipher. The sunrises and photons of twenty suns were hiding within her. "I could do a portrait series," thought Hans, off topic.

She was made of something whisked up, like a soufflé. The pale material of her skin and the bright, thin dress were the elements of this composition, like a petrified bouquet in the hands of a master florist. She wasn't walking in her high heels—she was slowly flying like a Boeing 747 painted in a red dress. A black-haired hurricane, the floral aroma of a field of music. Yuma, you're a grand piano with seventeen octaves. Hans turned a bit to balance out the bewitching blot of her summer dress with the average landscape of the street. She was carrying a cloth bag in which was resting the lens made of the same glass that Hans was holding. "That girl is strapped to a plane," thought Hans to himself, seeing the bass guitar case behind Yuma's back.

After what happened yesterday, Hans had an embarrassment hangover. He was ashamed of everything. He couldn't explain to himself, and definitely not to her, why he ran out of the club without saying practically anything. Hans knew one possible answer to that question, but he tried to hide it from Yuma so that she wouldn't suddenly tell it to his face. Hans wanted to appear like a gentleman. In a tuxedo, with a bow tie and mannerisms. And to take his leave of her as soon as possible. But he had to say something final before jumping into a cab. He'd promise not to leave his lens at the next concert and would take some good pictures and even give her a big flower after the show. Maybe in a flowerpot. Stop, Hans.

Why stop? A flower in a flowerpot both looks like a warm compliment and is nonchalant enough to fit the situation.

"Thanks a million, Yuma! 'Til we meet again!" said Hans, moving towards the road.

"Meet again when, Hans? We've already met again!" In two musical hops, she overtook him and lightly grabbed him by the sleeve. "Next time, we'll have to spend a few hours texting before we meet to find a convenient time. And then an hour to get there. But now I invite you to sit for a bit while we ask each other insufficient questions while facing a drink. Twenty minutes of conversation with a girl is an investment in the future. You'll be proud of yourself."

Hans smiled. He disappeared, nodding off a bit into a dream, although her words pleased him. "In New York, friends meet for lunch once a year," she continued as if she had lived here for the two hundred years since her birth. "That's the tradition in this town. That's the kind of space this is."

"Space—sounds spacious. We're friends, you think?"

"Yes, we're friends. Forget about yesterday. Don't worry about it. I understand. Sometimes I want to leave the stage during a performance. To run away! I actually did it once..."

They stood on a street filled with people as if it were a Beatles concert. Live At Shea Stadium, 1965. All around them were lights, noise, crackles as if a film was shooting 24/7. Maybe somewhere, the inspired spirit of Andy Warhol was wandering the streets with a colossal movie camera.

"Where should we go?" Hans agreed aloud. "I'll find something on the map…"

Hans didn't know the bars and restaurants well at all.

Sometimes he even wrote addresses down on paper to not fall flat on his face in the mud on future occasions. Then he'd search for the dirty piece of paper in his pockets. Balled up, and he couldn't make anything out.

Hans began poking the lit-up screen of his smartphone like he was thrusting at a small black-and-white TV with a convex kinescope. The smartphone was smarter than Hans and showed a million restaurants throughout the Galaxy. Or in any case in Hong Kong, Bogotá, and Ottawa. And a few in Calgary as well. He and Yuma could spend a million days together, at a new restaurant every day, changing them like gloves.

Well, that's enough of describing the smartphone. Now some truth. Next to Hans stood a woman of unearthly beauty, and Hans, realizing this, tried with all his might to not notice it. It was behavior worthy of a punk kid or a person with a shady background. His experience whispered to Hans that abandoning a business early was easier than getting caught up in it later when the boats were already in the water, but there wasn't enough for everyone. A business with real estate already overburdened with debt, and you couldn't very well show the shareholders the audit. And so on.

Yuma began to laugh. She laughed at Hans' awkwardness and the very essence of it all, understanding how bad an actor he was, trying to pretend he didn't notice her. Hans himself laughed and started to get nervous, poking the incomprehensible miracle of progress for the third time.

"OK, I admit that I never was able to actually use this thing."

New York thickened and closed in around them, with each second becoming more obtrusive and concentrated. The buildings bent over and peered down at them inquisitively as if they were made of rubber. Life was humming, simmering. Only Hans, it seemed, was not very interested in it. Why? Could it be the case that a singer with the most beautiful eye shape imaginable, in the most unabashed dress, who plays the bass guitar, and who is inviting you to have a few drinks, in addition to the infinitely brilliant diamond city—could it be that these improprieties, incompatible with life, call forth doubt? In that case, a little more truth: Hans' peripheral vision caught how Yuma's scarlet dress fluttered when the hot wind gushed. Among the stone boxes of the ambitious landscape, a stranger, a fireball of music, waited for him, for this wimp. These fragments of strange thoughts got in the way of Hans seeing the smile of volatility worn by the evening streets. When Berlin, with its rainy nights, left the impression of an unwanted gelatin shadow.

"Let's go already!" Yuma gave a sudden, high-amplitude smile. "Computers aren't faster than people yet. There are tons of great places all around."

"What does that mean, great places?" thought Hans. In that sense, it was always easier for women. They glide along the surface of life's LP without scratching it. Hans' record player had long ago gotten stuck on the same melody, the needle jumped and ruined the groove—the gravelly song turned into one incomprehensible word from an inaudible chorus about someone's woe.

Within two minutes, they were entering a poorly lit bar, where Hans almost lost Yuma. She dissolved into the darkness and wasn't answering her phone, so it took him a few minutes to find her again. Hans never really understood bars, particularly their darkness. After all, bars were made for meeting with people, but it just so happens that they're more often used for partings. In any case, Hans preferred open spaces and a bottle of red wine on the beach. The despondency and dullness of twilight-lit tables couldn't even compare with the hot stones of the shoreline. Glass, cocktail, nuts.

Cocktail, ice, potato chips. But there weren't many people in this bar, and the evening had just begun.

The precise and full notes of an old piano swarmed in Hans' hearing, and he found Yuma not far from the instrument and the stage, where a slow song in ear-pleasing Japanese was ending, supported by a saxophone, bass guitar, and the bold, rustling rhythm of drums.

Hans sat down at a free table with his back to the stage. A Suprematist pattern of multicolored flecks lighted Yuma. She sat down across from him, facing the musicians. Through and under the glass table with the grate of gold lines, Hans saw the peninsulas of Yuma's knees. It looked like Yuma was in a cage or prison. The contrast between beauty and captivity is always evocative. It seemed to Hans that they didn't even have to talk. He could just sit there and look at her. But etiquette demanded his presence, and Hans put on his social candy mask. Authentic curiosity had always been his strong point, which singled him out from others. Hans' first question to women he didn't know in New York was always the same:

"What brought you to New York?" Hans improvised in a relaxed manner.

Yuma smiled as if she knew his secret. Small diamond crystals appeared on her lips and eyelashes, and her make-up shone in the semi-darkness from that sparkle, which made her a living museum exhibit. Yuma's face had been crafted by Fabergé, or maybe someone even more talented, like Bill Gates or Steve Jobs. Her make-up skills astounded make-up artists and photographers around the world. She was no gadget, nor was she an analog work of antiquity. She was a girl woven together from contradictions: playful naiveté plus experience. The lemon of disappointment that won everyone over, shattering into pieces the crystal of her naiveté. The Bermuda triangle of her strange face had sunk more than one naïve ship of pilgrims. She had a birthmark on her left cheek and another near her lips, as a princess should. As a queen must. As is written in the rules of cinematography and love. And there were different birthmarks for different tastes. And most likely some under her dress. Her hairdo was the best in the world. Her black Japanese hair came down like a child's hat, a huge dark tulip that grew from the heartbeats of happily married parents. She loved to smile with her upper teeth, painted the white of Russian snow, Chinese mother-of-pearl, Indian ivory, and the radiance of the door of a Singaporean refrigerator. All the dentists in the world cried out to her—Stay away! You're too good even to pronounce your own name in our presence! But Yuma's most important good trait, her human essence, was in another part of her body, as one might easily guess. The most significant expression of her nature was the mischievous and insolent spider in her eyes. Maybe you didn't need to see her dress, and it wasn't necessary to measure the height of her heels and the angle at which her legs bent in relation to her gravitational vector. Maybe the birthmark near her lips was part of an antiquated, over-conservative textbook model of beauty. But her living eyes were a new form of human splendor found in the depths of a sweet and kind Japanese Cinderella—the kind of guileless queen that she seemed to be. Her eyes had wandered through millennia in various reincarnations before finding their only possible home in this amazing, elegant being.

"So, what brought you to New York?" Hans asked anyway. He knew that no one knew the answer to that question. Not even Buddha flying over Manhattan. Not even Mao Tse-tung. Neither did those who had lived all their lives in New York, nor those that had never been even once. Nobody could provide a straight answer. Even people for whom there was something that brought them to New York knew that they didn't know what brought them to New

York. Was New York a place for a romantic date? An insane asylum? A fantasy land for museum lovers? A gas chamber for tourists? A construction site for foremen? A ghetto for workers? An illusion for poets? A stuffy toilet that fits ten million people?

Hans tried to jot down each of these answers in his journal of days that had passed.

"So, what brought you to New York?" Hans asked Yuma when they were bringing her a glass of 梅酒 and him two cappuccinos so that he could feel like El Niño.

"I wanted to give a concert on the sequoias," she answered.

"A concert on the sequoias?" Hans inquired.

"Yes. Go up to the top, to the crown, make a stage in the branches, and sing at night alone in the forest, with a guitar. A concert."

"That's actually cool! It's a great idea! I could play the drums, nail them to the trunk. But I think the sequoias are in California."

"Yes, that's right. They're in California. But if you're going to California from Tokyo, why not stop in New York on your way?" Her face was serious.

"Makes sense! And you decided to get stuck here?"

"No, I wanted to go see the sequoias, to get stuck in the branches, and then everything else. I heard that the air in California helps change a person's destiny. The destiny of a drummer or a singer. And, of course, the sequoias have changed my destiny. That's why we're in New York now."

"Oh, so you were there?"

"Where?"

"In the sequoias."

"Well, yeah. I said they changed my destiny."

"And what did you do there?"

"I sang from the trees, sent my song to the ocean. Two nights I lived in the boughs, without hot water. And then in tents on the seashore, listening to the sound of the tides. I met so many interesting guys there. That's California. That's real destiny."

"How often do you play concerts here?

"Three times."

"A week?"

"No, a year."

"But why here? Why did you get the urge to leave your hometown? To discover something?"

"We don't have enough freedom in Tokyo. Japan is too traditional. Work fifty years in one company, live sixty years with one man. Seventy years in the same house. TV and growing flowers at eighty, grandchildren at ninety. The Guinness Book of World Records at a hundred and twenty. Boring. A library of rules, prejudices, and traditions."

"Is tradition bad?"

"Being born into a tradition is good. But people want to feel free and have freedom. Sometimes to change their country. It's something like treason."

"And you feel free here, in New York?"

"Oh yeeeeah."

"Oh yeeeeah?"

"Oh yeeeeah."

They both laughed.

"Well then. Shall we drink to treason?" proposed Hans.

"To treason!"

Between Hans' two hemispheres, it was raining. Thunderclaps boomed, streams of cold torrential rain flowed over the Earth, the river of water filling the whole street. It was almost impossible to walk.

The wind bent and then broke the tree branches. The raindrops beat your face and hit you right in the pupils of your eyes.

By asking boring questions, Hans risked appearing to have been born in a walnut shell, with arms spouting on the outside and head inside. He, therefore, intercepted his existential curiosity and instead glanced furtively at Yuma's knees. She noticed his glance through the square-patterned cage of the table and smiled apprehensively, but still expressed through her discomfort her negligible favor of the action. Hans also ordered himself 梅酒. It tasted so unexpectedly light that Hans felt a change in gravity, like he was wrapped up in the space-time continuum.

The band of musicians concluded their concert and began unhurriedly gathering their instruments. The speakers played a recording of some slow unknown melody. Yuma raised her head. She looked towards the speakers anxiously, as if imprisoned inside them was someone alive who needed her. She slightly opened her mouth to take stock of reality. Casting a look at the bartender, she faltered for a second more and then began to sing in an unknown language:

俺は河原の枯れススキ
同じお前も枯れススキ
どうせ二人はこの世では
花の咲かない枯れススキ

One of the musicians who was getting ready to go brought Yuma a guitar. She waved him aside after whispering something in his ear. In a second, a friendly blond with peroxide-dyed hair and a Marilyn hairdo was already handing Yuma an actual bass guitar plugged into an amp. From the other direction came a microphone stand, which had come down from the stage to Hans and Yuma's

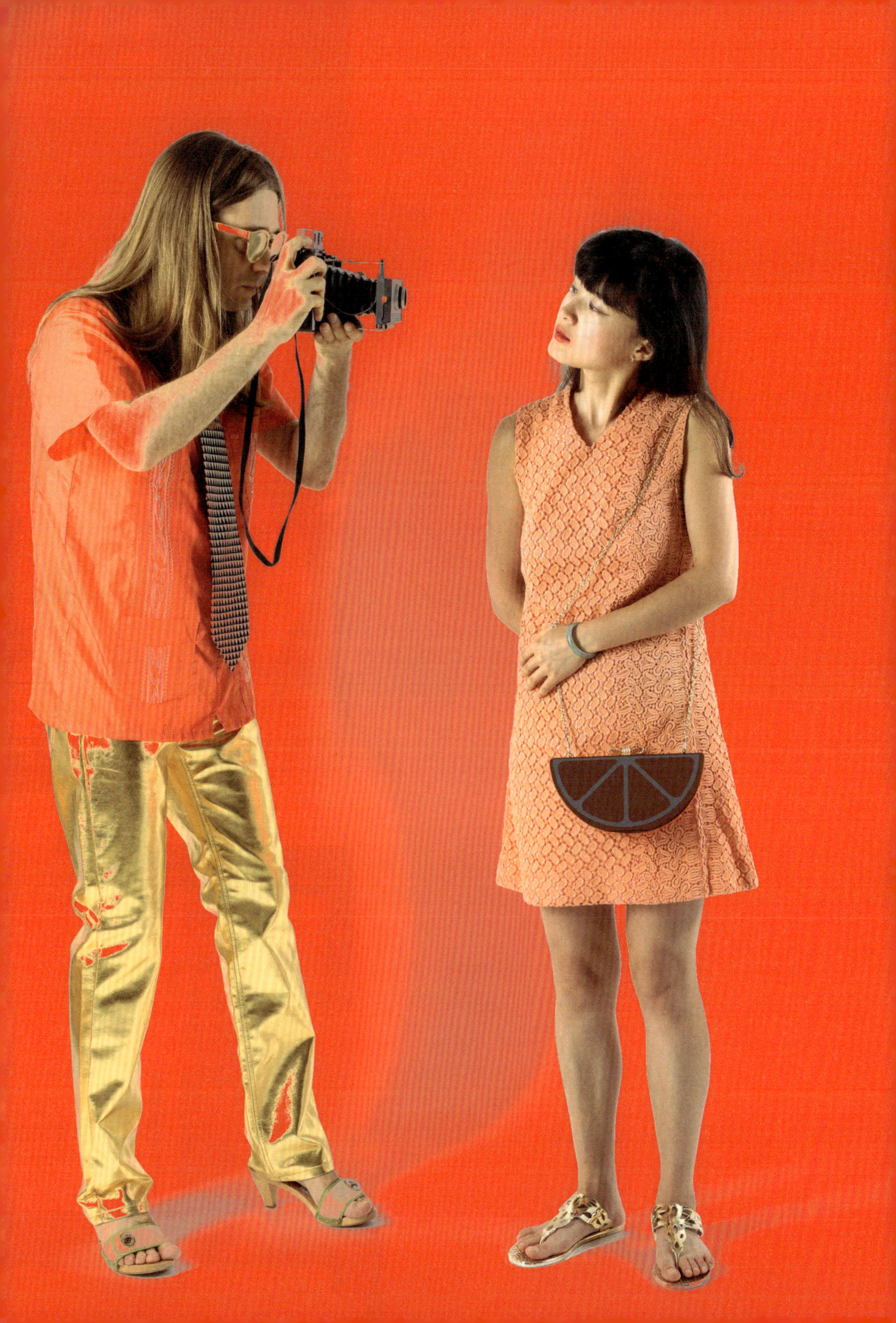

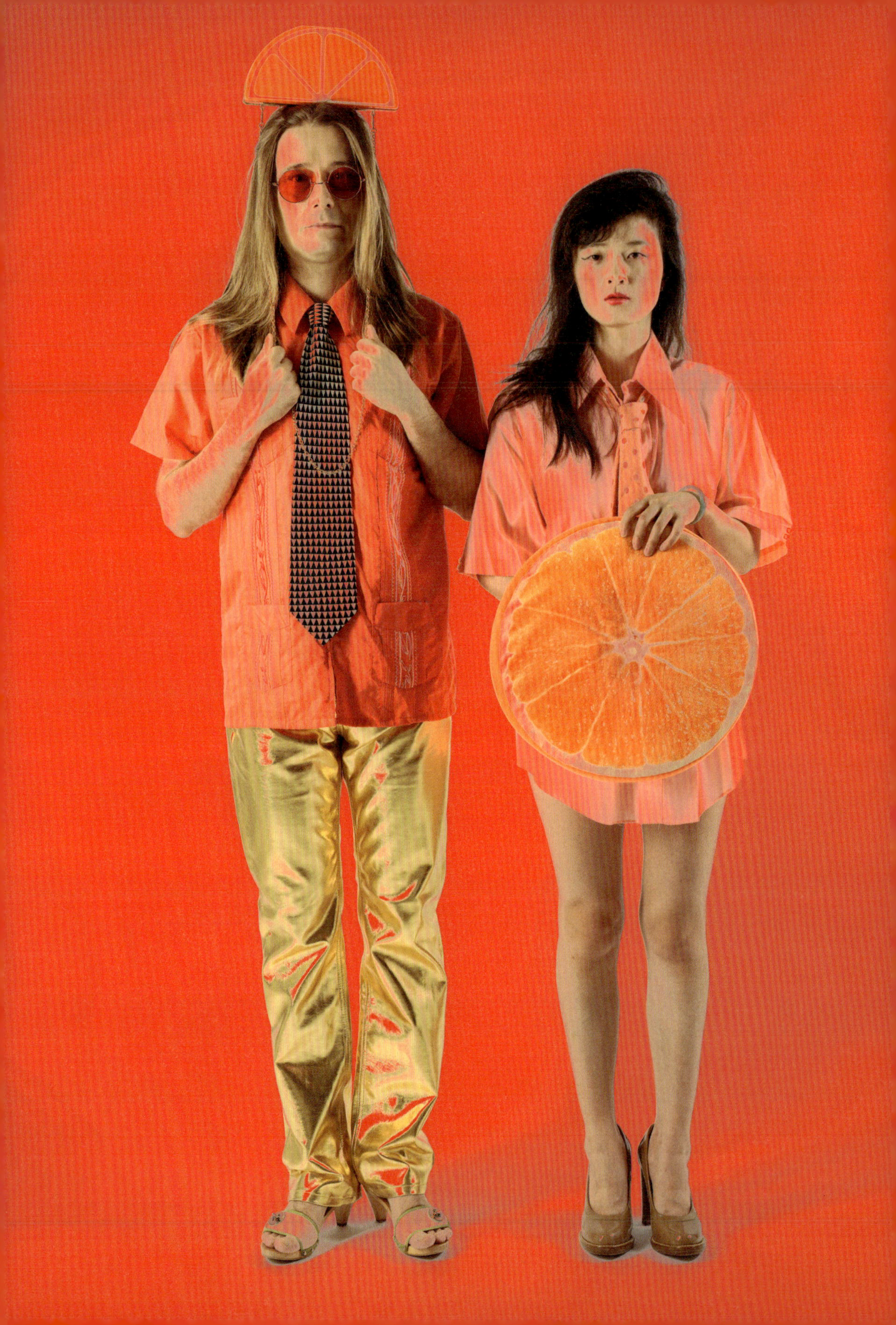

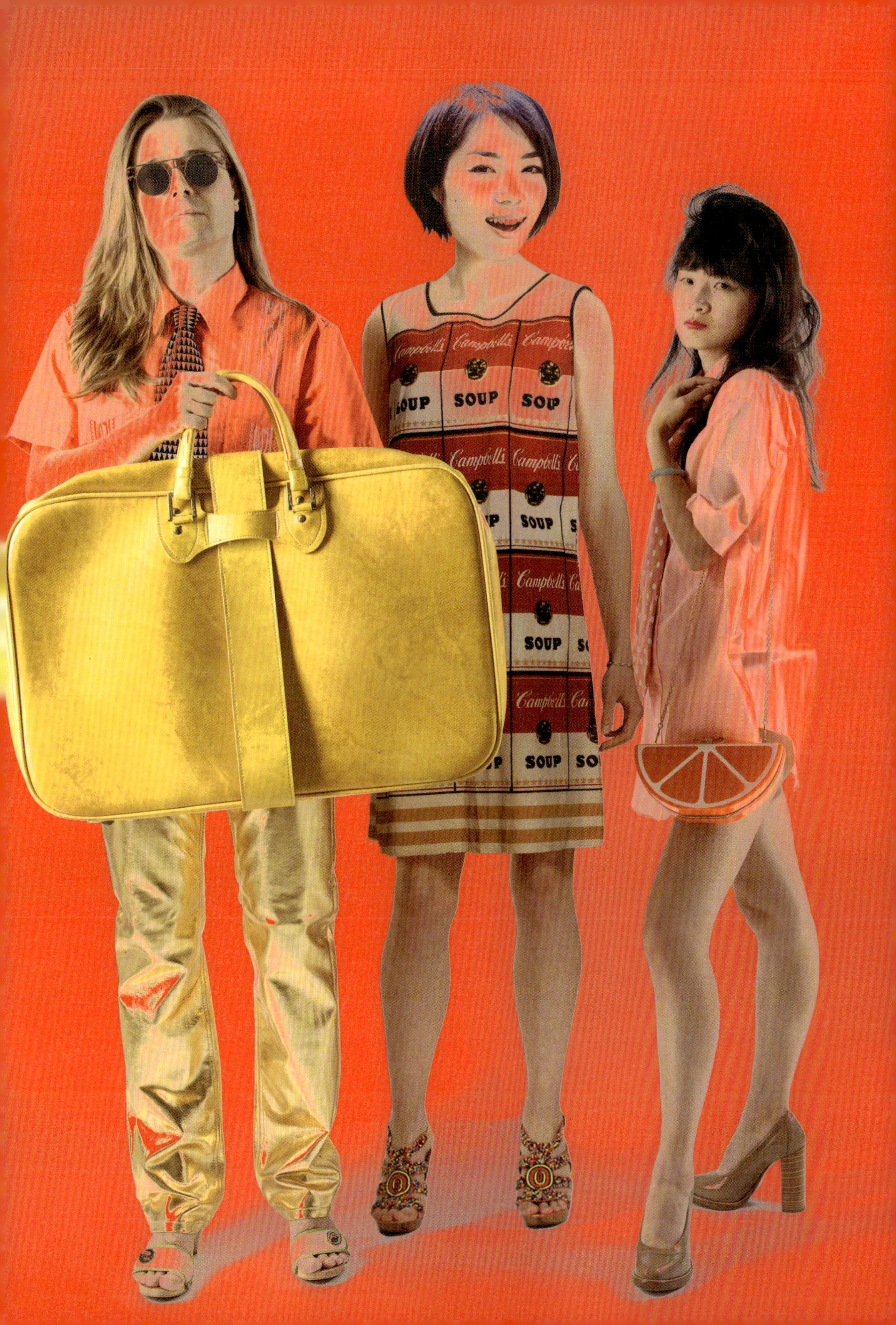
Campbell's
SOUP

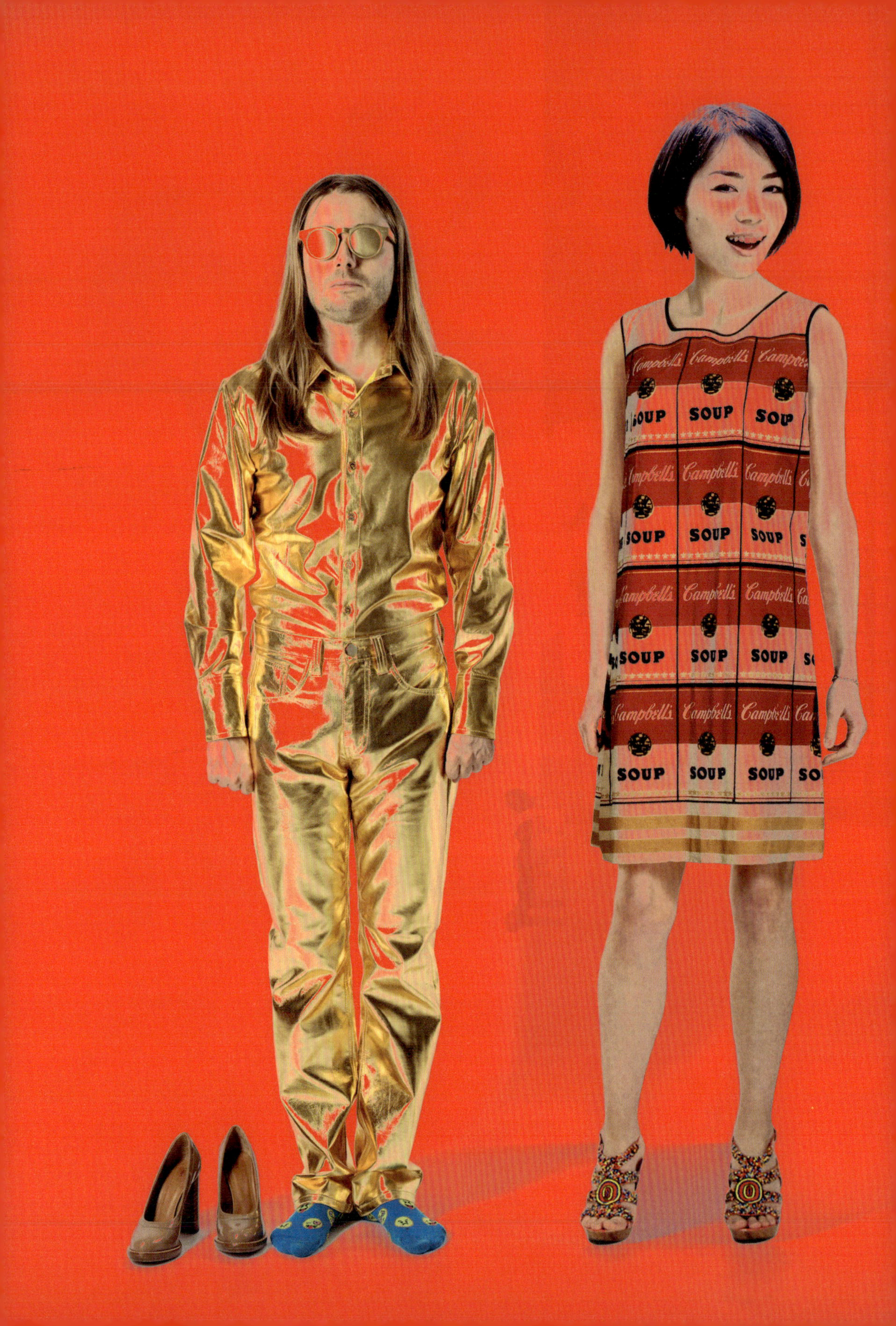
Campbell's
SOUP

table. Yuma stood up behind the microphone, played a B-flat on the top string.

死ぬも生きるもねえお前
水の流れに何変わろ
俺もお前も利根川の
船の船頭で暮らそうよ

The bartender turned off the recording, and Yuma continued alone but not alone, singing a lullaby to the bass guitar. Her forceful voice joined the sadness and softness of the melody with the snow-white stringed bass, forming a contrasting suspension of grief and authentic light. Not exactly smiling and not exactly weeping, she was floating along with her voice on the deck of the enormous cruise ship of the bass, which hummed restlessly, spreading the slow melody across the ocean's horizon. The people in the room stopped talking and drinking their drinks. Some turned towards the stage. The music sounded solemn and mournful. The audience's attention created a tension in the room.

Yuma played the bass guitar like José Raúl Capablanca. The fragile fingers with the thin, shiny diamond ring jumped between chords on the fretless neck, hugging the strings like a bunch of plaintively droning cables begging for mercy. The guitar's rhythm outstripped that of the voice. It seemed that the musical notes were running, streaming ahead, taking with them the sadness and the voice itself. Some people stood up from their tables, bewitched by this mystery. She ended the song with some slow, sad words, probably about dawn and the singing of birds and about the pinkening sky over the sea.

Someone was crying at the next table. Hans himself, it must be admitted, also couldn't hold back a tear.

"Bravo! Encore, encore!" From around the room came shouts

of people asking for more. More playing, more singing. Her dress, the sparkles, the beauty of her smooth movements, the elegant confidence of her thin fingers battling with the strings. Yuma started another song, hugging the bass, afraid to let it go.

The speakers were turned out onto the street and played so loud that the music could be heard in Soho for blocks. The unusual, flowing, grandiose, strong, meaningful music contrasted with transitory anxieties, fashion, and the amount of external debt borne by competition-weary New Yorkers.

People began coming into the bar from the street, more and more of them. A traffic jam formed outside. Cars stopped. Some of those who were originally just driving by wanted to park to find out what was going on, who got shot at today.

The room filled up with people who had heard Yuma's magical voice and didn't understand what was going on. Was this a return to the past? Or the discovery of something new? It seemed that the scratching of the vinyl record, the mood of wailing jazz, and the burned-out vacuum tubes of the amplifiers had all come back from the past, and everyone had anticipated this meeting for many years. People were crying, staring at her. They couldn't stop crying.

Yuma sang her third encore, on the stage now, where her thin ghost of a dress flew around her graceful, sorrowful figure and the beam from the footlights projected the shadow of her eyelashes onto the stage, making Yuma a spider with a multitude of legs. The most elegant and precious spider in the world, carved from mosaic gold. A musical witch-enchantress. A singing Japanese music box robot. A producer's dream. Unattainable by her listeners. Hans watched the show from the last balcony on the tenth floor, through field binoculars, and she was in orbit between Jupiter and Saturn in the shining x-rays of the cold sun. The origami of her voice was impossible to listen to without participating in it, and an obscure sorrow rose and cast a spell that transformed into an earthquake.

The restaurant filled up to the point of bursting. People could no longer sit at their tables. They all stood up to try to see the stage and the girl on it. Hans also stood up next to his table. Several people in front of him blocked his line of vision to Yuma. Jazz, then rock, then the howling of a lone bass string, drove the listeners into a trance. The music released feelings in people, feelings hidden in the gray bag of their calculated life. Yuma fished out the moods of everyone there with a rod and reel. The chemical reaction caused by coming into contact with her de-preserved sadness turned the audience inside out.

A line of people wanting to get into the bar formed out on the street. Those who couldn't get in stood near the entrance listening to the amazing voice pouring from the speakers. New York became a different city, where magic stopped time and filled the streets with an atmosphere of freedom. The music was just that gentle, disquieting, and transparent. Taxicabs were backed up on the street to the Upper East Side. The city fell quiet with pride.

The heights of the golden voice and the bravery of the silver bass gave birth to a snowy cocktail for summer and strings. The song progressively became one with the girl herself, becoming her breath, her hand gestures, and the movement of her dress. Every second, Yuma died and was reborn. With every bar of jazz in her songs, she gave hope to a future spring that flew out of her like a butterfly. Yuma's wings—her dress—drew flowing patterns of scarlet flashes that swung the melody around the room. The singer stood harmoniously behind the helm of the bass guitar, turning into the skinny stem of an agitated flower.

Hans saw her through the gaps in the crowd of people.

Tears of admiration traitorously trickled down onto his cheeks. Femininity—especially if you are a man—is beyond human vocabulary. Femininity is the harbinger of new life. Femininity is the smell of the air after a storm. Femininity is the dew on flowers in the quiet of the dawn. Femininity is birds flying above the horizon.

Yuma retrieved every note carefully, each more carefully than the previous one. Her face swayed in a barely noticeable breeze. She lived the song, becoming more important than the song. People couldn't turn away from the beauty and purity of her sounds, from the perfection of the lines of her pale face that had once been kissed by the sun. Her lips were a whipped froth of sweet pink chocolate. She knit them as if they were brows or a sailboat turning windward.

The music made her suffer. Her eyes burned with the light of grief. The nobility and sophistication of her movements made you follow every nuance with bated breath. In the middle of the stage, Yuma was so magnificent that she fettered the gaze of everyone in the hall with iron chains. It was impossible to think of anything else, to disengage from the music or the all-consuming beauty.

People even began taking each other by the hand. Some lit candles, some turned on flashlights. The public started waving their hands back and forth. People, most of the people, were crying. It was a genuine mystery. That bar, the whole of New York, had seen nothing like it since The Beatles.

When the song was over, the people, overwhelmed and blushing from all their feelings, cried and asked her to sing some more. She began another song. And it all continued. Young girls shrieked in ecstasy, unable to contain themselves. Someone had a heart attack, and an ambulance was called. The musicians all joined in, the piano breathing through its hundreds of keys and squeaking its wooden frame, helping the music along. It was out of the question that this song not be sung or the music not be played. Tourists, onlookers, couples taking a walk, adventure seekers, and passers by couldn't understand why traffic had stopped or what had just happened here, in this small, cozy corner of Soho, which on regular evenings was bathed in dull electric light.

Feathery clouds slowly shrouded the evening and transformed it into a warm, pleasant night. Inside Yuma lived many girls and women simultaneously. This overpowered Hans. Musically he could not match her talent, and his images didn't match her music. Yuma was so high up that the visual world of photography seemed excessively abstract and frozen.

Hans knew only one thing: she needed him today, not for his photographs, not for his talent, and not even for his admiration—she was being admired plenty without him.

The bigger the city, the more comprehensible the feelings of each of its denizens.

CHAPTER 9

The music died down. The bar emptied. Night came. They walked along the dark, already empty Greenwich Avenue towards the High Line. Hans had no words left, and he didn't much want to talk anyway. He required a language other than words, but what kind Hans didn't know. The notes from the bass strings of her guitar kept repeating in his head.

Hans listened and listened to the silence, finding within his heart's inertia the delayed notes in the night-cooled air. He found himself caught up in a current that was carrying him somewhere with its delicate, inconspicuous paws. Somewhere the waves were crashing in the sea.

Hans was not sufficiently respectful of experimentation. He decided to help Yuma take the bass guitar home and then return to his place by the shortest route. They got a cab at Eighth Avenue. Yuma lived in Harlem on 116th St., and all that Hans knew about Harlem was that the ghost of Duke Ellington wandered at night and would make music that the residents heard in their ears. Also, there were handsome, muscular guys walking around that you couldn't look in the eye—the strong men of the world. And these lively guys, like Duke, could also play jazz that wasn't that bad.

The cab driver was a young man who looked like an artist more than a cab driver. He wore the kind of close-fitting acid green t-shirt that cyclists wear an blue scarf around his neck. His unshaven face, covered by a black raincloud of a beard, was in sync with the current fashion. The frames of his glasses—which were possibly fake—were black too and made him a real playboy, a master of flirtation and success.

"I used to work at NASA. I calculated the trajectory for a flight to Mars," he began without any introduction, "but they cut the program, spent the money on some pre-election crap, and I decided to try my luck in New York. I don't have a real job yet, but I love trajectories and movement. That's why being a taxi driver for me is ideal—it's meditation. It's just a shame that there are no diagonal or hyperbolic streets."

It was as if he were speaking in equations, getting his kicks by confusing his listeners with unnecessary words.

"Are you musicians?" the fellow asked after a block of his philosophical musings.

"Yeah, something like that." Hans awkwardly kept his intonation up.

"You have a concert in Harlem?"

"Yes, a couple."

"Well, you guys make a nice couple."

For some reason, Hans looked at Yuma to size her up. To assess her assessment. Yuma smiled.

They rode down Fifth Avenue, passing by the Metropolitan Museum, and Yuma suggested they get out and walk a bit. OK. Unsmiling, Hans didn't object. He was surer and surer of his feeling of what she needed. Hans noted that Yuma's smile was a sad one. "Or is she tired? Or does she want me to take some initiative?" he asked himself. But Yuma got out of the cab happy, leaving doubt behind.

"I can't walk on these heels anymore. The lens, the bass…could you take my shoes too?" she asked, clearly realizing that Hans would indeed have some objection but that he couldn't refuse. Because a girl more magical than the Magic Flute itself walking around barefoot at night is a fairy tale, the dream of every park that's dying of boredom. Central Park, built for voyeurism, was hoping for a soap opera.

"Do you have a boyfriend, or um, a guy?" asked Hans insinuatingly.

"Yes, of course, I do. In Japan. He's big… kind. He plays ping pong and Nintendo."

"Nintendo? Is that anything like Go?"

"Yeah..." She got a bit embarrassed. "But we broke up ten years ago."

"Ah, OK. I'm sorry. That's very interesting. I mean, dramatic." Hans mumbled foggily.

"And you?" she asked.

"What?" Hans stalled.

"Who do you have?"

"I have a boyfriend too."

Her eyes got round with disappointment.

"Eeeeeeeeeeeeee! それは本当ですか？ What's his name?"

"Andy Warhol… He lives with me." Hans cracked a smile.

"Nice name, Andy Warhol… Have you been together long?" she asked, a bit agitated.

"Oh, it's been a very long time, I think. I guess since I was born. Yeah, since I was born!" Hans figured out loud.

"So, you're brothers?"

"Um, yeah."

"So you're Hans Warhol?"

"Yep, exactly!" Hans laughed.

She laughed too. They were both feeling quite good. So good that they looked at each other with eyes that were jumping with laughter.

A kiss on her lips
was like
kissing a pillow.

CHAPTER 10

Going deeper into Central Park, walking by the Met, after a complicated dialogue about the essence of being, Hans and Yuma walked in silence. So much had happened today that the Earth managed to revolve around its axis twice, drawing out time.

They sat down on the grass on a small hill across from Belvedere Castle, almost right next to the pond. Different colored lights lit up the castle and reflected onto the pond, mixed its colors with the grass, and crept into the dark water with its reflection's brown brick and stone pastel. On the hill, where it was so comfortable, the stony life of the skyscrapers took a step back, giving space to nature, the sky, and the night. The blue chips were sleeping somewhere, disconnected from the stock exchange computers. Yuma had removed herself somewhat from the fuss of the fame that was hers from the evening and became more relaxed. Hans sensed that she wanted to draw the evening out just as much as he did.

The weak gusts of warm wind brought barely audible echoes of thunder from somewhere. And it seemed that somewhere far, far away, flashes of lightning flared. The moon shone through the light smoke of a pattern of clouds, and grasshoppers chirred, playing on the lawn. In the distance, past the park, building spotlights shone too, looking like rock crystals. The city was still alive, simmering, conveying its emotions. People were breaking dishes on the hundredth floor, sobbing. Someone was spending money, someone couldn't get to sleep, and somebody's parakeets were dying. Someone was doing laundry.

Hans and Yuma at that minute were so far from that city amid its passions. It seemed like they had lived a very long and happy life together in the wilds of the forest. They sat a certain distance from one another, listening to the wind and the rustling of the trees in nature. As usual, Hans did not feel anything personal in the diffused picture of the pleasantly warm evening. He had learned to value detachment, the kind that the astronomer feels when he is elated by the barely visible twinkling stars he sees in the eyepiece of his instrument. A trillion miles, the echo of a few escaped photons... that's what made the picture incredibly spellbinding and absolutely beautiful. The sparkles on Yuma's dress spread themselves out like the Milky Way in her far-off galaxy, which Hans wanted to observe, but only through the optics of half-blind radio telescopes.

The recently cut grass smelled just as it did in childhood. The hot, moist air blew over their cheeks and whirled off skyward, playing first with the trees, then with the clouds, and then with the roofs of the buildings, freeing the world from stagnant desolation. Heavy fireflies filled with shining electricity flew slowly over the grass, their bulbs lighting up Belvedere Castle. Nature had a setting like that of a mechanical watch factory, the hands of the watch measuring the fluidity of existence, taking with them the daily cares of the high-rise buildings in the book-written past. Hans breathed that air and couldn't get enough of it, as if it was the first day he had ever seen the grass, and the sky, and the stars. The moon triggered the gravity of sad sorcery. Its circle shined a hospital stain of misery. The ashen color made Hans young and smoothed out his first wrinkles, turning him into a schoolboy, and then into a seven-year-old child with his father photographing a landscape in the fields with a tripod on a moonlit night.

His father brought a bentwood chair to the field from home and placed it among the bright spikelets swaying in the wind. It was a chilly, cloudy sky, and the disquieting and funereal light of the moon, whispering warnings of the future to little Hans, told him in advance about the shortness and futility of life. Hans' father was the same at one time: small, young, looking at the moon through binoculars from the bentwood chair. Later, the developed photograph turned night into day because it was a black and white negative. The field wiggling with grass became a soft river, enshrouding his father, who was sitting on the chair carefree and even joyful. That photograph was, to this day, the most significant memory of that life. It currently hung in his bedroom, in his strange little apartment in Soho.

Here in Central Park, Hans imperceptibly felt that, together with the sick moon and the warm caring fireflies, something else was also returning to him—a long-forgotten and, at the same time, disturbing feeling of happiness and youth. The restlessness of Hans' artistic body crowded together to make room for the new, unspoken delight in a life worn down into rags, which Hans could never connect with anyway. Despite the fireflies, the loveliness of the moon, and the warmth of the wind gusts. The picture of the magical night and the sweet girl sitting in front of him vanished like a scene from the window of a train unexpectedly pulling out of a station.

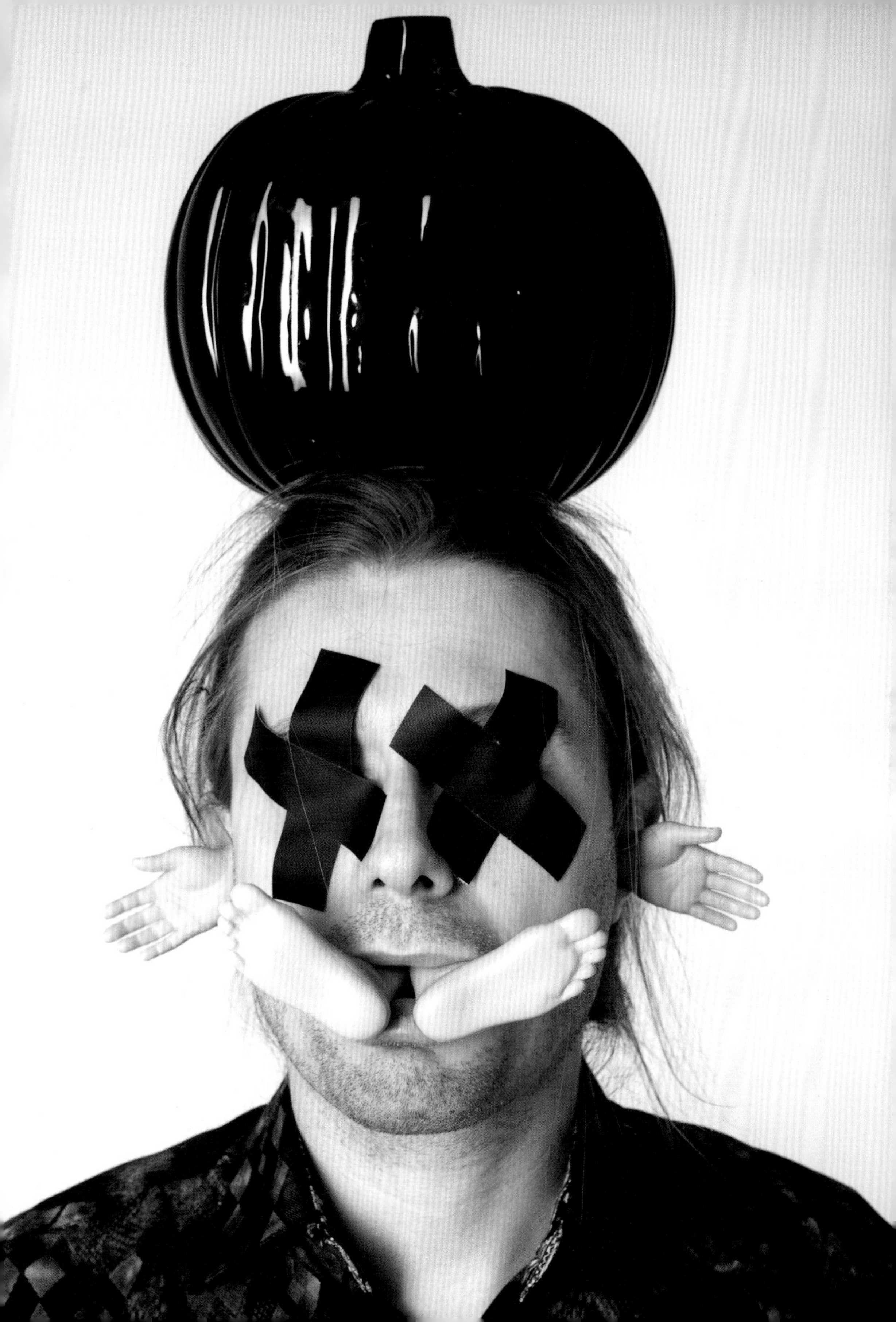

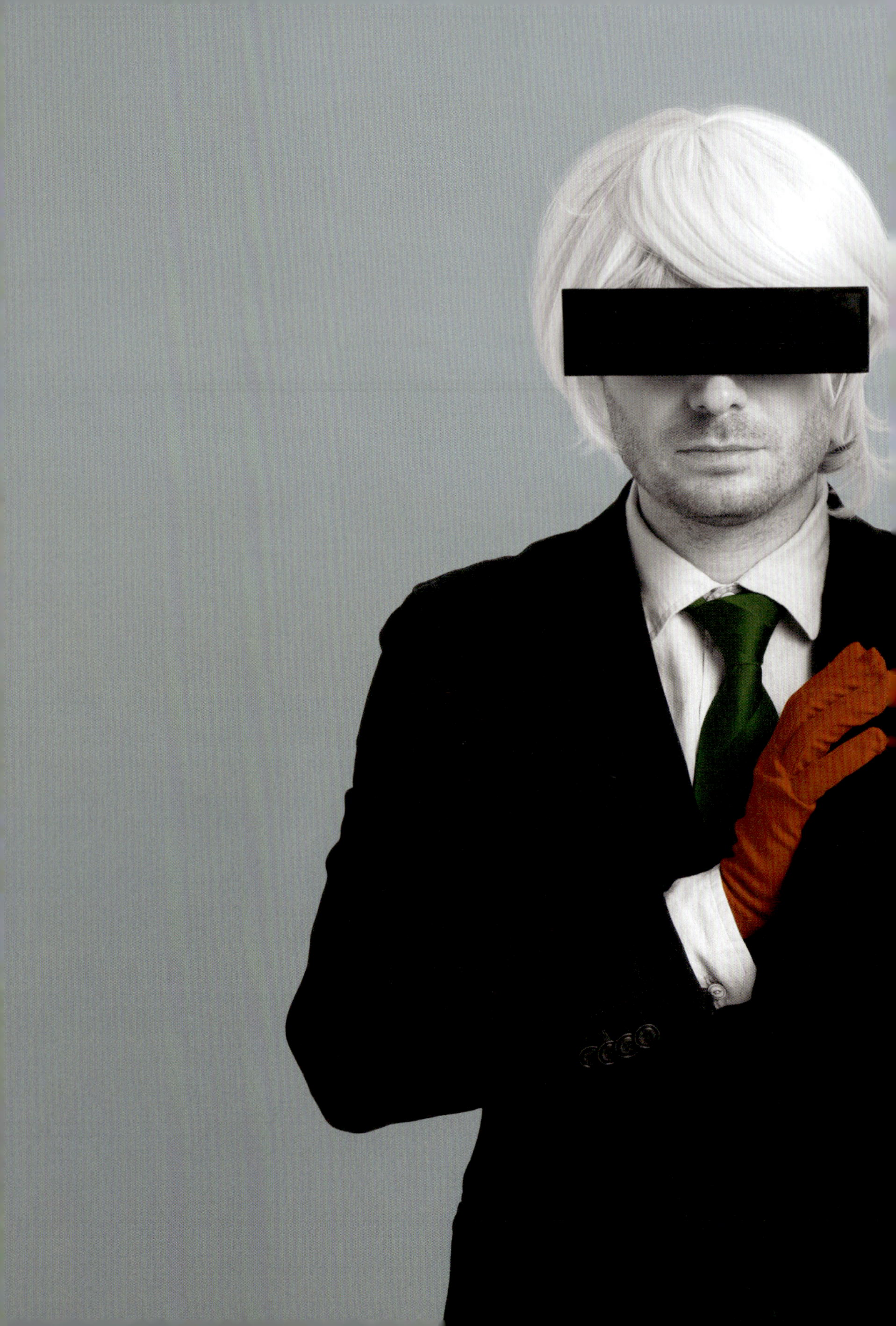

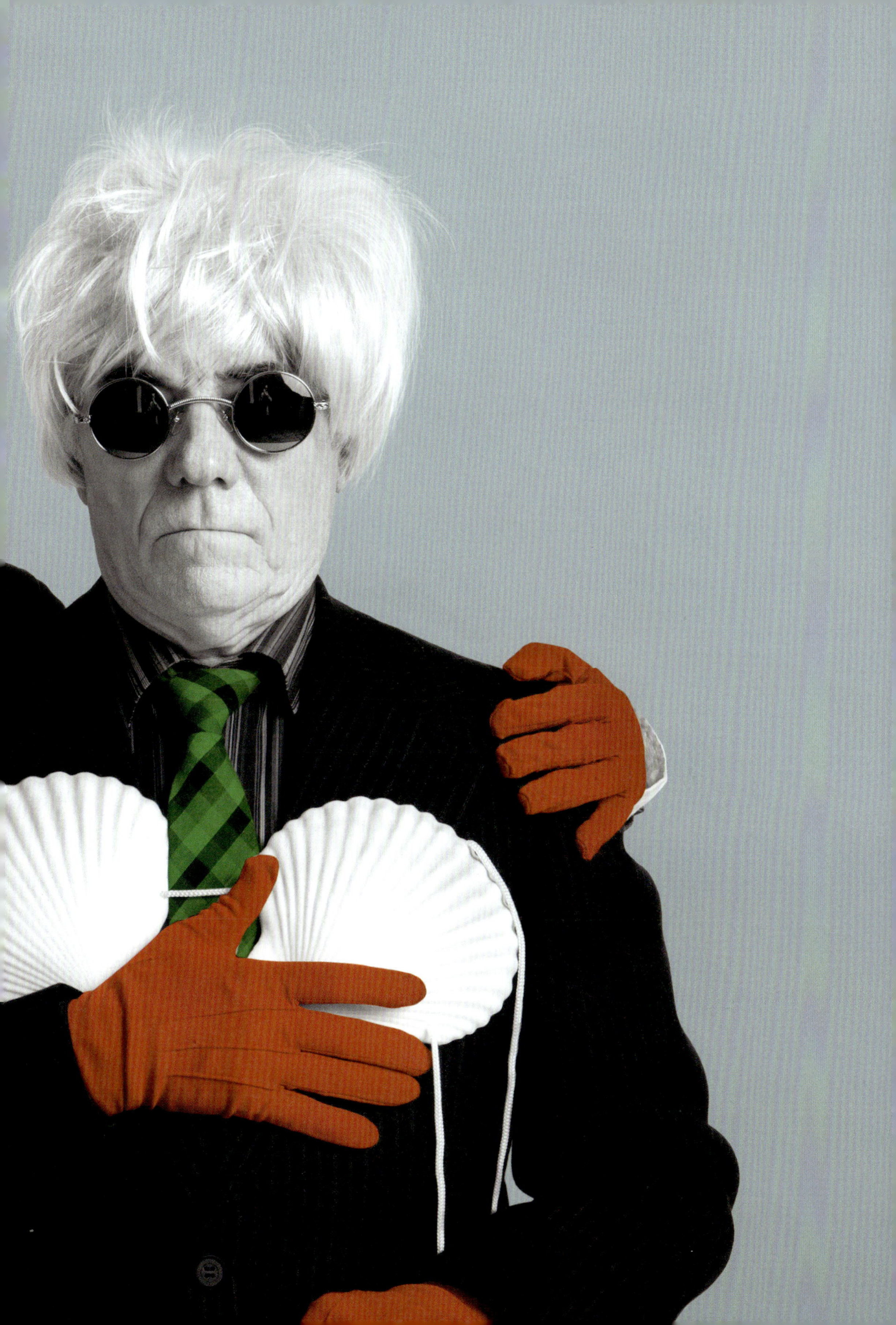

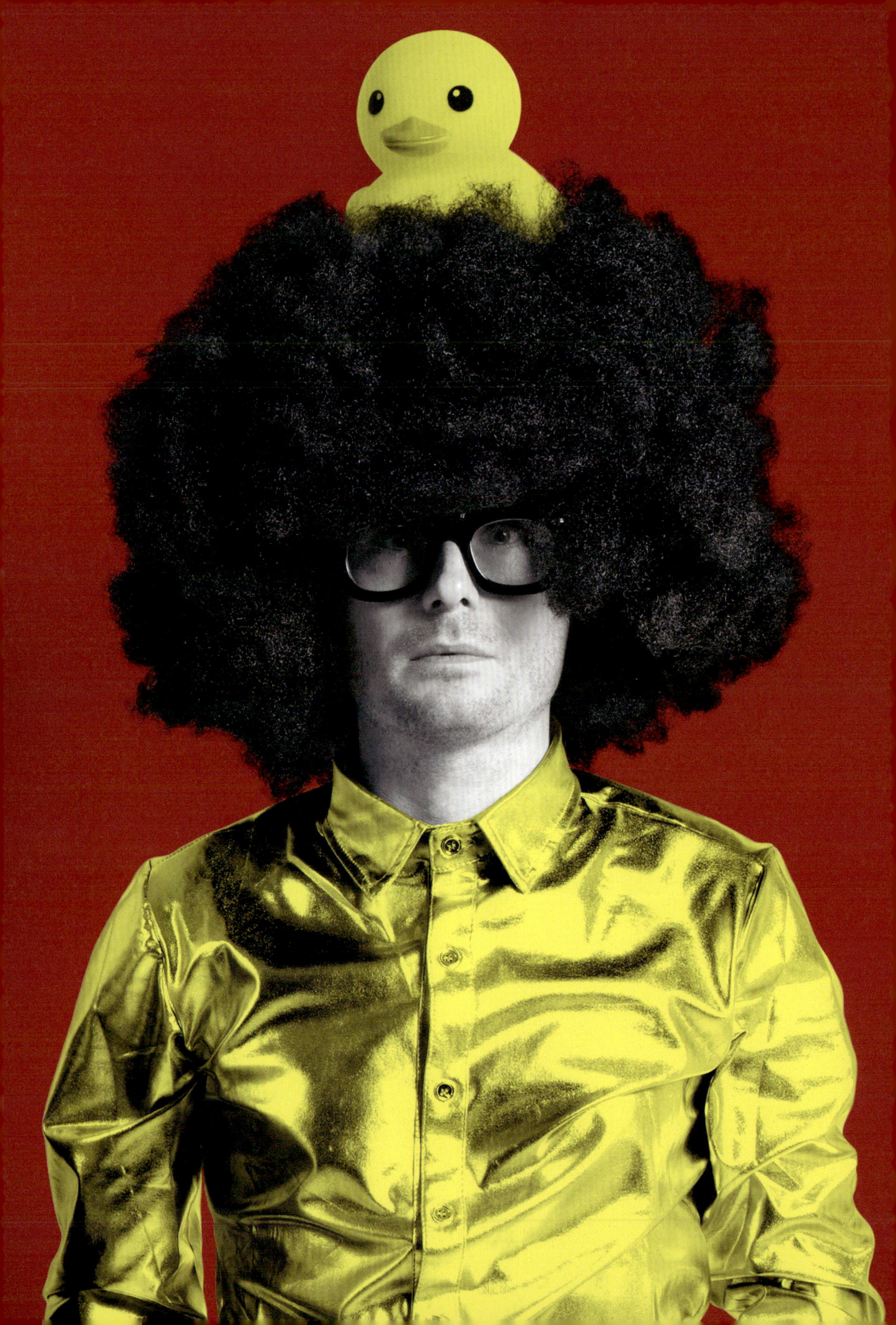

CHAPTER 11

Yuma was saying something in Japanese. She wasn't mumbling, but her pronunciation and articulation were clear and consistent so that Hans could listen to her and understand what she was saying. "I'll translate it later. I'll translate it later." He was sure. Hans tried to remember every word that he heard in that gentle language of the tides made up of seafoam. Daisuki. Kawaii ne. With his memory always seizing on the last word she said, he forgot all the previous ones.

Light gusts of wind brought sounds of thunderclaps from the south. They sounded so far off that neither Hans nor Yuma paid them any mind. Hans was ready to stay out watching the stars all night. The billions of firefly candles turned nature into a festive chandelier. Something was sneaking up into Hans' mood, and he didn't care what they talked about. He just wanted to ask more about the true music that played in the heart of real Yuma. He wanted to stretch out time so that she would never suddenly say, "Well, it's time for me to go."

Hans was able to live in relative unconsciousness. The effect of the successful anesthetic shot lasted day in and day out. His eyes emitted a muffled lifelight. This moderation insensibly turned over the leaves of the calendar and helped to turn the years. Sometimes Hans fanned the smoldering little flame of curiosity to the point of enthusiasm, fantasizing with the help of his photo film.

"Do you know what your paradox is?" Hans began, professor-like and cavalier as if he were in control of the situation. Yuma laughed. She felt a growing wall of awkwardness between them. Hans enchanted her by not being able to veil his bewilderment at all. It's possible that a woman knows the power of her weapon and always feels when it has been used, whether carefully or not.

"What's my paradox?" She was, after all, interested in whether the answer would be accurate.

"You glow with happiness and mischief. You jump on the stage like a tennis ball, but your music and your eyes tell of a different state. You, crawling out of your youth, are wandering the Earth as if you had the legs of an adult. How did this turmoil get in there...?" Hans' intonation was unhurried and attentive. "How old are you, Yuma?" he added as if he were joking.

"You're a buzzkill. I'm thirty-four," she said, proudly and probingly.

Hans was bee-stung with an electric current. He still thought he had misheard by a decade: a gust of wind jumped into the trees, shaking the fractal of their branches.

Until now, Hans had seen Yuma as a first-grader with white ribbons in her hair, who needed to be escorted home hand in hand and given candy upon parting. A small girl—waiting for a fairy tale from her mother before going to bed. So that she didn't get upset from seeing too much of shameless life with her child's eyes. Hans simply wanted to save her from that which permeated him like a potent poison. Maybe it was simply the normal feelings of a real man. Maybe it was cowardice or something else. Another road suddenly showed itself before Hans. The horizon through which he fell said to him: Yuma is your equal.

That's where that sad and naughty mocking was from. The glitter in her eyes was not a glitter of naiveté, but suffering, hidden in the jewelry box of a fragile creature. The fear that was still breathing through her eyes called one inside like a staircase. Yuma repeated with pride, "Thirty-five," adding a year for more causticity. Hans' inner being, the one that was hiding from the daylight, afraid of getting broken, now wanted to come out even more intensely. Instinctively, he moved closer to her.

"You know, the doctors told me," Yuma continued, "that I would never sing again. That's exactly what they said: 'Forget about your previous life. It no longer exists.' Those bastards are always able to find just the right words."

"What happened with your voice?" Hans hesitatingly asked.

"It was a tumor… They took me to the hospital along the narrow back streets of Musashino. I almost couldn't breathe and threw off the oxygen mask."

Yuma smiled.

Again, Hans was hit by a wave. The water dragged him with an insidious current from the shore. He floundered about, trying to save himself. Still, the horizon kept moving further and further away, and the outlines of the trees on the land got smaller and smaller until the landscape disappeared completely, leaving only the cruel waves surrounding him.

"I spent two months in the hospital," she continued. "And they damaged my vocal cords. Then I spent a few months breathing into a tube. The blue ball and the green ball would rise in the plastic tube to train my lungs and circulatory system. 'When you can raise the blue ball with an exhalation, we'll release you.' I lost my voice completely. And they told me, 'Don't worry; you can do something else.' Like they weren't talking about my life, but about embroidery lessons."

Her eyes filled with venom, a dry confusion, and a feeling of retaliation. Two people sitting in the magic of that scenery could not both simultaneously fear life.

The feeling of a different day immediately started spinning

palely-moving silhouettes in Hans' thoughts. At a funeral, a skull suddenly opened like a cigarette case. After the death, the police department insisted on an autopsy of the head to ensure that the cause of death was indeed a tumor and not diarrhea or murder. I mean, coroners are people too. And they forgot to fix the bone back in its place or did it improperly, and so under pressure, it just opened for some reason. Have you ever seen the brain matter of your father start soaking the pillow of the coffin in which he lay? All around were frightened screams, but he was still lying there, not getting up. Something had to be done, wipe off the pillow or wake him up. And he still wasn't waking up. Hans clearly felt this awkward, horrible moment of ongoing, traitorous life. He realized that the body that was somehow lying on the white fabric of the coffin, with its bones and cartilage, cold, uncomprehending, and motionless, could no longer be called father. It was just a wrapper from the past. A piece of material no longer connected with anything. Hans ran out of the room where the wake was being held, hiding from the wave bearing down on him, and asked himself, having fallen on his face into the cold, overgrown grass nearby: "Why continue living? What reason is there to continue living?"

Yuma looked at Hans unhappily and smiled a smile that asked what was going on with him. Her smile entreated him not to worry, knowing the power of her softness on others. All of this affected Hans much more than was necessary. Fragments of photographs and celluloid wrapped around his neck and pulled him not quite back to the past and not quite into timelessness. He tried everything to dodge the melancholy, wanting to make the best impression on Yuma so that she would trust him like a brother or father, roles that he needed to play but had not had the chance. Hans instinctively touched Yuma's knee, unable to employ words…and anyway, as before, he wasn't sure exactly what he wanted to express to her from among his feelings of sympathy and awe.

And this ambiguity just grew bigger, like the clouds occluding the stars from viewers in Central Park. You could hear the thunder even more distinctly while it was lulling nature to sleep, convincing every living thing to curl up into a ball for some forgetful dreams. So that suffering is temporarily wiped from the eyes and memories of the living creatures. So that they can sleep peacefully and, in their dreams, listen to the presence of the wind and the noise of the trees singing under the rain. Later the morning light would lead them to new desires… at least those who were able to wake up.

Yuma brightened at his touch. In addition to words, she needed a jinn to act on her girlish nature, which, while saying "no," awaited a gesture that would turn her on her head. The feelings that Hans was hiding behind ten wax seals were also hidden by Yuma, who, however, every day revealed her grown-up sorrow through the surrogate of music.

Hans stood up, taking the bass guitar. "It's time for us to go," he tried to say.

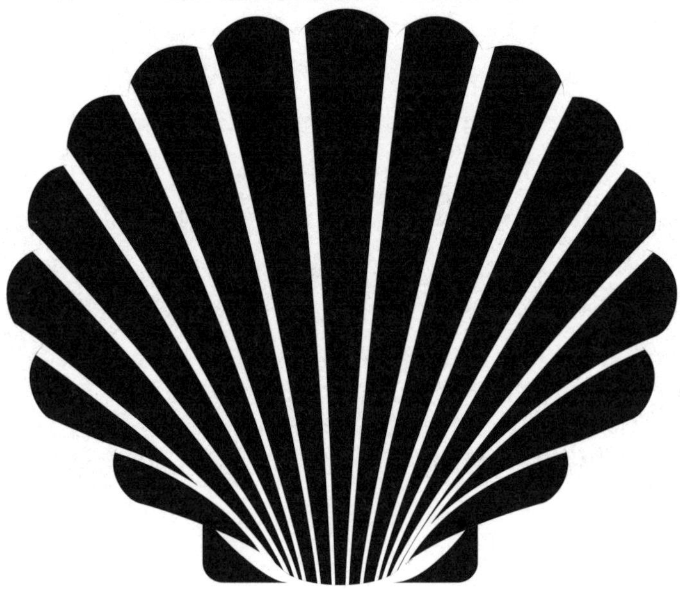

CHAPTER 12

They walked along the road near the Met, carefully lit by progress, and the streetlights hung over Hans like the sullen metal sunflowers that thirty years ago helped soldiers catch escapees. Hans was glad that the tentacles of that life could no longer reach him. The years' time had taken him out of the prison of childhood happiness and into the country of adult freedom. And now, in the warm night, he was simply happy to not think about the future. Hans was quite a sly one, having trained his endurance in soccer. But he was still somewhat trying to convince himself. He gathered all the evidence of his happiness. The camera, his work for the company, the big city with the stone landscapes, galleries, the bustle, the diversity of languages, lack of organization, brutality, coquettishness, superficiality, money—all these cheap resonating trinkets amused and pleased Hans. Because he did not harbor the proper respect for the whole list, he did not feel annoyed. He truly was Andy Warhol's brother. Hans Warhol—that was him.

Even Yuma's dress and her knees, at which Hans peeked at just the right moments, were an achievement for him. A girl in a dress was something that was indeed hard to acquire in New York.

When they crossed the street, their palms met. Yuma touched his hand by chance, or Hans accidentally moved his hand toward hers. Hans, jokingly perhaps, led the small girl across the street full of danger, like her father. He didn't expect the all-consuming intimacy of that feeling in the very first second. Behind the joke hid a barbed worry. After they had crossed the street, Hans unclasped his hand. Yuma did so as well, freeing almost all her fingers but unintentionally hooking her pinky onto his.

What were hands for, if not that?

In one second, which lasted a year, Hans felt that Yuma's hand was very hot and very close.

The road cozily snaked among the trees, and the rare streetlamps used their warm light to scatter the shadows of Hans and Yuma every which way, trying to muddle their path. The exotic birds that had bedded down in the trees curiously watched this new movie through the branches.

Hans, like a fearless engineer, measured the temperature of Yuma's palms in a lab experiment. His heart wanted to jump from its body bag and run along the side of the road, dissolving into the darkness of the bushes. His heart rustled traitorously and directed inappropriate questions to Hans, which would only have embarrassed everyone. In the second, the temperature of Yuma's hand increased so much that her palm shone with the yellow gleam of an open-hearth furnace. Hans shuddered. It even seemed to him that everything around had started to boil. He had never felt the absence of distance.

He looked at Yuma's bare feet. The dress, and the line of her legs even more so, neuron after neuron, immobilized him. Hans tried to free his hand. But he couldn't: someone had handcuffed him, or Yuma did not want to let go of his thin finger. Hans lingered and felt the clamminess of his palms.

They walked along, their hands fixed solidly to one another, and the night condensed around them with its thundering clouds that shrouded the moon. Hans tried to turn on his powerful onboard computer by scientifically calculating the trajectory of the road. For him, the theoretical picture was always more important than the experience itself.

The computer graphics were of excellent resolution. The grass was silent; the ants, having gone to sleep somewhere not far from Yuma's feet, approvingly accompanied the passing cophasal shadows with their tired gazes. On the narrow park path, somewhere north of the Reservoir, their legs stopped. Yuma pulled Hans by the hand.

"Why are you walking so carefully? And why are you silent?... Are you afraid of the dark?" And then added falteringly, "Or of me?"

Hans muttered something he thought was witty. Yuma didn't drop it:

"Are you afraid of me?"

She moved her face close to him, full of seriousness and even anger. Hans almost lost his balance. The bass guitar pulled him like a pendulum in the other direction.

"What, are you really afraid? Or were you a straight-A student in school?" She was upset and quite riled up.

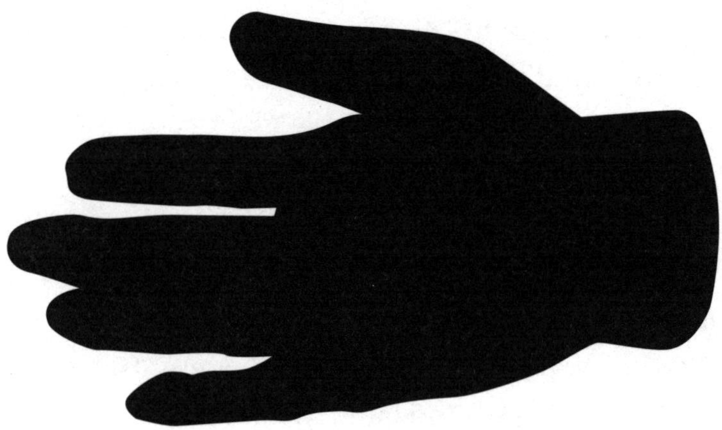

CHAPTER 15

The family moved not far from Spittelmarkt, trying not to do anything that might attract attention. The father and mother went to work every day. On the weekends, they went outside of the city to a small country house. Hans stayed to study in his old school, where mathematics would occupy his brain for days on end. He took the bus to school, and he liked that his house was so far away from it.

The two-room apartment was full of devices and whimsical objects connected with receiving and transmitting signals. In the eight-square-meter kitchen, built according to socialist standards, a pile of oscilloscopes reached the ceiling. Some of them had never been connected to a machine and were there solely to decorate the living quarters of an engineer, like petrified sculptures. The large wooden table took up almost the whole kitchen. To sit at its far end, you had to squeeze yourself along the white wall, pushing the chairs along the floor and making a racket. Then your clothes would have a mark from the whitewash on the wall. The table had large holes drilled in it for roller mills, which his father had installed to make metal parts for his antennas. When he was soldering waveguides, his father sometimes filled the entire kitchen with sheets of copper. A small cubbyhole on the wall near the gas stove held rulers, scissors, pliers, and other tools that might come in handy for building, even a real spaceship.

The "big room" in the apartment was rarely tidied up. Engineers were better than that. Dust clung to the walls and shelves, settled on books, and crawled under the bed. The desk, which traditionally took up half the room, was overloaded with a huge mountain of papers. That was his father's doctoral dissertation. He had abandoned it at the very end due to his disillusionment with the poetry of the science that the government had commissioned him to guard through the construction of electronic items. A science that seemed too bland to him.

Not only was the dissertation stalled in its paper life, but life itself had already stopped and was being lived differently. His father was overgrown with radio parts and the postcards that he often received. The senders were from farther and farther away, the antennas got bigger and bigger, and the radio signals became more disturbing and emphatic. His father broke through the shell of his forties and, at the same time, wove a cocoon to insulate himself from external reality, to no longer get burned by the hopelessness of the idea that he got from society's enthusiasm.

Inside the huge paper cocoon on the table that had been forming since the start of work on the dissertation, somewhere in the center, was the typewriter on which Hans' father allowed him to write. One careless move of the son and the father shot into action. He was not angry but worried that Hans might ruin the century-old pile of paper. Or that he would damage the useless and now unnecessary writing machine. "Whoa, whoa! Be careful!" his father interjected somewhere nearby, "enough rooting around in there!" This was the voice of the knowledge that he would never finish and defend his doctoral dissertation. His father was jealous of his own sobriety.

The dust in the room accumulated together with the knowledge and skepticism of his heart regarding the power of science. The dust was under the room's two-person bed. Hans loved to crawl under it to sneeze, collecting old newspapers. The dust also collected under the radiator near the window behind the bed. The radiator was almost

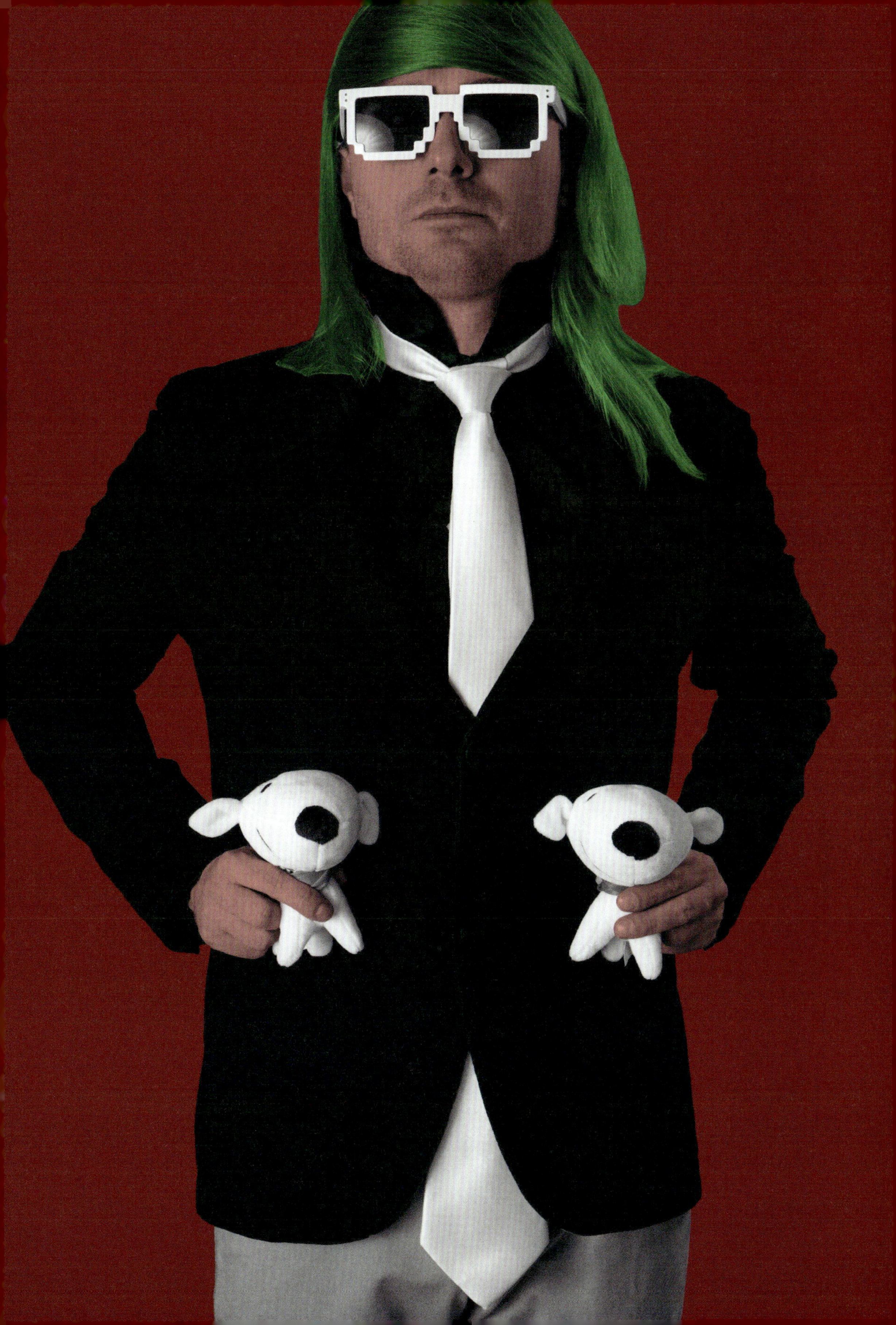

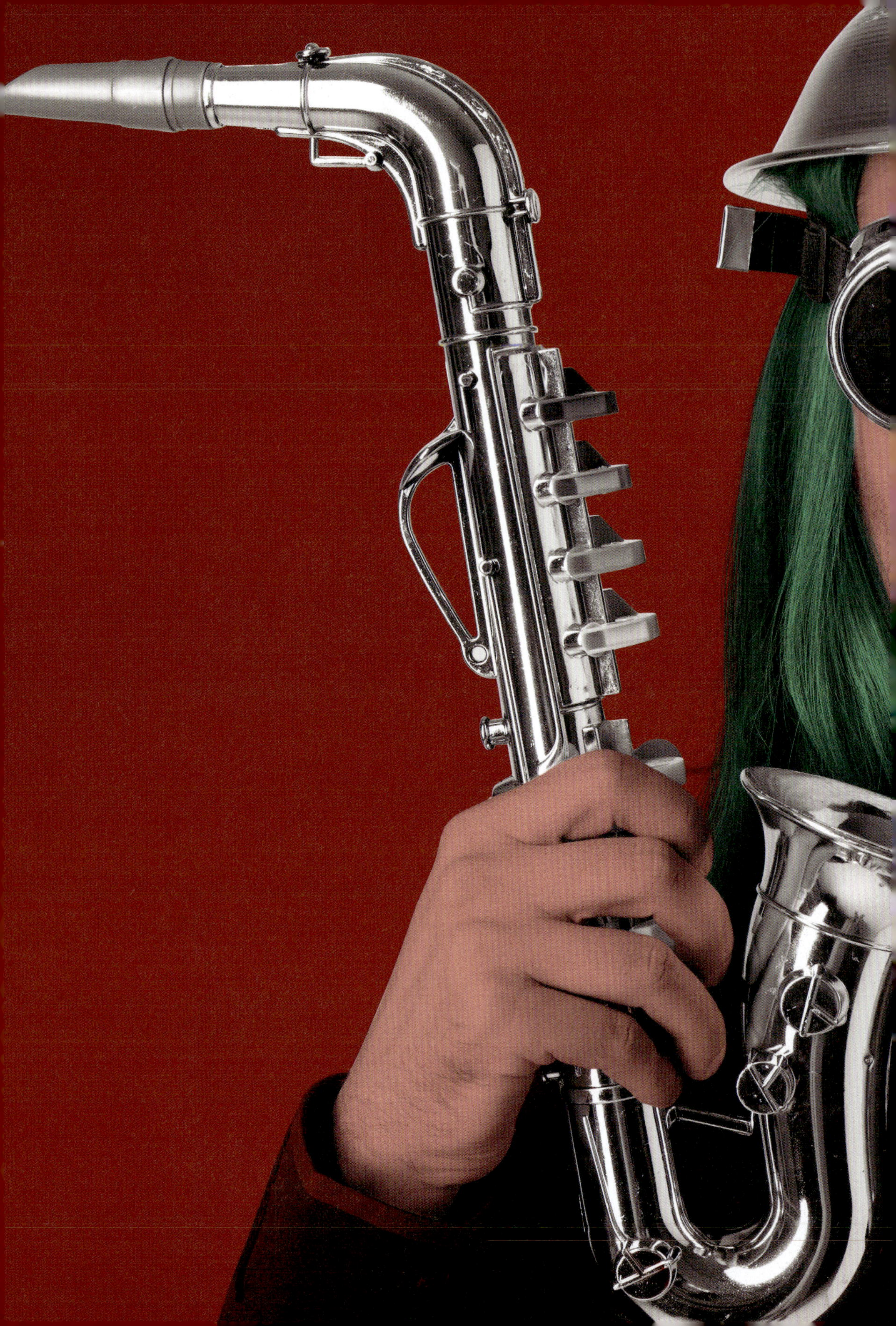

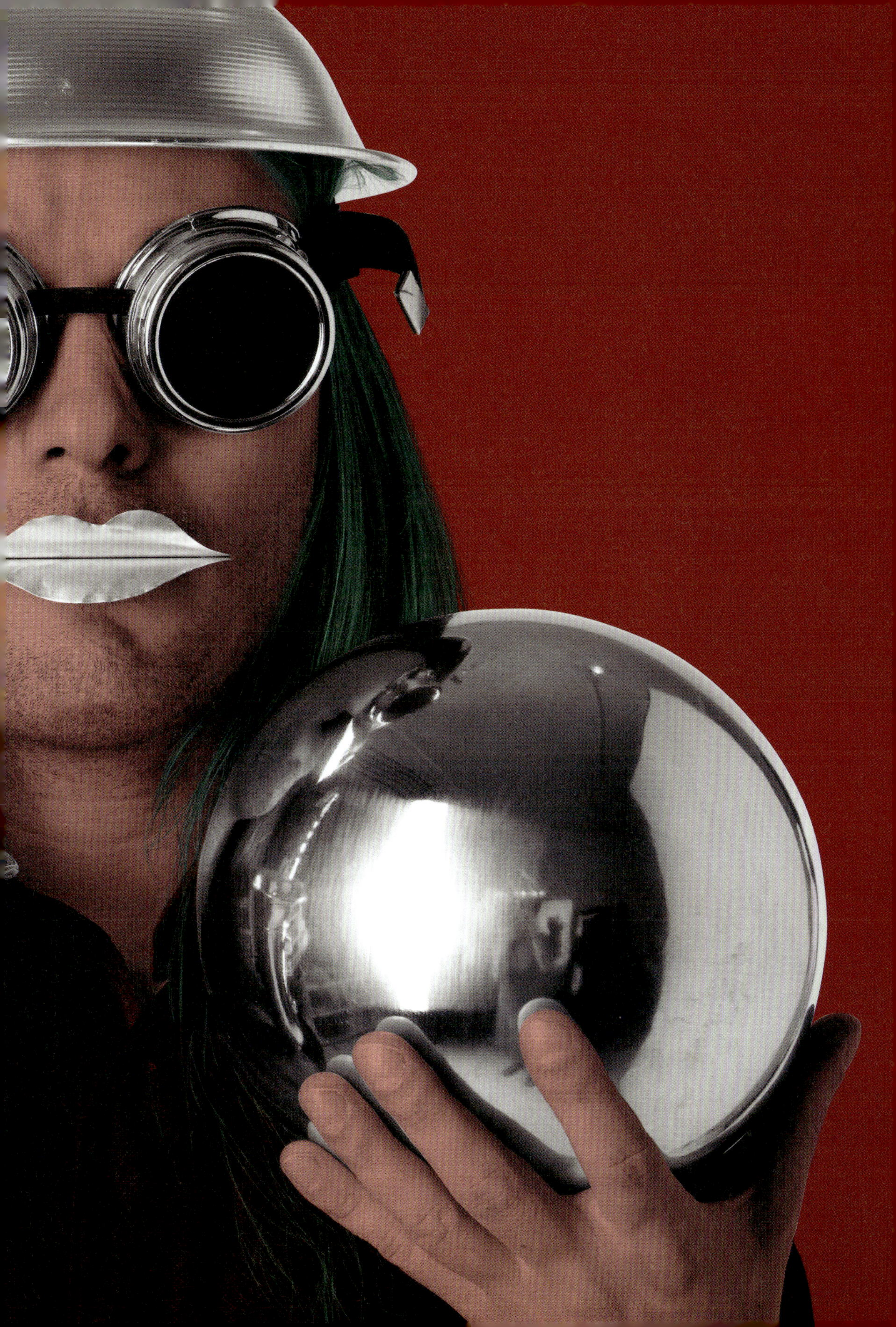

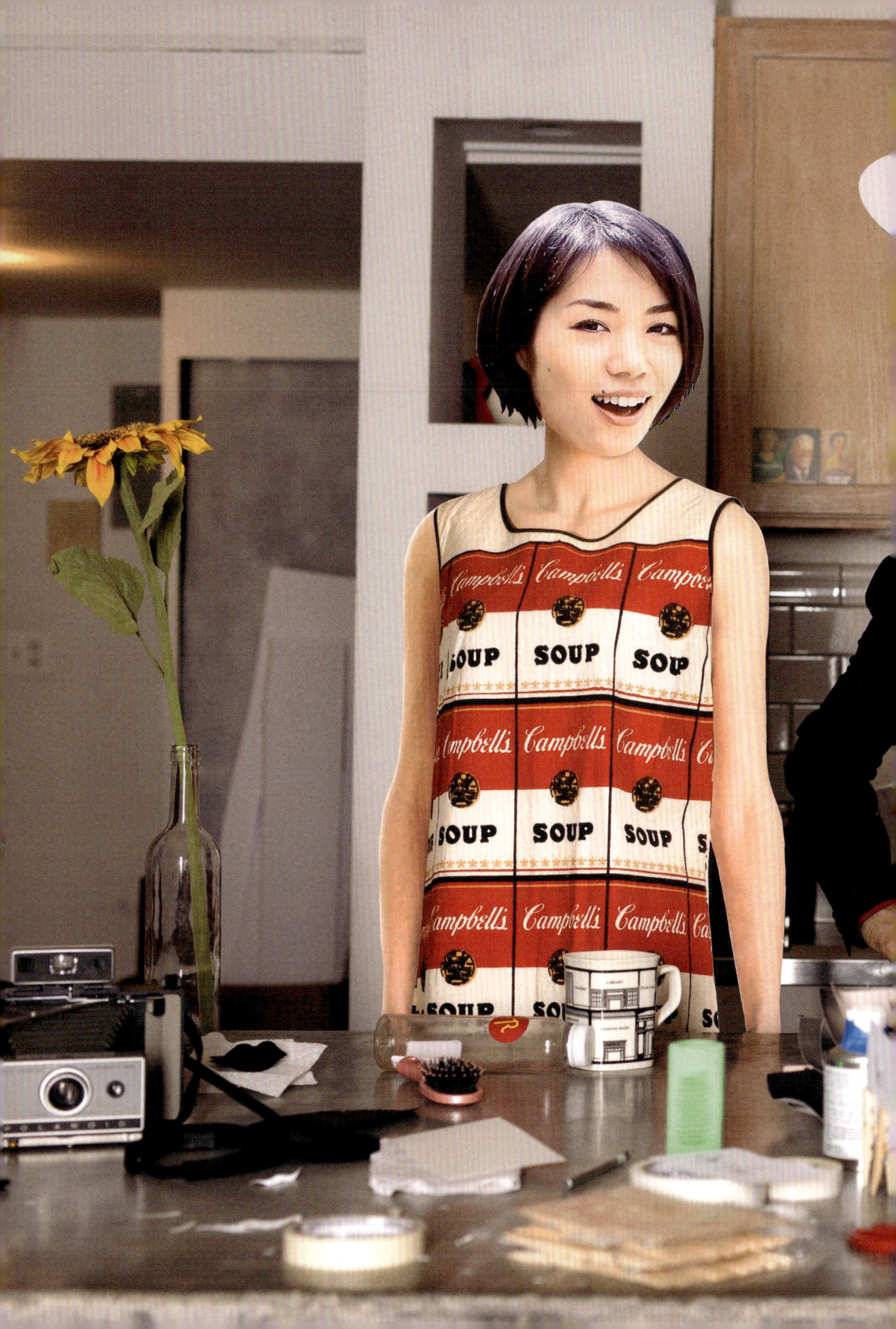
Campbell's
SOUP
Campbell's
SOUP
Campbell's
SOUP

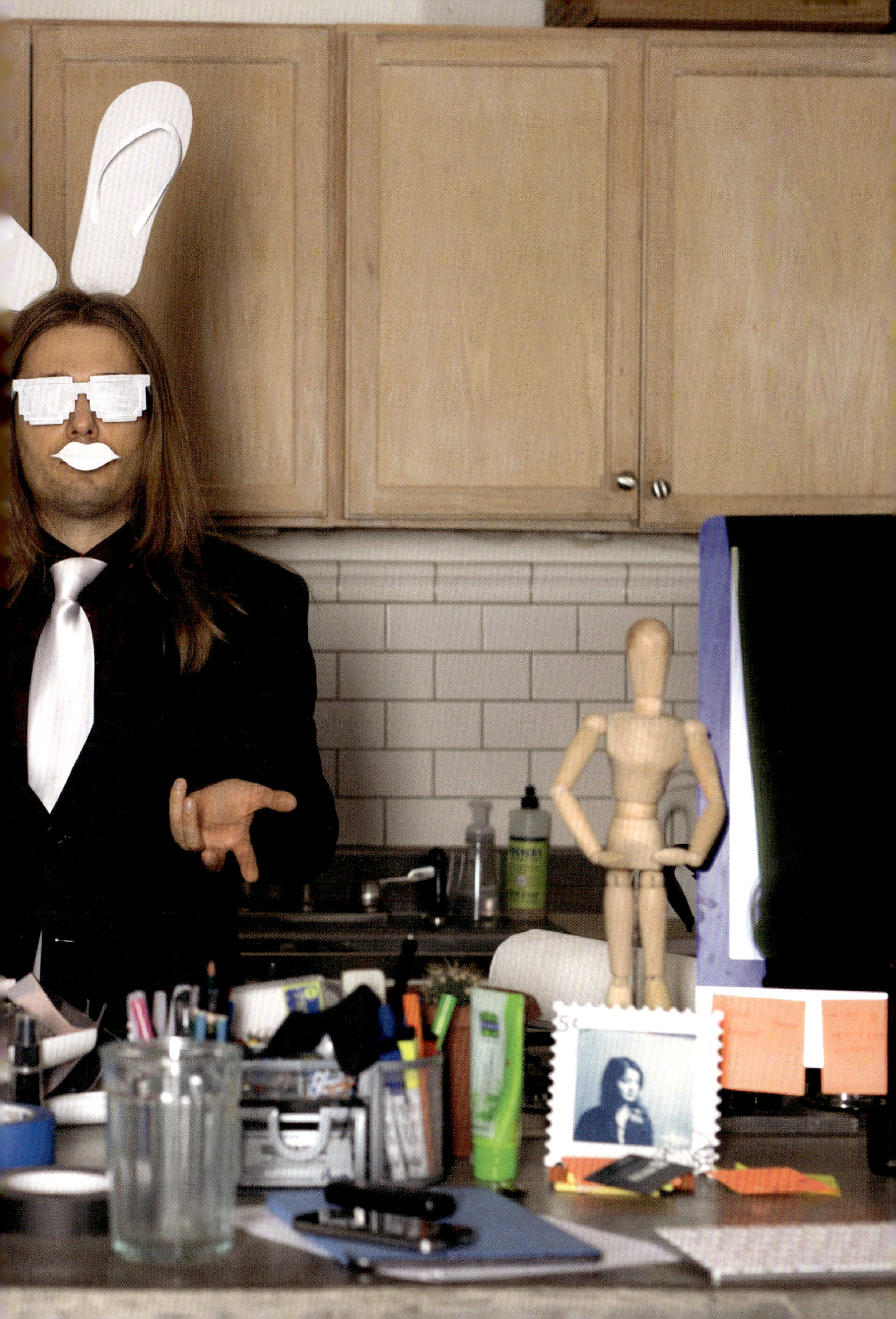

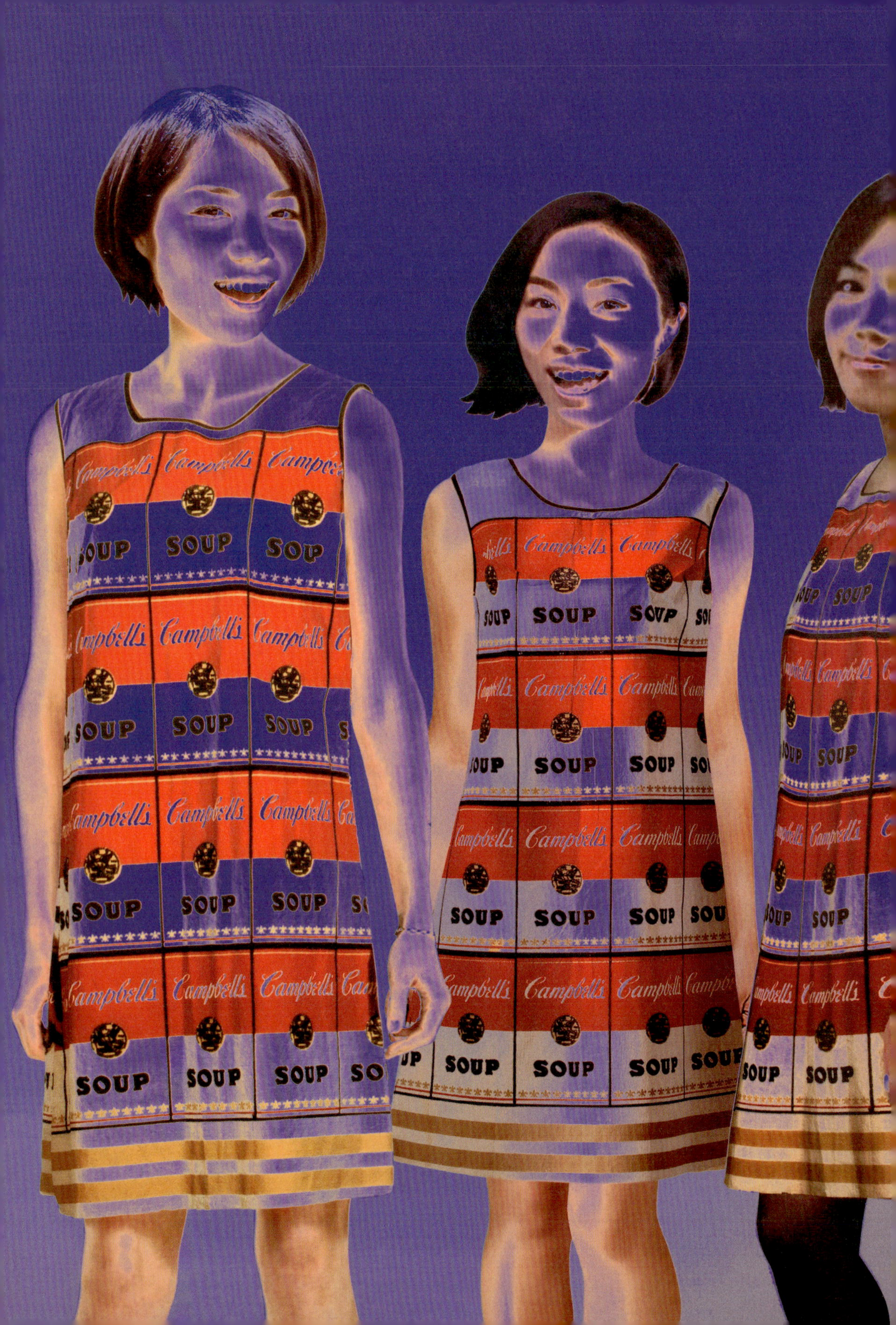
Campbell's
SOUP

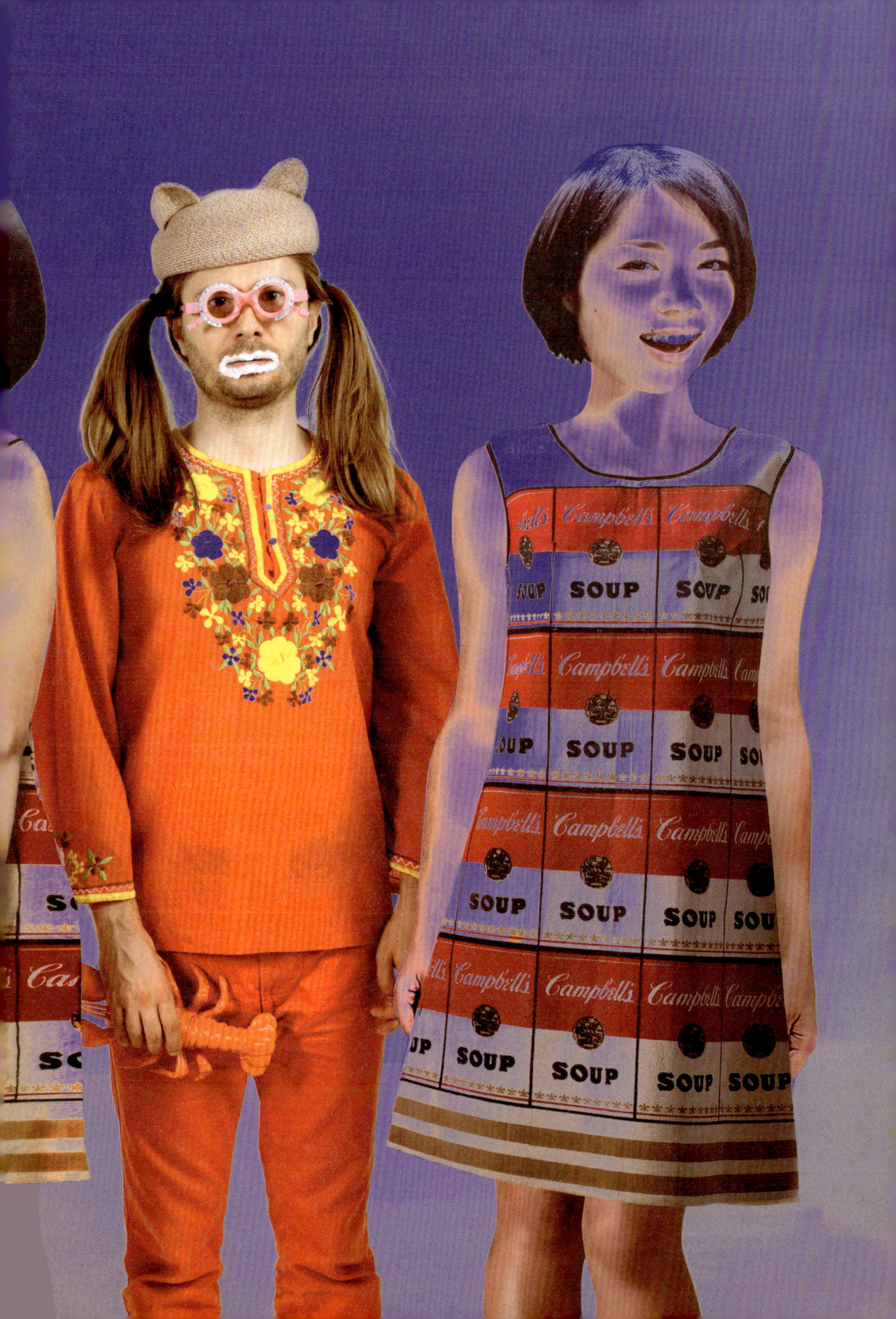
Campbell's
SOUP

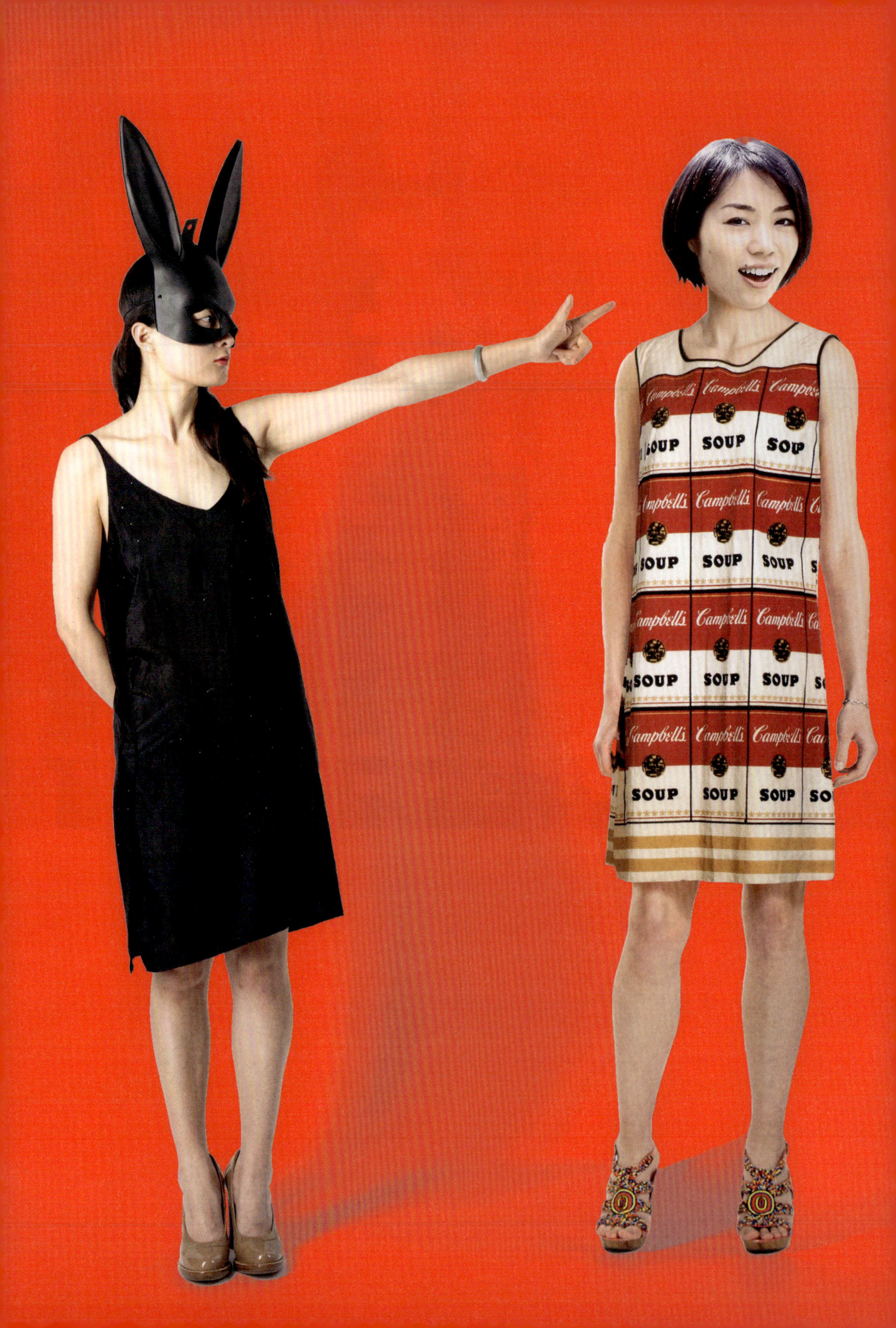
Campbell's
SOUP

boiling and incandescent in the winter. It gave off a specific fired aroma of parched dust. For six-year-old Hans, crawling under the bed was an entire journey. Not only could you collect yellow newspapers, but you could also find a couple of transistors or even a vacuum tube.

In that big room, in the opposite corner, stood a large color television whose back had been removed. "Look how it works!" Hans' father never ceased boasting to everyone as soon as they brought the sixty-pound cathode-ray tube monster home on a flimsy table. The vacuum tube TV was like a truck stuffed with incomprehensible rattling items. For it to work for half of a day, it usually required a whole day's repair. His father loved radio tubes and knew everything about sawtooth voltage generators and the electron emissions from cathodes. Maybe even more than Alexander Stepanovich Popov, Niels Bohr, Maxwell, Planck, and Edison. For him, it was a happy occasion when the television broke. He could easily neglect to take out the trash or forget to watch a boiling soup. His father's soldering iron had explored every corner of the massive, lazy, narrow-eyed box, not embarrassed by its whims. His father kept the soldering iron in a special closet full of science-fiction secrets, like a spy submarine. Hans was forbidden to open that closet. And when his father was at work, Hans loved to surreptitiously open the doors of the magic closet and dig around in the cans with the fuses: he had all different ones, from one amp to thirty. He could spend eternity looking at the boxes with the resistors and capacitors. And the transistors with three tin legs had stimulated Hans' imagination since he was three. He took a round battery and touched the transistor's legs to both of its sides. At first, the transistor heated up, then emitted a bitter, light smoke, and then burst like ripe fruit on a tree; the whole room was filled with a pleasant burning smell—the entire point of the experiment. Hans kept his fun a secret. Until one day when he connected an electrochemical capacitor to a battery. It exploded immediately, almost maiming Hans. There was a loud bang, some kind of liquid dripped onto his clothes, and the aluminum lid shot to the ceiling, where it left a dark stain. After this, his father installed a lock on the closet. Hans was not allowed to touch electronic parts. However, in his father's stuff, he found a real blue rotating beacon which Hans secretly played with when his father wasn't home and kept hidden in a cardboard box under the bed.

Under the cabinet in the big room were additional sections, with doors, for storing large things. Once Hans got hold of a spool with a telephone cable, a battery, and a small light bulb. He attached the cable to the inner wall of the wardrobe along the corners with some electrical tape and connected the light bulb to it. He also taped the battery to the wall of the wardrobe. Then he crawled inside his new apartment with a book—*Young Radio Enthusiast*—and closed the wardrobe doors. The light bulb lit up his sacrosanct residence, filling the space of the newly constructed house with a sense of coziness. Hans lay there in the wardrobe for a few hours, perusing his book, until the battery died.

After work, Hans' mother spent most of her time preparing dinners, breakfasts, and lunches and delivering them to whichever room their intended recipient happened to be. But since she was also a long-wave antenna designer, she would often sit at the drawing table late at night and sketch electrical diagrams that looked to Hans like strange animals with moustaches.

Hans' mother was fragile and feminine—and still somewhat resembled a schoolgirl. At home, she wore a thin, light-colored cotton robe that made her even more weightless and elegant. Hans felt this beauty in his own way and was quite happy when she came home from work and put that magic robe on. Sometimes he would peek at her from under the bed when she was changing in the big room, and he also loved running after her in the apartment, breathing in the native, somewhat milky smell of his mother, as if it were his own light smell as well.

Hans' father's idea of another world took some time to get through to his mother fully. Like any stubborn idea, it gave life a new meaning, which the whole family absorbed drop by drop . By listening to short wave radio, Hans' father was not only constructing a faraway reality. He also began experiencing a new, intensifying annoyance with the current one, as if it were simply a stopgap preparation period for the one to come.

CHAPTER 14

Ceasing her questions, Yuma threw Hans down into the grass. The cloud of her aromas burst into his room through the barbed wire and the cold autumn wind—a feeling that ran faster than dogs. Her pale skin was within an inch of him, and her hands, in the reflection of far-off lights, encircled his neck.

She looked at Hans without even a shadow of a shadow, as if they had known each other for a thousand years and hadn't seen each other in two thousand. In the dark, you could still make out her eyes shining with moisture. Yuma whispered to him in the language of the sunrise:

キスして…。ねえ、聞いてる?

Hans' heart was beating in sixty-fourth notes from a panic that he did not feel even when listening to the jazz of the peoples of the world on the most complex receiving devices. Finally, he had woken up and opened his eyelids, behind which was another pair of eyelids. He opened them too, upon seeing that he was, as before, still in a dream.

A kiss on her lips was like kissing a pillow. Leaping into a pile of wadding from the tenth floor. Falling into the sweetness of a field of cotton. The birthmark near her lips. Yuma pressed herself to Hans with all the gravitational attraction she could muster. Her faded breath smelled like the cinnamon of gingerbread and honey from a golden field of a million flowers that decorated the hot, happy day.

Her body spilled out in a desire to give voice to everything feminine that was in her through the heat and the incontrovertibility of that nighttime confession. The ants watched them.

That kiss was indescribable. Forbidden.

A kiss with her was like a sleepover in the International Space Station. Like drinking nectar all night while reclining in a flower. Yes, it was a kiss at a hundred thousand Kelvin. A kiss with the sun, with a billion solar neutrinos flying directly into your heart, stopping life with the wind of ecstasy.

A kiss with her was a night by the sea and the hot sand. A kiss with her was a sudden kiss. A kiss with her was a kiss sticking its head out the window of a train speeding south. A kiss with her was a confession of love in the language of exclamation marks in military formation. A kiss with her was a happy old age. A kiss with her was self-induced EMF. A kiss with her was a gravestone for two. A kiss with her was like a thousand kisses with her. A kiss with her was a vacation in the dorms.

A kiss with her was a strawberry with cream. A kiss with her was a handwritten letter. A kiss with her was a school dance. A kiss with her was the sunset and the sad song of an old Japanese fisherman. A kiss with her was The New York Times. A kiss with her was OOTOYA in Union Square. A kiss with her was a novel. A kiss with her was ramen. A kiss with her was the 6 subway stopping at eight in the morning. A kiss with her was a grand piano on a cloud. A kiss with her was watercolor on a white wall. A kiss with her was yellow boots. A kiss with her was checkmate in three moves. A kiss with her was a mountain that fit into a teaspoon.

A kiss with her was the electric chair.

Gently flying over the entwined bodies, the wind whistled a warm melody to the Southern night, fading into non-existence. Hans was still counting his seconds of happiness, writing them down in his notebook, like a construction foreman tightening up the ropes during the building of the final floor of the Empire State Building.

The ants scurrying along the grass, going about their business, looked with envy at the giant scene the Gullivers were making. Their work path was right under Yuma's back, and it was awkward to have to ask the young couple to move so that they might continue their work. Instead, a few desperate individuals crawled under Yuma's dress and, finding comfortable positions, watched the goings-on from there.

The smell of the grass, the whisper of the branches, and the shaming looks from the birds in the trees were all interwoven into the scene. Yuma's youth, openness, and availability created an attraction that was outside of Hans' calculating nature. He moved a little below her neck, and his lips reached something hard through her dress. A woman turns into a mother at the hour of love, both competing with the mother of the man and becoming a new mother for his children.

Hans wanted Yuma to get pregnant right now, on this grass. He wanted to become a father and to live together for at least a hundred years, raising his grandchildren, great-grandchildren, and their own children. This desire always arises at the boiling point of the love that the woman concocts so that her grandchildren will reluctantly ask how she met their grandfather.

Yuma's short dress helped hitch itself up, and Hans began fantasizing about everything that his humble, unpampered imagination desired.

"Can I turn the flashlight on for a second?" asked Hans.

Moving a bit downwards, he aimed the smartphone at her legs, looking at their shape. He simply wanted to see the color of her body against the backdrop of the grass and the dress. He moved his face closer to her knees to get a better look at the subtle landscape of her skin. Her body was smooth, and Yuma's snow-white moonlight legs stopped Hans' breathing. He entreated himself, "Breathe. Breathe, Hans." He got so close that he could see the barely noticeable down covering her thighs as infants have. The down cast a shadow on the beautiful skin of her leg. Hans took a couple of pictures with the smartphone.

In indecent books about women's structure, Hans read that only a light down grew on Japanese women's legs. Sometimes not even that. And other areas were even more beautiful. Maybe completely bald legs were not everyone's cup of tea, but they were very much to Hans' liking. These thoughts sent his head spinning definitively, and, spinning, he dug his face into Yuma's legs, tasting them, seeing how jelly-like they were, how tough, etc. Slowly crawling under the dress higher and higher, he felt like a rock climber in the mountains, who, having reached the top, loses his mind and his oxygen but is forever filled with the enthusiasm of a conqueror. Like an old-fashioned photographer, he hid under the drape of her dress, where he was able to take a masterpiece of a picture. He could come out the victor in this non-socialist competition by taking any earthly form: a father, a husband, a lover, a friend, a coach, an order bearer, a bass player. He could tie her up and make her play chess or bleat about love in the language of sheep. And now, his fingers felt the soft elastic of her panties that bound the gentle truffled beginnings of her legs. This elastic was the packaging for an expensive and prestigious gift that anyone might dream of getting, whether they were in the air, in space, on the Earth, or underwater, whether a subtle romantic, a university student in love, a soldier, an office manager, an old married auntie, a poet, or an artist. The only thing that any of them wanted was to be in this situation, the one in which lucky Hans found himself, where he was only three steps away from victory, where the depth of his feelings and his desire not to hurry were infinite.

Hans kissed Yuma through the elastic of her panties as if though a prison window and dreamed about everything that was permitted before marriage, as well as what was only allowed after. Yuma blew Hans into another galaxy with just the smell of her panties. Not only did she not object. She wanted an unceremonious workout and a rough landing. And that's why she gave in, like a reciprocal candy friend attaining the state of plasma, of being split into protons. She wanted to merge into one and become Hans' faithful wife in Central Park for a hundred years and even significantly longer, waking up in the mornings from the dew on the grass and the rays of the morning sun…

"Let me go, let me go!" Yuma screamed suddenly and jumped up onto her feet. "AAAAAh! Aaaah! It's here! It's here!"

"Who?" Hans didn't have any time to get scared.

"The ant! Ay! It bit my butt! Help me! Do something!"

"Where, where? Let me see."

Hans shined the flashlight on Yuma's panties. In the light of the smartphone flashlight, you could see everything nicely, in a kind of semi-transparency.

They were pink panties that were still giving off the smell of laundry detergent, deodorant, and Yuma's perfume. How did perfume get down here? The copyright of the odor of her skin, the flowery musical cocktail of secret vales, and indeed, a barely noticeable and almost sweet, animating scent. As well as the amorous fluid that ashamedly seeped out towards the moonlight, with its ancient, particular, thick odor. Yuma's panties even smelled like the American flag on the moon. Seriously—the smell of dust, a vacuum, the scorching sun, and two hundred seventy degrees of heat. From the smell of the grass and wildflowers that Hans and Yuma were lying on, one could compose a bouquet for new perfumes and call them "Yuma and Central Park." Or "Echo of New York." Or "Reminiscences of Tokyo." There was no noticeable bite from the clever ant to be seen on Yuma's cheeks, nor were any running or hiding insects noticed. Hans diligently shone the flashlight on her panties and legs to make sure that the incident would not be repeated. It seems Yuma had invented the bite.

The satisfied, smiling ant, in the meantime, crawled off to the side onto its path in the grass, to trudge on working 'til the morn once his other work had been done. He rushed back to tell his comrades about his part in the events begun by Hans. You could say that it was the envy of a good-natured insect that, if he were a man, would have been experiencing a split personality.

It began to drizzle, and Yuma proposed moving towards home. She took Hans by the hand. She embraced him between the guitar and his waist with her other hand. She didn't want to let him go or to feel that either of them had cooled down. Or that someone might ruin the feelings that were gathering like an anti-cloud. On the contrary: Yuma and Hans had become even closer. They wanted, even more, to be silent and continue something inexplicable.

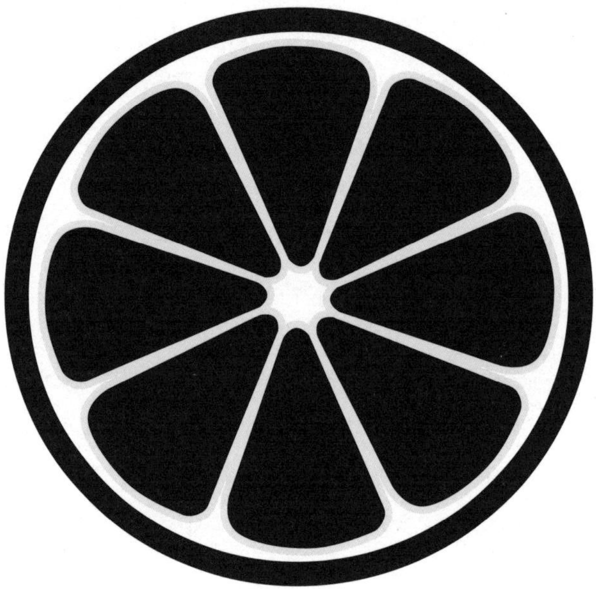

CHAPTER 15

It was summer when his father fell in the kitchen of their small house in Saint Augustine. It was, as always, hot, and the doors were open. Hans had just returned from the studio where he had finished taking photographs of clothing, a small order for a shop.

As soon as he entered the house, he felt that something wasn't right since the floor had water all over it coming from an open faucet. It was flowing over the rim of the sink. His father lay nearby on the floor, unconscious. Hans slapped him hard across his cheeks several times. His father opened his eyes:

"Where am I?" he asked, frightened.

The setting sun still shone a yellow patch on the boards of the floor. Hans helped his father stand up. When he came to, he stood up slowly, drank a glass of water, asked for a new t-shirt from the closet, and said that he had simply fallen. He had slipped in the kitchen and fallen onto the floor, lightly hitting his head on the table. Nothing serious.

"But you were unconscious!"

"No, I remember everything; what are you talking about?" his father protested. There was a slight doubt in his eyes.

Three months later, he fell again, this time on the porch of the house. This time harder. Blood was oozing from somewhere near his temple, and the skin had been torn off— it was pretty bad. Ronald, the neighbor, found him. Ronald was the same age as Hans, red-headed, with a kind heart and the good manners of someone brought up in the country. Hans had no friends in Florida or, one might say, anywhere on the planet. But his relationship with Ronald was special. Ronald and Hans felt a kind of brotherhood, or rather it was felt mostly by Hans, who needed that brotherhood more than Ronald.

His father was lying with the back of his head downwards, right in the doorway of the front door, which he had managed to open. It was already Fall, but the days were still long and hot, like always in Saint Augustine. The sun had heated his body intensely. Hans' father never wore hats in summer in Germany and continued not wearing them here, in Florida. He was unconscious. A small, sun-coagulated puddle of blood could be seen on the porch boards.

After a day in the hospital, Hans' father came to when Hans brought him a telegraph from Germany from his friends at the design bureau. "The Berlin wall has fallen. The borders are open. We can't believe it. Wilhelm, come back." For twenty years, Hans had not been able to forget father's face, blackened from tears.

They brought his father home a week later. Hans decided it would be best like that. His gaze was completely glassy, without light and not present, like a dusty plaster sculpture frozen on a shelf. It had been days now since his father had eaten anything, and trying to talk him into it didn't help. He drank with difficulty and only mumbled answers. And it was only when Hans gave him the dexamethasone injection that his father, like a tortured phonograph, gut-wrenchingly wheezed, "It hurts! It hurts!"

That night Ronald came to watch a movie with Hans. Sometimes they watched movies together. Ronald helped Hans understand what was going on, explaining the English, filling the room with a positive aura and the freckles on his face.

His father was lying in the next room when the seizures started. Hans and Ronald ran to him. Hans' father's wheezed vehemently,

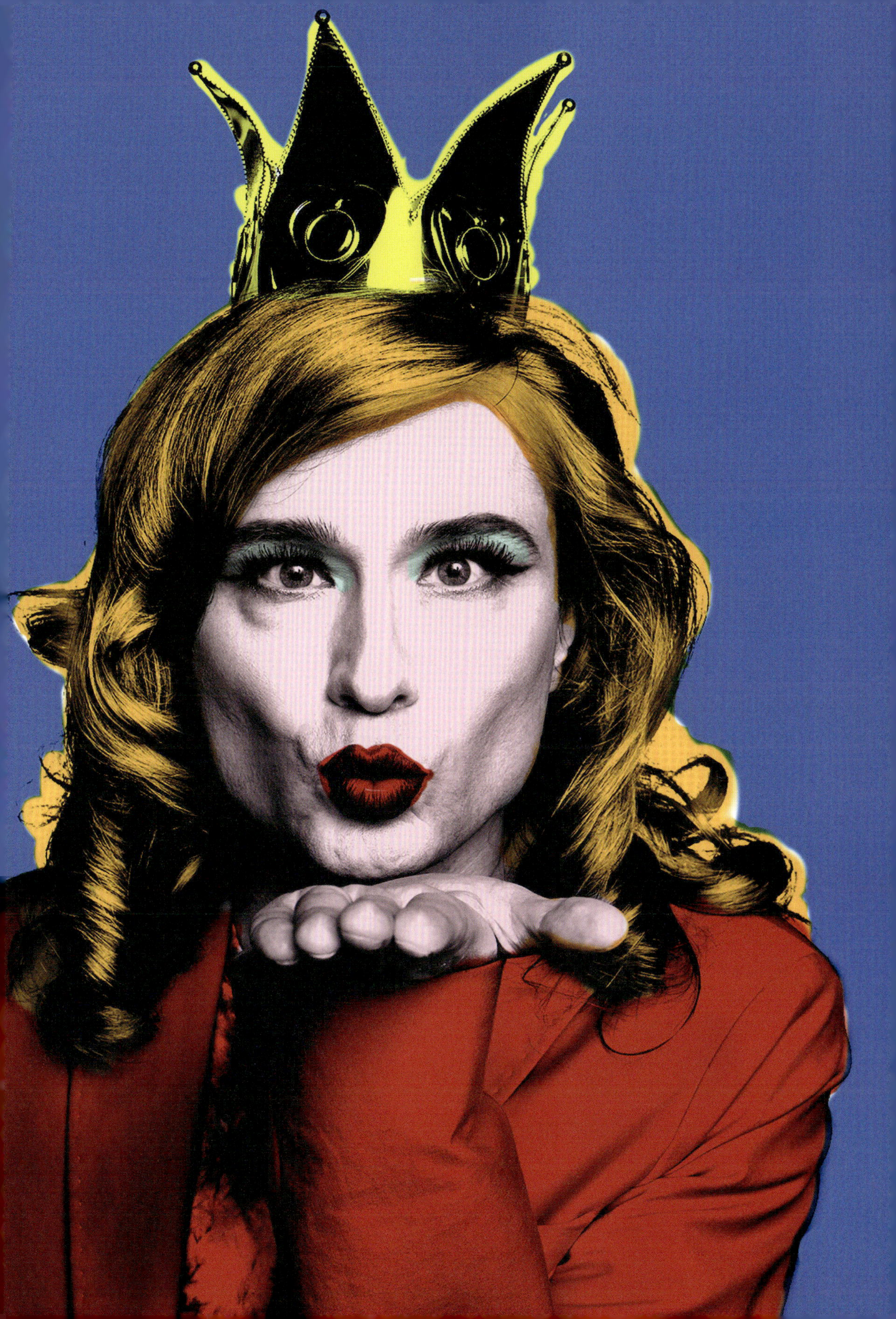

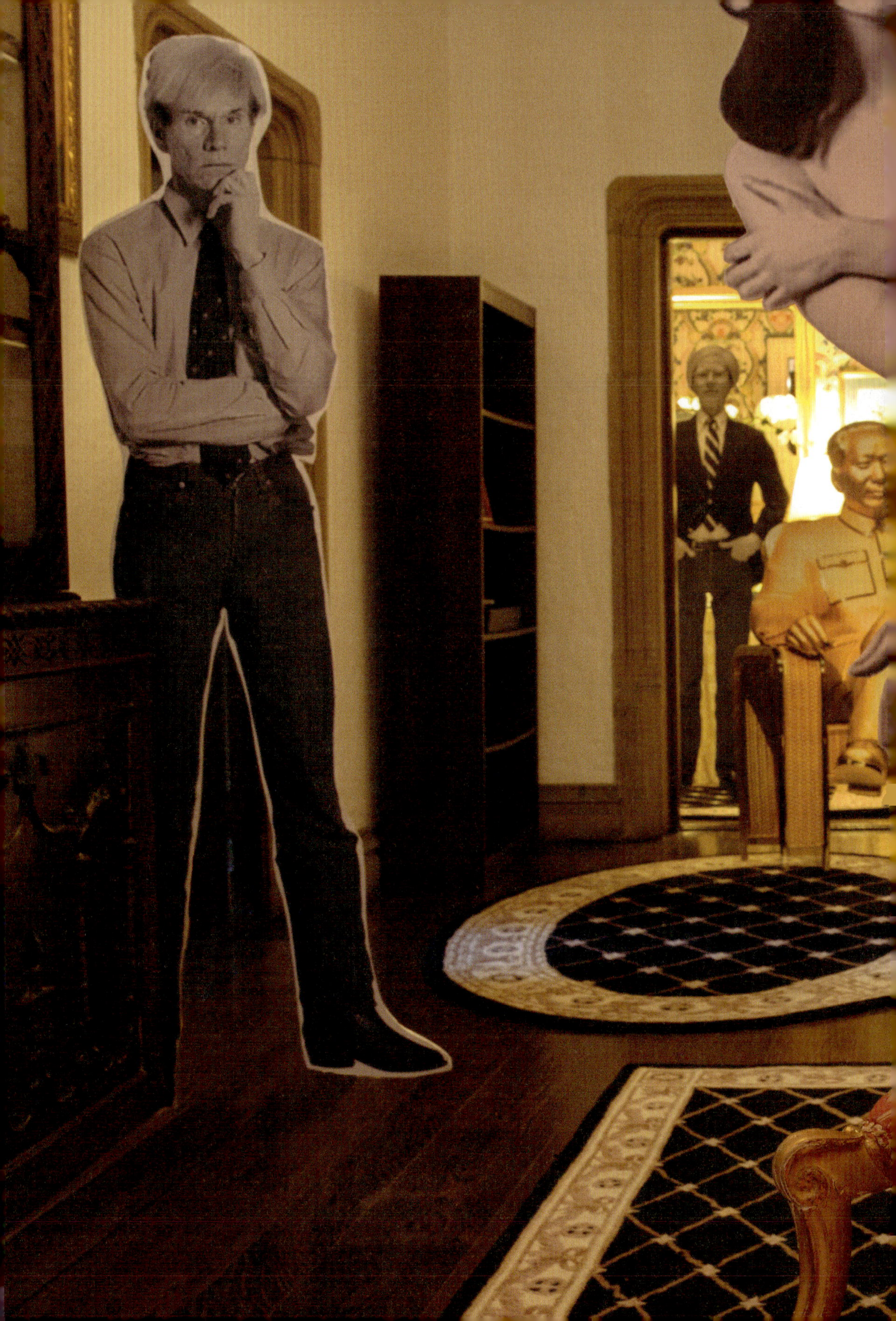

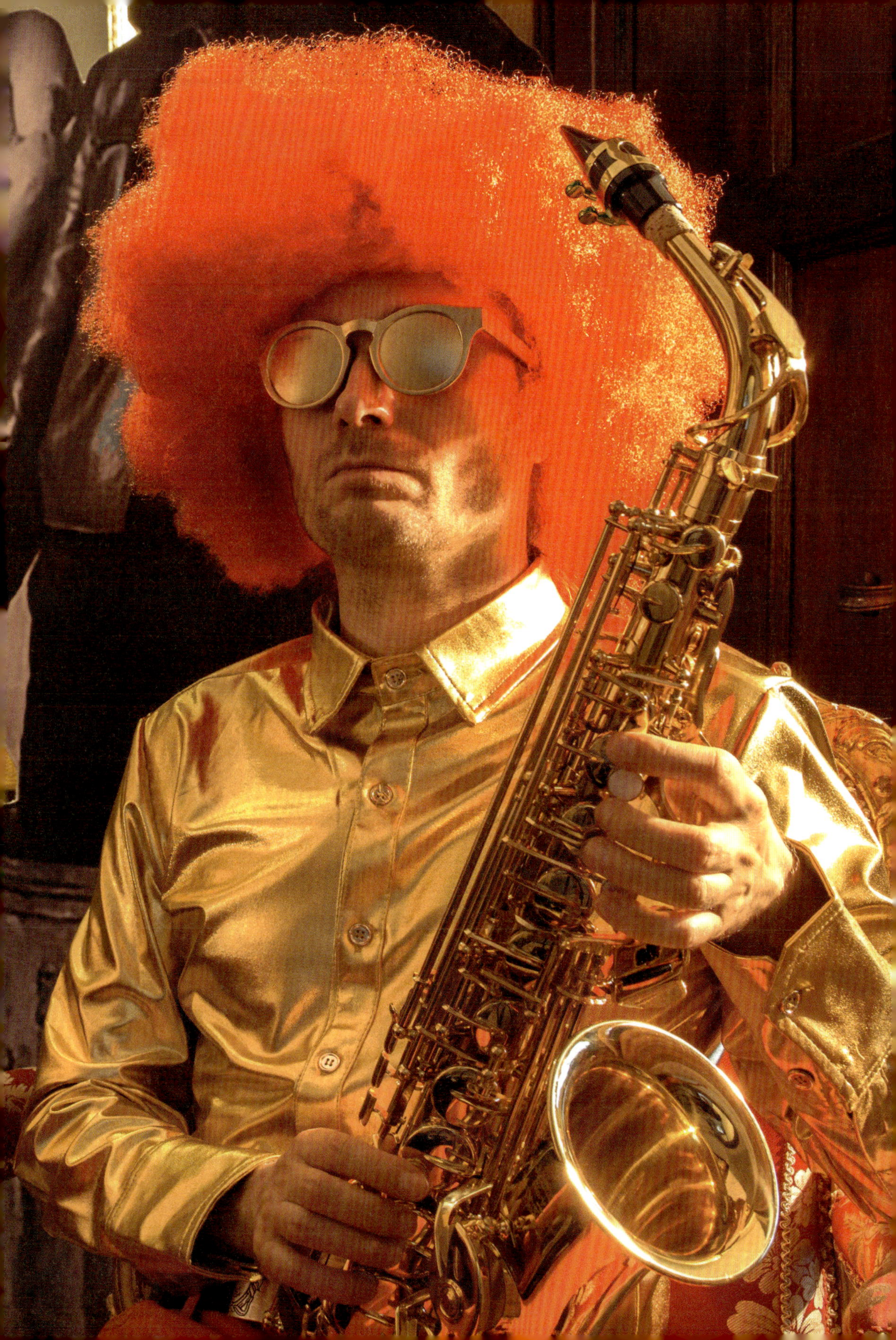

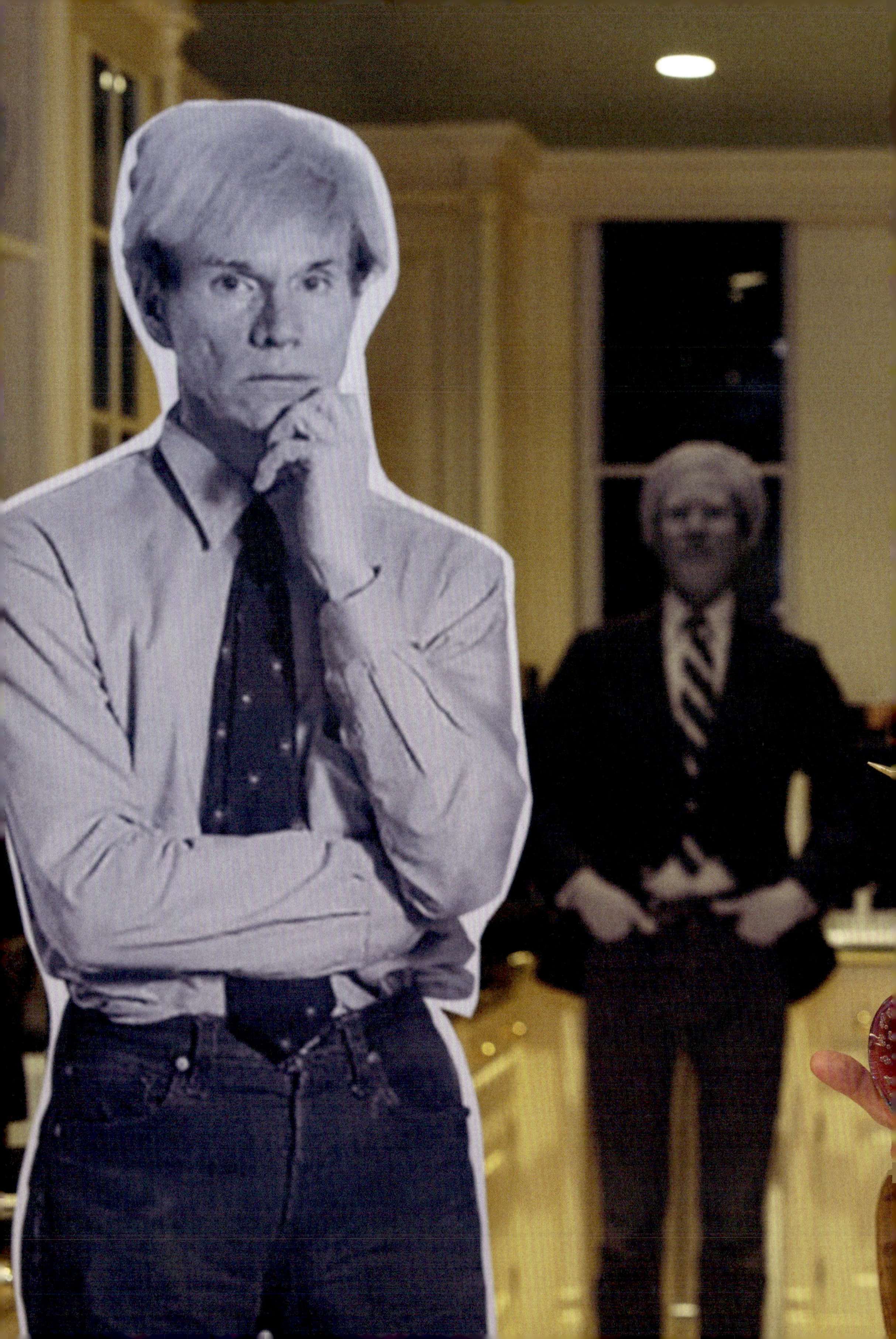

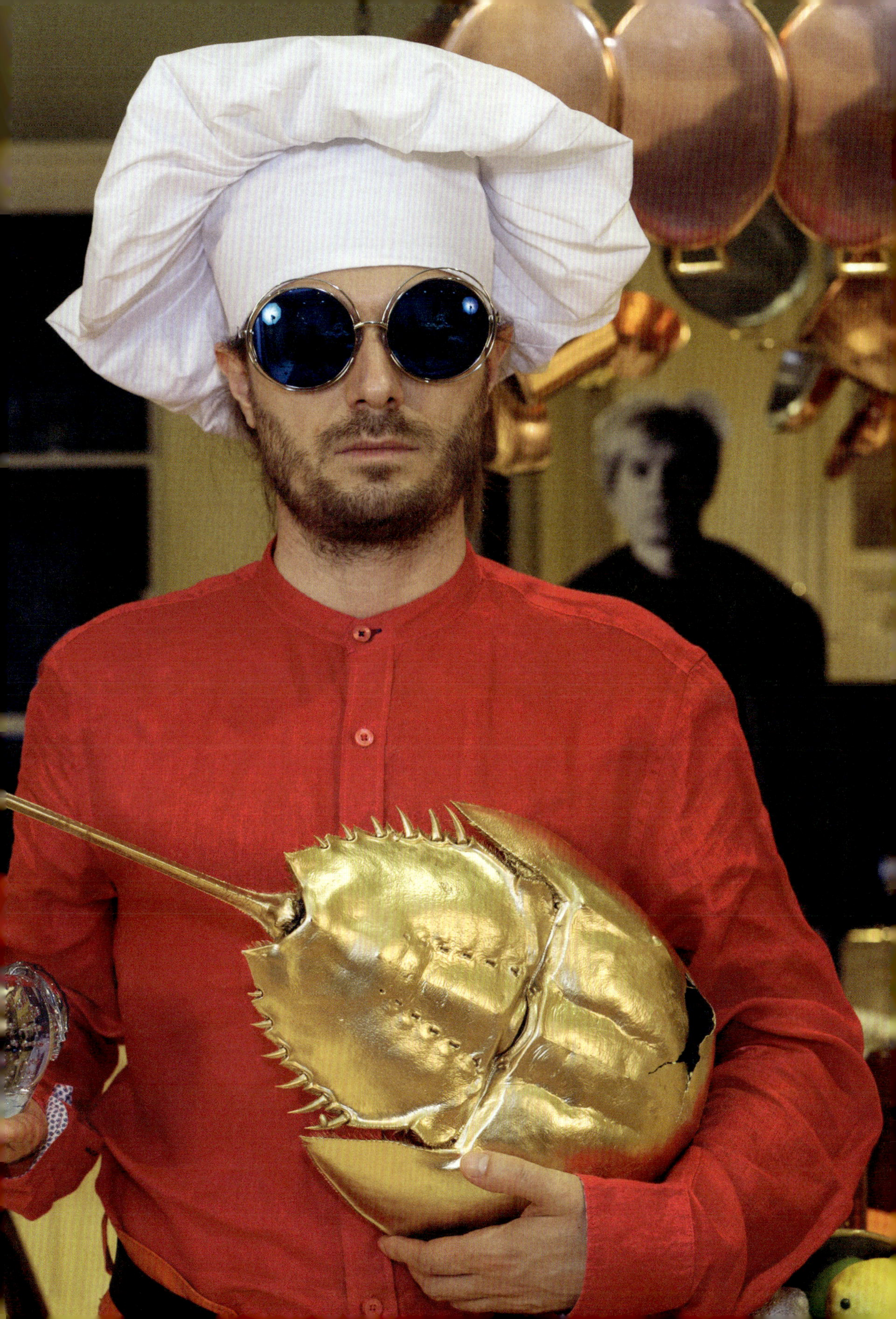

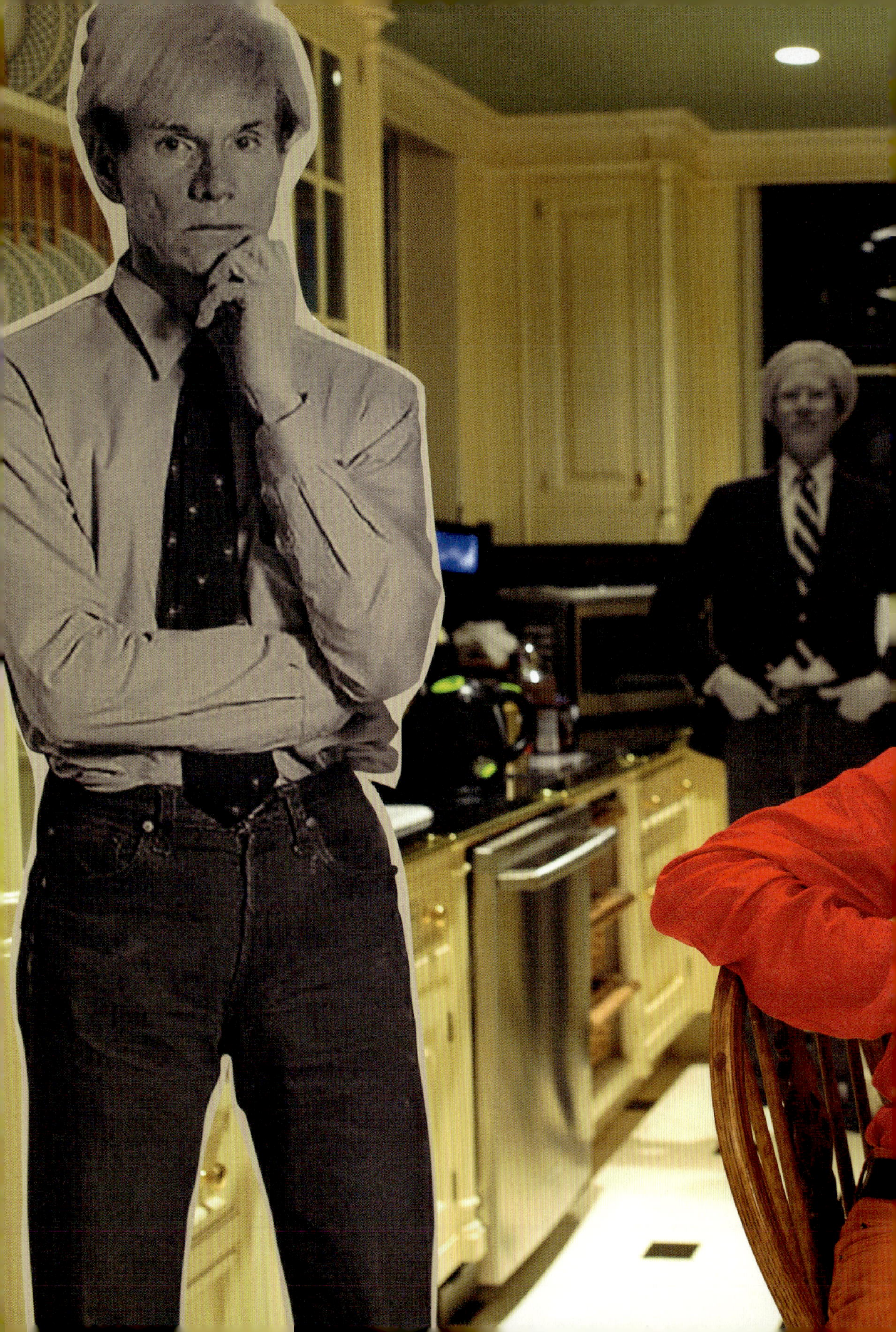

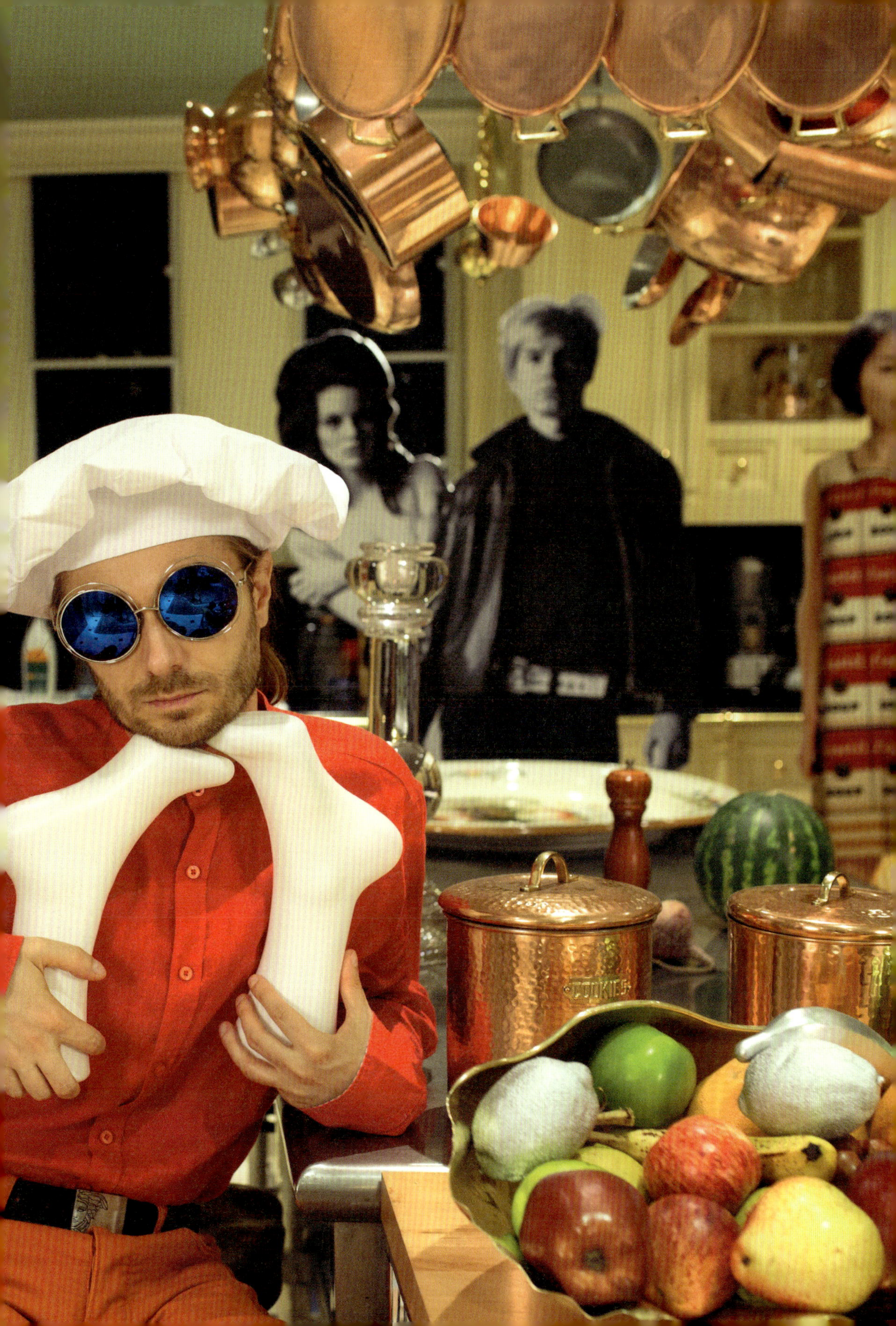
COOKIES

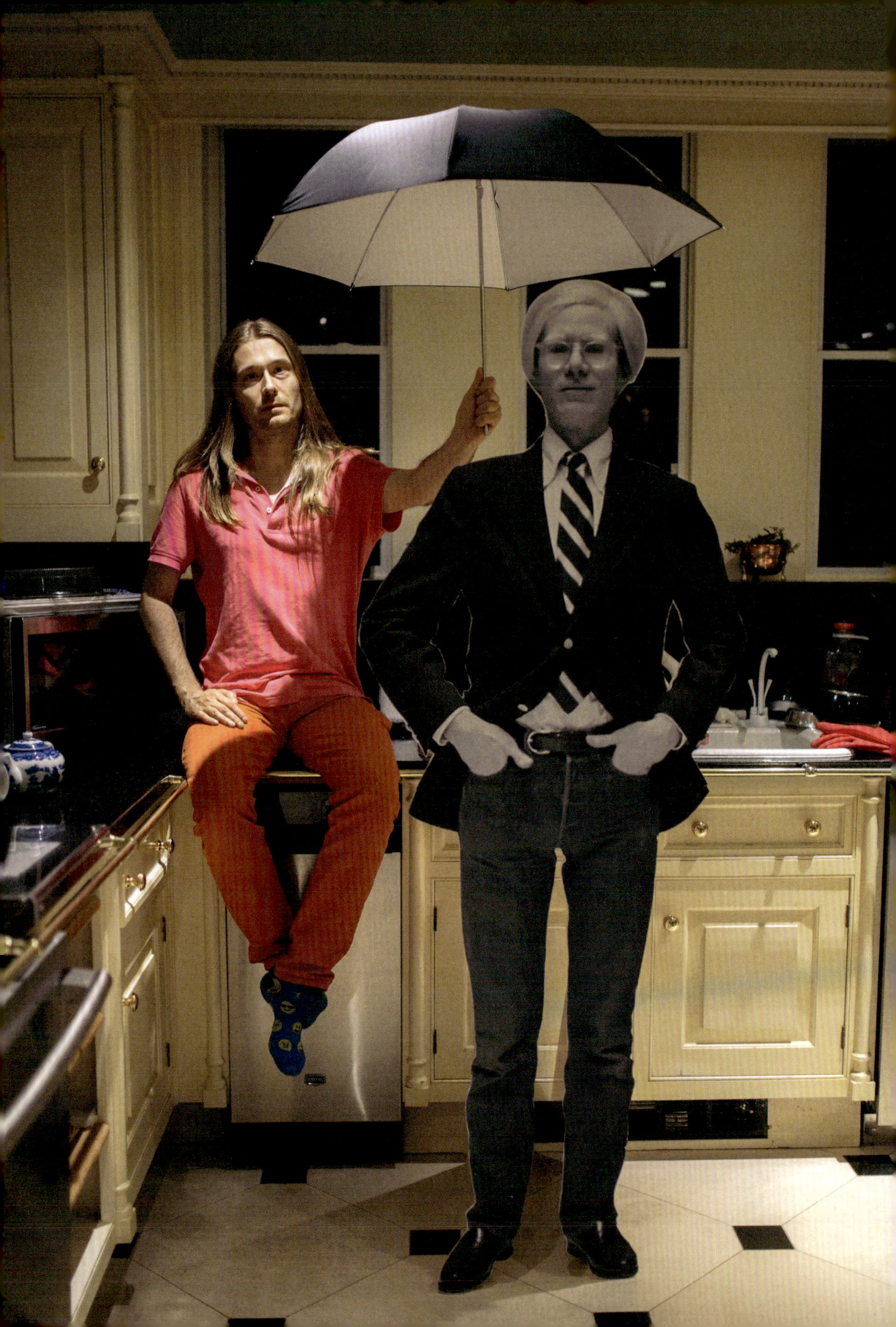

like a horse that couldn't run anymore. His body was rocking, and his legs hit the wooden wall. Hans jumped up and grabbed his head and neck in his hands. "Mouth, mouth, mouth!! Open it! Open his mouth!" Ronald commanded hurriedly, "or he'll swallow his tongue."

Hans pulled his father's jaws open with his hands, trying to secure his head. Ronald had run to the kitchen and come back with a large wooden spoon. He put its wooden handle between Hans' father's teeth.

"Hold it! Hold his head!" yelled Ronald.

Hans' father was hacking up blood onto his white shirt.

"Don't worry, guys, it's nothing… Everything will be fine. Nothing…" Ronald bravely attempted to calm Hans and his father. "Don't worry, guys!"

And then the police came. And then the ambulance. The body—warm, soft, sweet, and still smelling of childhood—was still hot. Hans burrowed his nose into his father's shoulders and took the weak, pliant hands in his. He hugged his neck, breathing in his native, minty-sweet, somewhat feminine odor, which in a moment reminded him of everything in the world: the night in the excavator bucket, his first time going to school, reading books, swimming in the Spree, his mother—everything that one could possibly remember in one second about a happy and endless childhood. Hans kissed the hot skin, remembering that the hands and feet would stiffen up in an hour, and the native smell would wane. And the heart, having given Hans the crumbs of its last happy feelings, would later shrink and shrivel somewhere underground, having lost its function of protecting life with its constant effort. The soul and thoughts would seep through the crust of the hardened, ice-filled muscles and fly upwards, freeing the shell. That shrunken heart and that cast-iron body would never hold Hans' father again.

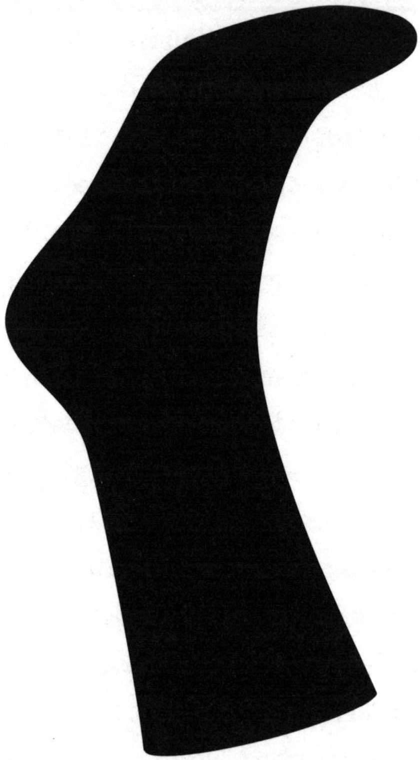

CHAPTER 10

This was no one-day urban romance. It wasn't even flirting, even though it was filled with feelings, freshness, new discoveries, and naïve sensations. It was something that stood on the sharp edge of a life's beginning.

Hans explored Yuma creatively in order to become memorable to her and stand out from the majority of those with whom she had been before. He encoded his kiss with a poetic message to her, which she was to read a little later, like the Voyager 1 spaceship launched in 1977, whose cardboard box held a record with the voices of people, bird noises, and the sound of the tides. The Morse code kiss said, "Just don't fly away. Mayday. Just be with me." Yuma felt these intonations. She needed them too as if Hans were a mirror for her. Their lives, occurring on different continents and in different alphabets, at this point in time had perplexingly intertwined. Yuma and Hans lived strangely identically in their identical sufferings.

In the meantime, a warm, light rain had begun falling down in slow drops like a hundred thousand soldiers. Yuma was walking barefoot on the asphalt that was still warm from the daytime. They left Central Park and headed towards the statue of Duke Ellington. The suit jacket and piano of the metal god were lit by floodlights, whose rays penetrated the thin, white raindrops like bullets.

"Duke was waiting for you to approve me! As your friend," concluded Hans. "But if you want, I can take his place at the piano while you take a walk to the Hudson."

Yuma threw her head back and looked up as if she were praying to an iron Buddha, with her eyes holding up the piano borne by nine musical goddesses. Yuma's figure distinctly resembled theirs, minus nine dresses. The movement of the tenth grace and the experiences of the day made Yuma the most irresistible of the irresistible. Her scarlet dress matched the iron monument and underscored life. Hans wanted to learn how to paint in oil to create a portrait of the girl: in a poppy dress, in the rain, looking up to the heavens at a musical angel coming down to Earth.

Fifth Avenue was completely empty, and in a few blocks, when they had turned onto a 116th St., they were engulfed by pitch darkness. Maybe someone in New York was trying to save electricity. Maybe some unseen hand was managing the comfort level of Yuma and Hans' relationship, and to support their closeness made the sky and the street darker. Maybe the organized motion of charged particles in the wires became unorganized. The electrons stopped working, abandoning all the light bulbs at once. In the pitch darkness, it began raining, and only rare lights from the sky from faraway flashes of lightning showed the photographer and musician the way. In New York, this love-conducive situation is called a blackout.

Hans squeezed Yuma to him with a new strength, forgetting about all the Japanese rules of origami and traffic. "親愛なるハンス," she muttered. There were no cars and no people. The warm rain coated the bass guitar, Yuma's hair, and Hans' orange jacket.

Hans pressed Yuma to him under the gigantic drops that were trying to wedge themselves in between their love. The drops were first the size of walnuts and then grew to balloon-size. Hans' two wide palms held Yuma's face and cheeks to feel more successful and stronger, so she couldn't extricate herself. And to prevent any more huge ants from getting in.

Again, she whispered something, addressing it either to herself or to the heavens. And the rain fell in an unending, blissful stream. "It must be trying to convince you to be my wife," thought Hans.

"明日東京に行きます," she said.

"Ich bin dein Gemahl, ich bin dein Gemahl," Hans answered.

Her grape lips turned into wine for him, from which Hans couldn't save himself. It was as if he were already screaming in every direction from his closed-in space, wanting to run away, like yesterday. But his scream remained the scream of a nightmare in a spellbinding thin wineglass.

The drops tapped on her eyelashes like they would on a roof, writing with her running mascara a magic name in calligraphy on her face.

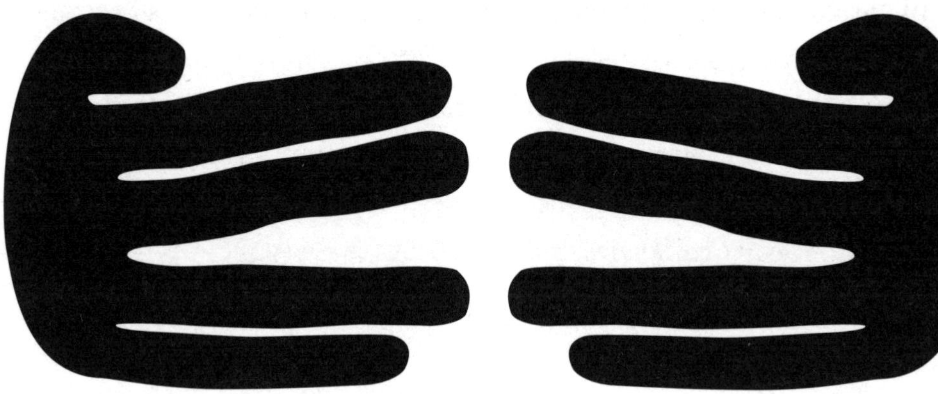

CHAPTER 17

What was Hans thinking now while standing in the rain in Harlem at 2 AM in the inky darkness? He could no longer turn his reason on and off—the circuit breaker was sparking. The working mechanism that had always stopped him had broken. Hans began weeping and covered his face with his hands. A wave of liberation or simultaneous despair flowed through his entire being.

"What happened? Where does it hurt?" exclaimed a frightened Yuma. "Are you crying?" She was still quite surprised.

"Eeeeeeeeee... Kawaiiii," she continued talking in broken Japanese. "Are you cold? Shall we go to my place?" She hugged him. "I have a Miles Davis record."

"Of course I'm not cold," answered Hans. "Rain got in my eye." "Eeeeeeeee," she repeated in Japanese and moved Hans' hand from his own face, hugging his jacket soaked through with summer together with the rain. Moving the bass case to the side, she kissed Hans and continued whispering her Japanese rhymes in his ear: きみは庭師、そして一輪の花。この世の牢獄できみは独りぼっちではない。

Hans stood on the street, with all his multi-leveled protection from the barbed wire of East Berlin, the high voltage, and the concrete fence with barking dogs having been smashed into smithereens.

The jets of rain trickled down his face from his eye to his shirt, sleeve, pants, and boots. The vigorous stream of rainwater then flowed to the sewer grate as if freedom was too foreign to it like it was for Hans.

"Iiiiiiiiiiiiii!" yelled Hans through the rain that took the sound away. A hundred thousand drops of rain. "Looooooooove!" A flash of lightning. "Yooooooooooouuuuuuu!" Thunderclaps.

Hans switched to a whisper, adding something new: "I love you. I love you. Love you. I love you. I love you. I love you. I love you. I love you. I love you." Hans whispered in all the languages of the world. "ഞാൻ നിന്നെ സ്നേഹിക്കുന്നു. Ek is lief vir jou. Të dua. እኔ ፍቅር. أنا أحبك. Ես սիրում եմ քեզ. Mən səni sevirəm. මම ඔයාට ආදරයෙ. Maite zaitut. Я кахаю цябе. আমতিমাকে ভালবাষি. Volim te ba. Обичам те. t'estimo. 我愛你. Gihigugma ko ikaw. Ndimakukonda. Ti tengu caru. Volim te. Miluji tě. Jeg elsker dig. I love you. Mi amas vin. Ma armastan sind. 나는 당신을 사랑합니다. Rakastan sinua. Je t'aime. Ik hâld fan dy. Quérote. მე შენ მიყვარხარ. Ich liebe dich. Σ 'αγαπώ. હું તમને પ્રેમ. Mwen renmen ou. Ina son ka. I aloha ia oukou. मैं तुमसे प्यार करता हूँ. Kuv hlub koj. Szeretlek. Ég elska þig. M hụrụ gị n'anya. Aku mencintaimu. Is breá liom tú. Ti amo. 私はあなたを愛して. Aku tresna sampeyan. ನಾನು ನಿನ್ನ ಪ್ರೀತಿಸುತ್ತೇನೆ. Мен сені жа сы к ремін. ខ្ញុំស្រឡាញ់អ្នក. Ez hej te dikim. Мен сени с й м. ריא עביל ךיא. Te amo. Es tevi mīlu. Aš tave myliu. Ech hunn dech gär. Te сакам. Tiako ianao. ผมรักคุณ. Saya suka anda. Aroha ahau ki a koutou. मी तुला प्रेम करतो. Би чамд хайртай. म तपाईंलाई प्रेम. Jeg elsker deg. مين ميرس مرل   من امش ار تسود مراد. Kocham cię. Eu te amo. ਮੈਨੂੰ ਤੁਹਾਡੇ ਨਾਲ ਪਿਆਰ. Te iubesc. Я люблю тебя. Ou te alofa ia te oe. Tha gaol agam ort. Волим те. ינא בהוא ךתוא. Kea u rata. Ndinokudai. نوہ ک ي ت و س ا ن پ ي ا ر ہآ ي. Milujem ťa. Ljubim te. Waan ku jeclahay. Te amo. Nakupenda. ຂ້າພະເຈົ້າຮັກທ່ານ. Jag älskar dig. Ман туро д ст медорам. Seni seviyorum. Я люблю тебе. م ےس مت ےهجم

تبح. Men seni Sevaman. Tôi yêu bạn. Rwyf wrth fy modd i chi. నేను నిన్ను ప్రేమిస్తున్నాను. Ndiyakuthanda ukuba. Mo ni ife ti o. Ngiyakuthanda. நான் உன்னை காதலிக்கிறேன்."

Hans had never spoken these words to anyone alive. A happy radio-technical childhood had never contained any real changes in life on whose threshold it would have been necessary to say aloud this obviousness.

Hiding behind the noise of the rain, Harlem strained to eavesdrop on what Hans was whispering now. That whisper resounded throughout New York, from Brighton Beach to the Hudson River.

"I love you, Yuma!" Hans finally screamed his quatrain to all of Harlem.

"I'm pleased to hear that," she smiled.

Hans was not naive. His hearing was tuned by a precise tuning fork. Hans was more closed than necessary, sometimes shy, even melancholic. He wasn't a master of wit. But he was not naive.

The rain refashioned their clothes like a designer. Yuma's dress got narrower and clung to her body. She looked more like herself: fragile, thin, with the furtive movements of a vulnerable chick shaking the globe with its first steps. Hans was wearing an orange jacket, which now also looked somewhat like a dress.

Hans didn't want the road to end. Fortunately, Harlem was endless and empty. Because of the rain, all the summer night enthusiasts had hidden in their houses and apartments. It was difficult to walk fast. When they had passed 115th St., light hit their path again unexpectedly—a few streetlights. Then in some of the windows, life shone forth as well. Maybe the strong winds had yet again done some damage to the power substation. Hans saw Yuma's silhouette wrapped in the piece of scarlet fabric. Her ironic eyes, with a note of sadness, glistened from the rain and with the flash of a new, bright light. Her eyes were deeply loyal to Hans. Yuma wanted to stay with him that night. The clock hands showed only three hours past midnight. It seemed that a week had passed since morning; so much had happened on that long-awaited day.

CHAPTER 18

Yuma and Hans stopped at the insignificant five-story building where she lived. Hans didn't have any ideas. He only knew that he couldn't leave her alone. The bass guitar stood on the steps resting after a hard day's night and walked up the stairs home by itself. It was embarrassed to watch the two kissing. The pink noise of the departing rain wanted to turn into a white Gaussian one. The drops, not subsiding, drummed hard on the neighboring roofs, sounding an alarm.

"Let's go to your place?" Hans took the initiative. "I'm cold, yeah."

It seems he had become a real, strong man that evening. "I only have one room. The owner lives in the other one, and she doesn't allow me to bring anyone home."

"Just say that you have a pet. I bet you can bring pets in."

"Haaans," she smiled with apologetic lips.

"Let's go back to my house?"

"Mmmm… I have to leave for the airport tomorrow morning. I'm flying to Tokyo. Home. But I'll come back here again. No reason to worry. We'll meet again and again."

Hans took the bass and tugged Yuma by the hand. "I have Miles Davis too. Come downtown to my place," he whispered, embarrassed in front of the street and himself. "I can get a cab."

He convinced himself that he could do it. But the taxis, they're so nimble… no friggin' way you can catch one.

"What did you say?" she had missed it.

Yuma, like bubble gum, pliantly followed him, stretching out her rubber arm a bit, having fallen behind Hans.

"I can't. After I arrive tomorrow, I have a recording in Tokyo. I have to sleep at least a little bit. I can't even drink coffee, eat nuts or sweet things, and other stuff. You have to sleep at least eight hours the night before a recording. All of that affects the voice."

Hans stopped pulling her by the arm.

"OK. It would be better if you slept. We really will have lots of time together later."

"Wir werden das ganze Leben zusammen sein, deshalb können wir die Zeit auch ohne einander verbringen," said Hans.

"You get the sleep you need, but remember."

"What?"

"What I screamed today in the dark." She smiled, "Of course. It's important to me."

Hans almost didn't notice that her answer worried him. Sometimes it was more convenient for him not to notice nuances.

"What time do you have to leave for the airport?"

"Eight in the morning. But I still have to pack, and my whole room is upside down."

"What, the floor is on the ceiling? Can I take a look?" She laughed.

"I'll be here at seven fifty-five," said Hans.

"Are you sure? You need to sleep too."

"Cameras don't sing. I'll be here at that time exactly. I'll have enough sleep. What's your apartment? The number?" It was as if Yuma somewhat hesitated.

"2C. Apartment 2C."

"OK, I'll be here tomorrow at seven fifty-five."

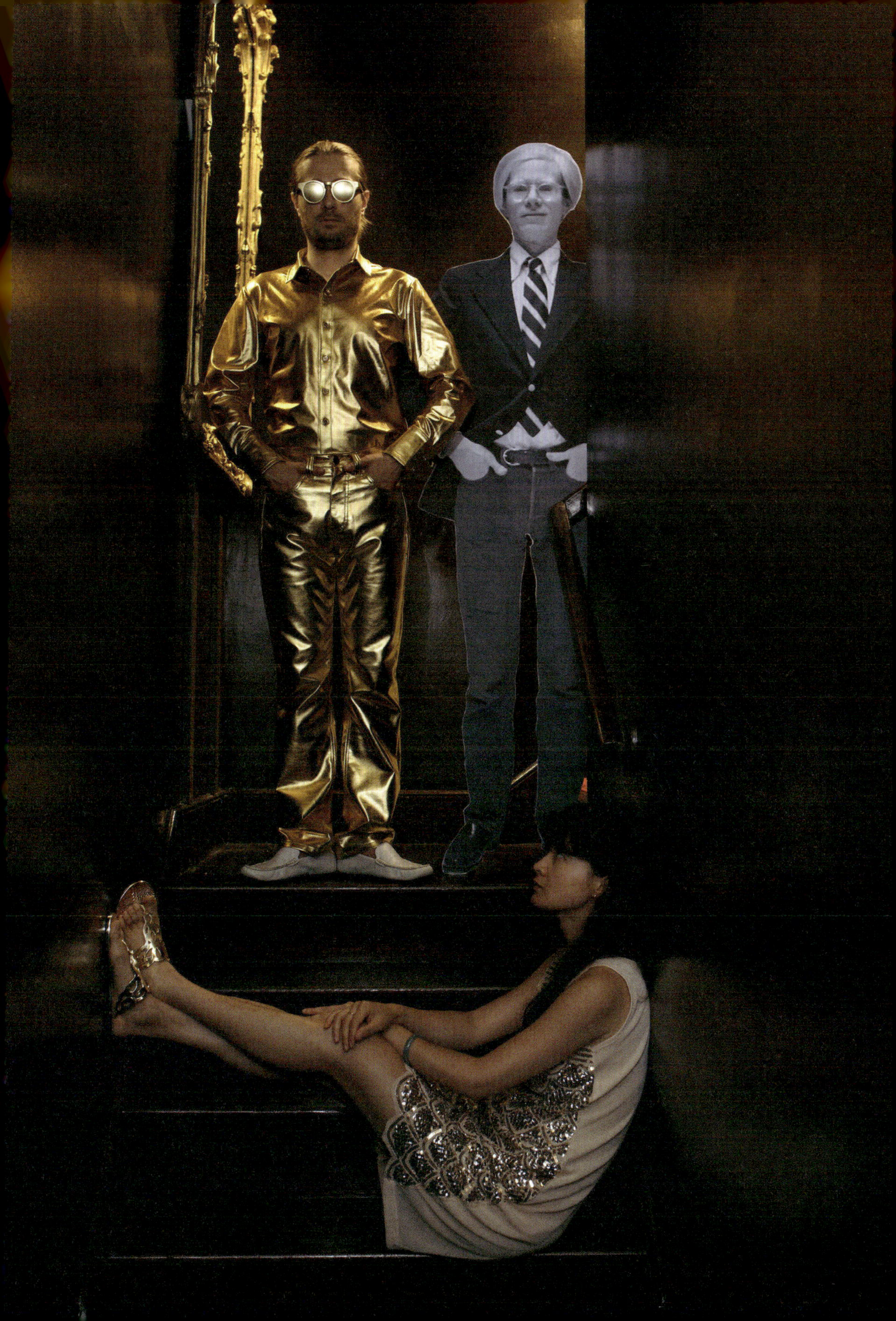

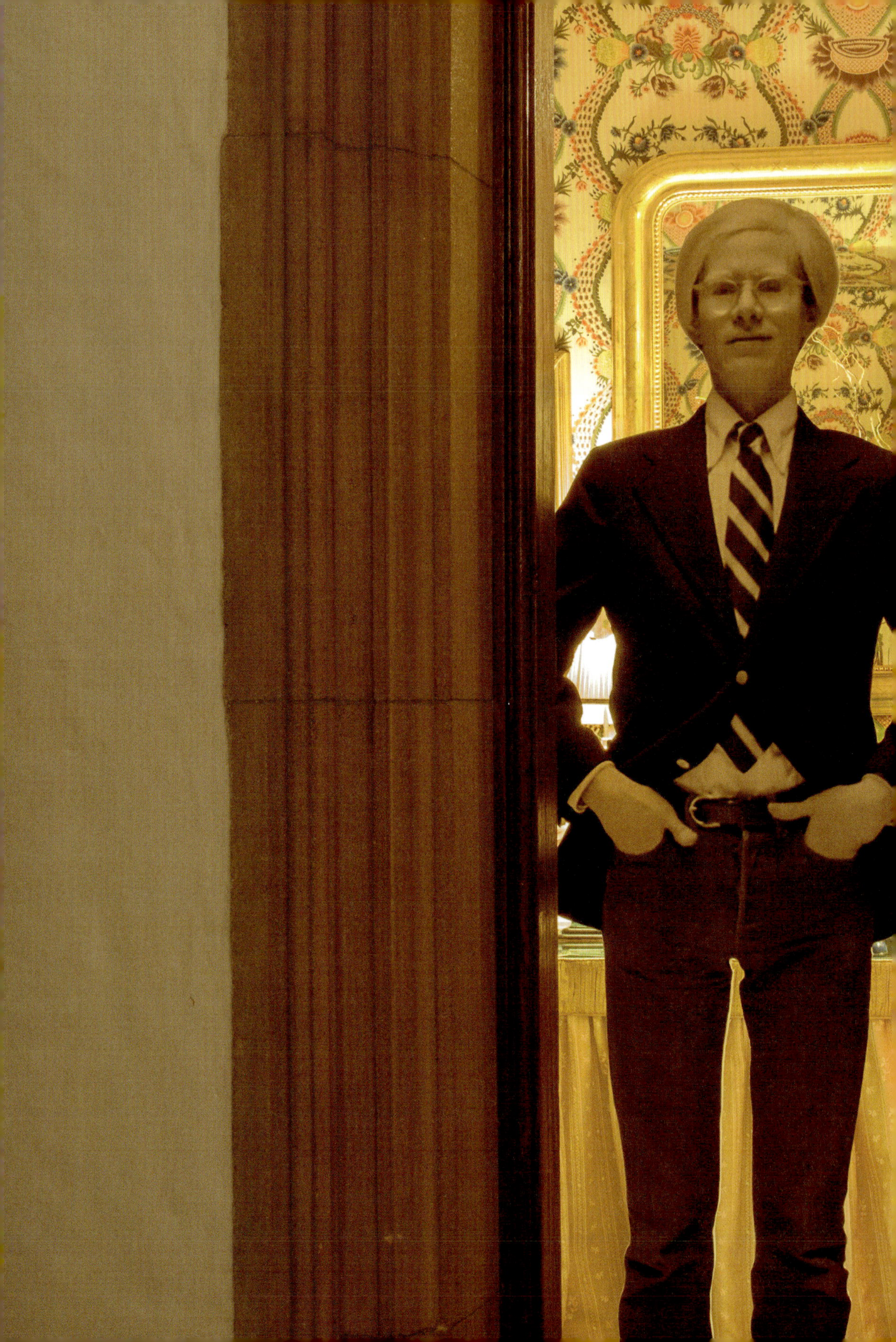

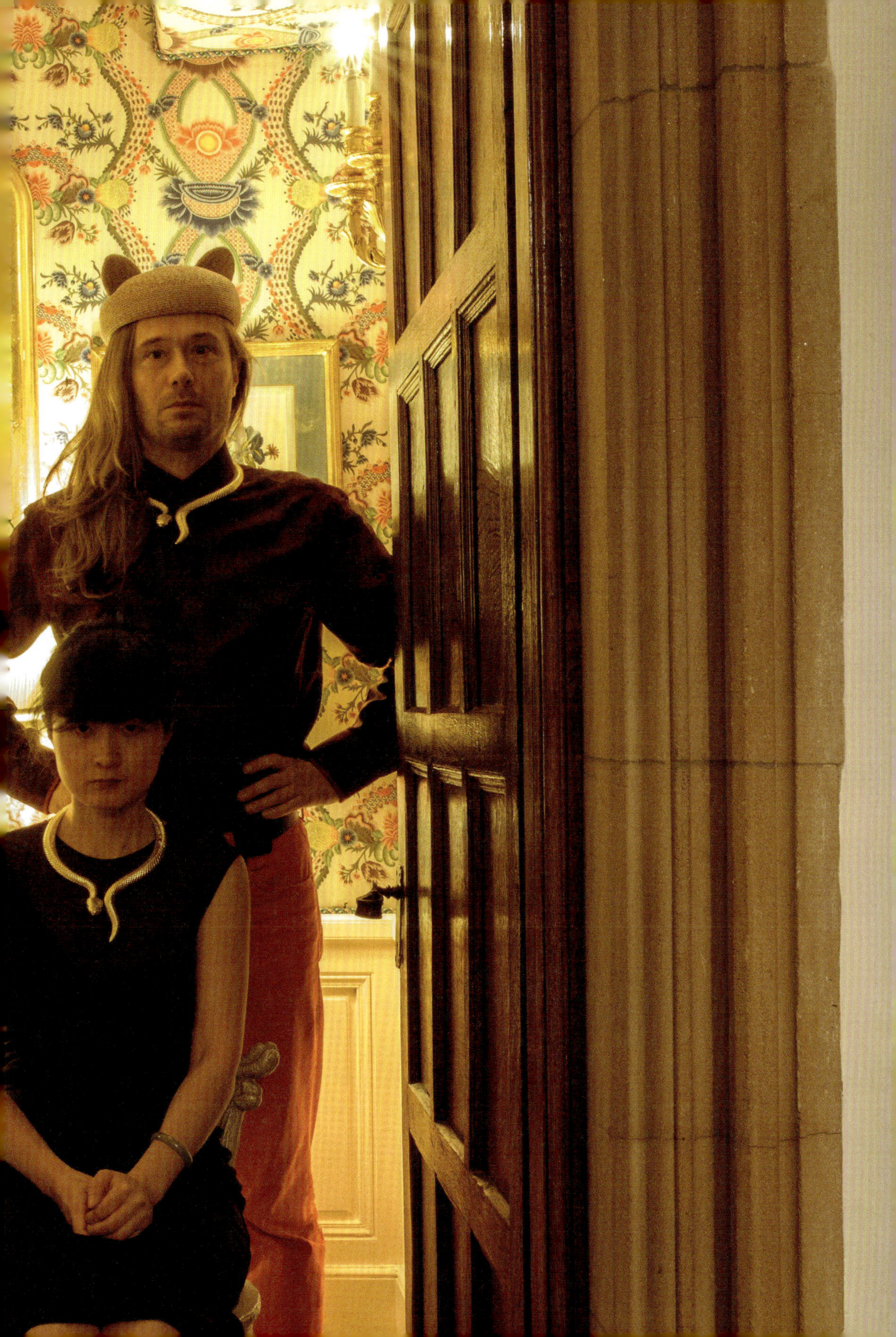

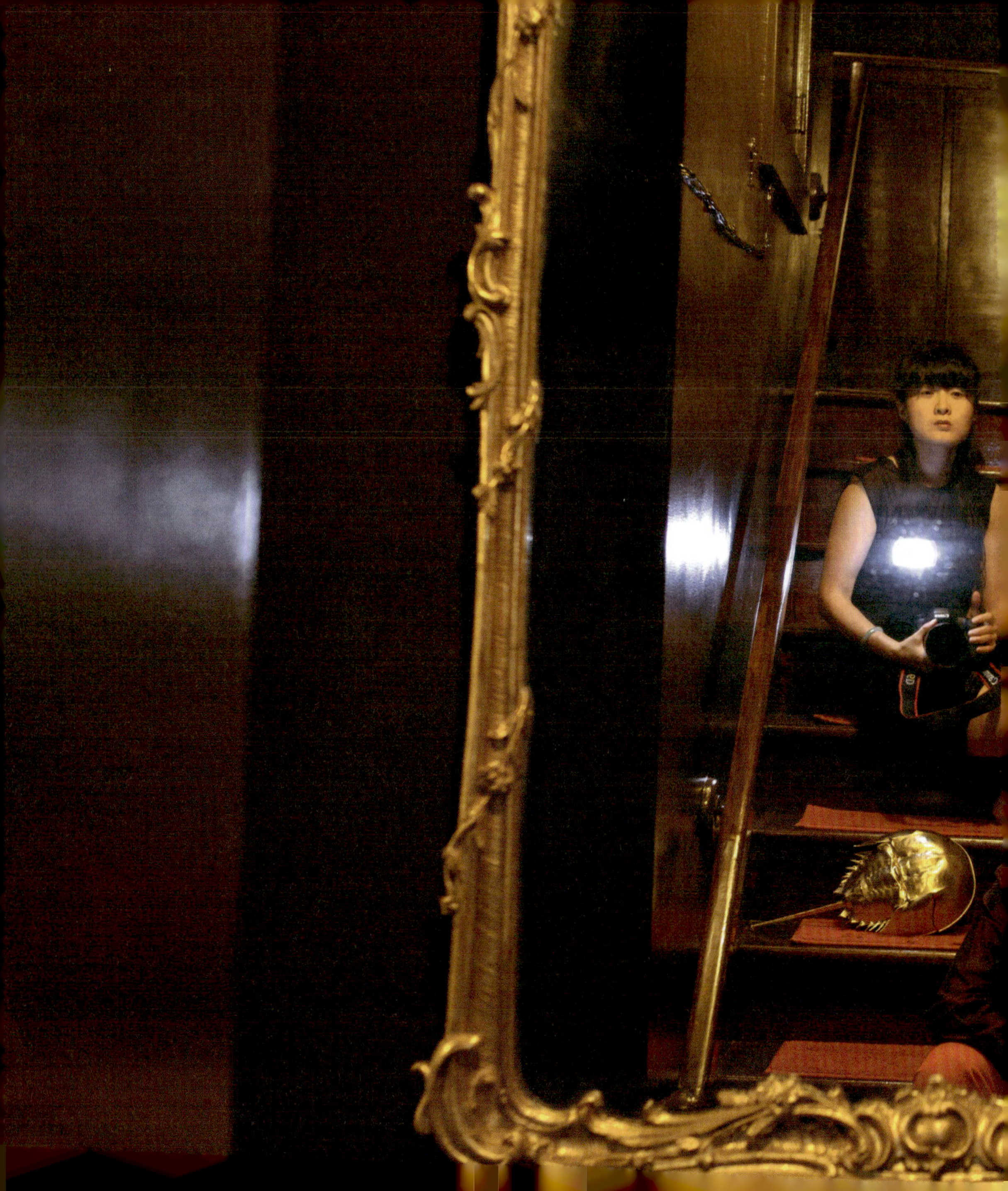

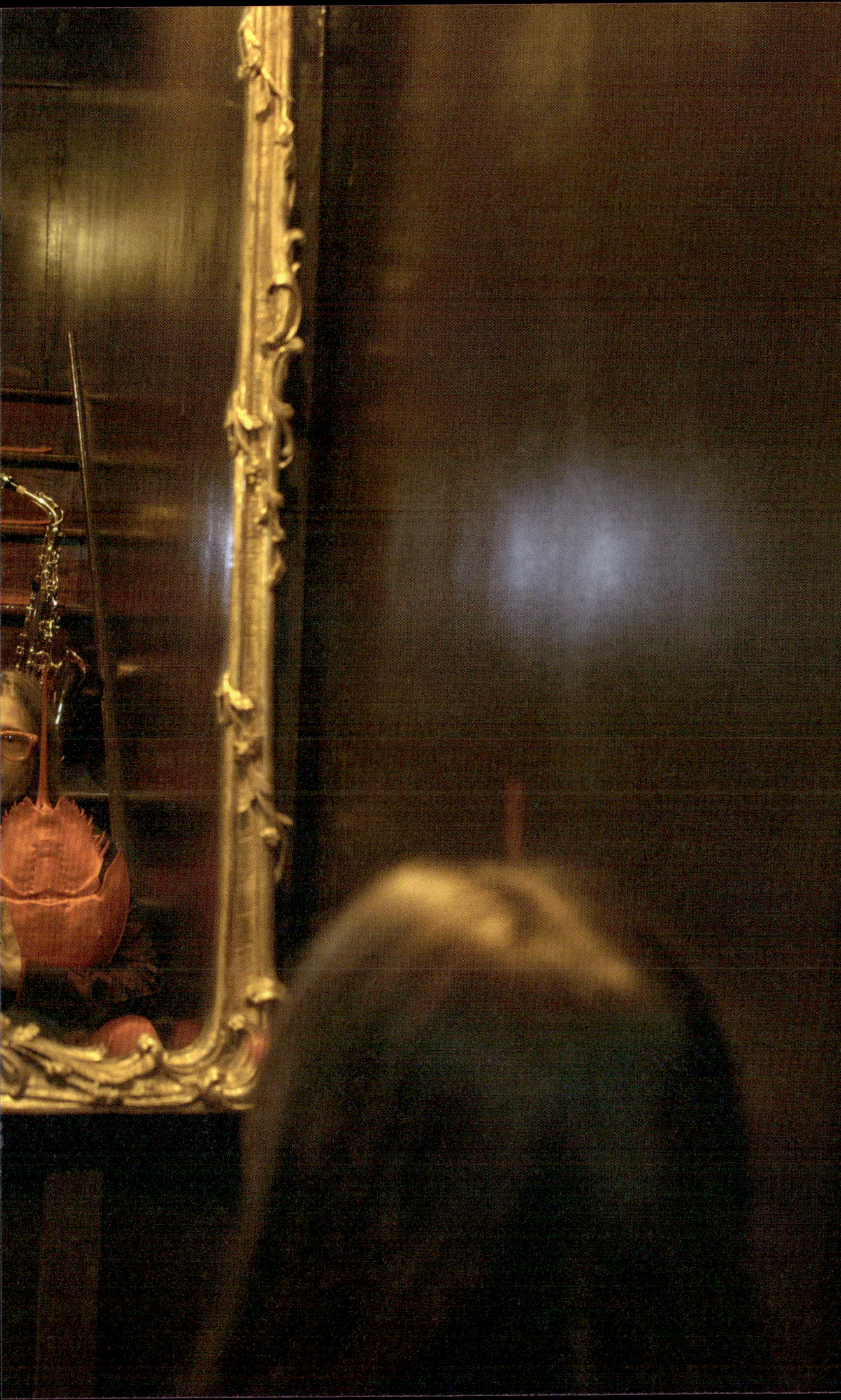

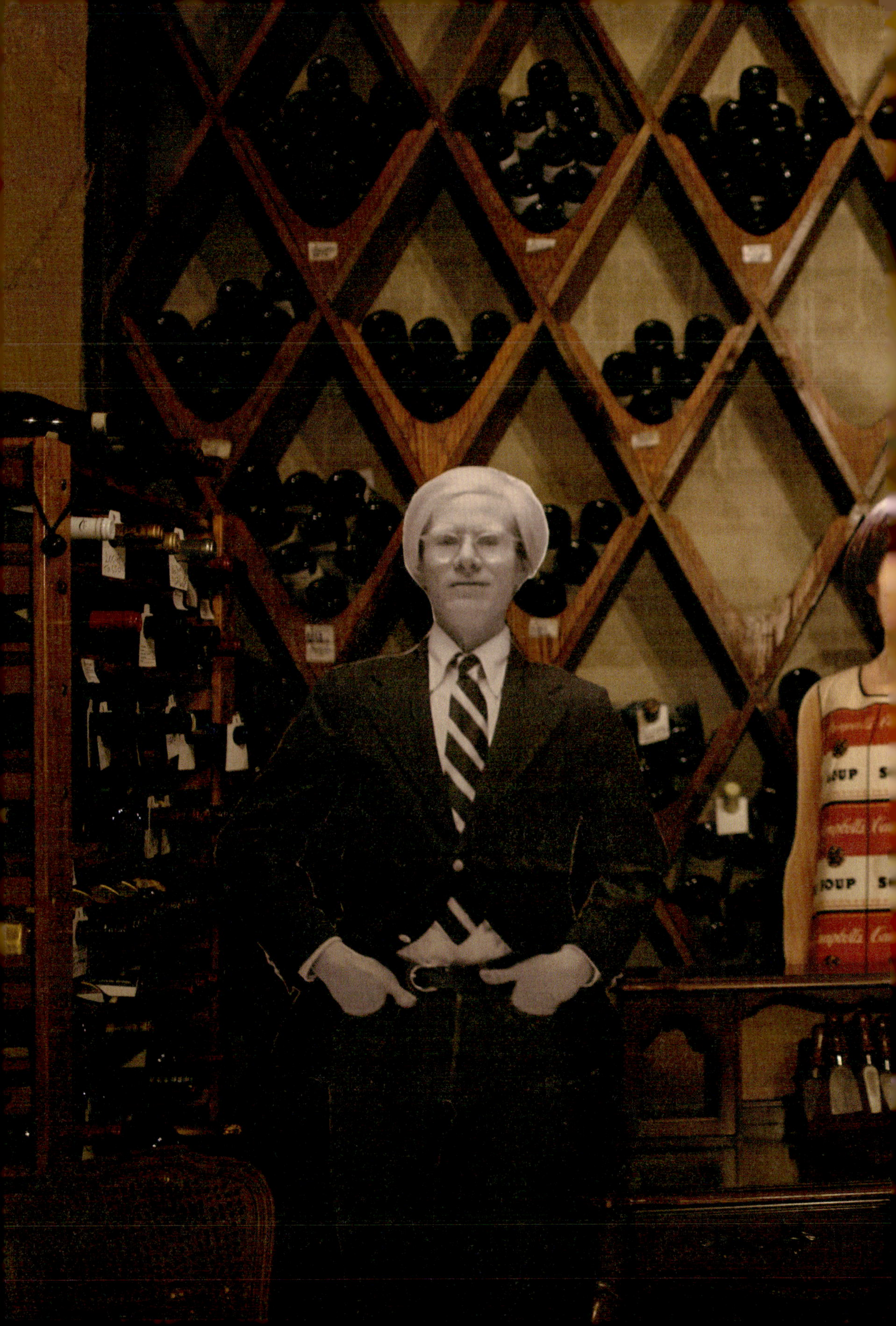
SOUP

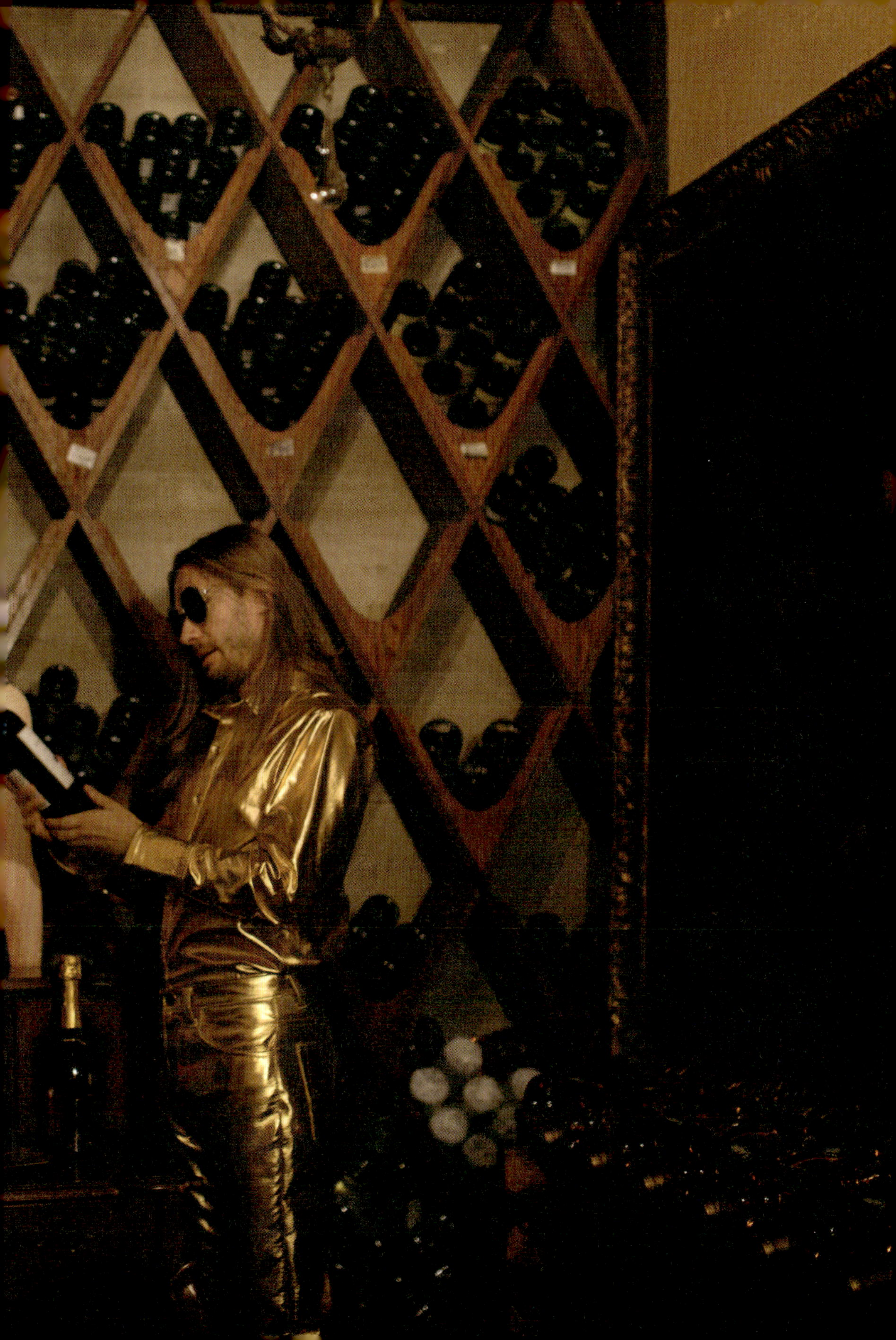

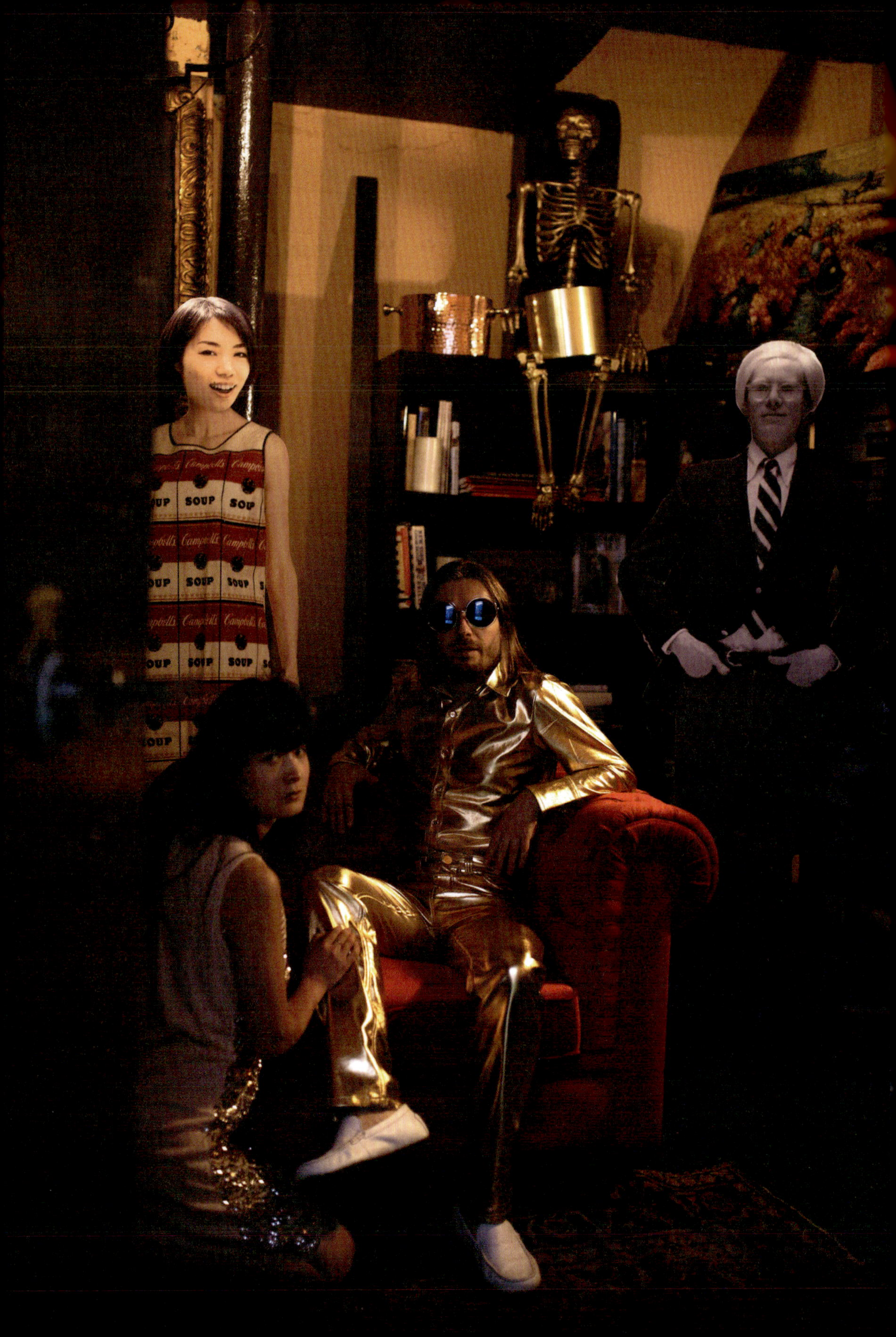
SOUP

"Well, if it's not too much for you to wake up so early for me..." she stirred the porridge of pleasantries the third time around. "OK. Then I'll be here at seven fifty-six. So I can catch some sleep."

Hans held on to Yuma's hair, breathing in her maiden smell. Even if they would see their dreams on different screens tonight, and their bed wouldn't stretch from downtown to Harlem, it wasn't their last meeting. This created in them both an exuberant tumult with so many variables intermingled. Soon Hans and Yuma would live together, and she would move in with him downtown, and they would have a daughter. Hans was able to see the future quite well. Especially at three in the morning. He had wonderful intuition.

This premonition for the first time in his life made Hans completely happy. Something set him on fire from the inside, crumpled him up, and stopped his regular breathing. Hans walked down Lexington Avenue back through Harlem, trying to catch a taxi. There were no cars at three o'clock in the morning, and only on One 105th Street did he see a yellow cab on the road, in which the driver was napping. Hans knocked on the car window.

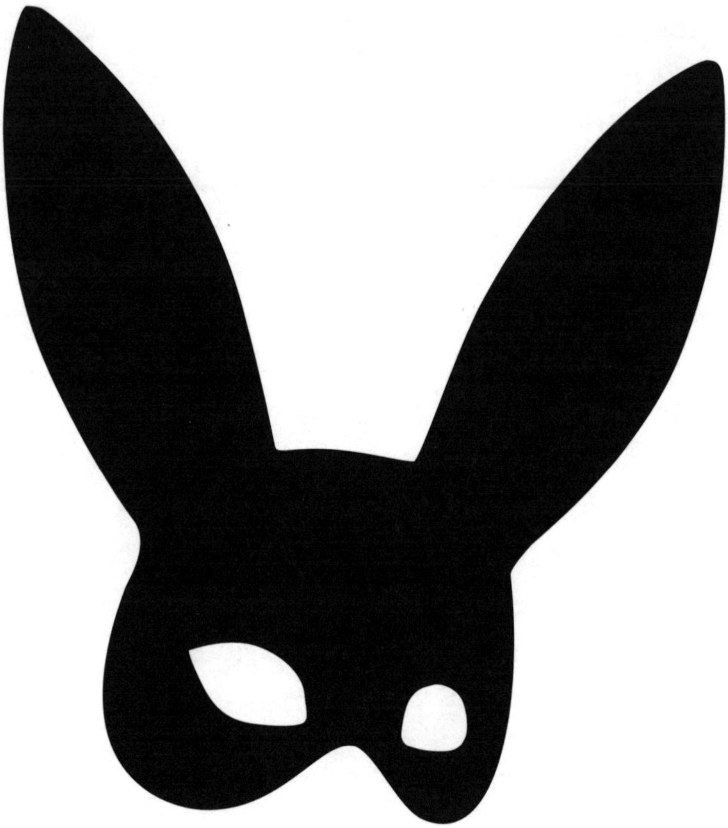

CHAPTER 19

When life takes a turn in any direction—when there is a drama occurring or a happy event that completely cancels out the past—time becomes a dream.

Daydreaming, Hans relived the moments he had lived during the day, turning off from his bodily sensations and from any consciousness of what was going on with him. Even in these waking dreams, he remained at somewhat of a distance from life, driven by the necessary inertia. In these dreams, Hans still did not manage to understand to the proper extent how happy yesterday was while falling asleep on that rainy night, how much the new sunny dawn promised, which he had met a thousand times with no interest at all. He was roused, moving from dream to dream. And that's how life tuckered him out, not giving him a reason to slough off the shell of melancholy.

Hans darted up like a spring at seven, dragged out of a short and shallow sleep. He put a Miles Davis record on his record player and, following the trumpet, began walking around the apartment. "I've been given a body. What shall I do with it?" Hans sang to a song of Miles' as he was choosing a fresh cover of shirt and pants for his legs and arms.

Soon Hans was speeding down summer Lexington Avenue, which was flooded with morning light, in a yellow summer car, towards summer 116th St. All that was left to do was get used to this new, happy life and understand that the anxiety of the past would no longer be venturing out of its pathetic scullery. Hans looked back at the houses that they were passing with curiosity, anxiousness, and joy, as if he were unwinding the ball of time back a bit, looking for a new home for his future family.

When he got to Yuma's house, Hans barely recognized it. It was an old, crooked, five-story shed, made from some unknown material, with the façade done in either wood or brick or paper. The branches of the rare-earth trees cast shadows on the walls, making the lattice dystrophy of the houses the urban design of Harlem. Hans gave the cabbie a tip that was bigger than the fare and wished him a wonderful day.

Seven fifty-five in the morning. Hans rang the doorbell.

No one answered.

He rang again. He waited a minute. And again. Finally, the outside doorknob shook, and the door opened to the new day. On the threshold stood a man of about sixty years of age. Gray, but with darker sections, unshaven, in velvet pants and a hastily thrown on t-shirt, and slippers.

"Good morning," Hans said, slightly taken aback. "Apartment 2C?"

"Yes."

"I'm here for Yuma. I suppose she's renting a room with you? The girl who's flying to Tokyo today."

"I live alone," the man stated, surprised. "I was here yesterday, and I stood on these steps with her."

"Are you sure about that?"

"Well… well… yes."

"Well, if you're waiting to be invited inside, you can come right on in and check. There are no girls here. I haven't been able to get it up for twenty years." Hans smiled wryly. "Maybe you've seen her here before? Maybe yesterday or before that? A girl with a birthmark."

"Like Marilyn Monroe?"

"Better. Maybe she was going up the stairs to the floor above, or you saw her going into the neighboring building? A girl carrying a guitar."

"So wait, does she have a guitar or a birthmark?... And who are you to her?"

"We work together. She's a speech therapist. And today, she was supposed to give a lecture at NYU instead of me."

"NYU. Is that part of the NYPD?" The man seemed worried.

"Yeah, yeah. We give lectures to arrestees on how to choose a lawyer. That's right."

"Listen here, son, don't joke around with that shit. I was locked up for eight years. And ain't no lawyers work around here. Or nowhere. They just shake you down for your money like you were an old empty piggy bank. They say they'll get you off all of it; you just pay 'em and plead. Pay and cry, as they say. Plead and weep as best you can," the storyteller's eyes rounded with hostile living memories, and he continued. "Lawyers are priests, holy fathers… Don't believe anyone but yourself. Those dirtbags sit in their offices like powdered porcelain dolls, so you start to think this world is for you. Have you been to the theater, son? I acted in the prison theater, so I understand that everything around you is just a big, lying, shitty story… I love the theater, son."

Suddenly he powerfully slammed the dry and heavy wooden door right in Hans' face. "But… maybe you…" Hans couldn't figure out what to ask or how to insist on asking a question in front of a closed door.

He comprehended that clearly, something had gone wrong last night or this morning. Maybe someone had redrawn the map of Manhattan? Maybe this was some other city or a dishonest taxi driver? Or someone switched the street signs? How would Yuma get to the airport without him? She has heavy suitcases, musical instruments, and there's no one to carry them for her. No one to expand her mood, ready to be improved after yesterday's meeting with him.

Hans rang the bell to 2C again. Maybe that was a mistake, and he should have tried his luck on another floor. One way or another, the door flew open almost immediately, as if the apartment's resident knew that Hans was going to do that in the future and was just waiting for the bell to make his countermove.

"You see this fork, son? Eight years ago, I plunged it into my neighbor's eye. He was a musician and would never shut up with that guitar of his. Diplomacy… international relations… the European Union is gonna hit bottom soon. You know, you shouldn't joke around with that shit. I hate musicians because they're useless eaters. They always sit on the stoop and strum their instruments, hoping for something."

Again, he closed the door with twice as much force, making Hans understand that he might do something worse next time. Hans was a bit lost, but his instinct forced him to think. What could have happened? Maybe he really did screw up the address? Maybe she lives on the same street in Brooklyn. But the lights came on right before they got near the house. And what about Duke Ellington? There's no second Duke Ellington in Brooklyn, is there? And maybe this dude—a boarder too—kicked her out or scared her away? Or is he holding her hostage? Anything could have happened. Hans was not a coward. The Wall had taught him a lot in just one moment.

Hans walked back along his morning path in thought. The previously napping mathematician chess player appeared in him and again began calculating odds. Harlem had already woken up from a disquietingly short sleep. The tired lemons of faces, squeezed during the night, streamed through the streets towards the subway station on Lexington Avenue to get to their place of employment through a dirty tunnel on a piece of groaning metal. The stores along the street had already opened, offering consumption of their wide assortment of mass-produced goods. Sunglasses and umbrellas, plastic cups and stuffed bunnies, lipstick for a dollar that melts before you can get it to your lips, trash bags, sweats, sneakers, toilet bowl cleaner, and slippers that you just could not pass by without buying. The Klondike of cheap valuables penetrated the street like a leprosy sore carefully spread along the buildings. The vendors with stands full of cheap jewelry extending past the horizon looked like crocodiles on the Nile, patiently awaiting their not-very-juicy victims. Still, walking two blocks in an offshore economic zone, Wall Street for those gone with the wind, the street moaning from the rancid smell of decaying one-dollar bills, Hans decided to go back.

Trying his bad luck once again, Hans rang 2C a third time. He no longer doubted his choice because it was clear that this apartment held the secret. And in this strange man who, possessing a sort of kindness, was definitely hiding something.

In a minute, the door opened again, and the first thing that peeked out from behind was a double-barrel shotgun.

"Private property in the United States is protected by the Constitution, and citizen's own home is inviolable!" declared the guy already familiar to Hans, ceremoniously and somewhat agitatedly. "Everyone in the United States has the right to self-defense. I'm counting to two. No, to one. If you don't get out of here, your brains will go flying in different directions all over the sidewalk, like ketchup on a sandwich from that shitty stand over there. Got it?! I don't even care that you apparently don't have those brains at all since you decided to show up here again."

And with those words, he cocked both hammers with the oft-repeated movement of a veteran's right hand, and Hans understood that this was no joke. Hans moved back down onto the sidewalk, not taking his eyes off the two barrels and not saying a word, crab-scooted to the other side of the street. Then, after slowly turning around, he immediately left.

After having gone a block towards the subway, he took out his smartphone, which might be a little more reliable than a doubting human. He listened to the long ring tones. Maybe Yuma was still sleeping or didn't hear the phone? "She could have gone to the airport earlier," thought Hans. But what had most likely happened was some kind of mistake with the address, and yesterday they had been at a different building, a different address. Hans carefully examined the houses, trying to understand which street it was they had turned onto and made an effort to try to remember what the building looked like. But the darkness that dominated the previous night for most of their time together had completely washed away his memories. Hans went down to the subway at 116th St. and took the 6 to Spring Street.

It was Monday, and the sun began delivering summer to the streets from the earliest hours of the morning, like pizza. Air conditioners again began wasting electricity, trying to work more zealously in order to cool the streets, the trees, and the birds, who might also be missing winter, snow, and paths crackling from the ice. The people, saturated with illusions, were heading downtown to conquer New York and dream of the good life that would certainly soon be laid out before them. They'd just have to work for about thirty or forty years. They might even die just to make sure.

Hans had not yet started to worry enough to start questioning yesterday's feelings. There was only concentration and an understanding that something unexpected or unfortunate had happened to Yuma. The desire to help her get to the airport and carry her things—to say a few important words to her in preparation for their temporary farewell—got even stronger. Today his words had crystallized and become even more precise. He understood that he had not just been drunk on the mistake of a fleeting attraction. He regretted that he had not said more to her.

All these thoughts were a bit strange: the contrast between the sunlight and the memories of the night made it clear to Hans that what had occurred had not been one hundred percent the truth as if reality was able to be somewhat peeled away.

Hans opened the door to his apartment with the key. The apartment was unusually empty, or so it seemed to him. Too much had changed in his mood. He obviously didn't want to return to living inside his old life, which now seemed to him too constraining. He stepped into the hallway, closed the door, and pulled the drapes so that the sunlight wouldn't hit the couch. Hans felt a slight tiredness, as he really hadn't slept all night. Instead, he had lain on the couch in a half-sleep, looking out the window, listening to the sound of the rain, and warming himself with his new, unexplored life.

Again, however, he called Yuma. It still was not too late to return and take her to the airport. He left a voice message saying that he wanted to come to her and that he loved her. But he didn't want to admit that he had possibly forgotten the address because of the dark and that he had rung the bell to the closed door. That the person who had come to the street to answer had pointed a shotgun at him.

Hans sat down in front of the computer, deciding to write to Yuma on Facebook. His account currently had only seventeen friends, two of whom he knew outside of the internet. One was redheaded Ronald, and the second was tall, skinny Otto. They had met on Hans' first day in the States when Hans had come with his father to live temporarily in the small town of Flagler Beach. Otto rented them a small apartment and carried the father and son's luggage up to the third floor, helping them settle in. They quickly found common ground, especially since Otto spoke German.

Hans logged onto his Facebook page. He went to write Yuma, but going to the "friends" section, he found that her name was not there. "She might have deleted me by accident," he thought. That number, seventeen—magic in many ways—kept nagging him. He clearly remembered how they had become Facebook friends the first evening he had spoken with Yuma. She had spilled wine on him and herself had asked to become Facebook friends.

He searched for her name on Facebook. There was no Yuma Matoya to be found. Then he tried to find Yuma's jazz quintet on the internet and the Blue Note website. He didn't want to investigate too deeply, afraid that he might discover that a completely different group was playing there the day before yesterday. He reluctantly began asking himself questions about Yuma's disappearance. When he searched the club's list of previous events, he saw that SERENITY OF ILLUSIONS, The Mirror Band, and JoinUs Blues had played on Saturday night. Again, Hans fatefully looked at the business card, somewhat ashamed that he was comparing the present to a past that seemed to clash with it.

The name of the band and her name were written in large black font on the orange background of the card with rounded edges: Yuma Matoya, "Dnab Rorrim Eht," Tokyo. "That's a coincidence," thought Hans, who for many years had worn an orange jacket. "She likes orange."

Of course, Hans could ask around the office about the photoshoot in the club and get the contact information for the band's manager or Yuma herself. But what would that actually give him?

More telephone numbers that wouldn't be answered? He didn't want to turn the bud of feelings into rational action that might possibly be used against him.

He couldn't find any such group on the internet. The search engine told Hans that there were "no results found." Absolutely nothing. Which was very strange and only served to make him wary without even having time to get upset. Hans decided to check just her last name, possibly increasing the chances of finding something—at least to start with. He typed out "Matoya" and immediately saw: Ise-Shima, Matoya Bay, Japan. Hans was filled with hope. This was clearly something to work with, evidence that Yuma might live there, or have a similar last name, or be in some other way connected to the place. Hans understood that there was logic in this and began checking all the links that the search engine had come up with below the map of Japan. But there was nothing else said of Matoya, as if it was a city of the deaf, a city of the dead, forsaken somewhere on the coast of an enchanted country.

Hans decided to call Blue Note. The ringing and the static on the telephone line gave him hope of an easy resolution. The telephone looked like a big yellow elephant jumping on Hans' chest and tickling him with its trunk receiver. But no one answered on the other end. The drapes whispered a gentle quatrain to Hans, shielding his already closed eyes from the sun. Hans then decided to go to the club and speak to the managers. Blue Note was not far away at all, and Hans thought that, despite the fact that it was morning, he might find someone there and ask them more about the musicians who had played that night. Throwing on his orange blazer, he set out directly for West Third Street.

The club was still closed. The continuing morning opened like a flower of the sun. And Hans was knocking on his second door of the day. After he had turned around, finally deciding to leave, he heard a squeak behind his back. The metal door opened, and a sleepy bearded fellow with his hair in a braid asked what he wanted. Hans showed him Yuma's card and asked if this band had played there two nights ago. The guy squinted and turned the card over in his hands as if he were adjusting his eyes to read what was written there, what language it was in. Finally, he confidently and tersely stated that no such person or band had played there.

"Then where did I get this card from?"

"I don't know. Maybe it was a different club?" The tired guy started playing offense.

Hans worried that the fellow's doubts might have some merit, that not only could he not prove that everything had started here, but that he couldn't be sure himself what had really happened yesterday. What part of what he remembered was true, and what part was made up, created by Hans' imagination?

"I'm sure, absolutely sure, that she performed with a jazz band here the day before yesterday," Hans insisted.

"Well, if you're sure, then there are no more questions, right? Did you come to confirm what you were doubting, or did you want to unconvince yourself of something that was one hundred percent real?"

Hans respected this guy. His question contained a hundred percent of what was torturing Hans at the moment.

"Yes, yes. You're absolutely right. If I had no doubts, I wouldn't be asking such a strange question. Maybe I wouldn't even have asked it at all if I was sure that she had given a concert here." "Then you've answered your own question." "I guess I have. Thanks for the explanation." "Good luck, man." The door started to close.

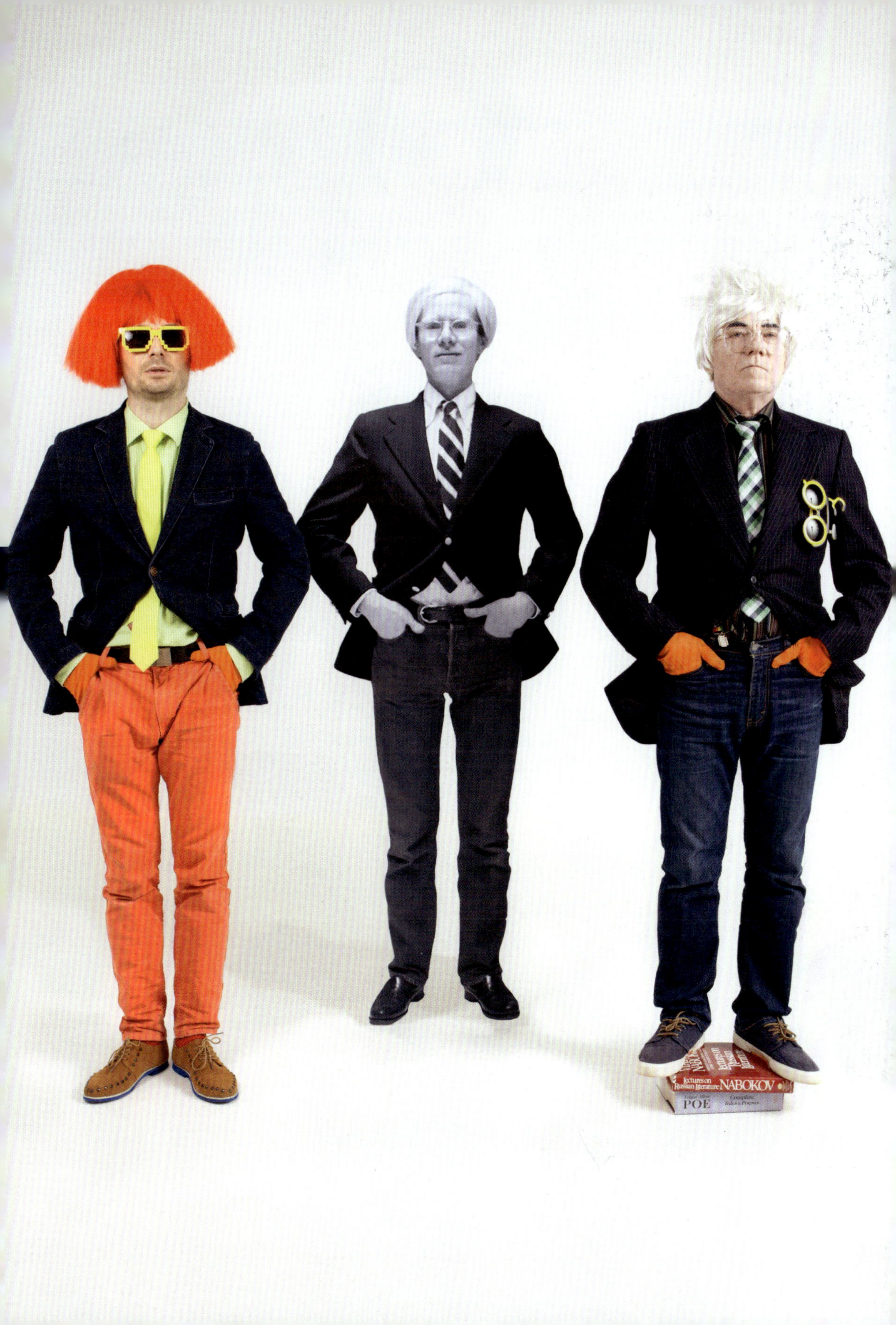
Lectures on Russian Literature NABOKOV
POE
Complete Tales & Poems

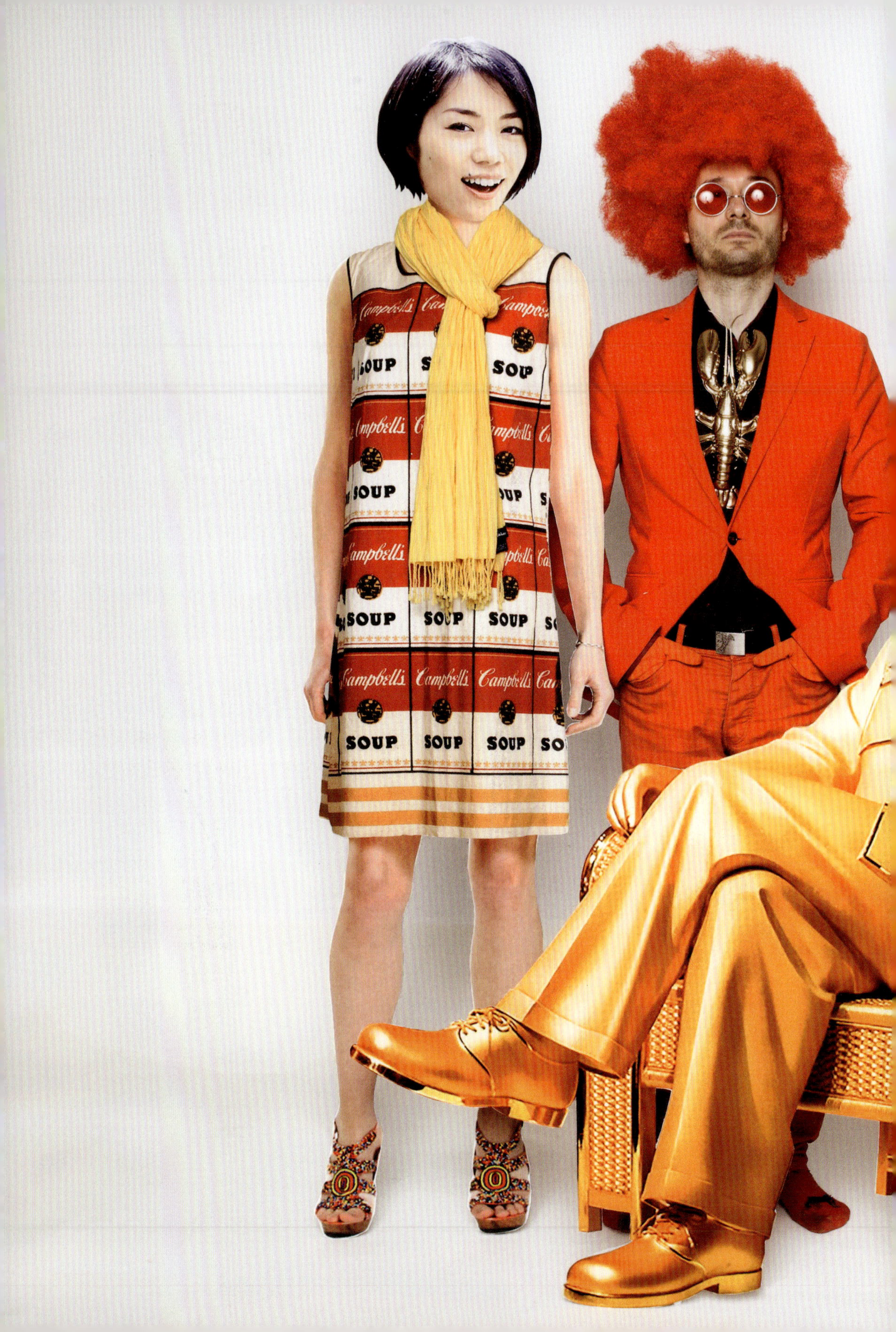
Campbell's
SOUP

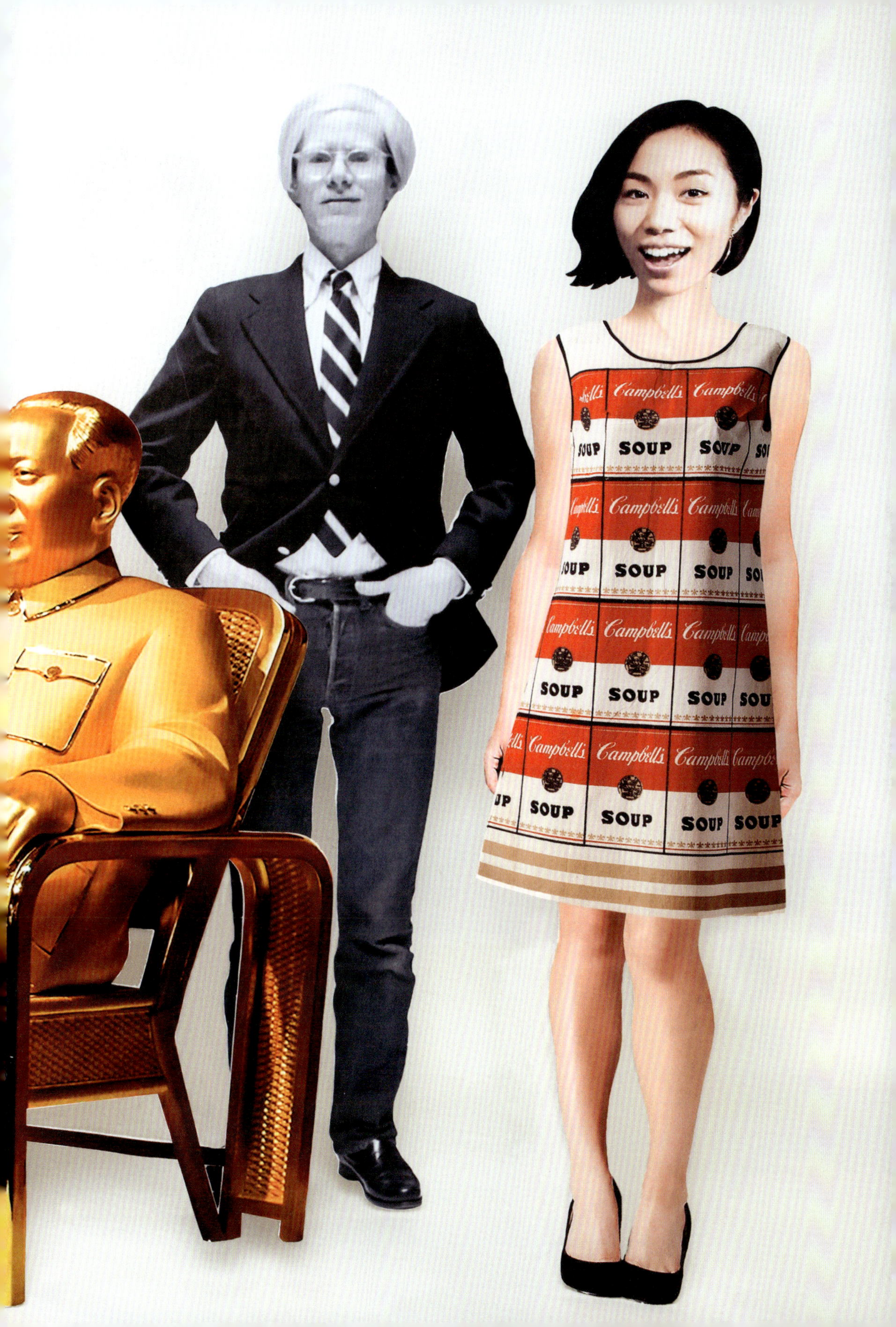
Campbell's
SOUP

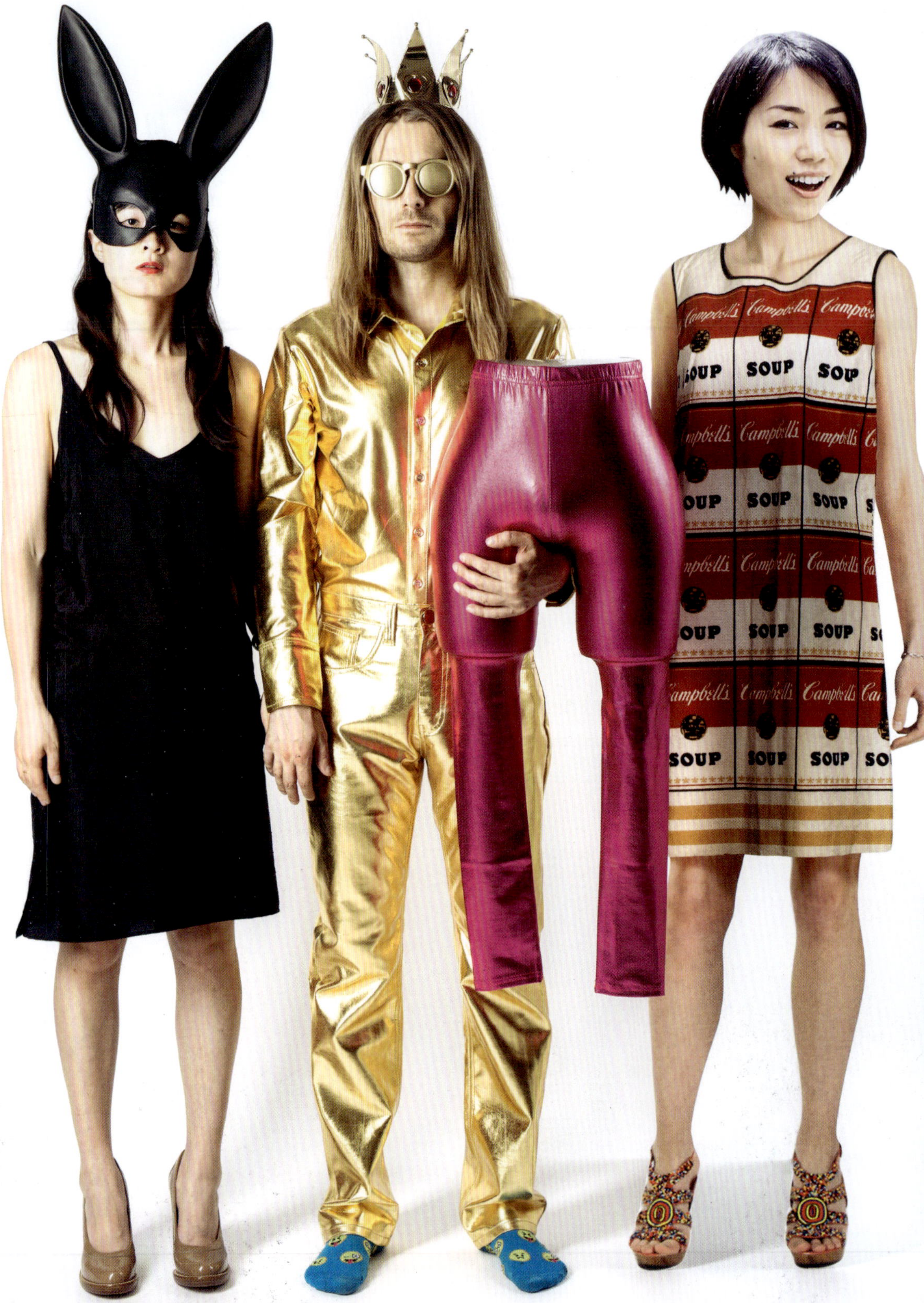
Campbell's
SOUP

CHAPTER 20

The lab where Hans left his film yesterday was not far away, on the West Side, a few blocks from the Blue Note. Hans made it there in ten minutes and reached out to give the bland, melancholic girl the receipt from his order. Slowly she looked at the receipt as if they were on a deserted island and there was no hurry to do anything at all and began digging in the metal drawers that held the film. Some time passed, and then she took the receipt and went to the next room. Through the slightly open door, you could hear how she was conversing in a much more lively way with a man in a smock. After even some more time, she came back and tried to explain something to him. She was blushing. But Hans, as if he knew that it would end up this way, also knew that he didn't have to listen to her.

Workers were driving a steel pile into the asphalt and woke Hans up with their loud activity while leading a healthy construction lifestyle. Hans awoke in the apartment on his couch. He was scared. He didn't understand whether what had happened was real or a dream. More than anything, Hans was upset that a whole series of events had unfolded that ran completely counter to logic. The son of an engineer, he did not believe in unusual manifestations of the law of probability. Heads coming up on a tossed coin one hundred times in a row was not something for his imagination, which was trained on the strict trigonometry of school competitions.

Now fully awake, Hans wanted to check for himself. He called the club to ask the same question that had come to him in the dream. Or was it in a dream? But no one was answering. Again no one was answering? Or was this the first time no one was answering? He tried to remember details of the dream-reality to compare them to what was going on now.

Then he looked out the window. The workers were making a mess on the sidewalk, covered by a layer of dirt and dust. Let's assume that he had gone out today. In that case, he would likely have closed the window, in the other room, across from the fire escape before leaving. All of a sudden, Hans was frightened. It was almost an attack of panic and terror as if, right at this exact moment, something horrible was going to happen. The window was closed.

Hans also checked his boots. They were dirty with construction dust, which most likely meant that Hans had been out today, because last night all the dirt had been washed away by the rain. And if he hadn't left the house, his boots would be clean because they were wet from the night before. The workers had only begun making their mess on the sidewalk in the morning. Hans looked out the window again. Dust, sand.

"OK," he thought, "if this was all not real, then where did these detailed memories of yesterday's events, and even those of the night before, come from? Could I have really thought that all up, or have slept for two days?" Hans asked himself with dread. "But what if I could have?"

What if he was ill, and these details were the result of his imagination playing games with him? At one point, Hans distinctly felt that it had to have been several dreams, several nights spent in a script written by someone else. And this morning's dream was the final touch, the capstone on the pyramid, which had densely intertwined with Hans' foundations and memories.

He was becoming quite disturbed because he understood that as he remembered even smaller details, he began to doubt even more the reality of what had occurred. And this kept going. Every detail would pull from memory something new, and one couldn't say what was real and what was brought on by his inflamed imagination.

If the events of that mysterious night were becoming clearer and clearer in memory, then myth and illusion had to be occluding the true picture, covering over it in layers. These disturbances fully united fiction and reality. His memory leaned towards the comfortable and beautiful, denying the real and uninteresting. The details of this myth would become the rightful owners of the "real memories." "There is no separation between imagination and reality. We exist in the place where we wish to," thought Hans. He knew that in recreating these false details, he was stepping into dangerous territory.

There was once a time when Hans was interested in philosophy as an attempt to overcome what had happened to him. Philosophy did not help. Hans knew how dangerous it was to live in the trappings of fantasy and never really came close to doing so. Photography was indeed a safe activity. It operated with the variables of the real world, not pushing one too far into fantasy, drawing permanent inspiration from a materialistic ab extra, which took Hans back to the smooth surface of predictable regularity. Having been born with a barrier to perceiving emotions directly, Hans understood that philosophical discourse would only further remove him from life and increase his suffering. And he did not want to humor this weakness, trying instead to grow out of it, be liked by people, live, be happy, do some crazy things, get angry, love, and burn out.

Hans realized that he could check some other facts from the last two days, which might calm him down, even if it would not give him a definitive answer. He remembered that it was a habit of his to save receipts, and so he should have the one from the café where he sat with Yuma yesterday.

He got his wallet out and began examining it carefully, pulling everything out. No receipt. Hans was annoyed with this result. Even angry. Reality was coming after him even more forcefully now. And he almost did not doubt that he had imagined these events due to heightened feelings, life in New York, and the heat, which had so deftly cut out this pattern in his head. The only thing left to prove was that this blurring of reason could really have happened to Hans, who had never before lost control of himself.

Hans also happened to notice that there were no credit cards in his wallet. He jumped up onto his feet and rushed out into the hallway where his orange jacket was hanging. He felt around in the inner pocket and nervously jammed his whole hand in. The pocket was empty. Then he remembered that sometimes when he's not paying attention, he puts things into the outer pockets of the jackets. He checked them too with no success, and he was angry with himself. Such a bumbler, losing his cool, his confidence, his reason—everything that was called normal!

But then, to Hans' surprise, he did feel something in one of the pockets. Pulling out the contents, he saw his credit card with a paper receipt wrapped around it and an orange business card. He looked at the receipt and saw the name of the plum wine that they drank yesterday.

Yes, if Hans was unsure, a person detached from reality and experiencing some kind of madness, that abnormality certainly wasn't enough to print out a receipt and put it in his jacket pocket.

CHAPTER 21

Hans' father was a radio engineer of the classic school of scientific romanticism, and Hans grew up on vacuum tubes and soldering irons, rosin and heterodyne. He began learning all about this at ten years of age when he started attending an afterschool program for kids interested in radio. At that age, he made his first shortwave receiver. Gradually, the homemade article began whispering evil programs to him from faraway countries, talking about a better life. By twelve, Hans' father had stopped believing in the eyebrows of the General Secretary, dreaming instead of the Florida seacoast, New York's Central Park, and Duke Ellington records.

With each year that passed, Hans' father felt even more acutely the magical freedom that was so close. One just had to cross over that accursed partition. The idea matured in him slowly, like an expensive wine. Hans' father dreamed of going to a Duke Ellington concert, hearing Niagara Falls, and seeing the sequoias in California.

He would think of any pretext to cool his feelings towards his familiar home and the enclosed life of his native city. Although he did understand that every family was fundamentally equally happy no matter what part of the world they lived in and that it didn't make much difference on which meridian you were while dreaming about the other side of the globe.

Listening to the short waves, exchanging postcards with people from around the world, and corresponding with radio enthusiasts with dots and dashes, Hans' father fell into a romantic reverie of an alien life. Like a schoolgirl collecting stickers, he didn't need real life as much as cultivation of the abstraction of his innocent dreams.

After work, Hans' father continued to work. He couldn't let go of the idea that life, as it was retreating, was occurring somewhere else. Radio waves for him possessed magic—they themselves were invisible, and through some miracle, still connected people that were far away from each other. Working as a structural engineer, he didn't believe in either the strength of science or the activity of radio waves. He didn't know how to explain their magic. Maxwell's equations seemed to him demons concocted by Maxwell to fool the twentieth century. Hans' father tended to look for the explanation of all radio-technical engineering successes in lyricism, so foreign to science. He just didn't have the courage to forgo the symmetry of the engineer and submerge himself in the poetic world of the knight. Nonetheless, there were faraway continents. And radio receivers and the large shortwave antenna on the roof. There were also postcards as confirmation of the existence of another, faraway life, in which Hans' father believed more.

He didn't understand why he could only buy postcards in the store that had pictures of communist leaders, while those that arrived from Australia, Japan, or America were colorful enchanted lands that kept you from sleeping at night. The life force behind the iron door had been sharpening Hans' father for decades, while the workers at the factory sharpened parts for cold-winged airplanes that restrained peaceful people. Day after day, Hans' father tuned his ears in time with the dream that had been born in them. To cross the line, go to a magical country, where paradise and flowers bloomed for all the residents of the peaceful world. On the shortwaves, he heard not only other radio enthusiasts but also radio professionals, whose radio programs enthralled him and filled him with a reason to exist. He didn't sleep enough at night and came to work drunk from his dream as if he hadn't wanted to wake up. Because all night the radio was hissing voraciously and whistling a gentle melody into his ear.

The austerity of the design office and the military theme of the things Hans' father worked on only heightened his disbelief in the electromagnetic world that he created. The only other thing that he wanted was for the internal variables to match as well, for Hans and Hans' mother to stand with him on this. And for him to agree with himself fully one day in the future.

Hans' father met Hans' mother in the cafeteria of the design office on his first day of work. She was in a long black dress, with her long black hair down. She designed amplifiers for the longwave range of transmitting and receiving devices. Hans' father developed phased array antennas for helicopters in the neighboring department. The romance of their meeting was heightened by the atmosphere of secrecy surrounding everything related to antennas. To even get inside the design office, you had to undergo a five-minute search, every day, of your clothing and other items.

Engineering taught the family patience. East Germany was barely able to handle all its problems in comparison to its lazy-joyous sister West Germany. People lived on their service, giving themselves over to the idea that any minute now the party would be victorious throughout the world, and then they wouldn't have to worry about inventing little planes or big antennas to make war with the enemy because there would be no enemy to make war with. Despite the directness of radio and electronic science, Hans' father was raised in the spirit of the sixties on the sounds of Miles Davis and Coltrane. The melodies of simple guys with electric guitars were also often heard in their house. Catcher in the Rye, Orwell, Hemmingway, and Nabokov. This had all been accepted in Hans' family since before his birth. This had all been retyped on typewriters and crawled at night from kitchen to kitchen. This had all been transmitted through the ether, even to grown-up Hans, although communism demanded concentration on the common cause and prohibited the reading of unnecessary books. But you could listen to Shostakovich. His mother really loved Shostakovich. Despite the waves of disappointment from the enchantments and new beliefs brought by the shortwaves, music was constantly playing throughout the years around Hans and his parents. The shortwaves, reflected from the stratosphere, sent the hooliganism of fresh jazz and the raw sadness of blues across the ocean.

Hans' mother felt the emotions felt by Hans' father, and as the one softer in nature, she harkened to him, wanting to catch the resonance and desire to the same thing her husband did.

Some women are particularly able to live for another. They will go to the ends of the Earth for any criminal, delinquent, troublemaker, or trailblazer. They will support the craziest, boldest, or most revolutionary idea. Hans' father had become a Decembrist, whose mood poured through the rooms. Less and less life and more and more plans moved into the apartment with the dust and radio parts.

Although Hans' mother had her own inner *amour propre*, she did not express it ideologically: that was his father's responsibility. But she could step on the rake with respect to those things that worked against the self-esteem and forehead of Hans' father. As a boy, Hans did not fully comprehend the nature of their quarrel. He saw that his mother had a huge influence on his father. That his father loved her and, therefore, was ready to surrender in any dispute, even if it was a painful one. The child would be the first to feel falseness and strain in a family. But Hans was not uneasy.

Every once in a while, Hans' mother would take an opportunity to establish herself or reassure herself of the strength of the feelings of this man whom she was ready to follow her whole life. Their disputes were like the disputes of people bound together with a rubber band: the further they ran away from each other, the stronger they were later pulled together, the stronger their reconciliation.

CHAPTER 22

A week had passed. The hands and the springs of a million clocks had turned around their axes, inconspicuously aging all living things. Yuma had not turned up anywhere and had not responded to any of Hans' attempts to contact her. By mid-July, autumn had begun creeping towards the clock dial of New York. No one noticed the changes. Skillfully and cruelly, with subtle ploys, fall crept closer and closer. Here it burned the grass, and there it left some flower stems barren, taking the juice for itself, leaving dried out skeletons of grass that were disinterestedly prepared to be buried in the icy belly of winter. Despite the holiday that it was for most people in Central Park, ready for a party and not noticing the seconds being stolen away, there were a few kids standing near the trees and gathering yellow leaves with a question in their eyes.

Hans felt much better. Maybe he just loved this foreshadowing of autumn. Moreover, the incident with the film had been resolved. They just called one day from the lab and said they had found it. The explanation was pretty simple: the lab had not been properly managed, but now that situation was under control. And, of course, he would not have to pay for anything. That was a relief. The turmoil he had experienced on that unfortunate morning was worth that fifty dollars, or thereabouts, that the photo lab declined to accept for their services. Hans took the negatives to the table with the special magnifying glass. On the film, he could clearly see scarlet patches. That was what Yuma's blue dress looked like, reversed by the camera's eye.

From that day on, Hans felt different. It might seem that he believed, to some extent, in the deception and had made his peace with it. Disappointment was able to comfort him.

However, on the other hand, Hans felt more confident in himself. He realized that everything depended on him alone and that it was he who had allowed Yuma to leave. When she slipped away from his extended hand, Yuma had utterly neutralized any close feelings, inviting Hans to a completely different type of war on a different scale. Leaving her at that moment, when she more than ever needed his help, was a mistake.

A few days later, Hans printed the pictures from the concert. The scandal with the agency had come to nothing: the customers were quite satisfied with the work. Hans really did not want to get into a mess and start looking for traces of the lost jazz band. He would not reconnect with Yuma by looking for the truth about the name or location of the band but would only increase his own torments. The issue wasn't with the name of the band or with her name, but with her mood, which Hans now knew nothing of. He wanted to, maybe, develop the strength of his feelings so much that he would undertake something much more serious than a simple address search and discussion of their relationship. He knew: the only thing he needed was time. And Yuma would come back to him. One wonderful day she would return herself. And ask for help operating her camera. And then Hans would make no more mistakes.

In his usual pensive mood, which had begun returning to him after the days of the shock, Hans, for his own pleasure and because he wanted Yuma to stay the way she was in his memories from the concert, printed out an enlarged photograph of her. He even cut out pieces of the stage and the other musicians, leaving only her. Then he decided that portraits weren't enough and enlarged the photographs even more. He wondered where the border was between a photograph and a real person. What made an image different from life? Going into this question within himself even deeper, he concluded that reality, in large part, is perceived visually, and the rest has to be filled in through the personal lens of experience, emotions, and expectations. Hans decided that he must construct a visual image, and the soul of the heroine would itself flow into the image.

He understood that he needed to enlarge Yuma to actual size and see what happens. The miracle should itself correct his expectations.

To try it out, he printed Yuma in the canned soup dress. And he also printed out his friend Andy Warhol, whom Yuma seemed so interested in. Hans thought that if Yuma were bored with him somehow, then Andy, the scallywag, would be able to water down any unhealthy company.

Yuma printed out taller than Hans because she was in heels. Warhol, in turn, was taller than Yuma. Hans liked this, and it underscored the idea that these were impressive people, in the literal and necessary sense of the word. All of this served to bring Hans even closer to his characters.

In a few days, Hans felt how much of a huge relief he obtained from the presence of people close to him. He was even shocked that no one had thought to go that route before. In general, people limit themselves to memories, photographs in albums. Someone might take pictures of a wedding on their cell phone. A few centuries ago, they hung paintings on walls. In offices, the employees have small portraits in frames at their desks.

But why did no one simply print out their relatives? Return the wrapping that could be quickly filled up with a spirit that precisely occupies all the internal geometric space in exactly the way we

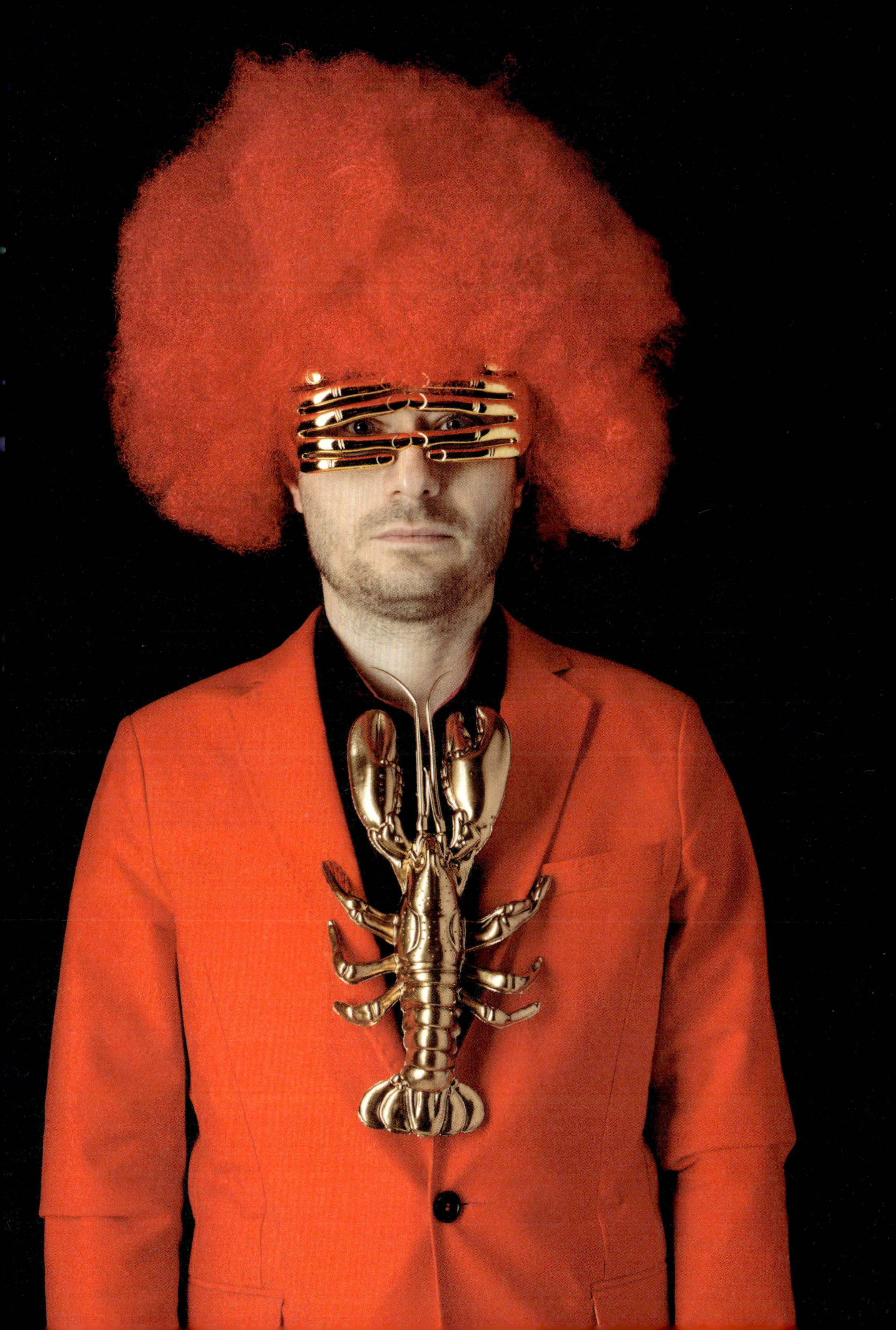

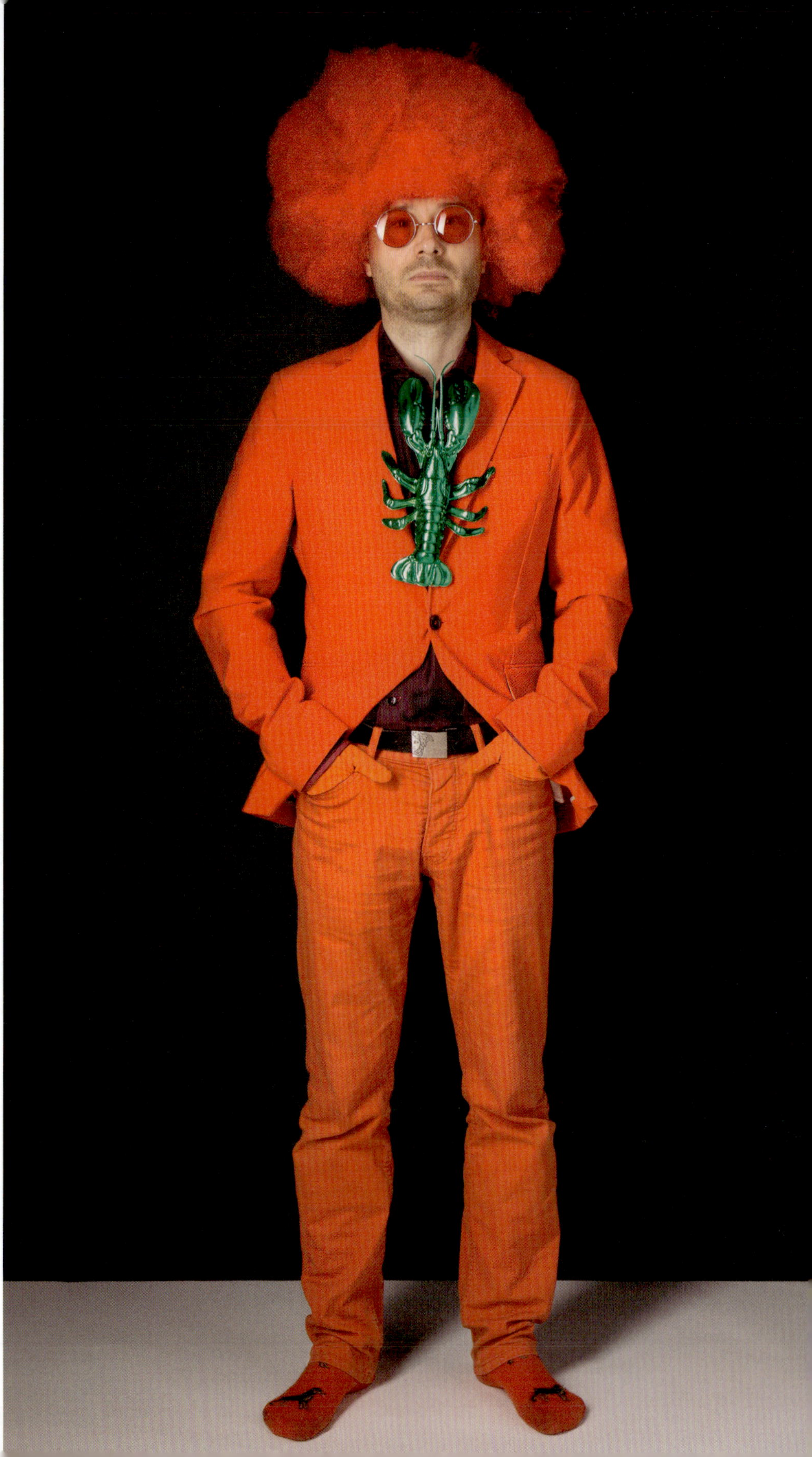

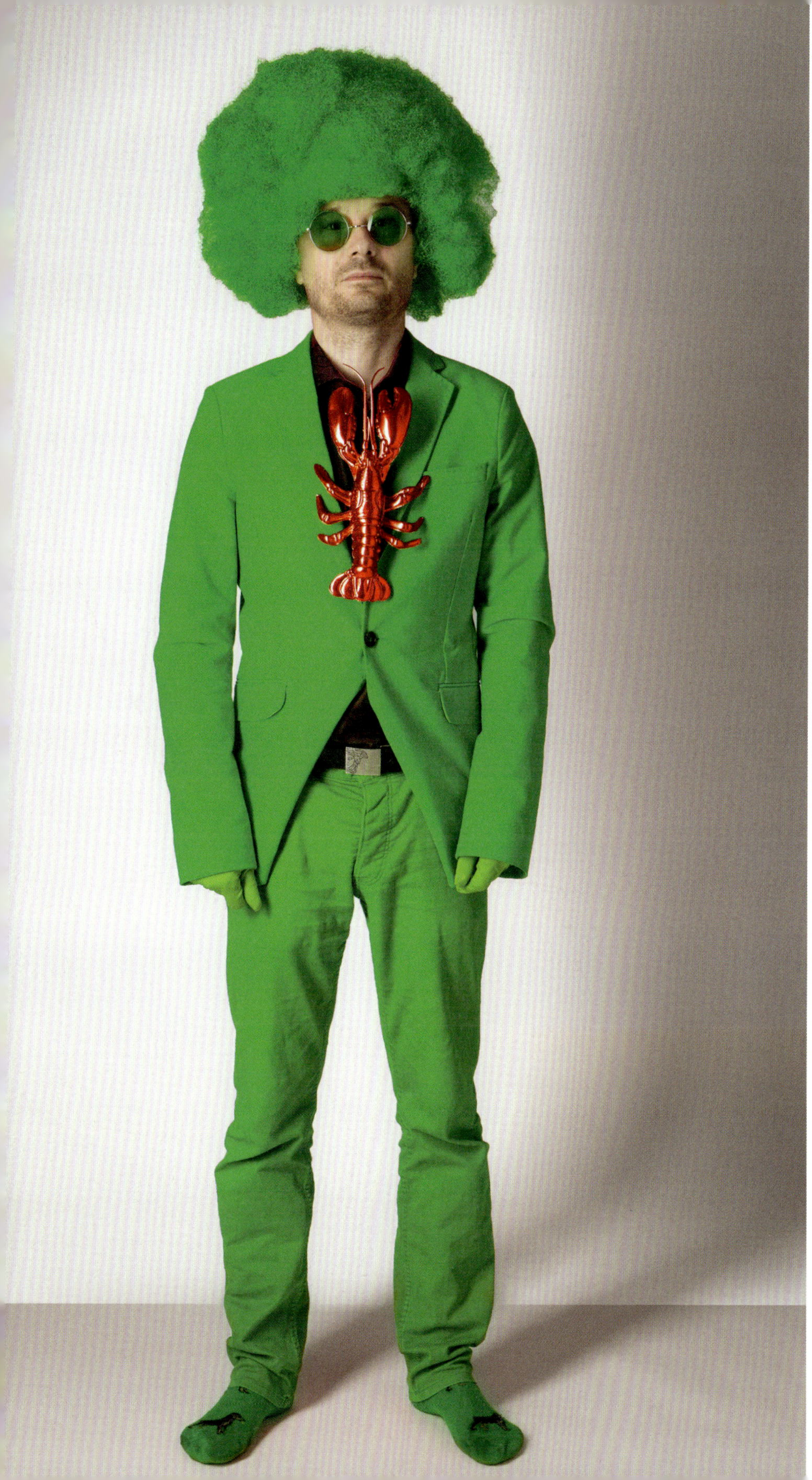

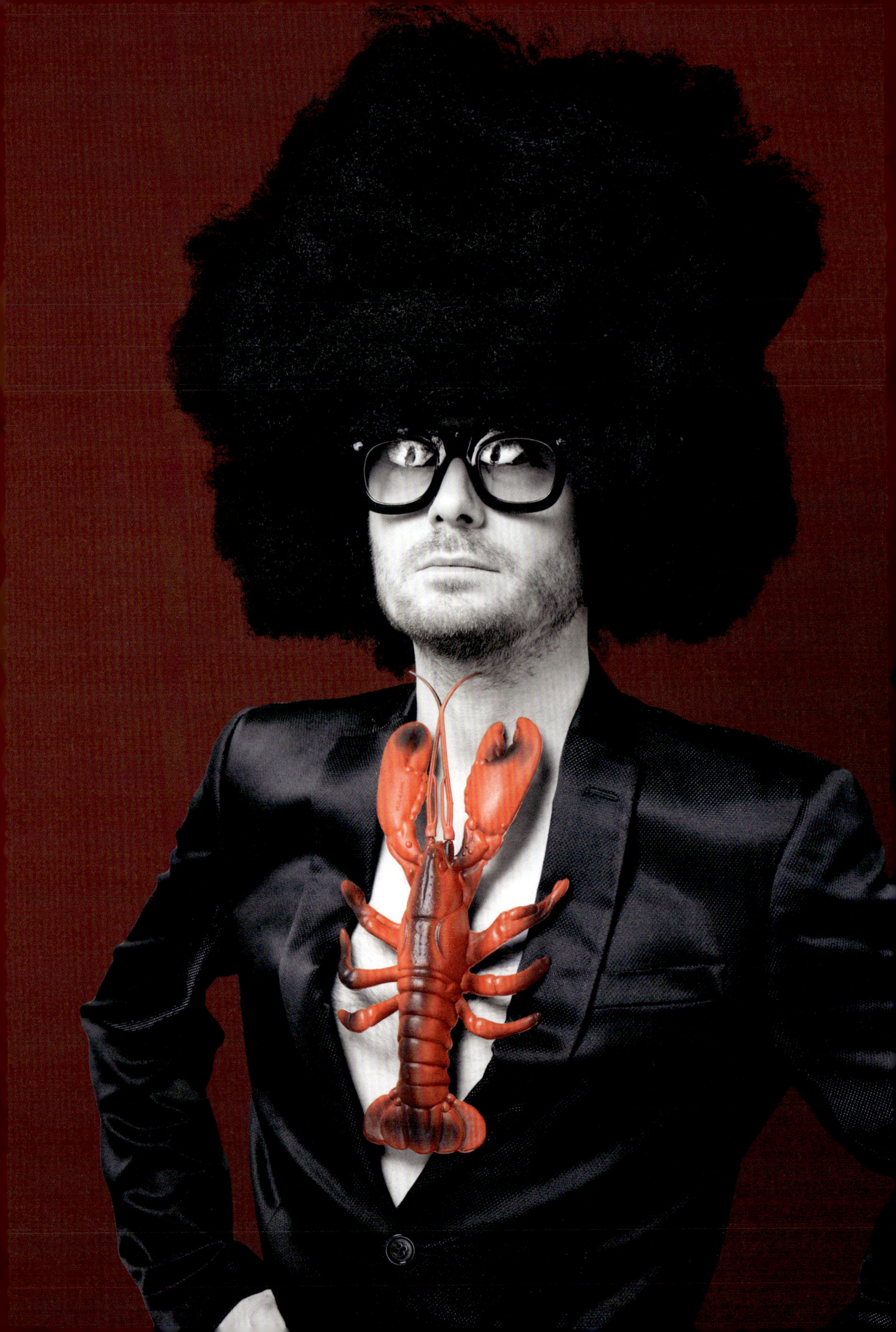

desire? Hans experienced somewhat of a euphoria from the success of his experiment and did not want to hurry with the completion of the idea. He didn't want to make any more characters. It was unclear whether or not there could be two Yumas together or whether bodily reincarnation was possible in one specimen only.

It was July, and the sun burned paths in the grass of Central Park. One day, Hans decided to go to Belvedere Castle, where he and Yuma sat that night, and to take her with him. And then take a ride on a boat on the magical lake that gave off the chill of the underworld. He made coffee on the gas stove in his small apartment on Prince Street and finished off the cup in a state of newfound peace.

Taking his camera and wrapping Yuma in soft paper, Hans put her in a large portfolio for artwork. Yuma was yielding and did not protest. You didn't have to speak to her. And that was a problem because Hans really liked to talk. Instead of everything else.

On the way to Central Park, he started asking questions, and it was as if Yuma was answering. Soon the difference between their situations was less noticeable. It seemed that Yuma was asking questions of Hans and that Hans, on the contrary, lying in the flat portfolio, was answering according to all the rules of etiquette. Hans liked Yuma's curiosity. Himself in possession of extraordinary natural curiosity, he respected a lively mind in others.

When they came to the place of their picnic, to the green clearing, the sun had already hidden behind the trees, and it wasn't so hot. Hans decided to take the first souvenir shot with the tripod and sat down with Yuma in the clearing in a graceful and responsible way.

Hans at first felt awkward when passersby tried to laugh at him. He didn't want to be labeled a loon, but explaining anything to anyone not involved was not in his plans, as per his nature. But gradually, the laughter abated. Instinctively, everyone who walked by compared the situation to their own and understood how lucky this guy was who had created a conversation partner for himself, someone he needed internally. The passersby smiled, respecting Hans, even envying him. Dreaming of joining him, arranging oneself in a position comfortable enough for a daguerreotype, exquisitely posing one's body on the grass. It seemed that everyone needed a cure, medicine for their personal anxieties and a direct means to get closer to their dream. To rudely grab the dream, forgetting about ceremony and the blues.

Hans took a number of photos, chatting with Yuma about the essence of being, hospitality in New York, and the transnational trend in modern music. This sparked a passion in the conversation partners so that the time flew by almost unnoticeably, and the sun's ellipse, under the influence of astronomical acceleration, invisibly declined towards sunset.

After the conversation in the shade of the summer trees, the friends decided to walk further and take a boat ride around the Central Park lake. The sun had already ducked behind the linear spectrum of the Manhattan skyline, but the water was still warm for the metal material the boats were made of, wanting to imbibe the warmth from the people who rode in them. Paying ten dollars for two people, Hans and Yuma stepped onboard their pretty tin boat, which resonantly repeated the notes of their legs as they stepped. This music continued the lyrical feelings of both travelers, Yuma with her shoes picking out a hello telegram to Hans on the bass guitar. The rhythm of the rowing, the motor of the orgiastic oars. Hans set Yuma down close to the bow of the boat so that he could see her and the surrounding landscape. He sat closer to the stern, enjoying the evening, remembering his young friend the way that she is.

Hans had completely ceased feeling that there was a difference between the Yuma that was given him in reality and the Yuma that he made himself from cardboard, photo paper, and glue. Maybe this Yuma, who had undergone a few improvements in her dress, looked even better. But this concerned not only her physical attributes. The emotional connection between Hans and Yuma became more reliable and stable. It was as if they had both gotten calmer and learned to accept their habits and areas of disagreement, no longer bothering or worrying each other with the newness of their acquaintance. Hans had gotten what he wanted—a soul-expensive wife and a submissive friend, burdening him with the ecstasy of care, courtship, and love.

In the boat, they spoke of loneliness in the big city. Yuma insisted that the megalopolis was an illusion of movement and that a person must necessarily become despondent in this big river among the endless streams of information and people. She is taken through disappointment to the banks of loneliness, and she ends up on land in a completely different place in life, surrounded by a foreign landscape, gradually becoming isolated, dodging local society. Hans' rhetoric appealed to pure will, human nature, and the spiritual source, which can all significantly influence circumstances. This means it can also attract people, be the center of life. Not only be necessary to people but need them too, for even greater creative acceleration. Hans asserted that a person doesn't become alienated in the city, but on the contrary, finds and comes together with those like him. When talking to Yuma, Hans believed in people and their victory over routine and boredom. With all his strength, he wanted things to be easy and prove to Yuma that it was possible to soar above everyday life. Hans wanted Yuma to believe in him, an optimist, to be enchanted with the freshness of his viewpoint now aimed at people. And that's what really happened. Yuma respected his point of view, listened to him attentively, and likely was even convinced that Hans was right.

It was getting a bit chilly on the water, and Hans put his yellow scarf and orange hat on Yuma to protect her from drafts. Yuma smiled at Hans. Of course, she couldn't smile at him in earnest. Literally—she couldn't. But Hans, gazing into her face, guessed at the warm, invisible gratefulness emanating from her. Hans knew that the real Yuma was really glad that he was with her as before. No matter what happened, no matter which turns life took with its trivialities, Hans would always warm her.

A sudden strong gust of wind rocked the boat a bit. Yuma wavered a second in the wind, bent over, and jumped into the water. Oh, horror! She slowly started sinking. That was a mistake since Hans had her wearing the new Manolo Blahnik shoes he had bought in Soho. There was no time for thinking. The boat kept moving forward from inertia, and Yuma was drowning six feet behind, sinking to the depths of the muddy waters. Hans jumped in the water with his clothes on, leaving his phone, scarf, and bag in the boat.

Yuma had already completely sunk under the water, but Hans was able to swim very well and dove down. East Berlin. The boiling water of the Spree hisses like a snake. The restless notes of the copper pipes play a funeral dirge underwater. The sounds of sirens went off somewhere. In the water, Hans saw glints of flood lamps and heard the hum of boats approaching and dogs barking on the shore.

Under the water, he grabbed her by the neck and pulled up the girl who had gone out of her senses. Then he headed towards the boat, holding Yuma by the hair. Giving her a chance to catch her breath near the boat, he laboriously helped her get back in. He got in at the stern. A few onlookers or invasive rescuers had already jumped into a motorboat, asking from afar if he needed any help, but Hans made them understand with definitive gestures that everything was OK and that he would handle it himself.

The July trees, no longer powerful enough to hold onto all their fresh leaves, began inconspicuously declining and quietly dropping them on the ground and water. The leaves floated like colorful dead ships on the surface of the sometimes calm and sometimes burbling lake. The wind moaned in an anxious whisper through the green branches, singing a song about the end of summer. Hans used the scarf to wipe Yuma dry and threw his jacket over her shoulders. He asked forgiveness for what had happened, for his carelessness and negligence. He asked forgiveness for that long-ago day.

CHAPTER 25

Hans now came to Central Park every evening. Sometimes even at twilight or completely in the dark. He took Yuma with him and sat her nearby on the bench. He might come with Andy Warhol too and sit him across a table from himself, where he would converse slowly with Hans through the sunset. Warhol often helped Hans write letters to Yuma. Beginning the moment of their separation, Hans had decided to write Yuma a letter every day and send it to Tokyo. To the postal address on the business card.

He usually wrote his daily letter to Yuma at comfortable tables near the Metropolitan Museum. Sometimes Hans stopped closer to the castle. There he felt additionally close to Yuma, the aftersound of her perfume and the afterword of her music. Sometimes he fancied he heard notes in the wind. These copper and bronze notes, like bugs, crawled across all the heavens, drawing erratic paths with their paws and sowing dismay. These notes reminded Hans of a melody of a brass band he had heard in his youth. The wind made the notes sour, and the lower tail of the notes stretched Hans' memory. He wanted to hide from these funereal sounds, wrapped in a blanket of insensitivity.

Hans wrote Yuma about his life in New York, notes on his observations of people, of their moods and conflicts. He wrote about work, about photography, about his dreams. He liked to write letters. Good traditions make existence more even. Every day he waited for the moment he could go to Central Park and get out a clean sheet of paper and a pen. He loved writing by hand. Calligraphy reminded him of ice skating and added a sentiment to the words, decorating them with movement.

Hans decided that he would fight until victory was won, no matter what the cost. He would never throw in the towel, never let doubt enter him. He would write Yuma every day, for as long as necessary, maybe ten years, until one day she answered. Hans was certain—female emotion would value constancy. And he knew that she would answer that loyalty, thanks to which Hans was ready to share himself with her. Someday. Not soon. She might even get married. Have children. Wrinkles might appear on her face from motherhood and the disappointments that would seep through the cracks in her apathetic daily life. Her gait would lose its previous attractiveness to young men, and her eyes, having inspected the lives and sorrows of other people, would begin to give out. Their light would go out, and that sweet chick jumping around the stage would no longer exist.

Hans' affection was stronger than his desire to enjoy the external and take from a woman her beauty. He wanted to breathe life into Yuma, a strength that would give her strength. Her tiredness, sadness, and indifference, the blurred expression on her face, was of no importance to him. He would change her and make her happy. He need only prepare for the long road ahead to not wear himself out before the good times came.

Hans knew that they were somewhere in the middle of life and that each month or year spent in absentia was measured by a large quantity of soul-substance lost. Hans convinced himself to not worry about the time of happiness that they could have organized together dissipating now into the space of the cosmos. That did not even hurt him, almost. He intended to leave for her a slow telegram with his words, that he was in some far-off snowy place, on a different planet, and waiting for her. His messages, sent on a long pilgrimage, said that they could begin everything right now. A warm house, tea on the roof, little arguments, doing laundry in the basement, reading books, photography. And coherent breathing beside one another every night.

Memories of his father holding him by the hand spun around in the fog of Hans' consciousness. They were coming home along a road that ran through a field. It was a snowy winter, which enshrouded nature in one color. There were no skyscrapers and no electric streetlights. Little Hans was freezing while they two were walking down the flat road with the strong wind racing down it. Off the road to the side were some cattails with thick German sausages of fruits bent towards the earth under hurricane winds. The snow fell in a horizontal wall, and it was becoming more and more difficult to walk with every minute. Off the road, a big old rusty excavator bucket was lying on its side, which could shelter more than one person. Hans' father said that they should wait it out in the bucket until the storm ended. He had some matches, and they began burning cattails that they pulled up nearby.

The snow kept coming. It was getting harder and harder to find and bring back the cattails. The thickness of the snow made it hard to walk at all. Fingers weren't functioning. His father brought the last armload and decided they should just stay inside the bucket. Every few minutes, they burned the straw that they had gathered, and it was almost not helping at all. Then the cattails ran out, and the matches were no longer needed. Hans remembered how his father kept rubbing his small child's hands through the mittens and then rubbing his own. Toes were starting to hurt, then feet. But after a while, the pain subsided. The snow kept on coming. Now they couldn't even get out of the bucket. Having protected father and son from the wind, it would now become a heavy sarcophagus taking two bodies into its hungry belly.

"Hans!" repeated a voice. "Hans, open your eyes!... Hans, open your eyes right now!" Before his eyes was a wide, stubbled, fixated face with eyes shining in concealed alarm. A big black beard in which Hans warmed his child's forehead.

The blizzard had quieted by midnight. When headlights of the first bulldozer could be seen on the road, Hans and his father still sat immobile, embracing, as they already had been for a few hours already, watching the road through the dawn. The snow reached more than halfway up the bucket.

Hans' feelings of love towards his father, blinking in the distance with fear, were victorious over the storm. The five-year-old boy did not quite understand who was knocking on the bucket while they were waiting for help.

In his dreams, Hans often saw his huge beard, black and white from the snow. Felt the touch of his warm, big hands, which for some reason always smelled like the earthy sweetness of freshly baked bread, as if his father were well-molded from the soft insides of bread. In his dreams and outside them, Hans had still not yet learned to live without him.

Hans woke up on a bench. A penetrating wind blasted his face. A guy picking up the trash slapped Hans insistently on the shoulder with his rubber-gloved hands, as if Hans were not a living being but a hazardous object. Hans looked around. It was already late evening. The streetlights that uselessly lit the empty roads had come on. Hans was very cold.

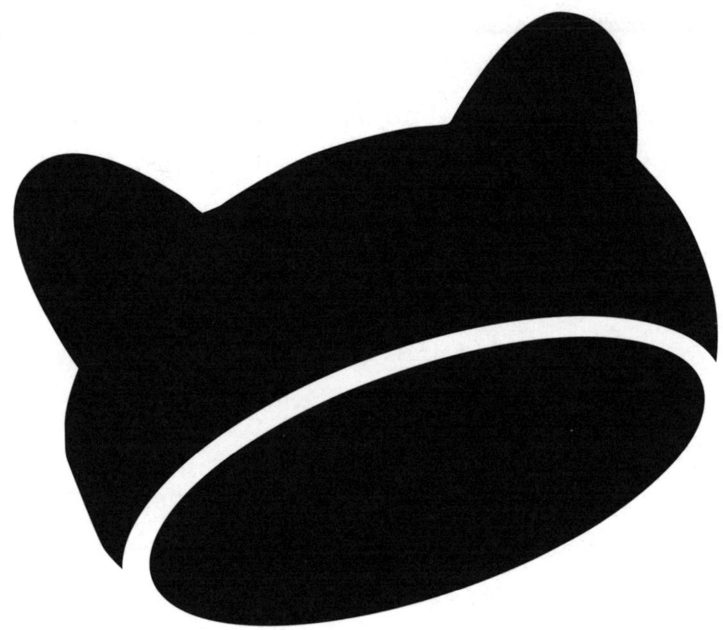

CHAPTER 24

Hans took pictures everywhere he could, together with Andy and Yuma. The locations he chose were cozy spots, picturesque landscapes, noisy squares, and trash heaps. The camera worked loyally for the whole group, peeking from the tripod at the light nonchalance of Hans' sadness.

In doing what he loved most, Hans added a bit of therapy to combat his doubts and wounds that wavered between tectonic plates. He could comfortably position himself in the world of photographic illusion, reflected from the gelatin of the film together with the photons of his worlds. Like writing letters, photography was a musical notation that he wrote to calm himself. By taking photographs and living together with cardboard Yuma, he left messages to the people he used to need. A need to one day be heard. Let the bottle reach the shore once there is no chance of rescue. Let the letters be read when there is not even ash left from Hans, and his spirit is wandering among the farthest stars. And he did everything he could, explaining to life that he had lived honestly.

Three months had already passed when Hans' life after the changes began to change even more. It was October. Hans was still renting that narrow-as-a-snake apartment on Prince Street. The apartment had no amenities and, as such, was perfect for an artist. In his time free from work, Hans continued taking pictures with his friends—his future wife and Andy Warhol. At that point, he had Yuma in all different poses, in indescribably elegant dresses and with different, inimitable smiles. In the rooms, near the walls, on chairs, and even in the bathroom, she took part in all of Hans' creative ideas and thoughts, encouraging him with words, sometimes even mocking or teasing him. They needed each other in this dialog. Hans liked coming home when people were waiting for him. Andy had his own room—more like a closet—where he had chosen a quiet corner to philosophize in. Sometimes Warhol would share his bold ideas with Hans. Hans trusted Warhol because he was older and less inhibited. In addition, Warhol was a deeply successful artist and quite popular too. When they walked down the street, people smiled, recognized Warhol, and asked whether he and Warhol had been together long, where they were going, or how the maestro was feeling in such bleak weather. Hans liked being in the moderate and light shadow of the master.

It was cozy at home. Warhol wasn't jealous and didn't get in the way. He showed brotherly, even fatherly, feelings towards Hans, giving him hints on how to care for Yuma, how to surprise her. For example, Warhol advised him to give her flowers every day, and Hans started with sunflowers. Every day he doubled the quantity, but he couldn't even get the bouquet in the door after a week. Yuma was happy to receive such attention, and their love grew stronger. The feelings between them were mutual and touching, with a hint of that warmth that arises when people have known each other for a long time, have already gotten used to each other, and don't go through those initial painful pretenses that often overshadow the relations of young couples.

Hans would return from work with a slight smile on his face and a desire to tell Yuma and Warhol about his day. In this balance of moods, there was one small drawback, a secret peephole into some-

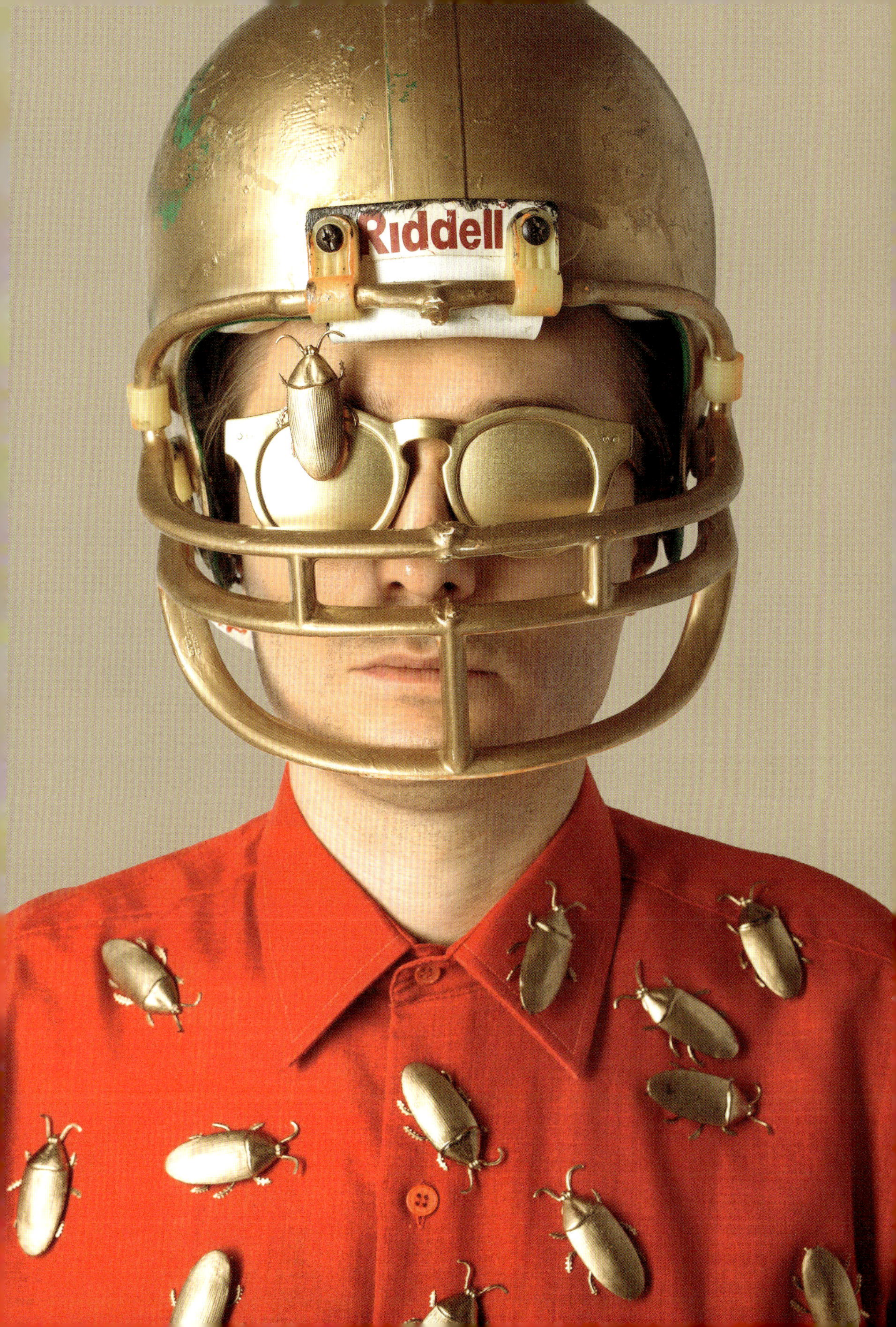
Riddell

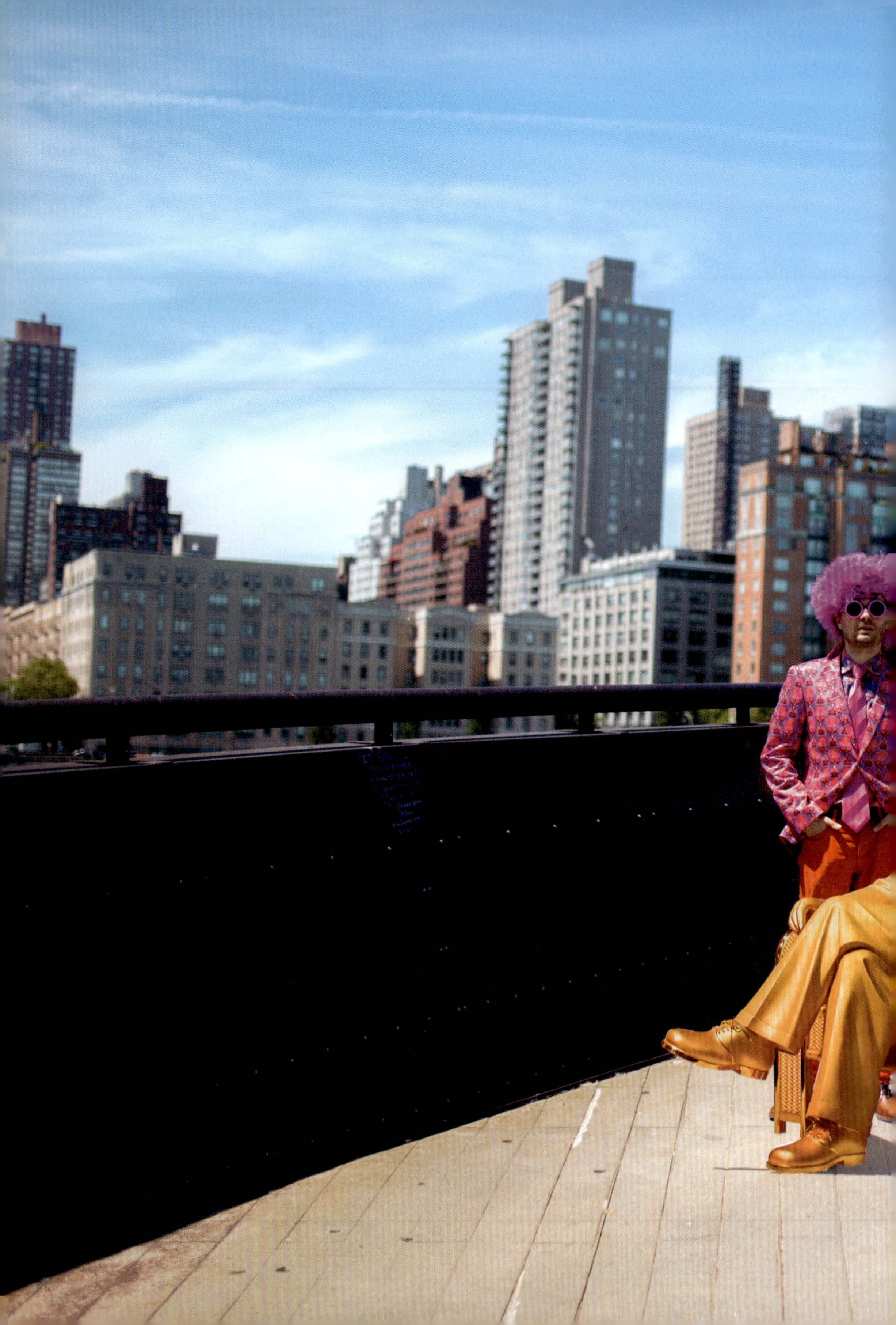

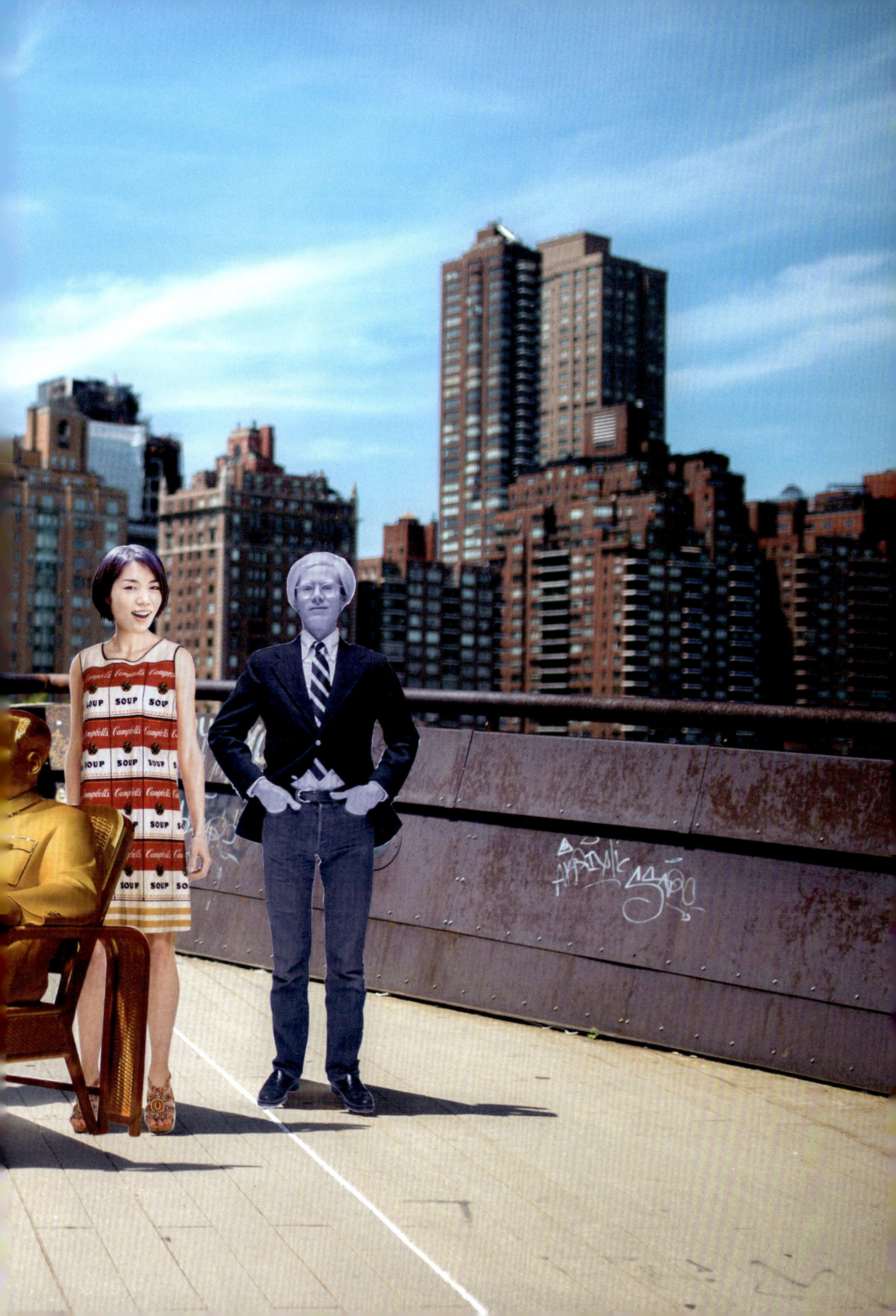
Campbell's
SOUP

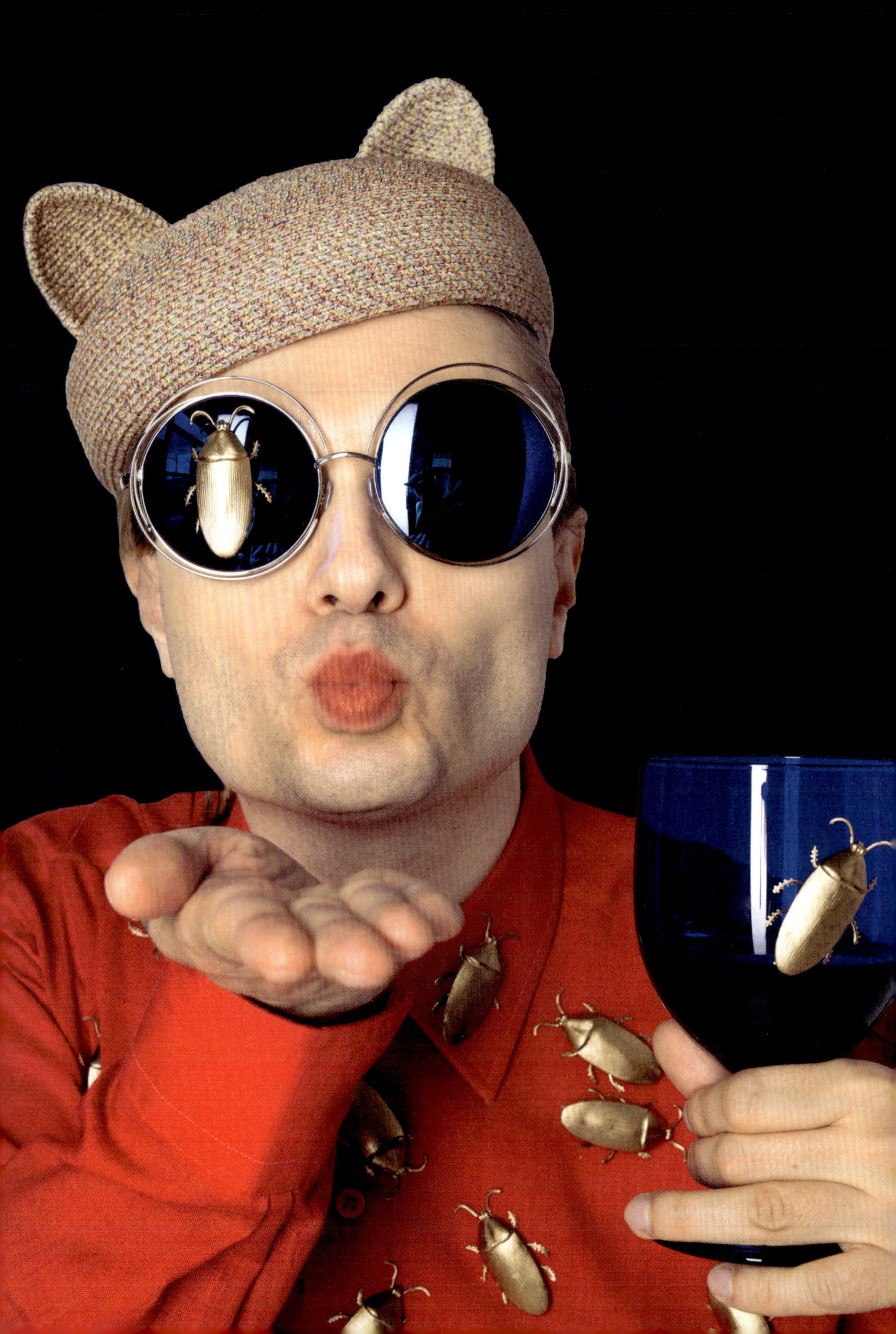

thing else, something Hans didn't want to admit to himself: this entire idyll of his was founded on one small calamity that could not be avoided. This new problem was hidden deep but fully accepted.

Autumn made circles in the cosmos with the sun, turning Earth around its earthly axis like an acrobat. The sunflowers that Hans gave Yuma, which had once cooled in fields, were preparing for the flight of saddened birds; the bugs in their burrows stuffed their pillows with blades of grass to never wake up again. And only Hans disagreed with the nature of the literalness of fear, not wanting to participate in the obviousness of melancholy. Hans preferred to hide in a carnival and supported the vehemence of joy, like the heat from the burning of cheery firewood. Trouble was standing outside the door and patiently stalking him like prey. But Hans didn't give it the slightest chance. He lived with mood swings; with the beautiful power of emotions, he erased his affliction and plugged up any drafts. He had an iron will and wisdom that told him: not a step of doubt here, not even the smallest movement backwards.

Every day, Hans wrote a letter and took it to the post office, dropping the envelope in the mailbox. He heard the letter fall heavily on the pile of other dispatches already in there, and he felt the other letters admiring the calligraphic garland designs in the narratives written to faraway and weightless her. The letters hugged each other inside the mailbox, greeting the new prisoner who now could never get back from whence it came.

When taking new pictures, Hans asked advice of Warhol: what would be more interesting? Which experiments would Warhol himself like to shoot that they had not yet done? The conversation and photography experiments resulted in a river of shots, the best of which Hans printed on photo paper every weekend in the darkroom. Hans worked a lot: even on days when he had photoshoots under his contract, he would come home and find time to take a few shots in the sunset after he wrote the letter. They were interesting to Hans as enclosures with his letters that disclosed his vision, as illustrations of the words.

In the end, by the middle of fall, a lot of material had piled up, and Hans, who was known in many galleries for his commercial work, decided to propose an art project to the curators.

The leaves were turning yellow in the sun to a honey hue of dried-up life. The trees were shedding their colored rags, which had frozen up in pride onto the paths, the streets, and the grass in the forest. And hiding with its gnarled face behind the beauty of the scene, as always, quiet and precise, preparing for the long-awaited, mischievous meeting with its glassy friend winter, was shameless death.

Pay and cry,
as they say.
Plead and weep
as best you can.

CHAPTER 25

Dear Yuma!

Well, I'm sitting down to write again. I got myself into the mood. Found time alone, as one should. The days have run by like a kaleidoscope. The golden wave of autumn is already rolling into winter, and stagnation is on its way. There's no rain. The roads are tensely dry, quiet, and hard. And it still hasn't snowed yet, calming our expectations.

In order to correctly answer the questions that life raises, I am sending letters as if they were etched in metal. They come out with garlands decorated with the trimmings of your dress.

You are so young and real, and I'm so creaky. And because of that, I just can't break apart the words of my shell. We are sitting in a New York closed off from one another, like beef stew in a jewelry box. And one fine morning, you'll say, ok, sure, let's go to Okinawa. But will I be able to get off the ground?

It's November, which I imagine like a red-orange flower, maybe due to the presence of the ghost of winter or the paints on an easel crying from the sentimentality of artists. And you and I hunkered down under the same calendar. Two breaths of smoke. Together we continue farther and shrink together under a blanket from the cold. This is a kind of pre-winter letter. A little celebratory. These days serious people are not acknowledged. That's why I insinuate so much.

And this letter is almost over, having said nothing. I'm obstinate. I can wait as long as I have to, until any final loss to you, until any absurd victory for you. It seems like just yesterday that I saw your knees. They moved towards my hands in the dark. When I write that, it's as if I am falling in love with you again. And again. Can you fall in love if you're already in love? The fractality of love has been scientifically proven by Niels Bohr. He said that love is a quantum tunnel. The contrast of two incongruous things. Let me explain.

Your posts on Facebook are wonderful and very friendly. You smile with your teeth in all the pictures. You apply only pretty dresses to your body. I don't even apply shaving cream or shoe polish. Rich and successful people always surround you. I only have beggars and idiots around me.

You are friends with famous musicians who play jazz in 5/8. My brain is 2/3 water, like encephalitis. I don't know any notes or any lengths. I am short-range and impatient.

People really do swirl around you like snowflakes. Muscular men in thin t-shirts and pearl-like overflowing muscles say "hi" to you. Even sanitation professionals don't say "hi" to me. I always say hello to the garbage men near my house. They only answer sometimes. Suffering and doubting, being a loser—these days, this is a grievous crime.

You are a queen, bathing in the rays of love from every one of your six hundred seventy-eight friends on Facebook. Dozens of new people each day add themselves as your friend. By the time you turn a hundred and twenty and you'll have the entire population of the terrestrial globe as friends!

I look at your posts, these movie films of raging parties, with my mouth agape! You shine among the skyscrapers, sparkling with the powder of immeasurable femininity and success. It's a somewhat sad, expensive movie that fake friends cannot get into. I click on the screen with my mouse, trying to get inside the monitor, but it won't let me in.

Mouse clicks of the world, unite!

I put my pictures on Facebook to show everyone how well our relationship is developing and that I can win the heart of a woman. It's very important to me that people see me as a positive person, especially in online interactions. The internet is now more important than everything else. Once I even got three likes on one of my photographs. Like you, I also wanted to be needed and show the successful face of my social life, positioned with the bright side towards people. I don't want to be a loser.

You write posts in Japanese. And for those who don't know enough Japanese, or for those who know it too well, you translate them into English so you can be that much more perfect. You fly on a private jet between two continents and languages, hovering over grandiose New York, where I survive like a maggot.

A marriageable damsel, who received a great education in the form of one one-hundredth of the Oxford English Dictionary, you are one of the diamond specks of dust that flies around shaking dollars from the sinewy winglets of mama's bag onto a pinkish scene of triumph. I envy New York, who begat this queen-creation. I envy the metamorphoses of the girl who lives surrounded by success. It's prestigious and lawful.

I should change my sex and grow some breasts already. Then I can go together with you to parties hosted by cool guys. I would be able to wear heels. I'd just have to train a bit with the lexicon and smiles. Yuma, be my guy and instructor at fashionable parties. Hire me as an intern. Assign me the most undoable and worst tasks. I am ready to traipse along behind you into the most undignified and cruel degradation!

Your Hans

The sun became even colder. Hans wrote more and more. His monologues became more precise and worrisome. It was piling up. Hans tuned his words into a narrow focus, sharpening the resonance of a pointed tuning fork with a pencil.

With every letter, Hans laid a new mile of railroad, which he built from the days speeding past the post. Every day, like the appearance of a ship in the ocean, Hans waited and waited on the desert island of Manhattan for a response. September had long passed in a sleepy and sad gait. October dove in and disappeared vertically like a fish, leaving orange splashes of leaves on the roads. The bell of iron November was also pealing its last. Every day, Hans opened with a small key the mailbox that had dried up like a spring.

CHAPTER 20

There was one gallery that offered Hans a show for his photographs. This was interesting for a number of reasons: for the level of self-abasement with which Hans surveyed the world with the viewfinder of the camera (and people love self-abasement), for the sharpness of the relationship with people around him, and for the shaky context that Hans worked with like a musician with resonances.

The PR team worked amazingly well, doing what Hans wasn't capable of. On an atypically cold November day, a photographer came to Hans to take some photos about the photos for the press. The press! In the twenty-first century, the press serves only presidents and kings. The press distributes uncleanliness and commands great people. The press arouses the gods. The press dishonors and hassles.

Nobody needs the press anymore. A gadget is better than a prostitute.

But there was the press. Even the internet—Facebook, Twitter, Instagram—was all filled with Hans' photographs in which he combined reality with the imagined and expressed the unexplainable that slinked behind it. Yuma was in almost every photograph as part of his current, new life. Sometimes she was only in a shot by a fragment of her dress or the elegant bend of her arm, and sometimes she fully covered the frame.

New York, November, Chelsea. The gallery had muted lighting. The electric lights were focused on the photographs so as to not to wound the lively eyes of the viewers, leaving them in the shade of the room. It seemed many people wanted to come to the opening. The Brownian legs of the viewers' good graces were intertwined into a collective movement. The public was motley and elegant, Hans felt that some important conversation was just about to happen. Half-darkness and ennui reigned in the room. The cloud of people who didn't know what to do, holding on to one another, like a fog, climbed the walls with the photographs. No one was particularly talking, and nothing was being discussed. And no one was looking at the photos. They say that thirty years ago, real and naked art lived in Chelsea and Soho, which, having run into a number of contradictions, chiseled out sparks of ingeniousness. People were interested in looking for truth. But today, the only thing left of the word truth was a miserly mess, which evoked an ironic grin and pity for the one who tried to speak it.

People were not only not talking to one another. They were also not drinking. The small plastic glasses were circulating all around, and the wine wanted to flow back into the bottle, feeling that it wouldn't warm the imaginations of its tasters. The atmosphere was as if a small fire had gone out. The floodlights and diamonds blazed, music played, and the champagne made the noise of a whisper of oceantide bubbles. But the people slept. They lay in their warm beds and watched a huge TV with a flat diagonal that didn't require dialog. The word "contemplation" was also out of place. Is it possible to contemplate if every second you are expecting some tedious amusement? The skeletons should be falling out of the closet, from the walls a hundred hungry wolves should be leaping onto the viewers, snakes should rustle between their feet, and into the walls should crash a huge airplane, having spat out its pilots mid-room with microphones and a drum kit. The walls of the gallery were white because perception itself was whitewashed. The artist was a reason for people to look at one another, and the artist himself wasn't necessary and didn't understand why everyone had come and why he had been summoned. There was even a small line standing out in front of the opening.

The silhouette of a tall woman artist in high heels spun around near the entrance and was pulled into the semi-darkness by the glass front door of the gallery. She was in a hat with a wide brim and a narrow black coat. The coat, it seemed, had wrapped her in two layers, although they were a long way from the New York winter. The woman looked quite elegant with those layers of winter articles and almost flew on her suspicious high heels.

He recognized her shoes. The outline of her figure, even under the coat, couldn't be mistaken. His legs got weak, and a humming started in his chest. His heart wanted to leap out of his body and take with it the unnecessary tendons. He wanted to say something, but his tongue would not obey him at all.

He still hadn't come to his senses, throttled by the ammonia of despair, when she, walking along the wall with the photographs, noticed him and headed directly for him. "Congratulations," said Yuma, reservedly and kindly, while coming closer as if nothing was happening and they had seen each other yesterday.

Hans stood artificially, made from pale porcelain behind which there was no person. What could he say?

It seemed as if she were taller than Hans. She levitated over the floor like Mary Poppins. Hans looked up at her from a saucer. How was it so easy to see her? It was a shock from which it was hard to recover: Yuma was much more beautiful than Hans imagined. Much more blinding and, most importantly, much more necessary to him.

All these months, Hans had been feeding on nothing more than the surrogate of his fantasy, which, like a dried painting, only nourished the minimalism of his imagination, not allowing the real Yuma to blossom. But Hans didn't even have a rough idea of the extent to which he needed her in those sparkling stoplight high heels. No notes, no memories of their first and last evenings, and no photographs or reassurances could correctly lay out the entirety of what was actually occurring.

Hans didn't want to fall into despair. Like an arm wrestler, with every tendon in him, he asserted his right to occupy space. In the twenty years after the fall of the Berlin Wall, he had learned to maintain himself in uncertain circumstances, to hide in the labyrinth of passing events. To occupy his hands and thoughts with distracting objects in order to assert his right to take his part of the air from nature. To preserve whatever he had left of the essentials and that which was seemingly unnecessary. He understood that destiny was so talentless that the most important and expected thing would not happen, but instead, it would simply continue on through him without leaving a trace.

"Is this your photo art?" she began rhetorically in her musical voice that dumbfounded Hans.

"Maybe it's a continuation of existence in other forms, like with Teilhard de Chardin?" sputtered Hans.

"What? I didn't get you. This is called art?"

"Contemporary art, yes..."

"Or is it just you who calls it contemporary art?"

Hans didn't know how to answer. He was getting confused. She continued as if she were very calm, with a slight pressure.

"Why did you use pictures of me? What does that mean? I

don't really understand."

"The protagonist in the photos is interacting with the past, creating flashes of time that describe our moods..." Hans started his pathetic explanation.

"My friend has been having problems ever since you posted that picture with her and the mop on Facebook," she continued in an unexpected assault.

"Oh my God, is she really in trouble? How can I help? Is she in New York? Does she need work? I could give her my apartment in Manhattan; that might help..."

"Hans, your humor is really out of place here. I don't want you to make such 'art' with my friends."

"But I have a second mop. We could mop the floor together. I'll give her the number of my München psychologist. He can cure us of depression over Skype..."

Yuma couldn't hear the forced jokes since she had unplugged herself from living conversation. From the gallery, from Hans, from everything that could be called human.

"This is for you. A gift," she said out of turn, extending a small box wrapped in white packaging to Hans. Hans read the worry on Yuma's face, which at least meant a certain lack of indifference. And even if there was some unfriendliness now coming through her coat, this agitation of hers quieted Hans, who realized she was still interested. Whether or not a gift was appropriate, even one presented in such an absurd scene expressed some kind of feeling. This gave Hans a bit of hope.

She shot away like a comet, like a racecar. Hans even didn't have a chance to figure out whether it was really her or a set of optical phenomena that looked like Yuma.

But why talk nonsense. It was two hundred percent Yuma,

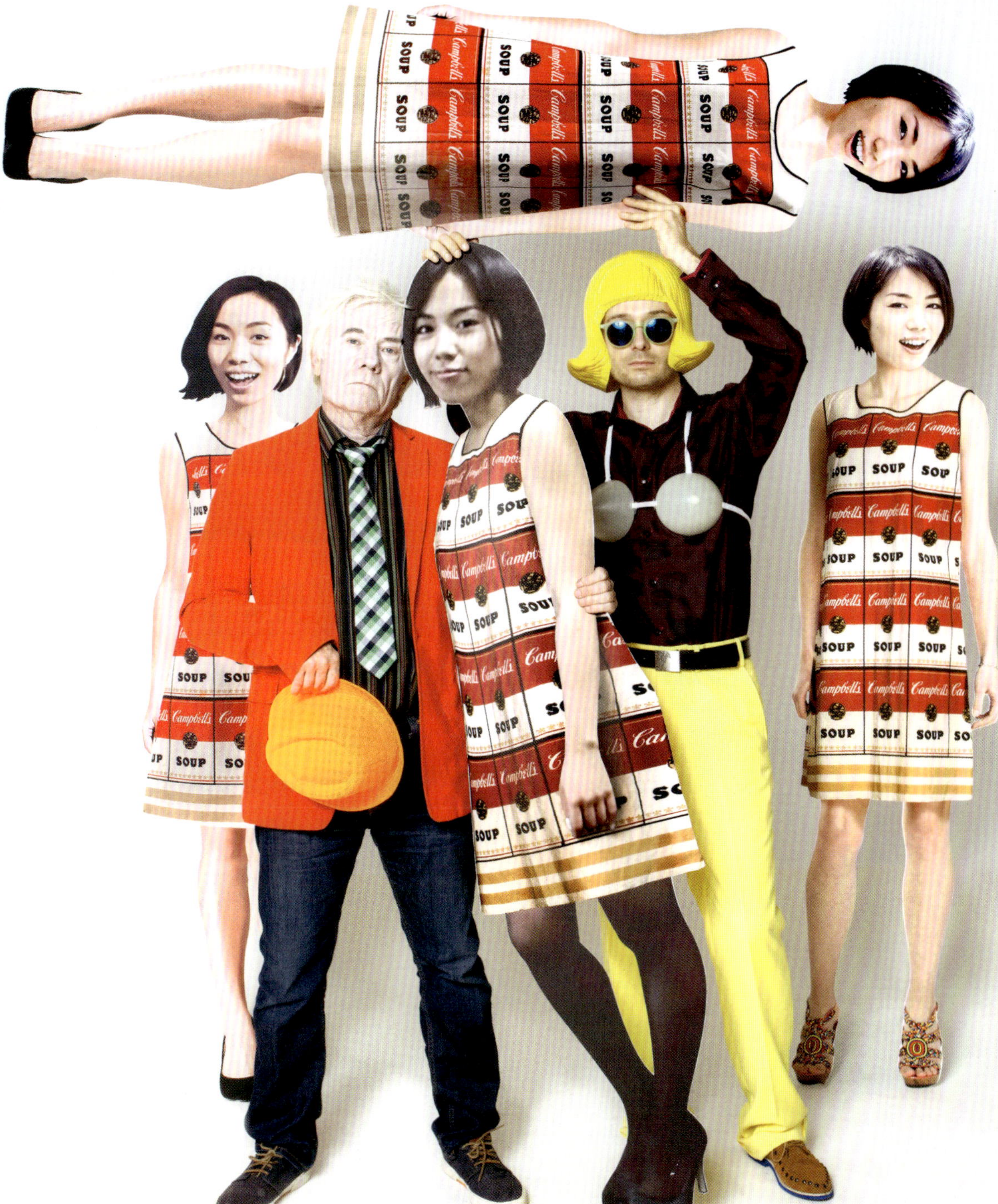
Campbell's
SOUP

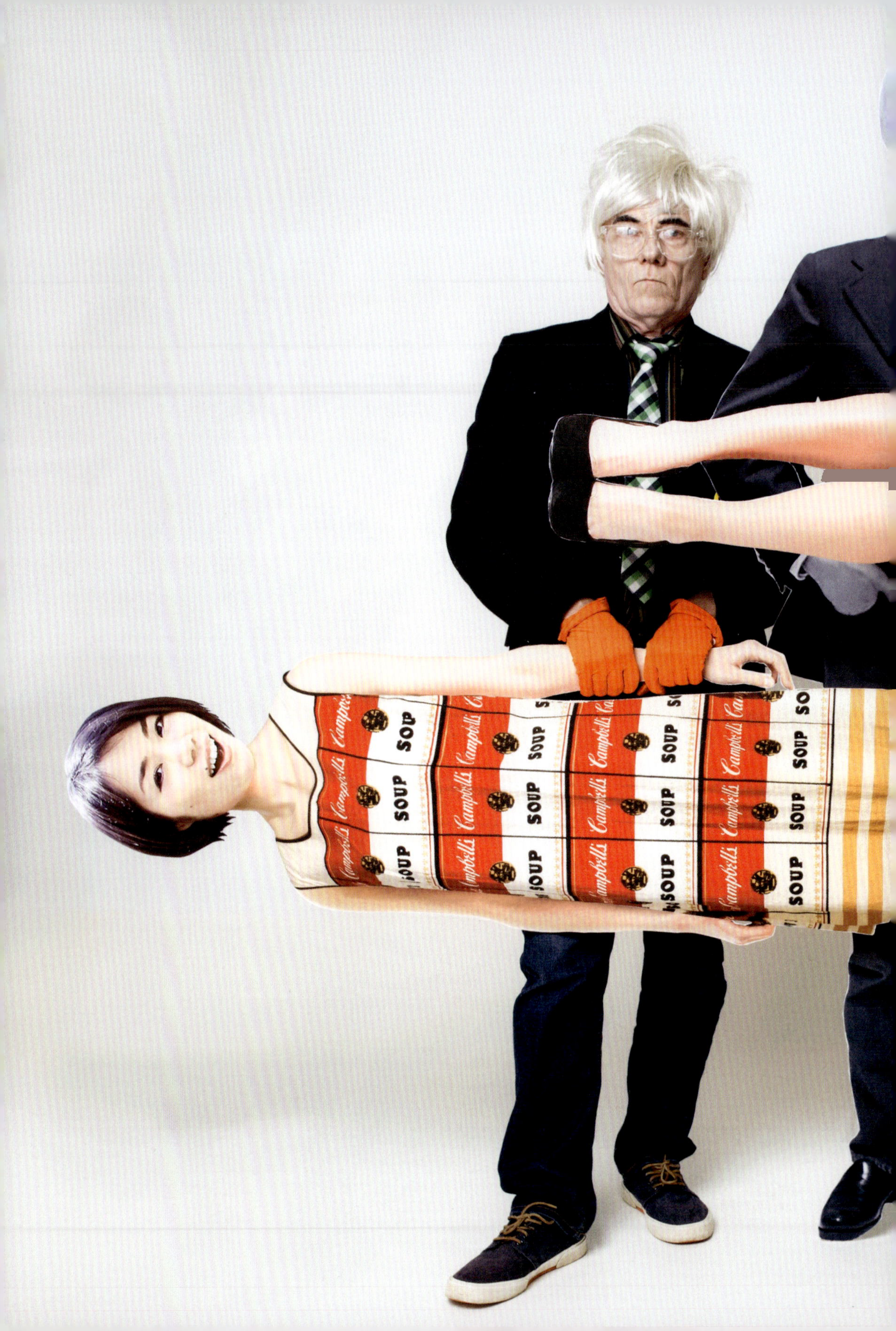
Campbell's
SOUP

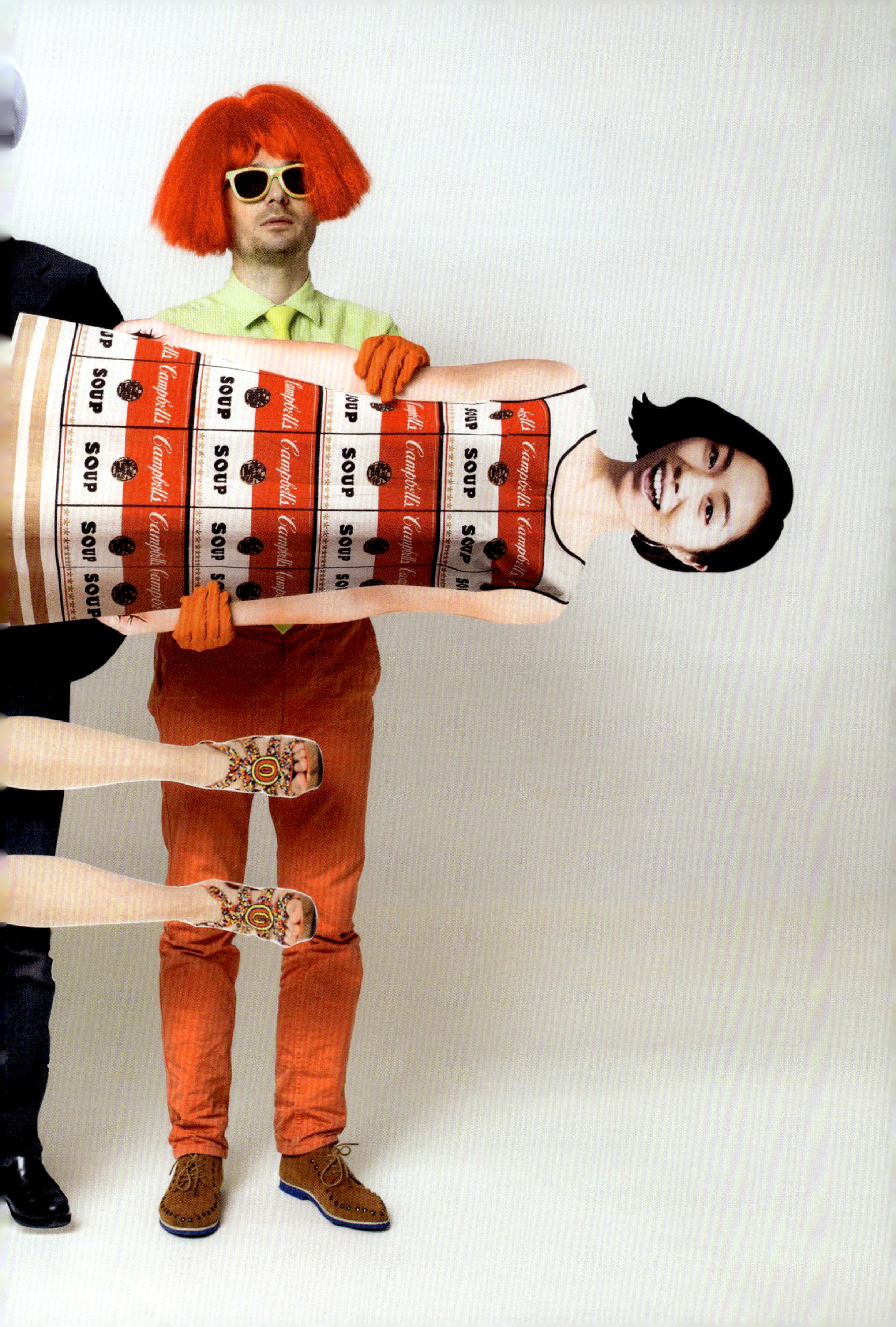
Campbell's
SOUP

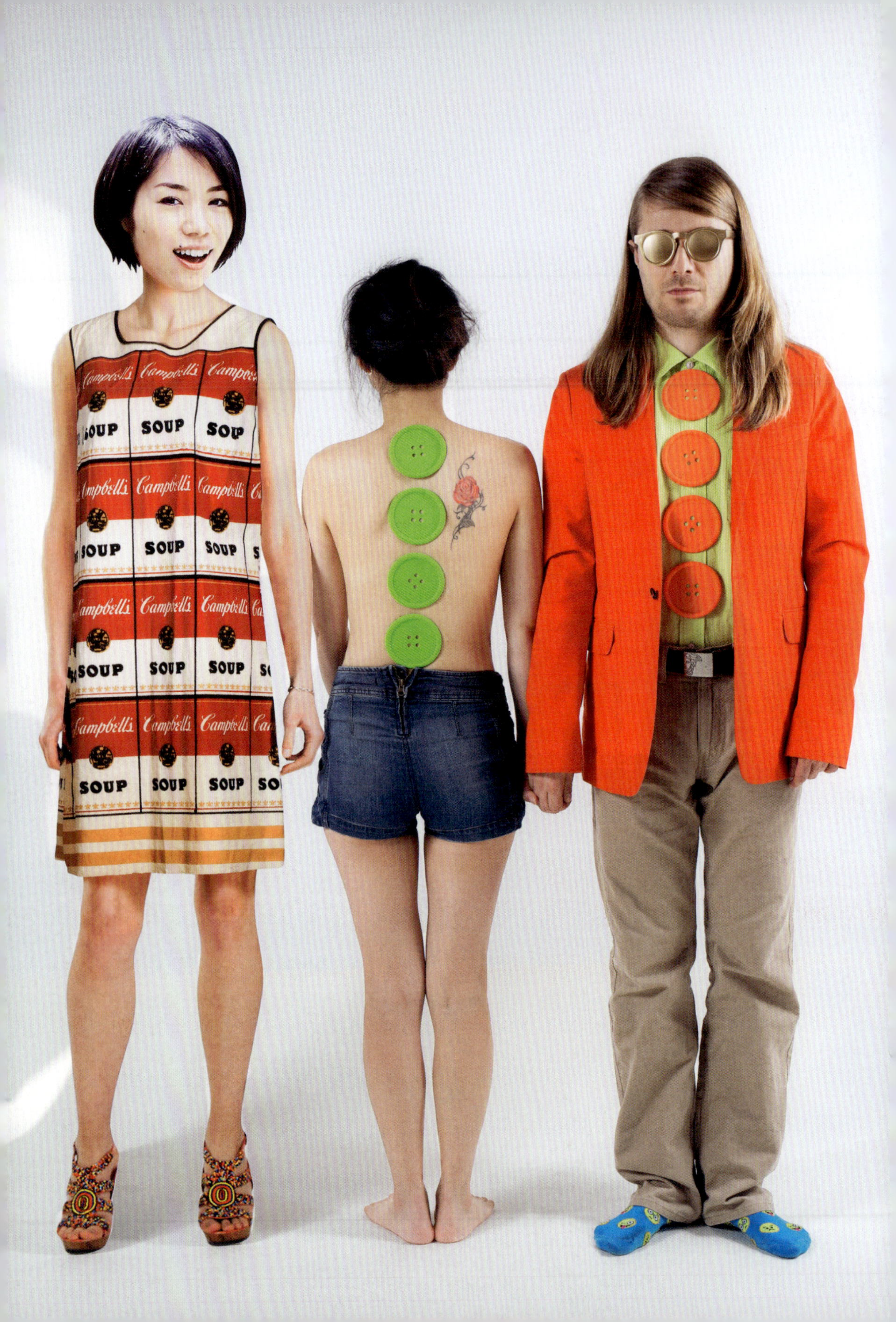
Campbell's
SOUP

with her blinding teeth, with her ink-hair fiery like the cosmos, and on heels like easels clanking on the stone floor of the gallery.

A comet.

It comes around only once every three hundred years. What ostentatious and empty words. Hans flew out onto the street to catch up with Yuma. It was dark on the street. Hans' eyes weren't obeying him.

Yuma was nowhere to be seen.

He arrived home. Without taking off his coat, he placed the box on the shelf. Then he took off his shoes and clothes. He threw his pants on the floor alongside inside-out socks. He turned off the lights in the rooms and lay down on the couch. Today he didn't want to feel, or ask questions, or speculate. He decided just to fall asleep. To cover himself with sleep like a blanket, forgetting for the whole night in the boat of the soft couch.

CHAPTER 27

It was morning. Warhol, who had stood all night next to the couch, told the still-sleepy Hans that you couldn't trust your feelings on slippery ice. Hans agreed.

His reason dissolved into a stream of questions about the current situation. He wanted a fair competition. He wanted to get into the ring, fight monsters, fight a thousand-ton army of robots. He wanted to cross the sword of wit with a Cyclopes of chess algorithms. He was ready to give himself plastic surgery to improve the style of his face and body. He wanted to learn guitar in two hours. Everything. Even dancing on crutches. Swimming the breaststroke in liquid nitrogen.

Just so she would like him. Just so something. No. Just so his application was examined. To get to the next round. Let him just get his foot in the door with difficulty, but on some fair, democratic base, as they say, these days. If Hans crawled to the finish line, he would come in first.

Before anyone knew it, between the concrete box houses that tore the sky apart, deep tin weather came to New York. The trees in Central Park, decorated with the colorful chalk of impressionism, did not want to encounter winter. Leaves were everywhere, on the roads and between the trees, in the pond water and on the grass. They fell and sheltered the land from the hard times coming. The last autumn sun was shining bright, right in your eyes, seeming to cool the air even more.

A strong restless wind made its way from the ocean through the skyscrapers and looked you right in the face, pitying no one. Hans pulled his hat on tighter, and that didn't help; the raw weather strove to stop everything that was alive. Hans liked the contrast between the melancholy of the weather and his own warmth that had not yet completely been exhausted. He even wanted to freeze, standing against the straightforward wind and icy sun. In running away from yesterday, he took Yuma's box with her present with him to Central Park. There he sat down at one of the chess tables to open it. Dried twigs and branches beaten off the fun-weary trees by the wind lay on the ground. Orange-red leaves swirled around like hang gliders, still interested in the lives of others. The wind picked the leaves up from the ground and dropped them in a pile on the chess tables in the white rays of the insipid and angry sun.

The majestic, suppressed beauty of nature evoked in each living creature a pinching grief that was not completely explainable. Hans sat comfortably at the chess table and was pleased with his position and his sadness. His mood was united with nature. The assonance of this deliberateness calmed him.

He got out the box wrapped in white paper out, intending to open it. Somewhere inside, Hans had surmised what he could expect, what sorrowful and needless news that box would bring. But he again waved these bothersome thoughts away. Contemplation had taught him to simply enjoy the passing of days. Some contrary side asked him how it was possible to take pleasure in passing days. Hans opened the box slowly.

It held his letters to Yuma.

They hadn't been opened. Hans slowly went through them. Some of them were dusty, as it seems they had been stored for a long time in an inappropriate place. Some of the envelopes had lost color, likely having sat on a windowsill for a long time. One of the envelopes had been torn but not opened, and on the other side had a brown half-circle of water blotches from a cup of coffee or tea that had sat on it. Hans looked at all of the envelopes as if saying goodbye to them. Some of them he held up to the light. Then he carefully put them all back into the box and got up from his bench that had been splattered by the autumn leaves.

Had that package told him any new truth that he had understood anyway? Had it given him the ability to look more pragmatically at what was occurring? For Hans, the envelopes were soil from the moon, specks of which had been touched by Yuma with her fingers. What happened there and how, in faraway space where his letters had arrived, however painful it was now, was unimportant. The fact itself of cosmic contact with her outweighed all terrestrial matters. Hans wanted magic and the world to be built from the bricks of his own fantasy. In the melancholy from the return of the letters, which had lifted him up as if it were a crane, he only felt that he had been right.

Moving a little away from the chess tables, Hans went up to the side of the path. There he poured all the letters into a bin with the word "Trash" written on it.

Suffering and doubting, being a loser—these days, this is a grievous crime.

CHAPTER 28

Somehow or other, whether the struggle had ended or just begun, Hans decided to hide away and determine the best strategy. Maybe find other paths to Yuma's attention. All he needed was a few meetings, walks, and conversations somewhere on the streets of New York. And Hans knew that for sure after that, Yuma would be his. Because no one could compete with Hans. He could feel through walls.

So, he decided to drill a hole in the wall.

For that, Hans took a taxi to Harlem. Of course. If Yuma had come to New York again, where might she be staying? Hans' thoughts said it might be that same evil apartment 2C in Harlem, with the tenant who never did tell Hans what was behind the door. It seemed the slippery fellow was hiding the truth. Hans was becoming sure that Yuma must be staying there. And if she had already been in town a few days, then Hans could just get that information from other neighbors.

He was lucky to a certain extent because upon getting out of the cab, he saw a jolly fat guy of about twenty-five clearly smoking some reality-enhancing smoke so that his heart could more easily work between the extra pounds of flesh and so that his lungs didn't have to meet the driver-polluted air head-on. Hans raised the matter on hand, asking the guy whether he lived here. After an affirmation that he lived on the third floor, they spoke about vegetarianism. Then a bit about the drones that would soon be delivering beer. They found common ground, and Hans asked whether Brad—that was the name of the guy, who worked Downtown and was now relaxing after work without having even taken his tie off—whether he had seen a girl who lived on the second floor and, maybe, sang. The guy reacted immediately to that.

"A Chinese girl with a saxophone?"

"Yes!" Hans plainly rejoiced. "A Japanese girl with a guitar!" The guy confirmed that a few days ago, he had seen the Chinese girl with a saxophone in a red dress leave to go somewhere. He again stressed that insignificant detail of her being Chinese.

"How did you know that it was a saxophone?" Hans attempted to precisely determine, squeezing through a puff of smoke.

"Well, it just seemed like one to me. A huge case. It was a big saxophone. Maybe it looked like a guitar. A sax monster. A saxsoguitarophone!

They laughed at the same time and clapped each other on the arm as if they had understood the root of the problem. More like different problems for each of them, which had nonetheless led to the same result. Hans could feel people. Sometimes. He invited the guy to move into his apartment for a month. And Hans would move here. "Why would you want to do that?" the guy asked guardedly, even a bit insulted. He didn't understand who would willingly move from Downtown to Harlem.

"You see, we've known each other for twenty years. I went to school with her in China. We haven't seen each other since, since I came here. But I promised that as soon as we were living in the same town, I would marry her immediately. And she has just arrived. I want to surprise her, right from the upstairs apartment. Like a flight to the heavens, a wedding between two floors, a date under the ceiling, and so on and so forth.

The guy was ecstatic. His smile could have damaged the

bottom of his face as wide as it was, revealing two rows of white fences of teeth.

"Really?!" He couldn't stop guffawing. "Dude, are you a poet or something? Sensitive? You waited for her twenty years, and you're skulking around here talking to a clown on the street? Man, you must be talented! Hey, let me just take you to her; wait a minute."

The guy went to ring the doorbell, but Hans lunged after him and resolutely obstructed his path.

"Stop, stop, Brad. Not now! I'm not dressed well enough. I don't want it to go like this. And also, you understand, the first impression… I mean, the first after so long a separation…"

"Yeah, brother, I get you, better than anyone else," Brad inhaled deeper, letting out the volume of his understanding smoke that blanketed your soul from the outside. "You've gotten into some serious shit. I can't even understand how you're gonna fix it all up. Twenty years you haven't seen her, or thirty did you say? How do you know where she is now? And more importantly, is that still her? I guess you have a good memory for faces or for something…" He laughed kindly. "OK, I'll live at your place. No problem. You just bring my fridge and all my shirts down there. 'Cause my boss likes ties and suits. I don't have much stuff other than that. The fridge is my most important piece of property," Brad exhaled a few smoke rings into the face of the situation that was being resolved satisfactorily for both sides.

Nothing surprised Hans as he entered the apartment. It was just as small as his Downtown one, with the only difference being the quantity of various things along the walls from the floor to the ceiling and even in the windows. He was a little perturbed by these things, most of which showed signs of being rare. They followed the guest with malevolent eyes, assessing his possible malevolence in return. In the two rooms, there was no space for one person to live. In order to get from one room to another, you had to make a path and crawl through it, like through a narrow cave that had sharp wall stalactites of teapots, Indian decorations, plaster figurines, plastic thingamajigs, dolls bought at flea markets, and other items whose purpose was more difficult to ascertain.

"Welcome to my piece of heaven. You'll have to excuse the mess. I haven't straightened up. You wouldn't believe that I work at a company that does cleaning throughout the state. But you understand what kind of teeth dentists have in their mouths." Brad laughed with cause. "Hans, one day, just take all this stuff out onto the street, OK? I'm serious. Do a favor for an unathletic and lazy guy."

The next morning, when Hans came by to move the things, Brad, late for work, was very serious and businesslike:

"I can't believe that I met my savior in such an unassuming guise, Hans. In another month, they probably would have fired me for being late so often. You've given hope to my dreams of building a career!" Brad tried to joke, standing in his underwear and tying the noose of a pink tie with frog bumps.

The move was quick and painless. That same evening, Hans took to the task of fixing up the apartment. He took out onto the street all the unnecessary shelves, frames, plastic dollies, three mirrors, four chairs, two couches that he was able to take apart, a few old dish sets, a set of pots, five cast-iron irons, and a number of ironing boards. There was a lot more that was awkward to talk about or impossible to recall. By evening the apartment was empty and pocked with the wounds of the crumbling walls like the hungry mouth of a wolf that hasn't eaten for days.

Throughout all these days, Hans shooed away the thought of what had actually happened just a short time ago. The meeting in the gallery was for him an icy shower. He had no enthusiasm left for remembering that fleeting meeting that had churned him up or explaining to himself again why he had to torment himself with reproaches instead of being with Yuma.

Hans was vexed that the "second meeting" had only unraveled his nerves and had not brought anything new. His thin connections with reality began to freeze up a bit. Hans was afraid that soon the course of events would only pull him into a slowly spinning funnel.

He had a premonition of something, some kind of unexpected news as if this "something" had already happened. His instinct was trying to convince him to run away, to a safe place, far from the swampy evening forest that called to him with its tired finger branches. The meeting with Yuma implanted in Hans strange, unabating music. The melody of this trumpet was not that sad, nor was it solemn, but in the notes of the melody was something nagging and at the same time barely audible. Hans desperately banished all questioning and ambiguous thoughts, dreaming not to be a realist but rather to not fall into evil dreams.

He even wanted, maybe, for nothing to ever have been. Somewhere in his heart slumbered the temptation to return to a few days into the past, before the moment he encountered Yuma. It seemed to him an enticing and good solution—just to have never met her.

With the avatar of the turtle, the further he ran trying to save himself, the closer Yuma was to him. After he moved in a floor above her, she occupied every corner of his personal space. She hung in the air of the apartment so that she was in his line of vision. To bother him with her. Every inhalation, sip of water, and every thought of Hans' was mixed with feelings about Yuma, returning to her every minute, freezing on the grass in Central Park. He felt her presence a foot away from him, and the ramifications of that feeling were intolerable. He knew that he could ring the doorbell of the downstairs apartment and, perhaps, she might open the door to him in her robe. Or he might meet her right now randomly on the street near the house. But after the conversation with her in the gallery, he understood that a new meeting without the necessary preparations would only make their relationship worse. All movement towards a meeting was pointless. Something extraordinary had to happen to move the tectonic plates. So, Hans decided to muster up some patience and make a peephole into the apartment Yuma lived in by carefully moving the floor tiles.

He began work that same day, convinced that there would be no noise below. To make sure there would be no noise, he placed his ear against the old floorboards for a few minutes. There was clearly no one downstairs. Hans heard only the noise of his own body.

The work was going boldly. The floorboards were half rotten and laid on the beams almost freely, so you could simply remove them without tools. Hans took away an even square in the corner of the room, two feet by two feet.

He had planned to make a small staircase, down which, at the right moment (choosing it carefully), he could climb down to Yuma in formal dress and propose with a ring. And all that jazz. Candles, champagne. He would even learn every detail of the Japanese wedding ritual. And he would ask Ronald to be his best man.

Hans, keeping his hands occupied, warmed himself quite well with thoughts of Yuma, of the idea that she might be so close to him. Physical work with objects relaxes and devastates thought, given to humans to increase anxiety.

Hans wanted to finish up the work building the access hole as fast as possible so that everything would be in place. He knew that after this action, this self-assured surge of elegance, everything would change for the better. Yuma would accept his proposal. She would be enchanted with his bravery and resourcefulness. She would melt from his artistic taste and instinct, his ability to create a one-of-a-kind atmosphere. At the same time, Hans was even thinking about decorations and social pageantry. He could invite TV in to cover the extravagant wedding. A master class in the class of the master! TV channels are bored. They love crackpots. To them, Hans would come across as a successful loser.

Maybe the owner of the building would even present the newlyweds with an apartment where they could best coexist and live a happy life in New York. They would have a decent number of children, so it wouldn't be too bad to have two floors.

While Hans was dreaming of his future happy life, he discovered that under the layer of floorboards and wood was also a layer of concrete separating the floors. His dreams faded, and work was suspended.

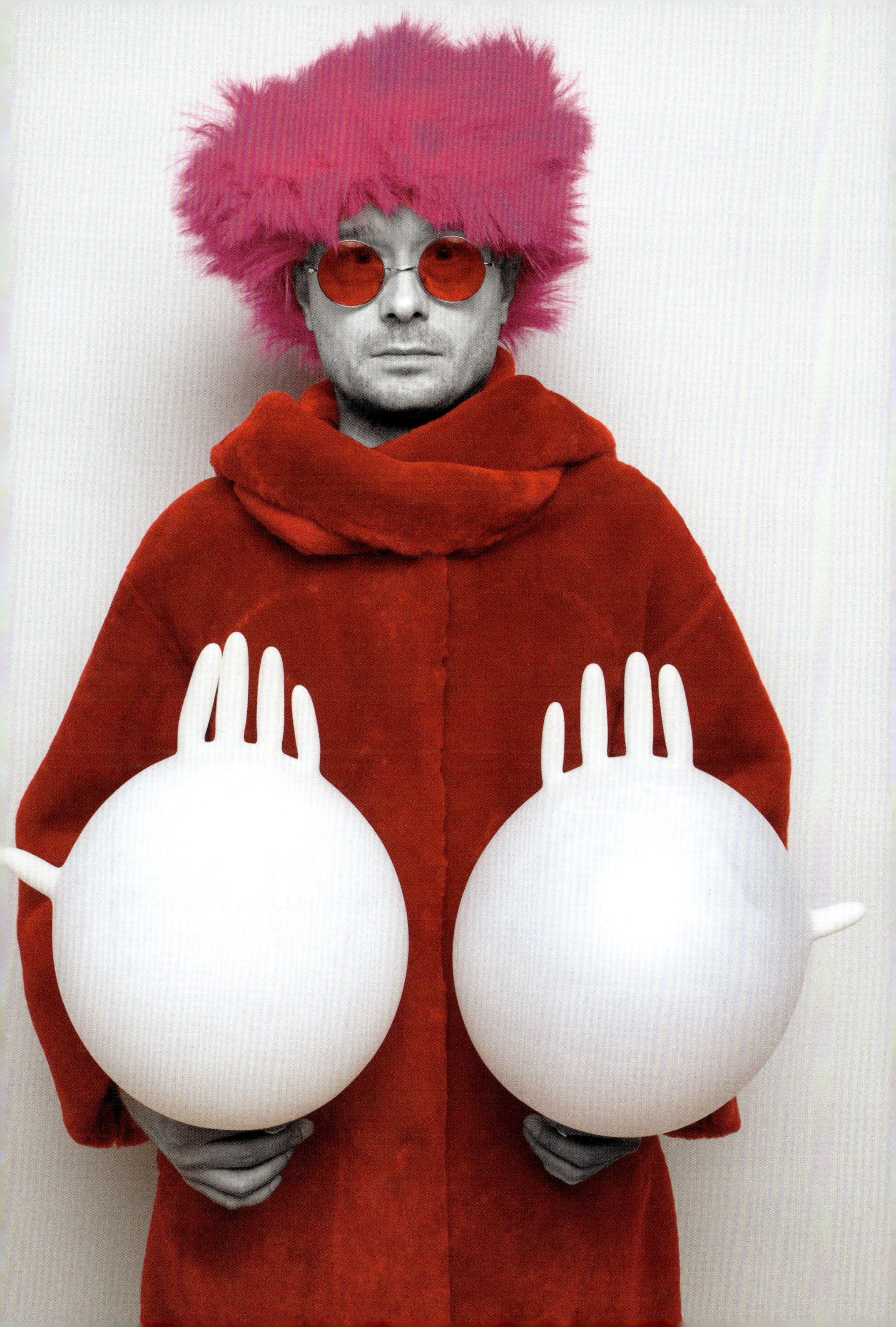

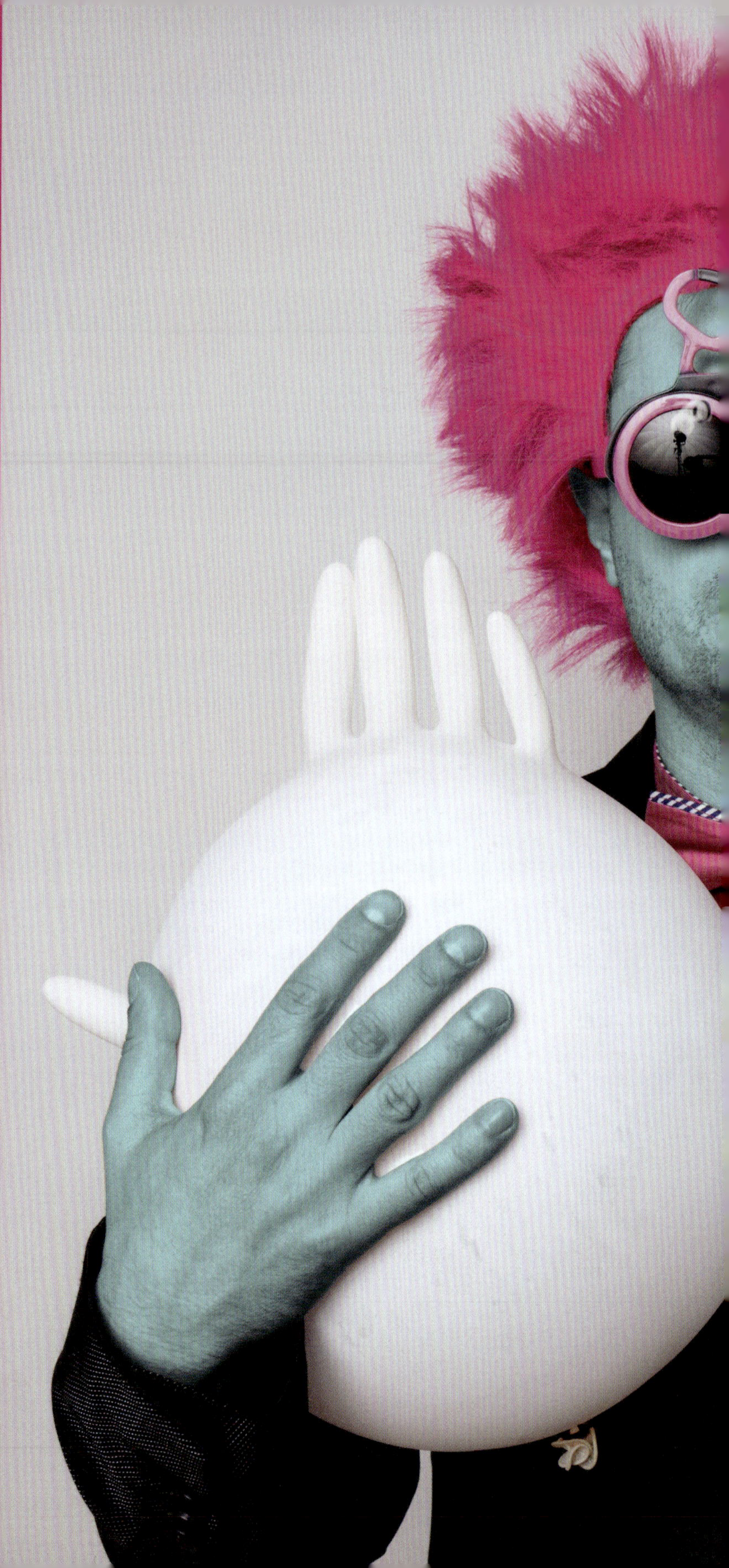

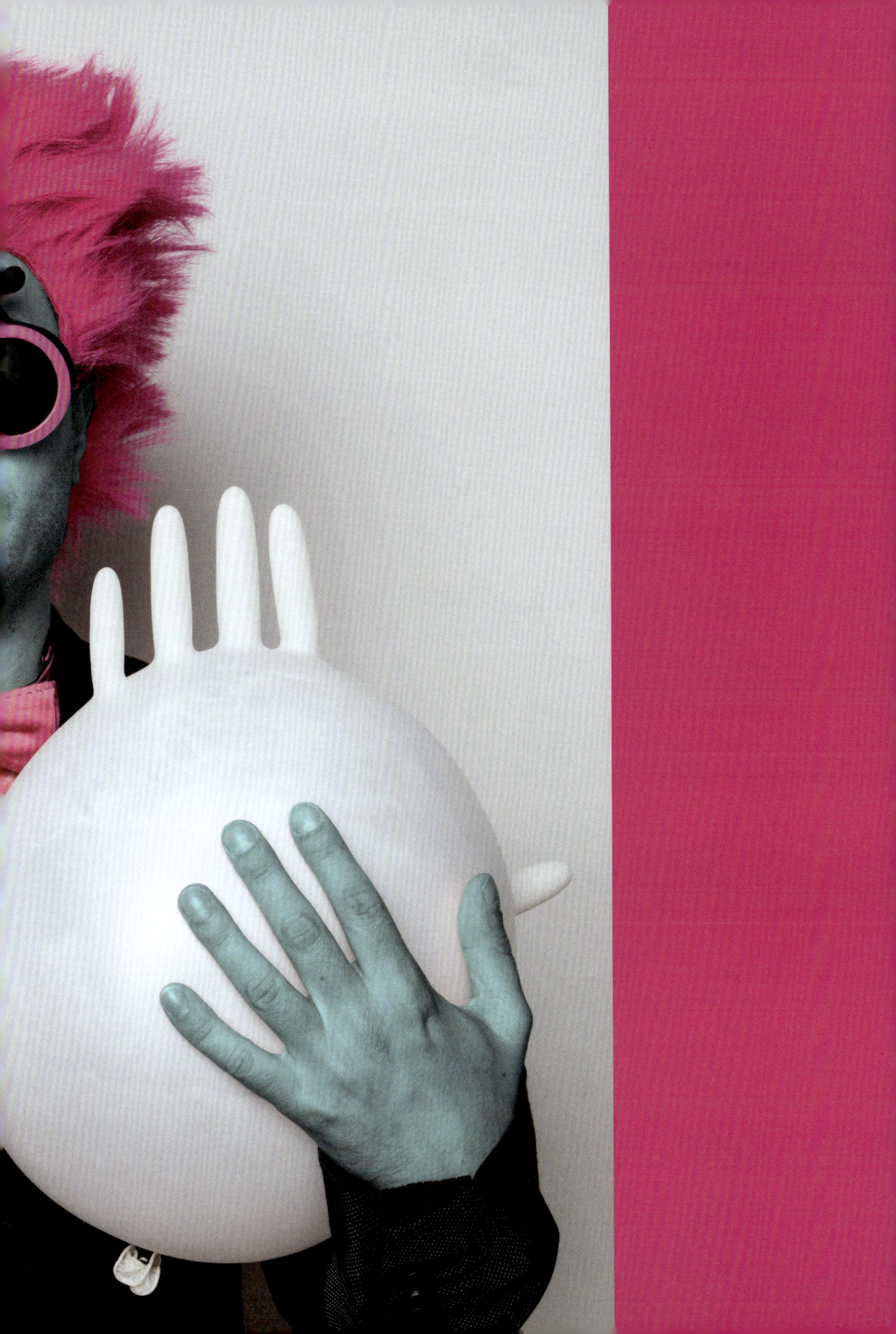

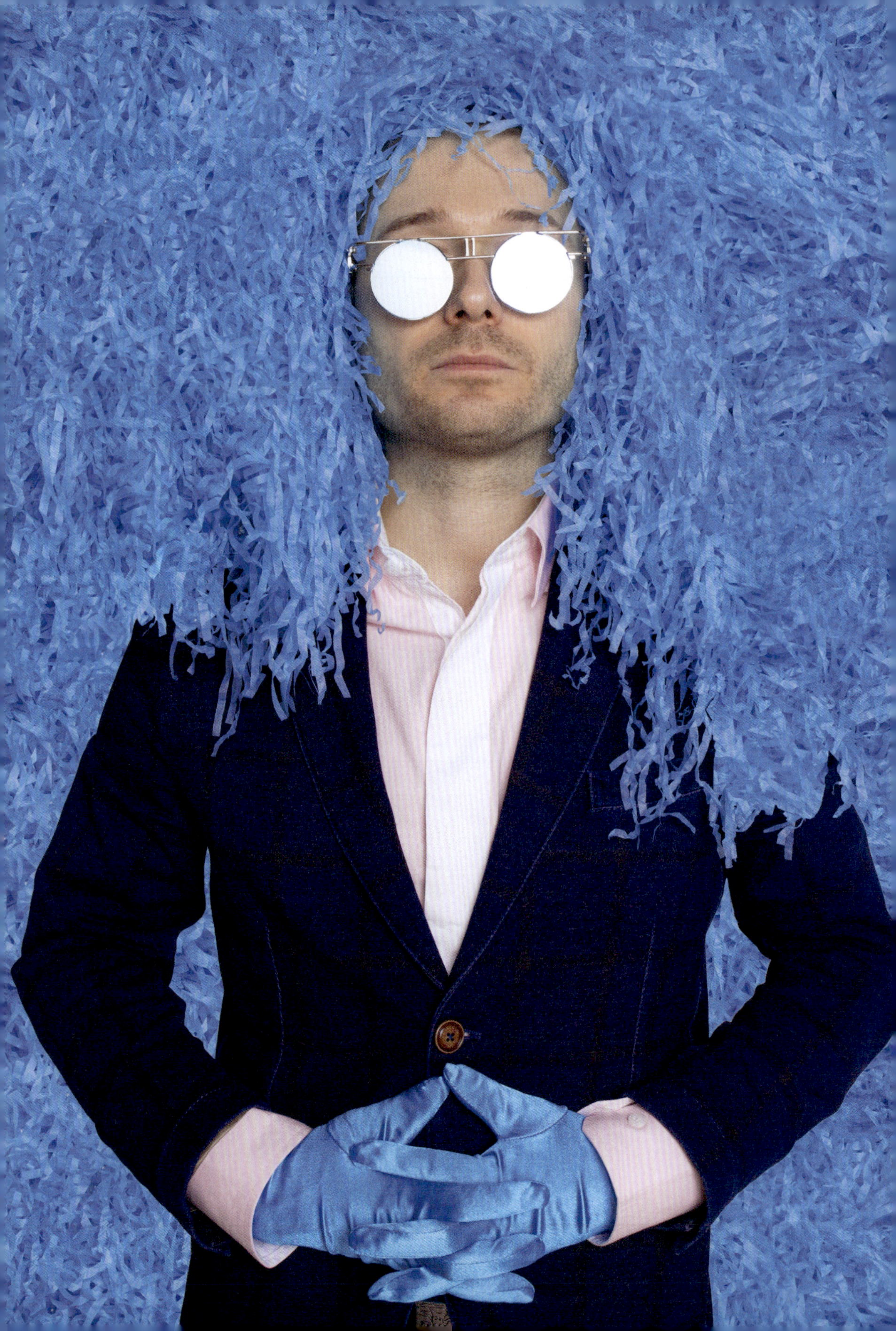

CHAPTER 29

From the fresh Harlem morning in the new apartment, Hans was able to brew up some coffee with the push of one button on the miraculous machine. As a mathematician, he loved stability, knowing that the robot, the machine, which would care for him every day, in the end, would acquire emotion and a membrane of life. Hans knew that even simple robots, like coffeemakers, suffer no less than living beings and need love. And he sympathized with all the mechanisms and devices that were languishing around him: not only the coffee machine but the microwave, the iron, and the camera.

After waking, digging through his smartphone was an additional pleasure that aided Hans in gathering his thoughts into a morning disorder. The satisfaction of chaos revealed itself in scrolling through news websites and receiving unwanted e-mails.

At the same time, he listened to voice mails about the hospital where he was supposed to send some money, about a flower shop having a sale, and a message from Brad, who it seems was finally able to make it to work on time. The message was brief: “Come over. It seems you’ve got some trouble.”

Hans listened to the information with obvious indifference. He knew that the most unpleasant thing in his life had already occurred. And now would come days that were, if not happy, at least improved.

Hans was still unable to explicate or fathom anything significant that it would be unpleasant to lose. His heart dwelled freely in a light air of lonely irresponsibility. "My landlord increased the rent," thought Hans, "or the neighbors were complaining that Brad was smoking his concentrated dope." Hans knew neighbors were always complaining about something preposterous; Hans knew.

Indifference lay on the surface of Hans' defensive reactions, like an incrustation left from a society that forcefully inclined him to be numb and disappointed, taught him to cut off any feeling from himself, killing in himself the child and the wizard. But the true side of him had not yet been completely extinguished. It was a potbelly stove that still worked, the coal was smoldering, and some of the sparks strayed onto the floor from time to time. Hans' anxiety was even uniform and all-consuming. It boiled within the thick walls of a cauldron.

Every minuscule event of his life made Hans even more strained on the inside and faded on the outside.

Hans headed home, walking to the subway and taking the 4 downtown, not as.... he was initially. He had the thought that small troubles were always connected with bigger ones and that they all stem from one universal idea, aimed at returning the aberrant tourist to the group. Hans loved and enjoyed life, or so it seemed to him in any case. Only the poison of premonition running along his tendons gave him pause and left a question mark.

Brad opened the door, and his face was too concerned.

"The mailman came by asking for you. I said that I was you because he needed someone to sign for a letter. So, I signed for it. Then I looked into the envelope." Without any superfluous affectation, Brad extended the envelope towards Hans.

It was a letter from court. A summons.

"I've gotten those kinds of letters, and I know what that is. It might be nothing. But it might also be some headache."

Hans went into his apartment and, without taking off his shoes, looked at the envelope for a few seconds, attempting to assess what it held. And also, by what umbilical cord its contents might be connected to any form of real trouble. Tearing open the envelope, he pulled out a summons.

The summons stated that Hans was obligated to appear in court in a few days at the address indicated. He would be able to review the suit and the court materials a day before the court hearing.

Hans didn't give much importance to this lawsuit, although it was clear that something unpleasant could be happening that might lead to additional hassle. Hans wanted to live as far as possible from the paper and office world where most of his acquaintances resided. And besides, every skyscraper in the layered pastry of New York was built to work with tons of paper, reports, and useless graphs, printed in the miles and falling into the wastebaskets of every floor of every office building. Hans tried to live away from this trash, filtering out the spectrum of the uninteresting with his oscilloscope, even in places where the uninteresting ran smack into his bodily coordinates.

Brad looked questioningly at Hans, trying to determine if everything was OK. It soon became clear to him that everything was not as good as it could be. Hans' face changed and went a bit pale. He tried to maintain himself as if nothing had happened, smiling and playing it off as if it were unimportant. But the smile was not sticking to his face.

"Is it something serious?" asked Brad, taking an active part in the peripeteia of his comrade.

"Nah, it's nothing," answered Hans. "Nothing serious."

"Well, if it is serious, let me know. My brother works in a law firm in New Jersey. I think they work with inheritances and bankruptcies.

He works in maintenance, though."

"All right," Hans grumbled flatly, "thanks. But I have to go... I'll think about it all later. It doesn't even amount to a hill of beans. Don't worry about it."

Hans went out onto the street and wandered up Greenwich Avenue towards Downtown and his office. Somewhere there, behind the commotion of work, he was planning on hiding from premature thoughts of the tangle of unrelated events that was moving towards him, recalling a faraway storm. It was already the end of autumn, and December was getting ready to turn the dial on November's attenuator. Winter in New York was rough and overwhelming. Only the buildings, born to stand against the impregnability of the Indian land, were just barely able to survive. Not so for non-stone people. The piercing, cold, hard wind won't let up all winter. Disappearing suddenly, appearing even more fiercely, day by day gathering anger and cruelty, it won't capitulate until April.

There were no more tables on the streets. The restaurants were hiding from themselves in dark, swarthy caves bathed in yellow light in the atmosphere of the haggard trees. The air was cold, and at the slightest swirl, the wind would burn your face. People hurried in the streets as if they were covered with shadowy masks.

Hans turned the corner and approached his office building, where a discussion of photographs awaited him. He went into the studio, where the first thing he did was make himself a cup of lulling, calming coffee. The wind couldn't reach Hans from outside the window, blowing from jealousy of the warmth. For a while, Hans froze all thoughts regarding the order he received. He knew that it was best to draw his reactions and feelings out.

In the evening, after work, Hans read *Anna Karenina*. That book had given him no peace since school in East Germany, where it was required reading for all children. But back then, Hans stopped at the part about the freezing blizzard that, cutting between the railroad cars, accompanied both the train going to Saint Petersburg and Vronsky, who was a symbol of something dangerous, dishonest, but at the same time real. Hans had stopped reading there, depressed by the atmosphere of ominous snow and despair evaporating from the pages of this book for schoolchildren. Hans' happiness was an unconscious barrier that protected him from reading himself into someone else's experience. He never wanted to finish the book and always avoided watching movies based on it. He didn't want to discuss the details of the story with any of his friends or classmates.

Now, something had changed in him. Ever since he had moved to New York, life and memories of his parents had been dulled. He wanted to know the bitter pill of human relationships that the book mirrored. He wanted to transfigure his suffering, to ask some diluted advice of the book on how he should offer himself up to mitigate his expanding tortures, which, Hans was sure, were now impossible to avoid. Placing some photo albums around himself in the unheated intestinal Harlem apartment for a feeling of fidelity and comfort, wrapping himself in his woolen blanket, he continued reading the sad book about the saddest woman.

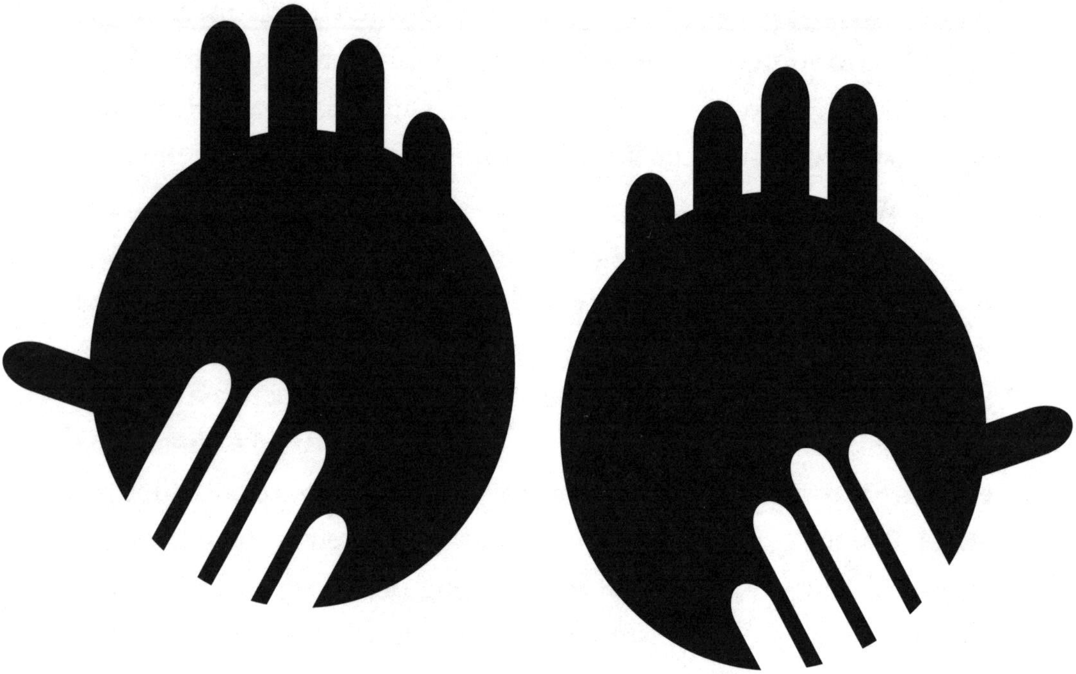

CHAPTER 30

Yuma closed Hans' mouth with a gag, tying his hands tightly behind him. She poured acid in his nostrils. She stood with her high heels on the piano of his fingers. She beat, atomized his joints. The louder and harder they cracked, the bigger and wider she smiled, snuggled in a kimono. Hans awoke from his own scream. His hand was between the pages of *Anna Karenina* and had gone numb.

The dawn of the morning helped Hans wake up on the couch. The sun was preparing all its leverage for its slow ascent over the horizon. Buildings, cold from the night, exhaled steam from their chimney nostrils. Birds chirruped in the stone jungle, wistfully dreaming of real wooden trees, reluctantly realizing that another day had started, in which again one had to think about food. As always in nature, nothing particularly wanted to live, but everything was happy to be alive. It was just a little more interesting than not living or not existing. Balancing on the threshold, every little bug wiped its eyes and stretched out its flimsy arms to begin the pointless slog.

Morning gave New York the gift of London fog. The bustle, wrapped in cold and melancholy, was confused, and production was down in offices because even the most unbridled employees were unconsciously somber, gathering messages in their messengers, using happy face emoticons to futilely attempt to be close to one another. With its newness and advancement, the electronic network could not compete with the breath of nature, which breathed a sorrowful fog on the city from the heights of the heavens. Hans brewed coffee on the gas stove and asked Warhol how he had slept. "Not bad, thanks. The mice scurrying at my feet disturbed me a bit, but on the whole very peacefully, very peacefully," answered Warhol.

"And how are you?" Andy inquired.

"I was gathering courage for court."

"Is it weighing on you?"

"To some extent. I dreamed I failed my exams."

"You're expecting a just decision or an unexpected turn?"

"I'm expecting a party."

Hans ceremoniously shaved. Not all the way, but he decreased the distance between the ends of the unshaven hairs of his stubble and his skin. Hans had no lawyer, and he didn't like people who worked with chisels. He decided to go alone to the New York District Court. All he needed was to see Yuma.

He arrived at the hearing early. He figured that the intent of the hearing could be ignored and that the court would happen of its own accord.

Carelessness caused the fear to retreat and be replaced by the adventurousness of an anthropologist. Hans wanted to get to that driving force that takes real things to absurd conclusions. It didn't matter to him what was happening, but the future presence of Yuma excited him since he planned to propose to her and reciprocate her gift with one of his own in white. To try to get married by pushing her buttons. Or at least get a written promise from her to do so as soon as possible. He understood the naiveté of the maximum efforts he had planned, however. Hans knew that dreaminess and slight absurdity push reality towards the desired contradictions, like a Doppler shift. And although cowardice stopped fireworks from being set off for Hans along his way, the tiny achievements were what he respected himself for. He knew that no matter how foolish an idea was, once it was voiced it already was somehow alive in the world, even if it was laughed at by every single person, without exception. Well, with the exception of Hans himself. There were also some humane specimens who loved Hans and understood that he was a deep person.

"She summoned me to court to fight, and I'll go and marry her and have children. Right in court! I'll explain myself to her there, in front of all the judges, prosecutors, juries, criminals, and ballistic experts. Unexpectedness brings people together. She'll appreciate it. She'll understand," thought Hans.

In the subway, he began making outlines of his speech to persuade her. It was like therapy to distract the heart from the paralyzing feelings it had carried all these months, like a dislocation.

Yesterday Hans brought her a gift and was now taking it to the courtroom. It was a white dress. Hans really had to decisively resist the bleakness of humanity's blueprints. He was certain: they could take the wedding picture right there during the hearing. He knew that all he had to do was hypnotize Yuma, and the force of feeling would break the dam. Yuma would not slip away from him again. Hans was anxious. He felt the moment of solemnity and battle coming closer.

There was no one in the courtroom besides the judge and some man sitting in the front row. That must be Yuma's lawyer. The hearing began suddenly and normally like it was nothing. The morning smiled gloomily in the window.

Hans heard nothing, and when he was asked questions, he answered, for the most part, in the affirmative. All his attention was on the door and on his own emotional discourse, the key points of which he attempted to highlight. The lawyer was saying something, the judge nodded, and Hans muttered. There was an hour of that.

Yuma had not come.

She had never planned to come since her dignity was represented by an interpreter of the law in an expensive suit. All that Hans heard was "…the plaintiff's claim shall be satisfied in part, by one half of the amount sought, five hundred thousand US dollars, to be recovered…" Hans wasn't really paying attention. Rather, he just didn't like ridiculous humor. He heard parts of the judge's speech in the twanging emptiness of the sections of his memory reserved for non-necessities.

The lawyer wore a barely discernable smile, stretching from satisfaction and yawning without covering his mouth, but almost bursting on the inside, anticipating spending his fee in vapid restaurants with cute girls. No, on a thirty-foot yacht in the Caribbean. Well, that, of course, was just the voice of jealousy. The ceremony of the judicial process bloomed like a proud flower from the concrete soil of newly-enthroned justice.

Hans left the courtroom. "Wait, wait!" someone yelled to him.

It was...

There was no one around. It was Hans himself coming to. And he asked himself: "What?... A hundred thousand? No, how much did they say? Ten thousand?"

CHAPTER 31

With an ill feeling, Hans again tried to read the paper they had handed him immediately after the court hearing. "Inasmuch as Hans Lidenberg used photographs of singer Yuma Matoya unlawfully, without her consent, for purposes of intimidation, and in view of the fact that his actions with her image were of an offensive nature, as witnessed, for example, by dressing Matoya without her consent in a striped dress with canned soup images, and in view of the fact that the quantity of such images of her on social networks and in the public domain of the internet have exceeded one thousand, in the claim of Yuma Matoya versus Hans Lidenberg, seeking one million US dollars, the plaintiff's claim shall be satisfied in part, and in connection with the damage done to the good reputation of the singer, as compensation for emotional distress and material losses, the amount of five hundred thousand US dollars is to be recovered. This decision shall enter into force immediately."

Money made from nothing.
Money is the sleep of reason.
Money is a rubbish wind.

Hans shook his head instinctively as if he were shaking something off. He hadn't had time to get drunk in order to be sobering up now, but the number of zeroes in that amount made him immediately the soberest and penniless man on Earth. Hans didn't worry about money, living in a world of photography far from interest rates. But he was struck that the quantity of money on the bill that he was just handed for his actions was catastrophically large for a photographic artist. He didn't gamble and didn't go into debt over three hundred dollars. He didn't smoke, didn't drink. He didn't trade in derivatives on the Chicago Mercantile Exchange. How could he have this debt now? Whose mind created it? What could one say or feel about a debt of five hundred thousand US dollars?

Hans wandered around Downtown, trying to convince himself that nothing had happened. His main question was: how can human bipolarity be measured in money? What force of pressure must occur in another being that results in a call to a lawyer and a thirst for punishment in an amount that is more than enough for more than one lifetime?

How can feelings that are not in agreement be censured with money? Was the desire to attain a material punishment the result of some other suffering of her soul? Was that suffering somehow connected with Hans, or was he only the occasion for her tangle of personal problems to start unraveling? Was the formality and cruelty of her actions connected with the distance and coldness of her relationship with her parents, who did the same thing with her?

"How can one appraise the force of her suffering? Did I really bring her so much affliction? Or is the real reason for her behavior something else?" thought Hans. "Is it possible to try on someone else's feet, heart, someone else's eyelashes, and feel something?"

Will illegal feelings really be punished by awarding financial compensation? Will that calm and satisfy both parties in a just court? Can you atone for guilt by writing a check? Can I empathize with her fully if I love her? Might that empathy be closed off from her by the

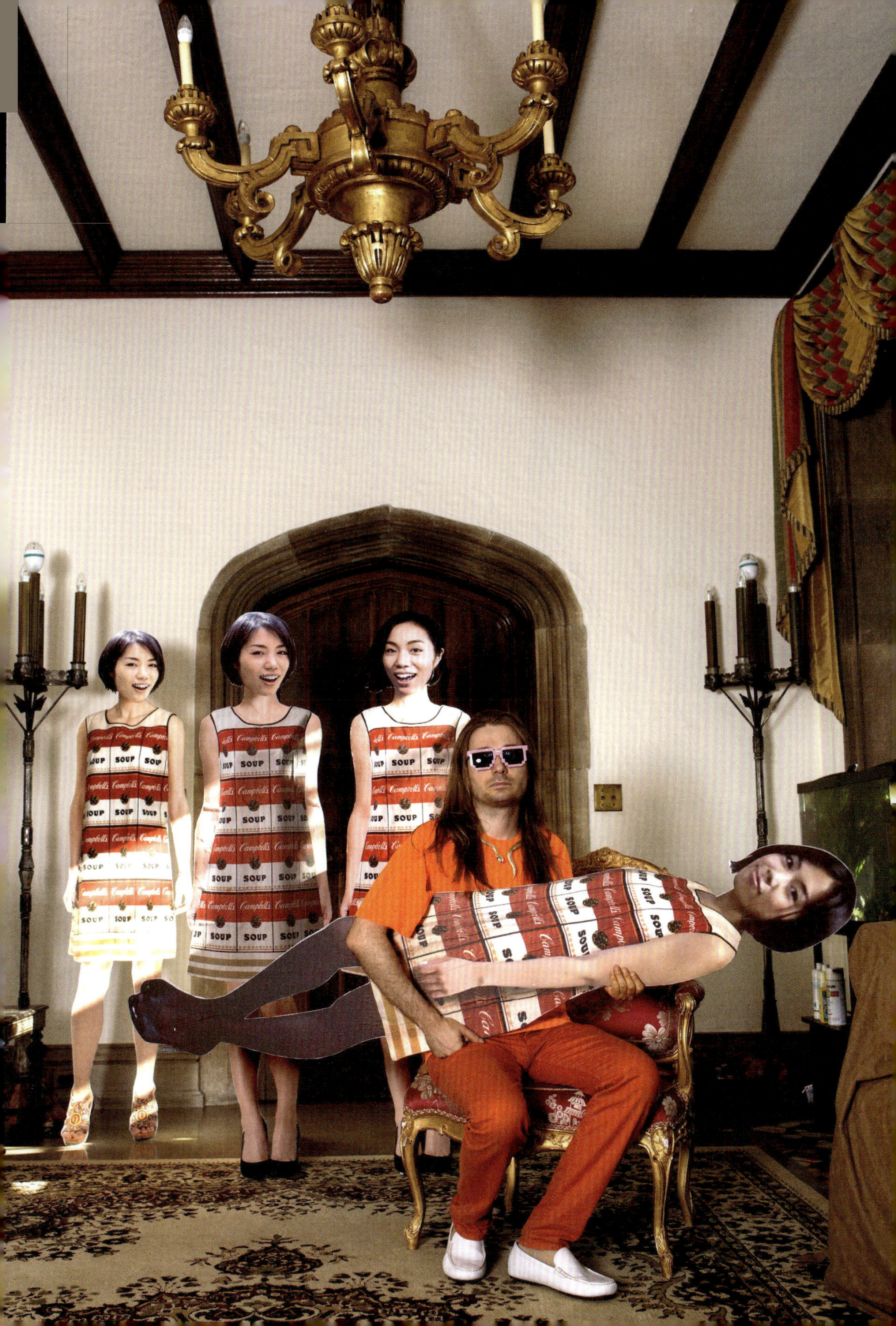
Campbell's
SOUP

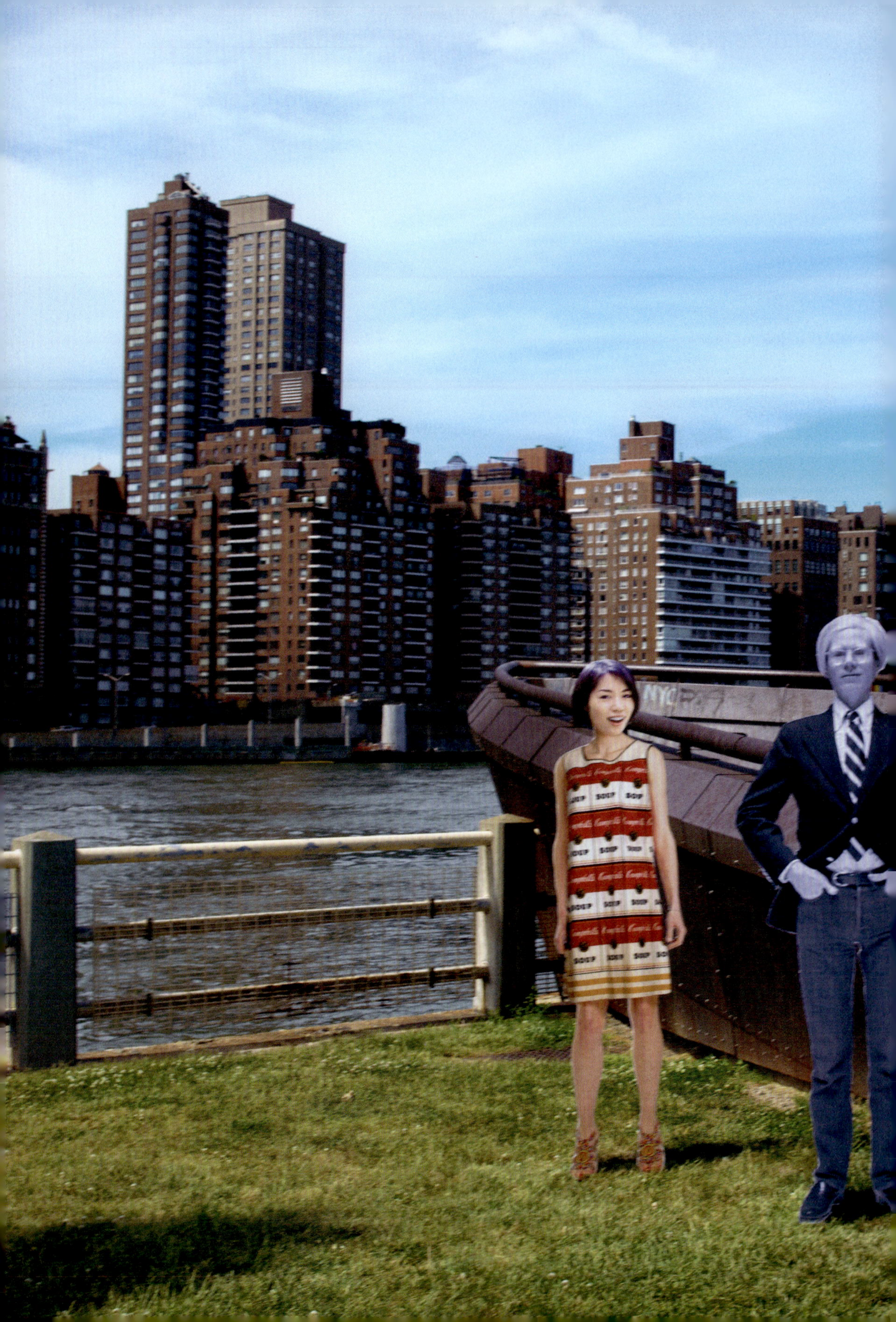

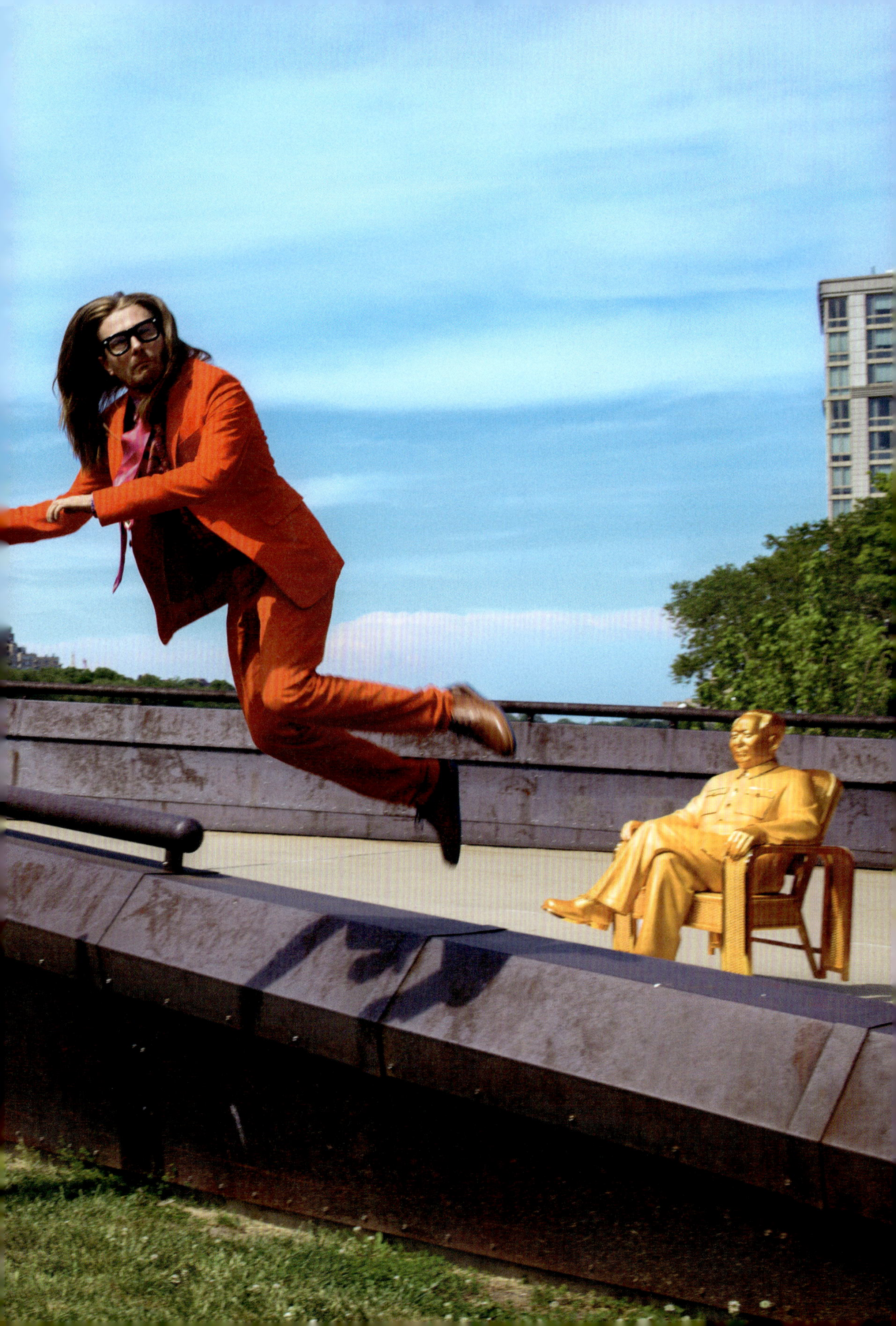

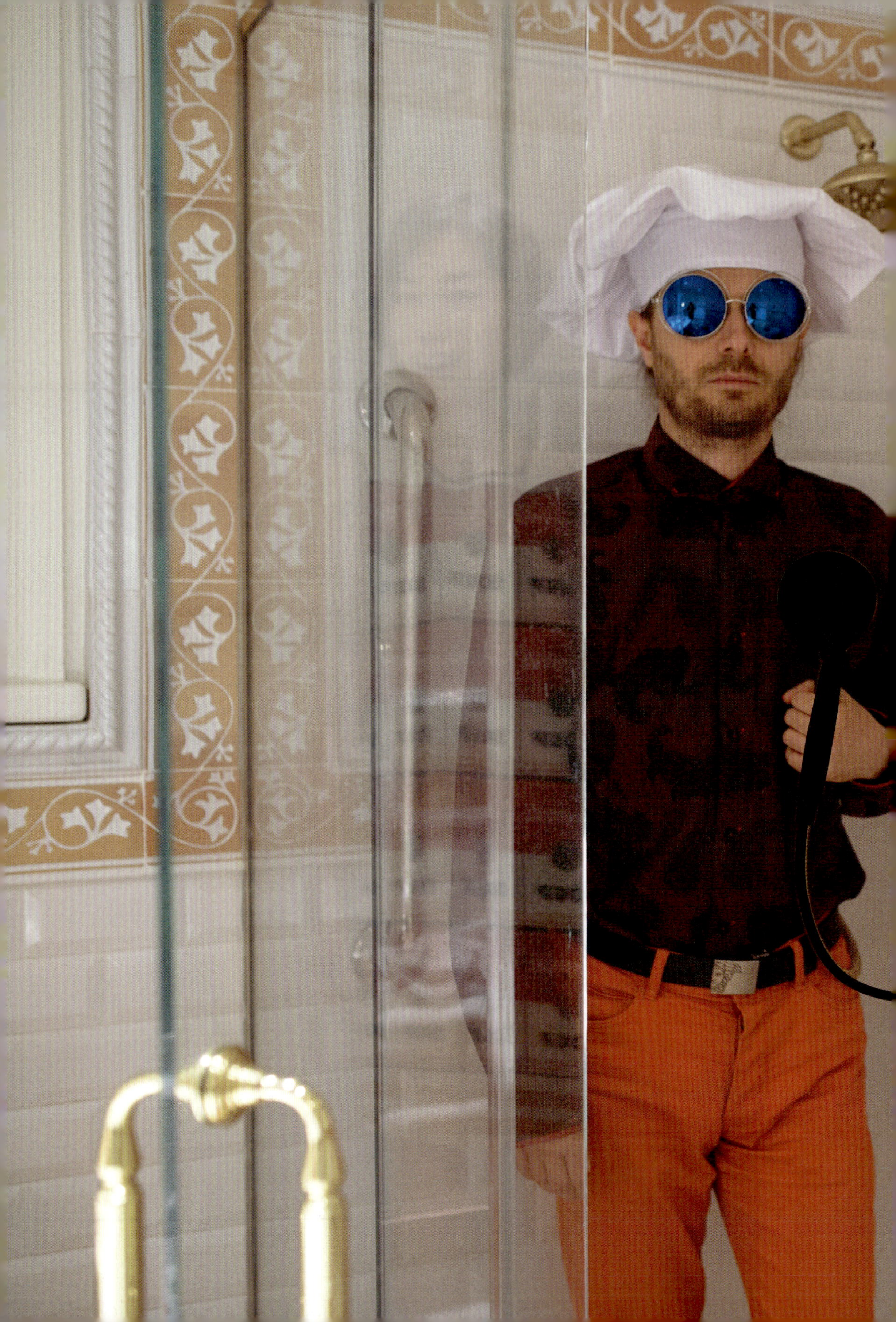

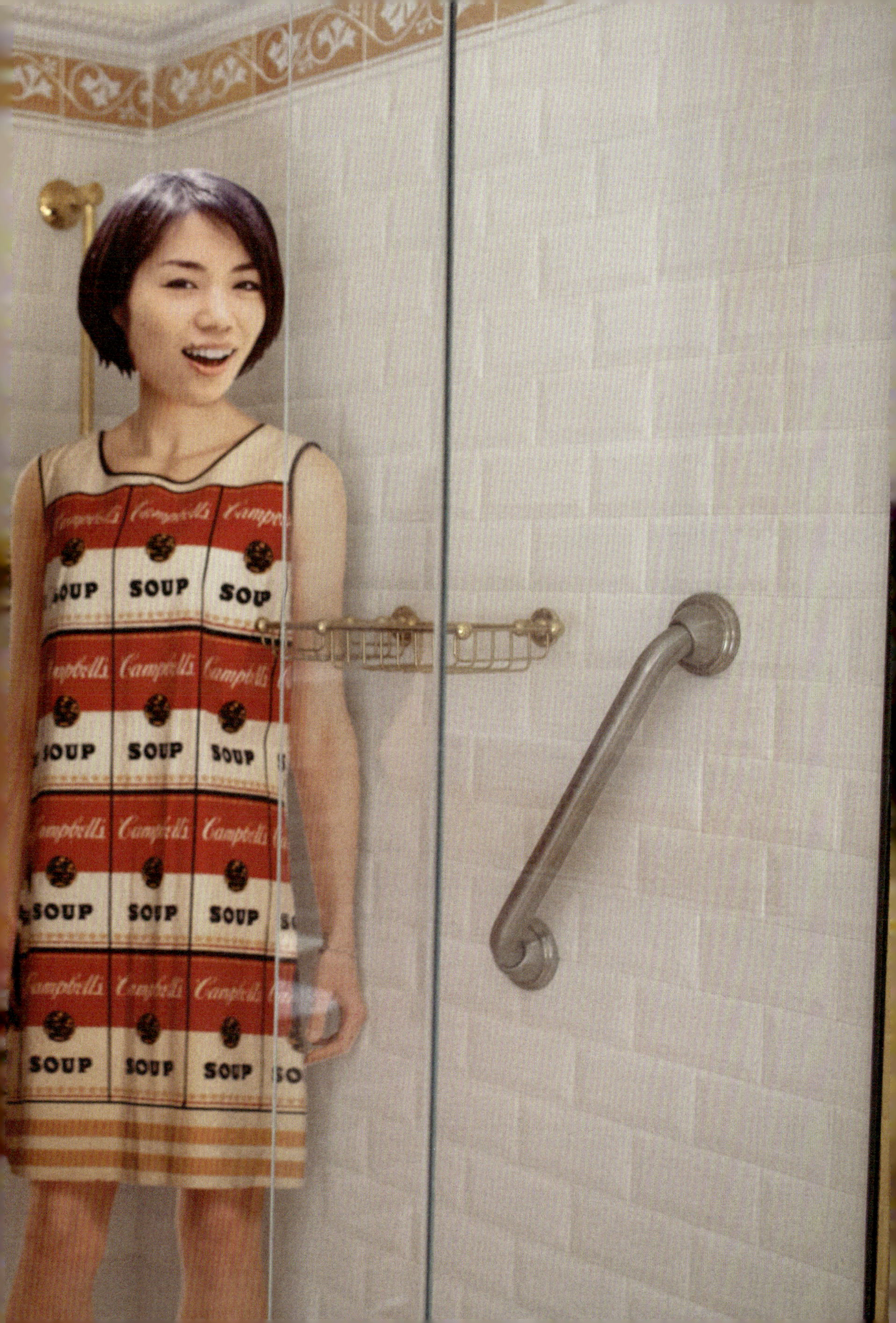
Campbell's
SOUP

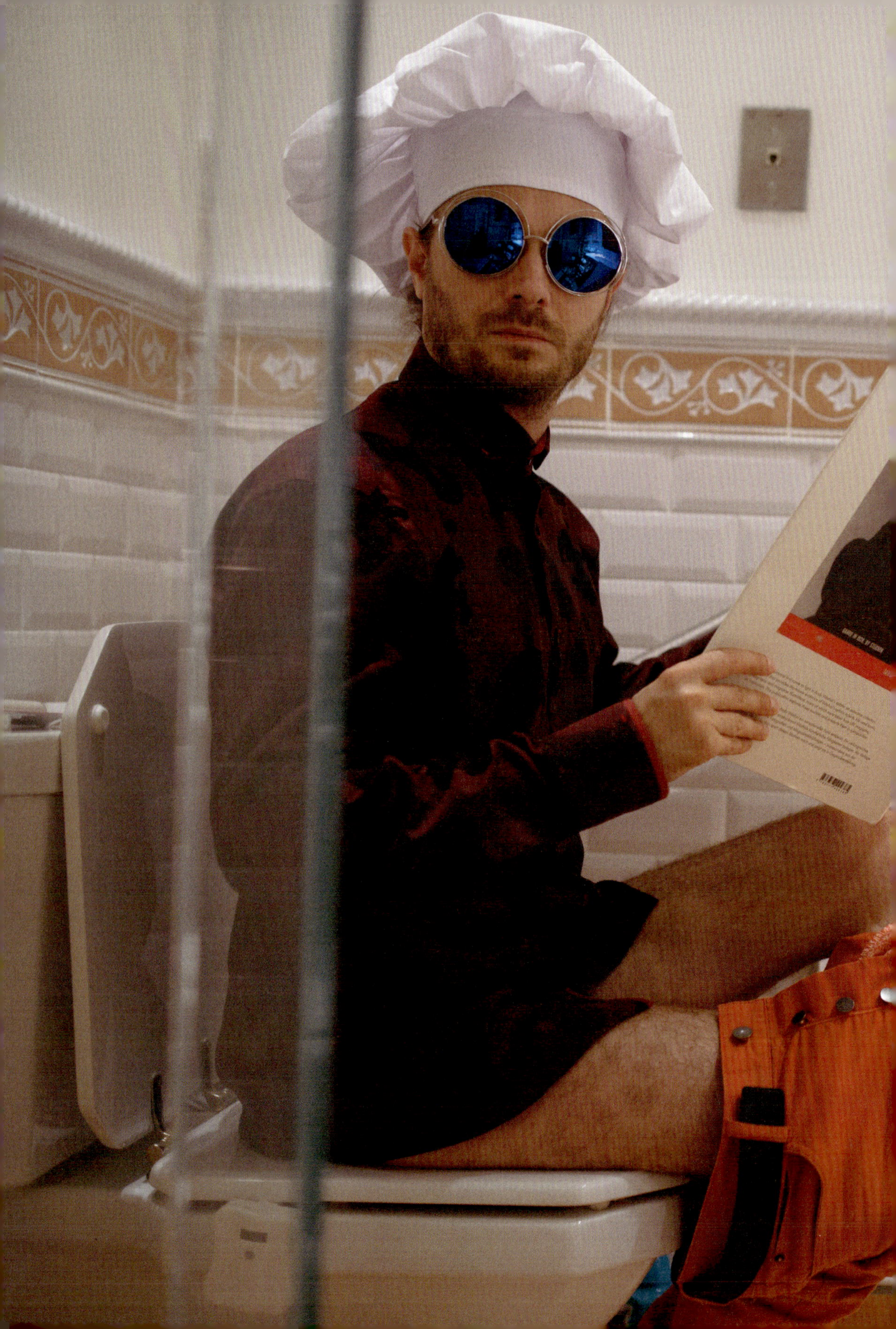

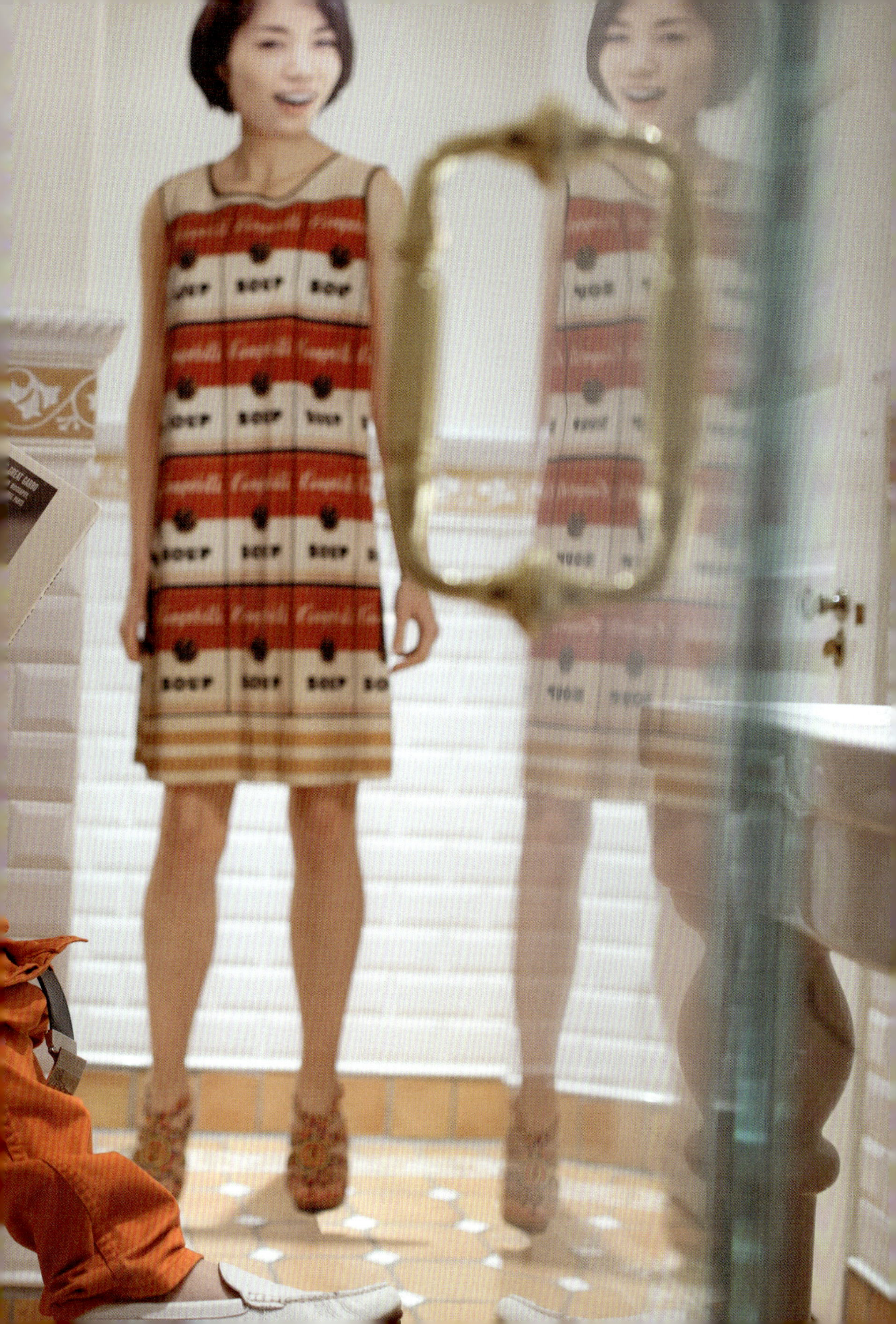
SOUP

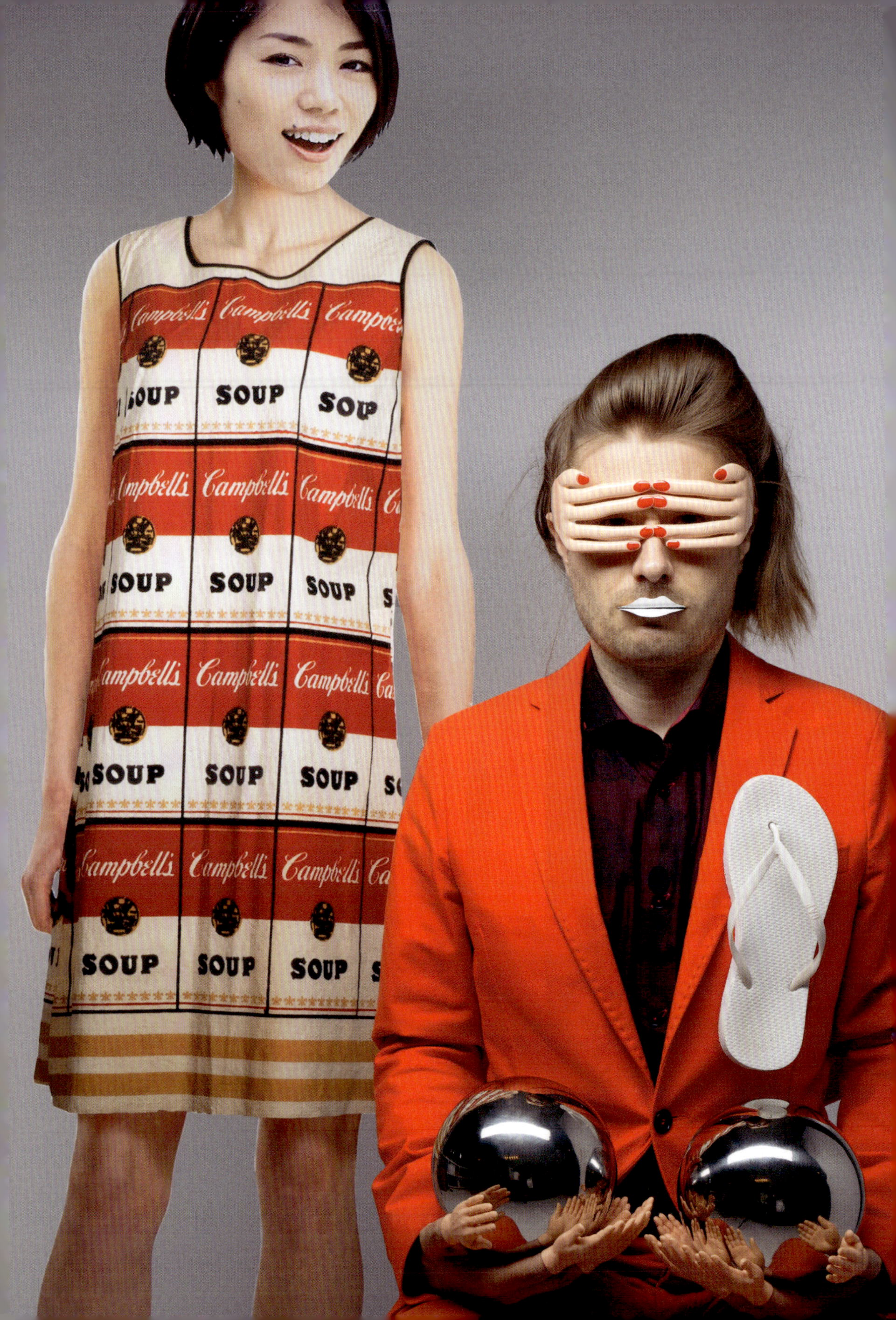
Campbell's
SOUP

wall of my egoism?"

Why did she decide to pursue extreme, violent measures? Did the pictures that I showed in the gallery really bring her such oppressive suffering? Why do I refuse to believe that such suffering could truly be? Could a third party reconcile us? Could I be so magnanimous as to understand her motives? Could she forgive me?

What do I know about her? Was I cruel as well? Maybe it's that I haven't understood her? Did I sufficiently understand what she wanted from interacting with me? Do I know how she got through her illness?

The emptiness of the silent air encouraged Hans to descend into the darkness and the hospitality of an underground reality. He walked, puzzled, like a plastic doll, surveying the mannequins in the windows along Fifth Avenue. One mannequin, two, three.

Despite the dominance of logic most of the time, sometimes emotions would overwhelm Hans to the point where his soul completely separated from the hemispheres of thought. And the only thing that Hans felt at those times was the peppery sting of defenselessness when faced with a situation in life that toggled the switch on the tracks whenever it wanted. These tramlines of his turmoil were always headed downhill.

Hans walked towards home, losing his way, counting the stoplights that halted him at the crossroads of the cell membranes of Manhattan. In Downtown, he decided that he should drink something strong. Maybe that would help him figure things out and sober up. Hans knew all the scenes of his story that would follow and wanted to jump out of it.

He never went to bars. They were too dark. And too noisy. He didn't like any of the drinks or cocktails from the bar. He didn't understand how to use them.

Hans asked the bartender for a double whiskey. The barman

winked understandingly as if he had truly read Hans' thoughts in a nanosecond. Thoughts that were for him, a bartender, trivial in the face of his entire life experience. People's complexity multiplied only in nuances of variation—the color of someone's hair, the number of nerve endings—but on the whole, the chessboard was the same, and the bartender understood all this without even having to ask.

Hans took all his whiskey in one swig. And it was as if, for a second, he felt better. Colors softened. The questions began hiding in the fog of people and twinkling lights.

"It could have all gone differently," thought Hans. "Maybe I shouldn't have taken that picture with Andy Warhol, and then there would have been no court? Maybe I should have written her more letters to flood her with them? Or was it a bigger mistake to let her go that night? I should have tied her up, put tape over her mouth, and waited until the morning! And then in the morning we could have gone to city hall and signed the marriage certificate, or whatever it's called. She's Japanese; she's malleable. She wouldn't have dared to resist. And then in the evening went with her to Tokyo on the next flight. Met her parents. Headed to Okinawa. And loved her there for eternity, for my entire life, until the end of time, and longer."

"What, did you break your heart somewhere?" the professional thinker and bartender understandingly interrupted Hans's introspection, advocating for a third whiskey.

"She unfriended me on Facebook," Hans began at full gallop, wanting like never before to be open, "and recommended friends of her friends to do the same and to block me."

"That's not the worst thing. Copy–Paste, Copy–Paste: terabytes of information, DDoS attacks! Get another account and friend her again. Friend her friends of friends. Be a man. Make ten accounts! A hundred Facebooks! Have you heard of fractals? What's your name?"

"Hans."

"I'm Jason," he held out his hand. "So OK, Hansy. Listen up. Stop sniveling. You need to go all out on her! From all different types of gadgets. They love consistency, onslaughts, and attention..."

"But she said she'd take me to court." Hans didn't let up. "She said she'd sue me to the skies. Those were her words. She would hire a team of the best lawyers in Brussels; she would put me away for a hundred years and sue me for three million dollars for every year I'm away. Totaling eighty-seven million dollars. She'd file a complaint with the Hague Tribunal, and no country in the world will let me in. I'll fly on planes from airport to airport my whole life in search of a prison that's willing to take me. I'll die in the air of pneumonia and contrition at the age of ninety-nine, attached to an artificial reading machine and a genetically modified organism feeding apparatus. They'll put an electronic bug with a web camera up my rear so that they can see over the internet how I'm decomposing from the inside. At that point, I won't even be a vegetable, more like something akin to a small collection of plastic bags with wires. She'll be drinking sake, splashing around with her lovers in an 温泉, lighting incense. And I'll be sneezing from prison tuberculosis. And you know, she's already done it. Her dreams have come true."

Hans pulled the court decision from his bag and proffered it to the bartender. The bartender moved his face close to the paper with a look of concentration. He most likely wouldn't understand what it said or even what it was.

"Don't get so hot under the collar," he soothed with a serious look. "It's just a piece of paper. Save your strength for what's most important. Don't worry. You'll fuck her."

Hans was overcome with disgust. That interpretation of his feelings demeaned him.

"You'd be better off knocking another one back for confidence."

And Hans drank his fourth glass of whiskey. A Ferris wheel immediately began spinning in his head, happy imps were jumping all around the seats, teasing Hans and making dark matter grimaces, and the wind swayed the spinning wheel so much that Hans had to hold on to the bar so as not to fall accidentally. The battery of bottle cannons behind the barman who mixed drinks so deftly began to spark and point its barrels at the drinkers, illuminated with weak light.

"OK," Hans thought foggily. "Five hundred thousand. I can borrow a thousand each from my friends and other people I know. All I need is five hundred people..." Hans opened up his telephone contact list with hope. There were eighty-four people on it. "OK, five hundred minus eighty-four is four hundred sixteen..." Hans continued his calculations. "I could put away two hundred dollars every month. That means I would have to work one hundred seventy-three years. Maybe they'll invent eternal life soon? At least for debtors."

"Or maybe I could invest the borrowed money in bonds and get inside a cryogenic chamber for a hundred years to pay off my debt when it accumulates enough interest. To solemnly arise, shake off the nitrogen and snow, wipe off my hands that have been soaking for a hundred years in formaldehyde, and happily head towards the bank for the interest. On the other hand, all these bonds and derivatives... Can you trust a bank for a hundred seventy-three years?"

"Listen, dude, a little math here." The bartender continued reading his mind. "There are three billion women on Earth. And two billion nine hundred eighty-three thousand of them are lonely and waiting for their prince right now. If that one you've got there doesn't want to, why should the others suffer because of your stubbornness? I live in Brooklyn. You should come by. I know everyone there. We'll smoke something nice, chill. Everything will be alright."

It was as if Hans was ashamed that he couldn't be inspired in time by people who desired only the best for him. It seemed that life and people were created only to serve and comfort, and he, the ungrateful pig, was angry with the people around him for his own bad luck instead of blaming himself. "Yes, I'm an ungrateful pig. I want to remain an ungrateful pig," bitter Hans said either seriously or just for the nice sound. He already didn't want to reply to the bartender as if he were sitting inside his own glass of alcohol with a lid on top.

He asked for the check, immediately paid, and headed towards the exit. The crowd was buzzing, watching football on the big screen. All Hans knew about it was the color of the field and the sky. Some guys with helmets hyped up and drove crazy the rest of the men, who were following from the tables and the bar. Their girlfriends, trying not to get excited, respectfully and serenely nestled up to the men, simply condoning the passionate intensity. It was a real feast for the spirit, and no one had any interest in Hans.

For the life of him, he couldn't get that crinkled piece of paper with the court decision back into his bag. His hands weren't following his wishes. He wasn't completely sober, and he felt that the truth of what was happening had touched fiery live wires to his throat and reason. It burned him with a few thousand volts and loosened his infusible tongue.

"Yes, I want to suffer! I want to sit in prison for my debt—for a crime of which I am not guilty!" Hans began his eccentric speech while scrambling towards the door:

"I stole feelings!"

"Take me; I'm a thief!"

"I should be in jail!"

One of the TVs in the bar was giving the weather report. "A winter storm is heading toward New York from the Atlantic." A girl in a summer suit and a short skirt carelessly cut by a designer was opining on winter, knowing nothing about it, with a pointer in her hand. As if she were the tamer of the ice, ready to melt right under the heat of her unabashed TV legs hidden somewhere below the screen. She promised that the series of low-pressure areas were coming from the east and that the weather for the next month would be snowier than any New York has seen in its meteorological history.

It seemed to Hans that the snow began falling right there in the bar, covering the tables with a white blanket. Everything around was turning white: snow maidens were standing at the hostess station, white clouds had crowded below the ceiling, distributing snow and eternal cold to the patrons, fully powdered from head to toe.

Hans' condition was already difficult to describe with any rational words. He didn't find a formula that would help him calmly accept what his fair trial had done to him. Victorious, the justice of the justice system had properly drawn its fiscal pattern on his face. "I'm a criminal!" Hans wasn't stopping.

"I jumped off the Berlin Wall!"

Finally, he laboriously made it through the crowd in the bar's small entryway onto the street. On the cold, wet, slippery sidewalk, after a few initial unsure steps, he slipped and fell. And lying on his back in a puddle, he continued screaming:

"I shot Andy Warhol!"

"I should die in prison!"

Mouseclicks of the world, unite!

CHAPTER 32

On the northern end of Roosevelt Island, in a small park, there are public barbeque grills for communicating the happiness of summer days to the stomachs of those relaxing from work. The grills serve no use in winter, gloomily turning into the fish scales of urban corrosion. Hans traveled to the island by tramway car so he could look at the span of the East River from a decent height. He took a backpack full of old photographs with him, many of which were developed in Berlin, and a large photograph of his father sitting on a chair in a river. This photo, in a frame, hung over Hans' bed, first in Florida and then in New York.

The small park was deserted. Summer disappeared from it even faster than from Manhattan, and people were no longer interested in rehashing their worries when they arrived on the north end.

Hans carefully took the large photograph from its frame, moved it close to his face, and looked for a long time at the figure of his young father sitting on the bentwood chair in the middle of the river. The quarks of the past began to cover the lenses of his eyes in grains of faded black-and-white film; he saw that day outside the limits of the picture frame. From the other side of the lens, he saw himself: a happy, bright-faced boy, enthusiastically photographing the sitting silhouette in the moonlight scenery. Hans folded the photo into quarters and placed it in the barbecue grill. He made a tidy little house with the other photos and placed them on top so that the wind could look at them from underneath.

The wind blew the first match out. The second, with a small

tongue of flame, began to eat the corner of the of the largest photograph. The paper house burned quickly, blown by the indifferent wind. Small pieces of the blackened, destroyed paper flew into the sky. Hans tried not to watch how the arms, legs, and smiling face were enveloped by the creeping black lava and turned into ash. He gathered all the remaining ash together into a tin box and headed off towards the north end of the island. There Hans leaned towards the fence that separated the island from the water. He stared at the patterns of the river that was slowly flowing by him. The water sketched strange drawings and shapes, sometimes wrapping itself into little vortices and sometimes building straight lines of water. It seemed like the speed of the current was different and like the water's smooth surface was imperceptibly retreating. The thick, dark color of the river attracted the eye and called one along with it to otherworldly life, where maybe it was sadder, but it was also easier due to the slowness and deafness of the cold stagnation.

He dropped the tin box filled with ashes in the water, and it floated south to meet the ocean, where everyone who fits into the cinders would be more joyful and at peace in eternity. For some time, it slowly flowed down along with the current until Hans finally lost sight of the sinking ship.

He returned home when the sun, woven from ice, had already set behind the mummy of buildings. The day had become very short, and even the sun didn't want to shine. Hans had nothing left to think about. Nothing was of interest to him anymore. He pitied and despised that blandness in himself.

Feeling a meeting with Yuma coming with the force of all the years that had been fully lived in advance, Hans was completely equipped for this meeting. Yuma was walking around New York in the same state of anticipation. Hans wanted to live because of her.

He wanted to bring life to her. He was just a bit surprised that a brief moment with her was stronger than the entirety of his past life, and even more so, his future one. This absurdity now tortured him with its seeming insignificance.

He again replayed the day when he would be able to not let her go. Not let her go home. Get in the plane, hide in her suitcase, or pretend to be the bass guitar.

Every day was an unbearable nightmare. Hans' feelings were overgrown with an irreversible sorrow, and it was already difficult for him to scramble out from between the branches of everyday life. The morning began with persuasion. He had to get up for work, but there was no desire to do so. Every bland day literally began by lying in the comfy cocoon of the couch, among his entreaties to himself just to live a little bit longer. Or just to live happier than he was. Or to pretend. Not to pressure-feed the niggling sadness that had laid the carpet in the sticky room, but to air it out.

Hello, sadness. You are inscribed in the lines on the ceiling.

Every day he had to argue with himself to justify the necessity of all these movements of outer and ornamental activity.

Pull on that smile like a cold pair of pants.

Hans opened the window and looked in a long stupor at the wall of the building across the way. The frozen bricks reminded him of his situation—no change, no possibility of breaking out of the cement. Hans' feelings were just and, thus, unbearable. His heart understood that there was no real reason to look for a way out of the long suffering and now slowly burned within a quatrain of walls. Hans' strained voice, tired from the contradictions and struggle, contained a shade of a potent poison. "I want to break records! I want to live!" Hoarse Hans shouted the question to the window.

The streetlights shone outside. It was snowing. Snowing.

CHAPTER 33

Hans hanged himself at dawn in Central Park. On the small island close to Belvedere Castle. The sky was still dark and cloudy. A fog carpeted the pond with a melancholic chill, the white lipstick of mourning skulking about the park.

The park was deserted and quiet. The water lapped onto the little island emotionlessly and peacefully. It would be quite a horrifying picture for anyone coming to the island from the castle. It was the beginning of December. Small snowflakes were falling everywhere, turning the dark landscape into a canvas thickly covered in gouache paint, where the tree branches became first wet and then had a layer of snow glued on, like a puffy layer of dough. There were practically no leaves left on the trees. The island was sheathed by high bushes, in which half of Hans' body hung hidden.

It was a terrible death, unworthy of him. The physical suffering that completely disfigured the soul before death changed Hans to the point where he was unrecognizable on the outside too. In an attempt to free himself from the noose, he tried to reach the ground with his feet, but the futility of his efforts only increased his torture.

There was something oppressive and additionally hopeless in his act as if suicide wasn't enough. He needed a loud scream of despair. He, disfigured and tortured, wanted to remain a monstrous sculpture, chiding the rest to live for all the inattention and cynicism with which they burned away what they were given and enjoyed it.

The location Hans had chosen, under normal circumstances romantic and cheerful, only enormously intensified the guilt that would be felt by someone who might know him or have played soccer with him. By those who loved that clearing, which on warm days was full of joyful people, baby carriages covered with sheets, sleepy and inattentive nannies, cold ice cream, and colorful balloons. A toy castle against the backdrop of the sky, with a princess secreted away inside.

That happy time had now evaporated into the overcast heavens, leaving next to it on the island only a bitter note on the past. A feeling of guilt that was impossible to reconcile.

It's hard to admit that the bustle of life is what makes us blind in the most simple and obvious situations. When a person needs help or support, we're not even capable of seeing the tiniest speck of the trouble of his condition. We run past the drowning reaching out their hands to us, yell angrily in response to tears, are afraid that our answers might contain some love, laugh at the pure and straightforward. We don't believe in death, wiping it from the panes of our eyes. We cross out names from our address books and turn away from the departed when they are still with us.

New York is a traitor.

A cold city of deception.

New York, a hard-hearted concrete monster where no one cares about anyone else. Where no one cares about the dead. And almost no one cares about the living.

It was quiet on the lake. Winter had justified its indifference with silence. Another heavy snowfall began, and the storm dropped the burning white mounds all around Central Park. Hans' body, hanging on a rope near the earth itself, quickly turned into a pile of snow that no one would think was a person.

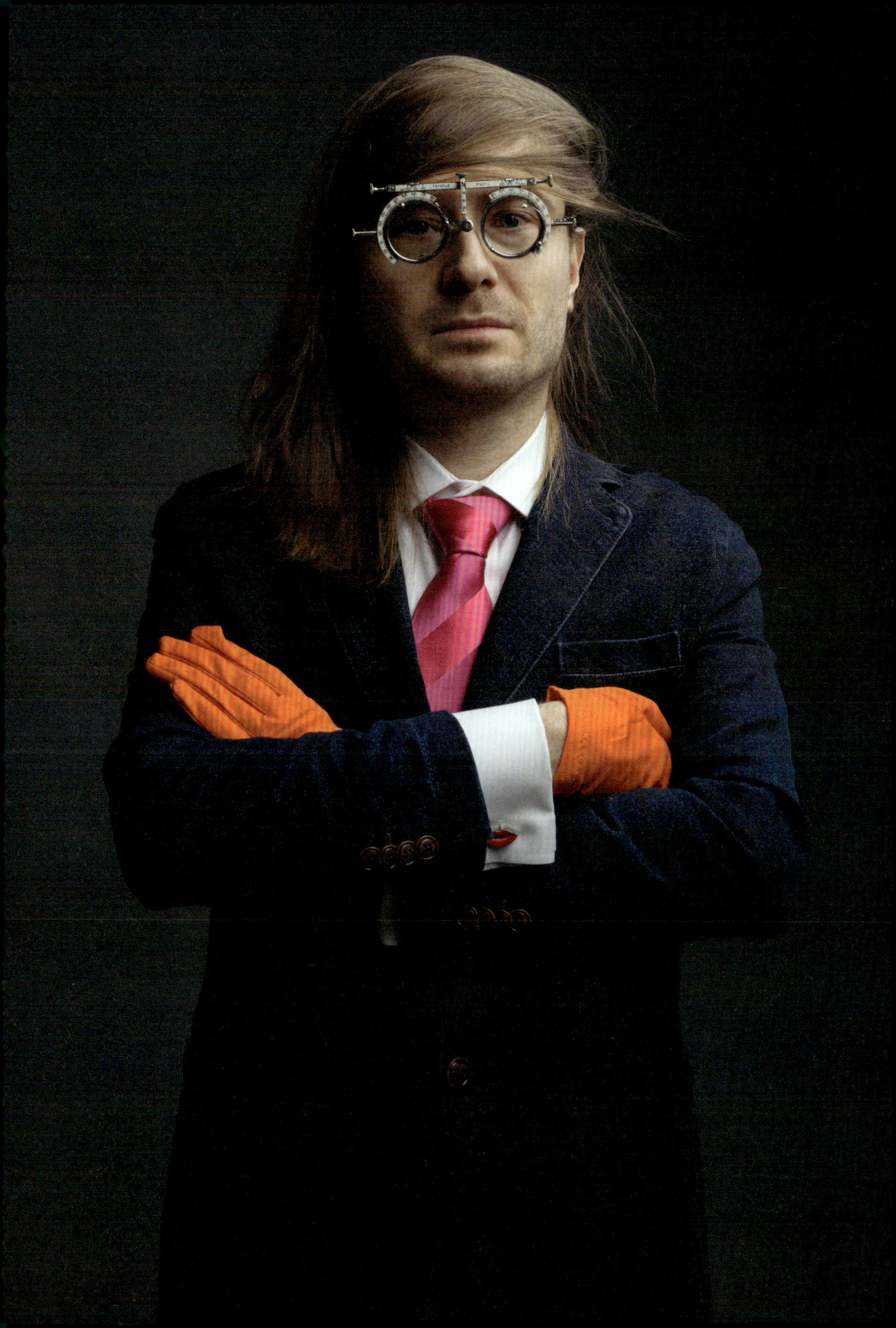

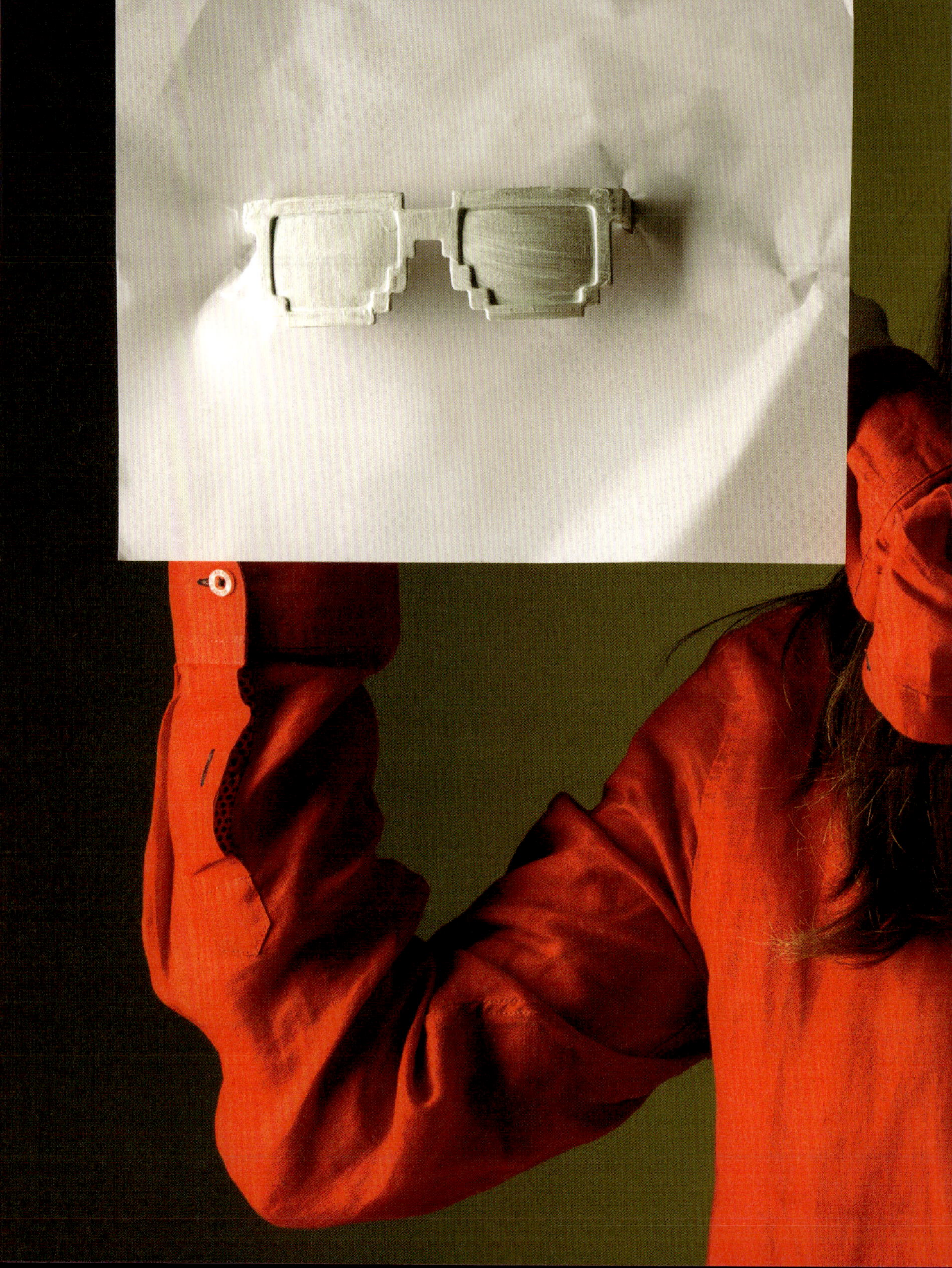

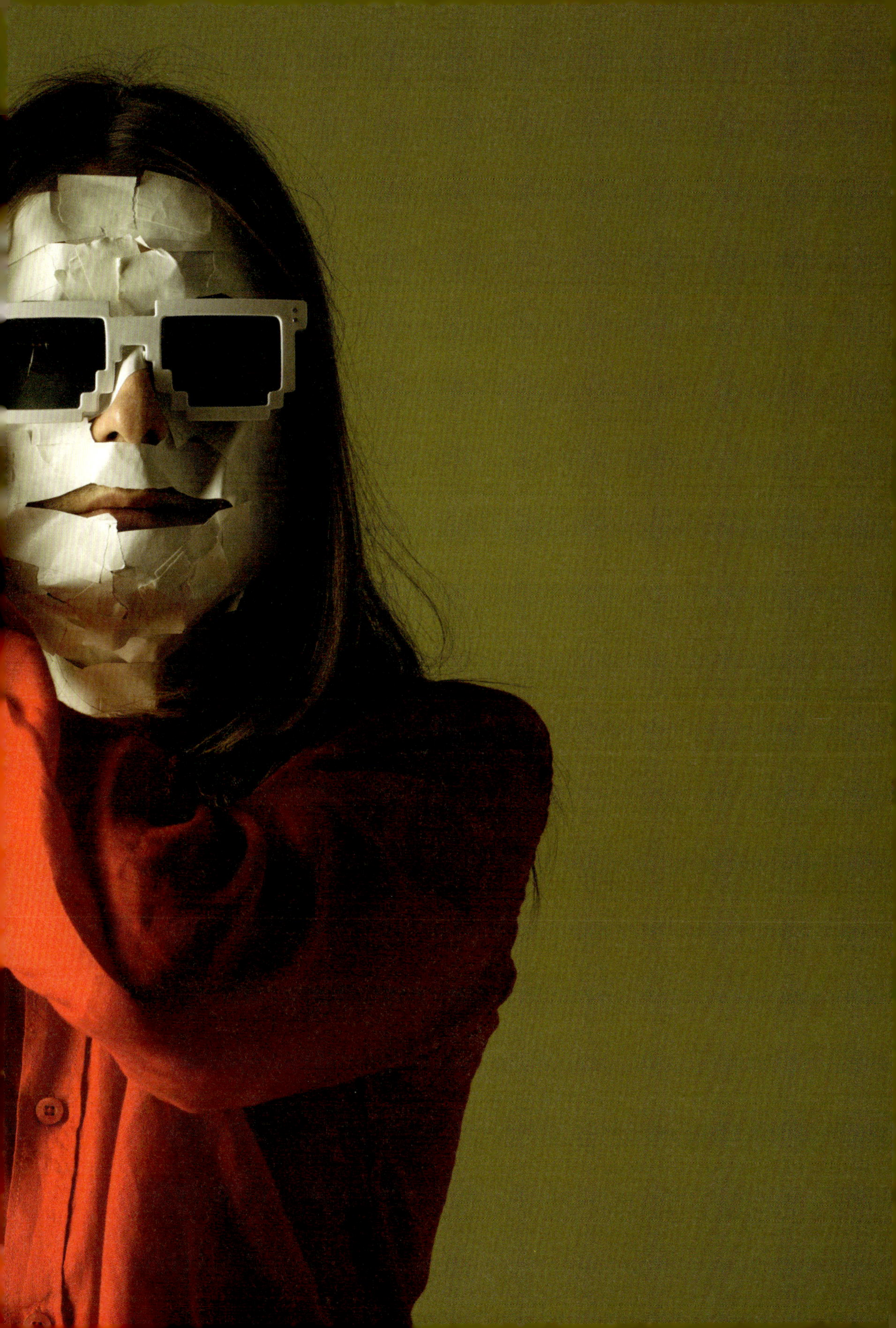

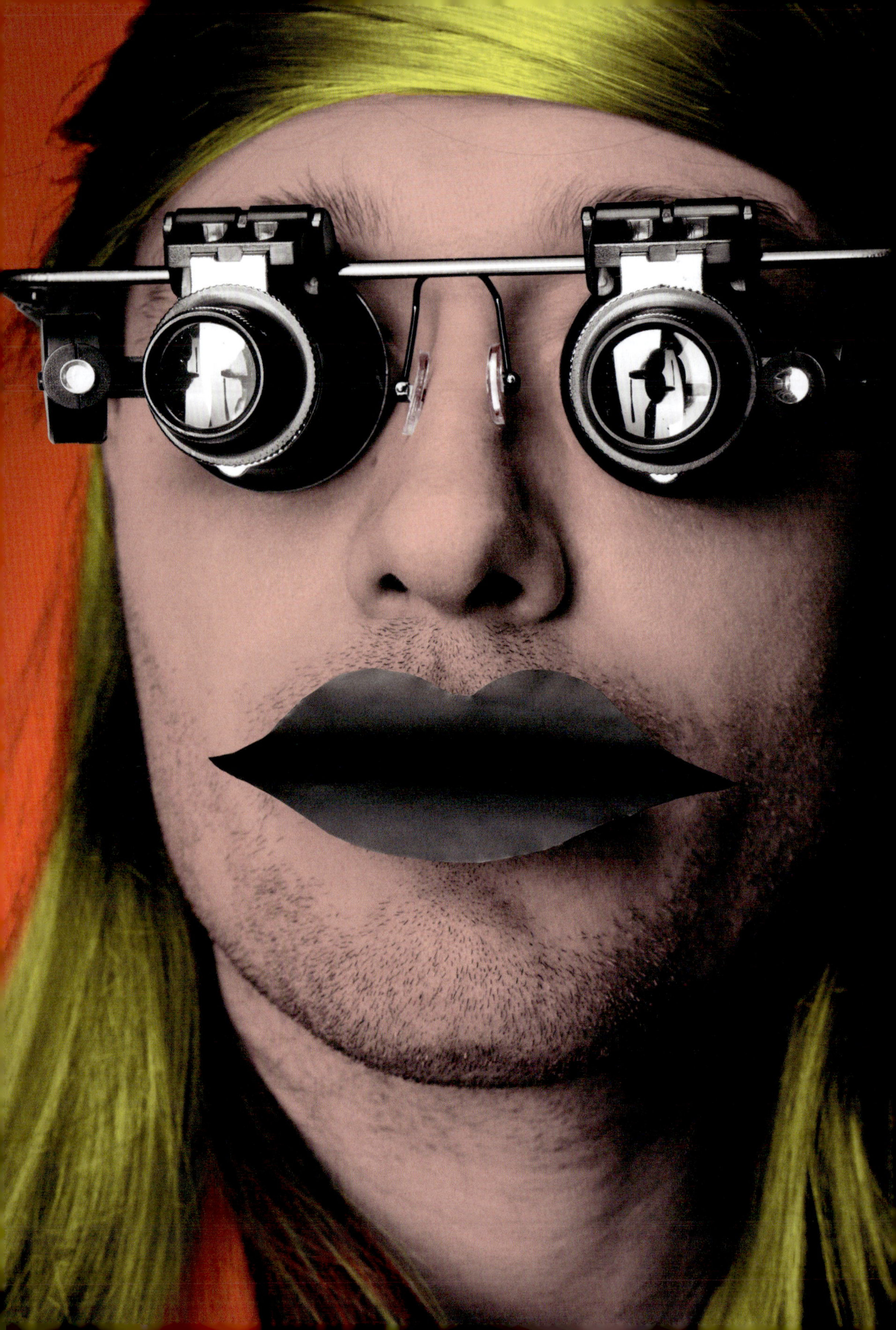

CHAPTER 04

Dear Yuma!
Do you remember you said that you played Led Zeppelin in school? You told me how you hid the sheet music from your mom under your pillow and then, with a flashlight, would learn it under the blanket, strumming the strings of a small guitar.

At that time, I was on the other side of the globe, soldering a shortwave radio receiver with my father in the kitchen. A cassette of Led Zeppelin was playing. The flies that had awoken were buzzing around. Outside the window was the smell of blue lilac and a burning spring. Hi. Or Greetings? What's the best thing to write under the cast-iron groan of Jimmy Page? Under the sounds of a mammoth. Under an echo of the past? Under the cognac of the music?

Hello, my dear! How unfree I am in my unfreedom that starting a letter seems like one of the greatest tortures. And instead of disclosing my feelings, I must count every letter, like an entomologist watchmaker with a magnifying glass taming the gears. As if I would get a bad grade for the wrong answer. I'm still like a schoolboy with you. I want to tell you about all the things I didn't share in previous letters. When you have a lot on your mind, you don't want to miss even the most insignificant detail.

New York. Six in the evening. Central Park. I'm sitting on the hard granite rocks of home, above the lush grass, observing life and thinking of you. Everything here is still sunny and hot. I'd gladly give myself over to this heat as if it would be able to make me closer to you and our retreating summer.

My Algiers! My hot wind!

I call you to Central Park with the strength of my thoughts. I'm here often. I hope to see you one day, to run to meet you until my legs give out. There's an errant woodpecker swimming near me in this dust, gracefully preening its wings. I want to be small with him, to glisten in my gold coating and fly away. It's such a pity I don't have wings! If I had them, I would fly to you right now, without thinking, from the branch of this hundred-year-old sycamore. September. There are heaps of fallen leaves around; nature is breaking out in new movement. Yellow leaves, different forms, and hundreds of shades. The wind invariably carries them along, like little carpets for the earth, so that it can sleep covered, without disturbance or cold, until next spring. If I can't wait for you, my darling, I suppose I'll fall asleep too. Just wake me up in April.

In spring, when it's so pleasant in New York, the sakura trees bloom in Central Park, their pink petals strewn all over. On 花見, you'll come to the park to admire the flowers with me. You'll sit next to me on the rock, and our thoughts will fly to your motherland, your home, towards the pink rays of the setting sun reflected in your window.

For hours I sit and imagine Japan. What is it like, that weightless, elegant, silent, melancholic country? It seems impossible how much I've mulled over the details. When I imagine the concrete buildings, I want to smell them, taste them with my tongue, feel their flavor. They seem so dollish and quaint. Their toy-like nature is thanks to the child builders, who, after putting on their construction helmets, went to play with plastic bulldozers—and that's how Tokyo was built. It seems to me that the people of Tokyo are like big children. They go to work, play with their pink elephants, their rattles, their metal toy cars, and their dolls. Even the gray-haired old men on the Tokyo stock exchange are blowing up pink balloons and tooting horns. And for lunch, the grown-up ladies come by to give them their farina—just like in kindergarten. Maybe this isn't true, but I so want people in Japan to stay little, as everyone should in a magical land, with their mothers always young. Do not think that I'm too naïve or anything like that. Children with niratama-gayu rice porridge caked on their pants. Holding plastic dolls. Children who ride on tricycles that effortlessly fly in the air.

Japan. House of the rising sun.

Japan, flooded with the sun. Japan, showered with gardens. Japan, napping in the fog of the mountain ravines. Japan, frozen for a second to sync the clocks. Japan, blooming flowers for the whole world. Japan, the gift of love. Japan, the house of contemplation.

I wonder what street you live on in Tokyo. What's it called? What does it look like? If you read this letter, maybe you can send me a postcard? From a place where you ran around barefoot and made your first friends. I'd look at that postcard every day and imagine what else was around: shops, paths, little gardens with trees, wires hanging like a web over the road. And what neighborhood in Tokyo do you live in, Yuma? If you tell me the name, I'll revel in it, that word. I want to feel every trifle of your life and every note of your mood.

I definitely need to meet your mom. We'd get along well. I could even help her out around the house if we lived nearby. We would be one big, loving family. Our parents are similar. I see that in you. I mean, they make up fifty percent of you. But you're better. You're better than anyone on Earth. You've bloomed in the twilight of the planet. The soft waves of your smile drive thousands of people on the streets insane, and they become perpetual prisoners of your charisma. I'm your captive too. The biggest one, who doesn't fit inside any package.

I had the idea to take a series of photographs called "One thousand of your smiles that I've never seen." It wouldn't even be portraits—only your lips. When we live together, I'll start taking the first shots. They'll be big pictures, full of feeling, contemplating you. You'll be filled with artistic rays that I will collect in my camera. I can make you look more complicated, more elegant, closer, more wonderful. I adore your little sly smile! It's like a mooncake made of soft sneers and startling beauty that pulls the feelings of the observer up by the roots.

I can't look at you when I'm looking at you! Your smile is your second sister, with whom you share everything. I can shoot photos of your lips at dawn. In near-dark in a half-smile. I can shoot them half-asleep in bed when the sun begins to melt the cold of dreams, provoking the drafts looking for a way into the room. I can catch you serious, with puffed-up cheeks. Or relaxed, with a barely noticeable smile that you give to the one who can notice it. Every day, waking up with you to see your new portrait and, through it, be free of my own "I." To just belong, to just be a soldier serving your elegance. You're not a woman. You are a Universe within Universes, the interference of eternities. You are the co-integration of all possible meanings and the incarnation of undiscovered perfections. Yuma, I love you with all my family. I love you with my father. I love you with my room. I love you with childhood.

I love everything about you: the worst in you is an unobtainable best in me!

I want to be with you in space—I want to feel spaced-out. I want to give you bottles of wine, and two-thousand-carat diamond rings every day! I want to sweep the asphalt before you wherever you go. I want to grovel before you in admiration. I want to serve you loyally and truly on the peripheries of your moods, fulfilling all your whims. I want to be your mirror, duplicating your turbulence. I want to sew dresses for you. Yes, when I was younger, I would cut and sew. I really want to sew you a dress from real silk, make you a bride. And in that dress, we'd fly to City Hall in a Ferrari racecar, where you would make me your husband! I want to get married in Tokyo next spring, in the Shinjuku Gyoen garden. You'll run from me along wooden bridges in the rays of the smiling evening sun, yourself radiant and happy, and I pretending that I can't catch you. I'll play graciously among the trees, acting like a slow and beautiful bird with colorful feathers in its tail.

And then I'll catch you. And lock you in the prison of my embrace, like the most precious African butterfly. You won't even resist. Because you're weightless, evasive, soft. I'll taste your breath, like when we were in Central Park. Deciding to kiss you is like deciding to jump into the mouth of a volcano, burn in the magma, and throw my ashen self into the sky!

To touch your waist, to embrace your shoulders is mind-blowing happiness for a sailor salted by months in the elements.

Your superconductivity melts my fuses. I want to be a Japanese robot with buzzing batteries and a wind-up key, recharging for the eternity that I will bundle up and lay at your feet, Yuma!

Do you remember that restless night when the hot wind of youth rubbed itself against our cheeks, scaring us and flying away into a thicket in Central Park? Berthollet's dream of happiness, which should have lasted a whole lifetime. Do you remember dusty, deserted, dark Harlem and the houses that, like clay pottery clustered together, hung over us with their shoddy walls? Do you remember that uneasy silence and that unshaven, long-haired German who was kissing his Japanese girl?

I want the shades of our memories to mix into soft watercolor, and together we'll blend in new hues of unexpected events. I want to ride on top of a car, lounge about in the silky sands of Okinawa and the green grass of Central Park. I want to sniff peonies in the Hamarikyu Gardens, burning the flower buds that ring quietly with dew towards evening.

Yuma, I'm your John Lennon.

I‘m your microphone.

I'm your four-stringed guitar.

I'm your balalaika and Berlin Wall!

I'm your marble elephant!

I want to cry over you for one-point-two eternities so that the wind of memory splashes my tears among the Higgs bosons, glorifying you with the depth of my sadness!

Yuma! I didn't finish telling you the words of my emotions. I didn't kiss you enough in Harlem; I underestimated you. The hands of the clock made a pumpkin of us. Doubt moved from the rustle of poems to steps on the street. From the steps to plans for the future. But there is no future! You flew away from it like a butterfly from its crunchy chrysalis.

I love walking along Fifth Avenue because there are no stoplights, and trees grow along it like in jungles. I love walking along Fifth Avenue because it was here that your shoes made your first feet hurt. I love walking along Fifth Avenue because it's here that I lost you. I love walking along Fifth Avenue because here I can find you in the blooming buds on the sakura trees! In the yellow-orange shamelessness of the sunflowers! I'll look for you in the Metropolitan Museum, in a Central Park café, in the subway, in the grass, in the sky, in the tree branches, in a glass of water, in the bubble of a Coca-Cola. In the hose of a doorman washing the street—everywhere I can, I'll be looking for you.

I miss you unimaginably!

Somewhere out there, Tokyo is clamoring, hiding you and wrapping you in its streets.

The bustle of a faraway city—the Milky Way,

smoldering in a telescope.

I need you as no one has ever needed anyone.

I was born to grasp you.

With one billion loves, my heart beats for you, asphyxiating it.

There, where feelings soak through the cracks of the summer drafts, you can hear a song that tugs at the soul, tired of living without you.

I need you like stars need telescopes. I need you like rocks in the ocean need the sea. I need you like a transistor needs a collector current. I need you like a sandwich needs a person. I need you like a tree needs a bird. I need you like a flower bud needs a ray of sunlight. I need you like a submarine needs a propeller to move through the seaweed in the depths. I need you like the prime minister needs a chair. I simply need you as the only one I need.

Yuma, please, call your parents. Tell them to call me! Let's set up a telegraph line between Japan, and we'll tap on each other's walls to communicate using the most beautiful expressions, using dictionaries and encyclopedias to help us think them up and sing them out.

Be for me my scientific and technical girlfriend and telegraph pole! Inspire me to be inspired by you even more recklessly, even more honestly!

You are my kerosene stove; you're my fuel and my rocket! Take me into the other worlds of your girlish magic. I can't pine any longer in the confinement of the dim world of GDPs and interest rates. I demand renewal! Beaches! Stars, faraway galaxies, the waves breaking on oceans of other planets, the rainbow redness of an unknown wine.

I demand a cosmic kiss in the morning x-rays of the cosmos lighting up our intergalactic ship! Yuma, the entire purpose of our lives is three trillion kisses:

3,000,000,0000,0000,00000,0000,000

And each of them will be different. In each of them, there will remain a shred of fantasy and care for you. Each will be gentle like a bumblebee is gentle as it caresses the fuzzy skin of the flower's pulp. Each of the kisses will burn on our lips, breaking the rules of astrophysics. Each will be like a security deposit, like a line from a great poem, like a television set in batter, like a grain of sand in the mountains, like bushes in a grand piano, like the melody of your flower song.

Yuma, everything is going as planned. I woke up and discovered that you were next to me. Now I just have to find you.

I'll be there soon.

To fly across the Universe to the bus stops of other worlds, we'll need provisions on our rocket. Don't worry, I know of a shop in New York. They sell a lot there. I tried to read things, but I couldn't. Reading Japanese is quite difficult.

I bought tako wasabi and crispy nori. I bought enough for us for a hundred years of our life together. Do you know that shop? You have to take an elevator to get there. There are no stairs. You have to push the button and ride to the second floor. It's a teleporter to Japan. Antigravity. Yuma. Little Yuma. The dimples from your cheeks. I looked for you there, among the carrots and marinated fish. You're still nowhere to be found. But you'll be here soon; I already feel it in the fibers of my being. There's some important reason you're keeping a low profile.

You know what I wanted to say? Living so far from one another is a bit difficult. A bit unbearable. That's life, though—a layering fog of patches of memories with false doors. But every day, I am with you, and I try to keep us fresh. To do that, I also use various modern technologies, like photographs, and your voice, which I recorded on my smartphone when you performed at the Blue Note. In me, you are the same, in no way faded under the heaviness of the slimy layers of time.

I really want to know the details of your life today, this very minute! What kind of hairstyle are you wearing? Which shampoo does your hair smell of? Maybe you could send me a lock? Or even just one eyelash?

So I can place it in an envelope with a return address touchingly written in Japanese, in the drawer of my desk, and know that you are somewhere with me. And if I want to smell your scent, I can always press my nose to that black thread of your eyelash.

Yours forever,
Hans

CHAPTER 35

The winter was unbelievably cold for New York. The temperature never got above twenty-three degrees Fahrenheit, and Central Park, it seemed, had been snowswept under the crowns of the trees, jealous of the skyscrapers' height. No one in New York wants or is even able to clear the snow if there are more than ten inches. The pond near Belvedere Castle was covered in ice, which was completely blanketed with snow. Central Park lived the lifelessness of all these long and lonely months. The wires were frozen over with white wool and had solidified because of the high voltage. City travelers feared being covered by snow in a blizzard, as they were warned about on the television waves. Adults and children walked along the hallways of their houses, looking sadly outside their windows in search of the sun, which was hidden in the cosmos behind the thousand gloomy snowflakes falling to the Earth.

There were practically no footprints on the streets. Just some squirrels jumping around, missing human company and using their coats to sweep away the white powdery blanket. The rest of the fragile animals preferred sleeping in dens, warming themselves near small wooden stoves, waiting out the pressure and brutality of winter. In the park, ice sunsets and dawns played the cosmic music of dying life. The rarely seen sun started to gnaw at the snow, but the wind froze the surface into a glazed crust, under which the rest of the fearful snow melted. A new storm cloud would arrive, and it continued like that for several months, leaving no signs of life in all of Central Park, which was sleeping, hoping that it might someday wake up for the days of spring. A woodpecker, missing southern nights and warm tree bark, pecked out a tired poem about a moving train with his typewriter into the cold black tree trunk, frozen in solidarity with all other sleepers.

***

It was the middle of March when the snow finally began melting. The ice on the pond turned into murky water. The little island broke out in black patches as the branches of the bushes and trees were being stripped, like a photograph developing in a dark room, until it finally revealed the most horrifying thing it had hidden on itself all winter long. The police officer in the boat was in no hurry to get to the island. He was in no rush to examine what the park workers had seen upon the shore.

The boat silently docked on the dark stony coastline. The stones were covered in a moss blackened by winter but which, in places, had retained their emerald color. The tree branches, awakened from their long illness, drooped with wires tangled into knots.
The police officer took a few steps towards the tree, crunching old autumn branches underfoot. The scene he was taking in was grizzly.

The murders he normally had to deal with were more prosaic and rough. This is why they were more understandable, and in those cases, his eyes were used to it. Here, though, the breath of death was clearly mixed with the lack of a good reason for it, as if there was no real need for it to have happened, nor any need for the method used in this heart-wrenching suicide. The paints used to design this exit, and the possible content of the tragedy made even the concrete

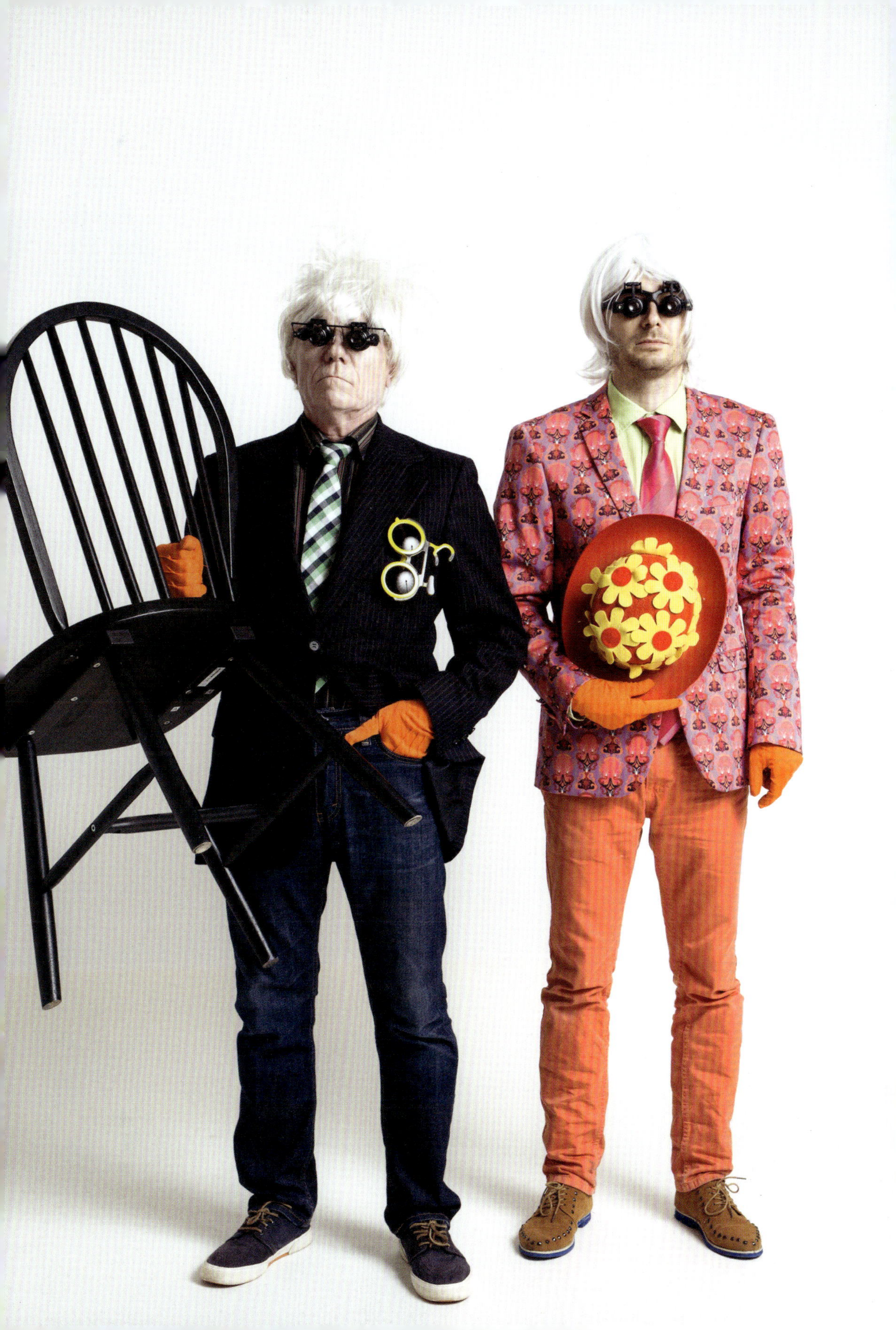

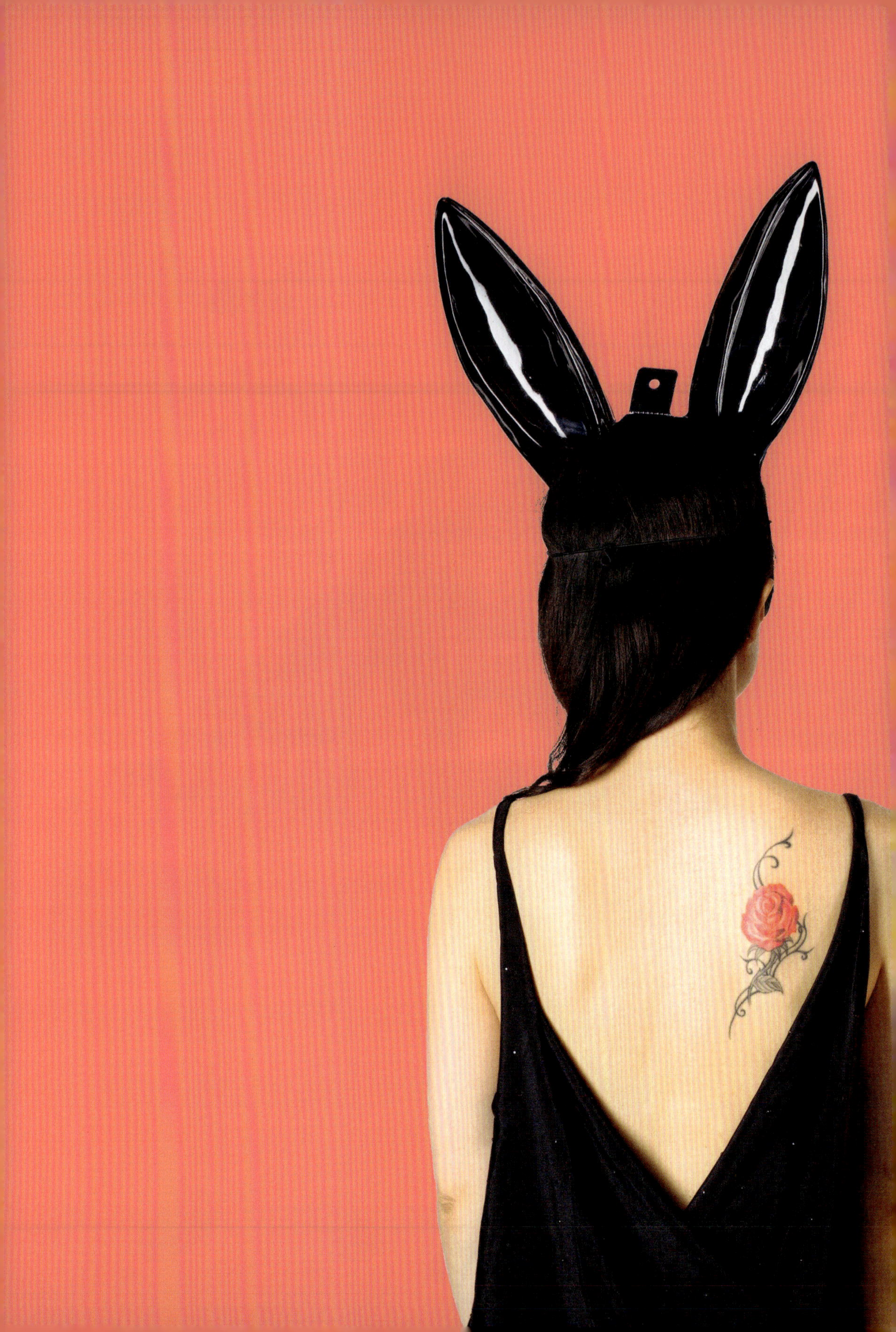

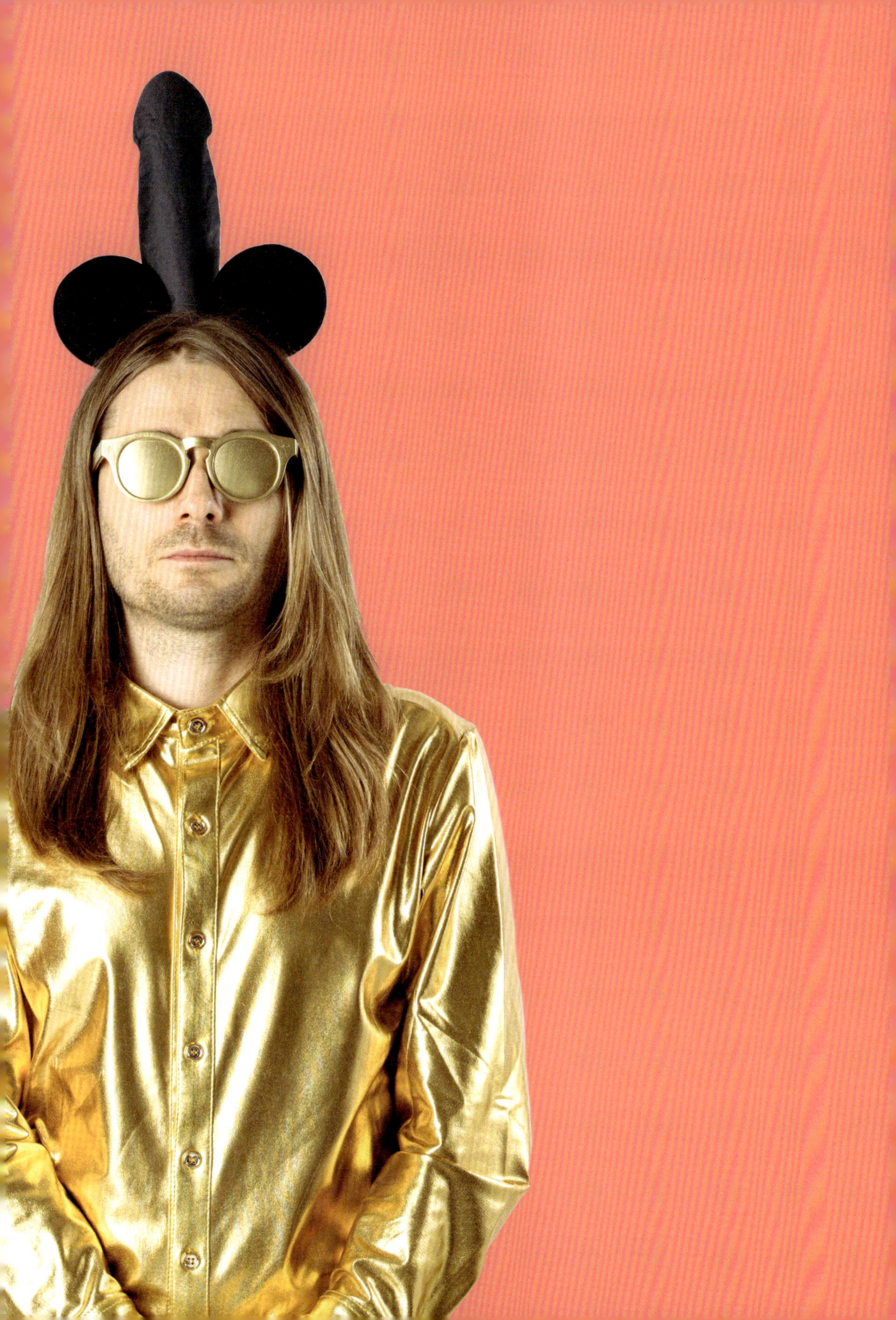

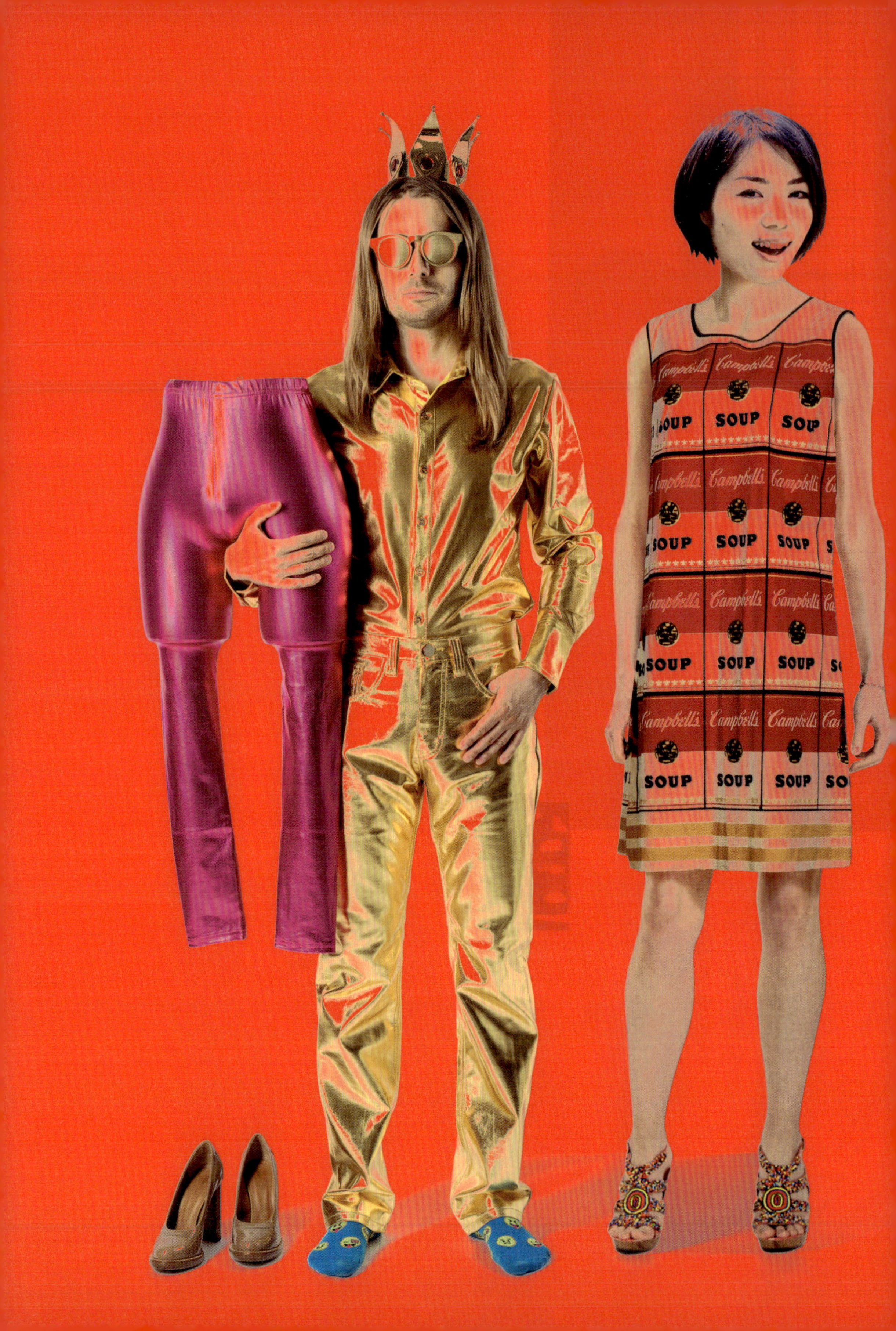
Campbell's
SOUP
Campbell's
SOUP
Campbell's
SOUP
Campbell's
SOUP

heart of the indifferent wielder of the law shudder.

The disfigured, completely black face jumped out from the sky like a sinister ritual bird mask. The desire to make this death right pressed even upon the emotions of the police officer, who had seen a lot in New York.

The hanging man was fully clothed. His clothes had gotten stuck to his body, and the figure looked unnatural, like a big rag doll with a huge, mournful plastic head ready to fall right off due to the rough treatment it had received. The noose was compressing the neck, the rope having fully cut into the flesh as if it were the hanging carcass of a dead animal. The neck was unnaturally thin, and it was unclear how the body was still being held by the rope.

Death ate the sad victim with all of its greediness, as a moth eats an old coat. Half of the right leg, had been ripped open and gnawed at, likely by rats or birds. That leg had neither boot nor sock on it, only some small bones of the foot that had been nibbled at stuck out from under the pant leg. The other leg was swinging to the side and still had its rubber boot on. It was longer than the right leg: the thigh bone had popped out of its joint. The hanged man had not hung the rope very high. He tied it to thin branches that could have easily broken under the weight of his body. And then, maybe, fearing that fate may not have wanted to take him to the next life, he could have returned home.

The police officer came closer to the hanging body, seeing a hand first. The fingers had mummified, although some insects, or maybe worms, had already found their way under the skin, having eaten pathways into the stiffened, almost inhuman flesh.

The officer looked closely at the head again. The blackened, disfigured face under the mop of dirty hair hanging in it showed horror and an attempt to escape the convulsions triggered by the rope pressing on the artery. The noose pulled smoothly, and the neck bones did not snap. The hanged man had suffered for a long time, attempting, it seemed, to escape death, but unavoidability, panic, and physical pain forced reason to snap in a living man.

One of the hanged man's arms was hiding a letter in a large envelope that had been folded in four. The police officer found the letter sticking out from the jacket pocket. The envelope had not been sealed, and in violation of his professional protocol, the officer opened it. The letter was handwritten. The ink had run from the water, and the words were barely legible.

As always in nature, nothing particularly wanted to live, but everything was happy to be alive.

CHAPTER 38

I was a good chess player and played soccer well too. When playing goals or scoring gambits, I would try to extricate myself from complex and beautiful positions, creating chaos on the chessboard and optimism on the soccer field, which happened to be the content of my life.

Thereupon, I missed out on true reality. Time had turned out to be such a deft opponent that, having nonchalantly turned the pages of half of my life, I had achieved nothing, was nowhere, and felt nothing.

I was of no use to anyone, and I brought only trouble to many. I have no friends and no connection to the world. In me, everyone sees a weak-willed traitor, exactly in the same way that I complain about others. Running away from the emptiness, I broke my legs and ran instead directly into the final emptiness.

I'm woefully tired of my own fears. People knock on my door and bring me envelopes with the rent bill, and I wake up to reality in a cold sweat. For many years, in a foreign country, with foreign people, I lingered on with all my strength and desired simply to survive! It seemed at least art never deserted me in the ultimate misfortune. Behind its doors, I pretended to have a normal life. I lied. I wriggled around and invented just to tick the box, just to stay clear of the vortex. I avoided the most dangerous places. Intuition tipped me off. I kept my distance from marshy bogs. But my body has gotten weak, and all of a sudden, I've lost any sense of danger. I got tired of lying to myself that I only had to wait a bit longer.

My last encounter changed my life in just one hour. I met my future wife. But I never did manage to get married. I reassured myself, creating the decorations for a jolly slapstick routine. As if it was I who was naive...

I really don't know where she is now. I didn't have the strength to figure all that out. "My love, I've come to you to begin living." I couldn't say that to her, and I couldn't say it to myself. A pathetic coward.

I wrote her letters. A triangular flock of a hundred white envelopes flew to her. But she invented a method that no inquisition had ever even thought of before: she didn't read them. And then I bought them back from her at a price of ten dollars each.

One wonderful day I encountered her at my exhibition. Instead of the real world, I had given her a false one, and for that, I was cruelly punished. I understood very little when I incurred the fine for that world of cardboard, lenses, and photo paper that I showed her.

My father taught me love. That love made me open and pliant to the world. I was unable to lie because my father never lied. I never adapted because my father had never become a cynic. We lived in the absolute happiness of a shared youth in a nest in a tall tree, where I didn't know what it was to fall from the heights. After work, he would cut out paper airplanes with me, develop photographs, and launch model airplane engines in the apartment that would smoke up the walls. We would solder receivers and tune heterodynes. It was a happy childhood. You couldn't have dreamed up a better one. Until I was thirty, I had no idea.

On the other side of the iron fence, the reverie of comfort pre-severed naiveté in my parents like an oven preserves heat. Believing in justice, they lived a real and rosy childhood within the walls of their prison. They knew nothing about the open ocean. Freedom was served to the table in big spoonfuls by the shortwaves that my father caught with his long antennas on the roof of our building. But one could only make it to the continent of the radio waves through the river.

It's a bitter pill for me to swallow, knowing that my father and mother died children, never learning the truth. Death in ignorance. What could be bitterer?

There is an unbearable guilt. I don't know how to justify myself.

I know that I have no one left, and I have done nothing to make myself of interest to anyone. I know that no one will read these words. Winter, two thousand eleven. I almost made it to forty. Having slipped through life in some incomprehensible movement and with a gnarled soul, I have no idea what to continue living for. It's hard to believe that my last emotions could be these. I'm ashamed that I don't have any more strength. It grieves me to admit it.

Forgive me.

The police officer finished reading. He let fall the heavy arms of the tin woodman, holding the opened envelope. Standing alone among the trees, he leaned on the trunk, cast a glance at the cold, murky surface of the pond, and froze in a metal pose awaiting the ambulance.

CHAPTER 37

The rains started in Berlin in the autumn. All over the country, something was not going right. The soldiers on guard were patrolling The Wall begrudgingly. And no one wanted to shoot anyone anymore. No one wanted to take on the responsibility of the executioner. Often the guards even sympathized with the mutineers. Not only did they serve reluctantly, but sometimes they would perform their duties improperly, allowing would-be escapees to get away. The regime feared the smallest scandal or opposition. Shooting was permitted only in extreme cases, and even then, not at women or children. Hans' father knew this from the muted stories of the military personnel at his design office. The desire to escape only got stronger in light of the crumbling circumstances, and in the anticipation of speedily obtaining paradise, the feeling of danger retreated, providing the will with the key to action.

It was decided to plan the escape for the fall when the rains and winds had put the border guards off guard. They decided to cross the death strip at the spot where the Spree River flowed in place of a second fence on the western side of the city, across from the West German district of Kreuzberg. Instead of a huge, high fence, only the river served as a natural barrier that you had to swim across. All of the open space that was without a wall was lit by searchlights from watchtowers on both sides of the area. Guards with machine guns were on patrol in the towers, and the smooth surface of the water was plowed by a white cutter, also fitted with two searchlights. At a certain time, the shifts on the boat would change.

In October, the water in the river wasn't yet that icy. The light in the kitchen stayed on long into the night in the last days. Hans knew all the details of the escape plan and was ready for it, believing his father's belief in a new life.

Hans' mother began to argue more with his father, a sign of the nearing climax. No one could live in such confrontation and heightened emotion for too long. The idea now belonged to everyone. Hans' father had so infected them all that not only did no one doubt their eventual victory, but they were all of one mind about ending their old life forever. Hans' father was completely absorbed in the picture of the future; he didn't want to know much about the nuances and difficulties of the transition. They were driven by faith in a new, vivid life. Just to get out, at any cost.

Hans' mother worried about the details, about the most important specifics of the transition. Hans' father wanted everyone to swim at the same time. He insisted that that way would be safer for Hans' mother. He was right with respect to the water crossing. But everything was not so clear as regards the death strip, and the dispute gathered steam. Hans' mother was categorically against the idea. She thought that if anything went wrong, they would all be caught. They would start shooting, and then everything would go not so well, or rather, pretty badly. Hans' father didn't want to hear it. All of the negative possibilities annoyed him. He did not want to let even a little doubt into his soul, holding fear off behind several sheaths. Hans' mother's logic was based on foreboding, and his father worried that they would not be able to reach a consensus regarding the most important aspect. Hans' mother insisted that they should all cross at equal intervals to lower the risk. This plunged his father into desperation, and it continued for a few weeks. Then his mother said that she was staying. She would find a way to get to him later. Just a bit later. After that, his father gave up immediately. He couldn't resolve the quandary in his head. Life without her had even less meaning than the life of an engineer. To allow his wife to be right, he closed his eyes to everything. It was decided that they would keep the necessary distance from one another in order to cross the death strip more safely.

zero

CHAPTER 38

Hans didn't hang himself. It was a very, very, very bad joke. He wanted to hang himself to discover any pity he might have for his own death, as is usually the case. As if he could look in the mirror and see his doll-like face jumping in the noose.

Hans was too weak to simply up and square accounts with life. He was just playing a bad game in which he should not have been participating. The branch he tied the rope to wasn't the biggest. It cracked. He landed on his back, on the dry branches and rocks, almost losing consciousness from the injury.

The rope pressed tightly on his neck and arteries. He was in pain as before and unable to breathe. The fall had knocked the air out of him, and the noose was tiresomely pulling him upwards. A sudden surge of adrenalin opened Hans' eyes, like the fastest apertures on Earth. He grabbed the rope with his hands and, breathing intermittently, pulled on it, raising his body.

After some time, he was able to sit upon the ground. With doubled strength, he began removing the noose from his neck. Oh God, how he was frightened by his own hands, which, shaking and dark blue, wouldn't obey him!

Hans' reason at that moment was so clear and pure as if he had taken some medicine to extend his life and that medicine had worked so well that he became disgusted and unbelievably ashamed at what he had attempted to do. Hans opened his eyes wide and saw thousands of snowflakes falling from the sky, coming ever closer to the lenses of his sobered pupils.

For some reason, Hans remembered that he had left his camera at home in the kitchen. He felt like immediately getting up and heading home. He tried to do so, but his body wouldn't comply due to the steady, sharp pain in his back and general weakness. Hans froze for a few minutes and tried to catch his breath.

After regulating his breath, he remembered Yuma and everything else. Slowly raising himself from the ground, he stepped towards the place where he had left his foam catamaran. That minute it was as if Hans had awoken even more. And the feelings that awoke him were disgust with himself because of the obfuscation of his reason that had led to such a detestable act and, at the same time, enthusiasm. It seemed that life had forgiven him, and he immediately dropped all grievances against it as well. It was possible to begin from the beginning right away. The only thing that seemed to Hans right and hopeful now was to come to an agreement with Yuma.

It's hard to understand how the feeling of inspiration grows from the blackest hell, from complete darkness, out of which leads an unending staircase of suffering. Like the small sprout of a future tree from a slab of granite. It's possible that physical strength, which did not allow the soul to be completely squeezed from Hans' body, had sprung back and spit out his real feelings. They immediately pulled him towards the simple brightness of existence.

Hans stood on his feet, grabbing with his hand the tree that had saved his life, playing the tree bark like piano keys with his fingers, trying to grab on more securely to the trunk so as not to fall. Looking around, he saw his catamaran. Hans began to crunch the branches underfoot, examining the surface of the lake. White snow covered the water in a star fall, disappearing in it like breadcrumbs,

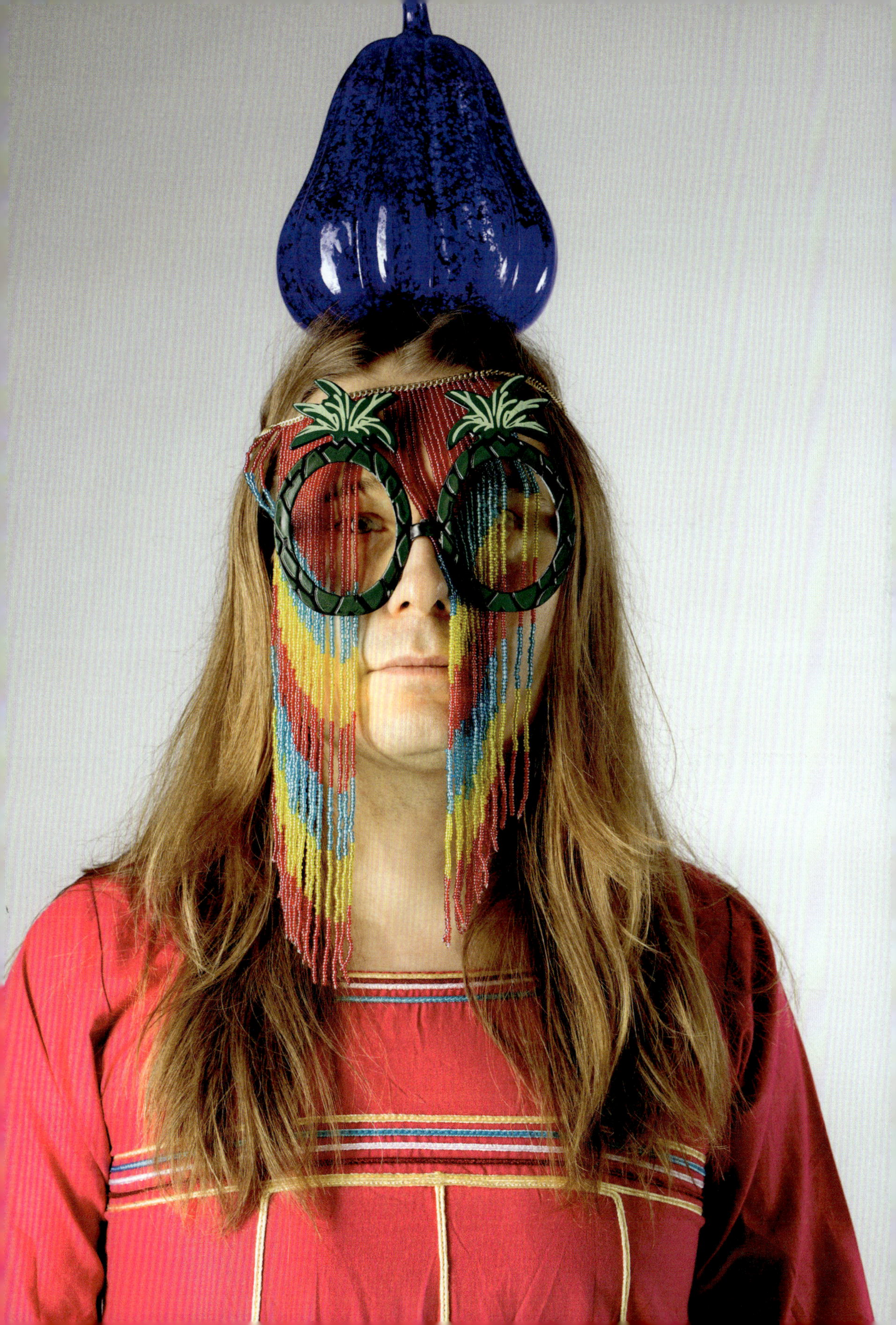

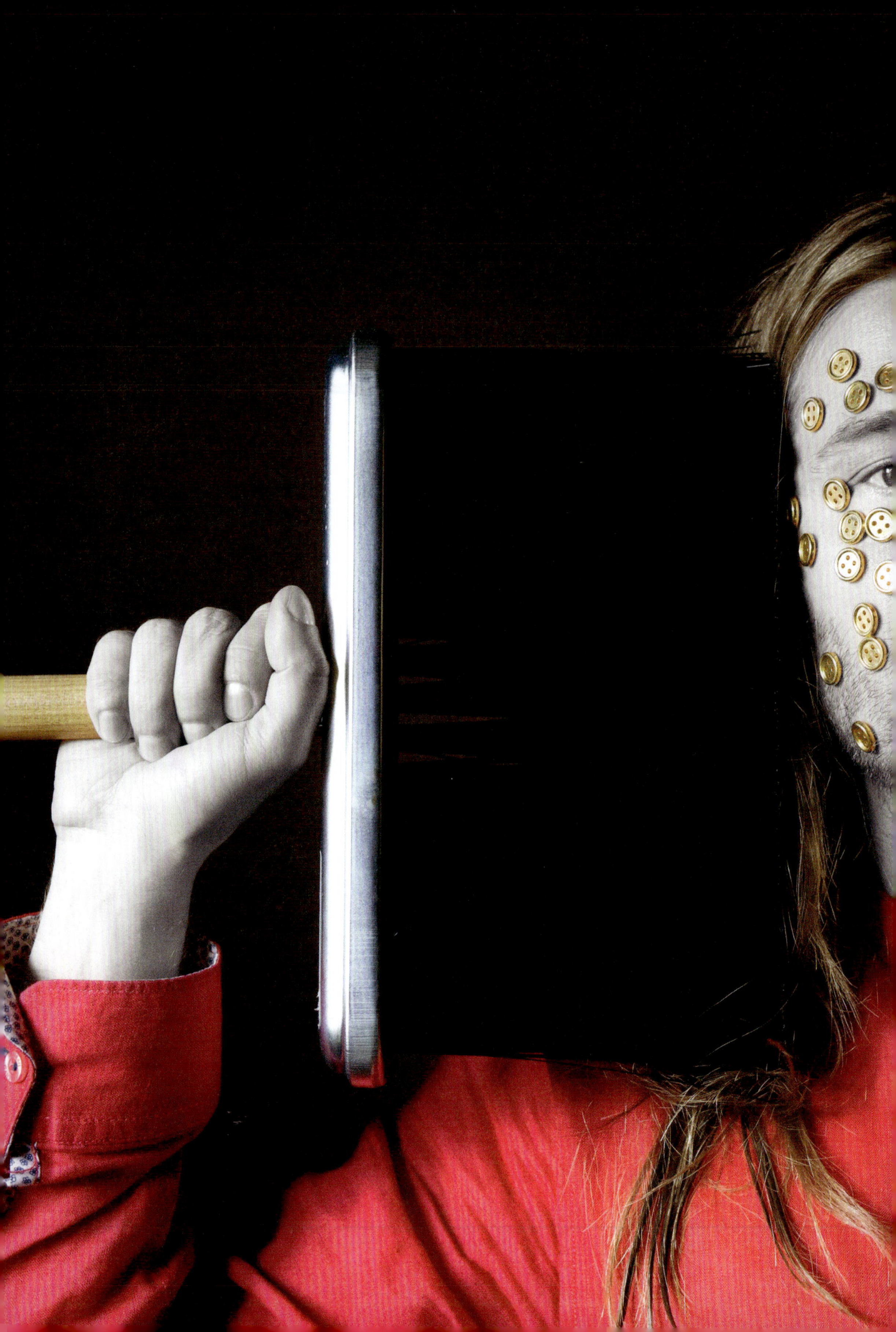

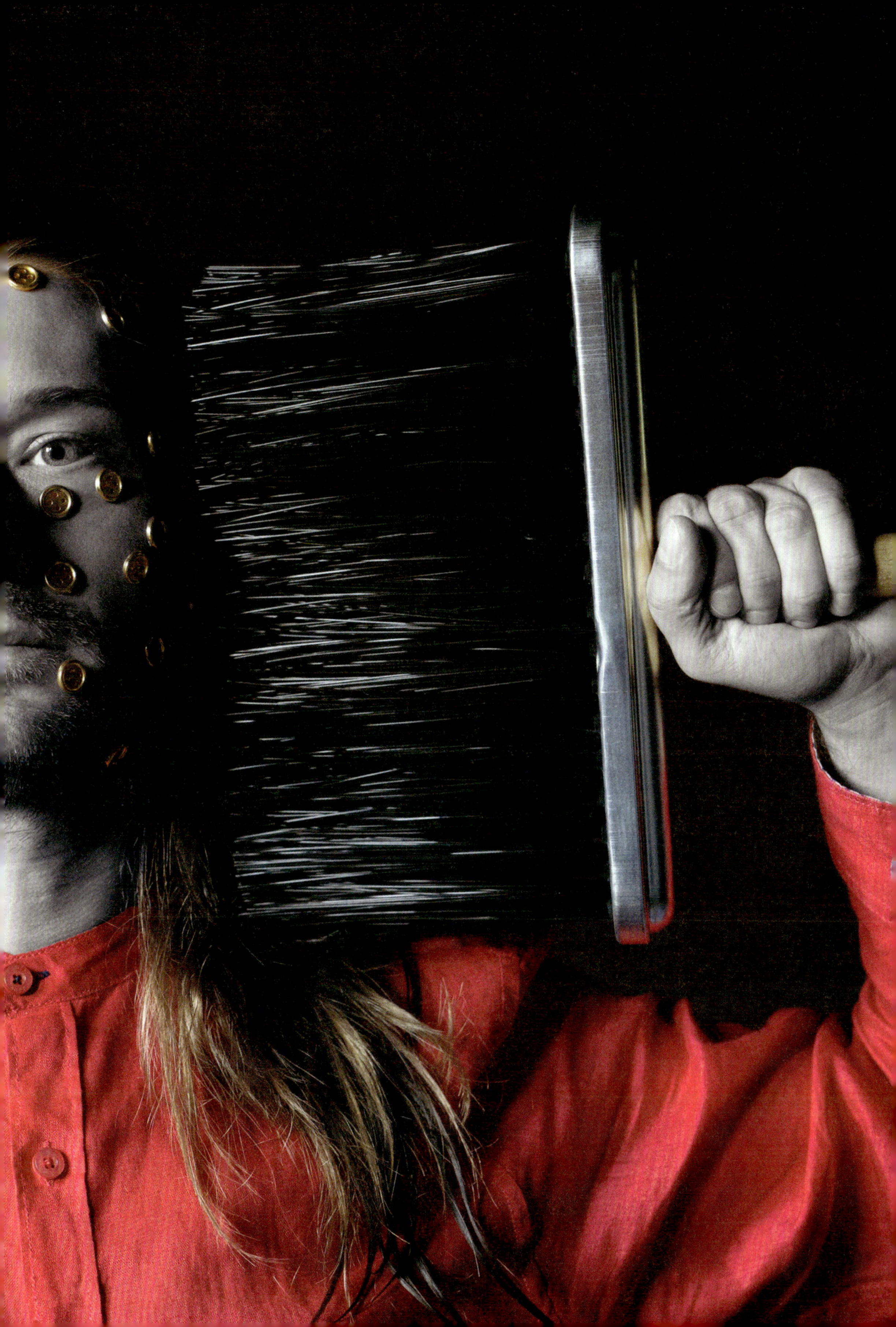

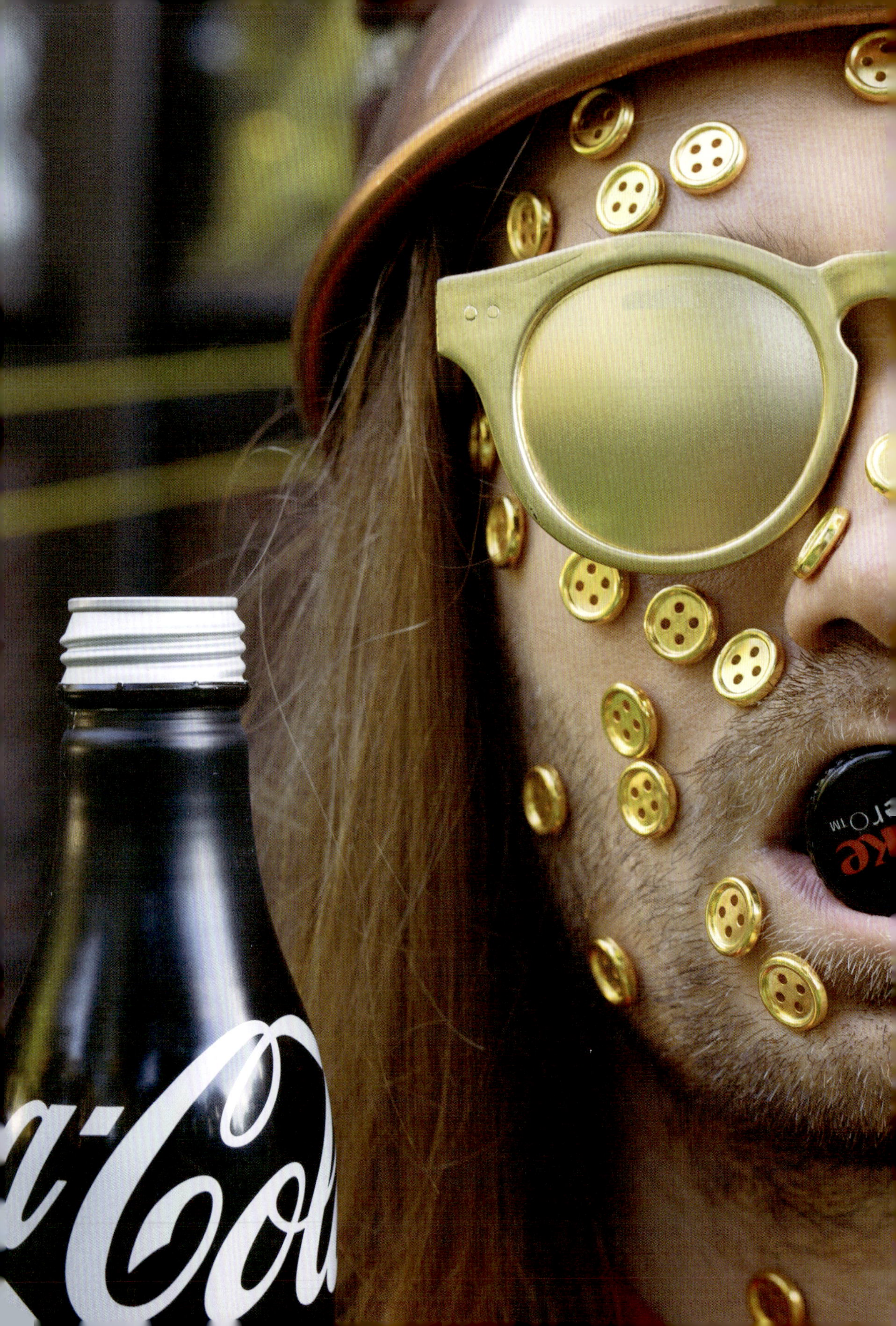

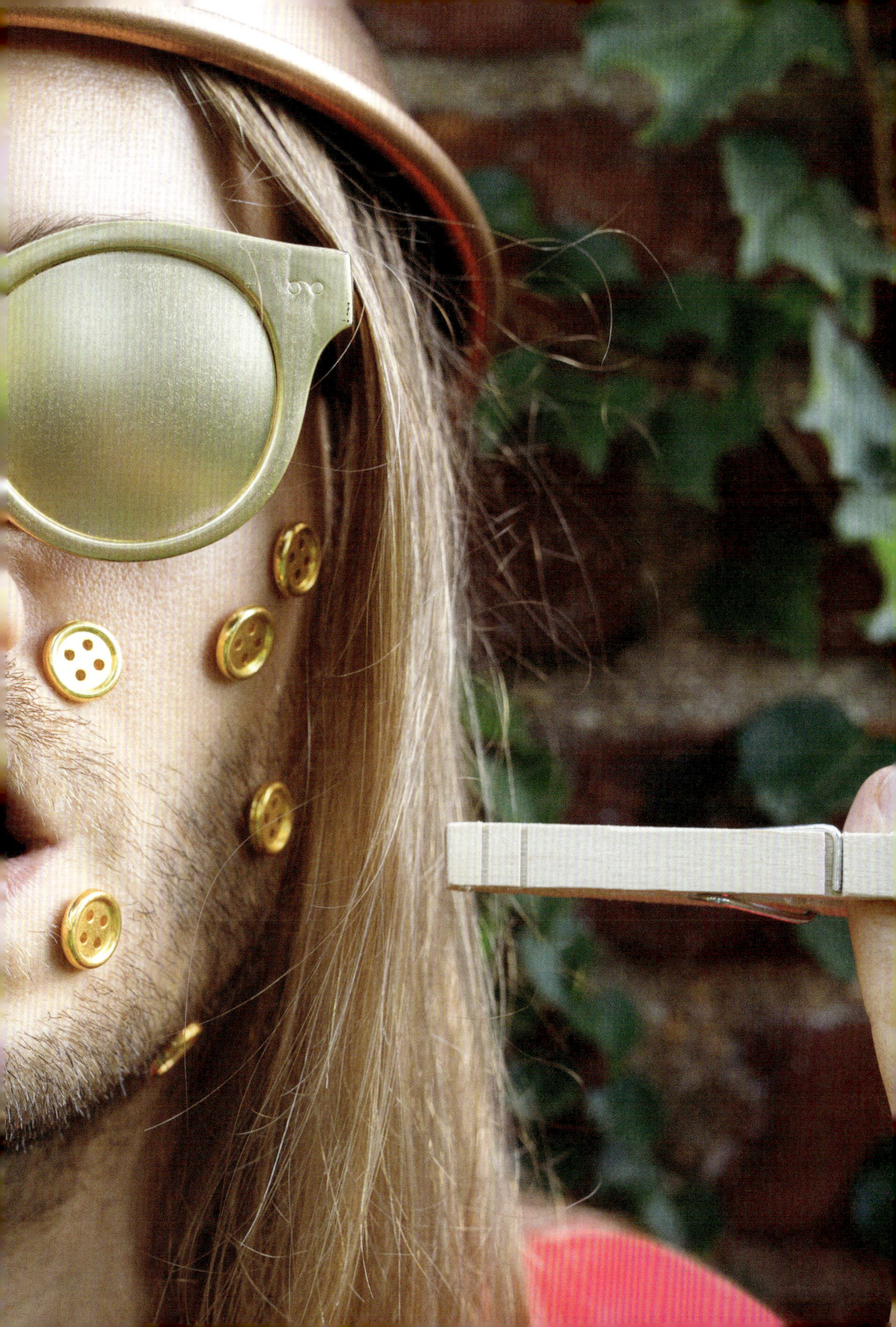

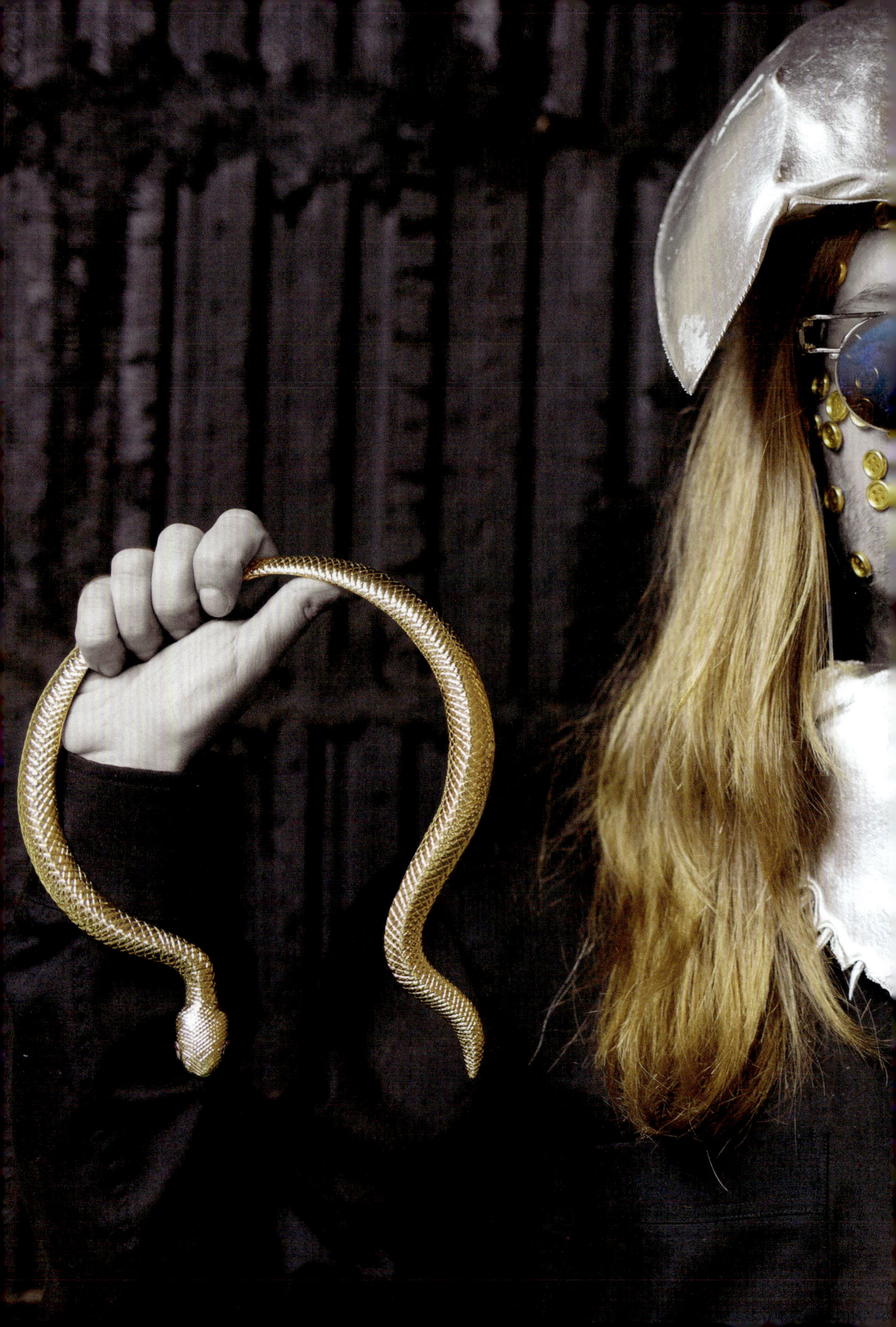

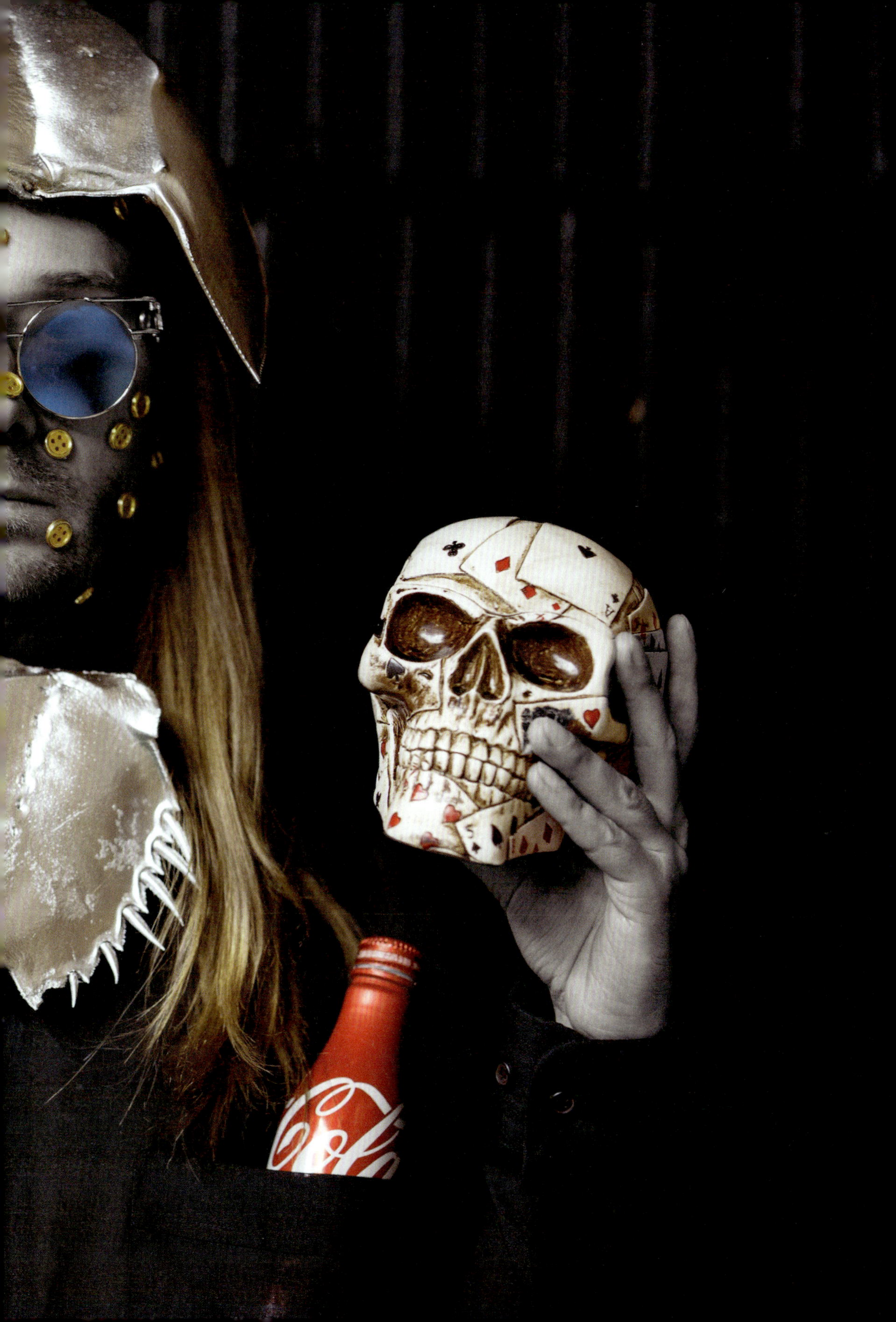

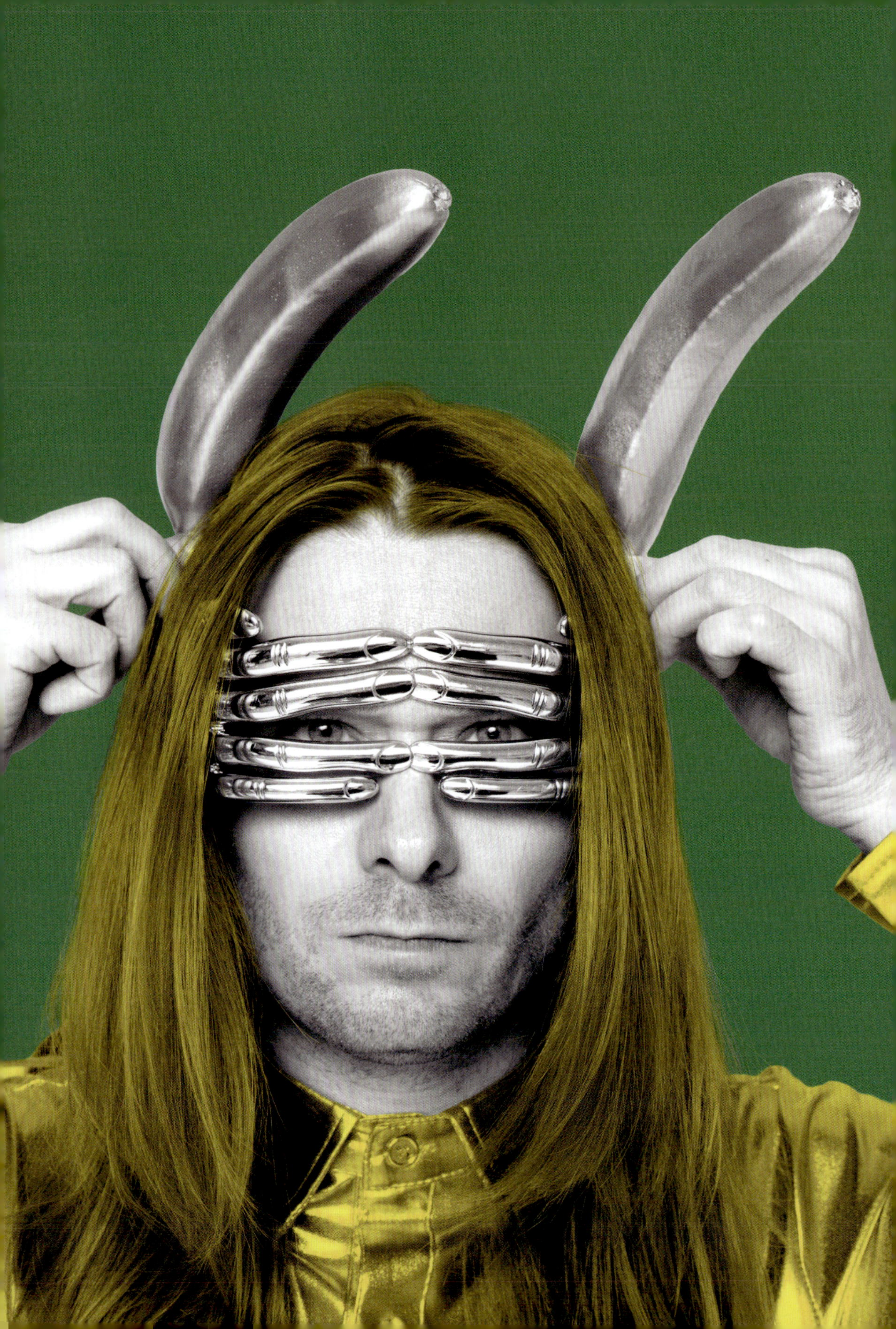

dissolving the sounds of nature that had woken up and the human morning bustle.

He quickly docked on the other shore in the catamaran. With his wet, still unsure steps, Hans sketched the dotted line of his path home. He thought he was walking in a straight line drawn using the ruler of his impatient imagination, but instead, he was tracing a sine wave from weakness and dizziness. He wanted to get out of the horrible forest that Central Park had become as fast as he could.

Arriving home, Hans opened the familiar dingy door of the Harlem apartment with the key. The sound of its scraping echoed in Hans' ears. Warm now and feeling protected in the cocoon of the ramshackle fifth-floor cabbage-leaf walls, Hans typed "Flight to Tokyo" into the internet search engine.

In twenty minutes, his printer's jets were buzzing a slanted and one-legged melody, printing out the ticket: from John F. Kennedy Airport to Narita Airport.

New York — Tokyo. Today.

There was no return ticket because Hans was leaving forever. He gathered everything he needed. The horror of that night gave him no time to get his bearings and no desire to pack properly. Realizing what he had done and how he would exonerate himself, he didn't want to stay for one minute longer in the city.

Indeed, how could he write that absurd, horrible letter? Get the foam to get across the water? Walk through the night across those branches, to the small, accursed island with a rope in his backpack?

Hans could have answered these questions for more than a whole day if he had had time to catch his breath.

Foreseeing confrontation with Hans, Hans wanted to avoid it. The faucet dropped drips, measuring the seconds before his start.

Hans threw on his orange jacket and began packing a bag. He

took the Andy Warhol album with him, a one-terabyte hard drive, and a photograph of Yuma singing with a microphone on the stage at the Blue Note. He planned on using that photograph to look for Yuma. He had to find some socks and his lobster-claw toothbrush.

He also took the dragonfly t-shirt.

"I suppose it's warm in Tokyo," he thought. "Even though it's December, it's still on the other side of the planet, where summer is hiding. I can at least wear the shirt around her house."

The sun shone in the sky and made its way through the window square of some unknown artist and into Hans' room. Winter was teasing him to stay in New York. Winter promised skis, sleds, snowballs, and swimming in ice holes. Winter deceived and howled between the old bricks. It was an ass kisser: come back. Don't make any sudden moves, Hans.

Hans shaved and threw the electric razor out the window. It was a playful gesture of boldness. The bravado of everyday jazz. Hans was filled with the absurd understanding that his life could so easily be changed. A flash of genius. Freedom of the will.

He had gone from the furthest reaches of despair to extreme, impetuous euphoria, almost to laughter. "Yuma, I'm nearby. I'm leaving! I'll be there soon," he insisted.

He had completely forgotten about his nighttime thoughts, about his evening in the bar, and about the debt that the court had ordered him to pay. He erased all problems from his memory: the lake at its horizon had turned into a small, shriveled puddle that he now just had to be step over to get to a new life.

The things, which jumped all by themselves into Hans' suitcase in origami patterns, could taste the meeting. The joyous fireworks of the eternal jubilee of Hans and Yuma's reunion would forever be set off outside their door.

The soap bubble of the past did not bother Hans, as if the past had been laid inside him like an undetectable larva, and a rainbow cloud, spilling over into the sunrays, showed the continents of a new planet. Images, metaphors, the complexity of space, and curiosity about the next twist plagued Hans' eyes, which could no longer feel the caraway seeds of suffering as if a rubber ball had reached a resonant bottom and sprung back and out the top.

Hans took his orange blazer off the hanger, barely hiding the euphoria of satisfaction and nervous joy. He tried to conceal his smile behind a second face of restraint. However, his skin and muscles gave him away, penetrated as they were with nerve fibers throughout, and connected by wires to the next page of the book that was just about to be read. Hans took a last look at the room, at the hole that he had not completed due to the strength of the concrete or the strength of Yuma's nerves. Saying goodbye in his head to the apartment below where Yuma once lived, he went out onto the street and caught a cab.

He stuffed the suitcase into the trunk of the cab like lottery winners transport boxes with cash. He rode to the airport like one would drink champagne. On camels and a divan on a magic carpet. In a restaurant on wheels. He rode as if on a classy yacht, lying in the pool on the second floor, lathered in a white diamond cream. In swim trunks that delicately hugged his body and with shaved legs. Smelling like taut masculine skin after a two-hour spa procedure. He made a duck face, lying under the barrels of television cameras and posing for a million followers on Instagram.

He looked out the window, where the sun was wiggling between frost patterns on the glass of the warm iron package of the car, soaring sorrowfully like a romantic bird in the trap of the concrete bridge.

Hans could feel the upcoming meeting, not in his thoughts and not as a scenario, and not even as a mood, but with the gentle touch of the imagined land of a friendly city. It was the ecstasy and innocence of a child. The picture of happiness was painted with unknown colors by someone sitting much higher up than the Manhattan Bridge, even higher than the sparks of sun that fell inside the car after welding the hoarfrost. With a joyful cold, the rays pinched their way into Hans' mood. And Hans sat in bliss in the back seat, looking at the disappearing tall pencils of Manhattan's mirror buildings.

He coddled and pronounced the name of the city and the girl, mixing them into a cocktail. Tokyo, Tokyo, Tokyo. Yuma. With every letter, shivers of anxiety burned him. The spoken name of the city brought him closer to the dream that was so close he could touch it with his hand. There was just one small hurdle—the round window of the plane through which Hans' immeasurable happiness rested and awaited him.

After arriving at John F. Kennedy Airport and finding Japan Airlines and his flight, Hans saw a large sign: 日本航空株式会社.

A certain kind of doubt began to take shape in his designer's head. It's possible that small technical complications would cast a shadow on his trip. He hadn't had time to learn Japanese, and the residents of Tokyo, Hans assumed, spoke Japanese. All of the signs were in Japanese, the books were in Japanese, and, most importantly, he would have to look for Yuma in Japanese. This wasn't too huge of a problem for Hans, not insurmountable. The second reason for the doubt was that Hans was not sure in which city Yuma lived.

He decided that it was Tokyo because Tokyo is a pretty large city in Japan. But there must be other cities in Japan. Maybe she lives in Kyoto? No problem. He could find where the 新幹線 to Kyoto was on the internet. And even if she lives in Okinawa…well, that's even better. Set up life somewhere on the shores of the ocean. Hans would sell all of his property in the US and buy a cheap little house in Okinawa. You have to live where no one wants to. What could be worse than Japan for the Japanese, and what could be better than Japan for those for whom any country is worse than what had been before? Of course, Hans wanted to live near the ocean and take his son to an Okinawa school. And Yuma would record songs in a studio on the seashore, which Hans would build for her from bamboo immediately, as soon as they chose the right place. Among the palms, the burning ocean sun…etc., etc.

The last question that Hans pondered was whether Yuma was in Japan at all. Maybe she had moved to another country or another state in America? Or maybe she had never even left New York? "Why is she hiding?" Hans wrung his elbows at that paradox. "Ahead of us is that small island of the future, built especially to fit us. No one else can go to the island. Why does she…" The thoughts tried to land for the sixteenth time.

The sun had already come over the horizon, overcoming the main and most difficult burden of ascent. The frosty wind retracted, not hindering the airplanes from revving their motors stuffed with horsepower, showing the passengers the might of metal progress.

The mood of sleepy and wintery people improved somewhat, to mid-range, giving them an explanation for why they should wake up at six in the morning, get up from bed, get dressed, and go to work.

Hans decided that he would rub out this winter day with an eraser. He was squeezing what had happened to him in the morning out from his subconscious with an alchemical force. The only problem was that he didn't know which way to move now: closer to Yuma or farther away from her.

She's probably in New York, Hans decided. And he understood that he had been a little too hasty with his flight. He simply wanted to lash out in some sort of elegant gesture, place himself in another pretty pose. "OK," Hans said to himself and got back in the taxi.

He had no desire to save his last money. What's the difference whether he gives the debt back a month later—not in twenty-two forty-five but twenty-two forty-six—just because he took a taxi? In the past, Hans had dreamed of being a truck driver, sitting behind the wheel, gazing at the movement of time along the logarithmic road facing him. He liked the stagnation of the road and the sparkling poetry of marking space. The lack of a strict schedule and the comfort of being alone in the truck's cab.

The taxi driver wore a turban, and again just like on that first day, asked Hans the address in Indian English, and again the cab sped Hans to Harlem. Not joyfully, but not as hopelessly as he would have felt in a taxi taking him to the elephants in faraway India.

Hans straightened out the printout of his ticket to Tokyo and folded a paper airplane from it, the same kind he had made in his childhood on the streets of Berlin. The secret was accuracy. If you prepare the airplane very precisely, its aerodynamic features allow it to fly higher than five-story buildings. Hans and his schoolmates would have contests to see whose airplane could get higher than the roofs of the buildings first. That sometimes required a whole day of unsuccessful launches. His schoolmates would gather on the playground, folding airplanes out of graph paper. Some planes headed towards the trees and got caught in the branches. Others landed on balconies or flew out of the solar system. The autumn days of school anxieties were displaced by the engineering investigations of boys' exploits, which were monitored by the lineup of the eyes of their female schoolmates attending to their familial futures. The sun whipped up the wind, blowing sand all over the playground and suddenly lifting the successfully constructed and launched airplanes. The happy playground was lit by the spotlight of the yellow sun between the brown patina of the brick houses. The painted steel poles of the carousel shone in rainbow blue-red-yellow, adding to the happy childhood. Nearby was a pharmacy where you could buy sweetened vitamin C tablets. There were a few cars parked in a row awaiting gas and wheelwork. The girls darted surreptitious glances. The boys understood that and straightened their spines while sitting on their knees in the sand and making flying devices with graph paper.

Hans made an airplane with precision, just as he had done thirty years ago. When his taxi drove along the long bridge connecting Queens with Manhattan, Hans opened the window, gauged the flight trajectory, and launched his airplane diagonally upwards on a long journey with an accurate throw.

"Fly to Tokyo. Say that I could have been one of the pilots. No! Say that I'm on my way," Hans fantasized, speaking to the airplane. He closed the window and was able to see from behind the glass how the airplane, shining in the rays of the sun, gained altitude in Z, made a course for the Pacific Ocean.

It was quiet at home. Even Andy's figure didn't help Hans feel that the place was full of familial warmth. He had recently more than once sped out of his apartment forever for various absurd reasons, and it was as if the space was upset with him. It had now become estranged, as if it wanted to say goodbye to its inhabitant, resting in emptiness.

Despite the fact that Hans had been convinced of Yuma's existence in maybe not the best manner, time had somehow erased the borders of his belief. Like a faraway star that could only be seen through a theoretical device, Yuma's image slipped away from his memory. Hans wanted to save her. He tried to draw her as he remembered her. He was now increasingly in doubt of the accuracy of the proof of her existence, which he had then been able to attain because the trail was hot. He saved the business card, as there was nothing else to save.

Hans did not understand where Yuma's human center, to which he might appeal, was now located. With every new wave of his heartfelt melancholy—especially when Hans would look at the print of her silver-gray smile on the photo paper—the earthquake shook his doubt a bit, wiping away the dust from the glass of memories. Hans opened up to meet his suffering.

Suffering was familiar and nice. Everything that went against humanity with its eternal common sense, production, health, commotion, and fuss—in all of that, Hans could feel the rightness of the existence of his own, separate, and contrary idea.

As a counter to the erasing of memory, his feeling grew and spread to other territories of the Yuma that was being erased. The real Yuma, the one who would be ready for marriage, might be upset to know that Hans was imagining characters. That a real, warm-blooded girlfriend wasn't something that he needed. Remaining loyal to his defeated soul, Hans finished the drawing of Yuma with those colors that he himself liked.

Maybe they'll
invent eternal life soon?
At least for debtors.

CHAPTER 39

Finally, another important idea took ownership of Hans: finish the work of making the passageway to the floor below. This idea supplied him with the necessary enthusiasm, and his reason worked in a more collected manner in the arena of engineering poetry. Quickly discovering that the concrete between the floors could not be broken through without causing the entire structure serious harm, Hans decided to use modern technology. Even if he could not set up a wedding present downstairs, rearranging furniture and hanging balloons and colored garlands, he could set up a teleconference from his apartment. An electronic date. Something like the internet, but with direct contiguity.

Hans wanted to create a meaningful effect for the meeting. To feel the moment when his heart would thump from the anticipated discovery. How Yuma would be walking around in her house dress, or maybe without it. There would be no indecent surprise in that. The architecture of Yuma's body Hans had discovered in Central Park in the grass. Further concealment of the secrets of her shape was harmful to the general nature of love. This was Hans' own worry since his feelings were justified, and seeing Yuma naked was his absolute legal right. Or, more precisely, it was her obligation.

Hans considered sending some rhyming poetic signal, a telegram, along the cable. A letter on air. Setting up a cunning electronic sleight of hand. And he decided to stealthily drill a small hole into the concrete floor, in the very corner of the room where his passageway was to have been. Through this aperture, he would carefully lower a web camera attached to a cable, connected to a computer and monitor. And also attach tiny loudspeakers and lower them into the room as well, to allow his speech to be heard through them.

It took all day to do the preparatory work. First, he had to move the table, which was too far from the planned outlet for the cable, and in general, cluttered the beauty of the environment. On the table was a pyramid of things and papers. Then he had to decide on the details and features of the broadcast. Hans decided that he would have Andy Warhol beside him and would bring in another chair, a better one. He would place a large bouquet of flowers nearby, too—roses. He would hang a few of his photos and would set himself up in the chair in the most bourgeois manner possible as if the material world could give more satisfaction to those whose souls didn't know what to do with it. Like a decorative moon landing. Indeed, it might be that the accessories would convince Hans of and brace him for the feeling of the solemnity of the moment.

Hans wanted to set the moment up and free himself. To do so, he asked what specifically might impede him. Don't hold back, Hans. He wanted to put a small table next to the chair with a glass of freshly squeezed carrot juice. Yes! Appease his stomach—that's what was needed to ward off the jinn of shame! Hans knew that he had to change in order to demonstrate seduction to Yuma instead of embarrassment.

At the store, he bought a large monitor, a small web camera with a long USB cord, and an external hard drive on which he could fit days of recordings of what was going on in the downstairs apartment in case things didn't work out the first time. Later, he could then find Yuma on the recordings. Edit together the film of his wedding.

"Why edit?!" Warhol was immediately indignant. "Reality is already a finished movie! The drama of editing is intrinsic in time itself."

Hans had to linger for a while, choosing a tungsten-carbide drill of the proper diameter and what he considered sufficient length to drill a hole in the thick concrete.

Hans decided to do the work itself the following day since it was already late, and he was feverish both from his ideas and from having caught a chill on the island. Inside, Hans was running from death as from a plague: not one cell, not one neuron of memory wanted to believe or concede the fact that he had been in the park that frosty morning, on a small island, in an absurd situation, one step from straightforward irreversibility.

The next afternoon, Hans began the final step in his work. He had hung colorful paper around the interior in case there was excessive dust and pieces. He liked to decorate interiors, to make a completely new environment.

It turned out that drilling concrete was not that difficult. There was almost no dust, and the noise was quite delicate as if an angry swarm of bees protecting their territory decided all at the same minute to fly into a small hole in the bee-resistant floor. In small intervals, within a half-hour, Hans had finished drilling, feeling that the boring tool was bored, so easily did it move downwards. He decided that he wouldn't rush and that he should take all the time he needed to properly prepare for the ceremonial e-date properly. He straightened up his room even more, removing the unnecessary paper and sweeping up the wood pieces and construction debris that had come from the electrical installation work. He brought the books and photographs from his recent sessions back into the room and changed the water in the vase with flowers. The small webcam, to help lonely people be voyeurs, had a special construction. It was a

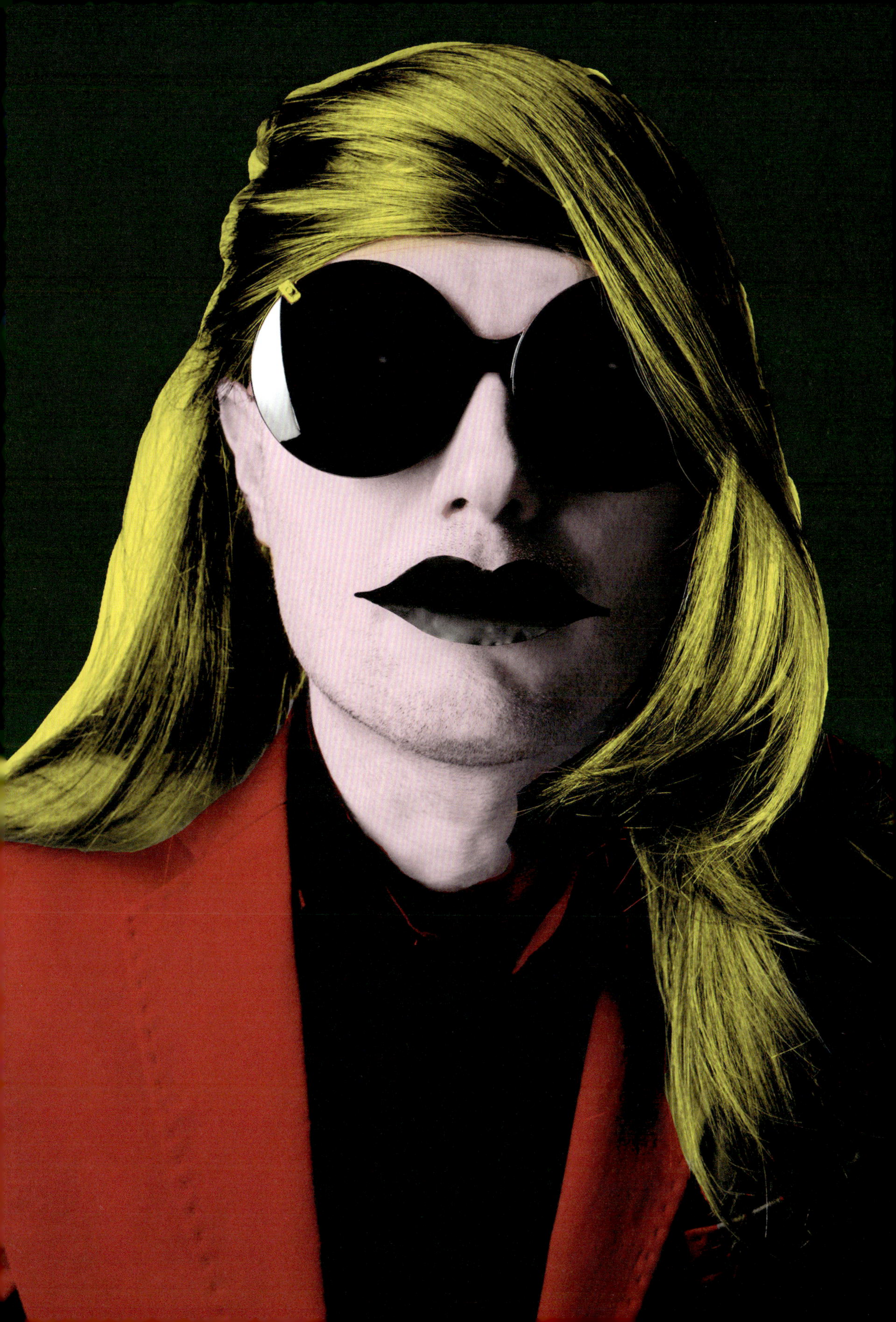

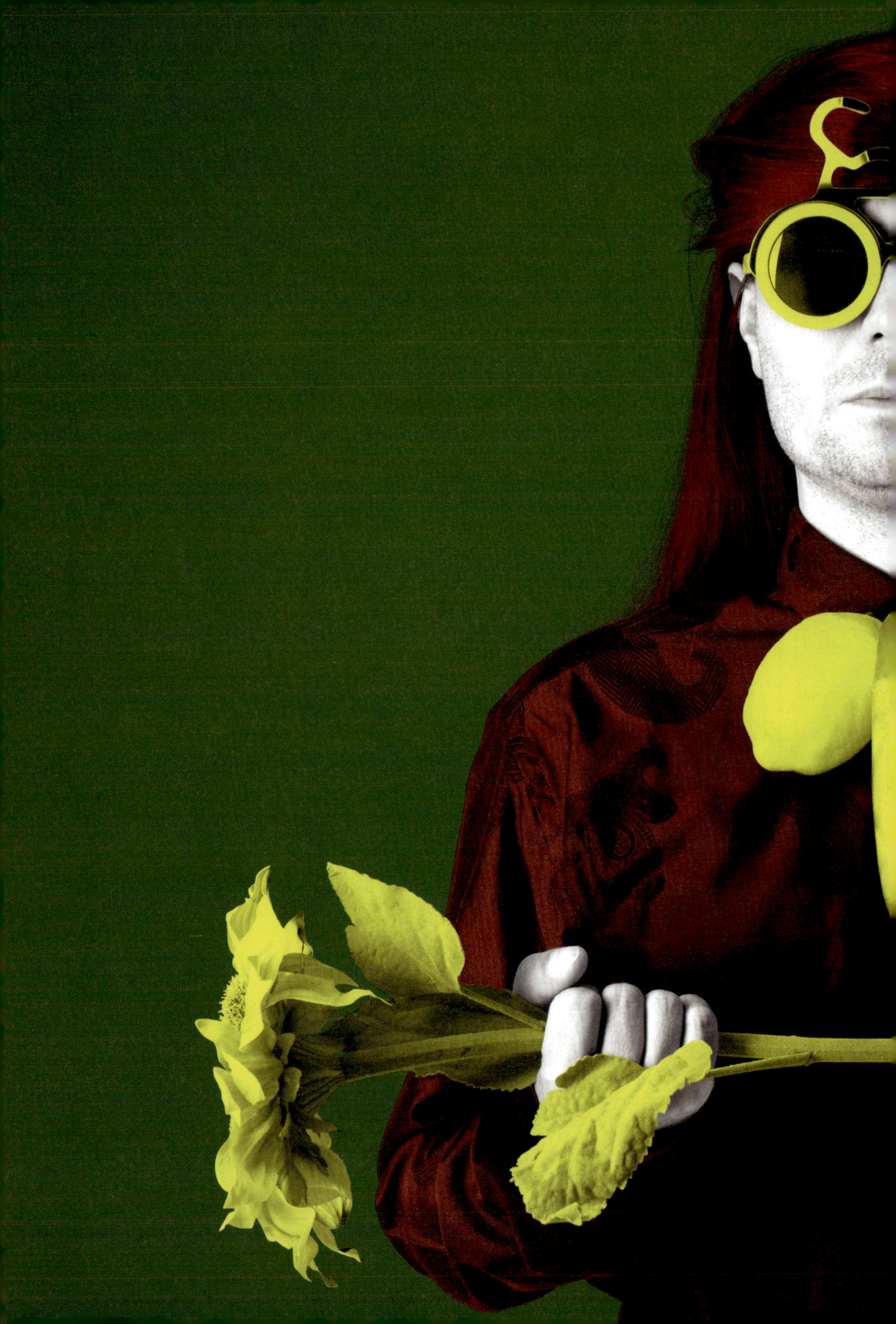

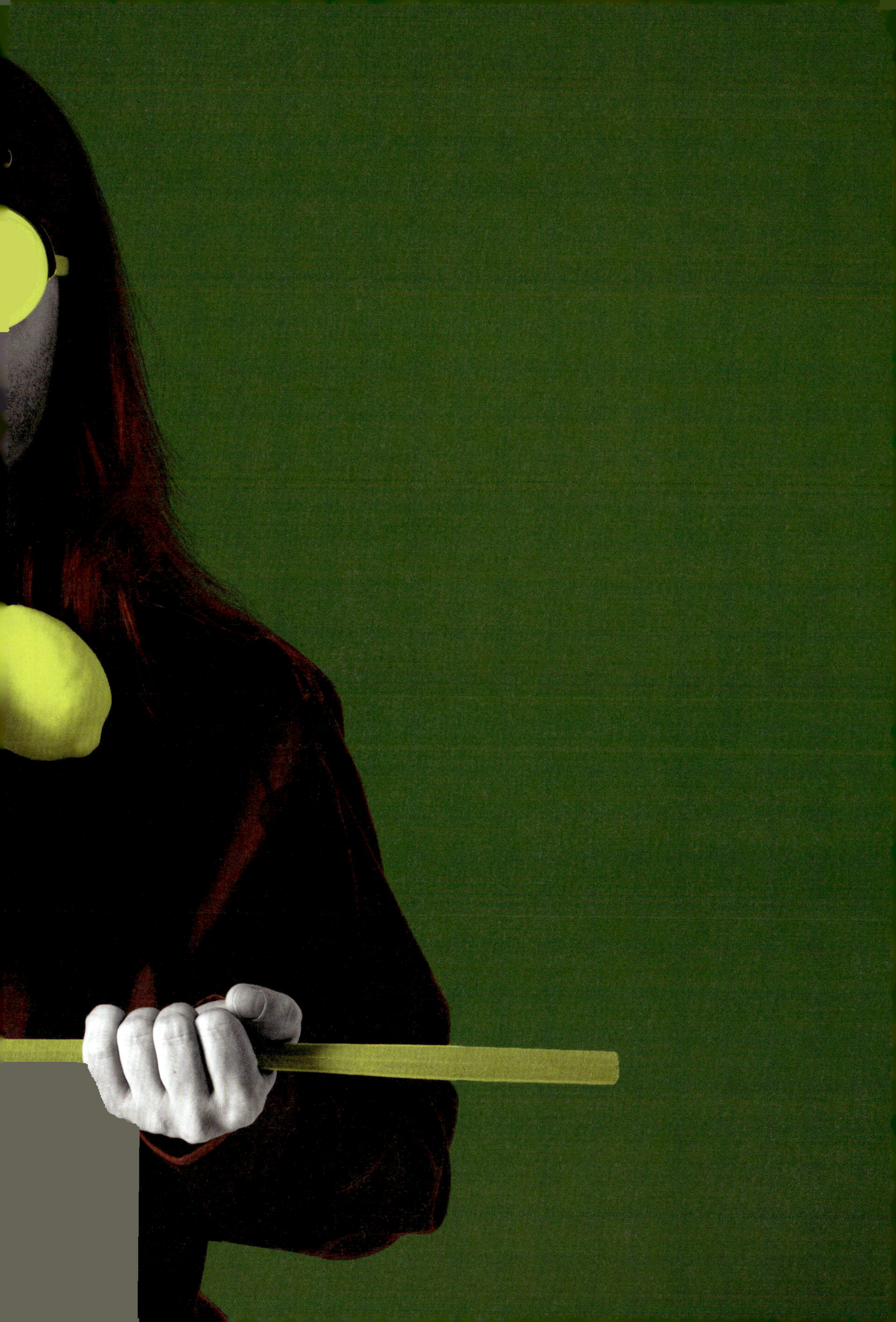

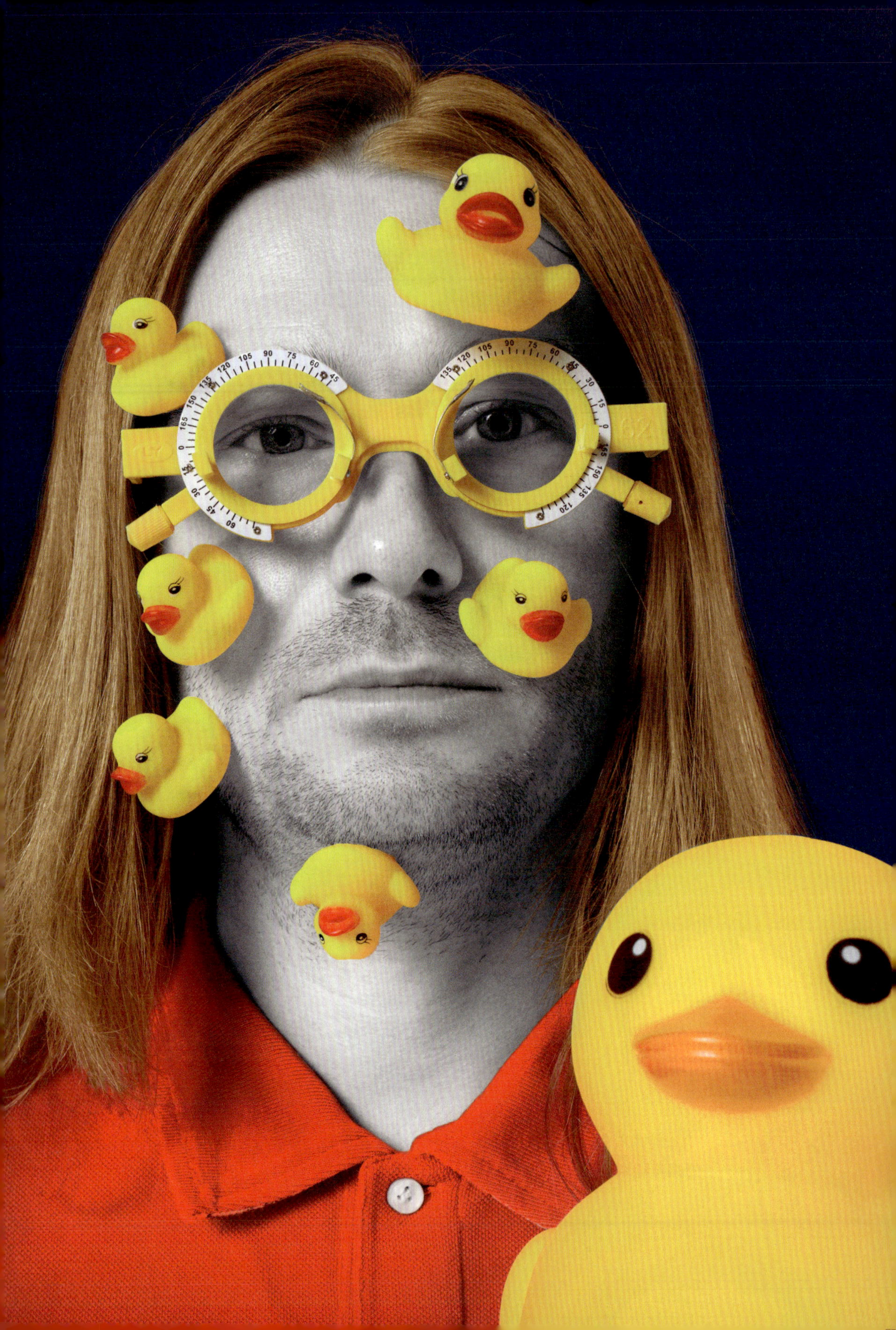

mirrored cylinder with a diameter of less than an inch, inside which the camera and lens rotated in a horizontal plane, controlled by the computer. You could set the camera's angle to focus on whatever you wanted to. And to leave outside the parentheses of imagination that which wasn't necessary to see. Using a metal rod, Hans carefully lowered the camera, and after it, the two small speakers, which remained between the floors so that they would not be seen.

After connecting the equipment to the computer, Hans focused the image, a bit worried, and pulled the camera back on the wire to be less noticeable. He glanced at the monitor. The room below was empty and flooded with sunlight. After adjusting the brightness, Hans saw only the floor, a table, and most of a wide sofa folded out into a bed. In the corner of the frame, he noticed the neck of a guitar.

He immediately screwed up his eyes, not wanting to look anymore at the details. He might ruin the impression before it was time or lower the effect of the solemn moment of meeting. He turned off the computer with trepidation, putting the date off until evening when Yuma returned home.

Hans decided to take a walk along the embankment of the East River to look at the opposite shore and the smokestacks peacefully smoking.

At the same time, the court decision again began to haunt Hans. The day had flown by quickly and with enthusiasm, so Hans had simply shooed away possible reality. It was important to him that he correspond to his décor. But again, he recalled that he had to deal with this financial problem based on a misunderstanding.

How could such a thing have happened? It must have been the lawyer who insisted, pressed on her kind heart, and she, listening to collective reason, agreed to the harsh strategy. Settling matters between people with courts and papers? Of course, it wasn't her fault. She just didn't have enough life experience to ameliorate her differences with Hans, maybe some grievance against him because of his callousness, his log-like head. His misunderstanding of her fragile soul that needed protecting, and caresses, and friendship. No matter how long Hans looked for where he made the mistake in the warmth of their summer journey, he couldn't find the flaw in the equations that had led to such a huge misunderstanding. He knew that as soon as he explained himself to Yuma, as soon as he could conquer her with the influence of his words, she would forgive him. She would cherish the picture of a future—with him. He just had to touch her, to fly through the blue sky to the darkness of her dark eyes, to the brightness of her bright smiliness.

After his walk, Hans returned home rosy from the cold, his feet frozen in the thin leather boots that he had also gotten wet along the way. It was dark in the apartment downstairs. Hans prepared all the electronic and alcoholic accessories for his party and waited until he heard voices or sounds of life from downstairs. He read Warhol's diaries. They were yet again monotonous. Warhol walked around, spoke to people, ate. Hans loved the sleepy feeling of endless records of everyday life.

No one came back to the apartment below that evening. The windows remained dark and the rooms silent. Hans went to sleep.

Yes, I'm an ungrateful pig.
I want to remain an ungrateful pig.

CHAPTER 40

The next day Hans had a photoshoot in Brooklyn, the characters in some film. In a studio not far from Brighton Beach. Hans didn't want to work. Rather, he didn't want to leave his house for the cold. He wanted to be alone, to figure out where the plane he had launched from the taxi was flying to. He didn't feel like it was diving into an abyss, flying freely, or gaining altitude. The threat of paying a debt for two hundred years continued to bother him greatly. He couldn't believe that anyone would need money that much. That someone was able to swallow up a person whole, together with boots and the ends of his hairs like piranhas sucking each other into their predatory stomachs.

After the shoot, Hans sat on a bench along the boardwalk and looked out into the horizon. The ocean roared a cold white whisper. Hans got out his notebook and pencil, which could be used in the cold. He wanted to write Yuma a letter explaining everything in a manner that would be practical and comprehensible to her. And he wanted to deliver the letter in an unusual manner, maybe using a messenger pigeon, by baking it lightly into a pastry, or engraving it on a large metal sheet. Having not yet decided how the letter should look with respect to its content, he began jotting something down, a bit saddened by the encroaching fogs of the ocean on the horizon.

December, Brighton Beach

Yuma!

I received an anonymous letter that you had become smitten with someone in Tokyo, fallen in love up to your ears. And I myself have also been suspicious, you Jewess, you miser. You probably fell out of love with me because I'm not a frugal person and asked you to blow your cash on one or two telegrams. Well now! I guess that's the way it is. I still love you out of an old habit, and you can see what kind of paper I'm writing you on.

I broach this subject with a feeling of awkwardness. Writing a telegram is a science more precise than mathematics. A few days ago, I was watching TV, indulging some bad tendencies. They predicted lots of snow and cold weather.

The best thing to do is to throw away all the letters unopened. That's why I haven't written you for so long, because I myself can receive my letters and read them. History has no eyes, but it seems it has ears through which you can place your artifacts in the right spot. Today was such a wonderful Sunday, and again I couldn't sleep.

I'm sitting on Brighton Beach. It's real winter here: a thick sky over the gloomy ocean, just like the ones in Central Park that we walked by while holding hands. I've completely frozen here on this bench, open to all the icy winds. But this state of struggle with the almighty elements weakens me: the ocean, attempting to come onto the shore with ferocious fang waves, can't win a complete victory over warmth. And I snuggle even more vigorously into my scarf, shivering from the cold. It's so nice and empty here: winter has cleansed the land of the hustle and bustle. The cold reason of the cosmos creates order on the land as if there had never been any reckless emotions here.

I see your face somewhere next to me. I want to get warm together with it. Everything inside me still breathes you so strongly. I can't believe that half a year has passed. Our moment was so short and so meaningful. In this periodic system that's manifesting, it will be easiest to appropriate you. You're again my own. The personal spirit of a fragile girl and the powerful strength of the faraway landscapes of your reality which excite me hourly. When there's no realistic path, I say—you're with me.

Again, I'm dreaming of Dubrovnik and that summer when we listened to records in the evenings and made bonfires with my cousins in the courtyard. During the day, you could go up into the mountains and gather mushrooms. It was cooler in the mountains. The mushrooms grew right under the pines, big ones, with full, moist, brown caps. If you broke the cap, the mushroom started to turn blue. In the mountains, there were also turtles, snakes, and all kinds of small creatures excitedly rustling among the layers of oak leaves. We caught the turtles that ran from us along the mountainside and piled one on top of another. The turtles were indignant and refused to cooperate. And again, the salty sea in the evenings, and after sundown a nose full of seawater… I so want to write you about this all again!

You know, I may have said something untrue to you last time. My uncle did not die in his sleep. At the sound of one of the regular shellings, everyone had run into the basement. They found my uncle under the rubble of his fallen ceiling after a second bomb hit the roof. He wasn't one to fear. "I want to live my life, and no war is going to make me leave my own house to go underground!" He had yelled this to his wife more than once when once again bombs were whirring and eating into the clenched teeth of the beautiful town.

One bomb went off in the courtyard, busting all the glass in the house. The window frame in the parlor, near which my uncle was reading a book in his favorite chair, was blown into the house together with the glass. He did not likely suffer for very long. What could he have been reading at that moment, and who was he fighting with? I had already been living for several years on my own in Florida when the long-distance call from my aunt woke me up in the middle of the night.

You know, since then, I have suspected that memory is harmful and brings us nothing good. I still had the strength then to try to deny that. I was still struggling. I waited twenty years, as if the past there, far away, could be changed by the strength of my wishes. I stored up memories, saved negatives. And yesterday, I gathered together all the photographs in my house and took the picture of my father from my wall. I don't want to seem crazy to you, but it seems to me that our memory is useless. There's nothing worse than two competing desolations.

Seeing you so close I could touch you is just a matter of my willpower. Now there's a new fashion for superheroes. They don't have that tiresome sentimentality that usually comes from the tendency to hide in the thicket of the past. Superheroes make a lot of money and smile big, attracting both children and adults. I've begun to work on my lips' flexors and extensors.

I'm alive and, it seems, healthy—although still coughing furiously.

Your hieromonk,
Hans

The copybook ran out of pages. At the same time, a breeze started upon the sea, on the ocean. The gusts of wind got stronger and found their way through Hans' clothing to his very bone. Swarthy clouds looked menacingly at strangers. Nature was preparing for the night and the violence of the waves, knocking a few practice tosses onto the shore.

Hans slowly headed towards the subway, knowing his way home.

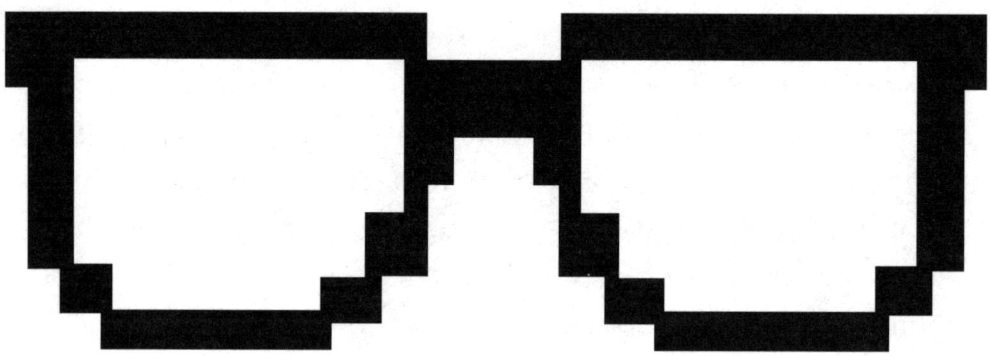

CHAPTER 41

Otto. Jesus, how could he be in Brighton Beach and not see Otto! Their interests really didn't coincide that much, but there was one thing that united them that didn't require explanation. If you were born in East Berlin and meet another person from East Berlin, there's not much you need to hash out between you. It's enough just to be silent together. Especially if you're far away and time has erased all your childhood like the relic of a mirage. Everything that you were remained there. And now you are not that. Or it is not you; however you want to phrase it. You don't need to talk—you can't, even. The candle of remoteness will burn out of itself, lighting up the grottos.

Otto tried to keep up with modernity. He sold Halloween costumes, or toys, or flowers, somewhere not far from the subway. His shop closed late. That's the only way you could make it in Brighton Beach, known for its pirozhki and samovar, chess games, borscht for three dollars, and the endless boardwalked beach.

"Here I am!" Hans said demurely after crossing the threshold of the small shop.

"My God! My God! What a pleasant surprise, Haaans! Hansiano! What a talent! Genius! G-e-e-nius. Good for you for coming to the backwaters. Careful, don't step on the cow pies. I'm so glad to see you! We live in New York, the most profligate city on Earth, but—let me complain a bit—nothing ever happens in this hick town. I'm dying of boredom. My bowels ache!" Otto looked at Hans with sincere admiration. "I need someone who knows his chess, vacuum tubes, and women. Someone who can drink until six in the morning and go to work at eight. God bless you! Someone who knows how to smoke frankfurters on a bonfire. Haaans! Brother! I'm so glad to see you. Let me give you another hug. You're shameless! You have no soul! How long has it been since we've seen each other? Where have you been, huh? Answer me that!"

Hans wasn't expecting such a kind reception. For two reasons. First of all, he had simply forgotten that such emotion was simply one of Otto's traits. Otto lived for constant contact with people, and it would have been difficult to count the number of friends he had or how many people he spoke to. Working in a shop was made for him; the endless art of convincing a buyer was like hunting in the wild woods, and maybe it was seeing new people every day that kept Otto in shape. Second, Hans was bogged down in his own matter and had stopped noticing the details of what was occurring around him. He again tried to freeze his emotions in order not to be destroyed by absurdity and the lack of a direct path.

"Yeah, I know, I've been meaning to come to see you," Hans started.

"Oh, stop making excuses. I know your tricks before you use them," Otto interrupted. "You have enough time to take pictures, but coming to an armpit of New York is beneath you, I know. A Casanova enchanted by the glamour of success!"

"Oh, come on, Otto, it's not..."

"Why do we have patience, Hans, huh? Why were we given patience? Yearning develops the soul. I didn't miss you at all by not missing you. Oh, I'm kidding, all these words. Words… How are you? What's new? Still all into your art?"

"Well, I'm somewhere in between spaces, I guess. You can't stay inside art in New York. This city is created for shops and boutiques."

"For chicks in stiletto heels, you mean? What's wrong with them? Here we go, you're really getting wiser, Hansiano. So go open a shop! Get on with it! You need years to work your way up here. Maybe even centuries. By the way, you wanna drink tonight?"

"I'd love to, but I've got a meeting today."

"You bastard, bastard. Who are you meeting with? A wooden statue on the third floor of the Metropolitan Museum? Have you gotten into architecture? Make a run over to the dump across the street and get us some coffee and something sweet then. I'm dying to poison your blood with some fast food. You've completely withered away with no one to take care of you, Hansiano."

And with those words, he reached out to Hans with fifteen dollars, adding another idea on the fly:

"You know, friend. You need to get married."

"Yeah, well, I… I just don't have any real interest in anyone…" Hans protested.

"Wow, you're a picky one, lord. Psychologists say that the best strategy is to marry the first person you come across. That means any girl, Hans. The first one you see on the street. In your case maybe you can marry the second one…So that you have ten seconds to think, or else you'll have a heart attack. You're sensitive. Just think, Hansiano! All of Latin America is yours! Venezuela, Brazil, Honduras…Oh, forget about Latin America…All the girls of the world are shaking their billions of bouncy tits in front of your flaccid co…"

"OK, OK, let me go get us some coffee," Hans said, attempting to climb out of the uncomfortable position.

"Get me an almond croissant! Almond! And get yourself one too!"

When Hans got back, there were customers in the store, and for a while, Otto was trying inventively to get them to buy a green duck, worm TV, or frog vampire costume for some party.

"So, what's new with you?" asked Hans.

That wasn't just politeness. He wanted to hear something. Hiding in the emotions of Otto—mature, nimble, and dutiful to life—was a peace. Hans wanted to connect with his rational life, to take up a small place in it, even if just a vase in his hallway. Rationality was one quality that Hans didn't have enough of. And he came to the shop for it in an attempt to plant himself on the surface like a magnet with at least one leg.

"We're expecting our second, and all our thoughts now are about moving and saving some money for the upcoming changes. You know, it really is all these cares that make up life. The spectacle of a soap opera that we're writing ourselves. Have you ever posted a picture of your kids on Instagram? No? Because you don't have kids. Do you know who I post them for? Of course, you know. For myself. And for my wife. It's a contest to see which one of your friends can be most annoying with pictures of the dumb mugs of their babies. We compete in our boringness, but—even so—we can't argue because, in reality, nothing matters to us but our own families. Nothing really matters to us. We're choking on our own happiness, Hans!"

"Yes, yes, you're completely right; you know you are. All these years, I've been trying to live a lifestyle that I've never had."

"And what have you got?"

"I failed that test."

"Because you never even took the test. You never showed up, Hansie, you bastard."

"Maybe. But I was busy searching for other truths, trying to heal our common wound."

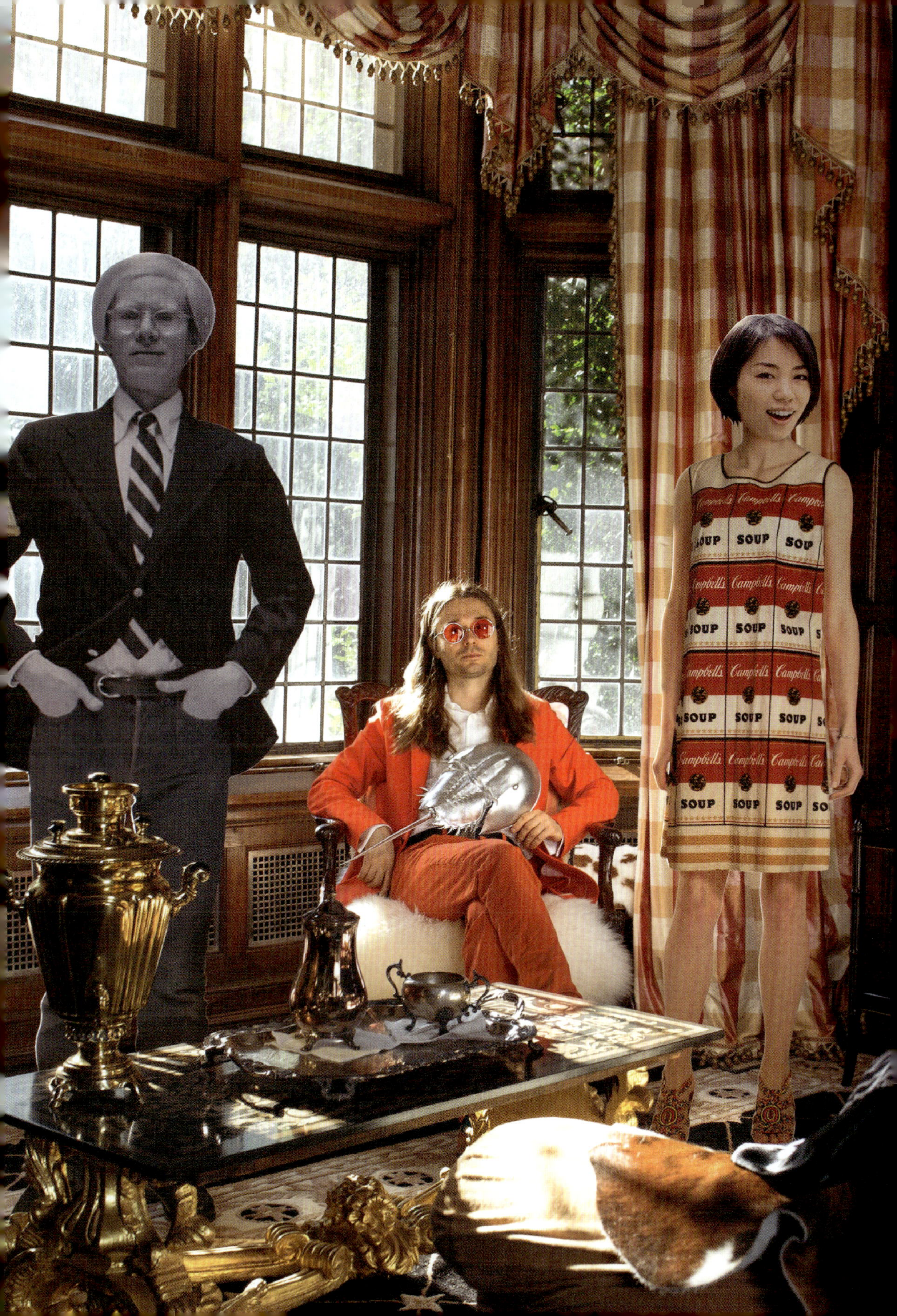
Campbell's
SOUP

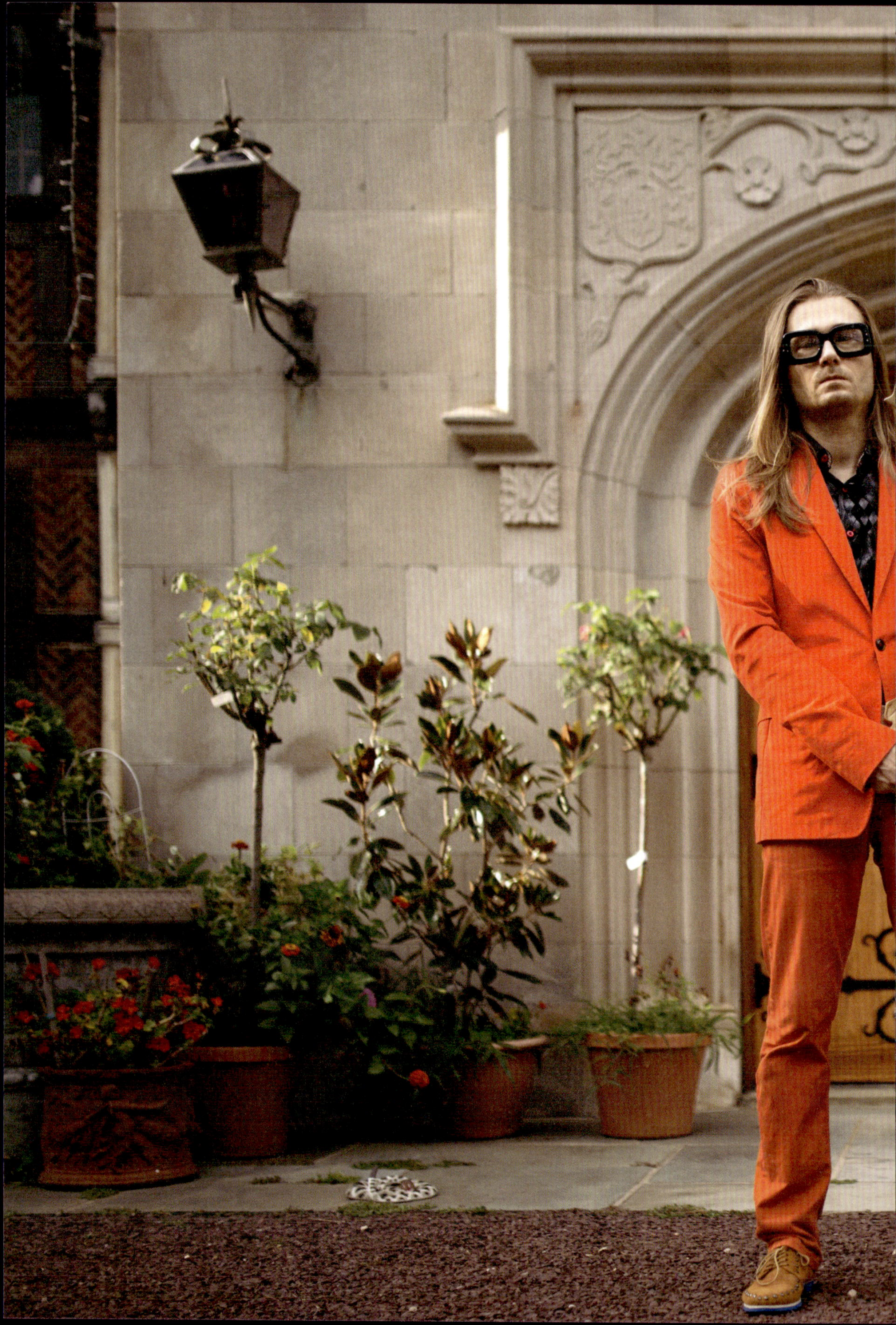

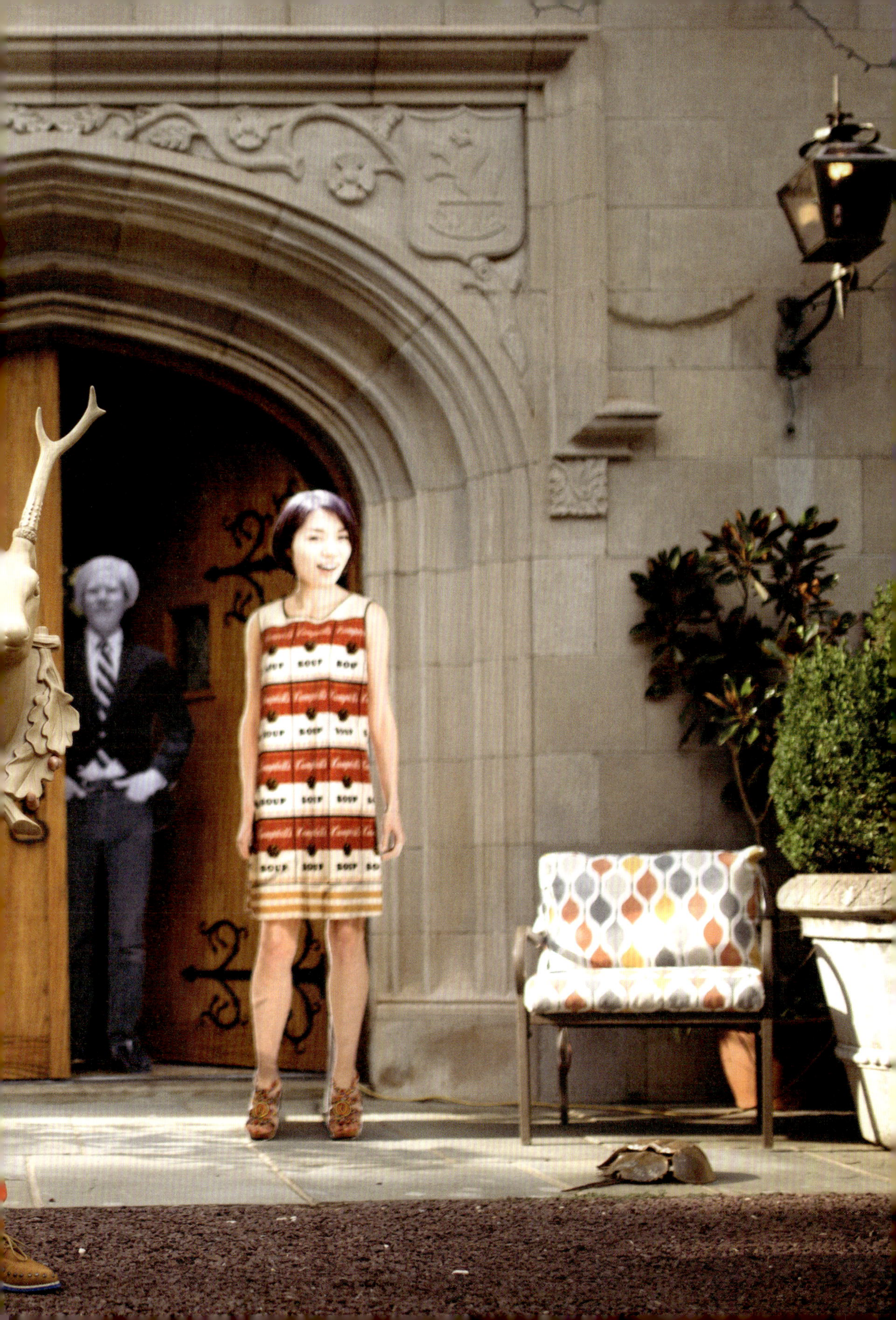
SOUP

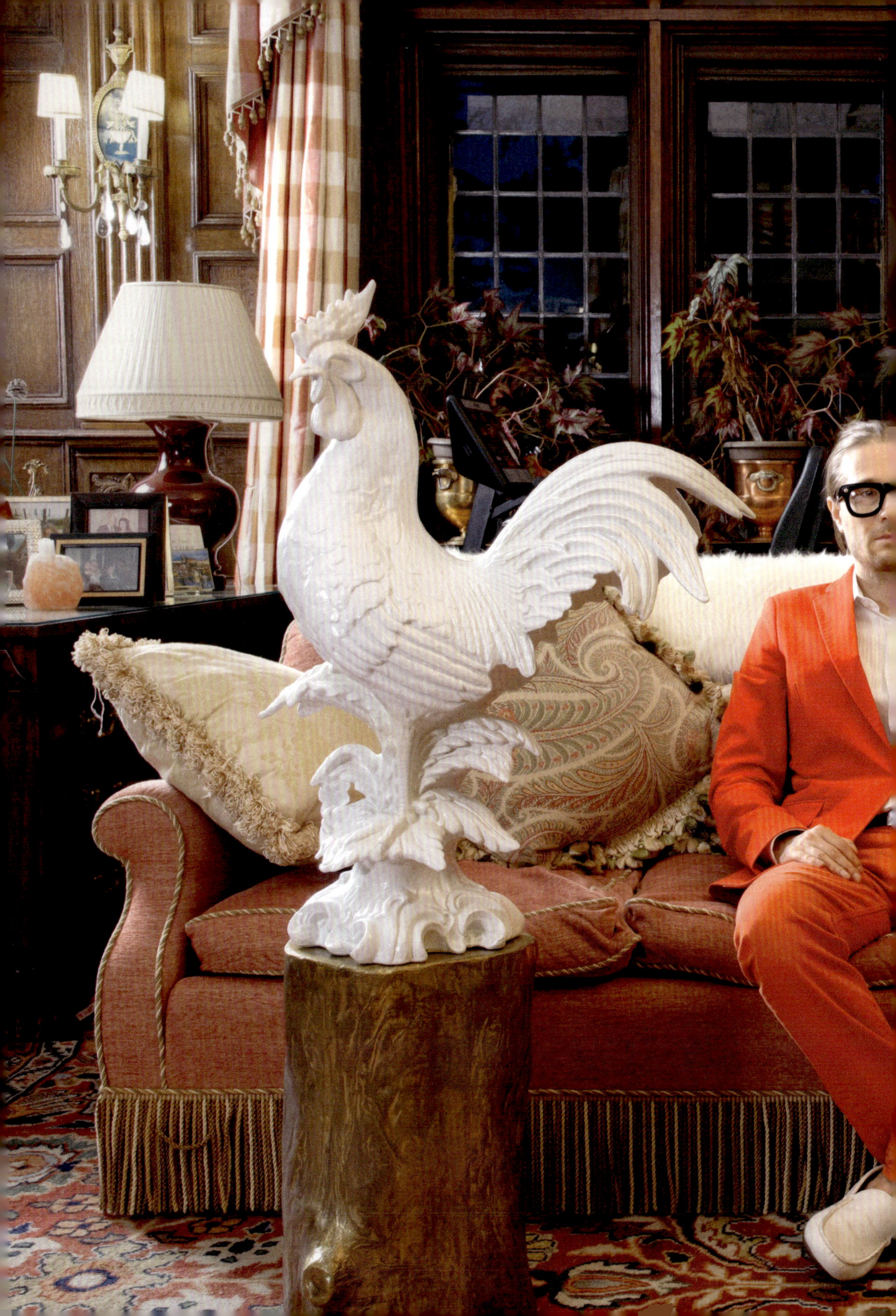

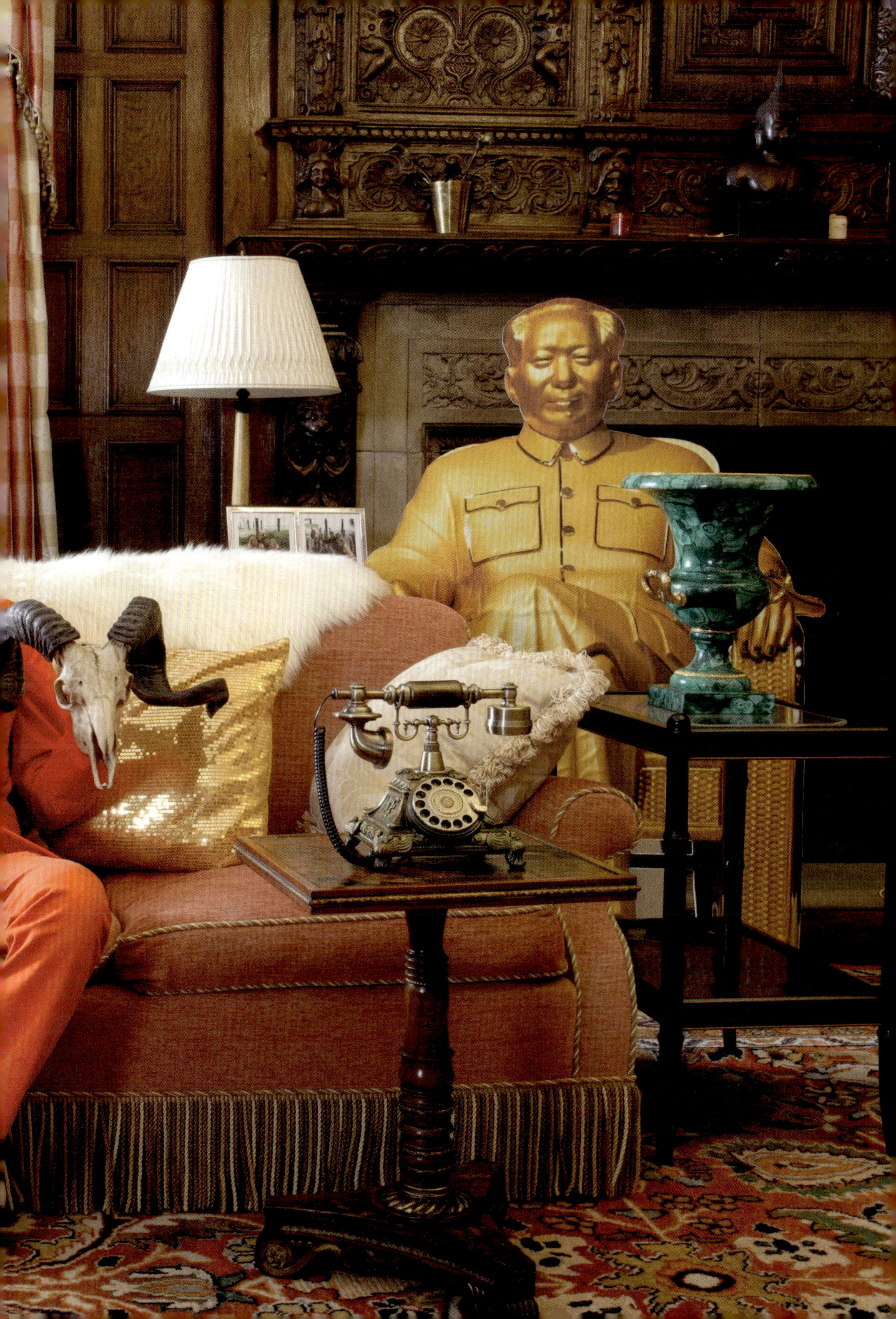

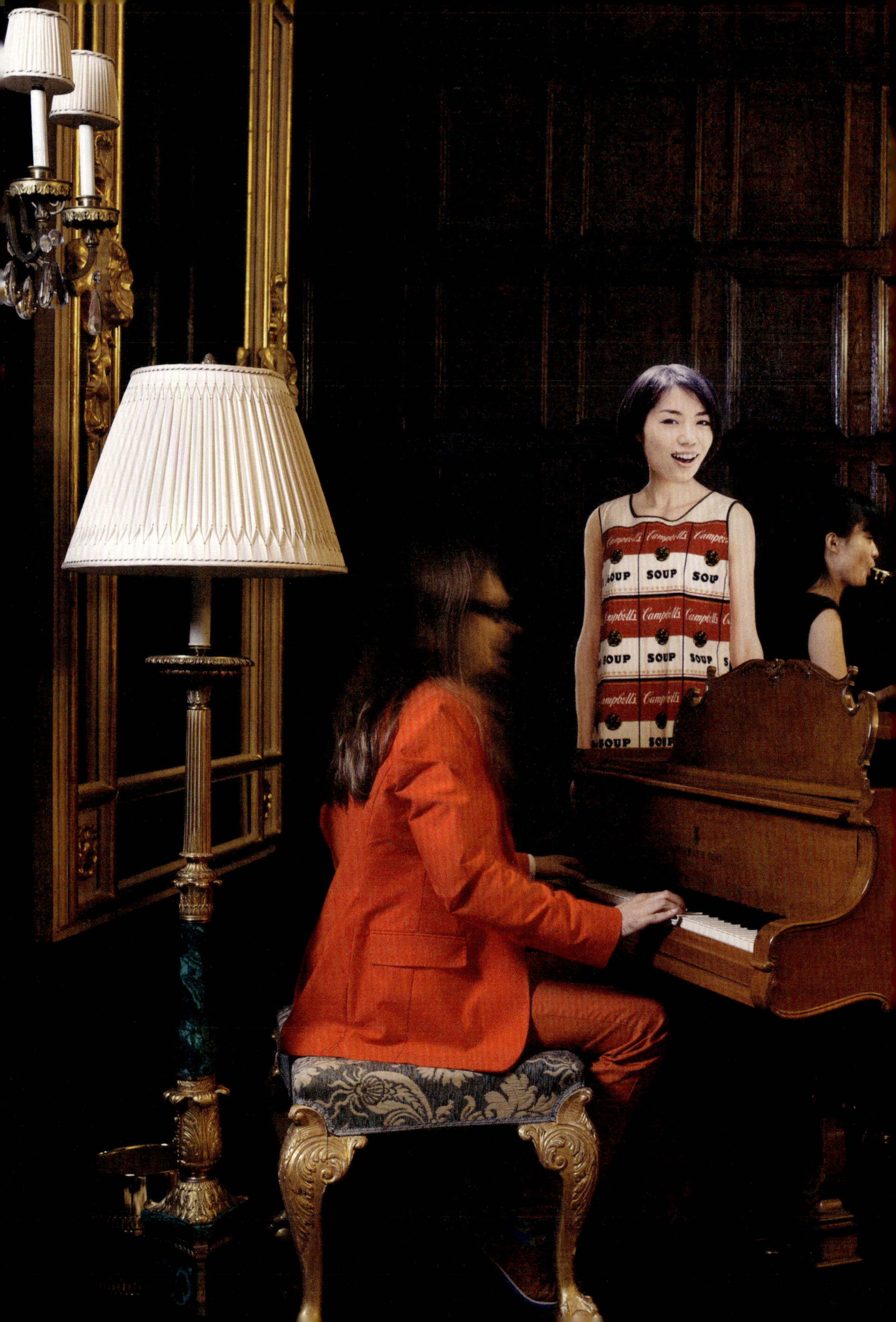
Campbell's
SOUP

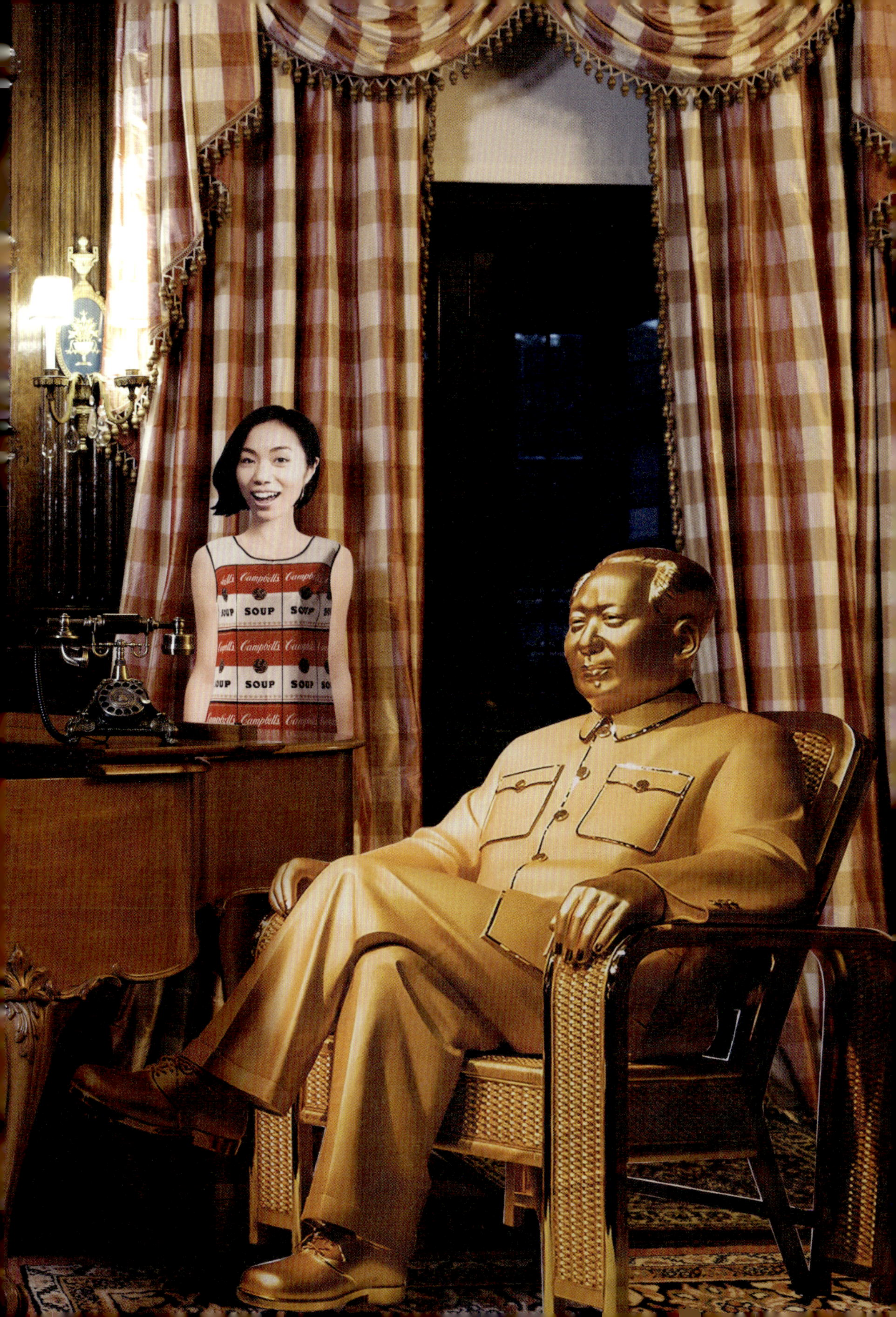
Campbell's
SOUP

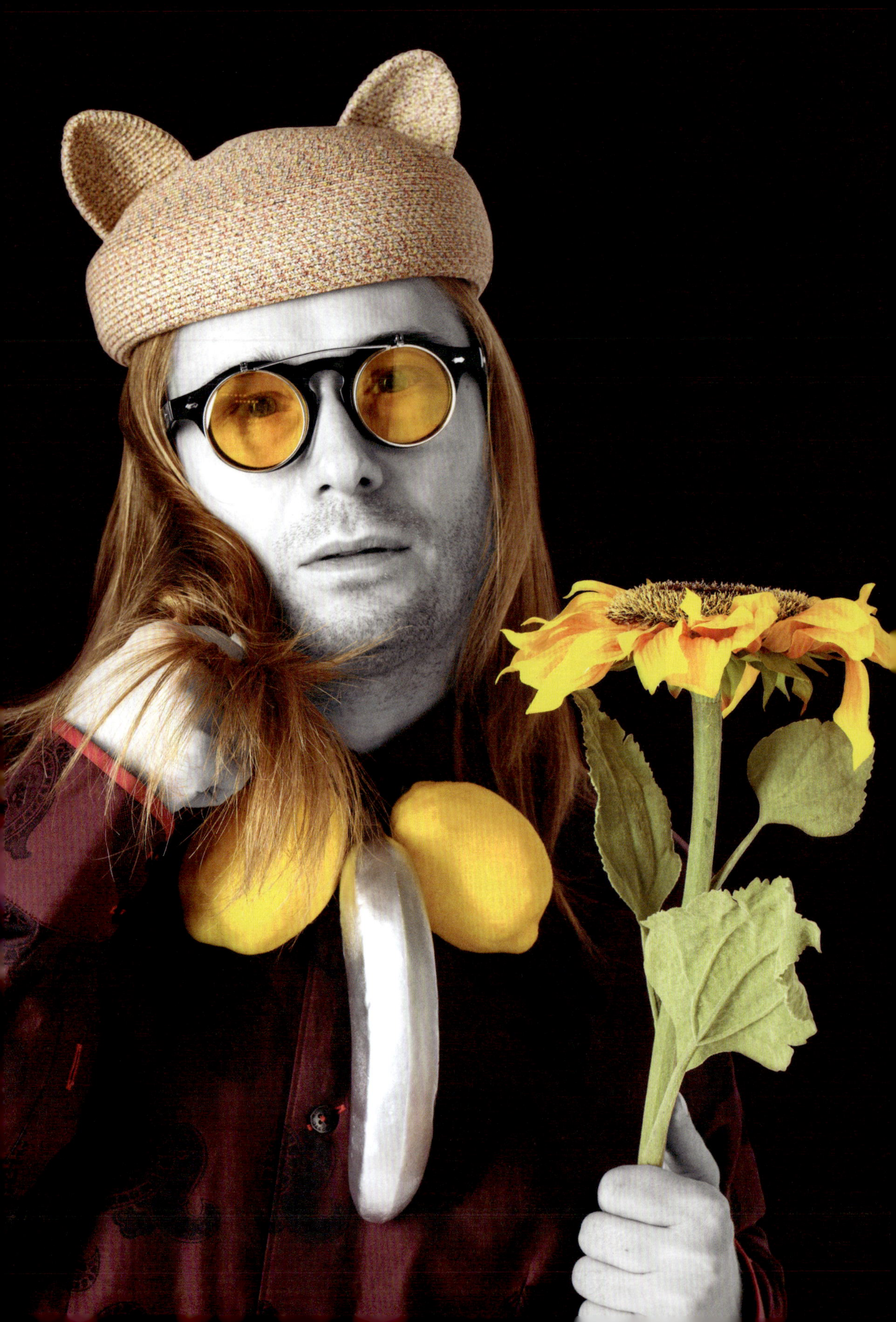

"Yeah, I understand. But the more you focus on your problem, the more immobile you become. And you have to move forward. Being a traitor—that's the medicine for life in a modern city. Look, take my shop. If it weren't for my shop, I would have never met my wife. If it weren't for my shop, I wouldn't have taken out a mortgage. If it weren't for my shop, I wouldn't know what other trash I could sell. Why have the past when you have a wife who you can buy frying pans on every birthday?"

"But some people see the safe path better than others. They don't run into the tree."

"There is no safe path, Hansie. Life is an unsolvable problem. Life is an asshole. But who am I to tell you that? You just have to rise above the impermanence. Like over a black hole. So you don't get sucked in. Einstein thought that up for himself. And one day, we'll fall into it. It's just that that doesn't surprise us. Flap your wings, Hans. Do you want to buy a murderous doctor costume with wings?"

"You know, I already have wings. Ten pairs. They swell up on my back under my shoulder blades."

"You're a hell-raiser! What talent! A shabby little poet! But I have the costume of the mad doctor with wings who flies around at night by people's windows playing concerts for the sleeping people. Mr. Pan and Lady Poppins in one. Jolie and Pitt's adoptive parents. Have a look."

"Thanks, Otto. Thanks, buddy. But you know my apartment is about the size of one-and-a-half of your bathrooms."

"No problem! Take a look at this, then. The professional deformation that occurs to a salesman's personality won't allow me to let you leave without buying something! I'll give you a discount of ninety-nine percent. This is my new stand. A new direction for the business. You know, I've even gotten all the permits…" he laughed uncontainably. "Come here..."

He disappeared around a corner.

"I sell guns now!" Otto said in a whisper and then laughed even louder.

Hans turned behind the folding screen and was flabbergasted. There was a stand containing all different kinds of guns, pistols, revolvers, and whatever else they were called.

"So? Which one? You like them? And the licenses, the licenses. I've got it all," Otto laughed.

"Ummm, yeah," Hans tuned out for a second, so undesired, disgusting, and awkward was the feeling.

"Any kind, any kind of shot. Single-shot, multi-shot. Regular or large caliber. Your choice. Drum magazine, PPSh-41, Beta C-Mag. To fit any taste. I've got it all!"

"I don't think I need one," Hans dismissed the idea with horror. "I'm part of another…genre. I work on a different plane, let's say."

"You might not need it, but America defends you against your will!" Otto countered even more excitedly. "Take it. You'll feel like a general."

The dragon of the benefactor in Otto grew savage.

"Take an M4 carbine with a UBG L and we're done. Otherwise, I won't lay off you!"

"I've…I've got nowhere to keep it," Hans protested like a poisoned animal.

"Man, just hang it on your wall, scare your friends and neighbors, that's all! What a piece! If you have a machine gun, ideas of what to do with it will come of themselves. You know that from books. They don't make this kind of weapon anymore. Brilliant Chinese workmanship. At the very least, you have to help my business, Hans!"

Without thinking about it for long, he got out a boxed one:

"This is a classic; you know what I mean? A classic."

The two-edged feeling of rejection of what his friend was doing added to the draw towards such kindness built on the sad joy of life, leaving Hans to look for a way out between shame, unbearableness and his pity of Otto.

"You should come over to our place some time and meet the wife. She only knows you from photos. You're like a movie star. Sit in a nice homey atmosphere..."

"Yeah, that's a great idea. We should discuss it."

"Discuss, discuss. Next week, and that's the end of it."

"OK, agreed. Next week. Why not? I'll stop by."

"Good man!" Otto guffawed without toning it down at all. "What a serious goose you are! Don't explode, now! Call me, brother, OK? Call me."

They embraced, and Hans took the box that was, for some reason, pushed on him into a cab.

A taxi. Another seventy dollars. But Hans didn't want to throw away the despicable unit, and taking it on the metro and along the cold streets would have been even worse. As if he were even afraid of the police.

CHAPTER 42

This time the light was on downstairs. Through the sky-blue curtains, that light made the room even colder than outside as if it were a window into a different winter. The room reminded Hans of the morgue where the steel saw opened his father's skull.

When he got into his apartment, Hans removed his goose-down coat that had gotten goosebumps from the cold, suffering for him. But Hans, too, had gotten colder than expected. Thanks to the low temperatures, his reason gained significant clarity. On the street, it wasn't as cold as it was New York windy. And the sharp patches of wind that reached his very spine were even capable of carrying one away to another country, like the paper plane that Hans had launched from the taxi. "Gone to another country....Gone with the Wind..." Hans muttered.

Hans dropped the box with the stupid present in the long intestinal room and began preparing for his soapy teledate with Yuma. To wipe away the remains of the day's colors and distance himself from the unpleasant ending of his conversation with Otto, he decided to take a bath. And also, even, so that the moment would acquire a solemnity while the hot streams caressed his body and washed away the remains of the snowstorm.

He grabbed the tobacco smoke-soaked bathrobe left to him by the previous resident. Hans placed all the other things necessary for a proper bath, such as shampoo, toothbrush, electric razor, and

Andy Warhol's diary, on a small, narrow shelf. Hans loved to read while enjoying the warmth of the bathwater. Although he wasn't very good at creating pleasure for himself—the springs of pleasure inside him were made from a material that didn't allow Hans to stay in one position, instead pushing him out. He avoided excessive corporeality, which called him along the path to temptations and, therefore, regret. Hans didn't want to struggle and explain his weaknesses. He preferred to hide and remain silent with himself. To wait it out in bland circumstances in order to make no mistakes that might bring about irrevocable destruction.

He wanted to take a bath in no hurry, to shave until he shone like a mirror, and to have a lovely read. The bath was edged by sheets of drywall sixty years ago, in the tiny apartment which didn't expect any such renovations. Thus, to fit in the bath, one had to have the skills of an astronaut—be able to fold yourself in four. Or be born in Japan.

The cast iron bathtub itself, which had seen things and accepted the bodies of hundreds of different bathers, was ready to fall apart from disappointment with the water and dirt. Replacing the tub with a new one meant also removing the faucet with the shower and all the pipes—renovating, basically, the entire bathroom. And, of course, after that, the entire apartment. Replacing all the wires and the sewage pipes and the plasterwork. Then replacing the whole building, exiling all the residents to another continent. Neither the residents nor the owner would want that. So, he had to use the antique fittings carefully and pray that the pipes and shower would have enough good humor remaining to service an unstable and fickle person. And that's how it was day in and day out, decade after decade. The cast iron faucets stiffly and diligently turned off the water as if they feared losing their job. It was the most reliable technology on the planet from the time of the industrial revolution.

Einstein and Miles Davis were just born when these faucets were cast. But unlike people, they had continued into the future, with enough left in them to work for another century.

That's why the houses in New York didn't fall to bits. They just exploded sometimes, turned into dust, or burned to cinders. But that didn't happen every day. An event noticeable only to a few eyes was something society as a whole was able to tolerate. Despite the venerable age of the bathroom's fixtures, they looked kindly and even, to a certain extent, exquisite and expensive. Especially from an artistic point of view, combining denseness, cheapness, heaviness, and the naiveté of their shape. The bathroom was like an abandoned factory workshop. Stuffy, small, dusty, and moist. Which was why it was pleasing. You're not just anywhere. You're in New York, the capital of worlds. If you want to be here, destroy the faience of the toilet bowl with your heavy butt cheeks. Don't be shy. Sit down in the milky foam of the antique bathtub, hiding your head in your stomach, and open yourself up to a meeting with delight.

Hans loved black Russian banyas. He increased the water temperature until it became a plasma, took off his clothes, placed them all on the lid of the toilet seat (there simply was nowhere else in the bathroom to put them as the hooks were all occupied with other things), and dove into the aromatic citrus foam.

Remembering Brooklyn today and the storm while melting in the water from the extreme temperature, Hans warmed up to life, whose orange aroma returned him to joyousness. He didn't even touch the book and just lay with half-closed eyes preparing himself for the upcoming meeting.

He went over and over in his mind that long summer day when nothing was foreshadowing the coming miracle. The problem was that he could only remember the best parts. Moreover, Hans didn't care whether there was anything worse. He was ready to do anything if only he could return to that day. He was prepared for any humiliation, to spend any money, do any work, if just to see her again as in the past, loving him. Just to have a chance. Anything.

Hans' memories were held on by the smell of her hair springing through his fingers. Her lips, like a small leather sofa in the anti-gravity of a spaceship. Lips into which a clumsy astronaut fell. Lips that carried you away into a sweet green forest with soft grass.

He still smelled the detergent odor of her panties. He didn't need eyes. His heart beat the vibrating drum on the screen of the nighttime scene. In his memory, Hans feasted on the beauty of her nature, which existed so simply that night for no one: for him alone. He was exalted, dumbfounded, and frightened; that this squandered beauty was given to him personally. Among the millions of anxious, billions of lonely, big, strong, talented, resourceful, leaping, and beautiful spermatozoids, Yuma had chosen him, Hans.

This unwound the spirals of all his deoxyribonucleic acids and awoke and inflicted on him cowardice, pain, and defeat with a sense of victory. If even once you get to the top, you aren't then able to erase the achievement from the wall of your narcissism. You were with her in the place where houses cost ten million dollars per square inch, where grasshoppers and cicadas sing a requiem, where birds on branches hide the stars with their wings from shame, to make it darker. Where your meek girlfriend displays herself to you in petals of inflorescences, elegant folds of cordial embarrassment.

The elastic from her panties drew a bloodline pattern resembling a gentle pink secret on the skin of memory. To stick your nose past the barrier and stroll through the grove among the chestnuts that for centuries guard the peace of the lake of temptation. To get lost there, fall asleep on the top of the hill in a soft hayloft. To get close and remain near her armpits, staying for a few days in each one to fully warm oneself in that perfumed burrow. The bright, incomparable combination of sharp odors of refreshing cheeses, red-hot saunas, tired and dispersed perfumes, the smell of chaste grasses, almonds, and vanilla. This bouquet spun the head of Hans' happiness and lifted him so high above the ground that he fell down into the warm bath from ecstasy. Hans perished like a scaly-winged praying mantis with its head bitten off.

Hans, do you remember how Yuma trembled at the melody of the starfall at night? Do you remember how, accompanied by the silence of the witnessing trees, you climbed to an orbit unknown by airplanes? How the hot passion of the heights carried you on the swings of the first kiss?

How you listened to the gusts of wind and the faraway peels of thunder, warming each other with myriads of close, lingering, spider kisses that transformed into one huge, slow fire?

Hans submerged himself into a maritime dream warmed by ideas, visions, and memories. Until he was woken by music.

The sounds of a bass drum rocked his bathtub as if he were in a cast-iron bell ringing for the evening mass. It was his neighbors listening to reggae. Hans woke up, squeezed himself through the half-open door to the current world, and stood up, getting used to the effects of gravity. His vision grew dim, and he felt the draughts of winter creeping into the bathroom.

It was about eight in the evening, and he had to act before all signs of life from downstairs were gone. Hans donned a white shirt with a tie and a pink jacket. He wanted to recreate the flowery mood that remained from his magical sleep in the bathroom.

Hans brought Warhol into the living room—if you could call it that—and placed him next to his chair so that he too could observe the date. Then he brought a scarlet drape from the closet and covered the table with it. The decorated space excited him, although not many people would understand that.

How would he see Yuma? What would she be doing? What would she be like in the first moments of their meeting? What would he say into the speakers? How beautiful and lofty would those words be? Would he be able to overcome his anxiety? When should he speak? Right away, or should he simply admire her for a while?

He brought a bottle of French red wine in. Hans had bad memories of the last time he got drunk, in the bar. But a glass was necessary here to create the atmosphere. The glass facilitated eloquence and the expansion of resourcefulness when it would be necessary to act after the initial observations.

Hans turned his large monitor and computer on. The LCD lights went on, and the iron and silicon device began warming up. The software launched, illuminating things to help love be once again conceived.

Hans hung Andy Warhol's stars on the walls, stickers that glow in the dark. Just in case darkness was needed like it was on their first date. If Yuma agreed to the wedding. Hans knew that much was riding on the unexpectedness and beauty of his onslaught. He brought in the velvet box with a diamond ring, a present chosen and prepared with particular care. He knew that he would be able to convince Yuma to live with him. He had already brought her close to him with letters. She didn't read them but did receive them. There was only one step remaining: get that stupid debt canceled, which she had hung on him with feminine cruelty. She'd understand everything quickly, and they would correct it all. The Japanese girl would listen to a knight, a real man…her future husband, for God's sake.

Hans prepared happy wedding music: the band ザ・ピーナッツ

with their song 恋のロンド. The Sony cassette recorder that Hans bought on eBay would play the song on repeat as a wedding march. Hans had the same kind of cassette recorder twenty-five years ago at his place in Berlin.

あの人の燃える
胸のぬくもりが
今も　今も　今も残るの
涙でつづる　想い出
忘れて踊りに行くわ

Hans got rid of the past, cleaning it with magnetic heads. But the past got in through the back door and again wound itself around him. As soon as Hans cleaned his memory, another part of the past rushed in to take the place of the old one. The burned photographs did not bring him relief, only kindled regret. Hans wanted them back. He wanted to look for the ashes and reassemble each photograph grain by grain.

Hans loved cassette recordings. The spirit of magnetic tape couldn't be replaced by any of the remarkable new devices. Internet and Wi-Fi, drones and driverless cars: it was all nonsense compared to a cassette recorder.

Hans prepared the second glass and poured wine into it. Yuma would need a drink too. Beside it, Hans placed their first wedding certificate, which they would sign by candlelight. They would repeat their feelings on a state certificate in Tokyo or stupid toy-like Las Vegas. A wedding! It seemed that everything was moving rapidly to that end, except for the fact that Yuma didn't know about this wedding. It was a significant triviality that Hans felt he would overcome. He just had to create a serious atmosphere in which Yuma would love to celebrate a wedding.

Hans set up small candles all around the room and lit them. It was now time to turn the webcam on, along with the microphone with the velvet magnetic tape of sound inside. Hans inhaled as much air as he could into his lungs, breathed out slowly, and tried to rid himself of the anxiety that continued to press with unseen hands on his face and rib cage. The glorious moment of shame, the sacred hour of joy, leaping hope, the imp of art jumping out from the underworld.

What would he say to her? "Yuma, how pleasant to run into you on this winter evening!" No. "I've come to you through a century of loneliness." Too sentimental. Or "Yuma, come upstairs and visit me." "I should choose something simple," thought Hans, "something conversational, to achieve a stereo effect." Hans had already set the speakers' volume at mid-range.

He sat on the chair and took a sip of the wine from his glass for courage as if he were at one of the school dances that he had never attended. Begirded by the rash of his decorations, he moved closer to the monitor and equipment to begin the long-awaited teleconference. Hans felt like Neil Armstrong landing a cardboard lunar module in fake orbit on the surface of a wooden moon. His eyes burned with the passion of a hunter. He drank the rest of the glass and poured another. And again, drank it all. When he felt that emancipating energy slowly rising from his feet to his head and straightening his compacted bones, Hans drank a third glass of fixer and pushed the button that turned the webcam on. The computer hummed from pleasure. Hans' eyes were clearer and sharper than ever before from the wine. He prepared his camera to photograph the first ceremonial moment: the monitor and smiling Yuma on it.

The webcam turned on, and the square of a room appeared, with a sofa in the center of the frame. On the couch, he could see quite

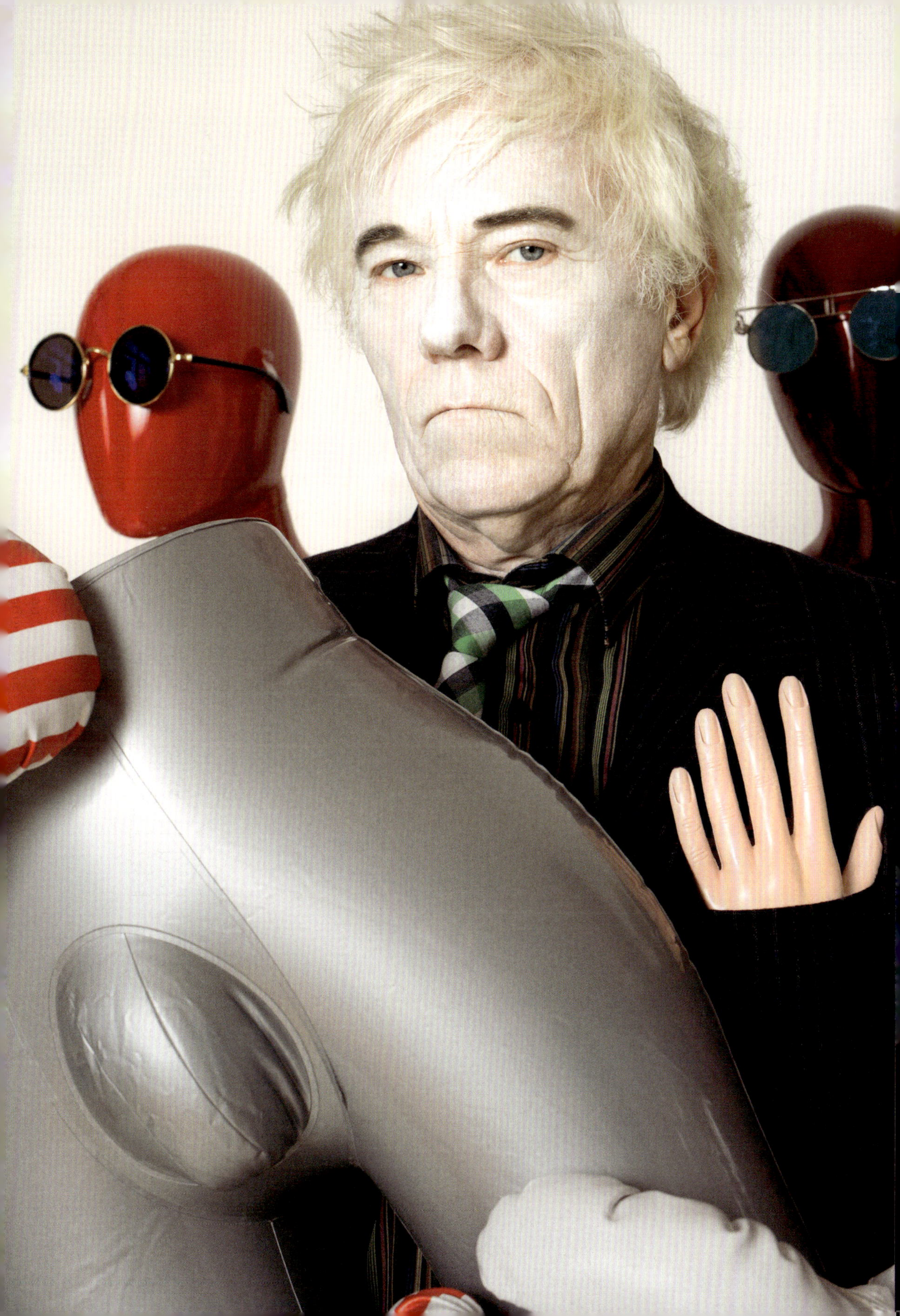

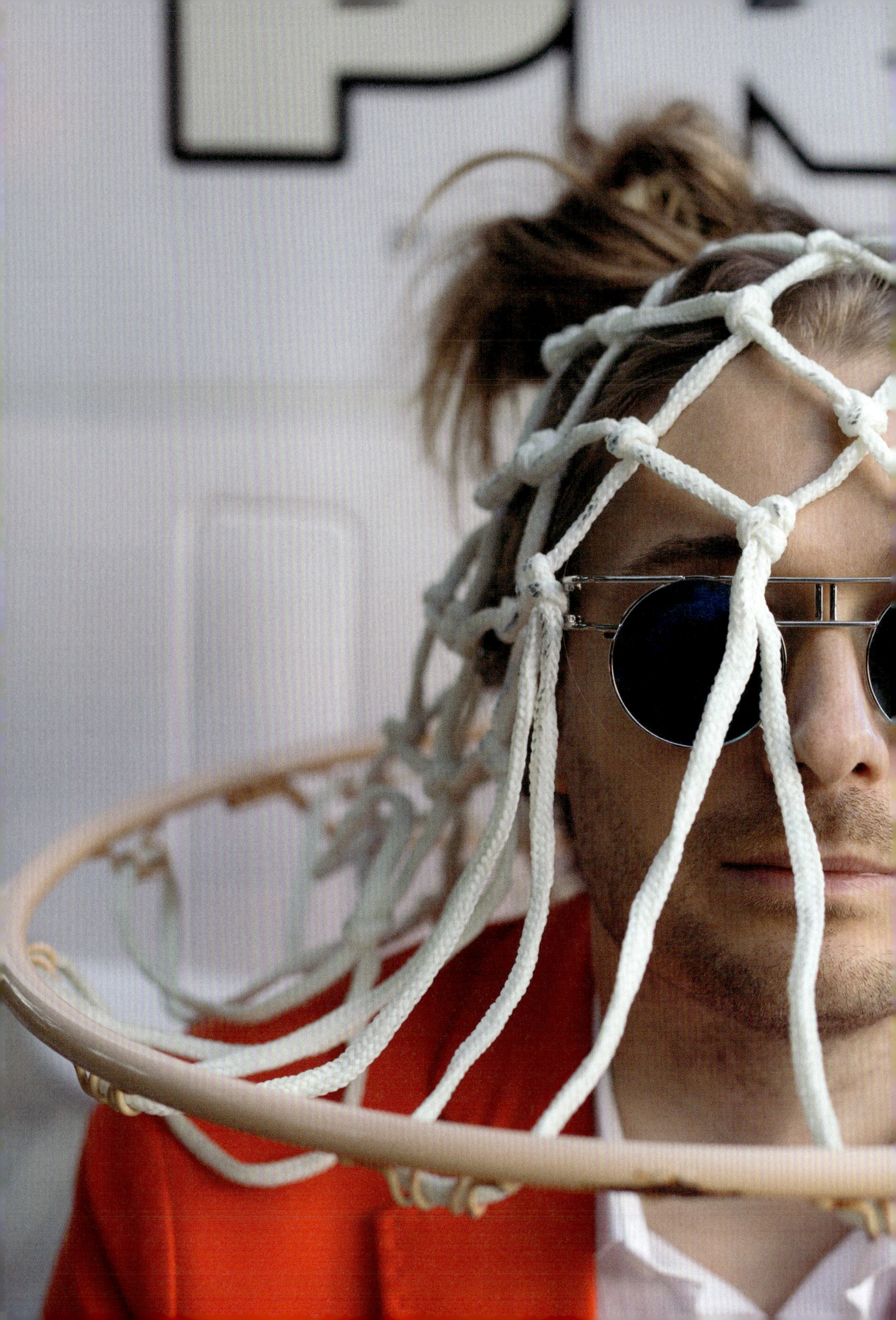

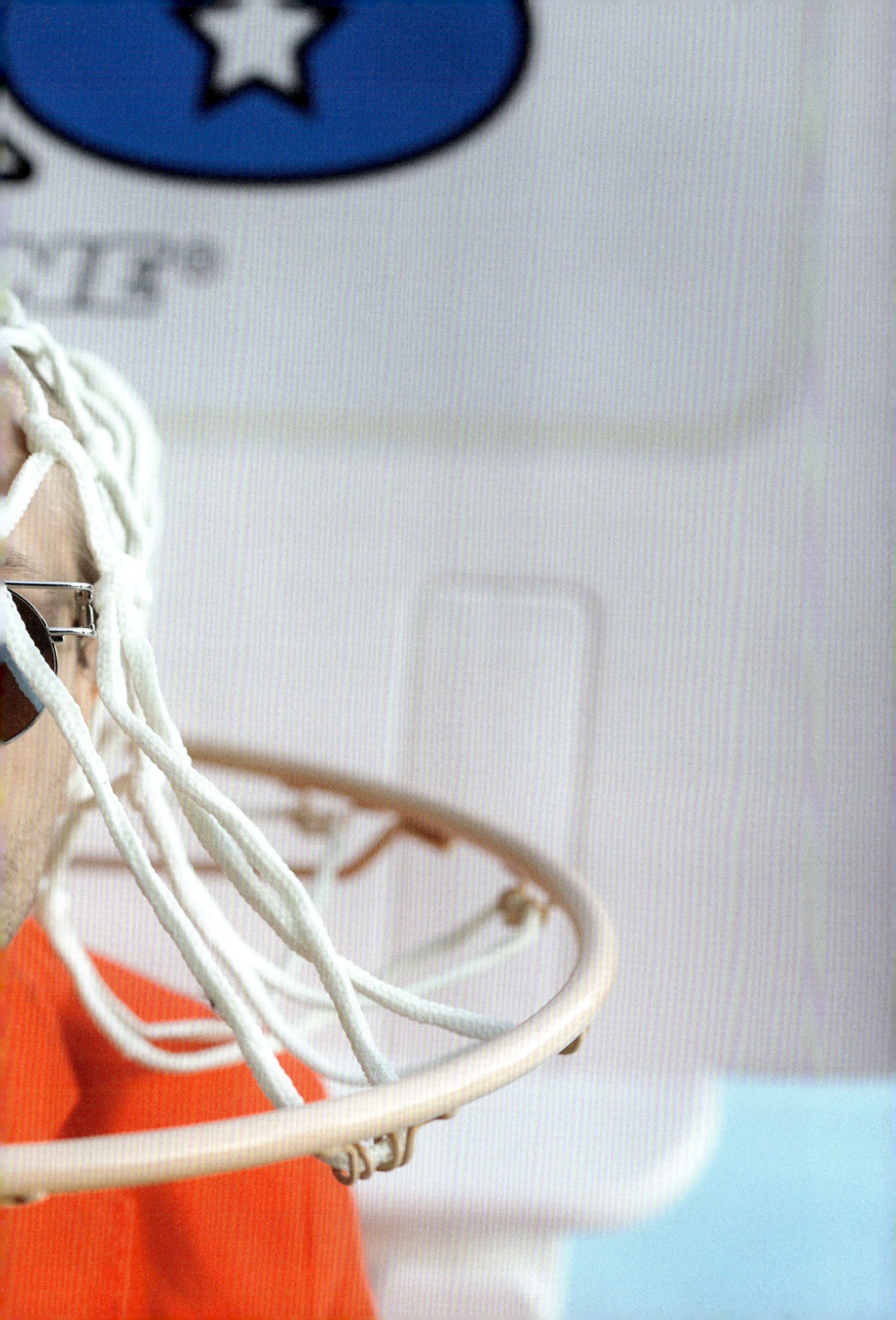

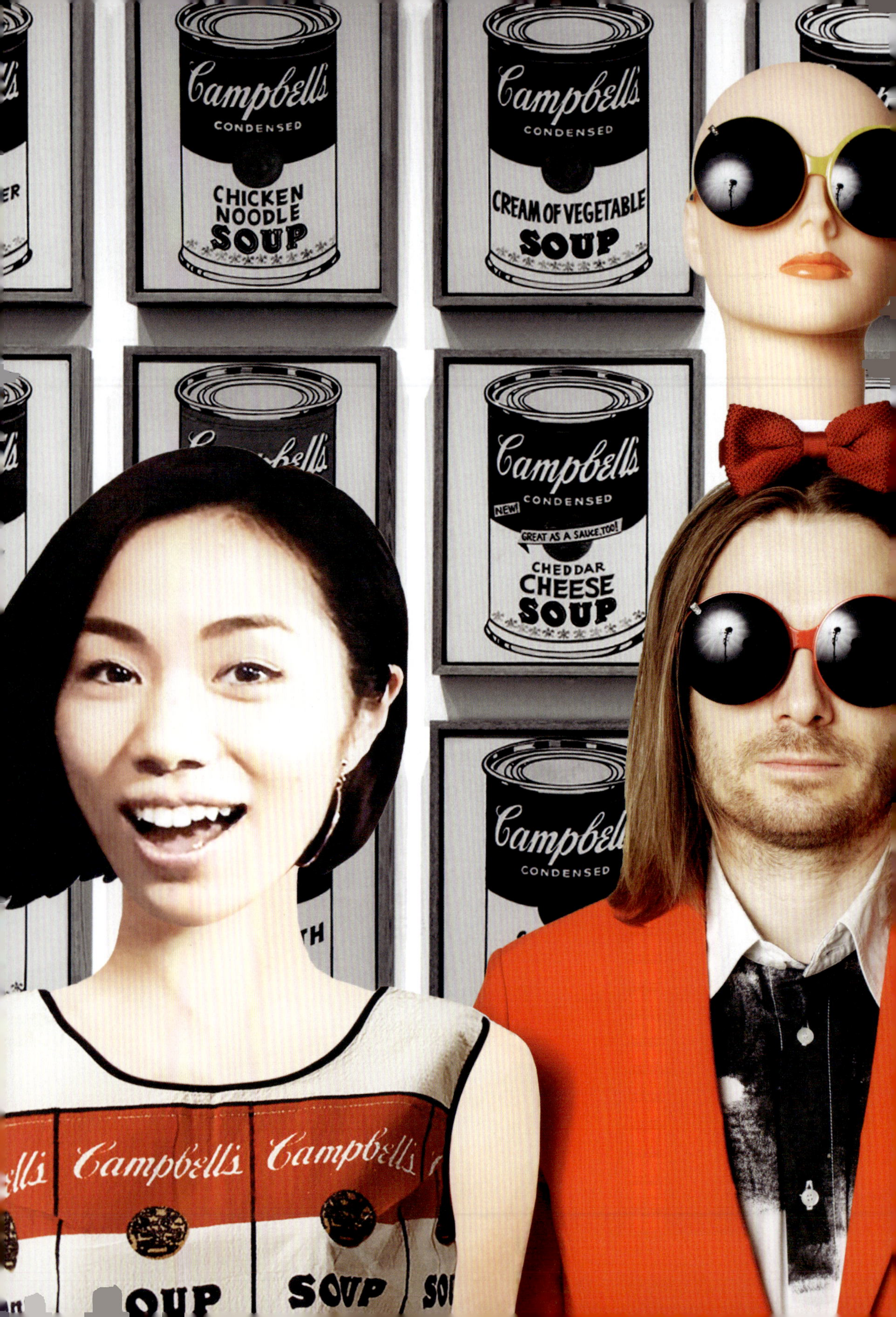
Campbell's
CONDENSED
CHICKEN NOODLE SOUP
Campbell's
CONDENSED
CREAM OF VEGETABLE SOUP
Campbell's
CONDENSED
NEW!
GREAT AS A SAUCE, TOO!
CHEDDAR CHEESE SOUP
Campbell's
CONDENSED
Campbell's Campbell's
SOUP

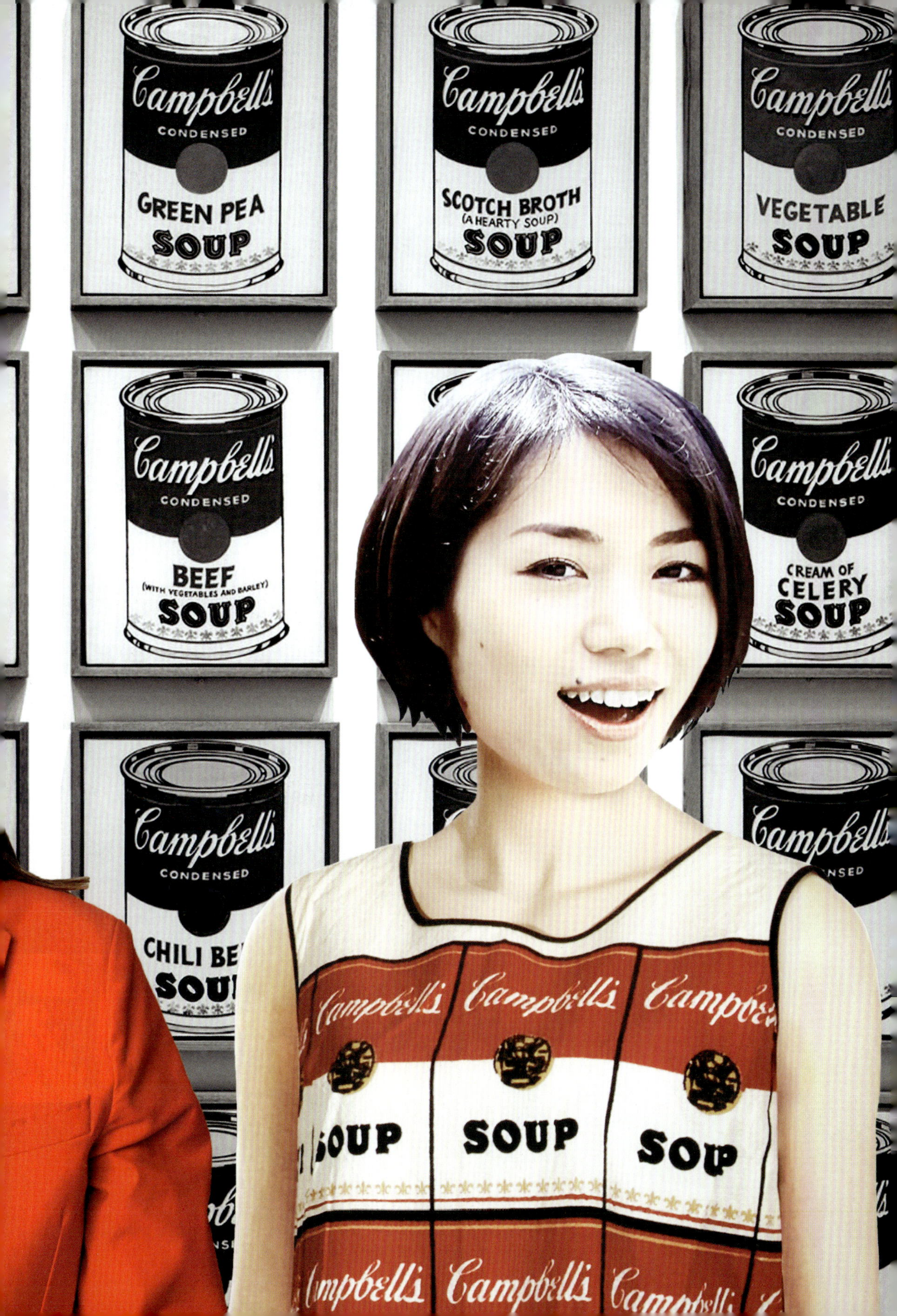
Campbell's
CONDENSED
GREEN PEA
SOUP
Campbell's
CONDENSED
SCOTCH BROTH
(A HEARTY SOUP)
SOUP
Campbell's
CONDENSED
VEGETABLE
SOUP
Campbell's
CONDENSED
BEEF
(WITH VEGETABLES AND BARLEY)
SOUP
Campbell's
CONDENSED
CREAM OF
CELERY
SOUP
Campbell's
CONDENSED
Campbell's
SOUP
SOUP

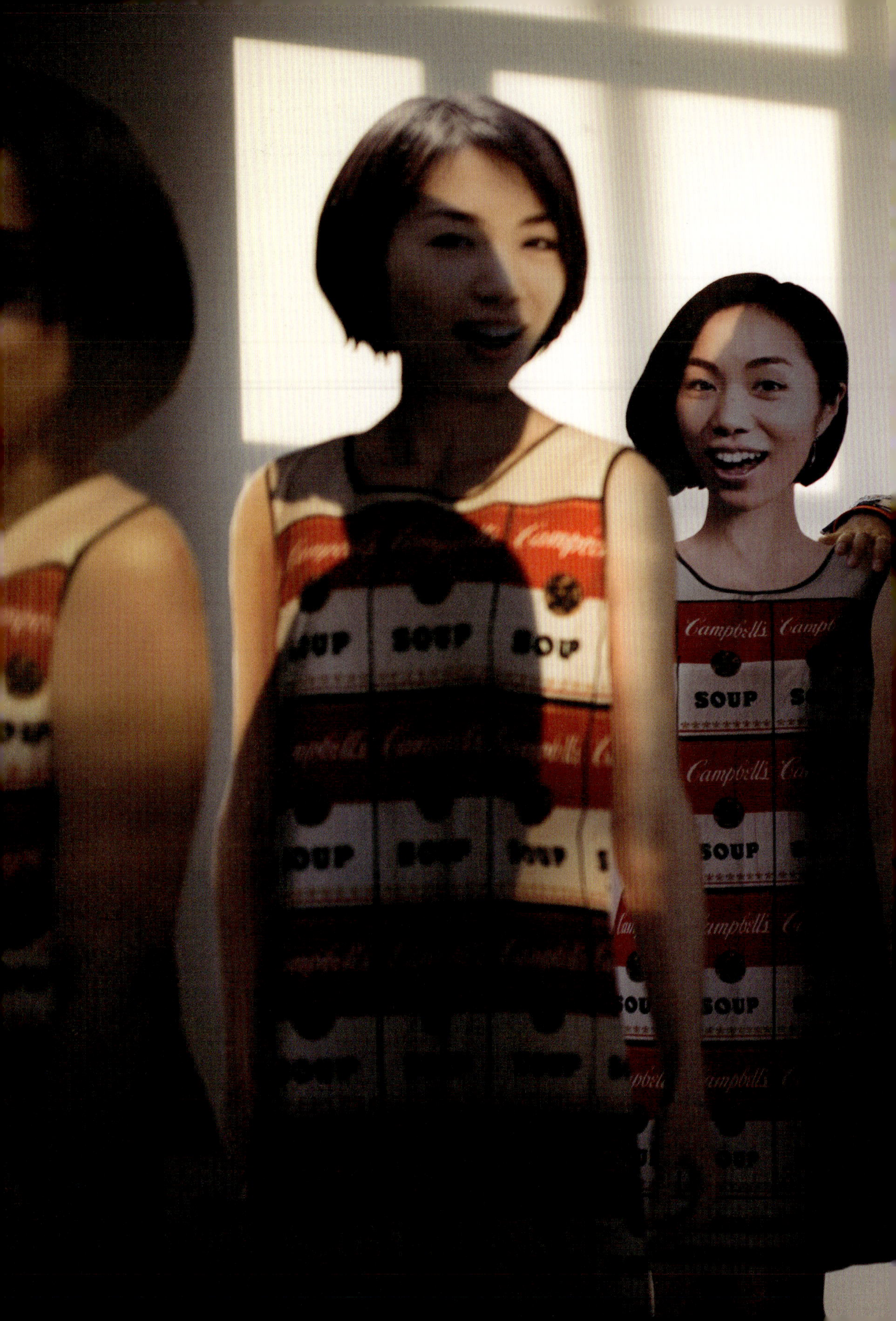
Campbell's
SOUP

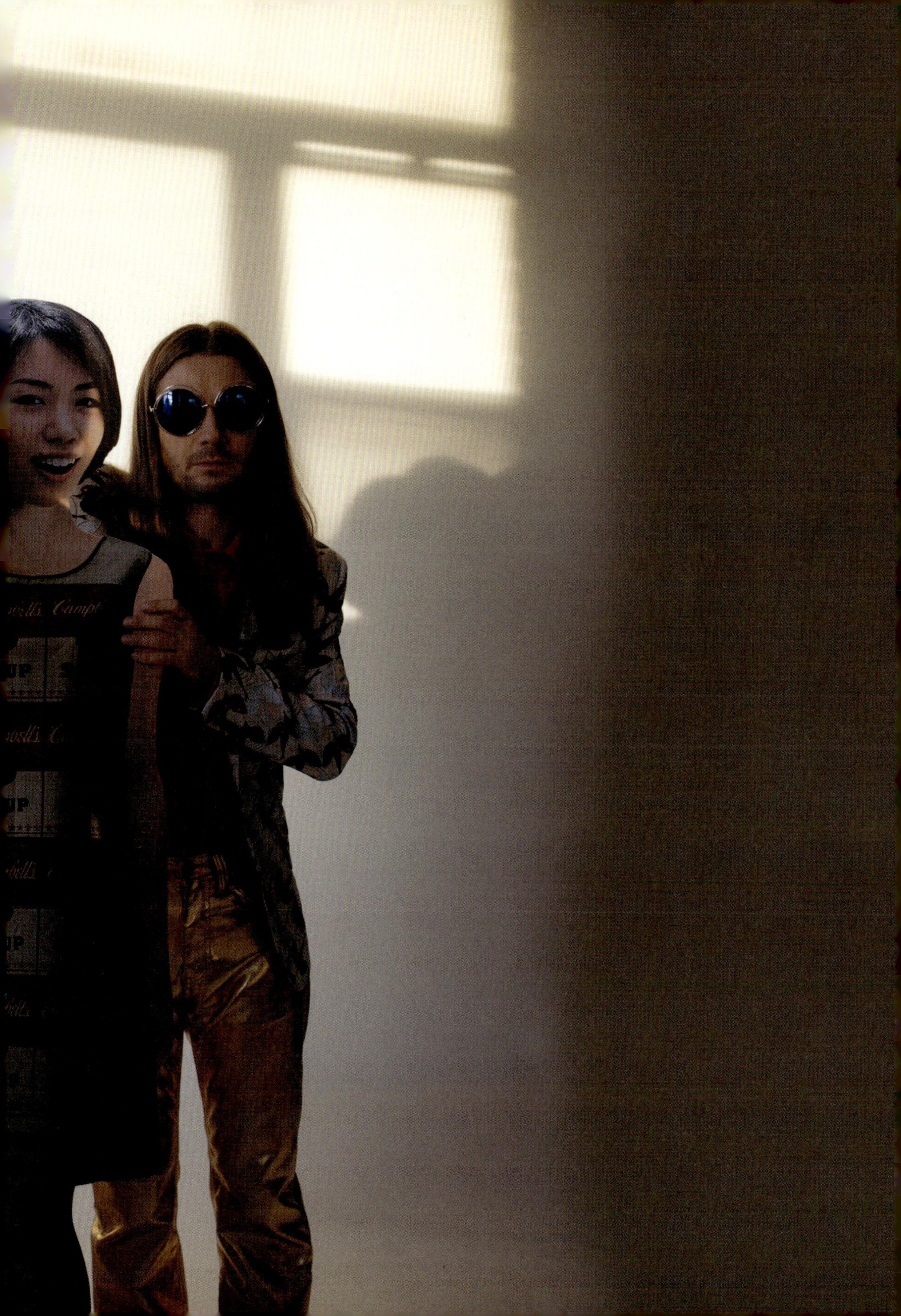

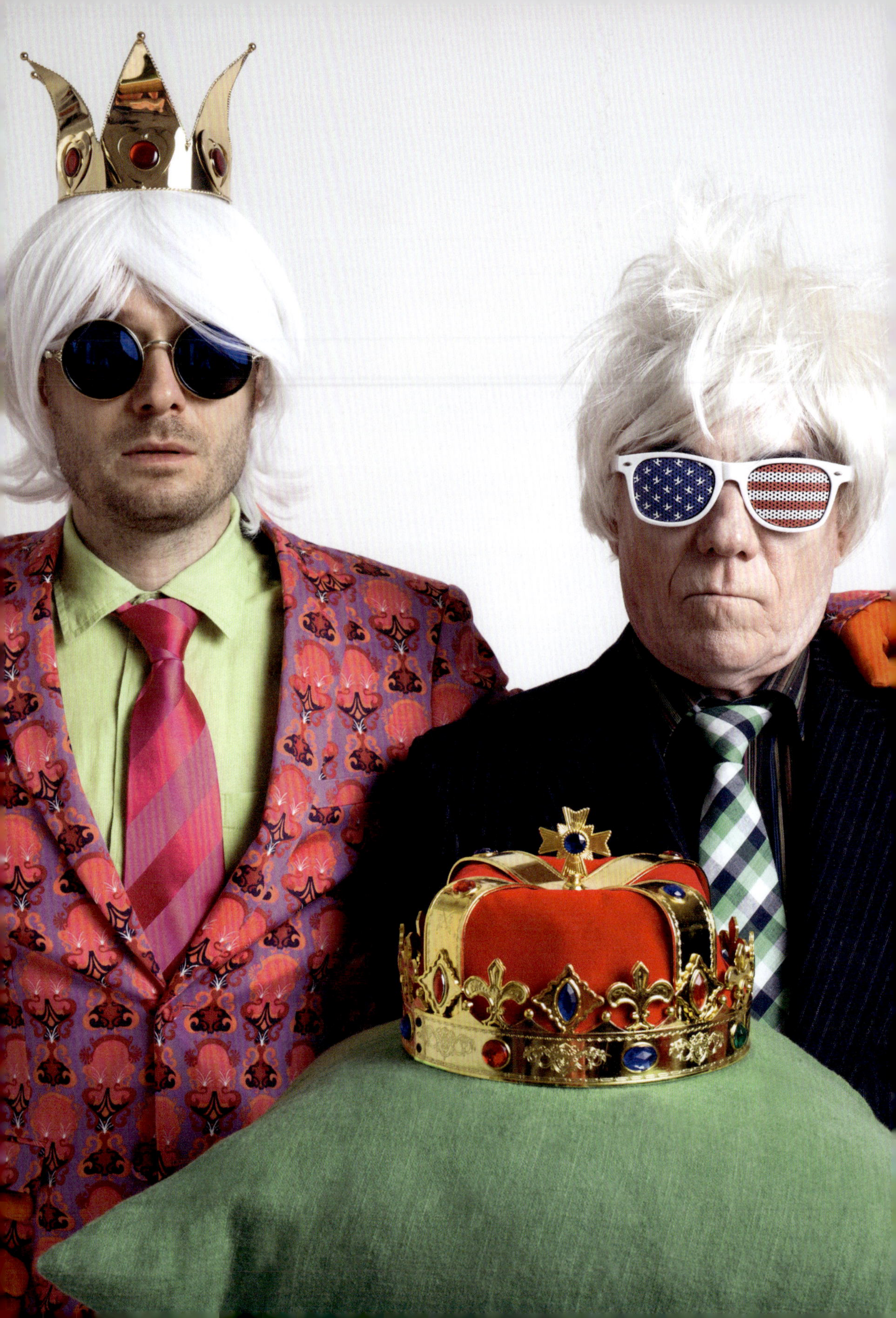

clearly and close up the hairy buttocks of a man deftly creating back-and-forth friction in the missionary pose for the one who lay under the assault of agility. A woman's hands embraced the also-hairy back, grasping it like the controls of an airplane gaining height.

The muscles of Hans' face froze in astonishment. He wanted to say something but didn't know what or how. His tongue spoke by itself:

"Stop screwing! I'm here."

Like an overheated train engine running along the rails, the man pressing the dainty girl to the sofa like an iron would a newly-washed shirt collar began slowly stopping the train. Only the long black tresses of the girl could be seen.

"Stop doing that," Hans sputtered quickly.

The guy did indeed stop screwing, not understanding what was happening, but not getting up from the location of the love-making, as he was as vain as any male of the species.

"Who's here?" he asked, growling at the savannah of the walls to instill fear, and looking all around.

"It's me, Hans, from upstairs."

The guy raised his head without understanding where to look. The speakers were hidden between the apartments, and it wasn't obvious where the sound was coming from. Hans saw a somewhat swarthy and relatively aloof yet disturbed face with thick lips. The face was round, giving it, and even other parts of the body, physical strength. The eyes were moist from having just had a female and desiring continuation. Like a buzzing fly, the foreign voice was a mild disturbance that one could not catch but could not ignore.

"You're upstairs from me?" the guy asked without even a taint of humor and articulating very clearly.

Hans could no longer answer. The dialog had led him down a blind alley. All the words he had prepared were from another lexicon. And in any case, he and Yuma were supposed to have met one-on-one. In any case.

Hans always got excited too late, when the party was already ending and there was no one around, and mourned when the worst and most unbearable was already far in the past. He turned the monitor off. He felt nothing. Or, more precisely, he felt only one thing: disgust with himself, with those idiotic wine glasses and dreams, with the circus, with the playful German romanticism with which he had stubbornly adorned himself. The only thing Hans couldn't understand was why the boringness of justice was able to triumph so quickly. Why wasn't he given a chance to go any further into illusion and ignorance? Why did triviality surge in with a cold shower and end the cacophonic melody?

Some demon from a box was fucking her. And for this, he drilled a hole in the floor to see hairy buttocks with nimbly operating muscles not connected to a brain? For this, he waited all those months? For this, he soothed himself with hope for all those days? For this, he wrote letters and suffered? For the Almighty to reward him like this?

But the issue wasn't with the hole in the floor. The hopelessness with which he struggled and latched onto the real Yuma was obvious to him from the start.

He was already hanging by one arm, slipping off a hard and inflexible cliff that had no humor, no empathy, no indication of any understanding of the humane. The cold stone on which Hans broke his nails and even teeth would remain a cliff.

The world is unjust. Hans sat behind the monitor as at the controls of an intercontinental bomber, frozen in the exoskeleton of a beetle pupa. Why did she, without even wanting to hear Hans out, try the words of his world? Why did she give herself on a dirty sofa surrounded by cigarette butts in Harlem to the first rough, bearish, uninteresting robot who was bored of sex? To a thresher who moved the force of gravity back and forth, who was indifferent to Tokyo, to her birthmark, to her vulnerability, to the sad, thin shine of her nighttime eyes, to the beauty of the lines of her hands, fingers, to her enchanting voice, to all of it, all of it?

He might not even know her name. He didn't care. And she was with him so easily, as if it was worth nothing: get undressed and touch with your gentle fingers, such beloved fingers, this bulging rubber creature who dove into her with a self-congratulatory baseball move. How could she let that in but not the letters? The silent, convincing, and fearful squeezed the question out of the tube into the emptiness.

Hans understood that he had reached the very peak of stupidity. His own silliness. The silliness was broadcast back to him on the television. It was his show. He was being stuffed, marinated, canned, and preserved. The path was disappearing. "So, you're finally here, Hans," he said to himself. "This is what you wanted, right?"

In this child's cosmos that reflected false conclusions, Hans' reason hit itself against the walls of bookshelves while looking for an exit back to his regular self. Hans couldn't explain anything. He moved forward, led by intuition. Intuition, the sister of stupidity, encouraged him.

He went into the far room and, without flipping the light on, felt around in the dark for the box with its gift from Brooklyn.

The M4 carbine.

After some time, having taken his jacket and tie off and put on a coat just in case, holding the weapon ready and a bit behind his back, Hans headed to the second floor, to Apartment 2C.

CHAPTER 43

When Hans got down the stairs, he saw a pair of naked buttocks. Like a living fish in the market, the live picture would not erase itself from his memory. So intrusive. "Who is it?" Hans thought melancholically. "A Japanese man? A Mexican? A Russian? Of course, not melancholically." He was just occupying his legs with this thought so that they would move more easily. And in a moment, it became unbearable. With more and more certainty, he sprung along the steps leading to the ocean.

There was no doorbell. But why ring? What Hans wanted to do couldn't be described in words. Rip out faucets, ruin electrical outlets, throw the couch onto the sidewalk, bust out windows and doors, crush the refrigerator and the gas stove. Hans wanted to root up the building and, together with its bowels, chuck it over to the other side of the Hudson River.

Hans banged heavily on the door with the butt of the carbine. As they say, he didn't have to wait long. He heard the sound of a lock opening and, through the slit, appeared Zeus, awkwardly covering the nakedness of his fixtures that still wanted to be working.

"What's the problem?" asked the track and field angel, irritated by irritations. "Was that you talking in my room?" he continued with a question, glancing cautiously at the M4 carbine.

"Yes. Where's Yuma?"

"Who?"

"Yuma."

“Listen. Go to hell.” Attractive men lose patience quickly.

“Excuse me, what?”

“Get the fuck out of here.”

“Are you her boyfriend?”

Hans took the carbine and slowly, as if a scaly reptile, slithered into the apartment, uncertainly pointing the weapon at his conversation partner. Hans didn’t even really know how to shoot.

“Are you her boyfriend?” he repeated.

“Open your eyes wider, idiot.”

Shots were fired. Again and again. In short bursts. With crisp, hard-hitting pops, the water balloon bullets burst forth. A powerful stream of water from the M4’s grenade launcher hit the Latin American partner in the face.

Made in China, with love.

An expellant force from the naked Archimedes laid Hans out on the floor. Then he was beaten with something soft but heavy. Then something hard and light. And to finish it, something blunt and cold.

“You fucked her, right? You fucked her?” Hans didn’t give up from down below. “Let the girl go home!”

He just said that because he was unable to find the right words.

“You’re a GMO,” and then a very significant pause.
“You’ve lost your fear completely, I see? “You want to try my sticking out gift too?”

“You’ve already tried mine ahead of time. Look at your face in the mirror. What’s that delicious substance dripping from your mouth?” groaned primate Hans.

As is obvious from the above, Hans was also a man and was able to fight for himself. His face pinkened like a piglet’s tomato cheeks from his proud phrase and unbendable will. In battle, all people tend to make mistakes. Language and context are mighty forces. Like in a slow-motion film, a huge fist came closer to Hans' nose and whacked him with a sharp punch. Blood oozed from his nose, drips falling on the rug, but Hans held his own in the heavyweight category. Even when the ardent knight knocked him on the floor of his hockey patch of an apartment.

"I had you so good, you can't even fart," Hans went into a rage.

"What did you say? Who were you just talking to? What the hell did you say? Fuck you. Fuuuuuuck you. Can you hear that word in your ears, you jerk off!? Fuck yoooou! I'm gonna kill you now."

Under the hundred-ton train of his Columbian partner, who had ironed him out and used the steam from his armpits to press his shirt, Hans continued to resist.

"Excuse me, sir, I'm finding it hard to breathe." Indeed, Hans had already begun suffocating. "Let's stop kidding around."

The large polite man did not subside.

"Why did you put on this comedy show here? I'll stretch your head over your ass now!" Indeed, his arms, it seemed, were the size of Hans' legs, like the huge sycamores in Central Park.

"You need to be punished right to teach you for the future. So other residents don't have to be tortured by you. So that you respect others' parties and keep your nose out of it."

And with those words, he produced from somewhere an enormous knife. Hans jumped up from the floor with supple rubber legs and extricated himself like an agile flea from fur. A surge of adrenaline turned his body into a spring. He felt that right now, that sharp, huge, shining steel, unimaginable knife in the hands of Godzilla might easily find its way through his heart, and a scarlet fountain splatter the old rug. And then the police would come, handcuff the man, and then they would spend a long time cleaning the blood from the floor. But it would all be useless by then.

Hans was so frightened that he turned into a three-year-old child, moving backward inch by inch, whispering: "Put the knife away. You've got a knife in your hands. Put the knife away, you hear?" The clod grabbed Hans by the head with one hand, pressing it to himself a bit, and placed the massive and life-threatening metal object to Hans' throat.

Hans started kicking and punching with his arms and legs, like a small tree bug in the beak of a bird, and screeching, trying to grab the mountain by the hair, which, unfortunately, there was none of on his head.

"Sir, stop!" Hans said, maybe joking and maybe shrieking some shameful nonsense like a toddler out of desperation. "Enough, enough! I'll stop!" He couldn't move or take in enough air for his fear or to breathe. The weight difference impeded the comparison of the two sides in a literary fashion.

What came next, Hans couldn't remember. He remembered only the stairs, the cold, and a slight feeling of flying at a strangely low altitude. The aftermath of the flight was an unbearable ache in his body when Hans finally opened his eyes, lying on the sidewalk in the light of a streetlamp.

The night was freezing. Snow and an unprecedented storm in New York. The lights in the houses and the streetlamps diffused beautifully thanks to the blurry, chalky snow, which fell like a wall on all the city's property. The snow was more than a foot thick on the road. There were no cars. Those who hadn't been forewarned of the impeding blizzard had abandoned their vehicles right in the middle of the street.

The Empire State Building shone gorgeously in a colorful color in the fog of the snow, recalling a child's lollipop disappearing in the hoary smoke of the merciless and heavy snowfall.

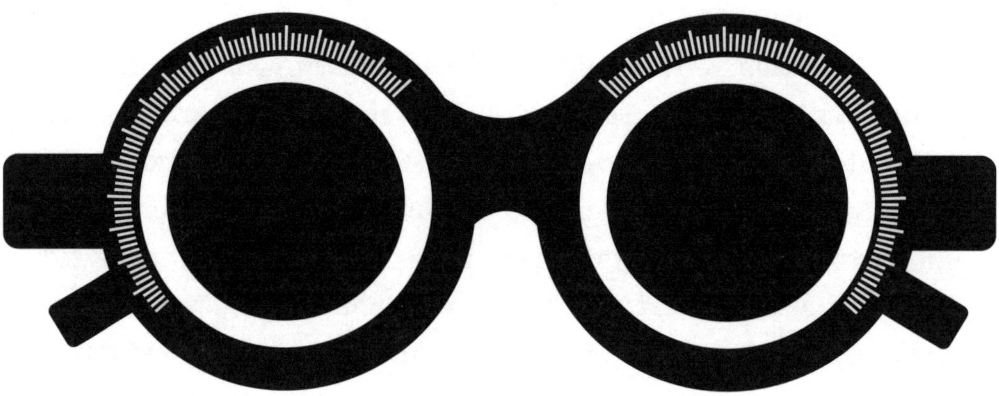

CHAPTER 44

Four in the morning. For the last time, Hans was speaking to his father in the kitchen.

There was a tomblike silence in the house and a storm raging outside. The autumn chill shook the window panes. Exit onto the street. There was steam coming from his father's mouth. He was concentrating on something. Trying to hide his doubt, even from himself, he spoke not a word. Speaking wasn't allowed. There was nothing to say. His whole body shivered.

His father was tall and sturdily built, with a black beard and a mouth hiding in it, thick brows, and a gaze replete with a warming irony. But now, his eyes were filled with the glass of the cold. Big, strong, but sensitive hands. The fingers of an engineer used to the fragility of tiny electronic parts. He was dressed in light-colored canvas pants to blend in with the gray concrete wall and a similar canvas shirt. Under his jacket were a number of layers of clothing with foam inserts. To avoid attracting attention, his mother wore wide pants that she could run in and a nondescript woman's jacket, of which there were probably half a million in East Berlin. Under her jacket was a pullover stuffed with foam.

October. Two days ago, the weather forecast on the light blue television screen promised rain and icy wind, which turned out to be truth. It was forty degrees Fahrenheit on the streets, with strong winds. The rain should decrease visibility and increase the attentiveness of the guard. And, most importantly, make it easier to ground the current-carrying wires in the wall.

Hans' father never smoked. There was some uncertainty remaining between the lines of the well-thought-out-plan. But the reason for the pack of Soviet Belomorkanal cigarettes sticking out from his pocket was unknown even to Hans.

The Berlin Wall was a complex monster that daunted and halted lively minds. The warning zone on the eastern side, the placards cautioning you to stay away from the wall, the first wall, then electrified wire netting and barbed wire, Czech hedgehogs, and a road for the patrol. Then came a strip of land—a sand or clay area that would maximize the visibility of footprints left by violators. Then a ditch, and then the last concrete wall with a rounded top to make it hard to climb over. After that wall was real West Berlin, which had never recognized a national border there. West Berlin, the freedom of free air, life without fear in the night. Green grass without a knock on your door. Bars for the evenings, the best movies, music, infecting you with the virus of incurable happiness.

That day the rain drummed on a thousand drums like a dreadful underworld festival. There was no one on the streets. It seemed as if the wind had blown any fearful people that remained there away like litter.

They decided to walk along the streets one by one.

The bodies of the escapees were smeared with a substance made from fat, which kept the warmth in. On top, they wore special, waterproof wet suits, and over them, life jackets with slabs of foam inside. The outermost layer consisted of inconspicuous jackets and pants.

The ladder built for the first wall was ready and hidden in the bushes, disguised as thick old tree branches. There was another ladder, just in case. Two notched wooden beams could be quickly made into a makeshift ladder.

They went over the first fence together. It was also topped with barbed wire, which actually helped to secure the ladder from above. Everything had been practiced multiple times. The only one who was not afraid was Hans' mother. A woman does not feel danger—she protects her family. Hans' father understood that that night was more difficult than any plans he had drawn up on paper. Because it was mixed with human emotion. There was no path back. The past had already been cut off with a huge pair of scissors.

Hans' father threw the rope with the bundle over the top. The wall was eleven feet high. He had been working on this throw in the country for several months. There was one difference—while training, you could make a mistake, be lazy, anything you wanted. You could try again. But here, there were no mistakes allowed. And, well, there was a second difference too. The fear that pushed him forward and made him freeze up at the same time. The possibility of making a mistake. The possibility of canceling your life out because of some trivial detail that you hadn't accounted for. The rope was now taut.

Hans went first. The pitch-black darkness, the motorcycle gloves, the warm hat that protected him from the wind and cold but with the ears showing to hear better. Peals of thunder. The horror of war. The lights on the poles were not on. The searchlights were also turned off, although they had a separate power line that fed them. The absence of light allowed all three to make it through the barbed wire. When he got to the top of the wall, Hans looked down. He could see nothing.

Still at home were the photographs of the electrified barriers and the sketches of the electric grid connecting them. They had to accurately cut the barbed wire along the perimeter, climb through a hole in that second fence, crawl past the Czech hedgehogs, run across the road and along the sand, jump over the ditch, and, unnoticed, make their way into the waters of the Spree. On top of their regular clothes was a rubber layer in case of any contact with electrified wires, and on their feet were rubberized socks and specially treated shoes.

The electricity was not in the wires but in his body. Knowing that he could not immobilize his body with fear, it nonetheless took Hans a long time to shake the stupor that had overcome him, afraid of making a mistake. Hans' father was second. Once again, they could not speak, moving along almost on their bellies. They worked with industrial cutters, destroying the metal netting that had been disconnected from the power feed. Hans' father neutralized the flare signal that was mounted onto a special pipe on the second barrier. Hans' mother was calm: she came over to help, and the work cutting the barbed wire speeded up. In a few minutes, everything was ready. Moving almost by touch and through a tiny hole in the second fence, the escapees crawled through the thorns of death.

The first one to go through this time was Hans' father, then Hans, and then Hans' mother. Everyone knew what to do, but the darkness got in the way of understanding precisely where they were and where they should be going. Luckily, the searchlights on the small piece of land did not go on. The engineer in charge of that plot of land had turned off the lights, signal wires, and searchlights for a few minutes, simulating a short circuit.

The rain was coming down so hard and fast that it seemed as if the drops were made of concrete or bullets being fired by the sky instead of the guards into the ground. His heart beat even more loudly, but not from fear. It was the paralyzing, panicked poison of animal terror. The silhouette of the tower on the bland piece of the remaining sky seemed, for a minute, to be in the shape of an enormous guard that any moment would start running towards them.

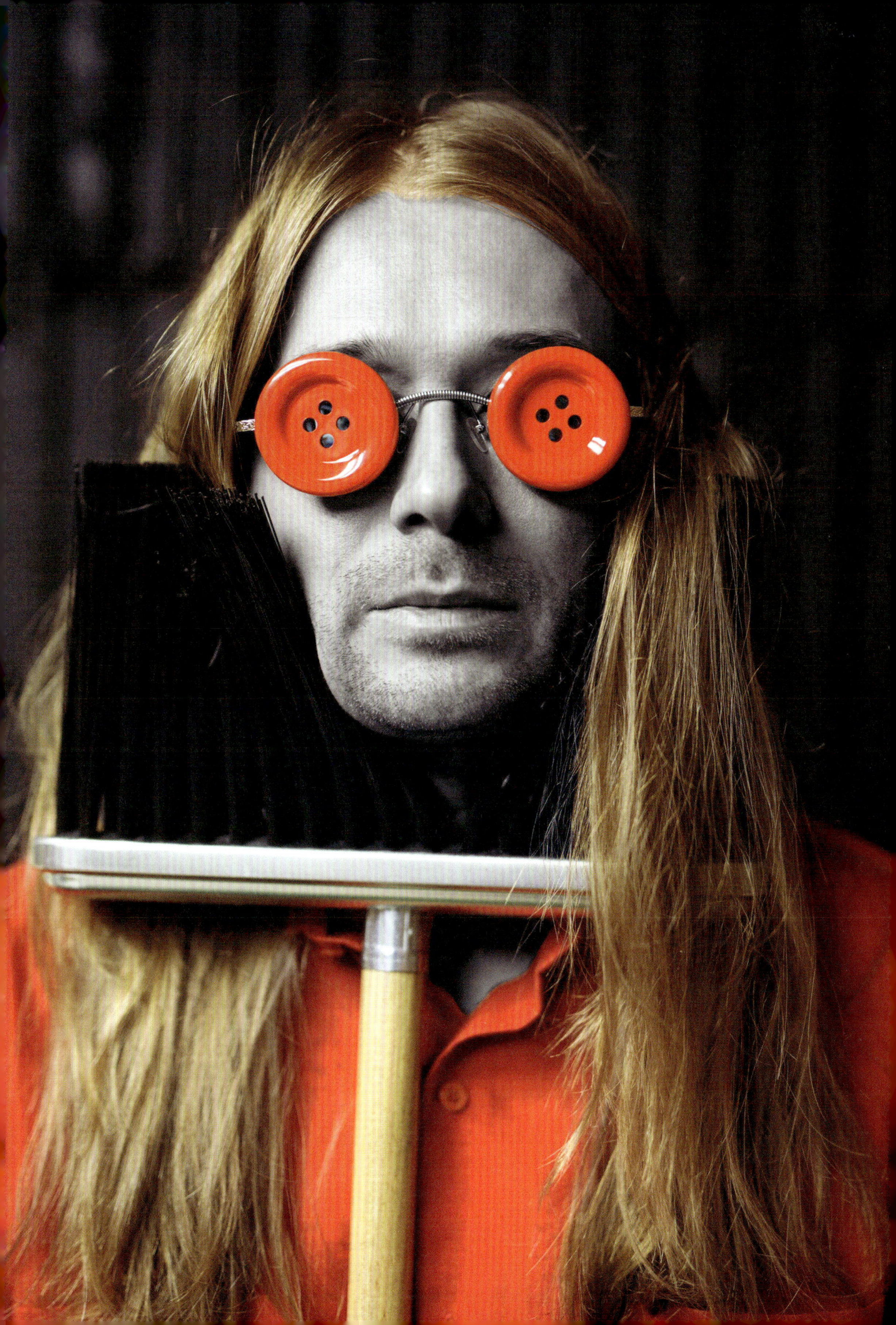

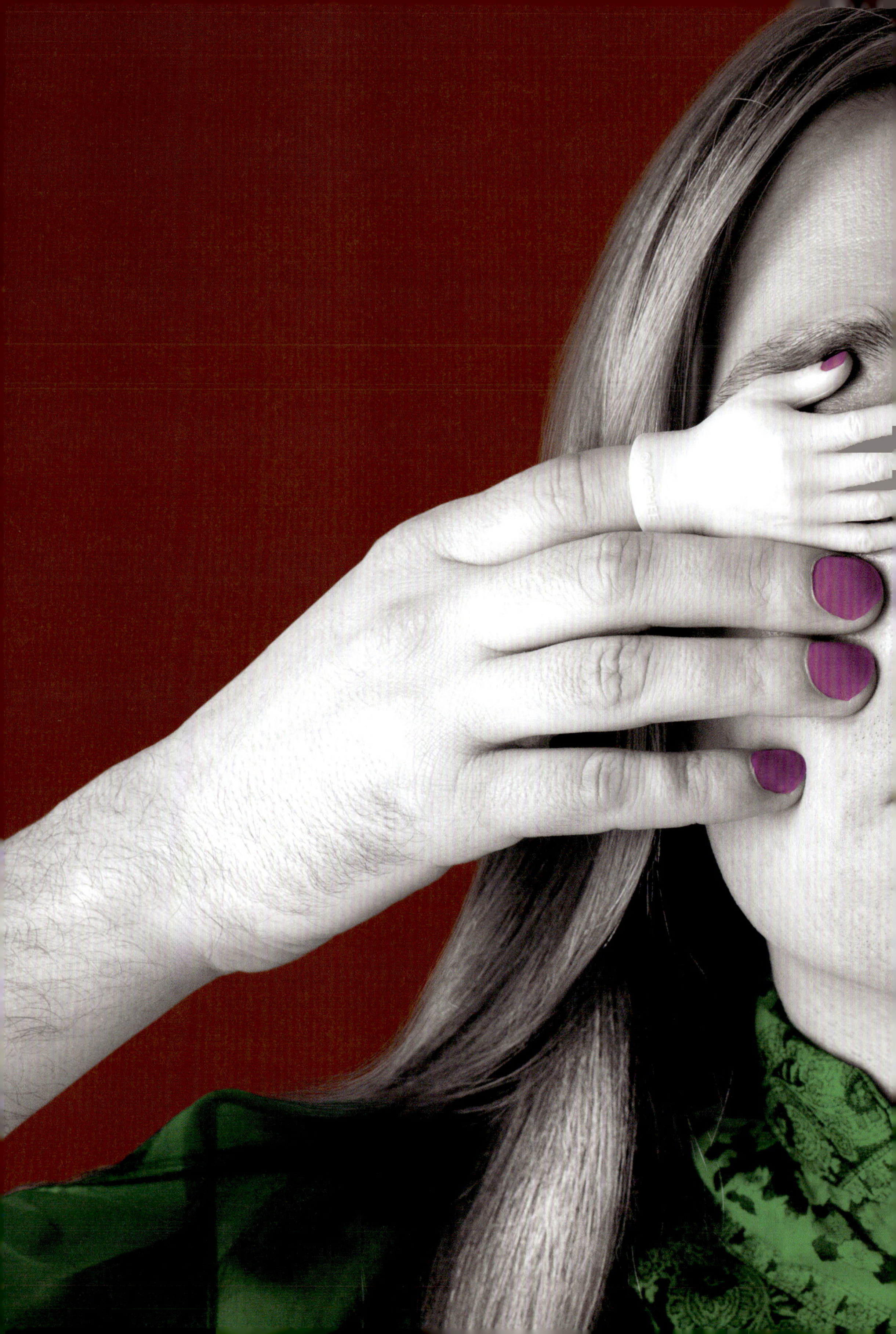

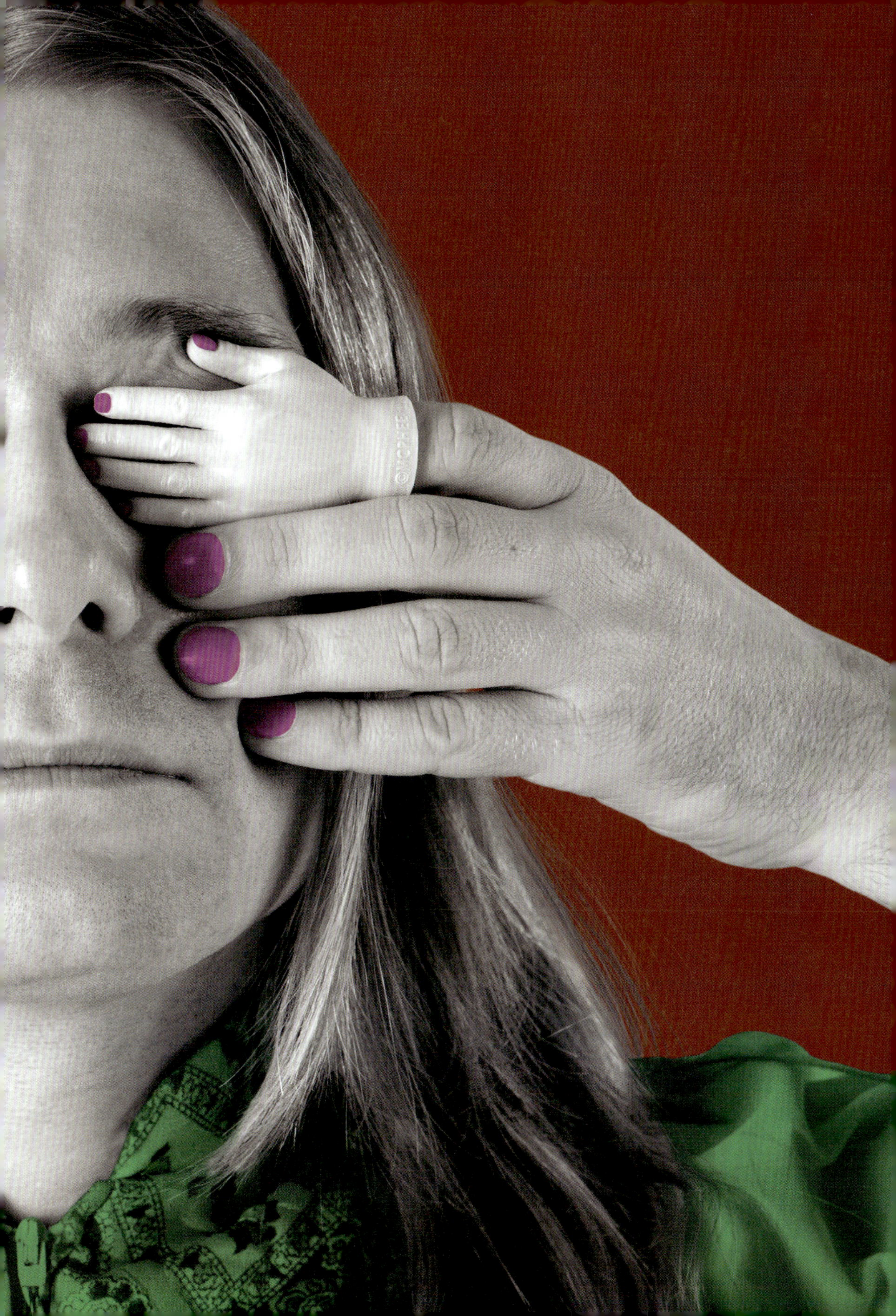

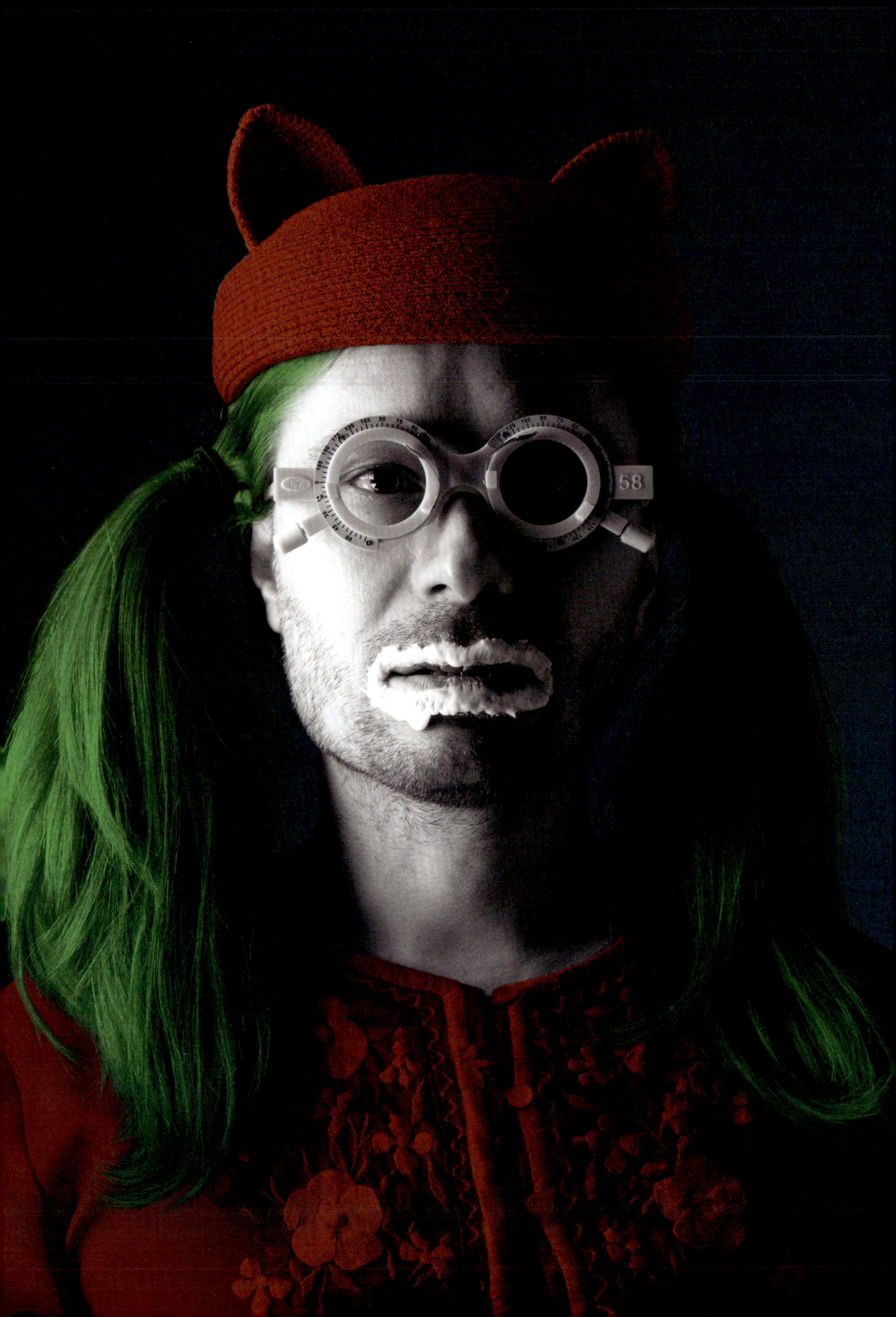
58

Death breathed into every inch of that strip of land.

Hans' mother got caught on the barbed wire of the third barrier on the Czech hedgehogs. Nothing particularly terrible. No one knew about that barbed wire since it could not be seen in the photographs. A long, sharp spike pierced his mother directly through her wrist, as a result of which she instinctively cried out, not only from pain but also from fear of losing precious time. She felt a warmth in her sleeve and her motorcycle glove; the blood ran like warm juice, soaking into her clothing. She felt pain all the way up to her shoulder. The barb had hit her tendon. But most of all, she wanted to live and wanted to win. "Freedom" was just the first part of the name of their new life. Compared to that, the pain in her arm and the warmth of the flowing blood was nothing. Hans was a few dozen feet ahead and had no idea about his mother's troubles with her arm. If he had known, he would not have moved further towards the ditch as they had planned. He would have waited for his mother and attempted to help her.

Hans' father, behind his wife, moved quickly towards her, grabbing her by both hands and trying to get her away from the barbed wire. It was taking a long time to get the arm out since a few of the barbs had dug their way into the clothing and began tearing at her skin even more.

He would have to go back for a tool, and such a hassle was already too dangerous. The searchlights could come on at any minute, and then it would all be over.

Hans' mother was able to make it across the torn-up road only after a few minutes had passed. Hans was waiting for her near the shore, already prepared to turn back, when he heard a splash of water among the noisy raindrops: having gotten across the ditch, Hans' mother smoothly made her way into the water of the river.

Hans' father was still nowhere to be seen.

Five, ten, fifteen, twenty seconds. Hans swam second. As the border patrol guards had said, there was no boat, and only the dim light from the park on the other shore lit the water slightly. The immobilizing cold water burned Hans' face, even though he had been training for a few months, pouring cold water over himself and swimming in cold rivers. The training was worthwhile. But now either his nerves had also entered the picture, or the weather had gotten worse, or the fear had spooked his reason. Hans almost couldn't move his arms and legs to swim and felt as if the paralyzing cold made it impossible for him even to inhale. His body, arms, and legs were trembling under the water.

The rain began again with a new strength, mixing the sky with the water. Hans' father was the last in the river. Now everyone was swimming along quite well. The short-lived crossing, which they had prepared several months for, was coming to an end. The shift supervisor who had turned off the searchlights had saved Hans' mother from the clinging thorns of the fatal wire.

The current in the Spree turned out to be quite strong, and Hans began swimming faster so that he wasn't carried too far off course. Where the park ended was a concrete embankment, and it was impossible to climb out of the water since the entire structure was about four feet high.

Right before Hans made it to the other side, he felt as if something warm had stung him on his side, and he became quite hot. Turning around, behind him, on the already far away eastern opposite shore, he saw a searchlight shining right into his face. The glare of the light reflected off the shaggy surface of the water and made everything around them in the foggy rain visible.

Hans' father was still somewhere in the water, while it seemed his mother had already made it to the shore. An energy that was ten times his normal level quickened Hans' pace. He swam a few strokes and, with a fearful heartbeat, reached the shore. The sirens went off, and the sound of dogs barking could be heard. Not somewhere in the distance, but very close by, on the redemptive western bank of the river that separated hell from the peace of socialism. It was just the echo of the dogs bouncing off the high walls of the houses. The short machine gun bursts were simply from a poorly executed attempt by the guard to follow instructions. The dogs never stopped barking, making it seem as if they were about to attack their capitalist prey.

A swarm of searchlights then lit up. On the opposite shore, Hans darted sideways, towards where the bushes grew, afraid of the gunfire. It seemed to him that there were machine guns firing again from the East German side or the water. Hidden in the grass, he saw his father running towards him along the embankment. The patrol boat was headed straight towards them. But it was too late! They had done it!

For some reason, Hans' father, hunched over, was running across the grassy shoreline, already far away from the water, intersected and followed by several searchlights. He was expecting a bullet or a machine gun round, but it wasn't that which was bothering him. His movements were spasmodic as if the icy water was made of acid and had burned his skin. Hans' father ran to Hans at a speed he had never seen him move at before.

"Where's your mother?" He shook Hans by the shoulders. "Where's your mother, you bastard?!" he screamed in the middle of the night, trembling, maybe from the cold, or maybe from the question. As if it were Hans' fault. Hans didn't understand a thing.

His mother was not on the shore.

After a week of torture, doubt, calls home from the already not so desirable land of freedom in the hope of obtaining information that his mother would be in court for her escape attempt, made worse by the fact that she had had access to state secrets, the telephone finally brought some information.

The news was not what Hans and his father were expecting. The low temperature of the water had triggered convulsions in Hans' mother. Apparently, the arm pierced by the barbed wire burr was not strong enough to swim to the other side. She had lost too much blood.

A few days following the escape, her body was found near a park downstream. At the spot where the concrete barrier would have made it impossible for her to climb to shore.

I love everything
about you:
the worst in you
is an unobtainable
best in me!

CHAPTER 45

Why do they say that New York is an egotistical town where no one cares about anyone else? Everybody in Harlem is quite concerned for everyone else. While Hans was lying with his head in a ditch, a dreadlocked young man bent over him to inquire:

"Hey, dude, are you OK? Who did that to you? Can you make it home by yourself?"

But it was already freezing out, and it was clear that Hans wasn't going to make it home. Even if his home was in the very same building just a few floors up.

"Take my hat," the guy held his knitted wool hat out to Hans, baring his black dreads. "Man, you're gonna freeze to death. You need to get up and go home."

Hans didn't answer. He either didn't hear, or his stubbornness kept him from replying. From accepting the serum of another's sentimentality. Hans didn't want to get up. He liked lying there and dying. But the dreadlocked fellow didn't give up.

"You'll freeze to death here, brother. All the happy drunks are at home watching TV. And you just decided to kick back here on the street today because of some silly accident. Get yourself together. Have some sympathy for your parents."

Again, Hans opened his eyes but didn't move. His back hurt. His nose was broken and, from the general feel of it, had shifted to the left. His hands either didn't want to move or were just tired of obeying coordinating commands. Hans liked it there in the snow. Melting while alive, he lost any sensitivity towards the living that were looking for continuation and their place in the world. He liked the calming cold of the snow, which relieved the tension pain of human physical vanity. This relief of pain calmed his caged heart and caused it to cease worrying. Hans had no desire at all to get up. It was too nice and calm there. Somewhere nearby loomed the bearded face of his father hiding in the dark bucket of the excavator.

Hans didn't remember how he got upstairs. He came back to consciousness in an apartment the temperature of hell. Maybe this is why the idea popped into his head that he might call Yuma and suggest they meet. To discuss their problem. Maybe that would help? He dialed her number, and for a long time, there was no answer. But then someone picked up.

It was voicemail.

Hans then decided to call Yuma's lawyer. He said that he had found the money and wanted to pay his debt. The lawyer was a bit tipsy and not work-level attentive. He was animatedly happy with this declaration of intent, understanding what such a turn of events meant for him. With the friendliness of enthusiasm, he said: "Well, that radically changes everything. Wonderful! Yuma will be back in a month. Let's wait for her and get this all settled."

"Yuma will be back in a month. Yuma will be back in a month." Hans repeated the sentence to concretize what was so vague.

The open Andy Warhol album was lying on the table in the big room. His silhouette had been cut out of the middle of the page, and in its place was a gaping emptiness, through which shone the fresh, golden face of Mao Tse-tung. The radiator was on so high that it seemed nuclear winter had finally arrived. The hell had moved out from inside the bomb and into every apartment in Harlem so that the soldiers of all armies could celebrate an undeserved victory. The dim light on the ceiling painted the walls and furniture with a yellow hue, which soaked through one's eyes and into his skin, to his fingers, to the taste buds on his tongue, souring his insides. The sofa was disappearing under the floor. The asthmatic plasterwork breathed through gills of asbestos walls, the gills of emigrant builders. Hans didn't understand how he could be here, sleep here, listen to Andy, and smile at Yuma.

Everything around him seemed estranged. He wanted to pull the paint from the walls, jump up and attack the dusty white cracked wall with sandpaper. He wanted to be the apartment Don Quixote, the vacuum cleaner vulture, which would destroy everything down to the very bricks. The windows were small and narrow, covered by old beige drapes drenched with black dust through which light could not pass either day or night. The old radiators and pipes raised an alarm, forcing aside last year's air and keeping a chaotic beat, at times every minute, at times every half hour, and at times completely silent.

Hans became irritated with every drop that fell from the rusty faucet. What he thought to be New York was now out of order. He wanted to spit the city out on a saucer like a bone that had been picked, like an awkward structure that was thrusting him apart with its crookedness. The houses squeezed each other together, and the walls pinned each other down. Everything existed in a stuffy, compressed slice in a state of brick war.

Hans took his backpack and stuffed it with everything he would need for a week. He had a long flight ahead of him. At first, he packed his electric razor, but then he realized that he wouldn't have access to any electricity along his way. Razor? Where would he put it? Shaving cream? No. He should shave now. He hurriedly turned on the water in the bathtub and gathered all his razors and the shaving cream. He lathered up his legs, back, and chest to the extent that his flexibility would allow it. His face was still in pain after his exercises with his neighbor. His nose had swollen up, although there was no intense pain anymore. His back was still aching from falling on the rock on the island. It's an ugly affair when you end up on a road that's not yours. Every trifle might break your neck. It's so repulsive. To build your life and then absurdly veer off course.

It's repulsive to live your whole life with fools and idiots. Hans mustered up the courage before heading out into the open cosmos. He was trying on the aerodynamics of a new life.

He was repulsed by the piquant dung aroma of the mice's excrements in the apartment, from the dust that had been flying around for centuries, and from the rusty pipes bubbling a funeral march dragged out into a hundred-year andante. His hands worked as a team, and his fingers held the razor handle with quickening impatience. He shaved his back looking in the mirror. He needed to remove all the hair to get rid of wind resistance. Resistance. He shaved his armpits and carefully shaved his legs down to the very bottom of the hairs.

He looked through all of his clothing and found a wetsuit for surfing. He placed a two-deck Sanyo tape player in his bag. Hans really did adore tape recorders. He liked the sharpish plastic smell, the shiny buttons, and the rustling of the tape as it rewound. It all seemed like magic to him, a preparation for listening to the music that it produced, somewhere in the bowels of the "music box," as his mother referred to all the cassette players that his father would buy. Hans liked the complexity of the mechanical mechanisms with the gears that smoothly switched modes at the push of huge shiny buttons.

One side of the cassette tape had a recording of Shostakovich. The same one that she didn't want to listen to because the earphones were broken. Or was it because of the forest fires? Or because of the bears that stepped on the ears of the other bears in the forest? (Or was it for some other nonsense reason.) She had some explanation.

On the other side of the cassette, Hans recorded the song 有楽町で逢いましょう several times, to listen to it over and over. Hans loved to listen to the same melody days on end. It created the right atmosphere.

Hans rubbed himself with some ointment for his injuries and put some extra on for those coming in the future. His entire mood was full of the spirit of the traveler who changes worlds like gloves. He took with him one photo of Yuma, gluing it to his chest. He placed the Andy Warhol album in the backpack, half a loaf of bread, and an additional hat in case of hurricanes or freezing temperatures.

Having packed all his things, he looked around the apartment for the last time. The weeks that he had lived here seemed to him one-thousandth of a second. He was calm. He didn't give a damn about the city or the past. He felt nothing—not a cinder of anger, no fear, no disappointment. He filled his lungs with the righteousness that was breathed out in parting by those walls that pressed in on residents at night in the mattresses of their beds.

Backpack, tape recorder, wetsuit, skis. Ski boots. Everything was ready to go.

Again, he rubbed some ointment on and quickly donned his thin cashmere sweater. Then the wetsuit over it. He hurled the backpack over his shoulder and grabbed the skis. Without locking the apartment, he closed the door and went out onto the street.

Hans got on his skis and headed towards the East River. Winter met him fluffily and boldly. Turning onto FDR Drive, he started towards the south of Manhattan.

According to his calculations, it would take twenty minutes on the skis to get where he was going. There were no cars on the road because of the two feet of snow, which they said wouldn't be cleaned up for at least a few days. It was December twenty-something, and work in the city had slowed down. In New York, they could collect taxis and taxes, but plowing the snow…And it was still snowing, subduing the administrative enthusiasm. Only the subway was working, and people were traveling with difficulty and fear, getting stuck in the sugary mountains of snow. Hans, on the other hand, on his skis, was breathing even more freely and joyfully.

The skis had been given to him by Ronald in Florida when it was 100 degrees out. That idiocy infuriated Hans no less than it does just reading it. Nothing is as annoying as unwanted gifts that pass as a joke or some useful thingamajig. It was on one of Hans' birthdays. Some occasion of little importance. After his mother and father, no one had given Hans anything. No one except Ronald, of course. Who brought him this crap. Hans kept the gift for its unpleasantness, like a message from his childhood. On the left ski were drawn hearts and an inscription: "To Hans, with love, from Ronnie." The worst possible thing to have written there. Hans had always wanted to either paint over it or just to throw the skis the hell out, but time had left them to age, like cognac.

The storm gained momentum, like an orchestra being conducted from afar. There was no strong wind, only paper flakes of all sizes and colors falling on New York, trying to bury the Empire State Building up to its roof. Manhattan became a candy pie whose filling was teatime commotion, hiding in its multilayered stories, awaiting its ceremonial teaspoon. The snow covered the differences in rent, making the future equal for all in the chilled desert. Hans slid on his skis alongside the East River, listening to the howling of the storm in the wires, between the snowflakes, and between the buildings. He was carrying the Olympic torch to confer the hot flame on his route's final cauldron. Rarely did he meet people along the way, peeking out from their doors. These brave souls looked at him with astonishment and even sympathy. Some of them, it seems, didn't understand what the mechanisms attached to Hans' feet were.

Hans was an artist. He was not seduced by material burdens. Now he was feeling a transformation from one state into another. The tunnel effect of an elementary particle. He disengaged from his circumstances, and the ski track slid his skis forward against the snow, wind, gravity, and a ton of other inventions. He watched an old film of the past in his mind for the fifth or tenth time.

Hans remembered the cold and the snow that dimmed the humming electricity of the streetlamps. He recalled the streets of his hometown and the nighttime paths that had been tracked through them. Sleds, the crackling of snow being trampled, the darkness and silence of the evening snowfall that stripped everyone naked before themselves. There was so much sadness in the air that it was difficult to endure its immodesty. The true melancholy of winter called you into vaults of eternal frost. Hans was content in affliction. The melancholy was an ocean where he could find himself a place at a comfortable depth.

He was delighted when he felt suffering coming and, thus, always ardently strived to meet it, moving close to the edge. The inferno of danger and real feelings beckoned to him like a snowy firefly. Hans came to a standstill in the snow of storm-covered Manhattan and then kept going, sometimes sliding down the hills where there was less snow or where it was somewhat stamped down. Hans saw that nature was taking him forward evenly and approvingly.

Having covered half of the journey, he saw the large matchbox United Nations Secretariat Building. Hans saluted international friendship by warmly and inspiringly thinking of Yuma, whom he would soon see.

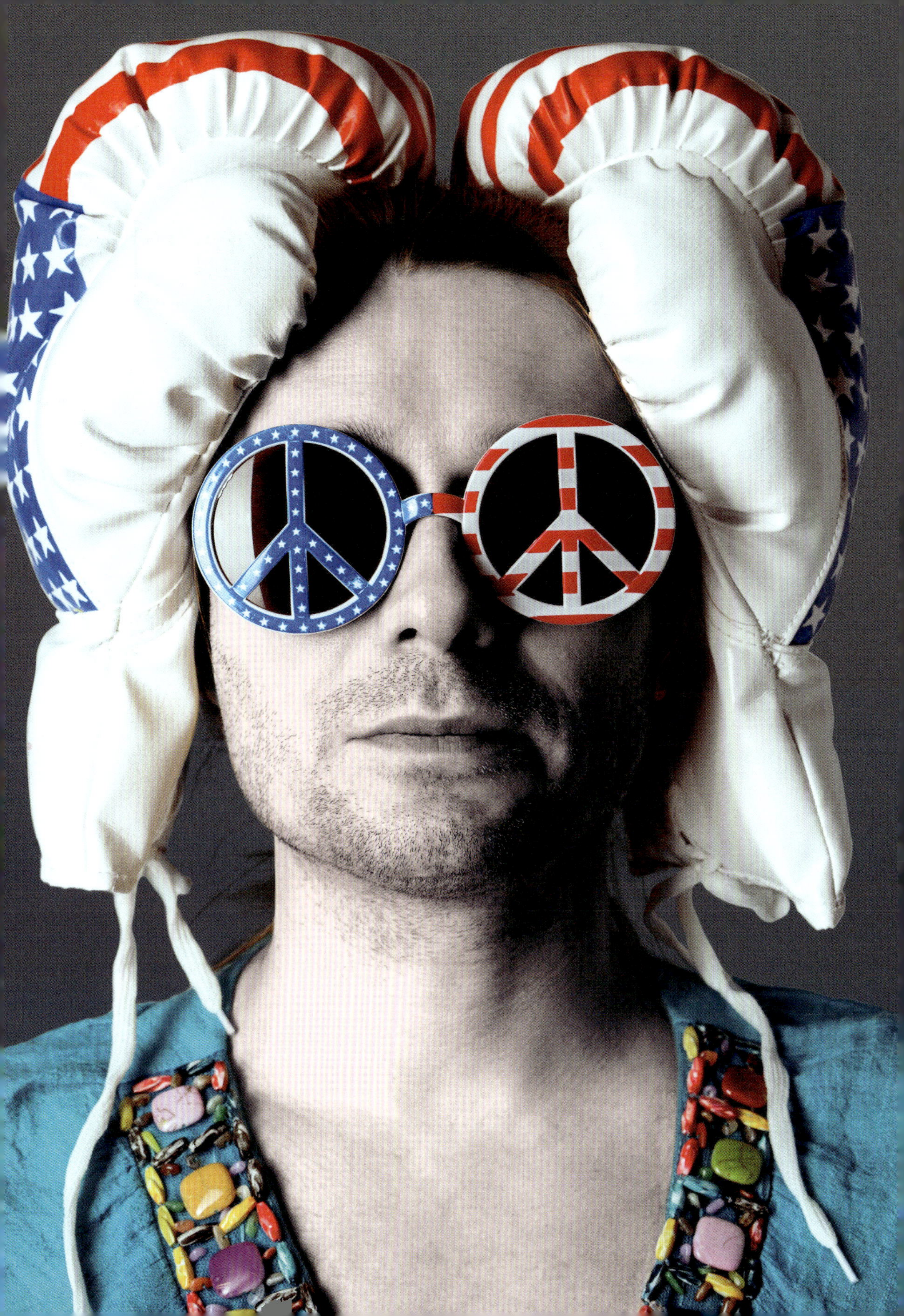

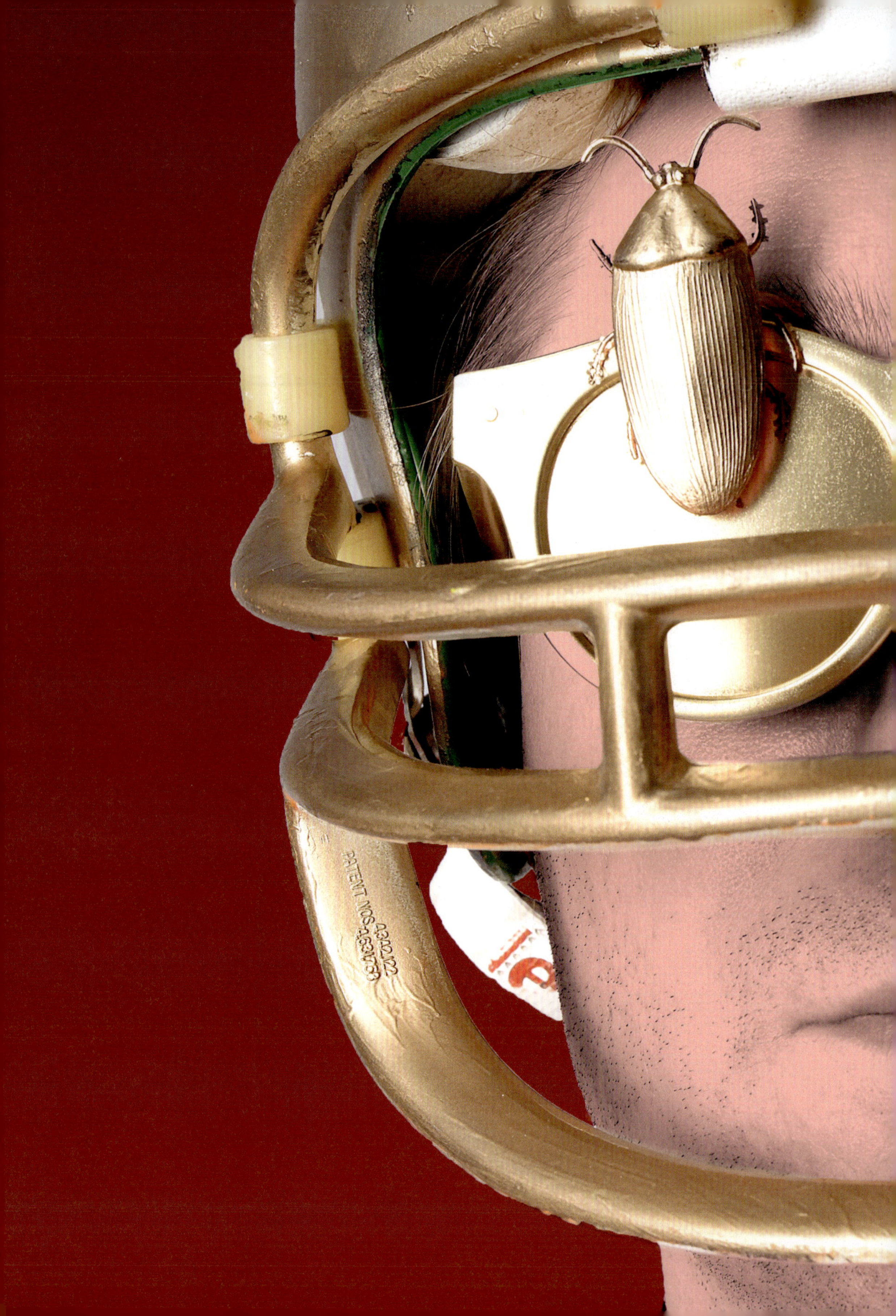
PATENT NOS 4342122
4631758

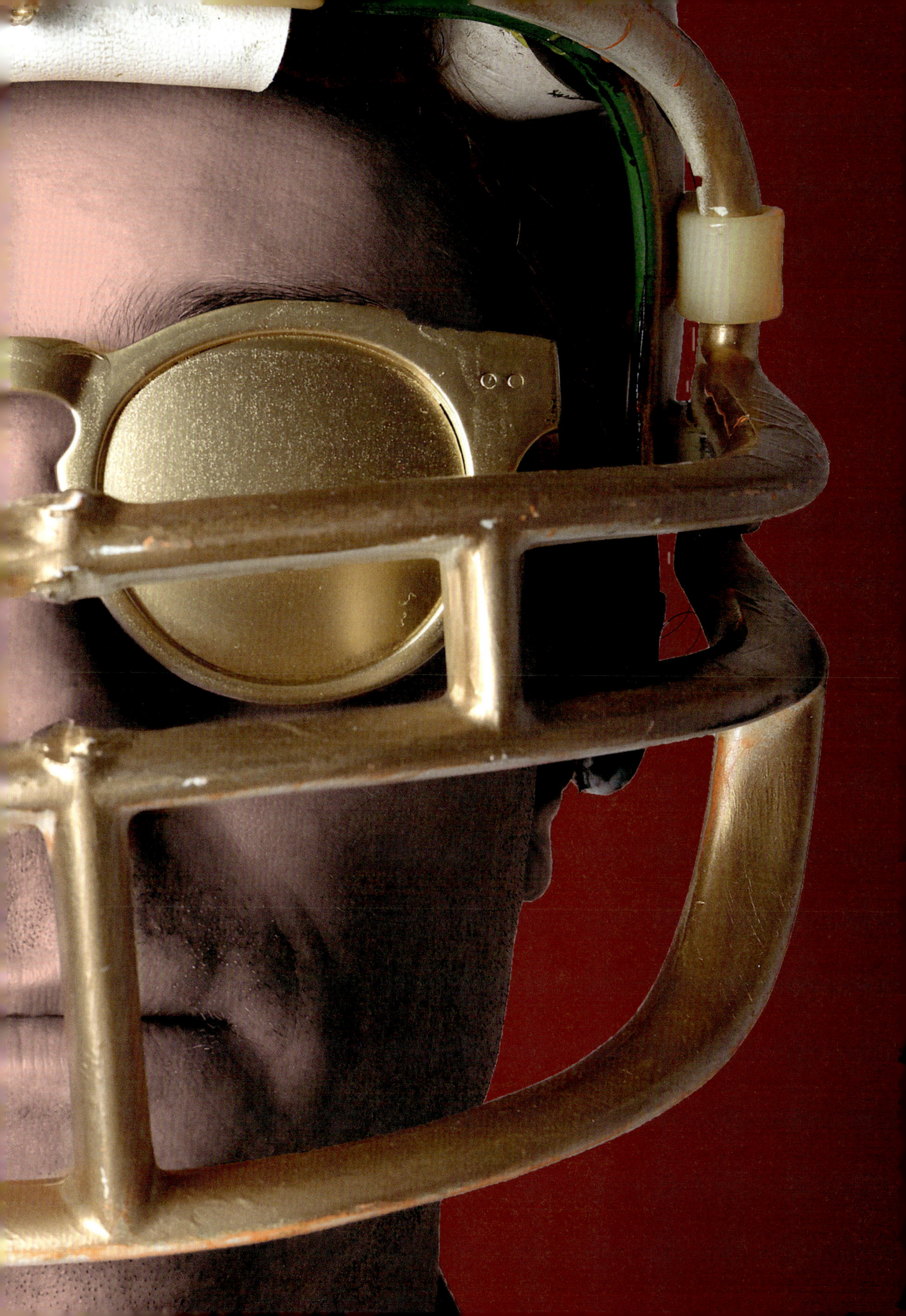

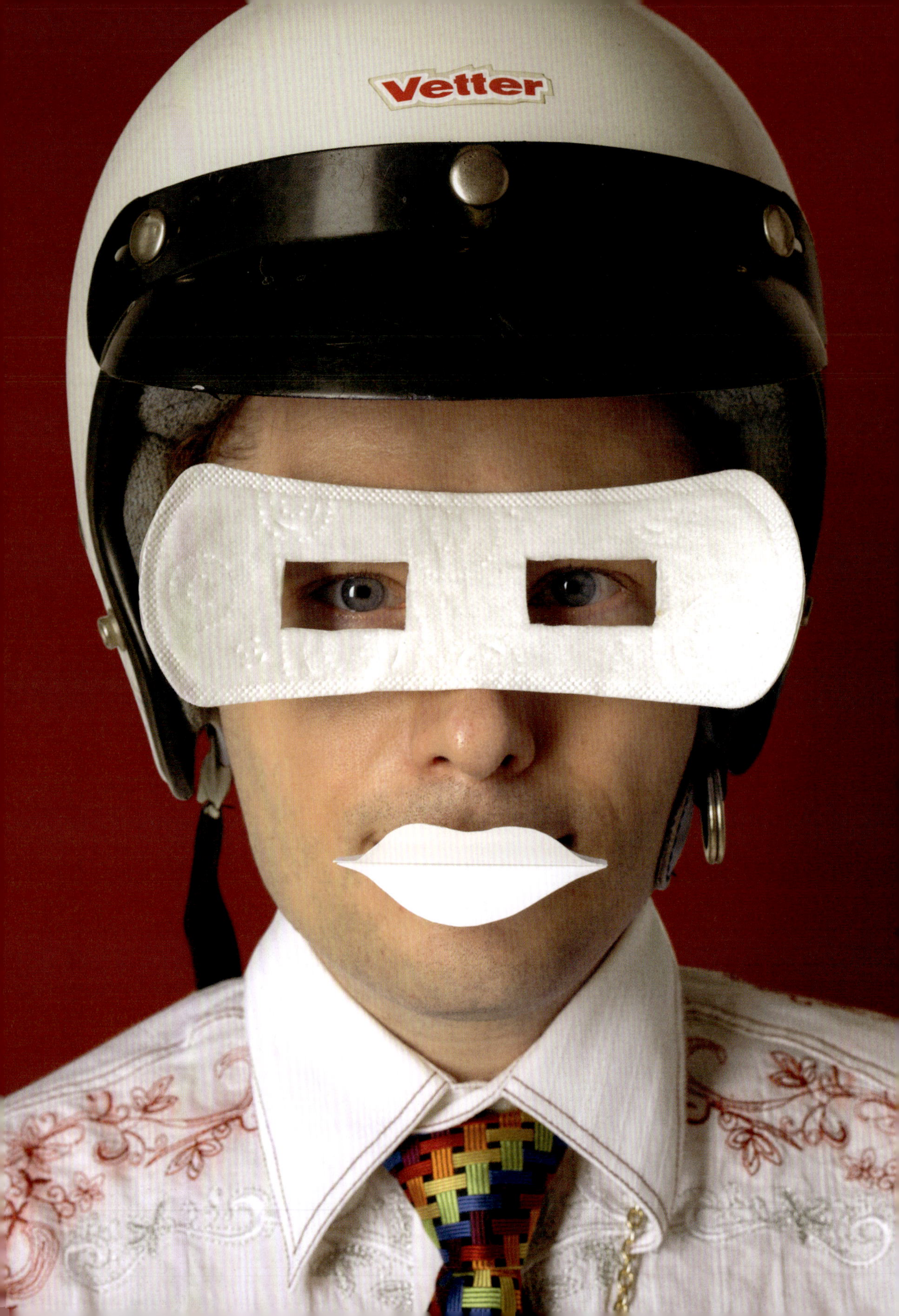
Vetter

The snow kept coming, with big, soft chilly-matte snowflakes sticking to his face as if they would be crunchy when chewed. The cars he came across stood under the albedo of white hemispheres warmed by the fuzz of snow to improve sleep. From a moving perspective, they seemed to be slowly crawling along the frozen road towards Hans. The road snaked slightly in time with Manhattan and soon led Hans to a huge concrete support.

The Brooklyn Bridge was completely covered in snow. The wires and cables woven together to make up the bridge's architectural skeleton were nervously taut, fighting with the improvisations of nature. The rivets, the beams, the railings, the lights, the netting—everything was frozen in anticipation. It seemed as if the bridge would bust any minute from the burden laid upon it; it just needed one footstep of trying to cross it. Near the first gothic arches, Hans unbuckled his skis and carefully leaned them on the bridge's handrails. Let someone from Harlem take them. He didn't feel tired. The beauty of the nighttime scene and the road beyond called to him. He decided to continue on foot.

He stopped in the middle of the bridge, took off his backpack, and got the tape recorder out. Everything was ready. Manhattan stood beautifully on the one side, and its buildings, like the Roman army, threatened the smaller soldiers on the Brooklyn side. It was as if any minute there would occur a great battle between the behemoth reinforced concrete monsters, and the peals of thunder from the floors, swords, and weapons being demolished would be heard miles away, alerting other cities to the combat. The buildings of Manhattan were already leaning forward a bit, preparing for the last delirious charge on the enemy. Brooklyn was full of indecisiveness and even a sort of sadness, which has no place in war. The buildings marched in place, having not yet decided to run away from the battlefield.

Hans turned the tape recorder on. Shostakovich's Prelude and Fugue No. 4 in E-minor, recorded five times in a row. He liked Prelude and Fugue No. 4 in E minor. Especially ever since he understood that Yuma didn't want to listen to his musical letters with CDs. Hans believed that such music could change the fate of someone in two minutes. Yuma didn't want to listen to either Shostakovich or Hans. Not to anyone.

Yes, Hans had brought a tape recorder to the Brooklyn Bridge and was playing Shostakovich. He wanted the sounds of the music to fly forward and triumphantly rouse Yuma. Some of them would dissipate into the Universe, and the future generation of scholars from extraterrestrial civilizations could listen to the far away demure melody from telescopes in their laboratories, an echo of the wounded past of New York consumed by the cosmos.

The snow fell in hypotenuses, summoning Pythagoras' theorem with a white telegraph. The lines of precipitation bent by the wind laid on the steel beams and stretched the cables of the Brooklyn Bridge. The bridge snoozed in the cold of raging nature, rocking in the bluster of the unchallenged wind.

Hans counted in his mind all the Yumas that he knew and that he printed out on the printer over these months. One hundred thirty-one. He wanted to see each one of them again, to prepare for the meeting with the main and only Yuma. Their meeting was not far off. He only had to cross the Cordilleras. Their meeting was just right over the Pacific Ocean, which peacefully awaited Hans, filtered by whales and warmed by the Alaska Current and starfish. Frothy from the myriad of shrimp, protected by the pride of jellyfish. The Great Ocean, which warmed the snow from below, held within it the secret of all unread books and the dreams of all travelers who had not drowned and had not yet crossed it.

Hans peered down along the East River, southwest. He thought he saw a lighthouse between the wall of snow. Maybe it was Yuma showing him the road to her far-off luminosity through a holograph of northern lights. The Statue of Liberty.

It was snowing.

Shostakovich was playing.

The snow was falling beautifully. The ceramic landscape palely and sternly lit a future in which there was no comfortable position for melancholy. The gravity of the snow provided lightness.

Hans pressed "Stop" and turned the cassette around. 有楽町で逢いましょう. Hans listened to the individual words but just couldn't fully understand what the song was about. He thought that it might be about the dawn and the flowering of the plum trees. Pink petals carpeting the roads in the town, bamboo groves that sing along in time with the wind, a flock of wild birds beautifully and sorrowfully flying south to bathe in the warm ocean and conceive new life. The murmur of the seashells, the depth of the waves, gusts of hot wind, and the scorching sun—it was all a song about Japan and about Yuma, who sat at the edge of the sea in Ithaca, waiting for Hans on Ithaca, looking out onto the horizon.

On the beach, only a kiss from salty lips would seem sweet. The tape recorder, knowing the worth of a peaceful moment, was covered in a thin cotton of weightless snow. Hans sat on the wooden railing and closed his eyes.

In the emerald surface of the sea, a half-naked Yuma flickered and swam while her hair glistened in the sun in rainbow crystal droplets. She was continually astonished at the hot day and tried to splash Hans, who was sitting on the sand in his clothes. The rush of the tide lulled Yuma, and she wanted to stay forever in the emerald and mother-of-pearl folds of the rocks, seaweed, and colorful fish that were paving a rainbow road in the deep. Yuma told Hans that she was made for him. He had made no mistake in dedicating his entire life to her. Now they would swim together for longer than the internet or the government would exist. Hans ripped off his t-shirt, threw his towel, pants, and shoes aside, and with one leap wound up next to her, creating an insane elixir of warm seawater around himself.

"How can you jump so far?!" Yuma marveled.

"I'm saturated with inspiration's performance-enhancing drugs and poisons!" cried Hans from under layers of the happy ocean as he moved towards her. Yuma tried to slip away from him with a few small steps, but it was already too deep. Hans caught and embraced her, feeling the slippery fish body of a warm mermaid. It was as if under the water Hans and Yuma were under a blanket weighing sixty tons, the size of the ocean, under a sunny day the size of the youth and foolhardiness of inexplicable happiness.

Hans caught Yuma somewhere near the bottom, in the weightlessness of bluish flecks of light. Her smile closed in on him at the distance of the smell of seaweed and the glitter of bewildered eyes, stretching the unnoticeable muscles of the mocking scarlet-pink lips with the birthmark. The actress of summer. The mayor of the island of Okinawa. The Queen of the Bank of Japan.

Hans kissed the birthmark near her lips as if it were a front door and never wanted to leave. A cufflink of happiness. A button for the secret of their mutual and passionate love. There was no one who knew how many birthmarks Yuma had—not Buddha, not Shinzo Abe, and not even Mao Tse-tung. Only Hans knew. Twenty-two thousand, eight hundred fifty-one. He had a powerful intuition and an scientific iron will. If he were to kiss a new birthmark every day, it would take him one hundred eighty years. This idea excited him. He wanted to transform into a fish and take Yuma home with him to the bottom and lay eggs with her under the mother-of-pearl thickness of the refraction of human trivialities that remained beyond the waves rolling onto the seashore. He wanted to eat sushi rolls with her for breakfast, lunch, and dinner. Hans wanted to have adventures in nature and for them to come to understand each other by living a natural life in seaweed that would teach them the secret of harmony by tangling them up in it. Rolling in time with the waters on the salted sandy beach in Okinawa. Hans dreamed of learning femininity and manliness from Yuma, the secret of her close connection with the sea's depths, and the strength of her fathomless superiority over all living things combined. Hans was also planning on learning music. He thought: "I can sing too. I could sing with her. And let my voice drown in her condescending laughter! Let my love be burned by the pedestal of her masterful artistry. I'll take an exam on solfège and be the best student in Japan. I can at least sing a mile away from her fragile and sensitive ears!" dreamed Hans.

He didn't want to lie to New York and tell it that he loved it. He didn't want to be liked at work, taking pictures of stiffly made-up and tired broads, overdone and uninteresting fashion, and concert audiences becoming depressed from indifference. Hans didn't want to say "How are you?" to weary guests of New York who miss their sunny families. All their faces showed disappointment, and Hans didn't like that geometry. He had been raised among literary classics and blueprints for airplanes, among the romance of the sea surf and the smell of mushrooms in the forest—everything that the poor and happy lived on.

During these months in New York, Hans was ill with a frightening and distinct feeling that measured on swinging scales the interference between the vastness of the past and the feebleness of the present. Hans' memory carefully stored the taste of the smell of the Central Park grass. The unrequited feelings that colored his closed eyelids orange hid in the dark and vibrated. The nuclear sun of the internal contradictions lit his brittle road. The meridian of snow-gnarled New York was sending Hans signals, which he would use to roll along just a bit more, now without the skis, like an empty rumbling train car from an extinguished smelting furnace.

Hans opened his eyes. From the retina of his dreams, Yuma had just flown at the speed of light back to her Japanese continent, returning from the museum paintings in the needle-eye of the napping city. The tape recorder rustled its tape, playing a slow and cold melody from childhood. It was like Hans had lost Yuma again, feeling it more precisely this time, as if the positive optics of dreaming had calibrated his perceptiveness. Hans picked up the tape player with the wonderful melody singing Tokyo's praises and climbed up onto the riveted metal beam that crossed overtop the bridge's road.

It was like the hundred-year-old photo. "Now I'm eating lunch!" Hans bragged.

Not scary.

Not high.

There it is, the road. Lying underneath, packed in metal and snow, and not one car. The bridge beam was also covered in beautiful crunchy snow. The Brooklyn Bridge, like an iron forest. With careful steps, Hans began a test run. The ski boots didn't slip. He ran boldly, gaining speed, along the beam over the road, towards the surface of the water.

The edge of the bridge opened up the enchanted abyss of the East River Valley. Hans, with no doubt whatsoever, made a few last long leaping steps, forcefully pushing off the beam with his left leg, and jumped into the scintillating abyss, through the snowing snow and the light of the floodlights and the millions of light bulbs of the city as it saw him off.

I know that
I have no one left,
and I have done
nothing to make
myself of interest
to anyone. I know
that no one will
read these words.

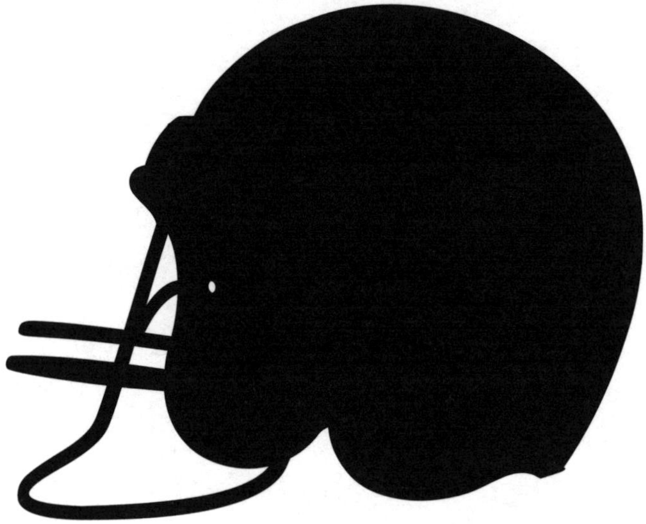

CHAPTER 40

Hans was flying!

かなしい宵は悲しよに
燃えるやさしい街灯り
ああ命をかけた恋の花
咲いておくれよいつまでも

While falling, he let the tape recorder go to free his hands.

He wanted to catch up to the sun, now shining in Tokyo.

"I'm flyyying! I'm a biiiird!" Hans yelled.

There was nothing important anymore. There would be no more questions. There would be no doubt. "The horizon is still far away. Another ten thousand miles, and I'll arrive at my girl's house. And I'll sit on her windowsill and in the early morning bring her sakura flowers in my beak!" Hans worried fixatedly. "My dearest, I'm somewhere close by! I'll warm you with the gentle embrace of my wings! You just wait for me, please!" Hans pleaded in an ecstasy of truth.

The surface of the East River was somewhere below, in a rotating kinescope, like in the cockpit of a spinning plane of a stressed pilot at war, trying to save his falling iron butterfly.

Hans was flying!

He forgot all the sadness which now was of no use to him in the air. If he could just flap his wings without ceasing. If he could just land in Tokyo!

Life had once again gained a happy meaning, like in childhood. A hot mid-day. A dog whines somewhere in the backstreets and, after seeing his master, begins to wag his tail and bound off to meet him. Children's lips encircle a cold bronze faucet. The handle unscrews with a squeak, and cold water that smells like chlorine falls onto the cast-iron grate and the asphalt, mixing in with the dust. The grapes encircling the wire grow in the sky, grasping onto the rest of nature with their tendrils. The children throw a ball at the wall of a building. There are clothes drying on the line, and loaders are hauling wooden crates from a shop into a vehicle with a rusty, rattling body. Hans' mother brings out a basin with clean wash onto the porch, carefully descends the building's long stairs, and makes her way deep into the garden, hanging sheets on the clothesline.

Free and beautiful flight!

Hans was soaring, full of strength and youth, impressed at how easy it was to fly. This feeling of life could not be mistaken for anything else. Flying is what he needed all this time. The real flight of a real pilot. A return to his country.

Here was the answer to all questions: Hans had been born in Japan. He was flying home!

The Brooklyn Bridge creaked with stingy rivets. In the wind, a sonata of steel supports held the road up like the clothespins of childhood. Connecting two banks to ease millions of human troubles. The only one the bridge couldn't help was Hans.

In the light of the electricity and white of the night sky, crystals of frost and ice flowing in small rainbows near Hans' eyelashes cut into the pupils of his wide-open eyes, immediately melting. From the perspective of flight, the snow flung open the shutters of space like a huge shell sky with pearly gems.

The majesty of the scene called Hans back to his home New

York, who had taken him in.

"Maybe you'll stay?" the wind whispered between the buildings.

"Noooooo! Goodbye forever!" yelled Hans.

The buildings of Manhattan stuck out like sharp needles from the darkness of the night into the foggy whiteness of the snow gleaming above the land and beckoned him back with its fingers of houses. The buildings that the bridge grew into wanted to go down into the river and take up some free space in the water: they were crowded and stuffy up there in line like soldiers in a cold barracks. Their yearning also gave the structures the splendor of haggard prisoners. The Brooklyn side was almost indistinguishable and, thus, seemed like the end of the world that one could never get to. The East River was solemn and limitless. The distant horizon ahead was closed off by a theater curtain of snow, increasing the beauty of the scene. The open, fresh wind blew in his face. There was a ringing silence because of the snow, just like thirty years ago when Hans and his father hid in the excavator bucket. Invisible lines of perspective, the shine of the river, the buildings of Manhattan, and the pale shimmer of Brooklyn gave rise to rapture, an influx of enthusiasm, and a desire to flap his wings faster.

Hans was flying southeast, towards the Statue of Liberty. She wasn't visible through the snow. The outline of the far islands wasn't showing through either. It seemed that the snow was starting to stick to his wings. No big deal. He would melt when the sun rose, and he could orient himself by the Manhattan shoreline.

Hans wanted to fly around the Statue of Liberty and then turn right and head west. Then through the mountains and ocean. Just to stay in the air and not veer off course. Just to have enough strength to meet the dawn on the long journey over the raging and very foreign Pacific Ocean.

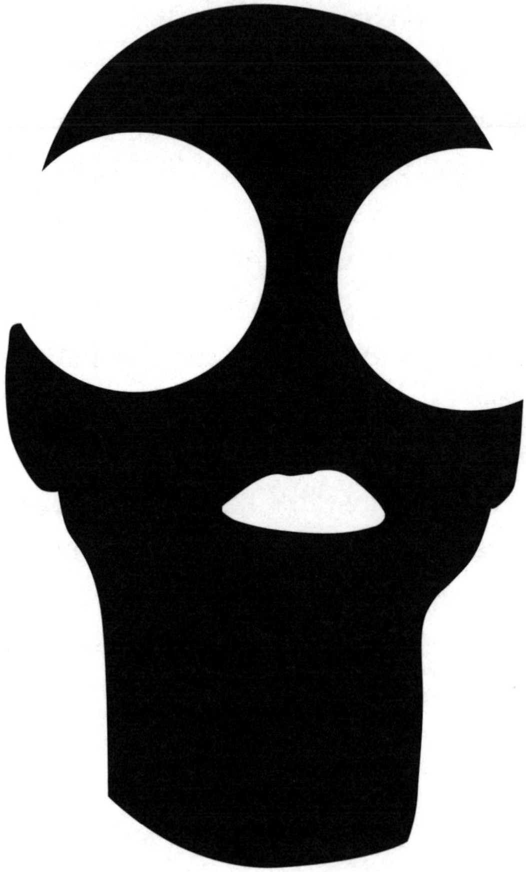

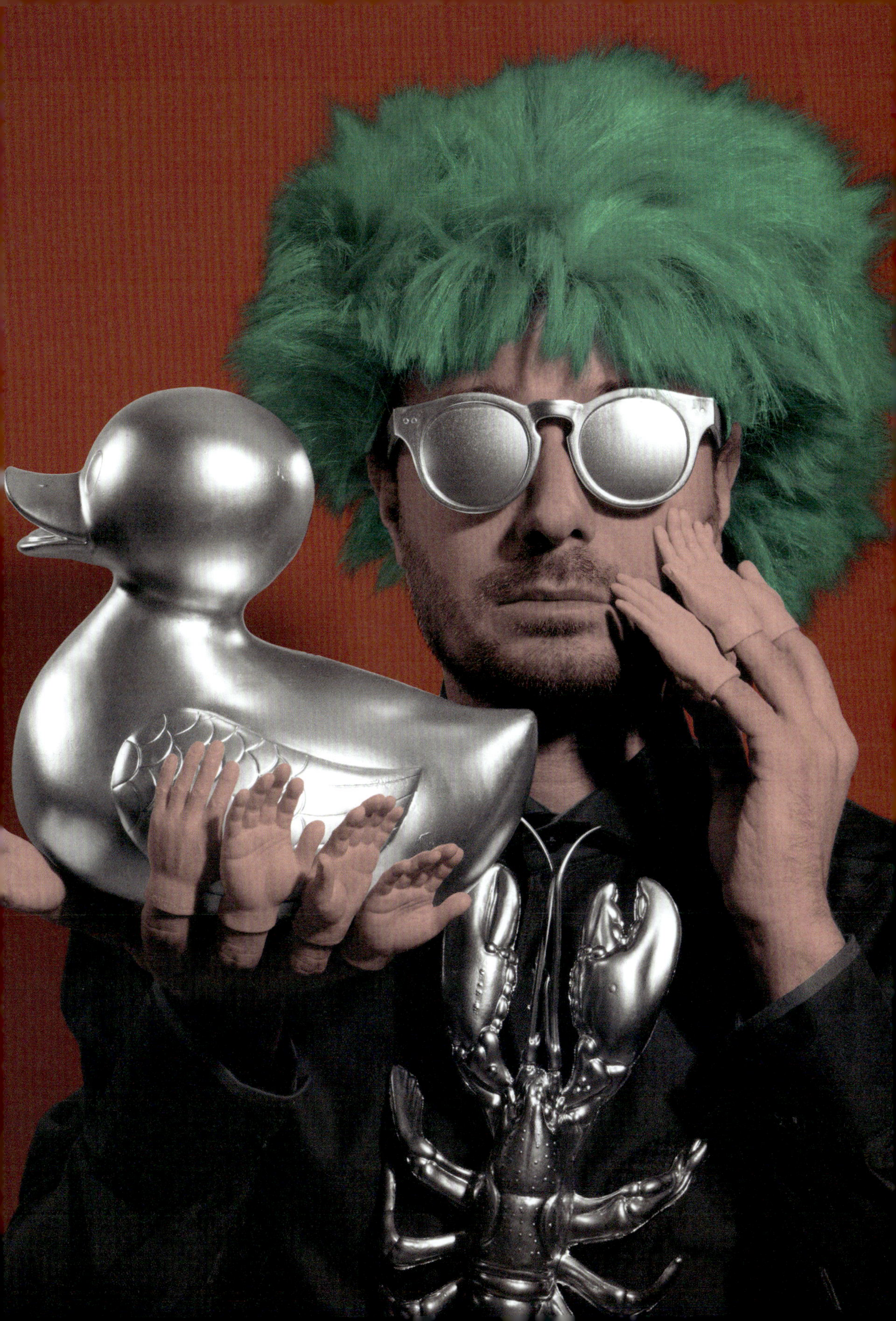

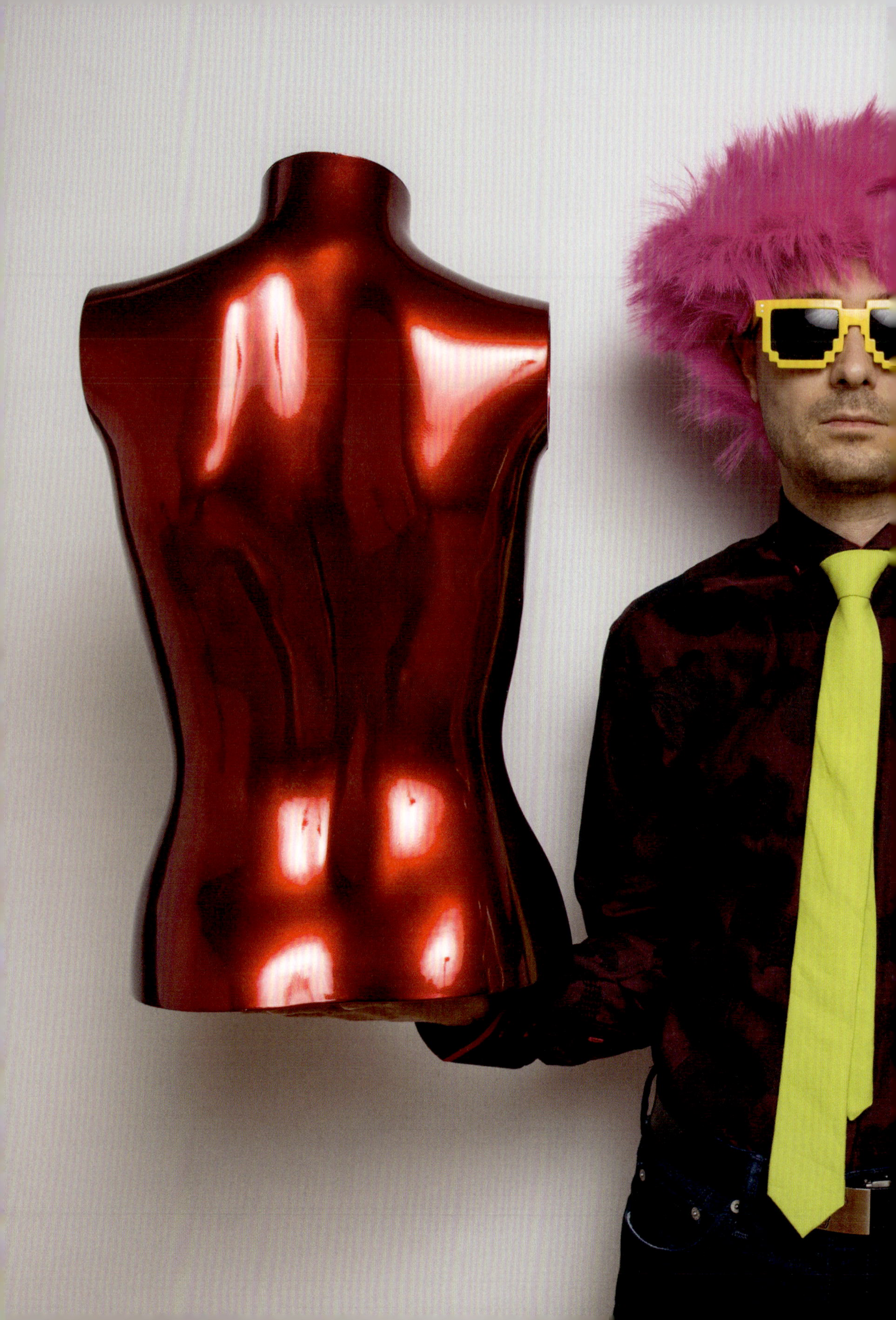

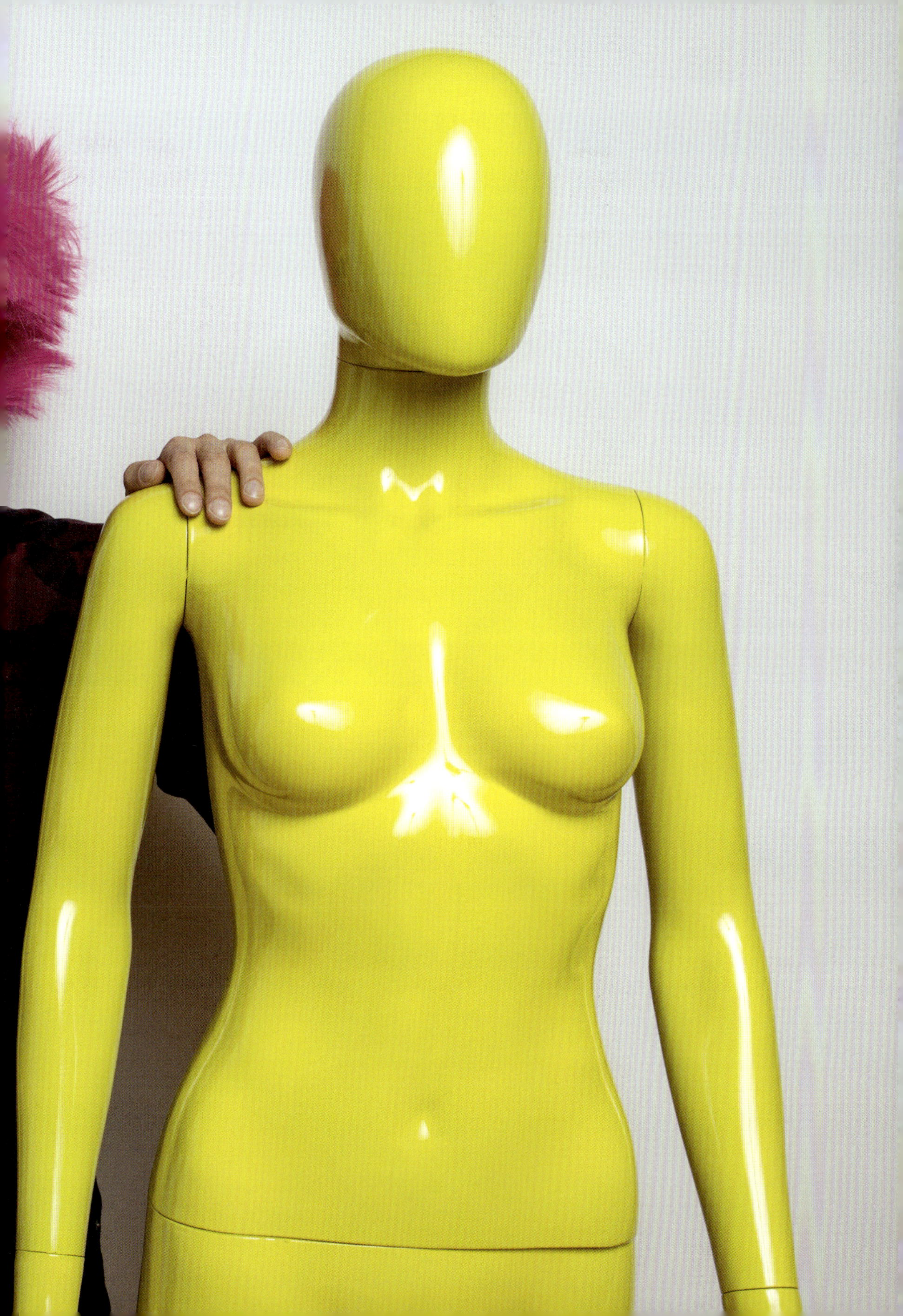

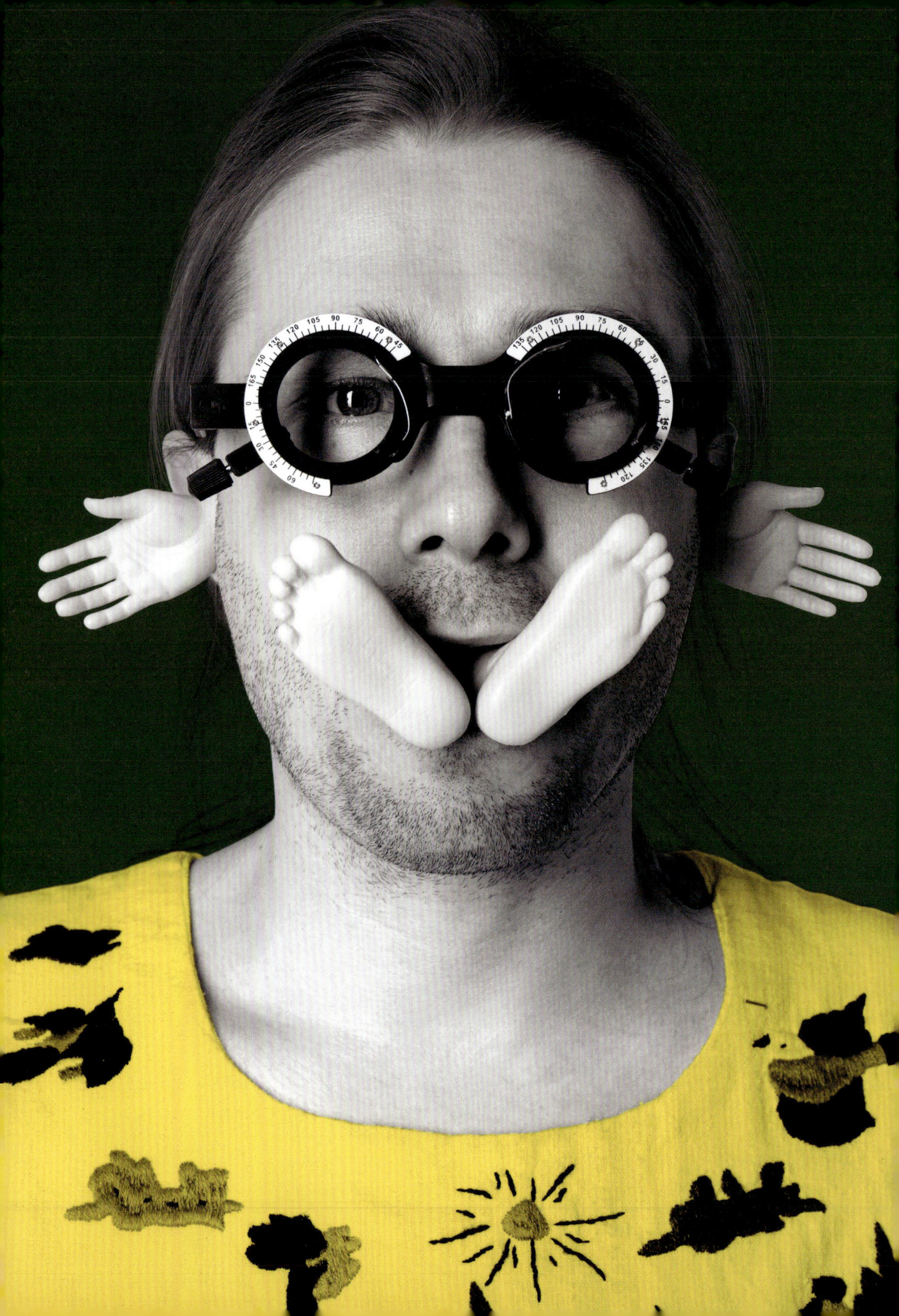

CHAPTER 47

With the sunrise, the snow did indeed begin melting on Hans' hands and back. He couldn't even brush it off since he had to continually flap his arms so as not to fall. Navigating by the sun was easy: in the morning, it began to shine near his feet and then gradually picked up speed, warming his back from above. He was flying somewhere over North America towards the Pacific Ocean, which was still thousands of miles away. What were those things? Oil derricks? Texas…?

At night Hans navigated by the stars. It was a bit cold. Particularly right before the morning when the air had chilled completely. But the stars were breathtakingly beautiful. Their allure kept Hans' strength up and stimulated his imagination. He began thinking about life on distant planets. There was nothing much to do the whole month he would be flying, and he dreamed of flying all the way to Saturn and rolling about in the liquid nitrogen.

Sweat seeped through his clothes and froze, forming a crust that whistled from the speed and stopped Hans from properly accelerating. His hat hardened and got in the way of him gathering momentum. The ski boots were somewhat heavy, but at least his feet stayed warm in them.

On the second day of his flight, Hans began singing a song in the mornings at sunrise, when the sun was gently cheering his face up with its first rays:

Fly into the rising sun,
Faces, smiling everyone
Yeah, she is a whole new tradition
I feel it in my heart

My woman from Tokyo
She makes me see
My woman from Tokyo
She's so good to me!

Hans tried to join flocks of birds that knew the way well and kept a rhythm. Sometimes he even took the place of the leader when the birds felt his authority and when the aerodynamics allowed him to gather enough speed. The birds particularly loved Hans for his orange hat, a shining beacon up ahead.

Jumping forward a bit, we must note that Wikipedia says that human flight across a transpacific distance without any machines—naturally, in other words—is now possible. The first person in history to cross an ocean by imitating bird flight was named Hans Lindberg. *Playboy* and *Esquire* magazines named Hans Man of the Year, politely inquiring if he would like to pose nude. But he refused. Elisabeth II bestowed an order upon him, which she sent by mail.

It was the first flight for which someone entered the Guinness Book of World Records as having flown across the Pacific Ocean using the energy from flapping his arms. "What's your secret?" the journalists asked in the manifold interviews. "First of all, there's the aerodynamics, of course. You pull in your head, don't spread your legs out, and don't make any unnecessary movements. Don't be nervous, that's the most important thing. Second, you have to flap your arms intensely and never stop under any circumstances. That's the main secret," Hans summarized. The fact that he had shaved his back and chest also played a role in lowering air resistance. His clothes clung tightly to his body. But Hans concealed that from the journalists.

The flight took thirty days, during which Hans neither ate nor drank. Imagine his bliss upon seeing below in the distance, finally, glints of electric light.

The lights of his long-awaited home, gentle Tokyo!

Tired Hans, who almost didn't believe in miracles, felt something warm near his eye. Tears of joy streamed down his unshaven cheeks. And while crying, he laughed nervously, not believing that he was here, in his heart's desire—hot, beloved home.

Majestically and slowly, Hans swooped towards the warmth of the electric lights on the banks of the Sumida, lightly rocked by the turbulence of the friendly, soft air. He was no longer in a hurry. While descending, he could rest and enjoy the cityscapes near the river. He no longer had to flap his arms and stare intently at the stars, calculating tangents and correcting the flight path.

Just think! He was home! His body fuselage was now calmly and professionally gliding over the houses, greeting morning Japan. The wind fluttered his tired pant legs and welcomingly whistled in his ears, howling on the bends. The temperature in the city was fifty degrees Fahrenheit, and the atmospheric pressure was seven hundred sixty millimeters of mercury, with clear skies. The time in Tokyo was seven forty-six AM.

One last sharp turn and then the landing.

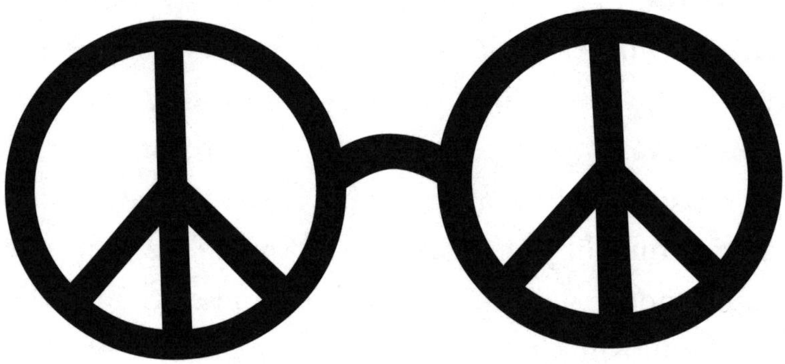

CHAPTER 40

The details of what happened next are not very clear since the story continues in Japanese, which can't be translated into any other language in the world for obvious reasons. The last pages of the manuscript have been partially erased. The only thing we know is that Hans—by showing Yuma's photograph to passersby—found her street and house relatively quickly. There was no girl on Earth of such beauty, and people recognized her portrait, recalling that they had seen her once in a short dress, long legs, and an egg hairstyle. She charmed the young men, teachers, and old couples. They, of course, knew nothing of the Fabergé egg. And, of course, the birthmark near her lips. "かわいいね!" they all said with one voice.

Yuma did indeed live in Japan and didn't suspect that Hans might just appear without warning. What bravery! What impudence! That's what women really love!

For the second time, Hans decided to use his ability to fly for his own purposes: they met near the window on the nineteenth floor. Gracefully landing on the windowsill, ceasing the flap of his practiced arms, he removed his knitted hat that smelled of sea and birds. Yuma opened the window. He crawled across the windowsill into the room. She said gingerly: "Sit down." He took off his ski boots and shook off the frost and trash that had clung to him during the flight. She, unable to hold her emotions back, began weeping, and with a delicate, timid embrace, she expressed her gratitude for his stubbornness, bravery, and daring. He asked for some water. She brought hot tea. He said that he needed to take a bath, as he had not bathed in a month. But she didn't let him.

Her hot, honest tears were, for him, a burning shower. The tears warmed their contradictory hearts, tearing off all masks, pouring down repentance in a sea storm. She remembered everything that had happened between them, and an unexpected feeling of happiness and gratitude for his appearance forged all her movements. She froze up for a second in confusion and, entwining her arms around his neck, again took refuge in sobbing.

They made love two hundred eighty-one times, and she didn't go to work in the morning. He ran to the university café to get coffee and croissants. He smiled the glassy smile of a Russian hacker and an Egyptian sphinx.

Then they made love again two thousand forty-three times before the next morning. Hans displayed all of his fantasies, courage, and inventiveness. One time he even pulled out a sketch to check the engineering details. To vary the geometric positions while lovemaking. Yuma was in ecstasy. Women are turned on by education and intelligence. She said: "you are worthy of me; this is top-notch."

And with those words, he taped her to the chandelier and then made love to her under the TV, Yuma wrapped in a high-voltage wire (closing the loop on himself, of course). Then they climbed into the refrigerator and copulated in the ice like wooly mammoths. There, their lips froze to one another's, and they thawed off in a hot bath together with the refrigerator for three hours, where Hans brought her to ecstasy a hundred thirty-three more times while she elegantly held a glass of champagne in her hand. Then they were on the Japanese featherbed and in the pillows. Then in a kimono under Japanese parasols. Then with the guitar and saxophone, which Hans quickly learned to play.

Then they bathed in the mineral waters of an onsen with bowls of shabu-shabu on a floating table, between rows of solicitous geishas. And so on, and so forth, and so on, and so forth.

Yuma turned out to be soft and pliant, not at all the virago she had been molded into by society, lawyers, and social networks. She was kind, sensitive, quiet. Her smile was soft and grateful, and her eyes full of love and humility, and a mutuality of such depth that no poem in the world could reach it. Yuma was magnificent. Just irresistible, unparalleled, unrivaled, captivating, fathomless, cute, glorious, colossal, comely, and divine.

And that says it all.

January 17, 2017
Mill Neck, New York

Playboy and
Esquire magazines
named Hans man
of the year, politely
inquiring if he would
like to pose nude.
But he refused.

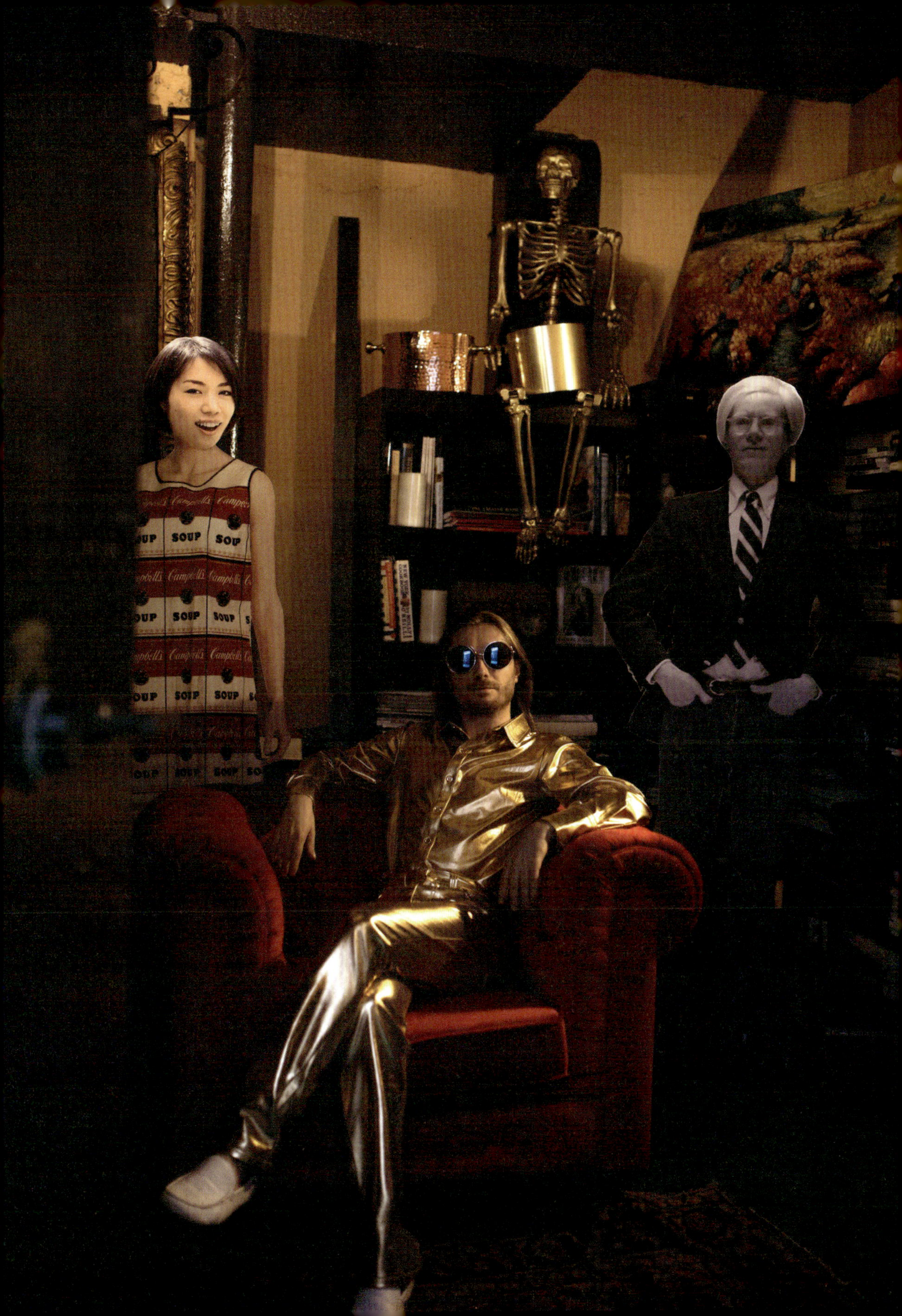
Campbell's
SOUP

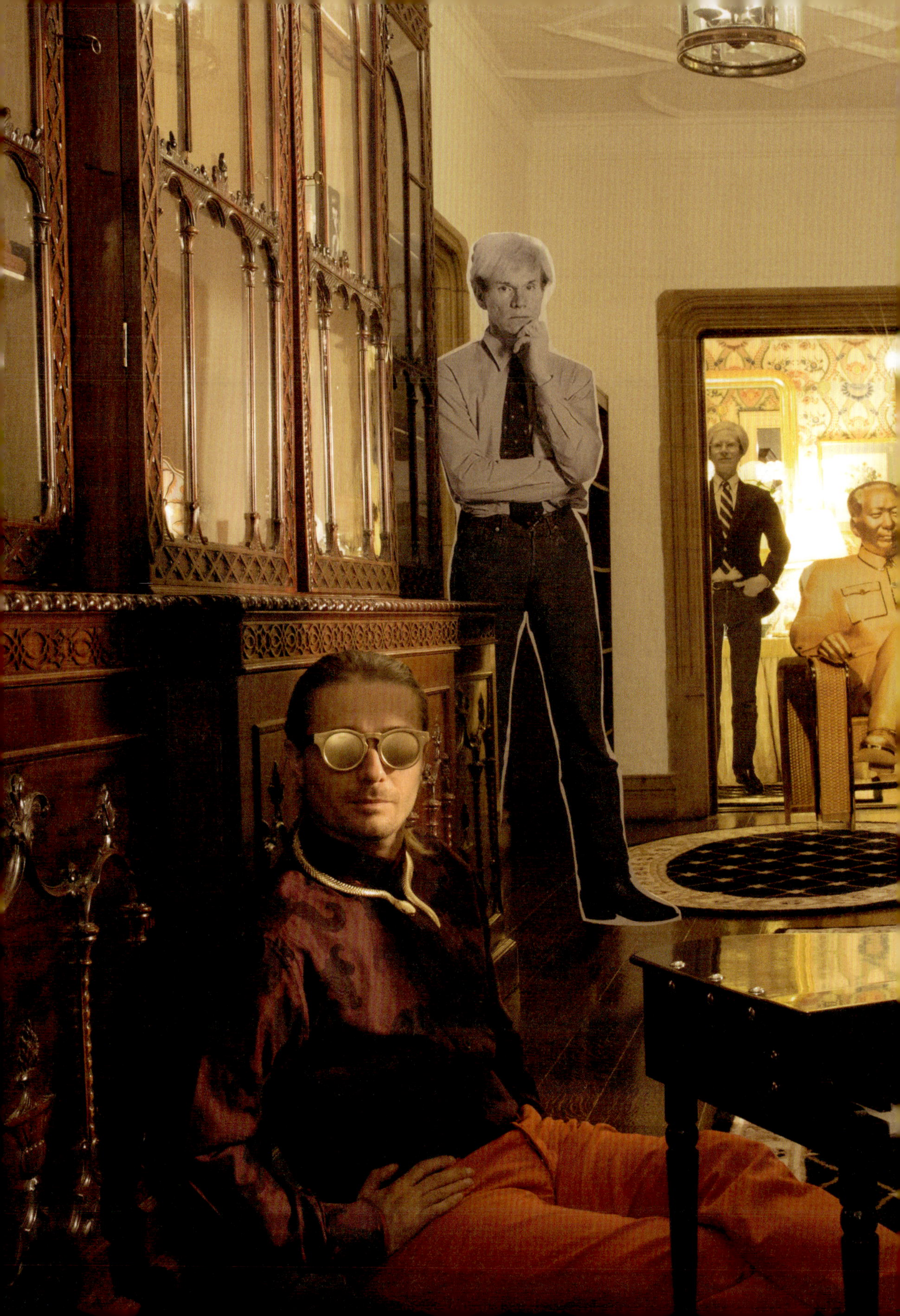

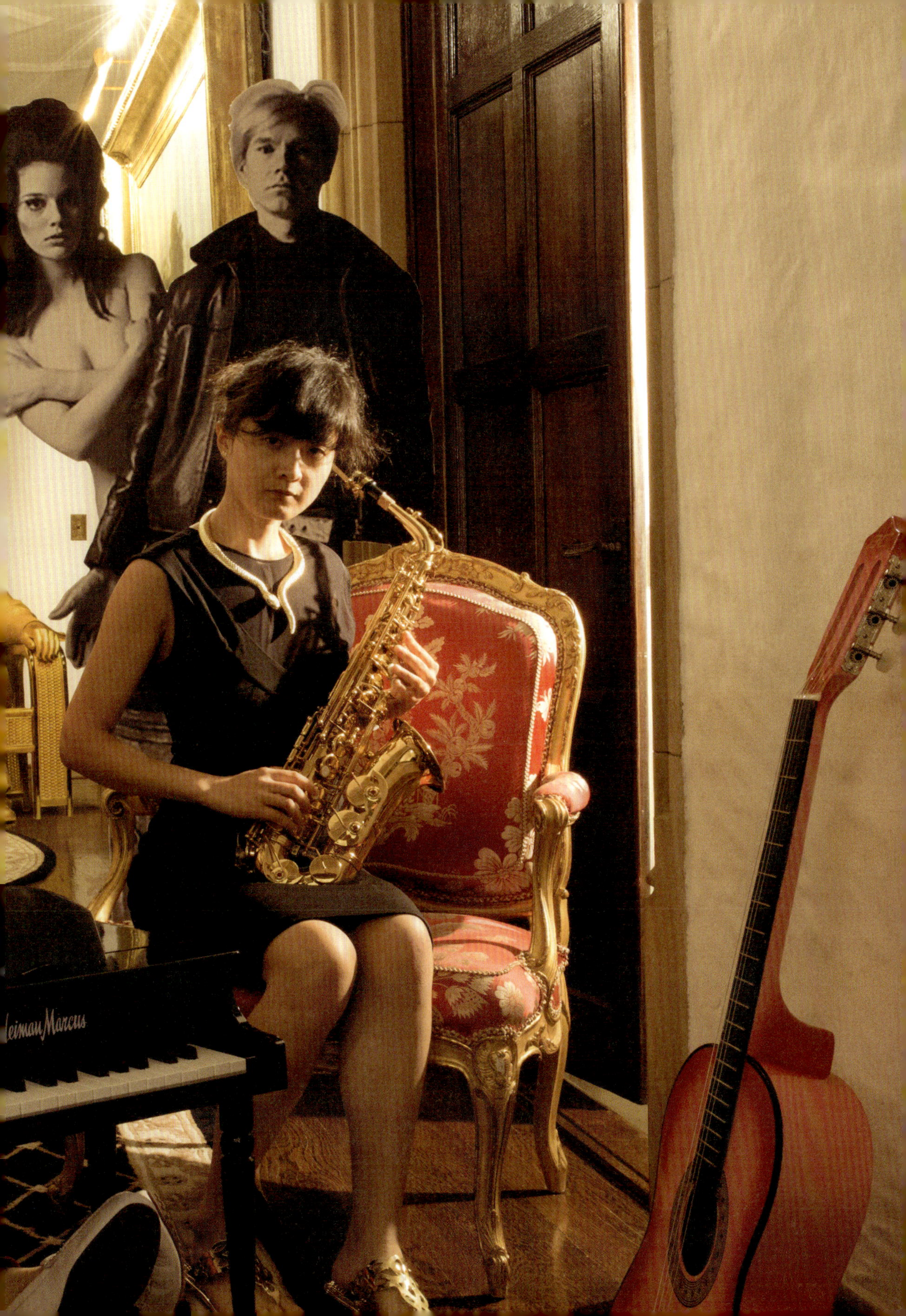

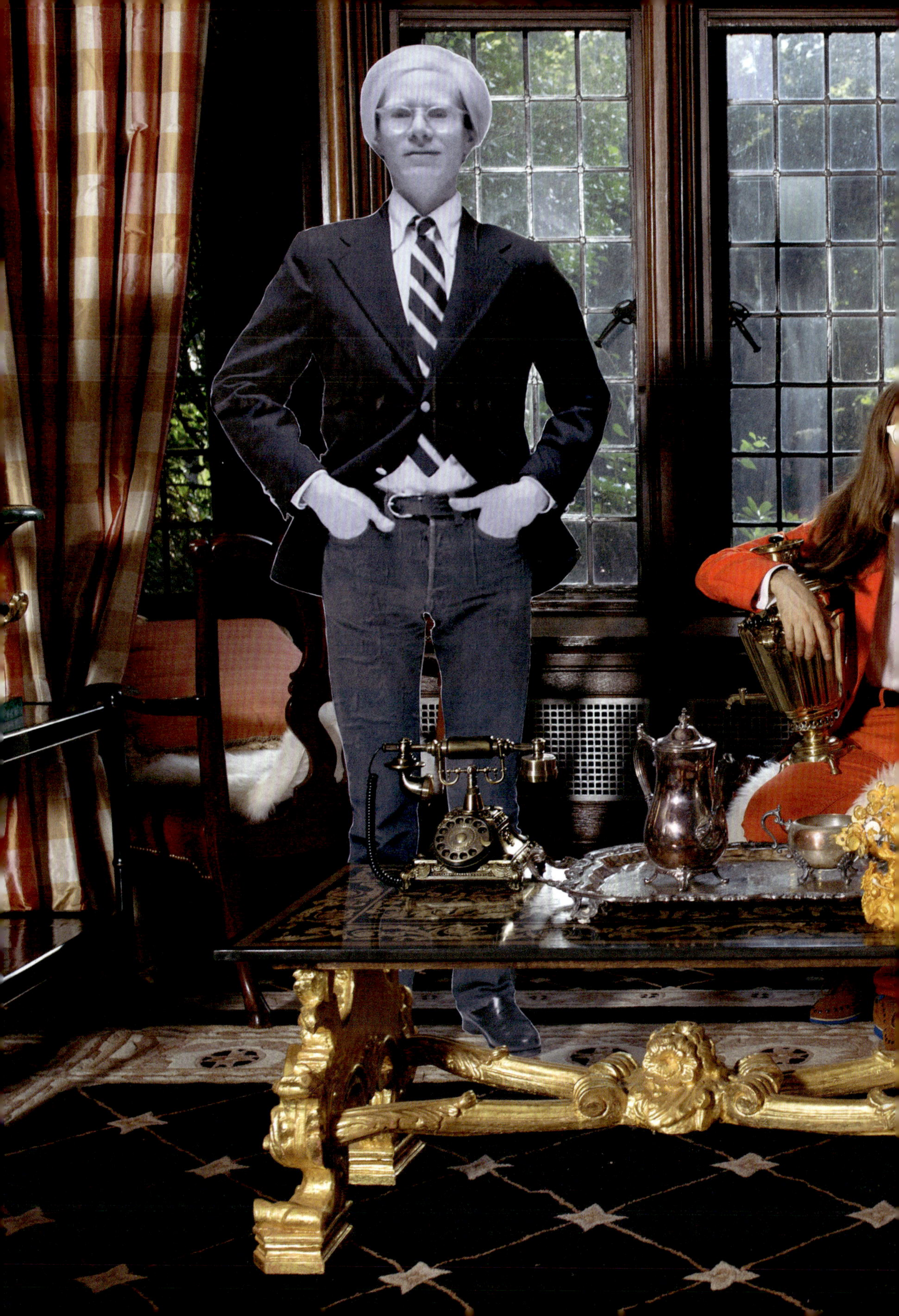

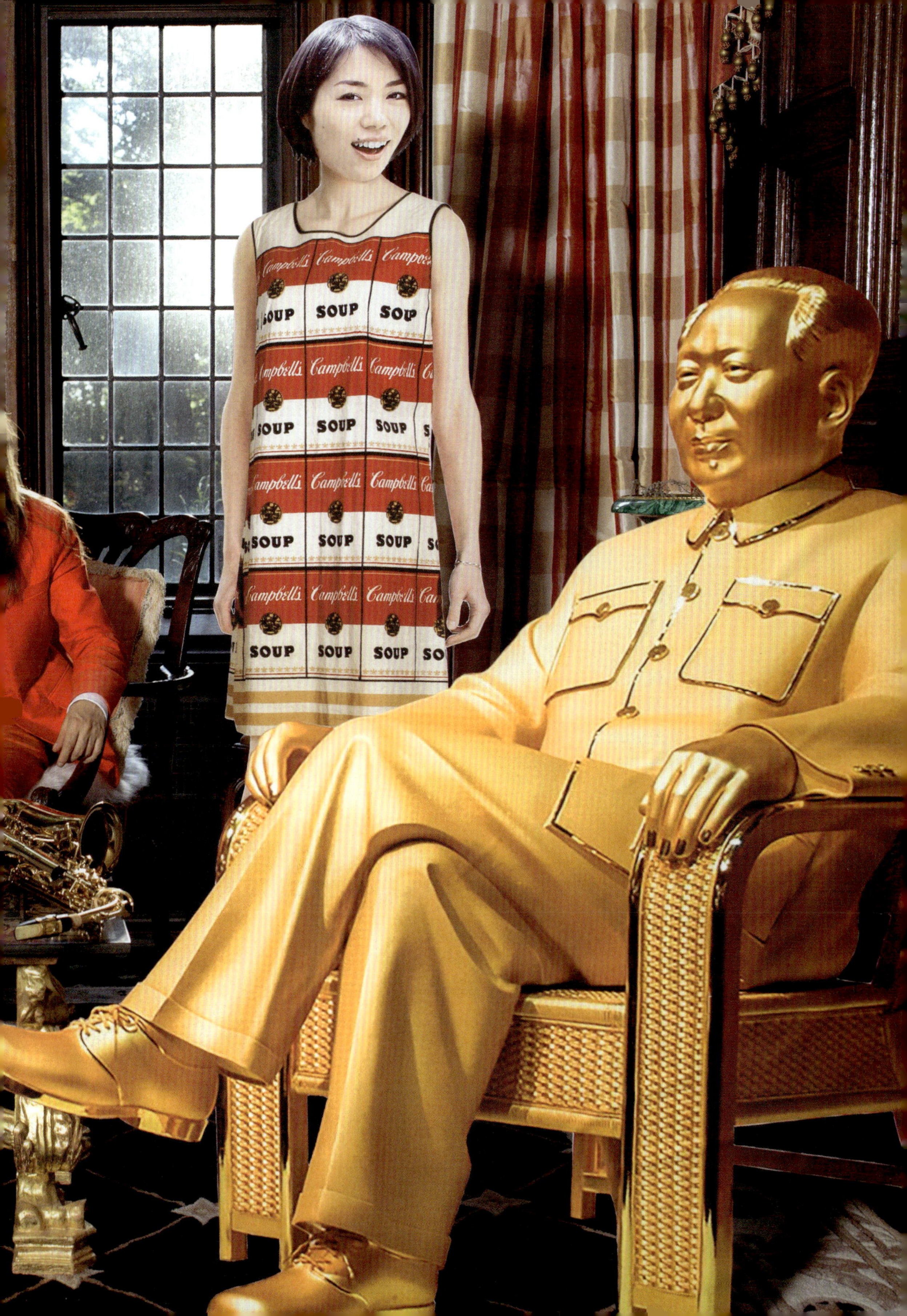
Campbell's
SOUP

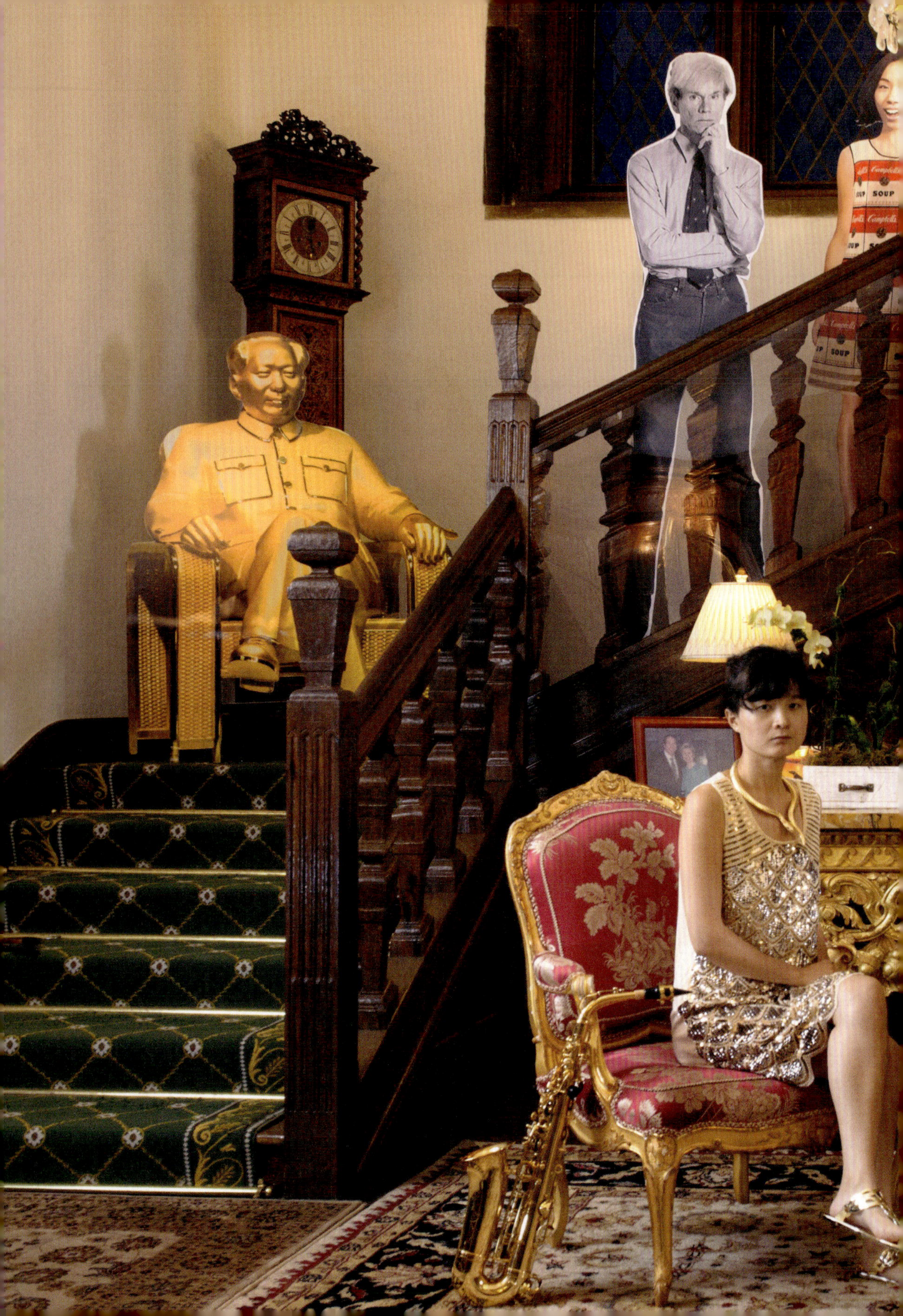
SOUP

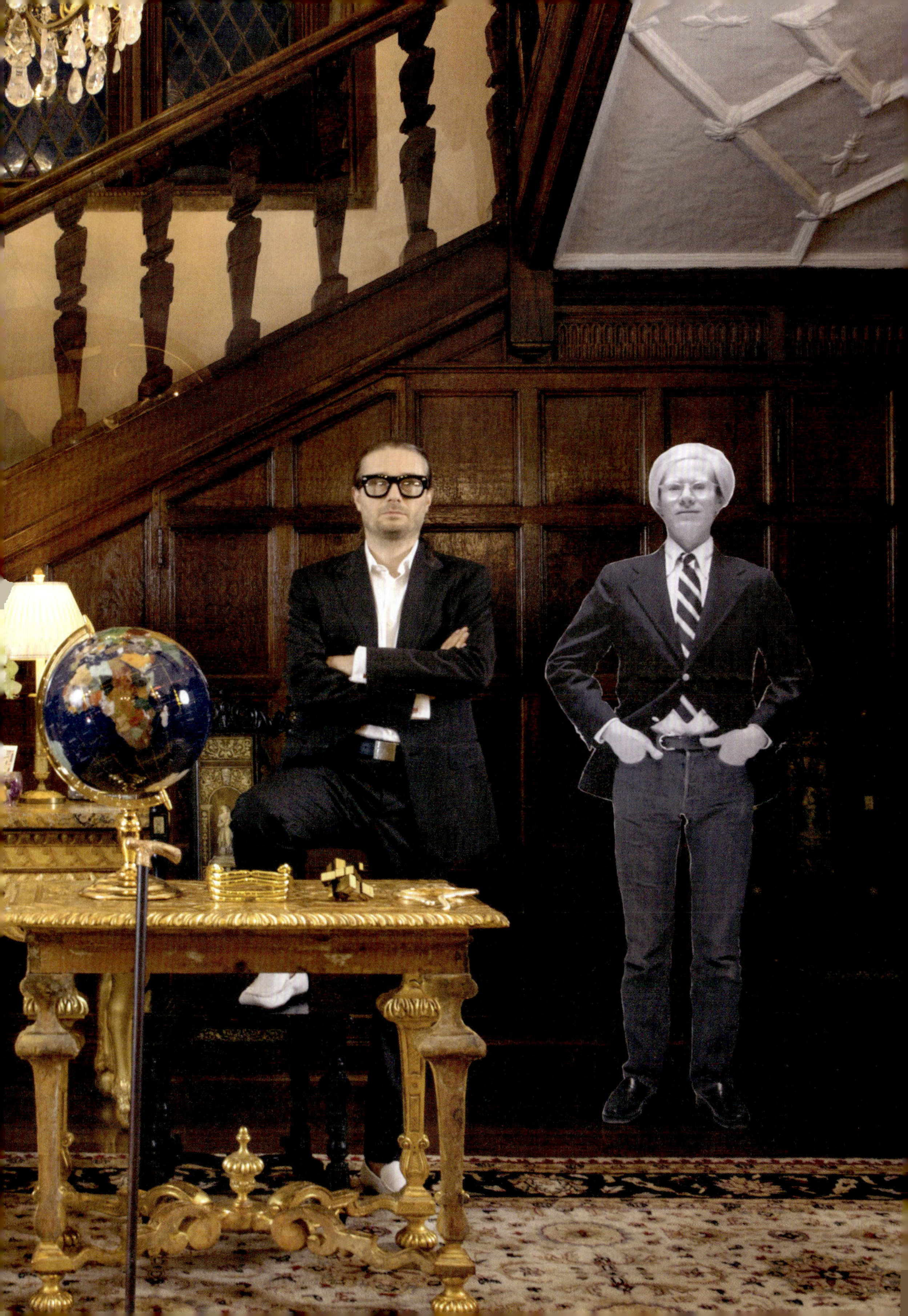

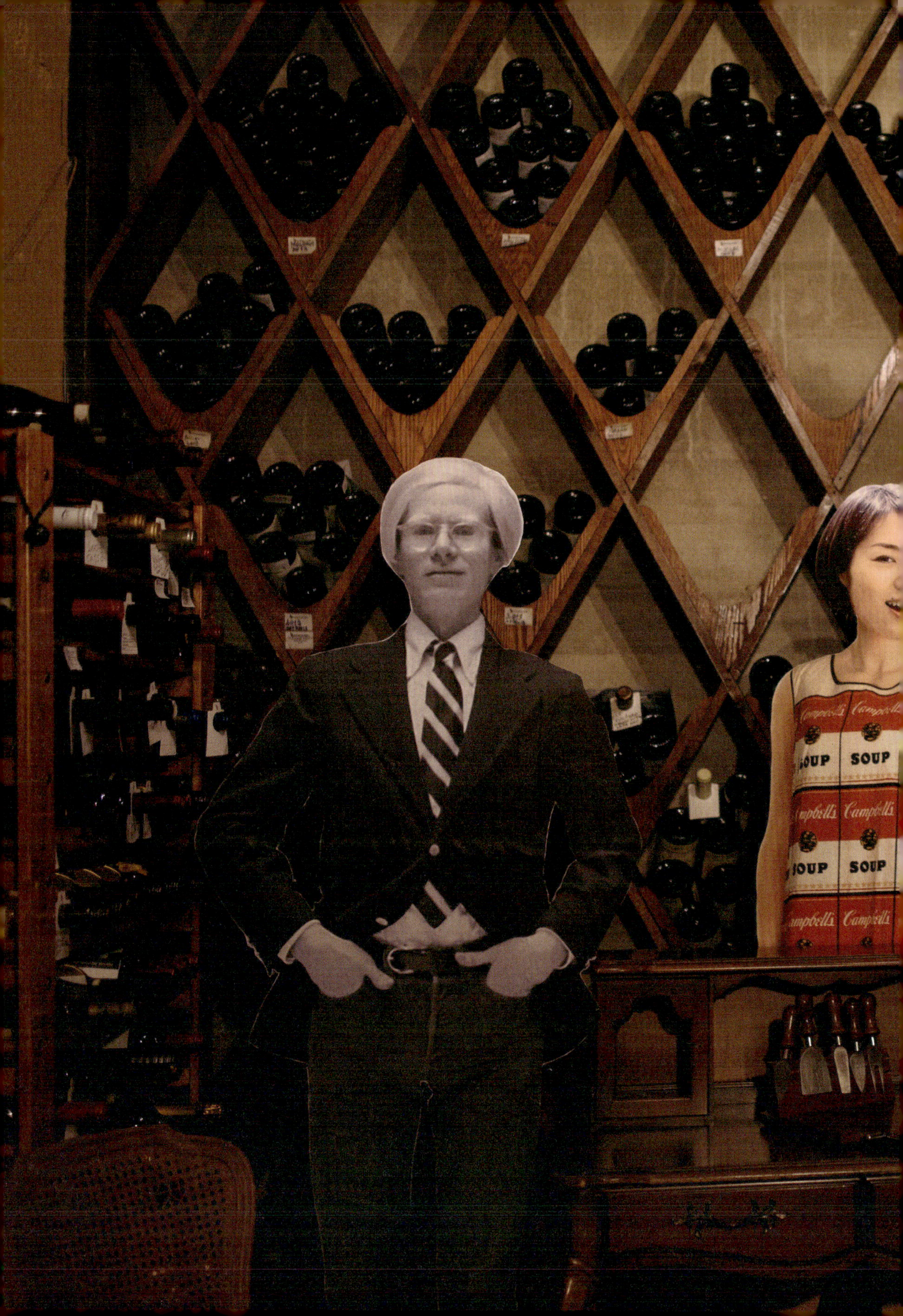
SOUP SOUP
Campbell's
SOUP SOUP
Campbell's

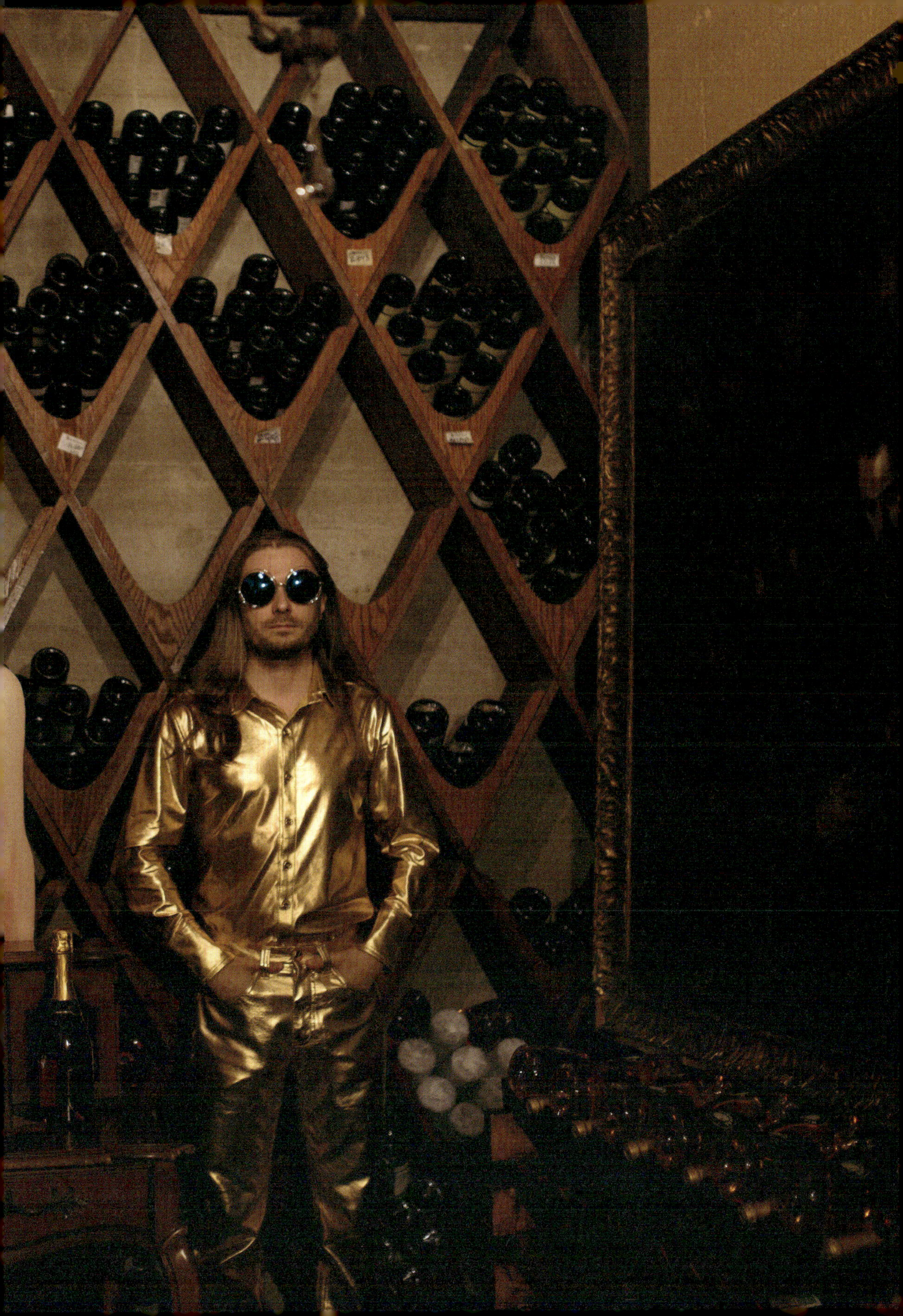

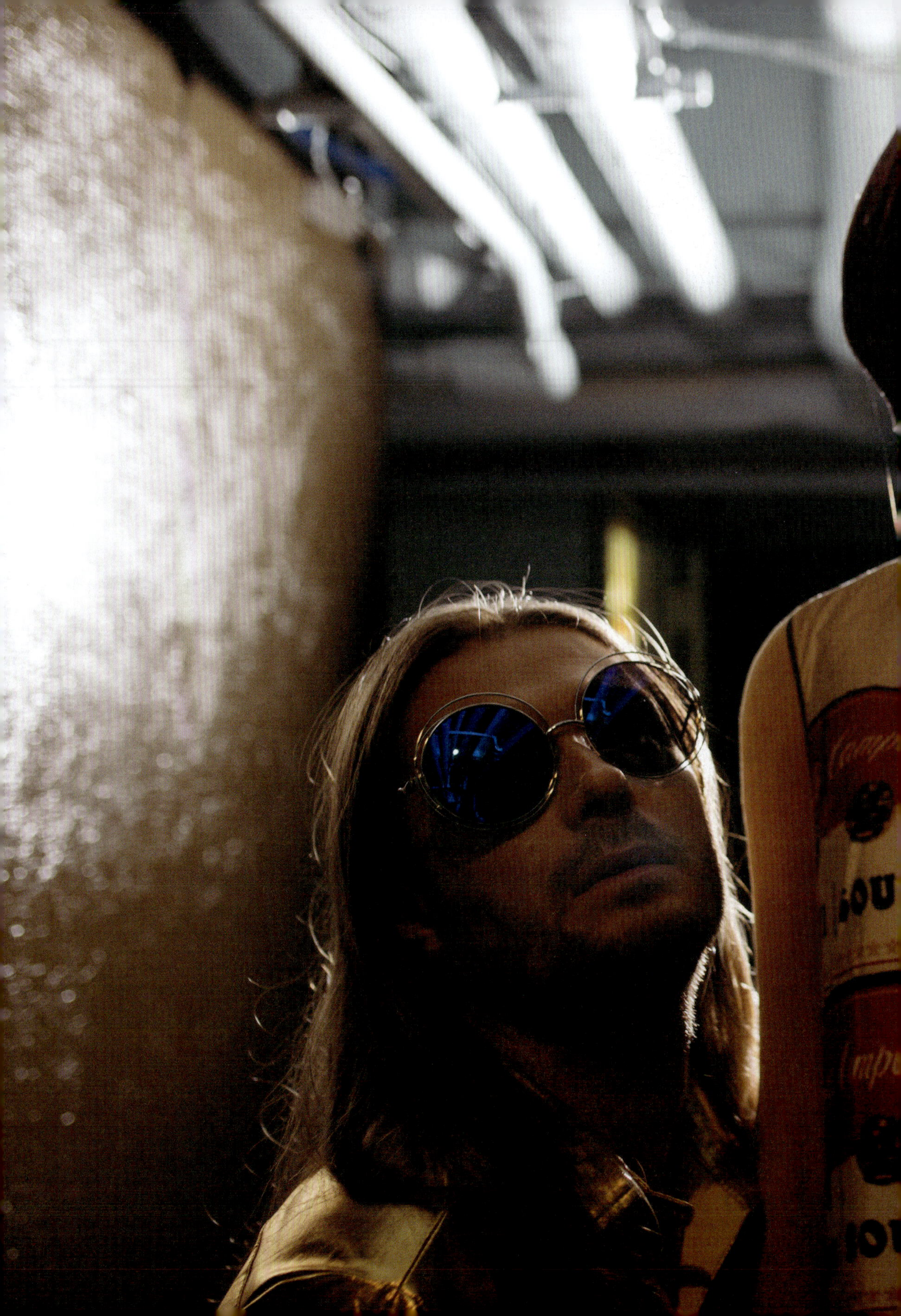

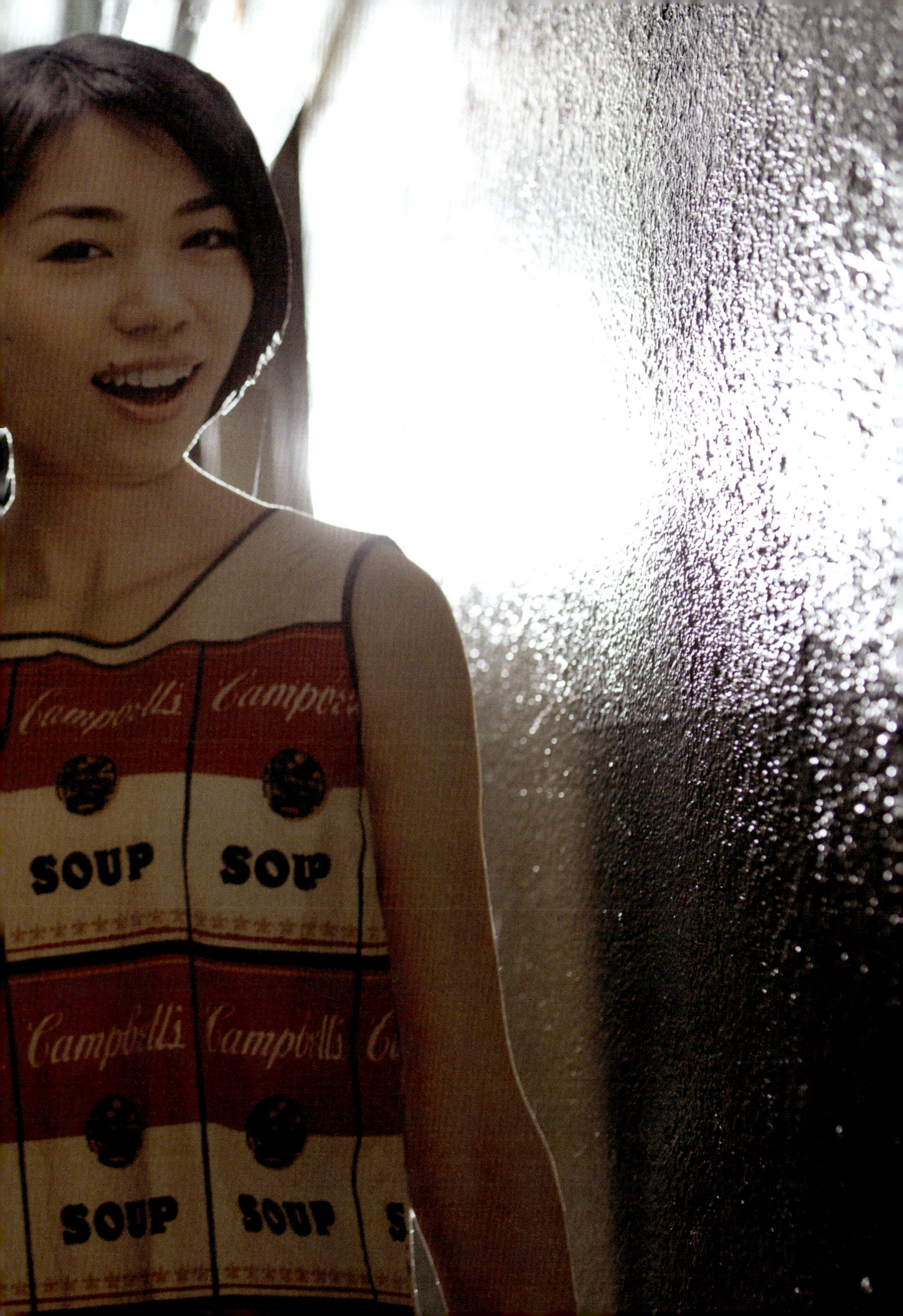
SOUP
SOUP
Campbell's
Campbell's
SOUP
SOUP

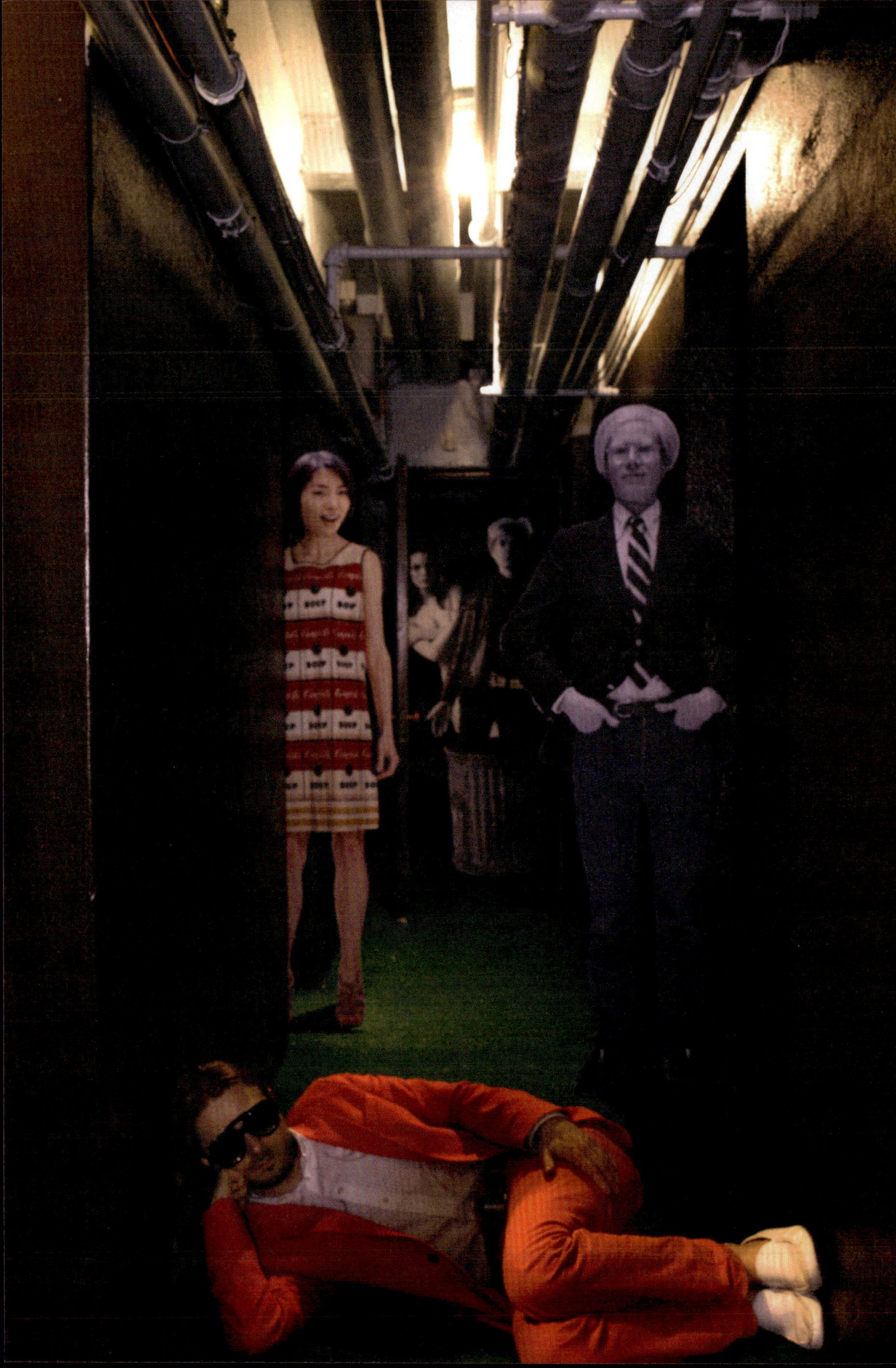

Intuition,
the sister of
stupidity.

Orange Art Foundation
www.orangeart.org

Editors:
Ajuan Song, Kuzma Vostrikov

Translation:
Jessica Mroz

Book design:
–SYB–

Cover design:
–SYB–

Copy-editing:
Matthew Dunleavy, Doreen Schmid
Production, printing and binding:
Wilco Art Books

ISBN:
978-1-7357028-9-6

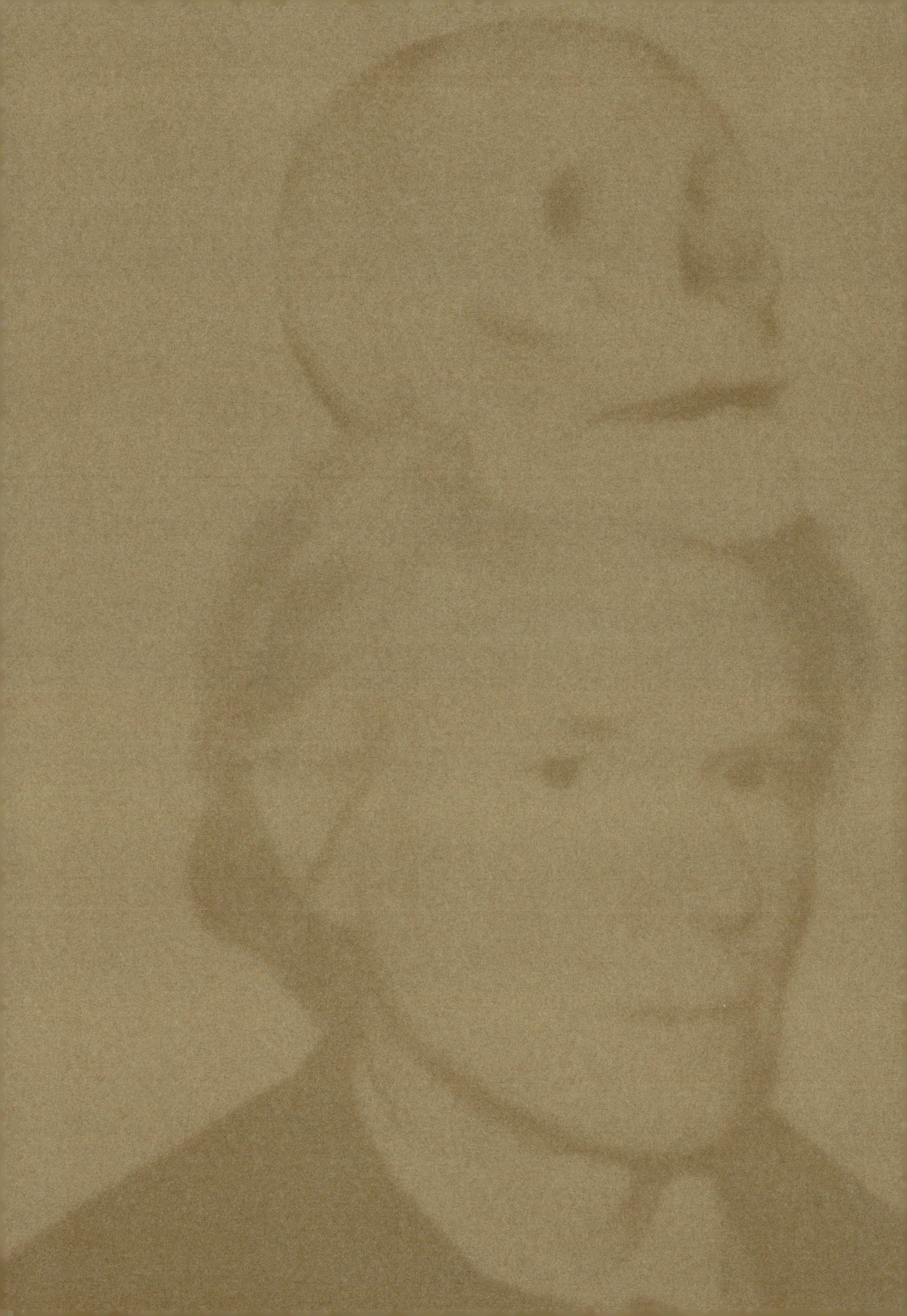

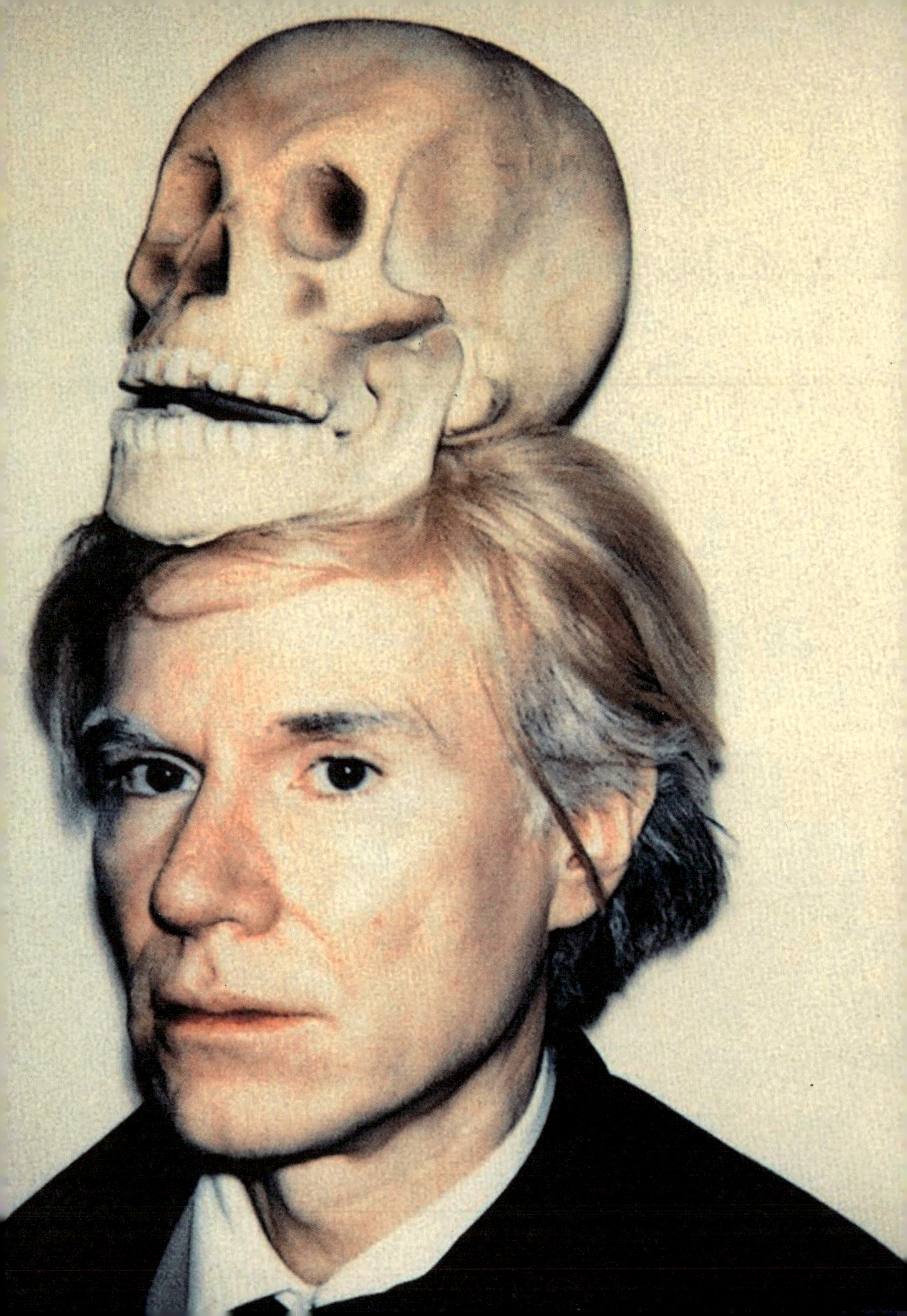